James Hogg (1770–1835), 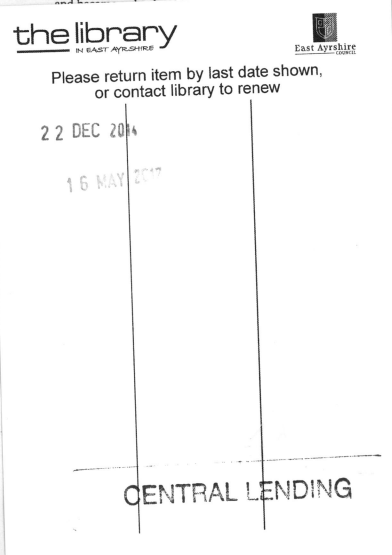 on his father's
farm in the Ettrick Forest near Selkirk in the Scottish
Borders. He left school for farm work at the age of seven

the library
IN EAST AYRSHIRE

East Ayrshire
COUNCIL

Please return item by last date shown, or contact library to renew

2 2 DEC 2014

1 6 MAY 2017

CENTRAL LENDING

THE
THREE PERILS
OF MAN

War, Women and Witchcraft

BY

JAMES HOGG

Edited with an Introduction,

Textual Notes and Glossary

by

DOUGLAS GIFFORD

CANONGATE
CLASSICS
74

First published in 1822. This edition first published
as a Canongate Classic in 1996 by Canongate Books
Ltd, 14 High Street, Edinburgh EHI ITE.

Introduction, notes and glossary copyright © Douglas
Gifford, 1989, 1996.

The publishers gratefully acknowledge general sub-
sidy from the Scottish Arts Council towards the
Canongate Classics series and a specific grant
towards the publication of this title.

Set in 10pt Plantin by Palimpsest Book Production
Limited, Polmont, Stirlingshire. Printed and bound
in Finland by WSOY.

Canongate Classics
Series Editor: Roderick Watson
Editorial Board: Tom Crawford, J. B. Pick and
Cairns Craig

British Library Cataloguing in Publication Data
A catalogue record for this book is available
from the British Library.

ISBN 0 86241 646 9

ACKNOWLEDGEMENTS

Canongate wish to acknowledge the kind assistance of the Association of Scottish Literary Studies for granting permission to reproduce the text of their edition of *The Three Perils of Man*.

Canongate also wish to thank Professor Douglas Gifford for his editorial work and for giving permission to include his notes to the A.S.L.S. edition in the present volume.

Contents

Introduction

Until fairly recently James Hogg has been known mainly as a poet. But he wrote several very different novels of astonishingly high quality; he is one of the finest of Scottish short story writers; and in *The Three Perils of Man* he created a work which goes beyond any of these categories – a work which he rightly called a Border romance. The fact that this comic, fantastic, and extravagant epic was dismissed as a trivial production in 1822 by Edinburgh literary circles, and by Walter Scott himself, can only be understood by looking briefly at the prejudiced and discouraging way in which Hogg's fiction (and indeed Hogg's presence) was received in polite Edinburgh. For its rich and varied living examples of folk lore and legend alone, his work should have excited at least the antiquarian interest of Scott and his contemporaries, yet the truth would seem to be that from the moment of his entry into literary Edinburgh in 1810, Hogg, as a serious writer of fiction, was doomed to misunderstanding and misdirection. This was tragic for Scottish literature since his genius was, in its unique way, as remarkable as that of Scott himself. Hogg was a victim of the ever-growing Edinburgh and Scottish upper- and middle-class snobbery of the late eighteenth and nineteenth centuries. Ramsay, Fergusson and Burns had met this snobbery – indeed that feature common to them all, what David Daiches has called a 'crisis of identity', arose directly out of these writers' unsureness as to where their audience and their significant critics were to be found. There has indeed been much discussion about the general Scottish cultural background to Hogg and his contemporaries, but the significance of his personal and literary relationships is only now being recognised.

In his influential *Scott and Scotland* (1936) Edwin Muir

claimed that no complete and healthy critical awareness existed in Edinburgh at the beginning of the nineteenth century, and that this was replaced by the doctrinaire disagreements of the great periodicals of the day, the Whig *Edinburgh Review* and the Tory *Blackwood's Magazine*. Contemporary criticism now challenges such a sweeping and denigratory view of Scottish literature in the period, but nevertheless sees real harm to creative effort coming from the adverse effect of the new genteel and Anglicised standards of taste and politeness which then held sway in the polite circles of the capital. Scott's unique and yet popular vision commanded, of course, the admiration of all classes. Susan Ferrier, on the other hand, abandoned fiction after 1832 because of a sense of the activity being socially unacceptable. The same sensibility made her refuse to read John Galt's fiction because its vulgarity 'beats print'. John Gibson Lockhart's two considerable attempts at serious investigation of the darker aspects of Scottish psychology, *Adam Blair* (1822) and *Matthew Wald* (1824), caused shock and disapproval to a degree which we now find difficult to understand, and which may have persuaded him to try other forms of writing. The refined Edinburgh which admired the fiction of John Wilson ('Christopher North') was bound to find Hogg's tales offensive, with their rude Border health and their directness of expression.

In 1810 Hogg came into this society like a bull into a china shop, with his plan to run a weekly magazine, *The Spy*. With his Border background of rich oral poetry and story, and his wholeness of attitude, which integrated manual labour and poetic vision, the 'Ettrick Shepherd' was an anachronism in nineteenth-century Edinburgh. His directness and honesty of approach attracted patrons at first, and then embarrassed them. And a curious and distasteful element emerges from his relations with some of his patrons. They kept up the pretence of being his friend, when they were in fact exploiting him.

While Walter Scott was not one of these false friends, and did help Hogg frequently, it was nevertheless always as Hogg's cultural and social superior. His letters are littered with allusions to the 'great Caledonian Boar' and the 'hog's pearls' (referring to Hogg's novel *The Three Perils of Women*). Hogg was annoyed at how Scott would manage him in public; and on one occasion the great man's help was offered on the condition that Hogg put his poetical talent under lock and key forever. Scott would give money and well-meant criticism about the lack of planning in Hogg's stories, but in terms of a full and frank interchange of ideas between literary and intellectual equals he failed him. The Scott of Hogg's *Domestic Manners of Sir Walter Scott* (1834) had 'a too strong leaning to the old aristocracy', 'a prodigious devotion for titled rank, amounting almost to adoration'. This Scott was bored at shepherds' discussions and quizzed his simple hosts in superior fashion, and supervised Hogg's table manners on public occasions. The relationship is found in a nutshell in Scott's dinner joke – 'If ye reave the Hoggs o' Fauldshope / Ye Harry Harden's gear . . .' – that is, you insult Scott's vassal.

And if Scott, the counsellor of writers the world over, could often ignore or fail to see the real talent of Hogg, it is not surprising to find lesser Edinburgh figures following his lead. Hogg's highly complex relations with *Blackwood's Magazine* illustrate this perfectly. He appears to have had a major hand in starting the magazine in 1817, beginning the famous parody of biblical writing in the scandalous 'Chaldee manuscript', which lampooned most of the Edinburgh notables of the time. His new friends, John Wilson and John Gibson Lockhart, fresh from Oxford, lacking Hogg's geniality, then reworked this, and allowed the savage note which came to be attributed as much to Hogg as to themselves. It is ironic in the light of this and later exploitation, that in 1817 Hogg had advised William Blackwood that

> Wilson's papers have a masterly cast about them; a little custom would make him the best periodical writer of the age – keep hold of him.

It seems that as Wilson and Lockhart grew more friendly with Blackwood, Hogg was increasingly viewed through glasses coloured by snobbery. Lockhart was not so bad

– indeed he paid a marvellous tribute to Hogg's 'un-affected simplicity . . . modesty and confidence such as well becomes a man of genius', along with his 'noble consciousness of perfect independence', in his *Peter's Letters to His Kinsfolk* (1818). But is there not still something here of the ritual of praising the Scottish peasant-poet that was enacted with Burns? There is no doubt about the attitude of John Wilson, whom modern critics increasingly identify as an embodiment of unhealthy and pre-Kailyard develop-ments in Scottish literature of the period, with his warped genius, his double-dealing, and his sentimental verse and politically biased and melodramatic fiction – all the more influential in the 'twenties and 'thirties for Wilson's being editor of *Blackwood's* as well as the politically appointed and sadly underqualified Professor of Moral Philosophy at Edinburgh University from 1820. Here is a typically ambiguous Wilson treatment of Hogg in *Blackwood's*:

> You, James, are the rough diamond he [the author of an article on Hogg in *The Scots Magazine*] proposes to describe with mathematical exactness. Really, I felt, during the solemn note of preparation, much as one feels in a drawing room, when, the stupid servant having forgotten to announce the name, the door slowly moves on its hinges, and some splendid stranger is expected to appear; but when, to the pleased surprise of the assembled company, in bounced you yourself, the worthy and most ingenious shepherd, rubbing your ungloved hands (would I were a glove on that hand!) as if you were washing them, with a good humoured smile on your honest face, enough to win every heart, and with a pair of top boots . . . instantly recalling the shining imagery of Day and Martin's patent blacking.

This combines the depiction of Hogg as buffoon with an appearance of affection in a way which the *Noctes Ambrosianae*, that series of imaginary evenings of drink and wayward discussion involving Wilson as 'Christopher North', with assorted friends and the Ettrick Shepherd, was to continue throughout the 1820s, a treatment particularly poisonous in its exploitation of its victim's good nature. Hogg wrote about this to Blackwood:

> I am almost ruing the day that I ever saw you. I have had letters, newspapers, and magazines poured in upon me . . . The country is full of impatience. No-one has any right to publish aught in my name without consulting me . . . It is confoundedly hard that I should be made a tennis ball between contending parties. If you can find out by the writ or otherwise who the shabby scoundrel is that writes the enclosed, pray return it to him in a blank cover.

Wilson could be even more direct. In 1821 he wrote:

> Pray, who wishes to know anything about his life? Who indeed cares a single farthing, whether he be at this blessed moment dead or alive? Only picture to yourself a stout country lout, with a bushel of hair on his shoulders that had not been raked for months, enveloped in a coarse plaid impregnated with tobacco, with a prodigious mouthful of immeasurable tusks, and a dialect that set all conjecture at defiance, lumbering in suddenly upon the elegant retirement of Mr. Miller's back shop . . . What would he [Hogg] himself have thought if a large surly brown bear, or a huge baboon, had burst open his door when he was at breakfast?

Wilson's statement about the country lout lumbering in on a scene of elegant retirement represents polite Edinburgh's heartfelt attitude to Hogg. And Hogg in his turn was bound to clash with the Edinburgh *Literati*. Of the trio who wrote the 'Chaldee manuscript', he alone managed to stay friendly with the Whigs who were satirised therein. Of an older generation, straightforward and without affectation, he was incapable of snobbery. This is charmingly revealed in the description by a contemporary of a typical Hogg gathering of the kind he used to hold in later life whenever he came up from the Borders to Edinburgh: Grassmarket meal dealers, genteel and slender young men from Parliament House, printers from the Cowgate, book-sellers from the New Town, all rubbed shoulders.

> Between a couple of young advocates sits a decent grocer from Bristo Street, and amidst a host of shop lads from the Luckenbooths is perched a stiffish young probationer who scarcely knows whether he should be here or not . . . jolly, honest-like bakers in pepper-and-salt coats give great uneasiness to squads of black coats in juxtaposition with them; and several dainty looking youths in white neckcloths and black silk eyeglass ribbons are evidently much discomposed by a rough type of horsedealer, who has got in amongst them and keeps calling out all kinds of coarse jokes to a crony . . . Many of Mr. Hogg's Selkirkshire store farming friends are there with their well oxygenated complexions and Dandy-Dinmont-like bulk of figure . . . If a representative assembly had been made up from all the classes of the community, it could not have been more miscellaneous than this company assembled by a man to whom, in the simplicity of his heart, all company seemed alike acceptable.[1]

Hogg's first fiction appeared in his magazine *The Spy*, which began in 1810 and lasted for only a year. In a way that is reminiscent of the polarised English and Scots roles adopted in their work by Ramsay and Burns, he wrote in a dual persona. In one role he was 'the Spy', inventing a background of gentle birth fallen on evil days, taking an observer's interest in psychological quirks, showing already his acute interest in morbid thought and action. Here also, however, was a contrived point of view, which, in its attempt to be at one with polite Edinburgh, produced unconvincing stories of rakes' progresses and vice punished. But defiantly another persona quickly followed, that of the robust and honest teller of country tales, 'John Miller', the Nithsdale Shepherd. Insecurity about his social and cultural position had created a form of split creative personality.

Criticism of Hogg's magazine followed shortly. It was considered too coarse; when girls were pregnant Hogg said so directly. This, amongst a lot of lively as well as hack writing, is all that can be found to account for the desertion of Hogg's generally deserving magazine by his subscribers. He admitted his mistake in one of his autobiographical accounts.

> I despised the fastidiousness and affectation of the people . . . the literary ladies in particular agreed . . . that I would never write a sentence which deserved to be read.

And in the final number of *The Spy* he wrote that

> The learned, the enlightened, and polite circles of this flourishing metropolis disdained either to be amused or instructed by the ebulitions of humble genius. Enemies, swelling with the most rancorous spite, grunted in every corner . . . Pretended friends . . . liberal in their advices . . . took every method in their power to lessen the work in the esteem of others by branding its author with designs the most subversive of all civility and decorum . . .

Thus from the beginning of Hogg's fiction adverse criticism was to inhibit his instinctive creativity. Already critics had adopted an attitude to Hogg which accepted his pleasant country songs, his moments of poetic genius, his sketches of the shepherd's life, but advised him not to attempt more. But Hogg was resilient in these early years in Edinburgh. He decided not to give in to the literary ladies and sensitive gentlemen, and between 1810 and 1821 added to and amended the early *Spy* stories for his collection, *Winter Evening Tales*. It is fascinating to compare the later with the earlier versions. Ghost stories are cut down to a stark simplicity, and their sense of threatening mystery deepened. And a recurrent theme emerges of dark inscrutable forces, powerful and aristocratic, surrounding and trapping an innocent protagonist. This may echo Hogg's own feelings about a 'conspiracy' of the gentry against him; but it could be argued that *Literati* criticism of Hogg's work and personality for once (and accidentally) contributed positively here, as it is predominantly this sense of inexorable and unknown powers conspiring against a vulnerable protagonist which makes so many of his stories compelling, from *The Justified Sinner* to *An Edinburgh Baillie*.

One story is remarkable for its time. Hogg extensively added to a *Spy* story called 'On Instability in One's Calling' to create the short novel *Basil Lee*. This was the tale which had caused most offence with its frank declaration of pregnancy. It illustrates admirably the direction Hogg was moving in, and should have been encouraged to move in. The original was a short description of the misadventures of a young fellow psychologically incapable of settling to any one job. Hogg capably linked a genuine interest in abnormal psychology with a very funny anti-romantic account of how his anti-hero continually dreams of new roles. Basil sees himself as a shepherd, taking lassies under his plaid, making up songs, living an Arcadian tradition – but the rain pours down, the job proves a dirty one, Jessie slaps his face. He tries life as a grocer – but sells vitriol by mistake for whisky. After trying many jobs, exhausting his father's patience, Basil gets sent abroad. He meets a beautiful young lady on the ship – who turns out to be an Inverness prostitute. Hogg reversed all conventions here by sensitively and effectively making her the most genuinely dignified person in the story and defining her relationship with the braggart Basil with a delicacy of control and insight unusual for the time.

In other ways, too, *Basil Lee* mocks the conventional romance. Basil becomes a hero of the American Wars when he gets entangled in the British flags while fleeing. He tries to kill the standard bearer, and when the smoke of battle clears he is mistaken as the saviour of the colours and promoted for valour. And much of this spirit of subversion, parodic mockery and satiric fun lies behind *The Three Perils of Man*, with its fundamentally anti-romantic bias. But Edinburgh was not ready for a story where the ending had the prostitute as the real heroine, redeeming a worthless good-for-nothing, with the pair squabbling happily ever after. The *Winter Evening Tales* (1820) in which this appeared were not unsuccessful; but invariably Hogg was reproached for the 'indelicacies' of stories like this, and applauded for the collection's simple Border anecdotes of the shepherd's life, with the occasional ghost story permitted. Social satire and rumbustious anti-heroics were not appreciated by literary Edinburgh.

By this time Hogg must have begun to wonder if there existed a significant prose form in which he could succeed; for in 1817 his first major novel had appeared (although it was in fact written after most of the stories which became *Winter Evening Tales*). *The Brownie of Bodsbeck* tells of Claverhouse's atrocities during the 'killing time'. The action is terse and vivid, the horrors described in a realistic, shocking and dramatic style, while the Border characters are as good as anything of the kind created by Scott. Moreover, Hogg experimented with techniques nowhere else found so early in the development of the novel. He used flashbacks and sudden cuts from time past to time present, admittedly causing some confusion to the reader, but occasionally achieving vivid moments of real success. His novel deserved a better reception than it received. Critics assumed that the shepherd was trespassing on the grounds of historical fiction, and Scott for one did not like Hogg's adoption of a view of the period so different from his own. He called it 'a false and unfair picture of the times and the existing characters, altogether'. Hogg replied: 'I dinna ken, Mr. Scott. It is the picture I have been brought up in the belief o' sin' ever I was born, and I had it frae them whom I was most bound to honour and believe . . .' and, alleging the atrocities to have happened, he continued, 'and that's great deal mair than you can say for your tale "Auld Mortality".'

Hogg certainly had some cause for annoyance in the

casual way his efforts at fiction were dismissed, when the more conventional and melodramatic historical novels of Sir Thomas Dick Lauder, and John Galt's treatment of the same topic, the qualitatively comparable *Ringan Gilhaize* (1823), were taken seriously. *The Brownie of Bodsbeck* may not be as good as *Old Mortality*, but it is better than Scott's lesser Scottish historical romances like *The Abbot* or *The Monastery*. Indeed, Scott's attitude speaks worlds in his letter to Laidlaw at the time, when, referring to *The Brownie* and its companion pieces, he says, 'The cubs have not succeeded well . . . but they are sadly vulgar, to be sure.'

Thus by 1822 Hogg had tried to break into historical romance, and to develop a vigorous vein of psychological anti-romance. His efforts were not appreciated, but he still wanted to write full-length, serious fiction. For his next effort he decided to join a loose historical background with his deep knowledge of Border legend and tradition, and to place both within the perspective of his fantastic imagination. The result was the astonishingly under-estimated *The Three Perils of Man* (1822). The *Noctes Ambrosianae* of the period set the tone of casual prejudgment: 'I dare say 'twill be like all his things, – a mixture of the admirable, the execrable, and the tolerable . . .' This was probably Lockhart, as Wilson said elsewhere that he would 'write a page or two rather funny on Hogg's romance' – obviously not in praise, as he went on to say, 'though averse to being cut up myself, I like to abuse my friends.' Hogg was lucky that Wilson did not follow this up.

What is more difficult to understand is Walter Scott's dislike. The man who had himself used goblins, astrologers and the devil in his poems and tales, told Hogg that he had ruined 'one of the best tales in the world' with his 'extravagance in demonology'. One would have thought that even for the romance's use of legend and folk lore alone the favour of Scott, the antiquary, would have been secured. But it would appear that his conception of the kind of supernatural material permissible or desirable for a novelist underwent considerable change throughout the 1820s. Hogg remarked on Scott's turning 'renegade' with his stories 'made up of half-and-half, like Nathaniel Gow's toddy', that is, with the supernatural content watered down to such a point that its very existence became ambiguous.

In a review of John Galt's *The Omen*, in *Blackwood's Magazine* in 1826, Scott made this change of view explicit, when he laid down a clear distinction between two kinds of fictional supernatural. Galt's novel presented an aristocratic protagonist whose sensitivity of soul is such that he receives mysterious and mystic premonitions which allow him to 'gaze beyond the curtain of futurity'. This Gothic supernatural sensibility, the product of good breeding, Scott approves; Byron and Sheridan shared it, he claims. But for the other kind of supernatural, that of folk tradition and legend, Scott by 1826, surprisingly, has less time. Now he condemns as unworthy of a man of breeding and education 'any belief in the superstition of the olden time, which believed in spectres, fairies, and other supernatural apparitions. These airy squadrons have been long routed, and are banished to the cottage and the nursery'. – Poor Hogg! The living connection of his romance with the Ballad tradition, with folk-tale and the world of vividly realised and colourfully diverse creatures of the folk tradition, is here by implication condemned. Arguably, Scott's attitude stands as a watershed in Scottish literature – with Hogg on the wrong side.

Now, uncertain and casting about for yet another fictional mode to try for success, Hogg wrote the three tales which form *The Three Perils of Women* (1823). It is possible that for the first tale, on the perils of love, he began by adopting as his model the novel of manners; and to an extent the result was a grotesque parody of Jane Austen's and Susan Ferrier's modes of social satire. In this, the main tale, what started out as a light-hearted study of the relationship of two girls, Gatty Bell and Cherry Elliott, became rather horrible, as if Hogg were already moving on to the gloomy ideas of *The Justified Sinner*. Gatty steals Cherry's lover and marries him; the betrayed Cherry dies of grief, and as punishment for her man-theft Gatty falls into a coma for three years, in the course of which she gives birth to a healthy boy, and lies uncorrupted till she awakes abandoned by whatever demon or mental disturbance had possessed her. As with *The Justified Sinner*, psychological sickness and supernatural agency are allowed to co-exist; in his afterword to the 1995 edition of the novel, David Groves finds a realistic depiction of the psychological state of catatonia, and it is unusually true of Hogg's fiction that it allows men and women to sin and suffer alike. In addition to this unique variation on the novel of manners there are two other tales: one, on the peril of 'leasing', being a savage assault on middle-class Edinburgh's appetite for slander, and the other, on the peril of jealousy, becoming a strange mixture of parodic Highland comedy and post-Culloden tragedy.

Hogg's aims in these tales are complex; in addition to their women protagonists suffering from the conventional symptoms of romantic love like jealousy and swooning, they foreground the perils of death from prostitution, adultery, and pregnancy. It is not surprising that the novel, ostensibly aiming at the readership of the polite ladies of Edinburgh, received damning reviews, Wilson being particularly vicious on this occasion. However justified their dislike – and modern critics are divided as to the intentions and achievement of the work as a whole – Hogg was demoralised. By this time, as well as frequently asking Lockhart and Scott to advise him and to read his proofs, Hogg finally admitted to loss of self-confidence.

> I am grown to have no confidence whatever in my own taste or discernment in what is to be well or ill taken by the world or individuals. Indeed it appears that were I to make my calculations by inverse proportion I would be oftener right than I am . . .'

And yet, even with this evidence of creative unsureness, the following year saw publication of the astonishing *Private Memoirs and Confessions of a Justified Sinner*. Brilliantly it fused together all Hogg's previous kinds of fiction, yet avoided falling into any one of the categories that critics had hitherto attacked. Consider the supernatural treatment. Always there is the possibility that the devil and other supernatural apparitions exist only in the mind of Wringhim. Thus to the critic who would attack the novel for its 'diablerie and nonsense', Hogg could reply that the story was a psychological study of a religious fanatic. Conversely, if the novel were attacked as the distasteful study of a lunatic, Hogg could reply that his work was in fact a supernatural tale, a nightmare *Pilgrim's Progress*. Hogg thus hoped to ride with the hares and hounds of contemporary criticism. It may be that Lockhart, with whom Hogg had joined before in literary trickery, and to whom he dedicated his previous novel, helped him think out the plan. Lockhart's fiction of this period shows an overlap with Hogg's in its interest in morbid psychological conditions. But there is nothing in the novel that is not prefigured in many of Hogg's stories before this. It was a clever, brave, and predictably sly attempt by Hogg to break free of the 'conspiracy' of critics against him. Nevertheless, further condemnation was his reward; for example, *The Westminster Review* regretted

> . . . that the author did not employ himself better than in uselessly and disgustingly abusing his imagination, to invent wicked tricks for a mongrel devil, and blasphemous lucubrations for an insane fanatic . . .

—and generally his novel was seen as a boorish aberration and a betrayal of his 'sweet land of poetry'.

Hogg could develop no further. For the rest of his life he retreated into sketches, short ghost stories, and occasional poems. Some of the stories in his 1829 collection, *The Shepherd's Calendar*, are excellent, but they merely illustrate how grievous a loss the Scottish novel had suffered. The final sign of his demoralisation came when he was encouraged in 1832 to collect his work. It is an indication of the shallowness of contemporary criticism and of his own lack of self-confidence that he decided to savage *The Three Perils of Man*. He cut it to one third of its original length. He stripped away all the magnificent folk lore and colourful supernatural extravaganza, leaving merely the Border skirmish which he called, for the purposes of the collection, *The Siege of Roxburgh*, the only version published till 1971, when The Association for Scottish Literary Studies chose to produce the full *Perils of Man* as its inaugural annual volume.[2]

The Three Perils of Man is Hogg's most ambitious work of fiction. Its range, its variety of characters, its wealth of fast action, are all on a scale far beyond even *The Justified Sinner* or *The Brownie of Bodsbeck*. But more significant still, it marks Hogg's courageous and epic attempt to work in the oral and popular tradition which had produced the Ballads, folk-tales and legends. It also marks the passing of this tradition as a living force. Ironically, the society which had been wildly enthusiastic about MacPherson's 'translations' from the Gaelic of the ancient bard Ossian, and which marvelled at the colourful natives of 'Scottland', had little time for the genuine and living popular tradition which Hogg represented. The stimulus for Hogg's new novel-romance may owe much to Scott's marvellous poetry (in particular, *The Lay of the Last Minstrel*, 1810), or to one of the first and most influential historical epics (which Hogg would certainly know and admire for its giant folk-heroes and forceful disguised heroines), namely Jane Porter's seminal *The Scottish Chiefs* (1810). That said, Hogg is too original to be seen as seriously indebted to his predecessors. In the context of Hogg's own development, *The Three Perils of Man* represents the burgeoning of his deep interest in that other class of the supernatural, the world of 'diablerie' and demonology, the world of Barnaby's tales in 'The Wool-gatherer', or 'The Hunt of Eildon', the world which he had treated with rationalistic reservations in *The Brownie of Bodsbeck*. It is the world of Will o' Phaup, his grandfather, who had spoken on sundry occasions with the fairies; not just of 'spectres, ghosts, fairies, brownies . . . seen and heard . . . in the Glen o' Phaup', but a larger imaginative world which included long tales of 'kings, knights, fairies, kelpies . . .' where history is transmuted to legend and recorded in the Ballad idiom of timeless, racy, understated simplicity. It is important to understand how solid a foundation this is to the romance. To dismiss the work as mere cloak-and-dagger nonsense is to betray ignorance of the difference between the traditional and folk treatment of things supernatural and the neo-gothic treatment of a production such as *Melmoth the Wanderer* (1820), an ignorance that critics in Hogg's time and since have frequently betrayed in assessing his fiction. The opening of the novel is in Scott's manner:

> The days of the Stuarts . . . were the days of chivalry and romance. The long and bloody contest that the nation maintained against the whole power of England, for the recovery of its independence – of those rights which had been most unwarrantably wrested from our fathers by the greatest and most treacherous sovereign of that age – laid the foundation [of this chivalry] . . . The deeds of the Douglases, the Randolphs, and other border barons of that day, are not to be equalled . . .

This is indeed Scott-like, but there is a difference, for Hogg's unnamed editor (basing his account on a manuscript inherited from old Isaac, the curate of Mireton) is altogether more racy and terse and more recently critics like de Groot have pointed out the contrast between the modern 'editor's' voice and that of the chivalric and romanticising curate. Isaac is the biased Borderer, seeing the King of England as 'treacherous', remembering epic stories of the Randolphs and Douglases, as Barbour, Blind Hary, and the Border Ballads told them. He describes how anti-English and chivalrous games spread from barons to schoolboys, even to the very ploughmen and peasants. And thus the whole of his story of the chivalric Game of the Siege of Roxburgh is based on 'national mania', beginning an ironic commentary which runs as a major counter-theme, mocking the superficial romance of chivalry. This pattern of romance offset by realism begins immediately. First we are given the romantic and fairy-tale opening:

> There was once a noble king and queen of Scotland,

as many in that land have been, beloved by all their subjects . . . and loved and favoured them in return; and the country enjoyed happiness and peace . . .

This is Isaac's voice, but it is surely how Hogg's mother began her stories too. And the signs of a traditional mode of storytelling are abundant. There is, for example, the Ballad emphasis on number; the castle of Roxburgh – though history tells very differently –

. . . had been five times taken by the English, and three times by the Scots, in less than seventeen months, and was then held by the gallant Lord Musgrave for Richard King of England.[3]

The King of Scotland's daughter, 'of exquisite beauty and accomplishments', is 'the flower of all Scotland'. The Game of Chivalry is set in motion by the folk-tale condition Margaret lays down for the winning of her hand. The King, as in Sir Patrick Spens, 'sat gloomy and sad', and asks which of his nobles will revenge him on Musgrave, the English captain of Roxburgh castle. Predictably, the price of failure is to be the forfeiture of 'lands, castles, towns and towers'. And the richness of detail of the folk-tale is there too – Margaret's left arm swings a scarf of gold, while her right 'gleamed with bracelets of rubies and diamonds'. This is the world of romance and nobility. But as in so many folk-tales and Ballads, the action now moves on to more down-to-earth and forceful characters. We meet Sir Ringan Redhough and his Border reivers, with their blunt realism. On being asked to help in the Game, Ringan's attitude is in explicit ironic contrast with the previous chivalry.

What, man, are a'I my brave lads to lie in bloody claes that the Douglas may lie i' snow-white sheets wi' a bonny bed-fellow? . . . Tell him to keep their hands fu'; and their haunches toom, an' they'll

soon be blithe to leave the lass an' loup at the
ladle . . .

The 'flower' of Scotland is reduced to a 'bonny bed-
fellow', while romantic love is seen as a curable disease.
Women, even royal princesses, are recognised as physical
and sexual beings in contrast to the stylised paragons of
conventional romance. Ringan's recommendations are to
use 'wiles' instead of chivalric methods. And in the savage
irony of the juxtaposition of 'bloody claes' (death) and
'snow-white sheets' (sexual pleasure), the one being the
price of the other, we meet again the idiom of Sir Patrick
Spens, with its ironic juxtaposition of the 'fingers white'
and 'goud kaims' with the floating hats and feather beds at
the ballad's end. Similarly, when we meet the main 'hero' of
the romance, Charlie Scott of Yardbire, the amiable giant,
he is breaking up the courtly pattern of the Game. With
colossal strength he hurls a knight *and* his horse backwards;
and his 'tak ye that, master, for whistling o' Sundays'
exactly sums up the reductive idiom of much of Hogg's
anti-romantic theme. It is all in the peasant tradition of
wry humour and worldliness found in the Ballads, the
chapbooks, and the *fabliau* tales of medieval Europe, with
something of the pace and ferocity of Smollett's action;
while, to late twentieth-century readers, it must surely
anticipate postmodernist notions of parody and subversion and Bakhtinian carnival. But it would certainly have
seemed 'vulgar' to most of Hogg's literary contemporaries.
There is one question to be asked concerning Hogg's
contrast of these two worlds. How sure is he of his
artistic intentions and of his own sympathies as he deals
with Douglas and Musgrave on the one hand, Redhough
and Charlie on the other? While it is valid to identify an
ironic attitude to chivalry in Hogg's comments through
Redhough, the Chisholm family, or Charlie, it may be
wrong to conclude that Hogg intended us to mock at the
world of kings and knights *in toto*. Sometimes it seems that
real sympathy for Douglas or Margaret is intended, and
that certain aspects of their chivalrous undertaking are
at least countenanced by him. The opposing attitudes

of Isaac the curate and the 'editor' may go some way
to explaining these inconsistencies of moral and artistic
position, with Hogg (as so often) utilising fictional nar-
rators to safeguard himself against charges of bad taste
and loss of control. Contemporary defenders of Hogg
would argue that it is precisely Hogg's refusal to allow
binary opposites to destroy each other in his fiction, that
is his unique strength. Contrarily, the irony is perhaps
simply less controlled, more local and episodic, than that,
say, in Scott's *Waverley* and may reflect Hogg's own
divided loyalties and insecurity about his social position.
Whatever the source of this insecurity, it blurs the dividing
line between straightforward presentation of romance and
ironic comment upon it. But it would be a parsimonious
reading of Hogg's romance that failed to realise that its
unity lies not in aspects of plot structure, or carefully
planned revelation of character through action, but in
something looser, larger, and much more uncommon
in the nineteenth century. C.S. Lewis made a special
plea that another Scottish writer of profound and vivid
imagination, George MacDonald, should be assessed on
the special consideration that his work went far beyond the
conventions of fiction, to become myth. Hogg is just such
a special case. And the strange unity that his work possesses
comes, not from qualities of myth (although it occasionally
attains to this) but from its sheer extravagance and fantastic
gusto and the obvious enjoyment of the author in allowing
his imagination free rein. Thus most readers will not object
to the ridiculous disguises of Princess Margaret and Lady
Jane Howard when they arrive at the Chisholm's house;
and thus Hogg gets away with the more serious ambiguity
underlying the later scene when Margaret, discovering who
'Sir Jasper' is, sends her prisoner, in the care of Charlie
Scott, to Douglas.

This is a typically difficult and ambiguous passage. On
one side it would seem that Hogg is ironically reducing his
knights and ladies to the level of barbarians and fishwives,
as when the two girls coarsely and spitefully attack each
other and become merely spoiled brats. Similarly Douglas,
knowing full well the identity of his captive, ignores her

appeals to his 'honour and generosity as a knight', threatens to strip her and later promises to cause her to be 'exhibited in a state not to be named' on a stage erected in sight of the western tower, raped publicly ('disgrace which barbarians only could have conceived'), 'and then to have her nose cut off, her eyes put out, and her beauteous frame otherwise disfigured'. How are we to read this? It is tempting to find here a rich anti-romantic irony; but on the other hand there is plenty of description of Douglas and the ladies as genuinely noble and romantic creatures, while the end of the novel has Charlie and Sir Ringan rewarded by these very princes and ladies. Perhaps, however, we should read such noble descriptions and endings as parodic? Perhaps, too, the final case for the greatness of the work lies beyond consideration of the sophistication or otherwise of the ironic structure, in the sheer carnival zest of the presentation and the speed of the metamorphoses and reversals of fortune. In the end the main grounds for the tale's worth may lie in its qualities as a tale to be told as Hogg's mother told him tales.

The irony is recognisably deliberate and fine at many other points. There can be no doubt of Hogg's meaning and where his sympathies lie in the hanging of the servants of Lady Jane. The Game of Roxburgh is death to the English peasant Heaton and his friends; the spoiled heiresses of Scotland and England have more or less murdered many like him by the time the Game is over. Immediately following this, as though to prove the point, is the passage involving the old Border fisherman, Sandy Yellowlees, one of Hogg's well-loved, independent heroes. Hogg tricks us into identifying with Sandy. His peasant humour, his comic fears when he starts finding sirloins of beef on the end of his fishing-line, and the fact that he is permitted to use the dramatic monologue to tell his story – a method Hogg generally reserves for favourites – contribute towards our shock at his sudden death and our revulsion against the chivalrous siege, when, with the sword-stroke suddenness of the Ballads, Sandy is captured and hung from the walls of Roxburgh castle.

And Part One ends on this cynical note. War is no longer

a game, if it ever has been. This peril has been shown to have a horrific and deadly reality. Savagery and madness dominate the starving castle. A group of mutineers are 'hanged like dogs, amid shouts of execration, and their bodies flung into a pit'; the remainder would eat their own flesh rather than surrender. Chivalry has become nightmare. Hogg now draws the English under Musgrave in a stylised, grotesque fashion, portraying them as bestial gargoyles, the very opposite of paragons of courtly love.

> There they sat, a silent circle, in bitter and obstinate rumination. Their brows were plaited down, so as to almost cover their eyes; their underlips were bent upwards and every mouth shaped like a curve, and their arms were crossed on their breasts, while every man's right hand instinctively rested on the hilt of his sword . . . a wild gleam of ferocity fired every haggard countenance.

The second part of the novel, that concerning the comic embassy's journey to the wizard Sir Michael Scott, introduces the peril of witchcraft (more properly the peril of wizards and warlockry) to the romance. This section releases Hogg from the juxtaposition of romantic and realistic attitudes. Indeed the term 'release' well describes the extended nightmare, comic and fantastic, which follows with the pace and spirit of Dunbar's 'Dance of the Sevin Deidly Synnis' and Burns's 'Tam o' Shanter'. Sir Ringan, needing to know something of the outcome of the struggle before he decides which side to favour, sends his representatives to find out. His embassy is grotesque, a collection of oddities and misfits freakish enough to please the unnatural tastes of Michael Scott. He sends

> As a bard, or minstrel. . . . Colley Carol, a man that is fit to charm the spirits out of the heart of the earth, or the bowels of the cloud . . . As a man of crabbed wit and endless absurdity . . . the Deil's Tam: As a true natural and moral philosopher, the Laird o' the Peatstacknowe: As one versed in all the mysteries of

religion, and many mysteries besides, or some tell
lies, we can send the gospel friar. All these are men
of spirit, and can handle the sword and the bow . . .
And as a man of unequalled strength and courage,
and a guard and captain over all the rest, we can send
Charlie o' Yardbire – and I will defy all the kingdoms
of Europe to send out sic another quorum either to
emperor, Turk, wizard, or the devil himself.

Add the captive maiden Delany, and the beautiful boy
Elias, and the embassy is complete. The motley crew on
its fantastic quest may be enjoyed equally as a parody of
the usual reiving party and as a travesty of a Canterbury
pilgrimage. The story has now become a mock-epic.
Not only is the medieval device of a journey used to
comic effect, but sometimes even the various characters,
the Deil's Tam especially, seem to be almost medieval
personifications of human qualities. Tam, standing for
Greed and Famine in one, takes part in a Dunbar-like
dance of sin, although, unlike Dunbar, Hogg mixes good
and bad in his increasingly wild movement. Adventure
follows adventure with the speed of Smollett; violence flares
suddenly and dies as quickly. There is little complexity of
situation now, apart from the pretty obvious hints that the
dour and mysterious friar is more than he seems. And
yet – probably because the embassy is mainly made up
of Borderers and dominated by the refreshingly unusual
hero, Charlie Scott – there is complete clarity of character
delineation within the group, even down to the mule, wilful
and almost human (and considered by Lockhart to be the
real hero of the romance).

We begin to have a feeling of significant completeness
in this group of contrasting characters. A pattern emerges,
with Charlie as Honesty and Strength, the Friar as Faith,
Gibby as Clownish Weakness (for which he is claimed
as temporary servant by Scott), and Tam as Greed and
Fleshly Lust (he signs his soul away to the devil). The
framework is at once definite and yet loose enough to
permit the contrasting idioms – the Friar's Chaldee style,
a mixture of the biblical and Ossianic, the poet's flowery

excesses, Charlie's blunt but compassionate realism, and Tam's crude, yet horrifically honest directness. We have moved from the world of chivalry, with its rules and conditions, to a world where these rules are subverted and turned upside-down; in this carnival of contrasts, Michael Scott and his master the devil will be the Lords of a Dance of Misrule. Hogg achieves the transition by capturing the unnatural atmosphere around Scott's castle of Aikwood at sunset:

> It was one of those dead calm winter evenings, not uncommon at that season, when the slightest noise is heard at a distance, and the echoes are all abroad. As they drew near to the huge dark looking pile, silence prevailed among them more and more. All was so still that even the beautiful valley seemed a waste. There was no bird whistling at the plough; no cattle or sheep grazing on the holms of Aikwood; no bustle of servants, kinsmen, of their grooms, as at the castles of other knights. It seemed as if the breath of the enchanter, or his eye, had been infectious, and had withered all within its influence, whether of vegetable, animal, or human life. The castle itself scarcely seemed to be the abode of man; the massy gates were all locked . . . and there was only one small piping smoke issuing from one of the turrets . . .

From now on metamorphoses occur on every second page. Gourlay is transformed by Scott by way of punishment into a hare, and frenziedly pursued by the attendant devils Prim, Prig and Pricker, who transform themselves with bewildering speed. An army of retainers marches from the wainscotting of the deserted castle to serve breakfast to the embassy, who are struck by their 'rattan faces'. And in one of the funniest of these transformations, the company are led from the raw and misty morning up into a tower room which blazes with light; the table offers a beautiful smoking sirloin of beef, with a gentle brown crust around it, and half swimming in gravy. Most of the embassy start without saying grace:

. . . the friar, later to enter, lifted up his spread hands, closed his eyes, and leaning forward above the beef so closely that he actually breathed upon it, felt the flavour of health and joy ascending by his nostrils [and] in that fervent and respectful attitude he blessed the beef in the name of Jesus. Never had blessing a more dolorous effect. When the friar opened his eyes, the beef was gone. There was nothing left on the wooden plate before him but a small insignificant thing resembling the joint of a frog's leg, or that of a rat; and perhaps two or three drops of gravy.

Metamorphosis dominates this part, from the curious use of the magic lantern (which, in its balancing with Michael Scott's genuine wizardry anticipates Hogg's juxtapositioning of rational explanation with supernatural horror in the devilish apparition by the Salisbury crags in *The Justified Sinner*) to the final banquet with the devil and Michael Scott, where hags with withered chops are transformed into beauteous ladies, and the men of the embassy into bellowing bulls. Slowly, from the apparently formless, though vastly entertaining, riot of diablerie and nightmare, the theme of this part emerges. We are witnessing an epic, yet still comic, struggle between the powers of light and dark. First of all the lieutenants meet. The monstrous Gourlay, Scott's seneschal-zombie, possessed of superhuman strength, clashes with the benevolent giant Charlie Scott. Their epic battle takes place in a vault where the giant bones of a previous victim lie gleaming in the moonlight. With an almost archetypal clash, like that of Beowulf and Grendel, they meet in titanic battle. Gourlay's back and ribs sound as they crack; his face grows hideous; they fall ponderously amidst the bones of the giant skeleton. The entire situation recalls Bunyan's *Pilgrim's Progress*, with Gourlay as Giant Despair.

Following this preparatory round, we anticipate the confrontation of the friar, that holy man of mysterious depths, and the satanic wizard. Both have epic features, but paradoxically it is Michael Scott who commands attention and even admiration, with his dignity, his respect for courage, his occasional sympathy, as when he hears the friar's tragic tale, contrasting with his unholy glee or despair, or his inability, like Faust, to repent. There is greatness in Hogg's imagination here; Michael is conceived on a superhuman scale, as is the account at the end of the romance of his cataclysmic exit from this world. His battle with the friar lives up to our expectations. Indeed, it may not be stretching the scene too much to find a deeper layer within it. The friar uses science: the magic lantern, tricks with chemicals, and finally his superbly fitting and comic removal of the monster Gourlay by blowing him up with gunpowder (which, as the exiled Roger Bacon, he is supposed to have invented). In contrast Scott uses sheer wizardry and the power of his master, Satan. Do we see here the division in Hogg's own allegiance to nineteenth-century rationalism and scientific achievement on the one hand, and to a belief in the supernatural forces of the past on the other, as in the subtler psychological and supernatural ambiguity of *The Justified Sinner?* In any event, although the friar is allowed a kind of victory, there is no doubt that Hogg's deepest sympathies are with Michael, goaded by the friar beyond endurance, to the point where he almost overstretches his remit from the devil.

Hogg's imagination blends here in superb fashion with his awareness of Border legend. He postulates a single and rounded Eildon hill, a great cone, prior to the battle. The wizard orders Prim, Prig and Pricker to twist it into three (as, of course, it is now). The ensuing storm is a colossal reversal of nature (significantly, it is the storm in which the Scots were attacked by the maddened English at the end of the first part). What makes this sensational 'diablerie' so acceptable is the comic but realistic and matter-of-fact way Hogg tells it all. It is exactly right for the extravagant, richly coloured imaginary world he has made, and sustains the supernatural so well that the effect has nothing of the neo-gothic melodrama of *The Castle of Otranto*. Hogg is saved from this by the fact that his own rich imagination is based firmly on folk tradition, which he uses in a vital and creative way. The Eildon hill scene is the best of these. Hogg's picture of the pallid, unnatural dawn following the turmoil of the night, with the friar and Charlie frozen in astonishment at the three peaks towering over new rivers is a magnificent climax, almost mythic in quality. His imagination sees it surely, and follows through without faltering:

> It was a scene of wonder not to be understood, and awfully impressive. The two rivers flowed down their respective valleys, and met below the castle like two branching seas, and every little streamlet roared and foamed like a river. The hills had a wan, bleached appearance, many of the trees of the forest were shivered, and towering up against the eastern sky, there stood the three . . . hills . . . of Eildon, where before there was but one . . .

The next part, which begins with the discovery that the embassy and Scott are trapped in the castle tower, perhaps looms too large in the overall story. It may be that Hogg, remembering his great success with a competition of raconteurs in *The Queen's Wake*, his long poem of 1813, tried to repeat it here. He certainly loved the exercise of adopting different styles and personae in storytelling (witness *The Spy* and the three points of view in *The Justified Sinner*) and poetry (witness his *Poetic Mirror* of 1816). Or it may simply be the case that he had some of these short stories already written, and decided to incorporate them, using the simple expedient of Scott's proposal, that they should relieve their plight by storytelling, the best storyteller winning Delany, the worst being eaten by the others. That said, it can be argued that these stories, like those of the *Canterbury Tales*, play a part in telling us something about the tellers. The friar's tale solves the mystery of the strange affinity between himself and the innocent Delany – she is the daughter of his sweetheart. And the Ossianic style has the function of contrasting refreshingly with the romance's usual, more direct idiom. Hogg's romance is loose enough in structure, and fantastic enough in content, to stand casual storytelling and highly coincidental revelations like this. Indeed, the story has a certain tragic pathos and power. It reveals yet again Charlie's sentimental nature. It causes the poet to change his mind about hating the friar. And when Delany reveals she is the friar's sweetheart's daughter, 'even Master Michael Scott once drew the back of his hand across his eyes . . .'.

In stark contrast is the savage tale told by the Laird of Peatstacknowe: harsh, unsentimental, chapbookish in its crude caricature of Marion's son Jock, who 'fought to be at meat, and Marion to keep him from it; and many hard clouts and claws there passed'. Jock is a recurrent type in Hogg's stories. There is something unnatural in his demonic hunger and his utter amorality, an unnatural and obsessive motivation which sets him alongside Basil Lee, or Merodach, the Brownie of the Black Haggs, or Robert Wringhim, the justified sinner. And Hogg is unsurpassed when it comes to describing sordid violence with sickeningly convincing detail. Jock's master wants to kick and beat him, and then murder him; he drags him to the lamb Jock has murdered, where again the remains, like those of a violated daughter, outrage him; he throws him down, kneels on him, and punches till Jock 'got hold of his master's cheek with his left hand, and his nails being very long, was like to tear it off. His master capered up with his head . . .' – and, unable to free himself, gets out his knife to cut off Jock's hand and then his head. The savagery is conveyed in the factual imagery, the bald statement of fact; the battle is 'like a battle between an inveterate terrier and a bull dog', and is ended suddenly and shockingly when Jock (whom we remember is, after all, little more than a child)

> . . . whipped out his own knife, his old dangerous friend, and struck it into the goodman's belly to the haft. The moment he received the wound he sprang up as if he had been going to fly into the air, uttered a loud roar, and fell back above his dead pet lamb . . .

The scene recalls the violent end of the sensual fox in Robert Henryson's 'The Fox, the Wolf, and the Cadger'. The slightly comic tone accentuates the violence (Jock uses his 'dangerous friend' to kill the goodman) as does the understatement. And, as in Henryson's *Fables*, the violence is all the more shocking, coming as it does in a pastoral setting; Jock's anxious mother, the scene in the goodman's cottage of the family eating, the shepherding, all assert the rhythms of peaceful countryside quietly repeating themselves. The violence is in horrible contrast to all this, as are the sensual descriptions of Jock's hunger and the goodman's nauseating and unnatural grief over his pet lamb. And all this is embodied in the main development of the surrounding story. Hogg reveals that Jock, this monster of carnal hunger, this unnatural child-demon, is in fact the Deil's Tam. With one easy move Tam's evil takes on a new depth and his fate grows darker. And again the reactions of the others reveal their characters. Charlie thinks it a good tale – 'o' the kind', he stresses; the poet, sensitive plant that he is, accepts the lamb-daughter equation, and is horrified at the eating of 'the flower of all the flock . . . her lovely form that's fairer than the snow'. And in fact many of the others accept this symbolism too; as Michael Scott says:

> The maid Delany is the favourite lamb, whom he wished you to kill and feast on and I am the Goodman whom you are to stick afterwards . . .

Charlie Scott's tale is a good example of Hogg's mastery of the story of action. Charlie Scott of Yardbire is a Border type Hogg loves, akin to the homely, honest, yet powerful giant hero of *The Brownie of Bodsbeck*, Wat o' Chapelhope. His tale illustrates the same qualities of stern bravery and feudal devotion that are found in the ballad of 'The Battle of Otterbourne'. It also serves to reveal Charlie's goodness, in his saving of a child in a raid – who turns out to be the poet. Thus like the others it relates to the main theme, in that it extends our knowledge of the characters in the embassy and supplies answers to Hogg's beloved mysteries. Its merits are such as recur abundantly in Hogg's story-telling, notably in the later 'Mary Montgomery' and 'Wat Pringle o' the Yair'. Then Tam's tale reveals that he is the 'Marion's

Jock' of Gibby's story. His character as personified Greed and Lust is completed by it. The story, with its savagery and cruelty and anti-heroic qualities, provides a contrast to Charlie's tale of healthy heroism, in the same way that Basil Lee and Robert Wringhim are utter opposites to that most natural of men, Wat o' Chapelhope. These types are recurrent polarities in Hogg's fiction, and Tam's story is one of Hogg's many horrifying pictures of amoral, lustful and utterly wicked men.

Nevertheless, although many of the tales are good in themselves (the poet's, ironically enough, being the weakest), and taken together contribute towards the development of relationships amongst the group, they do distract us from the main, hitherto swift-moving plot. And while Hogg may in this authorial self-indulgence be mocking the historical fiction of his time, it is nevertheless a relief for the reader, as well as for the trapped embassy, when Dan Chisholm and his Border friends arrive at the castle. Hogg now links his two projects, and we see Scott's wizardry through fresh eyes. Dan asks:

> Do nae ye ken that the world's amaist turned upside down sin ye left us? The trees hae turned their wrang ends upmost – the waters hae drowned the towns, and the hills hae been rent asunder . . . Tis thought that there has been a siege o' hell . . .

But the reign of Disorder is not yet over: Dan and Charlie now meet a mysterious friend of Sir Michael Scott. Unlike the friend Gilmartin, who is sinister from his very bland sophistication, this devil is in the best manner of Hogg's and Ballad demonology.

> It appeared about double the human size . . . its whole body being of the colour of bronze, as well as the crown upon its head. The skin appeared shrivelled, as if seared with fire, but over that there was a polish that glittered and shone. Its eyes had no pupil nor circle of white; they appeared like burning lamps deep in their sockets; and when it gazed, they rolled round . . . There was a hairy mantle that hung

down and covered its feet . . . every finger terminated
in a long crooked talon that seemed of the colour of
molten gold . . . It had neither teeth, tongue, nor
throat, its whole inside being hollow, and the colour
of burning glass . . .

It pursues them, vomiting burning sulphur, and, as the
nightmare climax of Disorder is reached, 'immense snakes,
bears, tigers and lions, all with eyes like burning candles'
threaten the heroes. Hogg here draws from sources as
diverse as Bunyan, the Ballads and contemporary Gothic
novels.

This supernatural climax, with its strange, glittering
beauty of imagery, so close to the clarity and concrete
visualisation of the Ballads, proves completely Hogg's
right to claim that he was 'king of the mountain and fairy
school' of poets. He achieves new heights of imagination in
its description of how Dan meets the Devil with his agents,
disguised as a Black Abbot and all on terrible white horses;
of how the Devil wanders in a village as a great shaggy
black dog, terrifying peasants; of how Dan and his friends
undergo a nightmare ride through the firmament; of how
the devil plays on the weakness of Charlie and his friends
for drink and lovely women, seducing their senses with a
superficial beauty such as Dunbar exposes in 'The Two
Mariit Wemen and the Wedo', with the essential foulness
of this beauty revealed when the drunken Borderers realise
that the lovely girls are hags with rotten teeth and wizened
faces. The Devil, in a final, glorious flourish of Disorder,
finishes the long dance by transforming them all into bulls.
All this is told with a dry attention to details, along with a
strange and beautiful description of the trappings of evil.
As in 'The Daemon Lover', with its fascination for gold
and silver, and the 'taffetie' of the sails, Hogg sees clearly
and enjoys the rich colours of his devils. This delight in
the physical and supernatural grotesque is a counterpoint
to the etiquette of chivalry elsewhere in the romance; the
horrors are vivid, but accompanied by a sense of release
through carnal and carnival enjoyment, so that the reader
almost shares the 'hellish delight' of the withered hags.

Yet for all this, Hogg does not forget more homely and human matters, such as Charlie's consideration for his horse, Corby, or his honest joy at realising that his Border lord and friends had not forgotten him. It is Charlie, of course, who characteristically persists through all terrors to secure the prophecy for Sir Ringan which is the point of his embassy, while Gibby is claimed by Sir Michael to replace Gourlay, and 'the Deil's Tam' fulfils his destiny in a scene which foreshadows the nightmare climax of *The Justified Sinner*.

There is nothing in the final part of the narrative to match this richness of fantasy and diablerie, but the return to the Siege of Roxburgh has at least two episodes – the affair of Dan Chisholm and the cattle skins, and the taking of the castle by Borderers disguised as cattle – which for sheer speed of action, racy dialogue and character, are as enjoyable as any of Hogg's short stories. This last episode marks the final irony of the Siege, for Douglas at last confesses that the chivalrous Game has beaten him. He has to descend to 'wiles' and beg Sir Ringan's aid. The chivalrous pattern has finally been wrecked. Musgrave, the dour defender of the besieged castle, has not been taken captive but has killed himself. Princess Margaret is believed to have been hanged. If Douglas finally obtains his desire, it is not in his intended chivalric way, nor by his own doing. And Lady Howard becomes the wife of the homely Borderer Charlie!

One aspect of this outcome that Hogg emphasises is its unity with the demonology of the middle parts. Sir Ringan acts because of the success of Charlie's embassy and Sir Michael's (and the devil's) advice; and his ruse of disguising his men as cattle connects with the metamorphosis of Charlie and his men into bulls. The wizard of the north and the devil have, in a manner, kept faith till the end. Hogg was aware of the strain imposed by his range of plots and characters, and he thought it necessary to make his 'editor' remind the reader that the final ironic burst of Border warfare which finishes the siege was

. . . wholly owing to the weird read by the great

enchanter master Michael Scott, so that though the reader must have felt that Isaac kept his guests too long in that horrible place the Castle of Aikwood, it will now appear that not one iota of that long interlude of his could have been omitted; for till the weird was read, and the transformation consummated the embassy could not depart – and unless these had been effected, the castle could not have been taken . . .

Thus the perils of War and Witchcraft are shown to be inextricably linked in the events and shape of the novel. There is of course a third peril, that of Women. While this peril is handled with humour and ambiguity, it is still true that women are throughout dangerous to men. They prompt to war, they disguise themselves, they turn out to be withered hags, and they use such deception for their own ends. They are also, however, given as rewards. Charlie, because of his goodness and strength, is given Lady Jane Howard, Douglas gains Princess Margaret, and Delaney is the prize for the storytelling contest. Hogg's fiction continually, and unusually for his time, emphasises the complexity and reality of women; and while the three heroic virgins of the poet's tale may be little more than the idealised feminine creatures of chivalric romance, in contrast Margaret, Lady Jane, and the Chisholm daughters, have full, sensual, and highly unconventional roles to play. The cross-dressing of these girls complicates both the action and the conventional notions of femininity presented by Isaac and the poet. Douglas's elfin page, Colin/Margaret, is one of Hogg's most teasing inventions, with his/her exploitation of male/female codes. The transformations of men are thus balanced with transformations of women, an important part of the rich and complex patterning of Hogg's epic.

In the end Hogg does succeed in holding together his three perils in this loose-woven romance, despite his many authorial and 'editorial' problems. His 'editor' had likened his problem in controlling his multitude of characters and situations to that of the waggoner who has to take his load up a steep hill in stages, going back to collect what had to be left behind. It is precisely the want of his waggoner's patience that has been most objected to in Hogg's immense undertaking. He tells us in *The Domestic Manners of Sir Walter Scott* that he and the great novelist discussed the romance, Scott accusing him of rushing impatiently on in random fashion, and thus spoiling a potentially good tale. Whether we agree with Scott or not, Hogg's statement in the same place about his method of composition is highly significant. He told Scott that when he started the first line of a tale or a novel, he never knew what the second was to be, and that this continued throughout. But he made an important qualification:

> When my tale is traditionary, the work is easy, as
> I then see my way before me, though the tradition
> be ever so short, but in all my prose works of the
> imagination, knowing little of the world, I sail on
> without star or compass.

In spite of the last statement there is a real sense of direction in *The Three Perils of Man*, and an impressive enough destination, but it is indeed at the several points where he has tradition to help him that Hogg sees his way best. These are found especially in the scenes set in the Borders and the scenes relating to Sir Michael Scott. It is in working out a path between one such familiar point and another that his uncertainties show. Yet paradoxically it is in the originality of such working-out which makes revaluation of Hogg in the twentieth century such an exciting and on-going process. Seen in the lights of post-structuralist criticism, revisions of Romanticism, Bakhtinian readings – and even feminist theories – Hogg's fiction generally, and not least *The Three Perils of Man*, reveals striking and challenging features which command respect and multi-faceted reassessment. And one particular implication of Hogg's statement few readers will be disposed to accept – seeming to give all the credit for his success to tradition, he belittles his own imagination and is grossly unfair to himself and his romance. For when one has pointed out Hogg's awareness of the Ballad and folk-tale tradition, when one has drawn parallels with *The*

Pilgrim's Progress or the chapbooks, one vital factor remains to astonish the critic. It is the sheer fecundity, immensity and colour of Hogg's imagination, which, working on all kinds of traditional material, creates a living world which needs no other justification than its own unique blend of irony, racy humour, fantasy and romance.

The final ironic reduction comes with the reader's dawning realisation (confirmed when a map of the Borders is consulted), after following the epic journey of the comic embassy through danger, darkness and leagues of Border mountains, that their entire romantic journey has been something of a storm in a teacup, and that a daylight's ride through passes in the hills would easily have sufficed to take Charlie and his companions the shortest route to Sir Michael Scott's castle. Hogg of course is fully aware of his grotesque inflation of the distance and the dangers: since when have the great journeys of imagination taken the shortest route? And conjecture as to the extent of Hogg's ironies leads the reader to a final and intriguing consideration concerning this troubled, love-hate journey to seek the advice of that medieval wizard of the north, Sir Michael Scott: given Walter Scott's complex and sometimes dubiously productive relationship with the shepherd, is Hogg playing games yet again, in variation of the *Chaldee Manuscript*, with his own quest for advice regarding his future development from his illustrious contemporary, that other wizard of the Borders and the north?

The achievement has no parallel. It is the last major effort of the dying, centuries-old tradition which produced the ballads, but it is something more. It is wonderful and refreshing entertainment, and is now recognised as an outstanding contribution, along with Hogg's other novels, stories and poetry, to the traditions of Scottish literature which the twentieth century has been recovering ever since.

Douglas Gifford

NOTES

1 This is the account of Robert Chambers, who attended at least one of these gatherings in his brother William Chambers's *Memoir of Robert Chambers*, Edinburgh, 1872, p. 258.

2 From Hogg's letters of the early 1820s it would appear that he at first thought the romance one of his happiest ventures – 'in my best stile indeed better than my best'. But by the time of the *Domestic Manners* (1834) his self-confidence was severely shaken by Scott's criticism. In addition to the self-deprecating account of the romance there, he says in his *Reminiscences of Former Days:*

> In 1822, perceiving that I was likely to run short of money, I began and finished in the course of a few months, 'The Three Perils of Man, viz. War, Women, and Witchcraft!' Lord preserve us! what a medley I made of it! for I never in my life rewrote a page of prose; and being impatient to get hold of some of Messrs. Longman and Co.'s money or their bills, which were the same, I dashed on, and mixed up what might have been made one of the best historical tales our country ever produced, such a mass of diablerie as retarded the main story, and rendered the whole perfectly ludicrous.

3 For an account of Hogg's use of history in the novel, see the Introduction to the Notes at the end of this volume (p. 540).

CHAPTER ONE

> There was a king, and a courteous king,
>   And he had a daughter sae bonnie;
> And he lo'ed that maiden aboon a' thing
>   I' the bonnie, bonnie halls o' Binnorie.
>
> But wae be to thee, thou warlock wight,
>   My malison come o'er thee,
> For thou hast undone the bravest knight,
>   That ever brak bread i' Binnorie!
>
> *Old Song*

THE DAYS OF the Stuarts, kings of Scotland, were the days of chivalry and romance. The long and bloody contest that the nation maintained against the whole power of England, for the recovery of its independence – of those rights which had been most unwarrantably wrested from our fathers by the greatest and most treacherous sovereign of that age, with the successful and glorious issue of the war, laid the foundation for this spirit of heroism, which appears to have been at its zenith about the time that the Stuarts first acquired the sovereignty of the realm. The deeds of the Douglasses, the Randolphs, and other border barons of that day, are not to be equalled by any recorded in our annals; while the reprisals that they made upon the English, in retaliation for former injuries, enriched both them and their followers, and rendered their appearance splendid and imposing to a degree that would scarcely now gain credit. It was no uncommon thing for a Scottish earl then to visit the Court at the head of a thousand horsemen, all splendidly mounted in their military accoutrements; and many of these gentlemen of rank and family. In court and camp, feats of arms were the topic of conversation, and the only die that stamped the character of a man of renown, either with the fair, the monarch, or the chiefs of the land. No gentleman of noble blood would pay his addresses to his mistress, until he had broken a spear with the knights of the rival nation, surprised a strong-hold, or driven a prey from the kinsmen of the Piercies, the Musgraves, or the Howards. As in all other things that run to a fashionable extremity, the fair sex took the lead in encouraging these deeds of chivalry, till it came to have the appearance of a national mania. There were tournaments at the castle of every feudal baron and knight. The ploughmen and drivers were often discovered, on returning from the fields, hotly engaged in a tilting bout with their goads and plough-staves; and even the little boys and maidens on the village green, each well mounted on a crooked stick, were daily engaged in the combat, and riding rank and file against each other, breaking their tiny weapons in the furious onset, while the mimic fire flashed from their eyes. Then was the play of *Scots and English* begun, a favourite one on the school green to this day. Such was the spirit of the age, not only in Scotland, but over all the countries of southern Europe, when the romantic incidents occurred on which the following tale is founded. It was taken down from the manuscript of an old Curate, who had spent the latter part of his life in the village of Mireton, and was given to the present Editor by one of those tenants who now till the valley where stood the richest city of this realm.

There were once a noble king and queen of Scotland, as many in that land have been—. In this notable tell-tale manner, does old Isaac, the curate, begin his narrative. It will be seen in the sequel, that this king and queen were Robert the Second and his consort—. They were beloved by all their subjects, (continues he,) and loved and favoured them in return; and the country enjoyed happiness and peace, all save a part adjoining to the borders of England. The strong castle of Roxburgh, which was the key of that country, had been five times taken by the English, and three times by the Scots, in less than seventeen months, and was then held by the gallant Lord Musgrave for Richard king of England.

Our worthy king had one daughter, of exquisite beauty

and accomplishments; the flower of all Scotland, and her name was Margaret. This princess was courted by many of the principal nobility of the land, who all eagerly sought an alliance with the royal family, not only for the additional honour and power which it conferred on them and their posterity, but for the personal charms of the lady, which were of that high eminence, that no man could look on her without admiration. This emulation of the lords kept the court of King Robert full of bustle, homage, and splendour. All were anxious to frustrate the designs of their opponents, and to forward their own; so that high jealousies were often apparent in the sharp retorts, stern looks, and nodding plumes of the rival wooers; and as the princess had never disclosed her partiality for one above another, it was judged that Robert scarcely dared openly to give the preference to any of them. A circumstance, however, soon occurred, which brought the matter fairly to the test.

It happened on a lovely summer day, at the end of July, that three and twenty noble rivals for the hand of the beauteous princess were all assembled at the palace of Linlithgow; but the usual gaiety, mirth, and repartee did not prevail; for the king had received bad tidings that day, and he sat gloomy and sad.

Musgrave had issued from the castle of Roxburgh, had surprised the castle of Jedburgh, and taken prisoner William, brother to the lord of Galloway; slain many loyal Scottish subjects, and wasted Teviotdale with fire and sword. The conversation turned wholly on the state of affairs on the border, and the misery to which that country was exposed by the castle of Roxburgh remaining in the hands of the English; and at length the king enquired impatiently, how it came that Sir Philip Musgrave had surprised the castle this last time, when his subjects were so well aware of their danger.

The earl of Hume made answer, that it was wholly an affair of chivalry, and one of the bravest and noblest acts that ever was performed. Musgrave's mistress, the lady Jane Howard, of the blood royal, and the greatest heiress of the north of England, had refused to see him, unless he gained back his honour by the retaking of that perilous castle, and keeping it against all force, intercession, or guile, till the end of the Christmas holidays. That he had accomplished the former in the most gallant stile; and, from the measures that he had adopted, and the additional fortifications that he had raised, there was every possibility that he would achieve the latter.

'What,' said the king, 'must the spirit of chivalry then be confined to the country of our enemies? Have our noble dames of Scotland less heroism in their constitutions than those of the south? Have they fewer of the charms of beauty, or have their lovers less spirit to fulfil their commands? By this sceptre in my right hand, I will give my daughter, the princess Margaret, to the knight who shall take that castle of Roxburgh out of the hands of the English before the expiry of the Christmas holidays.'

Every lord and knight was instantly on his feet to accept the proposal, and every one had his hand stretched towards the royal chair for audience, when Margaret arose herself, from the king's left hand, where she was seated, and flinging her left arm backward, on which swung a scarf of gold, and stretching her right, that gleamed with bracelets of rubies and diamonds, along the festive board, 'Hold, my noble lords,' said she; 'I am too deeply interested here not to have a word to say. The grandchild of the great Bruce must not be given away to every adventurer without her own approval. Who among you will venture his honour and his life for me?' Every knight waved his right hand aloft and dashed it on the hilt of his sword, eyeing the graceful attitude and dignified form of the princess with raptures of delight. 'It is well,' continued she, 'the spirit of chivalry *has not* deserted the Scottish nation – hear me then: My father's vow shall stand; I will give my hand in marriage to the knight who shall take that castle for the king, my father, before the expiry of the Christmas holidays, and rid our border of that nest of reavers; but with this proviso only, that, in case of his attempting and failing in the undertaking, he shall forfeit all his lands, castles, towns, and towers to me, which shall form a part of my marriage-portion to his rival. Is it fit that the daughter of a king should be given up or won as circumstances may suit, or that the risk should all be on one side? Who would be so unreasonable as expect it? This, then, with the concurrence of my lord and father, is my determination, and by it will I stand.'

The conditions were grievously hard, and had a damping and dismal effect on the courtly circle. The light of every eye deadened into a dim and sullen scowl. It was a deed that promised glory and renown to adventure their blood for such a dame – to win such a lady as the Princess of Scotland: But, to give up their broad lands and castles to enrich a hated rival, was an obnoxious consideration, and what in all likelihood was to be the issue. When all the forces of the land had been unable to take the castle by storm, where was the probability that any of them was now to succeed? None accepted the conditions. Some remained silent; some shook their heads, and muttered incoherent mumblings; others strode about the room, as if in private consultation.

'My honoured liege,' said Lady Margaret, 'none of the lords or knights of your court have the spirit to accept of my conditions. Be pleased then to grant me a sufficient force. I shall choose the officers for them myself, and I engage to take the castle of Roxburgh before Christmas. I will disappoint the bloody Musgrave of his bride; and the world shall see whether the charms of Lady Jane Howard or those of Margaret Stuart shall rouse their admirers to deeds of the most desperate valour. Before the Christmas bells have tolled, that shall be tried on the rocks, in the rivers, in the air, and the bowels of the earth. In the event of my enterprise proving successful, all the guerdon that I ask is, the full and free liberty of giving my hand to whom I will. It shall be to no one that is here.' And so saying she struck it upon the table, and again took her seat at the king's left hand.

Every foot rung on the floor with a furious tramp, in unison with that stroke of the princess's hand. The taunt was not to be brooked. Nor was it. The haughty blood of the Douglasses could bear it no longer. James, the gallant earl of Douglas and Mar, stepped forward from the circle. 'My honoured liege, and master,' said he, 'I have not declined the princess's offer – beshrew my heart if ever it embraced such a purpose. But the stake is deep, and a moment's consideration excusable. I have considered, and likewise decided. I accept the lady's proposals. With my own vassals alone, and at my own sole charge, will I rescue the castle from the hands of our enemies, or perish in the attempt.

The odds are high against me. But it is now a Douglas or a Musgrave: God prosper the bravest!'

'Spoken like yourself, noble Douglas,' said the king, 'The higher the stake the greater the honour. The task be yours, and may the issue add another laurel to the heroic name.'

'James of Douglas,' said Lady Margaret, 'dost thou indeed accept of these hard conditions for my sake? Then the hand of thy royal mistress shall buckle on the armour in which thou goest to the field, but never shall unloose it, unless from a victor or a corse!' And with that she stretched forth her hand, which Douglas, as he kneeled with one knee on the ground, took and pressed to his lips.

Every one of the nobles shook Douglas by the hand, and wished him success. Does any man believe that there was one among them that indeed wished it? No, there was not a chief present that would not have rejoiced to have seen him led to the gallows. His power was too high already, and they dreaded that now it might be higher than ever; and, moreover, they saw themselves outdone by him in heroism, and felt degraded by the contract thus concluded.

The standard of the Douglas was reared, and the bloody heart flew far over many a lowland dale. The subordinate gentlemen rose with their vassals, and followed the banner of their chief; but the more powerful kept aloof, or sent ambiguous answers. They deemed the service undertaken little better than the frenzy of a madman.

There was at that time a powerful border baron, nick-named Sir Ringan Redhough, by which name alone he was distinguished all the rest of his life. He was warden of the middle marches, and head of the most warlike and adventurous sept in all that country. The answer which this hero gave to his own cousin, Thomas Middlemas, who came to expostulate with him from Douglas, is still preserved verbatim: 'What, man, are a' my brave lads to lie in bloody claes that the Douglas may lie i' snaw-white sheets wi' a bonny bedfellow? Will that keep the braid border for the king, my master? Tell him to keep their hands fu', an' their haunches toom, an' they'll soon be blythe to leave the lass an' loup at the ladle; an' the fient ae cloot shall cross the border to gar their pots play brown atween Dirdanhead and Cocketfell. Tell him this, an' tell him that Redhough said it. If he dinna work by wiles he'll never pouch the profit. But if he canna do it, an' owns that he canna do it, let him send word to me, an' I'll tak' it for him.'

With these words he turned his back, and abruptly left his cousin, who returned to Douglas, ill satisfied with the success of his message, but, nevertheless, delivered it faithfully. 'That curst carle,' said the Douglas, 'is a thorn in my thigh, as well as a buckler on my arm. He's as cunning as a fox, as stubborn as an oak, and as fierce as a lion. I must temporize for the present, as I cannot do without his support, but the time may come that he may be humbled, and made to know his betters; since one endeavour has failed, we must try another, and, if that do not succeed, another still.'

The day after that, as Sir Ringan was walking out at his own gate, an old man, with a cowl, and a long grey beard, accosted him. 'May the great spirit of the elements shield thee, and be thy protector, knight,' said he.

'An' wha may he be, carle, an it be your will?' said Ringan; 'An' wha may ye be that gie me sic a sachless benediction? As to my shield and protection, look ye here!' and with that he touched his two-handed sword, and a sheaf of arrows that was swung at his shoulder; 'an' what are all your saints and lang nebbit spirits to me?'

'It was a random salutation, knight,' said the old man, seeing his mood and temper; 'I am not a priest but a prophet. I come not to load you with blessings, curses, nor homilies, all equally unavailing, but to tell you what shall be in the times that are to come. I have had visions of futurity that have torn up the tendrils of my spirit by the roots. Would you like to know what is to befal you and your house in the times that are to come?'

'I never believe a word that you warlocks say,' replied the knight; 'but I like aye to hear what you *will* say about matters; though it is merely to laugh at ye, for I dinna gie credit to ane o' your predictions. Sin' the Rhymer's days, the spirit o' true warlockry is gane. He foretauld muckle that has turned out true; an' something that I hope *will* turn out true: But ye're a' bairns to him.'

'Knight,' said the stranger, 'I can tell you more than ever the Rhymer conceived, or thought upon; and, moreover, I can explain the words of True Thomas, which neither you nor those to whom they relate in the smallest degree comprehend. Knowest thou the prophecy of the Hart and the Deer, as it is called?

> 'Quhere the hearte heavit in het blude over hill and howe,
> There shall the dinke deire droule for the dowe:
> Two fleite footyde maydenis shall tredde the greine,
> And the mone and the starre shall flashe betweine.
> Quhere the proude hiche halde and heveye hande beire
> Ane frenauch shall feide on ane faderis frene feire,
> In dinging at the starris the D shall doupe down,
> But the S shall be S quhane the heide S is gone.'

'I hae heard the reide often and often,' said the knight, 'but the man's unborn that can understand that. Though the prophecies and the legends of the Rhymer take the lead i' my lear, I hae always been obliged to make that a passover.'

'There is not one of all his sayings that relates as much to you and your house, knight. It foretels that the arms of your family shall supersede those of Douglas, which you know are the bloody heart; and that in endeavouring to exalt himself to the stars, the D, that is the Douglas, shall fall, but that your house and name shall remain when the Stuarts are no more.'

'By the horned beasts of Old England, my father's portion, and my son's undiminished hope,' exclaimed the knight – 'Thou art a cunning man! I now see the bearing o' the prophecy as plainly as I see the hill o' Mountcomyn before my e'e; and, as I know Thomas never is wrong, I believe it. Now is the time, auld warlock – now is the time; he's ettling at a king's daughter, but his neck lies in wad, and the forfeit will be his undoing.'

'The time is not yet come, valiant knight; nevertheless the prophecy is true. Has thy horse's hoof ever trode, or thine eye journeyed, over the Nine Glens of Niddisdale?'

'I hae whiles gotten a glisk o' them.'

'They are extensive, rich, and beautiful.'

'They're nae less, auld carle; they're nae less. They can send nine thousand leel men an' stout to the field in a pinch.'

'It is recorded in the book of fate – it is written there—'

'The devil it is, auld carle; that's mair than I thought o'.'

'Hold thy peace: lay thine hand upon thy mouth, and be silent till I explain: I say I have seen it in the visions of the night – I have seen it in the stars of heaven—'

'What? the Nine Glens o' Niddisdale amang the starns o' heaven! by hoof and horn, it was rarely seen, warlock.'

'I say that I have seen it – they are all to belong to thy house.'

'Niddisdale a' to pertain to my house!'

'All.'

'Carle, I gie nae credit to sic forbodings; but I have heard something like this afore. Will ye stay till I bring my son Robin, the young Master of Mountcomyn, and let him hear it? For aince a man takes a mark on his way, I wadna hae him to tine sight o't. Mony a time has the tail o' the king's elwand pointed me the way to Cumberland; an' as often has the ee o' the Charlie-wain blinkit me hame again. A man's nae the waur o' a bit beacon o' some kind – a bit hope set afore him, auld carle; an' the Nine Glens o' Niddisdale are nae Willie-an-the-Wisp in a lad's ee.'

'From Roxburgh castle to the tower of Sark—'

'What's the auld-warld birkie saying?'

'From the Deadwater-fell to the Linns of Cannoby – from the Linns of Cannoby to the heights of Manor and the Deucharswire – shall thy son, and the representatives of thy house, ride on their own lands.'

'May ane look at your foot, carle? Take off that huge wooden sandal, an it be your will.'

'Wherefore should I knight?'

'Because I dread ye are either the devil or Master Michael Scott.'

'Whoever I am, I am a friend to you and to yours, and have told you the words of truth. I have but one word more to say: – Act always in concert with the Douglasses, while they act in concert with the king your master – not a day, nor an hour, nor a moment longer. It is thus, and thus alone, that you must rise and the Douglas fall. Remember the words of True Thomas—

'Quhane the wingit hors at his maistere sal wince,
"Let wyse men cheat the chevysance."'

'There is something mair about you than other folk, auld man. If ye be my kinsman, Michael Scott the warlock, I

crave your pardon, Master; but if you are that dreadfu'
carle – I mean that learned and wonderfu' man, why you
are welcome to my castle. But you are not to turn my auld
wife into a hare, Master, an' hunt her up an' down the hills
wi' my ain grews; nor my callants into naigs to scamper
about on i' the night-time when they hae ither occupations
to mind. There is naething i' my tower that isna at your
command; for, troth, I wad rather brow a' the Ha's and
the Howard's afore I beardit you.'

'I set no foot in your halls, knight. This night is a night
among many to me; and wo would be to me if any thing
canopied my head save the cope of heaven. There are
horoscopes to be read this night for a thousand years
to come. One cake of your bread and one cup of your
wine is all that the old wizard requests of you, and that
he must have.'

The knight turned back and led the seer into the inner-
court, and fed him with bread and wine, and every good
thing; but well he noted that he asked no holy benediction
on them like the palmers and priors that wandered about
the country; and, therefore, he had some lurking dread of
the old man. He did not thank the knight for his courtesy,
but, wiping his snowy beard, he turned abruptly away, and
strode out at the gate of the castle. Sir Ringan kept an eye
on him privately till he saw him reach the top of Blake
Law, a small dark hill immediately above the castle. There
he stopped and looked around him, and taking two green
sods, he placed the one above the other, and laid himself
down on his back, resting his head upon the two sods – his
body half raised, and his eyes fixed on heaven. The knight
was almost frightened to look at him; but sliding into the
cleuch, he ran secretly down to the tower to bring his lady
to see this wonderful old warlock. When they came back
he was gone, and no trace of him to be seen, nor saw they
him any more at that time.

CHAPTER TWO

> This man's the devil's fellow commoner,
> A verie cloake-bag of iniquitie.
> His batteries and his craboun he deschargeth
> Flasche, not by airt or reule. Is it meet
> A Ploydenist should be a *cedant arma togae*,
> Mounted on a trapt palfrey; with a dishe
> Of velvatte on his heide, to keepe the brothe
> Of his wit warm? The devil, my maisteris,
> There is no dame in Venice shall indure itt.
>
> *Old Play*

WHILST THE KNIGHT and his lady were looking about in amazement for their mysterious guest, the tower-warder sounded the great bugle, a tremendous horn that lay on a shelf in the balcony where he kept watch. 'One – two – three,' said the knight, counting the three distinct notes – a signal of which he well knew the language – 'What can that mean? I am wanted it would appear: another messenger from the Douglas, I warrant.'

'Sir Ringan, keep by that is your own,' said the lady – 'I say, mind your own concerns, and let the Douglas mind his.'

'Dame,' said the chief, 'I hae gotten some mair insight into that affair than you; an' we maun talk about it by an' by. In the meantime let us haste home, and see who is arrived.'

As they descended from the hill hand in hand, (for none walked arm in arm in those days,) they saw Richard Dodds, a landward laird, coming to meet them. 'Oh,' said Sir Ringan, 'this is my officious cousin, Dickie o' Dryhope; what business can he be come upon? It will be something that he deems of great importance.'

'I hate that old fawning, flattering sycophant,' said the lady; 'and cannot divine what is the cause of your partiality for him.'

'It is his attachment to our house that I admire, and his perfect devotion to my service and interests,' said the knight.

'Mere sound,' exclaimed the lady bitterly: 'Mere waste of superfluous breath! I tell you, Sir Ringan, that, for all your bravery, candour, and kindness, you are a mere novice in the affairs of life, and know less of men and of things than ever knight did.'

'It is a great fault in women,' said the knight, making his observation general, 'that they will aye be meddling wi' things they ken nought about. They think they ken every thing, an' wad gar ane trow that they can see an inch into a fir deal—. Gude help them! It is just as unfeasible to hear a lady discussing the merits of warriors an' yeomen, as it wad be to see me sitting nursing a wench-bairn.'

'Foh, what an uncourtly term!' said the lady; 'What would King Robert think if he heard you speaking in that uncouth stile?'

'I speak muckle better than him, wi' his short clippit Highland tongue,' said the chief: 'But hush, here comes the redoubted Dickie o' Dryhope.'

No sooner were the knight and his lady's eyes turned so as to meet Dickie's, than he whipped off his bonnet with a graceful swing, and made a low bow, his thin gray locks waving as he bowed. Dickie was a tall, lean, toothless, old bachelor, whose whole soul and body were devoted to the fair sex and the house of his chief. These two mighty concerns divided his attention, and often mingled with one another; his enthusiasm for the one, by any sudden change of subjects or concatenation of ideas, being frequently transferred to the other. Dickie approached with his bonnet in his hand, bowing every time the knight and lady lifted their eyes. When they met, Sir Ringan shook him heartily by the hand, and welcomed him to the castle of Mountcomyn.

'Oh, you are so good and so kind, Sir Ringan, bless you, bless you, bless you, noble sir; how do you thrive, Sir Ringan? bless you, bless you. And my excellent and noble lady Mountcomyn, how is my noble dame?'

'Thank you,' said the lady coldly.

Dickie looked as if he would have shaken hands with her, or embraced her, as the custom then was, but she made no proffer of either the one or the other, and he was obliged to keep his distance; but this had no effect in checking his adulations. 'I am so glad that my excellent lady is well, and the young squires and maidens all brisk and whole I hope?'

'All well, cousin,' said the chief.

'Eh! all well?' reiterated Dickie, 'Oh the dear, delightful, darling souls, O bless them! If they be but as well as I wish them, and as good as I wish – If the squires be but half so brave as their father, and the noble young sweet dames half so beautiful as their lady mother – oh bless them, bless them.' 'And half so independent and honest as their cousin,' said the lady, with a rebuking sneer.

'Very pleasant! very pleasant, indeed!' simpered Dickie, without daring to take his lips far asunder, lest his toothless gums should be seen.

'Such babyish flummery!' rejoined the lady with great emphasis. Dickie was somewhat abashed. His eyes, that were kindled with a glow of filial rapture, appeared as with flattened pupils; nevertheless the benignant smile did not altogether desert his features. The knight gave a short look off at one side to his lady. 'It is a great fault in ladies, cousin,' said he, 'that they will always be breaking their jokes on those that they like best, and always pretending to keep at a distance from them. My lady thinks to blind my een, as many a dame has done to her husband afore this time; but I ken, an' some mae ken too, that if there's ane o' a' my kin that I durstna trust my lady wi' when my back's turned, that ane's Dickie o' Dryhope.'

'H'm, h'm, h'm,' neighed Dickie, laughing with his lips shut; 'My lady's so pleasant, and so kind, but – Oh – no, no – you wrong her, knight; h'm, h'm, h'm! But, all joking and gibing aside – my lady's *very* pleasant. I came express to inform you, Sir Ringan, that the Douglasses are up.'

'I knew it.'

'And the Maxwells – and the Gordons – and the hurkle-backed Hendersons.'

'Well.'

'And Sir Christopher Seton is up – and the Elliots and the Laird of Tibbers is up.'

'Well, well.'

'I came expressly to inform you—'

'Came with piper's news,' said the lady, 'which the fiddler has told before you.'

'That *is very* good,' said Dickie, 'My lady is so delight-fully pleasant – I thought Sir Ringan would be going to rise with the rest, and came for directions as to raising my men.'

'How many men can the powerful Laird of Dryhope muster in support of the warden?' said Lady Mountcomyn.

'Mine are all at his command; my worthy lady knows that,' said Dickie, bowing: 'Every one at his command.'

'I think,' said she, 'that at the battle of Blakehope you furnished only two, who were so famished with hunger that they could not bear arms, far less fight.'

'Very pleasant, in sooth; h'm, h'm! I declare I am delighted with my lady's good humour.'

'You may, however, keep your couple of scare-crows at home for the present, and give them something to eat,' continued she; 'the warden has other matters to mind than wasting his vassals that the Douglas may wive.'

'Very true, and excellent good sense,' said Dickie.

'We'll talk of that anon,' said Sir Ringan. And with that they went into the castle, and sat down to dinner. There were twelve gentlemen and nine maidens present, exclusive of the knight's own family, and they took their places on each side as the lady named them. When Sir Ringan lifted up his eyes and saw the station that Dickie occupied, he was dissatisfied, but instantly found a remedy. 'Davie's Pate,' said he to the lad that waited behind him, 'mak that bowiefu' o' cauld plovers change places wi' yon saut-faut instantly, before meat be put to mouth.' The order was no sooner given than obeyed, and the new arrangement placed Dickie fairly above the salt.

The dining apparatus at the castle of Mountcomyn was homely, but the fare was abundant. A dozen yeomen stood behind with long knives, and slashed down the beef and venison into small pieces, which they placed before the guests in wooden plates, so that there was no knife used at the dining board. All ate heartily, but none with more industry than Dickie, who took not even time all the while to make the complaisant observation, that 'my lady was so pleasant.'

Dinner being over, the younger branches of the family retired, and all the kinsmen not of the first rank, pretending some business that called them away, likewise disappeared; so that none were left with the knight and his lady save six. The lady tried the effect of several broad hints on Dickie, but he took them all in good part, and declared that he never saw his lady so pleasant in his life. And now a serious consultation ensued, on the propriety of lending assistance to the Douglas. Sir Ringan first put the question to his friends, without any observation. The lady took up the argument, and reasoned strongly against the measure. Dickie was in raptures with his lady's good sense, and declared her arguments unanswerable. Most of the gentlemen seemed to acquiesce in the same measure, on the ground that, as matters stood, they could not rise at the Douglas' call on that occasion, without being considered as a subordinate family, which neither the king nor the Douglas had any right to suppose them; and so strongly and warmly ran the argument on that side, that it was likely to be decided on, without the chief having said a word on the subject. Simon of Gemelscleuch alone ventured to dissent; 'I have only to remark, my gallant kinsmen,' said he, 'that our decision in this matter is likely to prove highly eventful. Without our aid the force of the Douglas is incompetent to the task, and the castle will then remain in the hands of the English, than which nothing can be more grievously against our interest. If he be defeated, and forfeit his lands, the power of the Border will then remain with us; but should he succeed without our assistance, and become the king's son-in-law, it will be a hard game with us to keep the footing that we have. I conceive, therefore, that in withdrawing our support we risk every thing – in lending it, we risk nothing but blows.' All the kinsmen were silent. Dickie looked at my Lady Mountcomyn.

'It is well known that there is an old prophecy existing,' said she, 'that a Scott shall sit in the Douglas' chair, and be lord of all his domains. Well would it be for the country if that were so. But to support the overgrown power of that house is not the way to accomplish so desirable an object.'

'That is true,' said Dickie; 'I'll defy any man to go beyond what my lady says, or indeed whatever she says.'

'Have we not had instances of their jealousy already?' continued she.

'We have had instances of their jealousy already,' said Dickie, interrupting her.

'And should we raise him to be the king's son-in-law, he would kick us for our pains,' rejoined she.

'Ay, he would kick us for our pains,' said Dickie; 'think of that.'

'Either please to drop your responses, Sir,' said she, sternly, 'or leave the hall. I would rather hear a raven croak on my turret in the day of battle, than the tongue of a flatterer or sycophant.'

'That is very good indeed,' said Dickie; 'My lady is so pleasant; h'm, h'm, h'm! Excellent! h'm, h'm, h'm!'

Sir Ringan saw his lady drawing herself up in high indignation; and dreading that his poor kinsman would bring on himself such a rebuke as would banish him the hall for ever, he interposed. 'Cousin,' said he, 'it's a great fault in women that they canna bide interruption, an' the mair they stand in need o't they take it the waur. But I have not told you all yet: a very singular circumstance has happened to me this day. Who do you think I found waylaying me at my gate, but our kinsman, the powerful old warlock, Master Michael Scott.'

'Master Michael Scott!' exclaimed the whole circle, every one holding up his hands, 'has he ventured to be seen by man once more? Then there is something uncommon to befal, or, perhaps, the world is coming to an end.'

'God forbid!' said Redhough: 'It is true that, for seven years, he has been pent up in his enchanted tower at Aikwood, without speaking to anyone save his spirits; but though I do not know him, this must have been he, for he has told me such things as will astonish you; and, moreover, when he left me, he laid himself down on the top of the Little Law on his back, and the devils carried him away bodily through the air, or down through the earth, and I saw no more of him.'

All agreed that it had been the great magician Master Michael Scott. Sir Ringan then rehearsed the conversation that had passed between the wizard and himself. All the circle heard this with astonishment; some with suspense, and others with conviction, but Dickie with raptures of delight. 'He assured me,' said Redhough, 'that my son should ride on his own land from Roxburgh to the Deadwater-fell.'

'From Roxburgh to the Deadwater-fell!' cried Dickie, 'think of that! all the links of the bonny Teviot and Slitterick, ha, ha, lads, think of that!' and he clapped his hands aloud without daring to turn his eyes to the head of the table.

'And from the Deadwater-fell to the tower o' Sark,' rejoined the knight.

'To the tower of Sark!' exclaimed Dickie. 'H – have a care of us! think of that! All the dales of Liddel, and Ewes, and the fertile fields of Cannobie! Who will be king of the Border, then, my lads? who will be king of the Border then? ha, ha, ha!'

'And from the fords of Sark to the Deuchar-swire,' added Sir Ringan.

Dickie sprang to his feet, and seizing a huge timber trencher, he waved it round his head. The chief beckoned for silence; but Dickie's eyes were glistening with raptures, and it was with great difficulty he repressed his vociferations.

'And over the Nine Glens of Niddisdale beside,' said Sir Ringan.

Dickie could be restrained no longer. He brayed out, 'Hurrah, hurrah!' and waved his trencher round his head.

'All the Esk, and the braid Forest, and the Nine Glens o' Niddisdale! Hurrah! Hurrah! Mountcomyn for ever! The warden for ever! hu, hu! hu!'

The knight and his friends were obliged to smile at Dickie's outrageous joy; but the lady rose and went out in high dudgeon. Dickie then gave full vent to his rapture without any mitigation of voice, adding, 'My lady for ever!' to the former two; and so shouting, he danced around, waving his immense wooden plate.

The frolic did not take, and Sir Ringan was obliged to call him to order. 'You do not consider, cousin,' said the warden, 'that what a woman accounts excellent sport at one time is at another high offence. See, now, you have driven my lady away from our consultation, on whose advice I have a strong reliance; and I am afraid we will scarcely prevail on her to come back.'

'Oh! there's no fear of my lady and me,' said Dickie; 'we understand one another. My lady is a kind, generous, noble soul, and so pleasant!

'For as pleasant and kind as she is, I am deceived if she is easily reconciled to you. Ye dinna ken Kate Dunbar, cousin—. Boy, tell your lady that we lack her counsel, and expect that she will lend us it for a short space.'

The boy did as he was ordered, but returned with an answer, that unless Dickie was dismissed she did not choose to be of the party.

'I am sorry for it,' said Sir Ringan; 'but you may tell her that she may then remain where she is, for I can't spare my cousin Dickie now, nor any day these five months.' And with that he began and discussed the merits of the case *pro* and *con* with his kinsmen, as if nothing had happened; and in the end it was resolved, that, with a thousand horsemen, they would scour the east border to intercept all the supplies that should be sent out of England, and thus enrich themselves, while, at the same time, they would appear to countenance the mad undertaking of Douglas.

CHAPTER THREE

'Come, come, my hearts of flint; modestly; decently;
soberly; and handsomely—. No man afore his leader—.
Ding down the enemy tomorrow – ye shall not come
into the field like beggars—. Lord have mercy upon me,
what a world this is! – Well, I'll give an hundred pence
for as many good feathers, and a hundred more for as
many scarts: – wounds, dogs, to set you out withal!
Frost and snow, a man cannot fight till he be brave!
I say down with the enemy to-morrow!'

Sir John Oldcastle

THE CASTLE OF Roxburgh was beleaguered by seven
thousand men in armour, but never before had it been so
well manned, or rendered so formidable in its butresses;
and to endeavour to scale it, appeared as vain an attempt
as that of scaling the moon.

There was a great deal of parading, and noise went on,
as that of beating drums, and sounding of trumpets and
bugles, every day; and scarcely did there one pass on
which there were not tilting bouts between the parties,
and in these the English generally had the advantage.
Never was there, perhaps, a more chivalrous host than
that which Musgrave had under his command within the
walls of Roxburgh; the enthusiasm, the gallantry, and the
fire of the captain, were communicated to all the train.

Their horses were much superior to those of the Scots;
and, in place of the latter being able to make any impression
on the besieged, they could not, with all the vigilance they
were able to use, prevent their posts from being surprised
by the English, on which the most desperate encounters
sometimes took place. At first the English generally prevailed, but the Scots at length became inured to it, and

stood the shocks of the cavalry more firmly. They took care always at the first onset to cut the bridle reins with their broad-swords, and by that means they disordered the ranks of their enemies, and often drove them in confusion back to their stronghold.

Thus months flew on in this dashing sort of warfare, and no impression was made on the fortress, nor did any appear practicable; and every one at court began to calculate on the failure and utter ruin of the Douglas. Piercy of Northumberland proffered to raise the country, and lead an army to the relief of the castle; but this interference Musgrave would in nowise admit, it being an infringement of the task imposed on him by his mistress.

Moreover, he said, he cared not if all the men of Scotland lay around the castle, for he would defy them to win it. He farther bade the messenger charge Piercy and Howard to have an army ready at the expiry of the Christmas holidays, wherewith to relieve him, and clear the Border, but to take no care nor concern about him till then.

About this time an incident, right common in that day, brought a number of noble young adventurers to the camp of Douglas. It chanced, in an encounter between two small rival parties at the back of the convent of Maisondieu, which stood on the south side of the Teviot, that Sir Thomas de Somerville of Carnwath engaged hand to hand with an English knight, named Sir Comes de Moubray, who, after a desperate encounter, unhorsed and wounded him. The affair was seen from the walls of Roxburgh, as well as by a part of the Scottish army which was encamped on a rising ground to the south, that overlooked the plain; and, of course, like all other chivalrous feats, became the subject of general conversation. Somerville was greatly mortified; and, not finding any other way to recover his honour, he sent a challenge to Moubray to fight him again before the gate of Roxburgh, in sight of both armies. Moubray was too gallant to refuse. There was not a knight in the castle who would have declined such a chance of earning fame, and recommending himself to his mistress and the fair in general. The challenge was joyfully accepted, and the two knights met in the midst of a circle of gentlemen appointed by both armies, on the castle green, that lay betwixt the moat and the river, immediately under the walls of the castle. Never was there a more gallant combat seen. They rode nine times against each other with full force, twice with lances and seven times with swords, yet always managed with such dexterity that neither were unhorsed, nor yet materially wounded. But at the tenth charge, by a most strenuous exertion, Sir Thomas disarmed and threw his opponent out of his saddle, with his sword-arm dislocated. Somerville gained great renown, and his fame was sounded in court and in camp. Other challenges were soon sent from both sides, and as readily accepted; and some of the best blood both of Scotland and England was shed in these mad chivalrous exploits. The ambition of the young Scottish nobles was roused, and many of them flocked as volunteers to the standard of Douglas. Among these were some of the retainers of Redhough, who could not resist such an opportunity of trying their swords with some rivals with whom they had erst exchanged sharp blows on the marches. Simon of Gemelscleuch, his cousin John of Howpasley, and the Laird of Yard-bire, all arrived in the camp of Douglas in one night, in order to distinguish themselves in these tilting bouts. Earl Douglas himself challenged Musgrave, hoping thereby to gain his end, and the prize for which he fought; but the knight, true to his engagement, sent him for answer, that he would first see the beginning of a new year, and then he should fight either him or any of his name, but that till then he had undertaken a charge to which all others must be subordinate.

The Laird of Yardbire, the strongest man of the Border, fought three combats with English squires of the same degree, two on horseback and one on foot, and in all proved victorious. For one whole month the siege presented nothing new save these tiltings, which began at certain hours every day, and always became more obstinate, often proving fatal; and the eagerness of the young gentry of both parties to engage in them grew into a kind of mania: But an event happened which put an end to them at once.

There was a combat one day between two knights of the first degree, who were surrounded as usual by twenty lancers from each army, all the rest of both parties being kept at a distance, the English on the tops of their walls, and the Scots on the heights behind, both to the east and

west; for there was one division of the army stationed on
the hill of Barns and at the head of the Sick-man's Path,
and another on the rising ground between the city and
castle. The two gentlemen were equally matched, and the
issue was doubtful, when the attendant Scottish guards
perceived, or thought they perceived, in the bearing of
the English knight, some breach of the rules of chivalry;
on which with one voice they called out 'foul play.' The
English answered, 'No, no, none.' The two judges called
to order, on which the spearmen stood still and listened,
and hearing that the judges too were of different opinions,
they took up the matter themselves, the Scots insisting that
the knight should be disarmed and turned from the lists in
disgrace, and the English refusing to acquiesce. The judges,
dreading some fatal conclusion, gave their joint orders that
both parties should retire in peace, and let the matter be
judged of afterwards; on which the English prepared to
quit the ground with a kind of exultation, for it appeared
that they were not certain with regard to the propriety of
their hero's conduct. Unluckily, it so happened that the
redoubted Charlie Scott of Yard-bire headed the Scottish
pike-men on the lists that day, a very devil for blood
and battery, and of strength much beyond that generally
allotted to man. When he saw that the insidious knight
was going to be conducted off in a sort of triumph, and
in a manner so different from what he deemed to suit
his demerits, he clenched the handle of his sword with his
right hand, and screwed down his eyebrows till they almost
touched the top of his nose. 'What now, muckle Charlie?'
said one that stood by him. 'What now!' repeated Charlie,
growling like a wolf-dog, and confining the words almost
within his own breast, 'The deil sal bake me into a ker-cake
to gust his gab wi', afore I see that saucy tike ta'en off in sic
a way.' And with that he dropt his pike, drew his sword, and
rushing through the group he seized the knight's horse by
the bridle with his left hand, thinking to lead both him and
his master away prisoners. The knight struck at him with
all his might, but for this Charlie was prepared; he warded
the blow most dexterously, and in wrath, by the help of a
huge curb-bridle, he threw the horse backward, first on his
hams, and then on his back, with his rider under him. 'Tak
ye that, master, for whistling o' Sundays,' said the intrepid

borderer, and began to lay about him at the English, who now attacked him on both sides.

Charlie's first break at the English knight was the watchword for a general attack. The Scots flew to the combat, in perfect silence, and determined hatred, and they were received by the other party in the same manner. Not so the onlookers of both hosts – they rent the air with loud and reiterated shouts. The English poured forth in a small narrow column from the east gate along the draw-bridge, but the Scottish horsemen, who were all ready mounted, the better to see the encounter from their stations, scoured down from the heights like lightning, so that they prevailed at first, before the English could issue forth in numbers sufficient to oppose them. The brave Sir Richard Musgrave, the captain's younger brother, led the English, he having rushed out at their head on the first breaking out of the affray; but, notwithstanding all his bravery, he with his party were driven with their backs to the moat, and hard pressed, Douglas, with a strong body of horse, having got betwixt them and the castle-gate. The English were so anxious to relieve their young hero that they rushed to the gate in crowds. Douglas suffered a part to issue, and then attacking them furiously with the cavalry, he drove them back in such confusion, that he got possession of the drawbridge for several minutes, and would in all likelihood have entered with the crowd, had it not been for the portcullis, the machinery of which the Scots did not understand, nor had they the means of counteracting it; so that just when they were in the hottest and most sanguine part of their enterprise, down it came with a clattering noise louder than thunder, separating a few of the most forward from their brethren, who were soon every one cut down, as they refused to yield.

In the meantime it fared hard with Richard, who was overpowered by numbers; and though the English archers galled the Scottish cavalry grievously from the walls, he and all that were with him being forced backward, they plunged into the moat, and were every one of them either slain or taken prisoners. The younger Musgrave was among the latter, which grieved his brother Sir Philip exceedingly, as it gave Douglas an undue advantage over him, and he knew that, in the desperate state of his undertaking, he would go any lengths to over-reach him. From that day forth, all challenges or accepting of challenges was prohibited by Musgrave, under pain of death; and a proclamation was issued, stating, that all who entered the castle should be stripped naked, searched, and examined, on what pretence soever they came, and if any suspicious circumstances appeared against them, they were to be hanged upon a post erected for the purpose, on the top of the wall, in sight of both armies. He was determined to spare no vigilance, and constantly said he would hold Douglas at defiance.

There was only one thing that the besieged had to dread, and it was haply, too, the only thing in which the Scots placed any degree of hope, and that was the total failure of provisions within the castle. Musgrave's plan, of getting small supplies at a time from England by night, was discovered by Sir Ringan Redhough, and completely cut off: and as Douglas hanged every messenger that fell into his hands, no new plan could be established; and so closely were the English beleaguered, that any attempt at sending additional supplies to those they had proved of no avail. The rival armies always grew more and more inveterate against each other, and the most sharp and deadly measures were exercised by both. Matters went on in this manner till near the end of October, when the nights grew cold, long, and dark. There was nothing but the perils of that castle on the Border talked of over all Scotland and England. Every one, man, maid, and child, became interested in it. It may well be conceived that the two sovereign beauties, the Lady Jane Howard and Princess Margaret of Scotland, were not the least so; and both of them prepared, at the same time, in the true spirit of the age, to take some active part in the matter before it came to a final issue. One of them seemed destined to lose her hero, but both had put on the resolution of performing something worthy of the knights that were enduring so much for their sakes.

CHAPTER FOUR

And O that pegis weste is slymme,
And his ee wald garr the daye luke dymme;
His broue is brente, his brestis fayre,
And the deemonde lurkis in hys revan hayre.
Alake for thilke bonnye boye sae leile
That lyes withe oure Kynge in the hie-lande shiele!

Old Rhyme

I winna gang in, I darena gang in,
  Nor sleep i' your arms ava;
Fu' laithly wad a fair may sleep
  Atween you an' the wa'.
War I to lie wi' a belted knight,
  In a land that's no my ain,
Fu' dear wad be my courtesye,
  An' dreich wad be my pain.

Old Ballad

ONE COLD BITING evening, at the beginning of November, Patrick Chisholm of Castleweary, an old yeoman in the upper part of Teviotdale, sat conversing with his family all in a merry and cheerful mood. They were placed in a circle round a blazing hearth fire, on which hung a huge caldron, boiling and bubbling like the pool at the foot of a cataract. The lid was suspended by a rope to the iron crook on which this lordly machine was hung, to intercept somewhat the showers of soot that now and then descended from the rafters. These appeared as if they had been covered with pitch or black japanning; and so violently was the kettle boiling, that it made the roof of Pate Chisholm's bigging all to shiver. Notwithstanding these showers of soot, Pate and his four goodly sons eyed the boiling caldron with looks of great satisfaction – for ever and anon the hough of an immense leg of beef was to be seen cutting its capers in the boil, or coming with a graceful semicircular sweep from one lip of the pot to the other.

'Is it true, callants,' said Pate, 'that Howard is gaun to make a diversion, as they ca't, in the west border, to draw off the warden frae the Cheviots?'

'As muckle is said, an' as muckle expectit,' said Dan, his first born, a goodly youth, who, with his three brethren, sat in armour. They had come home to their father's house that night with their share of a rich prey that the warden had kidnapped while just collecting to send to Roxburgh under a guard of five thousand men. But Sir Ringan, getting intelligence of it, took possession of the drove before it was placed under the charge of those intended to guard it.

'As muckle is said, an' as muckle is expectit,' said Dan; 'but the west border will never turn out sae weel to us as the east has done. It's o'er near the Johnstones, and the Jardines, and the hurklebackit Hendersons.'

Pate looked from under his bonnet at the hough of beef—. 'The Cheviot hills hae turned weel out for the warden,' continued Dan; 'Redhough an' his lads hae been as weel scrieving o'er law and dale as lying getting hard pelts round the stane wa's o' Roxburgh, an' muckle mair gude has he done; for gin they dinna hunger them out o' their hauddin, they'll keep it. Ye'll draw an Englishman by the gab easier than drive him wi' an airn gaud. I wad ride fifty miles to see ony ane o' the bonny dames that a' this pelting an' peching is about.'

'Twa wanton glaikit gillies, I'll uphaud,' said Pate, looking at the restless hough; 'o'er muckle marth i' the back, an' meldar i' the brusket. Gin I had the heffing o' them, I sude tak a staup out o' their bickers—. Whisht, I thought I heard the clanking o' horse heels—. Callant, clap the lid down on the pat; what hae they't hinging geaving up there for?'

The clattering of the horses approached, but apparently with caution; and at length a voice called at the door in an English accent, 'Hollo, who holds here?' 'Leel men, an' for the Scots,' answered Dan, starting to his feet, and laying his hand on his sword. 'For the knight of Mountcomyn, the Scottish warden?' – inquired the horse-man without.

'For the same,' was the answer. 'It is toward his castle that we are bound. Can any of you direct us the way?'

'Troth, that I can,' said old Pate, groping to satisfy himself that the lid was close down on the pot, and then running to the door; 'I can tell you every fit o' the road, masters: You maun gang by the Fanesh, you see; it lies yon way, you see; an' then up the Brown rig, as straight as a line through Philhope-head, an' into Borthwick; then up Aitas-burn – round the Crib-law – an' wheel to the right; then the burn that ye come to there, ye maun cross that, and three miles farther on you come to the castle of Mountcomyn—. Braw cheer there lads!'

'I am afraid, friend,' said the English trooper, 'we will make nothing of this direction. Is it far to this same castle of the Scottish warden?'

'O no, naething but a step, some three Scots miles.'

'And how is the road?'

'A prime road, man; no a step in't a' wad tak your horse to the brusket; only there's nae track; ye maun just take an ettle. Keep an ee on the tail o' Charlie's wain, an' ye'll no gang far wrang.'

'Our young lord and master is much fatigued,' said the trooper; 'I am afraid we shall scarcely make it out. Pray, sir, could you spare us a guide?'

Dan, who was listening behind, now stepped forward, and addressed them: 'My masters, as the night is o' darkness, I could hardly ride to Mountcomyn mysel, an', far or near, I couldna win there afore day. Gin ye dought accept o' my father's humble cheer the night—'

'The callant's bewiddied, an' waur than bewiddied,' said Pate: 'We haena cheer for oursels, let abe for a byking o' English lords an' squires!'

'I would gladly accept of any accommodation,' said a sweet delicate voice, like that of a boy; 'for the path has been so dreadful that I am almost dead, and unable to proceed further. I have a safe-conduct to the Scottish court, signed by all the wardens of the marches, and every knight, yeoman, and vassal is obliged to give me furtherance.'

'I dinna ken muckle about conducks an' signatures,' said Pate, 'but I trow there winna be mony syllables in some o' the names if a' the wardens hae signed your libelt; for I ken weel there's ane o' them whase edication brak aff at the letter G, an' never gat farrer. But I'm no ca'ing ye a leear, southron lord, ye may be a vera honest man; an' as your errand may be something unco express, ye had better post on.'

'It sal never be casten up to me neither in camp nor ha,' said Dan, 'that a stranger was cawed frae my auld father's door at this time o' the night. Light down, light down, southron lord, ye are a privileged man; an', as I like to see the meaning o' things, I'll ride wi' ye mysel the morn, fit for fit, to the castle o' Mountcomyn.'

The strangers were soon all on their feet, and ushered into the family circle, for there was no fire-place in the house but that one. They consisted of five stout troopers, well armed, a page, and a young nobleman, having the appearance of a youth about seventeen or eighteen years of age. Every eye was instantly turned on him, there was something so extraordinary in his appearance. Instead of a steel helmet, he wore a velvet cap, shaped like a crown, striped with belts, bars, and crosses of gold wire, and manifestly more for ornament than use. His fair ringlets were peeping in curls out from below his cap, and his face and bright blue eyes were lovely as the dawn of a summer's morning.

They were not well seated till a noise of the tread of horses was again heard.

'The warld be a-wastle us!' cried old Pate, 'wha's that now? I think fouk will be eaten up wi' fouk, an' naething for fouk's pains but dry thanks; – thanks winna feed the cat—'

He was stopped in his regretful soliloquy by a rough voice at the door: 'Ho, wha hauds the house?' The same answer was given as to the former party, and in a minute the strangers entered without law or leave.

'Ye travel unco late, maisters,' said old Pate: 'How far may ye be for the night?'

'We meant to have reached the tower of Gorranberry tonight,' said one of the strangers, 'but we have been benighted, and were drawn hither by the light in your bole. I fear we must draw on your hospitality till day.'

'Callant Peter, gang an' stap a wisp i' that bole,' said Pate; 'it seems to be the beacon light to a' the clanjaumphry i' the hale country. I tauld ye aye to big it up; but no ane o' ye heeds what I say. I hae seen houses that *some* fouk whiles gaed by. But, my maisters, its nae gate ava to Gorranberry – a mere haut-stride-and-loup. I'll send a guide to Bilhope-head wi' ye; for troth we hae neither meat nor drink, house-room nor stabling, mair about the toun. We're but poor yeomen, an' haud our mailin for hard service. We hae tholed a foray the night already, an' a double ane wad herrie us out o' house an' hauld. The warld be a' wastle us! I think a' the mosstroopers be abraid the night! Bairns, swee that bouking o' claes aff the fire; ye'll burn it i' the boiling.'

The new comers paid little attention to this address of the old man; they saw that he was superannuated, and had all the narrow selfishness that too generally clings to that last miserable stage of human existence; but drawing nigh they began to cye the southron party with looks of dark suspicion, if not of fierceness.

'I see what maks ye sae frightet at our entrance here,' said the first Scots trooper, 'ye hae some southron spies amang ye – Gudeman, ye sal answer to the king for this, an' to the Douglas too, whilk ye'll find a waur job.'

'Ken where ye are, an' wha ye're speaking to,' said Dan, stepping forward and browing the last speaker face to face: 'If either the ae party or the ither be spies, or aught else but leel men, ye shall find, ere ye gang far, whase land ye are on, an' whase kipples ye are under. That auld man's my father, an,' doitet as he is, the man amang ye that says a saucy word to him I'll gar sleep in his shoon a fit shorter than he rase i' the morning. Wha are ye, sir, or where do you travel by night on my master the warden's bounds?'

'Sir,' answered another trooper, who seemed to be rather a more polished man, 'I applaud your spirit, and will answer your demand. We go with our lord and master, Prince Alexander Stuart of Scotland, on a mission to a noble English family. Here is the king's seal as well as a pass signed by the English warden. We are leel men and true.'

'Where is the prince?' said Dan: 'A prince of Scotland i' my father's house? Which is he?'

A slender elegant stripling stept forward. 'Here he is, brave yeoman,' said the youth: 'No ceremony – Regard me as your fellow and companion for this night.'

Dan whipped off his bonnet and clapped his foot upon it, and bowing low and awkwardly to his prince he expressed his humble respect as well as he could, and then presented the prince to his father. The title sounded high in the old man's ears, he pulled off his bonnet and looked with an unsteady gaze, as if uncertain on whom to fix it – 'A prince! Eh? – Is he a prince o' Scotland? Ay, ay!' said he, 'Then he'll maybe hae some say wi' our head men – Dan – I say, Dan' – and with that he pulled Dan's sleeve, and said in a whisper loud enough to be heard over all the house – 'I say, Dan, man, gin he wad but speak to the warden to let us hae a' the land west the length o' the Frosty lair. O it wad lie weel into ours.' 'It wad, father, and I daresay we may get it; but hush just now.' 'Eh? do you think we may get it?' enquired the old man eagerly in the same whispering tremulous voice, 'O man, it wad lie weel in; an' sae wad Couter's-cleuch. It's no perfect wanting that too. An' we wad be a great deal the better o' twa or three rigs aff Skelfhill for a bit downfa' to the south – See if ye can speak to the lad.'

Dan shook his father's hand, and nodded to him by way of acquiescence. The old man brightened up: 'Whar is your titty Bessy, Dan? Whar are a' the idle hizzies? Gar them get something set down to the princely lad: I'se warrant he's e'en hungry. Ye'll no be used til siccan roads as thir, Sir? Na, na. They're unco roads for a prince—. Dan, I say, come this way; I want to speak to you – I say,' (whispering very low aside) 'I wadna let them ken o' the beef, or they'll just gang wi't. Gie them milk an' bread, an' cheese, an' a drap o' the broo; it will do weel aneuch. Hunger's good sauce. But, Dan – I say, could ye no contrive to get quat o' thae English? I doubt there will be little made o' them—. They're but a wheen gillie-gaupies at the best, an nae freends to us—. Fouk sude ay bow to the bush they get bield frae.'

'It's a' true that ye say, father; but we surely needna grudge an Englishman a piece o' an English cow's hip—. The beef didna cost you dear, an' there's mair where it cam frae.'

The old man would not give up his point, but persisted in saying it was a dangerous experiment, and an unprofitable waste. However, in spite of his remonstrances, the board was loaded with six wooden bickers filled with beef broth, plenty of bear-meal bannocks, and a full quarter of English ox beef, to which the travellers did all manner of justice. The prince, as he called himself, was placed at the head of the table, and the young English nobleman by his side. Their eyes were scarcely ever turned from one another's faces, unless in a casual hasty glance to see how others were regarding the same face. The prince had dark raven hair that parted on a brow of snow, a black liquid eye, and round lips, purer than the cherry about to fall from the tree with ripeness. He was also a degree taller than the English lord; but both of them, as well as their two pages, were lovelier than it became men to be. The troopers who attended them seemed disposed to contradict every thing that came from the adverse party, and, if possible, to broach a quarrel, had it not been for the two knights, who were all suavity, good breeding, and kindness to each other, and seemed to have formed an attachment at first sight. At length Prince Alexander inquired of his new associate his name, and business at the Scottish court, provided, he said, that it did not require strict secrecy. The other said, he would tell him every thing truly, on condition that he would do the same: which being agreed to, the young English nobleman proceeded as follows:

'My name is Lord Jasper Tudor, second son to the Earl of Pembroke. I am nearly related to the throne of England, and in high favour with the king. The wars on the Borders have greatly harassed the English dalesmen for these many years, and matters being still getting worse between the nations, the king, my cousin, has proposed to me to marry the Princess Margaret of Scotland, and obtain as her dowry a confirmation of these border lands and castles, so that a permanent peace may be established between the nations, and this bloody and desperate work cease. I am on my way to the Scottish court to see the princess, your sister; and if I find her to be as lovely and accomplished as fame speaks her, I intend to comply with the king's request, and marry her forthwith.'

This speech affected the prince so much that all the guests wondered. He started to his feet, and smiling in astonishment said, 'What, you? you marry m – m – my sister Margaret? She is very much beholden to you, and on my word she will see a becoming youth. But are you sure that she will accept of you for a husband?' 'I have little to fear on that head,' said the Lord Jasper Tudor jeeringly; 'Maids are in general not much averse to marriage; and, if I am well informed, your lovely sister is as little averse to it as any of her contemporaries.'

The prince blushed deep at this character of his sister, but had not a word to say.

'Pray,' continued Tudor, 'is she like you? If she is, I think I shall love her – I would not have her just like you neither.'

'I believe,' said the prince, 'there is a strong family likeness; but tell me in what features you would wish her to differ from me, and I will describe her minutely to you.'

'In the first place,' said the amorous and blue-ey'd Tudor, 'I should like her to be a little stouter, and more manly of frame than you, and, at least, to have some appearance of a beard.'

All the circle stared. 'The devil you would, my lord,' said Dan; 'Wad ye like your wife to hae a beard, in earnest? Gude faith, an your ain war like mine, ye wad think ye had eneuch o't foreby your wife's.' The prince held up his hands in astonishment, and the young English lord blushed deeper than it behoved a knight to do; but at length he tried to laugh it by, pretending that he had unwittingly said one thing when he meant the very contrary, for he wished her to be more feminine, and have less beard—. 'I think that will hardly be possible,' said Dan; 'but perhaps there may be a hair here an' there on my lord the prince's chin, when ane comes near it. I wadna disparage ony man, far less my king's son.'

'Well, my noble lord,' said the prince, 'your tale has not a little surprised me, as well it may. Our meeting here in like circumstances is the most curious rencounter I ever knew; for, to tell you the plain truth, I am likewise on an errand of the same import, being thus far on my way to see and court the lady Jane Howard, in order that all her wide domains may be attached to my father's kingdom, and peace and amity thereby established on the border.'

'Gracious heaven!' said young Lord Tudor, 'can this that I hear be true? You? Are you on your way to my cousin, the lady Jane Howard? Why, do you not know that she is already affianced to Lord Musgrave?'

'Yes, it is certain I do; but that is one of my principal inducements to gain her from him; that is quite in the true spirit of gallantry; but, save her great riches, I am told she has little else to recommend her,' said the prince.

'And, pray, how does fame report of my cousin Jane?' said Tudor.

'As of a shrew and a coquette,' answered the prince; 'a wicked minx, that is intemperate in all her passions.'

'It is a manifest falsehood,' said Tudor, his face glowing with resentment, 'I never knew a young lady so moderate and chastened in every passion of the female heart. Her most private thoughts are pure as purity itself, and her—.'

'But, begging your pardon, my lord, how can you possibly know all this?' said the prince.

'I do know it,' said the other, 'it is no matter how: I cannot hear my fair cousin wronged; and I know that she will remain true to Musgrave, and have nothing to do with you.'

'I will bet an earldom on that head,' said the prince, 'if I chuse to lay siege to her.'

'Done!' said the other, and they joined hands on the bargain; but they had no sooner laid their hands into one another's than they hastily withdrew them, with a sort of trepidation, that none of the lookers on, save the two pages, who kept close by their masters, appeared to comprehend. They, too, were both mistaken in the real cause; but of that it does not behove to speak at present.

'I will let you see,' said the prince, recovering himself, 'that this celebrated cousin of yours shall not be so ill to win as the castle of Roxburgh; and I'll let Musgrave see for how much truth and virgin fidelity he has put his life in his hand; and when I have her I'll cage her, for I don't like her. I would give that same earldom to have her in my power to-night.'

The young Lord Tudor looked about as if he meditated an escape to another part of the table; but, after a touch that his page gave him on the sleeve, he sat still, and mustered up courage for a reply.

'And pray, sir prince, what would you do with her if you had her in your power to-night?'

'Something very different from what I would do with
you, my lord. But please describe her to me, for my very
heart is yearning to behold her – describe every point of
her form, and lineament of her features.'

'She is esteemed as very beautiful; for my part I think
her but so so,' said Tudor: 'She has fair hair, light full blue
eyes, and ruddy cheeks; and her brow, I believe, is as fine
and as white as any brow can be.'

'O frightful! what a description! what an ugly minx it
must be! Fair hair! red, I suppose, or dirty dull yellow!
Light blue eyes! mostly white I fancy? Ah, what a frightful
immodest ape it must be! I could spit upon the huzzy!'

'Mary shield us!' exclaimed young Tudor, moving farther away from the prince, and striking lightly with his hand
on his doublet as if something unclean had been squirted
on it. 'Mary shield us! What does the saucy Scot mean?'

Every one of the troopers put his hand to his sword, and
watched the eye of his master. The prince beckoned to the
Scots to be quiet; but Lord Tudor did no such thing, for
he was flustered and wroth.

'Pardon me, my lord,' said the prince, 'I may perhaps
suffer enough from the beauty and perfections of your fair
cousin after I see her; you may surely allow me to deride
them now. I am trying to depreciate the charms I dread.
But I do not like the description of her. Tell me seriously
do you not think her very intolerable?'

'I tell you, prince, I think quite otherwise. I believe Jane
to be fifty times more lovely than any dame in Scotland;
and a hundred times more beautiful than your tawny virago
of a sister, whom I shall rejoice to tame like a spaniel. The
haughty, vain, conceited, swart venom, that she should lay
her commands on the Douglas to conquer or die for her! A
fine presumption, forsooth! But the world shall see whether
the charms of my cousin, Lady Jane Howard, or those of
your grim and tawdry princess, have most power.'

'Yes, they shall, my lord,' said the prince: 'In the mean
time let us drop the subject. I see I have given you offence,
not knowing that you were in love with Lady Jane, which
now I clearly see to be the case. Nevertheless, go on with
the description, for I am anxious to hear all about her, and
I promise to approve if there be a bare possibility of it.'

'Her manner is engaging, and her deportment graceful

and easy; her waist is slim, and her limbs slender and elegant beyond any thing you ever saw,' said Lord Tudor.

'O shocking!' exclaimed the prince, quite forgetting himself; 'Worst of all! I declare I have no patience with the creature. After such a description, who can doubt the truth of the reports about the extreme levity of her conduct? Confess now, my lord, that she is very free of her favours, and that the reason why so many young gentlemen visit her is now pretty obvious.'

High offence was now manifest in Lord Jasper Tudor's look. He rose from his seat, and said in great indignation, 'I did not ween I should be insulted in this guise by the meanest peasant in Scotland, far less by one of its courtiers, and least of all by a prince of the blood royal. Yeomen, I will not, I cannot suffer this degradation. These ruffian Scots are intruders on us – here I desire that you will expel them the house.'

The Prince of Scotland was at the head of the table, Tudor was at his right hand; the rest of the English were all on that side, the Scots on the other – their numbers were equal. Dan and his three brethren sat at the bottom of the board around the old man, who had been plying at the beef with no ordinary degree of perseverance, nor did he cease when the fray began. Every one of the two adverse parties was instantly on his feet, with his sword gleaming in his hand; but finding that the benches from which they had arisen hampered them, they with one accord sprung on the tops of these, and crossed their swords. The pages screamed like women. The two noble adventurers seemed scarcely to know the use of their weapons, but looked on with astonishment. At length the prince, somewhat collecting himself, drew out his shabby whanger, and brandished it in a most unwarlike guise, on which the blue-eyed Tudor retreated behind his attendants, holding up his hands, but still apparently intent on revenge for the vile obloquy thrown on the character of *his cousin*, Lady Jane Howard. 'Tis just pe te shance she vantit,' said the Scot next to the prince.

'My certy, man, we'll get a paick at the louns now,' said the second.

'Fat te teel's ta'en 'e bits o' vee laddies to flee a' eet abeet 'er buts o' wheers? I wudnae hae my feet i' their sheen for three plucks an a beedle,' said the third.

'Thou's a' i' the wrang buox now, chaps,' said the fourth. These were all said with one breath; and before the English-men had time to reply, clash went the swords across the table, and the third Scot, the true Aberdonian, was wounded, as were also two of the Englishmen, at the very first pass.

These matters are much sooner done than described. All this was the work of a few seconds, and done before advice could either be given or attended to. Dan now interfered with all the spirit and authority that he was master of. He came dashing along the middle of the board in his great war boots, striking up their swords as he came, and interposing his boardly frame between the combatants. 'D—n ye a' for a wheen madcaps!' cried Dan as loud as he could bawl: 'What the muckle deil's fa'en a bobbing at your midriffs now? Ye're a' my father's guests an' mine; an', by the shin-banes o' Sant Peter, the first side that lifts a sword, or says a misbehadden word, my three brethren and I will tak' the tother side, an' smoor the transgressors like as mony moor-poots.'

'Keep your feet aff the meat, fool,' said old Pate.

'Gude sauff us!' continued Dan, 'What has been said to gie ony offence? What though the young gentlewoman dis tak a stown jink o' a' chap that's her ain sweetheart whiles? Where's the harm in that? There's little doubt o' the thing. An' for my part, gin she didna—'

Here Dan was interrupted in his elegant harangue by a wrathful hysteric scream from young Tudor, who pulled out his whinyard, and ran at Dan, boring at him in awkward but most angry sort, crying all the while, 'I will not bear this insult! Will my followers hear me traduced to my face?'

'Deil's i' e' wee but steepid laddie,' said Buchan the Aberdonian; 'it thinks 'at 'er preeving it to be a wheer 'e sel o't!'

Dan lifted up his heavy sword in high choler to cleave the stripling, and he would have cloven him to the belt, but curbing his wrath, he only struck his sword, which he made fly into pieces and jingle against the rafters of the house; then seizing the young adventurer by the shoulder, he snatched him up to him on the board, where he still stood, and, taking his head below his arm, he held him fast with the one hand, making signs with the other to his brethren to join the Scots, and disarm the English, who were the aggressors both times. In the meantime, he was saying to Tudor, 'Hout, hout, young master, ye hae never been o'er the Border afore; ye sude hae stayed at hame, an' wantit a wife till ye gathered mair rummelgumption.'

The five English squires, now seeing themselves set upon by nine, yielded, and suffered themselves to be disarmed.

When Tudor came to himself, he appeared to be exceedingly grieved at his imprudence, and ready to make any acknowledgement, while the prince treated him with still more and more attention; yet these attentions were ever and anon mixed with a teazing curiosity, and a great many inquiries, that the young nobleman could not bear, and did not chuse to answer.

It now became necessary to make some arrangement for the parties passing the night. Patrick Chisholm's house had but one fire-place in an apartment which served for kitchen and hall; but it had a kind of *ben end*, as it was then, and is always to this day, denominated in that part of the country. There was scarcely room to move a foot in it; for, besides two oaken beds with rowan-tree bars, it contained five huge chests belonging to the father and his sons, that held their clothes and warlike accoutrements. The daughters of yeomen in these days did not sit at table with the men. They were the household servants. Two of Pate's daughters, who had been bustling about all the evening, conducted the two noble youths into this apartment, together with their two pages. The one bed was neatly made down with clean clothes, and the other in a more common way. 'Now,' said one of the landward lasses, 'You twa masters are to sleep thegither in here – in o' this gude bed, ye see, an' the twa lads in o' this ane.' The two young noblemen were standing close together, as behoved in such a room. On the girl addressing them thus, their eyes met each other's, but were as instantly withdrawn and fixed in the floor, while a blush of the deepest tint suffused the cheeks of both, spreading over the chin and neck of each. The pages contemplated each other in the same way, but not with the same degree of timidity. The English stripling seemed rather to approve of the arrangement,

or at least pretended to do so; for he frankly took the
other by the hand, and said in a sweet voice, but broad
dialect, 'Weall, yuong Scuot, daghest thou lig woth mey?'
The young Caledonian withdrew his hand, and held down
his head: 'I always lie at my master's feet,' said he.

'And so shall you do to-night, Colin,' said the prince,
'for I will share this bed with you, and let my lord take
the good one.' 'I cannot go to bed to-night,' said Tudor,
'I will rest me on this chest; I am resolved I sha'n't go to
bed, nor throw off my clothes to-night.'

'Ye winna?' said May Chisholm, who visibly wanted a
romp with the young blooming chief – 'Ye winna gang til
nae bed, will ye nae, and me has been at sic pains making
it up til ye? Bess, come here an' help me, we sal soon
see whether he's gang til his bed or no, an' that no wi'
his braw claes on neither.' So saying, the two frolicsome
queans seized the rosy stripling, and in a moment had him
stretched on the bed, and, making his doublet fly open all
at one rude pull, they were proceeding to undress him,
giggling and laughing all the while. Prince Alexander,
from a momentary congenial feeling of delicacy, put his
hand hastily across to keep the lapels of Tudor's vesture
together, without the motion having been perceived by
any one in the hurry, and that moment the page flung
himself across his master's breast, and reproved the lasses
so sharply that they desisted, and left them to settle the
matter as they chose.

The prince had, however, made a discovery that astonished him exceeding; for a few minutes his head was almost
turned – but the truth soon began to dawn on his mind,
and every reflection, every coincidence, every word that
had been said, and offence that had been taken, tended
to confirm it: so he determined, not for farther trial, but
for the joke's sake, to press matters a little further.

When quietness was again restored, and when the blush
and the frown had several times taken alternate sway of
the young lord's face, the prince said to him. 'After
all, my lord, I believe we must take share of the same
bed together for this one night. It is more proper and
becoming than to sleep with our pages. Besides, I see
the bed is good and clean, and I have many things to
talk to you about our two countries, and about our two

intended brides, or sweethearts let us call them in the meantime.'

'Oh no, no, prince,' said Tudor, 'indeed I cannot, I may not, I would not sleep in the same bed with another gentleman – No – I never did – never.'

'Do not say so, my dear lord, for, on my word, I am going to insist on it,' said the prince, coming close up to him, his eyes beaming with joy at the discovery he had made. 'You shall sleep by my side tonight: nay, I will even take you in my bosom and caress you as if you were my own sweet dear Lady Jane Howard.' Tudor was now totally confounded, and knew neither what to say for himself, nor what he did say when he spoke. He held out both his hands, and cried, 'Do not, prince, do not – I beg – I implore do not; for I cannot, cannot consent. I never slept even in the same apartment with a man in all my life.'

'What, have you always slept in a room by yourself?' asked the teazing prince.

'No, never, but always with ladies – yes, always!' was the passionate and sincere reply.

Here the prince held up his hands, and turned up his eyes. 'What a young profligate!' exclaimed he, 'Mary shield us! Have you no conscience with regard to the fair sex that you have begun so wicked a course, and that so early? Little did I know why you took a joke on your cousin so heinously amiss! I see it now, truth will out! Ah, you are such a youth! I will not go a foot further to see Lady Jane. What a wicked degraded imp she must be! Do not kindle into a passion again, my dear lord. I can well excuse your feigned wrath, it is highly honourable. I hate the knight that blabs the favours he enjoys from the fair. He is bound to defend the honour that has stooped to him; even though (as in the present instance I suppose) it have stooped to half a dozen more besides.'

A great deal of taunting and ill humour prevailed between these capricious and inexperienced striplings, and sorely was Tudor pressed to take share of a bed with the prince, but in vain – his feelings recoiled from it; and the other, being in possession of a secret of which the English lord was not aware, took that advantage of teazing and tormenting him almost beyond sufferance. After all, it was decided that each should sleep with his own page; a decision that did not seem to go well down at all with the Yorkshire boy, who once ventured to expostulate with his lord, but was silenced with a look of angry disdain.

CHAPTER FIVE

He set her on his milk-white steed,
    Himself lap on behind her,
And they are o'er the Highland hills;
    Her friends they cannot find her.

As they rode over hill and dale
    This lady often fainted,
And cried, 'Wo to my cursed moneye,
    That this road to me invented.'
                    Ballad of Rob Roy

O cam ye here to fight, young man,
    Or cam ye here to flee?
Or cam ye out o' the wally west
    Our bonnie bride to see?
                    Balled called Foul Play

IT IS BY this time needless to inform my readers, that these
two young adventurers were no other than the rival beauties
of the two nations, for whose charms all this bloody coil
was carried on at Roxburgh; and who, without seeing, had
hated each other as cordially as any woman is capable of
hating her rival in beauty or favour. So much had the
siege and the perils of Roxburgh become the subject of
conversation, that the ears of the two maidens had long
listened to nothing else, and each of them deemed her
honour embarked in the success of her lover. Each of them
had set out with the intent of visiting the camp in disguise;
and having enough of interest to secure protections for
feigned names, each determined to see her rival in the
first place, the journey not being far; and neither of them

41

it is supposed went with any kind intent. Each of them had a maid dressed in boy's clothes with her, and five stout troopers, all of whom were utterly ignorant of the secret. The princess had by chance found out her rival's sex; but the Scottish lady and her attendant being both taller and of darker complexions than the other two, no suspicions were entertained against them detrimental to their enterprise. The princess never closed an eye, but lay meditating on the course she should take. She was convinced that she had her rival in her power, and she determined, not over generously, to take advantage of her good fortune. The time drew nigh that Roxburgh must be lost or won, and well she knew that, whichever side succeeded, according to the romantic ideas of that age, the charms of the lady would have all the honour, while she whose hero lost would be degraded – considerations which no woman laying claim to superior and all-powerful charms could withstand.

Next morning Dan was aroused at an early hour by his supposed prince, who said to him, 'Brave yeoman, from a long conversation that I have had last night with these English strangers, I am convinced that they are despatched on some traitorous mission; and as the warden is in Northumberland, I propose conveying them straight to Douglas' camp, there to be tried for their lives. If you will engage to take charge of them, and deliver them safely to the captain before night, you shall have a high reward; but if you fail, and suffer any of them to escape, your neck shall answer for it. How many men can you raise for this service?'

'Our men are maistly up already,' said Dan; 'but muckle Charlie o' Yardbire gaed hame last night wi' twa or three kye, like oursels. Gin Charlie an' his lads come, I sal answer for the English chaps, if they war twa to ane. I hae mysel an' my three billies, deil a shank mae; but an Charlie come he's as gude as some three, an' his backman's nae bean-swaup neither.'

'Then,' said the counterfeit prince, 'I shall leave all my attendants to assist you save my page – we two must pursue our journey with all expedition. All that is required of you is to deliver the prisoners safe to the Douglas. I will despatch a message to him by the way, apprising him of the circumstances.'

The Lady Margaret and her page then mounted their palfreys and rode off without delay; but, instead of taking the road by Gorranberry, as they had proposed over night, they scoured away at a light gallop down the side of the Teviot. At the town of Hawick she caused her page, who was her chief waiting-maid and confidant, likewise in boy's clothes, to cut out her beautiful fleece of black hair, that glittered like the wing of the raven, being determined to attend in disguise the issue of the contest. She then procured a red curled wig, and dressing herself in a Highland garb, with a plumed bonnet, tartan jacket and trowsers, and Highland hose and brogues, her appearance was so completely altered, that even no one who had seen her the day before, in the character of the prince her brother, could possibly have known her to be the same person; and leaving her page near the camp to await her private orders, she rode straight up to head-quarters by herself.

Being examined as she passed the outposts, she said she brought a message to Douglas of the greatest importance, and that it was from the court; and her address being of such a superior cast, every one furthered her progress till she came to the captain's tent. Scarcely did she know him – care, anxiety, and watching had so worn him down; and her heart was melted when she saw his appearance. Never, perhaps, could she have been said to have loved him till that moment; but seeing what he had suffered for her sake, the great stake he had ventured, and the almost hopeless uncertainty that appeared in every line of his face, raised in her heart a feeling unknown to her before; and highly did that heart exult at the signal advantage that her good fortune had given him over his rival. Yet she determined on trying the state of his affections and hopes. Before leaving Hawick, she had written a letter to him, inclosing a lock of her hair neatly plaited; but this letter she kept back in order to sound her lover first without its influence. He asked her name and her business. She had much business, she said, but not a word save for his private ear. Douglas was struck with the youth's courtly manner, and looked at him with a dark searching eye – 'I have no secrets,' said he, 'with these my kinsmen: I desire, before them, to know your name and business.'

'My name,' said the princess pertly, 'is Colin Roy

M'Alpin – I care not who knows my name; but no word further of my message do I disclose save to yourself.'

'I must humour this pert stripling,' said he, turning to his friends; 'if his errand turns out to be one of a trivial nature, and that does not require all this ceremony, I shall have him horse-whipped.'

With that the rest of the gentlemen went away, and left the two by themselves. Colin, as we must now, for brevity's sake, term the princess, was at first somewhat abashed before the dark eye of Douglas, but soon displayed all the effrontery that his assumed character warranted, if not three times more.

'Well, now, my saucy little master, Colin Roy M'Alpin, please condescend so far as to tell me whence you are, and what is your business here – this secret business, of such vast importance.'

'I am from court, my lor'; from the Scottish court, an't please you, my lor'; but not directly as a body may say – my lor'; not directly – here – there – south – west – precipitately, incontrovertibly, ascertaining the scope and bearing of the progressive advance of the discomfiture and gradual wreck of your most flagrant and preposterous undertaking.'

'The devil confound the impertinent puppy!'

'Hold, hold, my lor', I mean your presumptuous and foolhardy enterprise, first in presuming to the hand of my mistress, the king's daughter – my lovely and queenly mistress; and then in foolhardily running your head against the walls of Roxburgh to attain this, and your wit and manhood against the superior generalship of a Musgrave.'

'By the pock-net of St Peter, I will cause every bone in your body to be basted to powder, you incorrigible pedant and puppy!' said the Douglas; and seizing him by the collar of the coat, he was about to drag him to the tent-door and throw him into the air.

'Hold, my lor'; please keep off your rough uncourtly hands till I deliver the credentials of my mistress.'

'Did you say that you were page to the Princess Margaret? Yes, surely you are, I have erst seen that face, and heard that same flippant tongue. Pray, what word or token does my dear and sovereign lady send me?'

'She bade me say, that she does not approve of you at all, my lor': – that, for her sake, you ought to have taken this castle many days ago. And she bade me ask you why you don't enter the castle by the gate, or over the wall, or under the hill, which is only a sand one, and hang up all the Englishmen by the necks, and send the head of Philip Musgrave to his saucy dame? – She bade me ask you why you don't, my lor'?'

'Women will always be women,' said Douglas surlily to himself: 'I thought the princess superior to her sex, but—'

'But! but what, my lor'? Has she not good occasion for displeasure? She bade me tell you that you don't like her; – that you don't like her half so well as Musgrave does his mistress – else why don't you do as much for her? He took the castle for the sake of his mistress, and for her sake he keeps it in spite of you. Therefore she bade me tell you, that you must *go in* and beat the English, and take the castle from them; for she will not suffer it that Lady Jane Howard shall triumph over her.'

'Tell her in return,' said Douglas, 'that I will do what man can do; and when that is done, she shall find that I neither will be slack in requiring the fulfilment of her engagement, nor in performing my own. If that womanish tattling be all that you have to say – begone: the rank of your employer protects you.'

'Hold, my lor', she bade me look well, and tell her what you were like, and if I thought you changed since I waited on you at court. On my conscience you look very ill. These are hard ungainly features of yours. I'll tell her you look very shabby, and very surly, and that you have lost all heart. But oh, my lor', I forgot she bade me tell you, that if you found you were clearly beat, it would be as well to draw off your men and abandon the siege; and that she would, perhaps, in pity, give you a moiety of your lands again.'

'I have no patience with the impertinence of a puppy, even though the messenger of her I love and esteem above all the world. Get you hence.'

'Oh, my lor', I have not third done yet. But, stay, here is a letter I had almost forgot.'

Douglas opened the letter. Well he knew the hand; there were but few in Scotland who could write, and none could write like the princess. It contained a gold ring set with rubies, and a lock of her hair. He kissed them both; and tried the ring first on the one little finger, and then on the

other, but it would scarcely go over the nail; so he kissed
them again, and put them in his bosom. He then read to
himself as follows:

'MY GOOD LORD – I enclose you two love-tokens
of my troth; let them be as beacons to your heart
to guide it to deeds of glory and renown. For my
sake put down these English. Margaret shall ever
pray for your success. Retain my page Colin near
your person. He is true-hearted, and his flippancy
affected. Whatever you communicate to him will be
safely transmitted to

'MARGARET.'

It may well be supposed how Colin watched the emotions
of Douglas while reading this heroic epistle; and, in the
true spirit of the age, they were abundantly extravagant.
He kissed the letter, hugged it in his bosom, and vowed
to six or seven saints to do such deeds for his adored and
divine princess as never were heard or read of.

'Now, my good lor,' said the page, 'you must inform me
punctually what hopes you have of success, and if there is
any thing wanting that the kingdom can afford you.'

'My ranks are too thin,' replied the Douglas; 'and I have
engaged to take it with my own vassals. The warden is too
proud to join his forces to mine on that footing, but keeps
scouring the borders, on pretence of preventing supplies,
and thus assisting me, but in truth for enriching himself
and his followers. If I could have induced him and his
whole force to have joined the camp, famine would have
compelled the enemy to yield a month agone. But I have
now the captain's brother prisoner; and I have already given
him to know, that if he does not deliver up the castle to me
in four days, I will hang the young knight up before his
eyes – I have sworn to do it, and I swear again to keep
my oath.'

'I will convey all this to my mistress,' said Colin. 'So
then you have his only brother in your hold? My lor', the
victory is your own, and the princess, my mistress, beside.
In a few hours will be placed in your hands the primal cause
and fomentor of this cruel and bloody war, the Lady Jane
Howard.'

The Douglas started like one aroused from slumber,

or a state of lethargy, by a sudden wound. 'What did you say, boy?' said he. 'Either I heard amiss, or you are dreaming. I have offered estates, nay, I have offered an earldom, to any hardy adventurer who would bring me that imperious dame; but the project has been abandoned as quite impracticable.'

'Rest content,' said Colin: 'I have secured her, and she will be delivered into your hands before night. She has safe passports with her to the Scottish court, but they are in favour of Jasper Tudor, son to the Earl of Pembroke; so that the discovery of her sex proves her an impostor, and subjects her to martial law, which I request, for my mistress' sake, you will execute on her. My lady the princess, with all her beauty, and high accomplishments, is a very woman; and I know there is nothing on earth she so much dreads as the triumph of Lady Jane over her. Besides, it is evident she was bound to the Scottish court either to poison the princess, or inveigle her into the hands of her enemies. All her attendants are ignorant of her sex, save her page, who is said to be a blooming English country maiden. The Prince Alexander bade me charge you never to mention by what means she came into your hands, but to give it out that she was brought to you by a miracle, by witchcraft, or by the power of a mighty magician.' 'It is well thought of, boy,' said the Douglas, greatly elevated – 'I have been obliged to have recourse to such means already – this will confirm all. The princess your mistress desired that you should remain with me. You shall be my right hand page, I will love and favour you; you shall be fed with the bread and wine, and shall sleep in my tent, and I will trust you with all my secrets for the welcome tidings you have brought, and for the sake of the angelic dame that recommends you to me; for she is my beloved, my adored mistress, and for her will I either conquer or die! My sword is her's – my life is her's – Nay, my very soul is the right of my beloved!' Poor Colin dropped a tear on hearing this passionate nonsense. Women love extravagance in such matters, but in those days it had no bounds.

It was not long till the prisoners arrived, under the care of muckle Charlie Scott of Yardbire and Dan Chisholm, with their troopers, guarded in a very original manner. When Charlie arrived at old Chisholm's house and learned that a *prince* had been there, and had given such charges about the prisoners, he determined to make sure work; and as he had always most trust to put in himself, he took the charge of the young English nobleman and his squire, as he supposed them to be. The page he took on his huge black horse behind him, lashing him to his body with strong belts cut from a cow's raw hide. His ancles were moreover fastened to the straps at the tops of Charlie's great war boots; so that the English maiden must have had a very uncomfortable ride. But the other he held on before him, keeping her all the way in his arms, exactly as a countryman holds up a child in the church to be christened.

The Lady Jane Howard had plenty of the spirit of romance about her, but she neither had the frame nor the energy of mind requisite for carrying her wild dreams of female heroism into effect. She was an only child – a spoiled one; having been bred up without perhaps ever being controlled, till she fell into the hands of. these border mosstroopers. Her displeasure was excessive—. She complained bitterly of her detainment, and much more of being sent a prisoner to the camp. When she found herself in muckle Charlie Scott's arms, borne away to be given up to the man whom of all the world she had most reason to dread, she even forgot herself so far as to burst into tears. Charlie, with all his inordinate strength and prowess, had a heart so soft, that, as he said himself, 'a laverock might hae laired in't;' and he farther added, that when he saw 'the bit bonny English callan', that was comed o' sic grand blude, grow sae desperately wae, an' fa' a blirting and greeting, the deil a bit but his heart was like to come out at his mouth.' This was no lie, for his comrades beheld him two or three times come across his eyes with his mailed sleeve – a right uncouth handkerchief; and then he tried to comfort the youth with the following speech: 'Troth, man, but I'm unco wae for ye, ye're sae young an' sae bonny, an' no' a fit man at a' to send out i' thir crabbit times. But tak good heart, an' dinna be dauntit, for it will soon be over w'ye. Ye'll neither hae muckle to thole nor lang time to dree't, for our captain will hang ye directly. He hangs a' spies an' messengers aff hand; sae it's no worth naebody's while to greet. Short wark's aye best i' sic cases.'

'He cannot, he dares not injure a hair of my head,' said Lady Jane passionately.

'*Canna!*' said Charlie, 'Gude faith, ye ken that's nonsense. He can as easily hang ye, or do ought else w'ye, as I can wipe my beard. An' as for the thing that the Douglas *darena* do, gude faith, ye ken, I never saw it yet. But I'm sure I wish ye *may* be safe, for it wad do little good to me to see your bit pease-weep neck rackit.'

'It was most unfair, as well as most ungenerous in your prince to detain me,' said she, 'as my business required urgency. I had regular signed warrandice, and went on the kindest intent; besides, I have a great aversion to be put into the hands of Douglas. How many cows and ewes would you take to set me at liberty?'

'Whisht, whisht, Sir!' said Charlie; 'Gudesake haud your tongue! That's kittle ground. Never speak o' sic a thing. But how many could ye afford to gie, and I *were* to set you at liberty?'

'In the first place, I will give you five hundred head of good English nolt,' said Lady Jane.

'Eh? What?' said Charlie, holding his horse still, and turning his ear close round to the lady's face, that he might hear with perfect distinctness the extraordinary proffer. It was repeated. Charlie was almost electrified with astonishment. 'Five hunder head o' nout!' exclaimed he: 'But d'ye mean their heads by theirsels? – cuttit aff, like?'

'No, no; five hundred good live cattle.'

'Mercy on us! Gude faith, they wad stock a' Yardbire – an' Raeburn,' added he, after a pause, putting his horse again slowly in motion; 'an' Watkerrick into the bargain,' added he, with a full drawn sigh, putting the spurs to his beast, that he might go quicker to carry him away from the danger. 'For troth, d'ye ken, my lord, we're no that scarce o' grund in Scotland; we can get plenty o' that for little thing, gin we could get ought to lay on't. But it's hard to get beasts, an' kittle to keep them i' our country. Five hunder head o' black cattle! Hech! an Charlie Scott had a' thae, how mony braw lads could he tak at his back o'er Craikcorse to join his master the warden! But come, come, it canna be. War somebody a Scots lord, as he's an English ane, an i' the same danger, I wad risk muckle to set him free. But come, Corby, my fine naig, ye hae carried me into mony a scrape, ye maun carry me out o' this ane, or, gude faith, your master's gane. Ha, lad, ye never had sic a backfu' i' your life! Ye hae five hunder head o' black cattle on't, ye dog, an' ye're carrying them a' away frae your master an' Yardbire wi' as little ceremony as he took you frae Squire Weir o' Cockermouth. Ah, Corby, ye're gayan like your master, ye hae a lang free kind o' conscience, ye tike!'

'But, my dear Sir,' said Lady Jane, 'you have not heard the half of my proffer. You seem to be a generous, sensible, and good natured gentleman.'

'Do I?' said Charlie, 'Thanks t'ye, my lord.'

'Now,' continued she, 'if you will either set me and my page safely down on English ground, or within the ports of Edinborough, I'll add five thousand sheep to the proffer I have already made you.'

'Are ye no joking?' said Charlie, again stopping his horse.

'On my honour I am not,' was the answer.

'They'll stock a' Blake-Esk-head an' the Garald-Grains,' said Charlie: 'Hae ye a free passport to the Scottish court?'

'Yes, I have, and signed with the warden's name.'

'Na, na, haud your tongue there; my master has nae name,' said Charlie: 'He has a good speaking name, an' ane he disna think shame o', but nae name for black an' white.'

'I'll show you it,' said Lady Jane.

'Na, ye needna fash,' said Charlie; 'I fear it wad be unmannerly in me to doubt a lord's word.'

'How soon could you carry us to Edinborough?' inquired Lady Jane, anxious to keep muckle Charlie in the humour of taking her any where save into the hands of Douglas.

'That's rather a question to speer at Corby than me,' said Charlie; 'but I think if we miss drowning i' Tweed, an' breaking our necks o'er the Red-brae, an' sinking out o' sight i' Soutra-flow, that I could tak in hand to hae ye in Edinborough afore twal o'clock at night—. Bad things for you, Corby.'

'Never say another word about it then,' said Lady Jane; 'the rest are quite gone before us, and out of sight. Turn to the left, and ride for Edinborough. Think of the five hundred cows and five thousand sheep.'

'Oh, that last beats a'!' said Charlie. 'Five thousand sheep! how mony is that? Five score's a hunder – I'm sure o' that. Every hunder's five score; then – and how mony hunder maks a thousand—?'

'Ten,' said the page, who was forced to laugh at Charlie's arithmetic.

'Ten?' repeated Charlie. 'Then ten times five hunder that maks but ae thousand; an' other ten times five hunder – D—n me if I ken how mony is o' them ava. What does it signify for a man to hae mair gear than he can count? I fancy we had better jogg on the gate we're gaun, Corby.'

'I am sure, friend, ye never had such a chance of being rich,' said Lady Jane, 'and may never, in all likelihood, have such a chance again.'

'That is a' true ye're saying, my lord, an' a sair heart it has gi'en me,' said Charlie; 'but your offer's ower muckle, an' that maks me dread there's something at the bottom o't that I dinna comprehend. Gude faith, an the warden war to suffer danger or disgrace for my greed o' siller, it wad be a bonny story! Corby, straight on, ye dog: ding the brains out o' the gutters, clear for the camp, ye hellicat of an English hound. What are ye snoring an' cocking your lugs at? Od an ye get company like yoursel, ye carena what mischief ye carry your master into. Get on, I say, an' dinna gie me time to hear another word or think about this business again.'

The young lady began here to lose heart, seeing that Charlie had plucked up a determination. But her companion attacked him in her turn with all the flattery and fair promises she could think of, till Charlie found his heart again beginning to waver and calculate; so that he had no other shift but to croon a border war-song, that he might not hear this dangerous conversation. Still the page persevered, till Charlie, losing all patience, cried out as loud and as bitterly as he could, 'Haud your tongue, ye slee-gabbit limb o' the auld ane. D—n ye, d'ye think a man's conscience is to be hadden abreed like the mou' of a sack, an' crammed fu' o' beef an' mutton whether he will or no? Corby, another nicker an' another snore, lad, an' we'll soon see you aff at the gallop.'

Thus ended the trying colloquy between muckle Charlie Scott o' Yardbire and his two prisoners; the rest of his conversation was to Corby, whom he forthwith pushed on by spur and flattery to the camp.

When the truth came to be discovered, many puzzled themselves endeavouring to guess what Charlie would actually have done had he known by the way what a treasure he had in his arms – the greatest beauty, and the greatest heiress in England; – for Charlie was as notable for kindness and generosity as he was for bodily strength; and, besides, he was poor, as he frankly acknowledged; but then he only wished for riches to be able to keep more men for the service of his chief. Some thought he would have turned his horse round without further ceremony, and carried her straight to Yardbire, on purpose to keep her there for a wife; others thought he would have risked his neck, honour, and every thing, and restored her again to her friends. But it was impossible for any of them to guess what he would have done, as it was proved afterwards that Charlie could not guess himself. When the truth came to be divulged, and was first told to him, his mouth, besides becoming amazingly extended in its dimensions, actually grew four-square with astonishment; and when asked what he would have done had he known, he smacked his lips, and wiped them with the back of his hand as if his teeth had been watering – and, laughing to himself with a chuckling sound, like a moor-cock, he turned about his back to conceal his looks, and only answered with these emphatic words: 'Gude faith, it was as well I didna ken.'

CHAPTER SIX

Some write of preclair conquerouris,
And some of vallyeant emperouris,
And some of nobill mychtie kingis,
That royally did reull the ringis;
And some of squyris douchty deidis,
That wonderis wrocht in weirly weidis;
Sa I intand the best I can
Descryve the deidis and the man.
Sir Dav. Lindsaye

Wald God I war now in Pitcary!
Becass I haif bene se ill deidy.
Adew! I dar na langer tairy,
I dried I waif intill ane widdy.
Ibid

IN THE SAME grotesque guise as formerly described, Charlie at length came with his two prisoners to the outposts of the Scottish army. The rest of the train had passed by before him, and warned their friends who was coming, and in what stile; for no one thought it worth his while to tarry with Charlie and his overloaden horse. When he came near the soldiers they hurra'd, and waved their bonnets, and gathering about Charlie in crowds, they would not let him onward. Besides, some fell a loosing the prisoner behind him, and others holding up their arms to release him of the one he carried before; and, seeing how impatient he was, and how determined to keep his hold, they grew still more importunate in frolic. But it had nearly cost some of them dear; for Charlie, growing wroth, squeezed the Lady Jane so strait with the left arm, that she was forced to cry out; and putting his right over his shoulder, he drew out his tremendous two-hand sword. 'Now stand back, devils,' cried Charlie, 'or, gude faith, I'll gar Corby ride ower the taps o' the best o' ye. I hae had ower sair a trial for heart o' flesh already; but when I stood that, it sanna be the arm o' flesh that takes them frae me now, till I gie them into the Douglas's ain hands. Stand back, ye devils; a Scott never gies up his trust as lang as his arm can dimple at the elbow.'

The soldiers flew away from around him like a flight of geese, and with the same kind of noise too -- every one being giggling and laughing – and up rode Charlie to the door of the Douglas' pavilion, where he shouted aloud for the captain. Douglas, impatient to see his illustrious prisoner, left the others abruptly, and hasted out at Charlie's call.

'Gude faith, my lord,' said Charlie, 'I beg your pardon for garring you come running out that gate; but here's a bit English lord for ye, an' his henchman – sic master, sic man, as the saying is. There war terrible charges gi'en about them, sae I thought I wad secure them, an' gie them into your ain hands.'

'I am much beholden to you, gallant Yardbire,' said Douglas: 'The care and pains you have taken shall not be forgotten.'

This encouraging Charlie, he spoke to the earl with great freedom, who was mightily diverted with his manner, as well as with his mode of securing the prisoners.

'There's his lordship for ye,' said Charlie, holding him out like a small bale of goods: 'Mind ye hae gotten him safe off my hand; an' here's another chap I hae fastened to my back. An a' the English nobles war like thir twa, I hae been thinking, my lord, that they might tak' our lasses frae us, but we wadna be ill pinched to tak their kye frae them; an' it wad be nae hard bargain for us neither.' So saying, he cut his belts and thongs of raw hide, and let the attendant lady, in page's clothes, free of his body. 'He's a little, fine, soft, cozey callan this,' added Charlie, 'he has made my hinderlands as warm as they had been in an oon.'

Douglas took Lady Jane off from before the gallant yeoman in his arms. He observed with what a look she regarded him; and he was sure, from the first view he got of her features, that the page Colin must have been right with regard to the sex of the prisoner. He likewise

noted the holes in her ears, from which it was apparent
that pendant jewels had lately been taken; and he hoped
the other part of the page's information might likewise be
correct, though how to account for such an extraordinary
piece of good fortune he was wholly at a loss. He led
her into the inner pavilion, and there, in presence of his
secretary and two of his kinsmen, examined her papers
and passports. They were found all correct, and signed
by the public functionaries of both nations, in favour of
Jasper Tudor, son to the Earl of Pembroke.

'These are quite sufficient, my young lord,' said Douglas;
'I see no cause for detaining you further. You shall have a
sufficient guard till you are out of the range of my army,
and safe furtherance to the Scottish court.'

The prisoner's countenance lighted up, and she thanked
Douglas in the most grateful terms, blessing herself that
she had fallen into the hands of so courteous a knight,
and urged the necessity of their sudden departure. Douglas
assured her they should be detained no longer than the
necessity of the times required; but that it was absolutely
requisite, for his own safety, the safety of the realm, and
the success of the enterprise in which he was engaged,
and so deeply concerned, that they should submit to a
personal search from head to foot, lest some traitorous
correspondence might be secretly conveyed by them.

The countenance of the prisoner again altered at this
information. It became at first pale as a lily, and immediately after blushed as deeply as the damask rose, while the
tears started to her eyes. It was no wonder, considering
the predicament in which she now stood; her delicate lady
form to be searched by the hands of rude warriors, her sex
discovered, and her mission to the Scottish court found out
to be a wild intrigue. She fell instantly on her knees before
Douglas, and besought him in moving accents to dispense
with the useless formality of searching her and her young
kinsman and companion, assuring him at the same time
that neither of them had a single scrap of writing that
he had not seen, and adjuring him on his honour and
generosity as a knight to hearken to this request.

'The thing is impossible, my lord,' said Douglas; 'and,
moreover, the anxiety you manifest about such a trifle
argues a consciousness of guilt. You must submit to be

searched on the instant. Chuse of us whom you will to
the office.'

'I will never submit to it,' she said passionately, 'there is
not a knight in England would have refused such a request
to you.'

'I would never have asked it, my lord,' said he; 'and it is
your utter inexperience in the customs of war that makes
you once think of objecting to it. I am sorry we must use
force. Bring in two of the guards.'

'Hold, hold, my lord,' said Lady Jane, 'since I must
submit to such a degradation, I will submit to yourself. I
will be searched by your own hands, and yours alone.'

They were already in the inner tent. Douglas desired his
friends to go out, which they complied with, and he himself
began to search the person of Lady Jane, with the most
careful minuteness, as he pretended, well aware what was
to be the issue of the search. He examined all her courtly
coat, pockets, lining, and sleeves – he came to her gaudy
doublet, stiff with gold embroidery, and began to unloose
it, but she laid both her hands upon her breast, and looked
in his face with eyes so speaking, and so beseeching, that it
was impossible for man to mistake the import. Douglas did
not mistake it, but was bent upon having proof positive.

'What?' said he, 'do you still resist? What is here you
would conceal?'

'Oh my Lord,' said she, 'do you not see?'

'I see nothing,' said he; and while she feebly struggled
he loosed the vest, when the fair heaving bosom discovered
the sex of his prisoner, and at the same time, with the
struggle, the beautiful light locks had escaped from their
confinement, and hung over her breast in waving ringlets.
The maid stood revealed; and, with the disclosure, all
the tender emotions and restrained feelings of the female
heart burst forth like a river that has been dammed up
from running in its natural channel, and has just got
vent anew. She wept and sobbed till her fair breast was
like to rend. She even seized on Douglas' hand, and
wet it with her tears. He, on his part, feigned great
amazement.

'How is this?' said he, 'A maid!'

'Yes indeed, my lord, you see before you, and in your
power, a hapless maid of noble blood, who set out on a

crazy expedition of love, but, from inexperience, has fallen into your hands.'

'Then the whole pretended mission to our Scottish court is, it appears, a fraud, a deep laid imposition of some most dangerous intent, as the interest that has been used to accomplish it fully demonstrates. You have subjected yourself and all your followers to military execution; and the only method by which you can procure a respite, either for yourself or them, is to make a full confession of the whole plot.'

'Alas, my lord, I have no plot to confess. Mine was merely a romantic expedition of youthful love, and, as you are a knight, and a lover yourself, I beg your clemency, that you will pardon my followers and me. They are innocent; and, save my page, who is likewise a lady, and my own kinswoman, all the rest are as ignorant who I am, and what I am, as the child that is unborn.'

'If you would entertain any hopes of a reprieve, I say, madam, either for yourself or them, declare here to me instantly your name, lineage, and the whole of your business in Scotland, and by whose powerful interest you got this safe conduct made out, for one who, it seems, knows nothing of it, or who, perhaps, does not exist.'

'Surely you will not be so ungallant as to insist upon a lady exposing herself and all her relations? No, my lord, whatever become of me, you must never attain to the knowledge of my name, rank, or titles. I entrust myself to your mercy: you can have nothing to fear from the machinations of a love-lorn damsel.'

'I am placed in peculiarly hard circumstances, madam; I have enemies abroad and at home, and have nothing but my own energies to rely on to save my house and name from utter oblivion, and my dearest hopes from extinguishment. This expedition of yours, folded as it is in deceit and forgery, has an ominous and daring appearance. The house of Douglas must not fall for the tears of a deceitful maiden, the daughter of my enemy. Without a full disclosure of all that I request, every one of you shall suffer death in the sight of both armies before the going down of the sun. I will begin with the meanest of your followers, in hopes, for the sake of your youth and your sex, that you will relent and make a full disclosure of your name, and all your motives for such an extraordinary adventure.'

Lady Jane continued positive and peremptory, as did also her attendant, who had been thoroughly schooled before-hand, in case of their sex being discovered, never, on any account, to acknowledge who she was, lest it should put Musgrave wholly in Douglas' power. The latter, therefore, to keep up the same system of terror and retribution first practised by his opponent, caused sound the death knell, and hung out the flag of blood, to apprise those within the fortress that some of their friends were shortly to be led to execution.

The first that was brought out was a thick-set swarthy yeoman, who said his name was Edmund Heaton, and that he had been a servant to Belsay, whom he had followed in the border wars. When told that he was about to be hanged for a spy and a traitor, he got very angry, even into such a rage that they could not know what he said, for he had a deep rough burr in his throat, and spoke a coarse English dialect. 'Hang'd? I hang'd? and fogh whot? Domn your abswoghdity! Hang ane mon fogh deying whot his meas, tegh beeds him——?' He was told that he had not two minutes to live, unless he could discover something of the plot in which his employers were engaged; that it was found he had been accompanying two ladies in disguise, on some traitorous mission which they would not reveal; and it was the law of war that he should suffer for the vile crime in which he was an accomplice.

'Nobbit, I tell you that won't dey at all; – n-n-nor it sha'n't dey neithegh. Do you think you aghe to hang eveghy mon that follows ane woeman? Domn them, I nevegh knew them lead to oughts but eel! If I had known they had been woemen – Domn them!' – He was hauled up to the scaffold, for he refused to walk a foot. – 'Wh-wh-why, nobbit speak you now,' cried he in utter desperation; 'why n-n-nobbit you aghe not serious, aghe you?' He was told he should soon find to his experience that they were quite serious——. 'Why, cworse the whole geneghation of you, the thing is nwot to be bwoghn. I wont swoffegh it – that I woll not. It is dwonright mworder. Oh, ho, ho!' and he wept, crying as loud as he could, 'Oh-oh! ho: mworder! mworder! Domn eveghy Scwot of you!' – In this mood, kicking, crying, and swearing, was he turned off, and hanged in sight of both hosts.

The walls of Roxburgh were crowded with spectators. They could not divine who it was that was suffering; for all kind of communication was forbid by Musgrave, and it was now become exceedingly difficult. Great was their wonder and anxiety when they beheld one trooper after another of their countrymen brought out and hanged like dogs. But it was evident to every beholder, from the unsettled and perturbed motions of those on the wall, that something within the fortress was distressing the besieged. Some hurried to and fro; others stood or moved about in listless languor; and there were a few that gazed without moving, or taking their eyes from the spot where they were fixed. Not one flight of arrows came to disturb the execution, as usual; and it was suspected that their whole stock of arrows was exhausted. This would have been good tidings for the Scots, could they have been sure of it, as they might then have brought their files closer to the walls, and more effectually ensured a strict blockade.

Lady Jane's followers were all executed, and herself and companion sore threatened in vain. Douglas, however, meant to reserve them for another purpose than execution – to ensure to himself the surrender of the fortress, namely; but of her squires he was glad to be rid, for fear of a discovery being made to the English that the lady was in his hands, which might have brought the whole puissance of the realm upon him; whereas the generality of the nation viewed the siege merely as an affair of Border chivalry, in which they were little interested, and deemed Musgrave free from any danger.

It was on St Leonard's day that these five Englishmen were executed; and as a retaliation in part, a Scots fisherman was hanged by the English from the wall of the castle; one who indeed had been the mean of doing them a great deal of mischief. And thus stood matters at that period of the siege; namely, the Earl of Douglas and Mar lay before Roxburgh with eight thousand hardy veterans, all his own vassals. The Redhough kept a flying army on the borders of Northumberland, chiefly about the mountains of Cheviot and Cocketdale, interrupting all supplies and communications from that quarter, and doing excellent service to himself and followers, and more to the Douglas than the latter seemed to admit of. Whenever he found the English gathering to any head, he did not go and attack them, but, leaving a flying party of horse to watch their motions, he instantly made a diversion somewhere else, which drew them off with all expedition. A numerous army, hastily raised, entered Scotland on the west border, on purpose to draw off the warden; but they were surprised and defeated by the Laird of Johnson, who raised the Annandale people, and attacked the English by night. He followed them into Cumberland, and fought two sharp battles with them there, in both of which he had the advantage, and he then fell a spoiling the country. This brought the Northumberland and Durham men into these parts, who mustered under Sir William Fetherstone to the amount of fifteen thousand men. Johnston retired, and the Earl of Galloway, to back him, raised twenty thousand in the west, and came towards the Sarke: So that the siege of Roxburgh was viewed but as an item in the general convulsion, though high was the stake for those that played, and ruthless the game while it lasted. Douglas now looked upon the die as turned in his favour, as he held pledges that would render the keeping of it of no avail to his opponent. The lady was in his power at whose fiat Musgrave had taken and defended the perilous castle so bravely – but of this no man knew save the Douglas himself. Sir Richard Musgrave was likewise in his hand, the captain's youngest, most beloved, and only surviving brother; and Douglas had threatened, against a certain day, if the keys of the castle were not surrendered to him, to hang the young hero publicly, in the view of both hosts; and in all his threats he had never once broke his word. We must now take a peep within the walls of Roxburgh, and see how matters are going on there.

CHAPTER SEVEN

I cast my net in Largo bay,
    And fishes I caught nine;
There were three to roast, and three to boil,
    And three to bait the line.

Old Song

Saw never man so faynt a levand wycht,
And na ferlye, for ouir excelland lycht
    Corruptis the witt, and garris the blude awail,
    Until the harte, thocht it na dainger aill,
Quhen it is smorit membcris wirk not rychte,
    The dreadfulle terrour swa did him assaile.

Pal. of Hon.

BERWICK WAS THEN in the hands of the English,
and commanded by Sir Thomas Musgrave, the captain
of Roxburgh's cousin; so also was Norham, and all the
forts between, on that side of the river. Notwithstanding
of this, the power of the Scots predominated so much in
the open field during that reign, that this chain of forts
proved finally of no avail to Lord Musgrave, (or Sir Philip
Musgrave, as he is generally denominated,) though he
had depended on keeping the communication open, else
in victualling Roxburgh he had calculated basely. The
garrison were already reduced to the greatest extremes; they
were feeding on their horses and on salted hides; and, two
or three days previous to this, their only communication
with their countrymen had been cut off, they could not
tell how. It was at best only precarious, being carried on
in the following singular way—. The besieged had two
communications with the river, by secret covered ways
from the interior of the fortress. In each of these they had

61

a small windlass, that winded on and let off a line nearly a mile in length. The lines were very small, being made of plaited brass wire; and, putting a buoy on a hook at the end of each one of these, they let them down the water. Their friends knowing the very spot where they stopped, watched, and put dispatches on the hooks, with fish, beef, venison, and every kind of convenience, which they pulled up below the water, sometimes for a whole night together; and though this proved but a scanty supply for a whole garrison, it was for a long time quite regular, and they depended a good deal on it.

But one night it so chanced that an old fisherman, who fished for the monastery, had gone out with his coble by night to spear salmon in the river. He had a huge blaze flaming in a grate that stood exalted over the prow of his wherry; and with the light of that he pricked the salmon out of their deep recesses with great acuteness. As he was plying his task he perceived a fish of a very uncommon size and form scouring up the river with no ordinary swiftness. At first he started, thinking he had seen the devil: but a fisher generally strikes at every thing he sees in the water. He struck it with his barbed spear, called on Tweed a *leister*, and in a moment had it into his boat. It was an excellent sirloin of beef. The man was in utter amazement, for it was dead, and lay without moving, like other butcher meat; yet he was sure he saw it running up the water at full speed. He never observed the tiny line of plaited wire, nor the hook, which indeed was buried in the lire; and we may judge with what surprise he looked on this wonderful fish – this phenomenon of all aquatic productions. However, as it seemed to lie peaceably enough, and looked very well as a piece of beef, he resolved to let it remain, and betake himself again to his business. Never was there an old man so bewildered as he was, when he again looked into the river – never either on Tweed or any other river on earth. Instead of being floating *down* the river peaceably in his boat, as one naturally expects to do, he discovered that he was running straight against the stream. He expected to have missed about fifty yards of the river by his adventure with the beef; but – no! – instead of that he was about the same distance advanced in his return up the stream. The windlass at the castle, and the invisible wire line, of which he had no conception, having been still dragging him gradually up. 'Saint Mary, the mother of God, protect and defend poor Sandy Yellowlees!' cried he; 'What can be the meaning of this? Is the world turned upside down? Aha! our auld friend, Michael Scott, has some hand i' this! He's no to cree legs wi': I's be quits wi' him.' With that he tumbled his beef again into the water, which held on its course with great rapidity straight up the stream, while he and his boat returned quietly in the contrary and natural direction.

'Aye, there it goes,' cried Sandy, 'straight on for Aikwood! I's warrant that's for the warlock's an' the deil's dinner the morn. God be praised I'm free o't, or I should soon have been there to!'

Old Sandy fished down the river, but he could kill no more salmon that night – for his nerves had got a shock with this new species of fishing that he could not overcome. He missed one; wounded another on the tail; and struck a third on the rigback, where no leister can pierce a fish, till he made him spring above water. Sandy grew chagrined at himself and the warlock, Michael Scott, too – for this last was what he called 'a real prime fish.' Sandy gripped the leister a little firmer, clenched his teeth, and drew his bonnet over his eyes to shield them from the violence of his blaze. He then banned the wizard into himself, and determined to kill the next fish that made his appearance. But, just as he was keeping watch in this guise, he perceived another fish something like the former, but differing in some degree, coming swagging up the river full speed. 'My heart laup to my teeth,' said Sandy, 'when I saw it coming, and I heaved the leister, but durstna strike; but I lookit weel, an' saw plainly that it was either a side o' mutton or venison, I couldna tell whilk. But I loot it gang, an' shook my head. 'Aha, Michael, lad,' quo' I, 'ye hae countit afore your host for aince! Auld Sandy has beguiled ye. But ye weel expeckit to gie him a canter to hell the night.' I rowed my boat to the side, an' made a' the haste hame I could, for I thought auld Michael had taen the water to himself that night.'

Sandy took home his few fish, and went to sleep, for all was quiet about the abbey and the cloisters of his friends, the monks; and when he awoke next morning he could scarcely believe the evidence of his own senses, regarding what he had seen during the night. He arose and examined his fishes, and could see nothing about them that was not about other salmon. Still he strongly suspected they too might be some connections of Michael's – something illusory, if not worse; and took care to eat none of them himself, delivering them all to the cook of the monastery. The monks ate them, and throve very well; and as Sandy had come by no bodily harm, he determined to try the fishing once again, and if he met with any more such fish of passage to examine them a little better. He went out with his boat, light, and fish-spear as usual; and scarcely had he taken his station, when he perceived one of a very uncommon nature approaching. He did not strike at it, but only put his leister-grains before it as if to stop its course, when he found the pressure against the leister very strong. On pulling the leister towards him, one of the barbs laid hold of the line by which the phenomenon was led; and not being able to get rid of it, he was obliged to pull it into the boat. It was a small cask of Malmsey wine; and at once, owing to the way it was drawn out, he discovered the hook and line fastened to the end of it. These he disengaged with some difficulty, the pull being so strong and constant; and the mystery was thus found out. In a few minutes afterwards he seized a large sheaf of arrows; and some time after, at considerable intervals, a number of excellent sides of beef and venison.

Sandy Yellowlees saw that he could now fish to some purpose, and formed a resolution of being the last man in the world to tell his countrymen of this resource that the enemy had. The thing of which he was most afraid was a discovery. He knew that the articles would soon be missed, and that his light would betray him; and then a flight of arrows, or even a single one, from a lurking foe at the side of the river, would put an end to his fishing for ever. Such an opportunity was not to be given up, notwithstanding of this danger; so, after much prying, both by day and by night, Sanders found that at an abrupt crook in the water, whatever the line brought up came close to the side, and when the water was low it even trailed them over a point of level sand-bed quite dry. This was a joyous discovery for Sandy. He had nothing ado but to sail down in his boat when it grew dark, and lie lurking at this crook in the water, and make a prey of whatever came within his reach. The very first night he filled his boat half full of valuable stuff. There was a necessity for disposing of a part of this, and Sandy was obliged to aver that he had discovered a hidden store belonging to the English; and, moreover, he hinted that he could supply the towns of Kelso and Roxburgh, the abbey of the one and the priory of the other, for some time to come. Great was the search, that was made about the banks of the river, but no one could find the store; yet Sanders Yellowlees continued to supply the market with luxuries, tho' no one knew how. Intelligence was sent down the stream, with the buoys, of the seizure of the provisions, and of the place where they were taken off, which they knew from the failure of the weight they were pulling to be always at the same place. The news also spread of Sandy's stores, and both reached the secret friends of the English, from whom the provisions were nightly sent to their beseiged friends and benefactors, with all the caution and secrecy possible, it being given them to understand that on that supply alone depended the holding out of the fortress.

Many schemes were now tried to entrap Sandy, but all without effect; for the Scots had a strong post surrounding that very point where Sandy caught all his spoil. It was impossible to reach it but by a boat; and no boat was allowed on the river but that one that belonged to the abbey At length an English trooper undertook to seize this old depredator. Accordingly, in the dead of the night, when the lines came down, he seized them both, twisted them into one, and walked silently up the side of the river until he came nigh to the spot where the Scots lines on each side joined the stream. He then put the two hooks into his buff belt, and committing himself to the water, was dragged in silence and perfect safety up the pool between the outposts.

The first turn above that was the point where Sandy lay watching. He had only seized one prey that night, and that was of no great value – for they had given over sending up victuals to enrich an old Scots rascal, as they termed honest Sanders. He was glad when he saw the wake of a heavy burden coming slowly towards him. 'This is a sack o' sweet-meats,' said he to himself:' It must be currans an raisins, an' sic fine things as are na injured by the fresh water. I shall get a swinging price from the abbey-men for them, to help wi' their Christmas pies.'

No sooner did this huge load touch the land, than Sandy seized it with all expedition; but, to his inexpressible horror, the sack of sweetmeats seized him in its turn, and that with such potence that he was instantaneously overpowered. He uttered one piercing cry, and no more, before the trooper gagged and pinioned him. The Scottish lines were alarmed, and all in motion, and the troops on both sides were crowding to the bank of the stream. A party was approaching the spot where the twain were engaged in the unequal struggle. To return down the stream with his prisoner, as he intended, was impracticable; so the trooper had no alternative left but that of throwing himself into Sandy's boat, with its owner in his arms, shoving her from the side into the deep, and trusting himself to the strength of the wirelines. As the windlasses were made always to exert the same force and no more, by resisting that they could be stopped; so by pushing the boat from the side in the direction of the castle, the line being slackened, that again set them agoing with great velocity; and though they soon slackened in swiftness, the trooper escaped with his prisoner undiscovered, and, by degrees, was dragged up to the mouth of the covered way that led through or under the hill on which the castle stood; and there was poor Sanders Yellowlees delivered into the hands of his incensed and half-famished enemies. It was he that was hanged over the wall of the castle on the day that the five English yeomen were executed.[1]

The English now conceived that their secret was undiscovered, and that their sufferings would forthwith be mitigated by the supply drawn by their lines. They commenced briskly and successfully; but, alas! their success was of short duration. Sanders' secret became known to the Scots army. The night-watchers had often seen the old

---

[1] As there can be no doubt of the authenticity of this part of the Curate's tale, these secret passages must have been carried under ground all the way from the castle to the junction of the two rivers; and it is said that a tradition still exists on the spot, that these vaulted paths have often been discovered by former inhabitants.

man's boat leaning on the shore at that point at all hours of the night; for he was always free to go about plodding for fish when he pleased. His cry was heard at that spot, and the boat was now missing: the place was watched, and in two days the Englishmen's secret, on which they so much relied, was discovered, and quite cut off; and that powerful garrison was now left with absolute famine staring them in the face.

As in all cases of utter privation, the men grew ungovernable. Their passions were chafed, and foamed like the ocean before the commencement of a tempest, foreboding nothing but anarchy and commotion. Parties were formed of the most desperate opposition to one another, and every one grew suspicious of his neighbour. Amid all this tempest of passion a mutiny broke out: – a strong party set themselves to deliver up the fortress to the Scots. But through such a medley of jarring opinions what project could succeed? The plot was soon discovered, the ringleaders secured, and Sir Stephen Vernon, Musgrave's most tried and intimate friend, found to be at the head of it. No pen can do justice to the astonishment manifested by Musgrave when the treachery of his dear friend was fully proven. His whole frame and mind received a shock as by electricity, and he gazed around him in moody madness, as not knowing whom to trust, and as if he deemed those around him were going to be his assassins.

'Wretch that I am!' cried he, 'What is there more to afflict and rend this heart? Do I breathe the same air? Do I live among the same men? Do I partake of the same nature and feelings as I was wont? My own friend and brother Vernon, has he indeed lifted up his hand against me, and become one with my enemies? Whom now shall I trust? Must my dearest hopes – my honour, and the honour of my country, be sacrificed to disaffection and treachery? Oh Vernon – my brother Vernon, how art thou fallen!'

'I confess my crime,' said Vernon; 'and I submit to my fate, since a crime it must be deemed. But it was out of love and affection to you, that your honour might not stoop to our haughty enemies. To hold out the fortress is impossible, and to persevere in the attempt utter depravity. Suppose you feed on one another, before the termination of the Christmas holidays, the remnant that will be left will

not be able to guard the sallying ports, even though the
ramparts are left unmanned. In a few days I shall see my
brave young friend and companion in arms, your brother,
disgracefully put down, and ere long the triumphant Scots
enter, treading over the feeble remains of this yet gallant
army. I may bide a traitor's blame, and be branded with a
traitor's name, but it was to save my friends that I strove;
for I tell you, and some of you will live to see it, to hold
out the castle is impossible.'

'It is false!' cried Musgrave. 'It is false! It is false!' cried
every voice present in the judgment-hall, with frantic rage;
and all the people, great and small, flew on the culprit to
tear him to pieces; for their inveteracy against the Scots
still grew with their distress.

'It is false! It is false!' shouted they. 'Down with the
traitor! sooner shall we eat the flesh from our own bones
than deliver up the fortress to the Scots! Down with the
false knave! down with the traitor!' – and, in the midst of
a tumult that was quite irresistible, Vernon was borne up
on their shoulders, and hurried to execution, smiling with
derision at their madness, and repeating their frantic cries
in mockery. It was in vain that the commander strove to
save his friend – as well might he have attempted to have
stemmed the river in its irresistible course single-handed.
Vernon and his associates were hanged like dogs, amid
shouts of execration, and their bodies flung into a pit.
When this was accomplished, the soldiers waved their caps,
and cried out, 'So fare it with all who take part with our
hateful enemies!'

Musgrave shed tears at the fate of his brave companion,
and thenceforward was seized with gloomy despondency;
for he saw that subordination hung by a thread so brittle
that the least concussion would snap it asunder, and
involve all in inextricable confusion. His countenance
and manner underwent a visible change, and he often
started on the approach of any one toward him, and
laid his hand on his sword. The day appointed by the
Douglas for the execution of Sir Richard, provided the
castle was not delivered up before that period, was fast
approaching – an event that Musgrave could not look
forward to without distraction; and it was too evident to
his associates that his brave mind was so torn by conflicting

passions, that it stood in great danger of being rooted up
for ever.

It is probable that at this time he would willingly have
complied with the dictates of nature, and saved the life of
his brother; but to have talked of yielding up the fortress to
the Scots at that period would only have been the prelude to
his being torn in pieces. It was no more their captain's affair
of love and chivalry that influenced them, but desperate
animosity against their besiegers; and every one called
aloud for succours. Communication with their friends
was impracticable, but they hoped that their condition
was known, and that succours would soon appear—.
Alas, their friends in Northumberland had enough ado
to defend themselves, nor could they do it so effectually
but that their lands were sometimes harried to their
very doors. The warden, with his hardy mountaineers,
was indefatigable; and the English garrison were now
so closely beleaguered, that all chance of driving a prey
from the country faded from their hopes. Never was the
portcullis drawn up, nor the draw-bridge at either end let
down, that intelligence was not communicated by blast of
bugle to the whole Scottish army, who were instantly on
the alert. The latter fared sumptuously, while those within
the walls were famishing; and at length the day appointed
for the execution of Sir Richard drew so near that three
days only were to run.

It had been customary for the English, whenever the
Scots sent out a herald, bearing the flag of truce, to
make any proposal whatsoever, to salute him with a flight
of arrows; all communication or listening to proposals
being strictly forbidden by the captain, on pain of death.
However, that day, when the Douglas' herald appeared
on the rising ground, called the Hill of Barns, Musgrave
caused answer him by a corresponding flag, hoping it
might be some proposal of a ransom for the life of his
beloved brother, on which the heralds had an interchange
of words at the draw-bridge. The Scottish herald made
demand of the castle in his captain's name, and added, that
the Douglas requested it might be done instantly, to save
the life of a brave and noble youth, whom he would gladly
spare, but could not break his word and his oath that he
should suffer. He farther assured the English captain, that

it was in vain for him to sacrifice his brother, for that he had the means in his power to bring him under subjection the day following, if he chose.

A council of the gentlemen in the castle was called. Every one spoke in anger, and treated the demand with derision. Musgrave spoke not a word; but, with a look of unstable attention on every one that spoke, collected their verdicts, and in a few minutes this answer was returned to the requisition of the Scots.

'If Sir Philip Musgrave himself, and every English knight and gentleman in the castle were now in the hands of the Douglas, and doomed to the same fate of their brave young friend, still the Douglas should not gain his point – the castle would not be delivered up. The garrison scorn his proposals, they despise his threats, and they hold his power at defiance. Such tender mercies as he bestows, such shall he experience. He shall only take the castle by treading over the breasts of the last six men that remain alive in it.'

This was the general answer for the garrison – in the meantime Musgrave requested, as a personal favour of the Douglas, that he might see and condole with his brother one hour before his fatal exit. The request was readily complied with, and every assurance of safe conduct and protection added. The Douglas' pavilion stood on the rising ground, between the castle and the then splendid city of Roxburgh, a position from which he had a view of both rivers, and all that passed around the castle, and in the town; but, since the commencement of winter he had lodged over night in a tower that stood in the middle of the High-town, called the King's House, that had prisons underneath, and was strongly guarded; but during the day he continued at the pavilion, in order to keep an eye over the siege.

To this pavilion, therefore, Musgrave was suffered to pass, with only one knight attendant; and all the way from the drawbridge to the tent they passed between two files of armed soldiers, whose features, forms, and armour exhibited a strange contrast. The one rank was made up of Mar Highlanders; men short of stature, with red locks, high cheek bones, and looks that indicated a ferocity of nature; the other was composed of Lowlanders from the dales of the south and the west; men clothed in grey, with sedate looks, strong athletic frames, and faces of blunt and honest bravery. Musgrave weened himself passing between the ranks of two different nations, instead of the vassals of one Scottish nobleman. At the pavilion, the state, splendour, and number of attendant knights and squires amazed him; but by them all he was received with the most courteous respect.

Sir Richard was brought up from the vaults of the King's House to the tent, as the most convenient place for the meeting with his brother, and for the guards to be stationed around them; and there, being placed in one of the apartments of the pavilion, his brother was ushered in to him. No one was present at the meeting; but, from an inner apartment, all that passed between them was overheard. Musgrave clasped his younger brother in his arms; the other could not return the embrace, for his chains were not taken off; but their meeting was passionately affecting, as the last meeting between two brothers must always be. When the elder retired a step, that they might gaze on each other, what a difference in appearance! – what a contrast they exhibited to each other! The man in chains, doomed to instant death, had looks of blooming health, and manly fortitude: The free man, the renowned Lord Musgrave, governor of the impregnable but perilous castle of Roxburgh, and the affianced lord and husband to the richest and most beautiful lady in England, was the picture of haggard despair and misfortune. He appeared but the remnant, the skeleton of the hero he had lately been; and a sullen instability of mind flashed loweringly in his dark eye. His brother was almost terrified at his looks, for he regarded him sometimes as with dark suspicion, and as if he dreaded him to be an incendiary.

'My dear brother,' said Sir Richard, 'what is it that hangs upon your mind, and discomposes you so much? You are indeed an altered man since I had the misfortune to be taken from you. Tell me, how fares all within the castle?'

'Oh, very well; quite well, brother. All perfectly secure – quite well within the castle.' But as he said this he strode rapidly backward and forward across the small apartment, and eyed the canvass on each side with a grin of rage, as if he suspected that it concealed listeners; nor was he wrong in his conjecture, though it was only caused by the frenzy of habitual distrust. 'But, how can I be otherwise than discomposed, brother,' continued he, 'when I am in so short a time to see you sacrificed in the prime of youth and vigour, to my own obstinacy and pride, perhaps.'

'I beg that you will not think of it, or take it at all to heart,' said the youth; 'I have made up my mind, and can look death in the face without unbecoming dismay. I should have preferred dying on the field of honour, with my sword in my hand, rather than being hanged up between the hosts, like a spy, or common malefactor. But let the tears that are shed for Richard be other than salt brine from the eyes of the Englishmen. Let them be the drops of purple blood from the hearts of our enemies. I charge you, by the spirits of our fathers, whom I am so shortly to join, and by the blessed Trinity, that you act in this trying dilemma as the son of the house you represent. Shed not a tear for me, but revenge my death on the haughty house of Douglas.'

'There is my hand! Here is my sword! But the vital motion, or the light of reason, who shall ensure to me till these things are fulfilled? Nay, who shall ensure them to this wasted frame for one moment? I am not the man I have been, brother: But here I will swear to you, by all the host of heaven, to revenge your death, or die in the fulfilment of my vow. Yes, fully will I revenge it! I will waste! waste! waste! and the fire that is begun within shall be quenched, and no tongue shall utter it! Ha! Ha, Ha! shall it not be so, brother?'

'This is mere raving, brother; I have nothing from this.'

'No, it is not; for there is a fire that you wot not of. But I will quench it, though with my own blood. Brother, there is one thing I wish to know, and for that purpose did I come hither. Do you think it behoves me to suffer you to perish in this affair?'

'That depends entirely upon your internal means of defence,' answered Richard. 'If there is a certainty, or even a probability, that the castle can hold until relieved by our friends, which will not likely be previous to the time you have appointed for them to attempt it; why, then, I would put no account on the life of one man. Were I in your place, I would retain my integrity in opposition to the views of Douglas; but if it is apparent to you, who knows all your own resources, that the castle must yield, it is needless to throw away the life of your brother, sacrificing it to the pride of opposition for a day or a week.'

Musgrave seemed to be paying no regard to this heroic and disinterested reasoning – for he was still pacing to and fro, gnawing his lip; and if he was reasoning, or thinking at all, was following out the train of his own unstable mind – 'Because, if I were sure,' said he, 'that you felt that I was acting unkindly or unnaturally by you, by the Rood, I would carve the man into fragments that would oppose my submission to save my brother. I would teach them that Musgrave was not to be thwarted in his command of the castle that was taken by his own might and device, and to the government of which his sovereign appointed him. If a dog should dare to bay at me in opposition to my will, whatever it were, I would muzzle the hound, and make him repent his audacity.'

'My noble brother,' said Richard, 'what is the meaning of this frenzy? No one is opposing your will, and I well believe no one within the castle will attempt it– '

'Because they dare not!' said he, furiously, interrupting his brother: 'They dare not, I tell you! But if they durst, what do you think I would do? Ha, ha, ha!'

Douglas overheard all this, and judging it a fit time to interfere, immediately a knight opened the door of the apartment where the two brothers conversed, and announced the Lord Douglas. Musgrave composed himself with wonderful alacrity; and the greeting between the two great chiefs, though dignified, was courteous and apparently free of rancour or jealousy. Douglas first addressed his rival as follows:

'I crave pardon, knights, for thus interrupting you. I will again leave you to yourselves; but I judged it incumbent on me, as a warrior and a knight of honour, to come, before you settled finally on your mode of procedure, and conjure you, Lord Philip Musgrave, to save the life of your brother—'

'Certainly you will not put down my brave brother, Lord Douglas?' said Musgrave, interrupting him.

'As certainly,' returned he, 'as you put down my two kinsmen, Cleland and Douglas of Rowlaw, in mere spite and wanton cruelty, because they were beloved and respected by me. I am blameless, as it was yourself who began this unwarrantable system, and my word is passed. Sir Richard must die, unless the keys of the castle are delivered to me before Friday at noon. But I shall be blameless in any thing further. I conjure you to save him; and as an inducement, assure you, by the honour of knighthood, that your resistance is not only unnatural, but totally useless; for I have the means of commanding your submission when I please.'

'Lord Douglas, I defy thee!' answered Musgrave. 'You hold the life in your hand that I hold dearest on earth, save one. For these two would I live or die; but, since thy inveterate enmity will not be satisfied with ought short of the life of my only brother, take it; and may my curse, and the curse of heaven, be your guerdon. It shall only render the other doubly dear to me; and, for her sake, will I withstand your proud pretensions; and, as she enjoined me, hold this castle, with all its perils, till the expiry of the Christmas holidays, in spite of you. I defy your might and your ire. Let your cruel nature have its full sway. Let it be gorged with the blood of my kinsfolk; it shall only serve to make my opposition the stronger and more determined. For the sake of her whom I serve, the mistress of my heart and soul, I will hold my resolution—. Do your worst!'

'So be it!' said Douglas. 'Remember that I do not, like you, fight only in the enthusiasm of love and chivalry, but for the very being of my house. I will stick at no means of retaliating the injuries you have done to me and mine, however unjustifiable these may appear to some – no act of cruelty, to attain the prize for which I contend. Little do you know what you are doomed to suffer, and that in a short space of time. I again conjure you to save the life of your brother, by yielding up to me your ill-got right, and your conditions shall be as liberal as you can desire.'

'I will yield you my estate to save my brother, but not the castle of Roxburgh. Name any other ransom but that, and I will treat with you. Ask what I can grant with honour, and command it.'

'Would you give up the life of a brave only brother to gratify the vanity and whim of a romantic girl, who, if present herself, would plead for the life of Sir Richard, maugre all other considerations, else she has not the feelings of woman? What would you give, Lord Musgrave, to see that lady, and hear her sentiments on the subject?'

'I would give much to see her. But, rather than see her in this place, I would give all the world and my life's blood into the bargain. But of that I need not have any fear. You have conjurors among you, it is said, and witches that can raise up the dead, but their power extends not to the living, else who of my race would have been left?'

'I have more power than you divine; and I will here give you a simple specimen of it, to convince you how vain it is to contend with me. You are waging war with your own vain imagination, and suffer all this wretchedness for a thing that has neither being nor name.'

Douglas then lifted a small gilded bugle that hung always at his sword belt, the language of which was well known to all the army; and on that he gave two blasts not louder than a common whistle, when instantly the door of the apartment opened, and there entered Lady Jane Howard, leaning on her female attendant, dressed in attire of princely magnificence. 'Lady Jane Howard!' exclaimed Sir Richard, starting up, and struggling with his fettered arms to embrace her. But when the vision met the eyes of Lord Musgrave, he uttered a shuddering cry of horror, and sprung with a convulsive leap back into the corner of the tent. There he stood, like the statue of distraction, with his raised hands pressed to each side of his helmet, as if he had been strenuously holding his head from splitting asunder.

'So! Friend and foe have combined against me!' cried he wildly. 'Earth and hell have joined their forces in opposition to one impotent human thing! And what his crime? He presumed on no more than what he did, and could have done; but who can stand against the powers of darkness, and the unjust decrees of heaven? Yes; unjust! I say unjust! Down with all decrees to the centre! There's no truth in heaven! I weened there was, but it is as false as the rest! I say as false! – falser than both! – I'll brave all the three! Ha, ha, ha!'

Douglas had brought Lady Jane the apparel, and commanded her to dress in it; and, perceiving the stern, authoritative nature of the chief, she judged it meet to comply. At first she entered with a languid dejected look, for she had been given to understand something of the

rueful nature of the meeting she was called on to attend.
But when she heard the above infuriated rhapsody, and
turned her eyes in terror to look on the speaker, whose
voice she well knew, she uttered a scream and fainted.
Douglas supported her in his arms; and Sir Richard,
whose arms were in fetters, stood and wept over her.
But Musgrave himself only strode to and fro over the
floor of the pavilion, and uttered now and then a frantic
laugh. 'That is well! – That is well!' exclaimed he; 'just
as it should be! I hope she will not recover. Surely she
will not?' and then bending himself back, and clasping his
hands together, he cried fervently: 'O mother of God, take
her to thyself while she is yet pure and uncontaminated, or
what heart of flesh can endure the prospect? What a wreck
in nature that lovely form will soon be! Oh-oh-oh!'

The lady's swoon was temporary. She soon began to
revive, and cast unsettled looks around in search of the
object that had so overpowered her; and, at the request
of Sir Richard, who perceived his brother's intemperate
mood, she was removed. She was so struck with the altered
features, looks, and deportment of the knight, who in her
imagination was every thing that was courteous, comely,
and noble, and whom she had long considered as destined
to be her own, that her heart was unable to stand the
shock, and her removal from his presence was an act of
humanity.

She was supported out of the tent by Douglas and her
female relation; but when Musgrave saw them leading her
away, he stepped rapidly in before them and interposed;
and, with a twist of his body, put his hand two or three
times to the place where the handle of his sword should
have been. The lady lifted her eyes to him, but there was
no conception in that look, and her lovely face was as pale
as if the hand of death had passed over it.

Any one would have thought that such a look from the
lady of his love, in such a forlorn situation, and in the hands
of his mortal enemy, would have totally uprooted the last
fibres of his distempered mind. But who can calculate on
the medicine suited to a diseased spirit? The cures even of
some bodily diseases are those that would poison a healthy
frame. So did it prove in this mental one. He lifted his hand
from his left side, where he had thrust it convulsively in

search of his sword, and clapping it on his forehead, he seemed to resume the command of himself at once, and looked as calm and serene as in the most collected moments of his life.

When they were gone, he said to Sir Richard, in the hearing of the guards: 'Brother, what is the meaning of this? What English traitor has betrayed that angelic maid into the hands of our enemy?'

'To me it is incomprehensible,' said Sir Richard: 'I was told of it by my keeper last night, but paid no regard to the information, judging it a piece of wanton barbarity; but now my soul shudders at the rest of the information that he added.'

'What more did the dog say?' said Musgrave.

'He said he had heard that it was resolved by the Douglasses, that, if you did not yield up the fortress and citadel freely, on or before the day of the conception of the Blessed Virgin, on that day at noon the lady of your heart should be exhibited in a state not to be named on a stage erected on the top of the Bush-law, that faces the western tower, and is divided from it only by the moat; and there before your eyes, and in sight of both hosts, compelled to yield to that disgrace which barbarians only could have conceived; and then to have her nose cut off, her eyes put out, and her beauteous frame otherwise disfigured.'

'He dares not for his soul's salvation do such a deed!' said Musgrave; 'No; there's not a bloodhound that ever mouthed the air of his cursed country durst do a deed like that. And though every Douglas is a hound confest, where is the mongrel among them that durst but howl of such an outrage in nature? Why, the most absolute fiend would shrink from it: Hell would disown it; and do you think the earth would bear it?'

'Brother, suspend your passion, and listen to the voice of reason and of nature. Your cause is lost, but not your honour. You took, and have kept that fortress, to the astonishment of the world. But for what do you now fight? or what can your opposition avail? Let me beseech you not to throw away the lives of those you love most on earth thus wantonly, but capitulate on honourable terms, and rescue your betrothed bride and your only brother from the irritated Scots. Trust not that they will stick at

any outrage to accomplish their aim. Loth would I be to
know our name were dishonoured by any pusillanimity
on the part of my brother; but desperate obstinacy is not
bravery. I, therefore, conjure you to save me, and her in
whom all your hopes of future felicity are bound up.'

Musgrave was deeply affected; and, at that instant,
before he had time to reply, Douglas re-entered.

'Scots lord, you have overcome me,' said he, with
a pathos that could not be exceeded: 'Yes you have
conquered, but not with your sword. Not on the field,
nor on the wall, have ye turned the glaive of Musgrave;
but either by some infernal power, or else by chicanery
and guile, the everlasting resources of your cursed nation.
It boots not me to know how you came possessed of this last
and only remaining pledge of my submission. It is sufficient
you have it. I yield myself your prisoner; let me live or die
with those two already in your power.'

'No, knight, that must not be,' replied Douglas, 'You are
here on safe conduct and protection; my honour is pledged,
and must not be forfeited. You shall return in safety to your
kinsmen and soldiers, and act by their counsel. It is not
prisoners I want, but the castle of Roxburgh, which is the
right of my sovereign and my nation – clandestinely taken,
and wrongously held by you. I am neither cruel nor severe
beyond the small range that points to that attainment; but
that fortress I will have – else wo be to you, and all who
advise withholding it, as well as all their connexions to
whom the power of Scotland can extend. If the castle is
not delivered up before Friday at noon, your brother shall
suffer – that you already know. But at the same hour on
the day of the Conception, if it is still madly and wantonly
detained, there shall be such a scene transacted before your
eyes as shall blur the annals of the Border for ever.'

'If you allude to any injury intended to the lady who is
your prisoner,' said Musgrave, 'the cruellest fiend in hell
could not have the heart to hurt such angelic purity and
loveliness; and it would degrade the honour of knighthood
for ever to suffer it. Cruel as you are, you dare not injure
a hair of her head.'

'Talk not of cruelty in me,' said Douglas: 'If the knight
who is her lover will not save her, how should I? You have
it in your power, and certainly it is you that behove to do

it; even granting that the stakes for which we fought were equal, the task of redemption and the blame would rest solely with you. And how wide is the difference between the prizes for which we contend? I for my love, my honour, and the very existence of my house and name; and you for you know not what – the miserable pride of opposition. Take your measures, my lord. I will not be mocked.'

Douglas left the apartment. Musgrave also arose and embraced his brother, and, as he parted from him, he spoke these ominous words: 'Farewell, my dear Richard. May the angels that watch over honour be your guardians in the hour of trial. You know not what I have to endure from tormentors without and within. But hence we meet not again in this state of existence. The ties of love must be broken, and the bands of brotherly love burst asunder – nevertheless I will save you – A long farewell my brother.'

Musgrave was then conducted back to the draw-bridge, between two long files of soldiers as before, while all the musicians that belonged either to the army or the city were ranked up in a line behind them, on the top of the great precipice that overhangs the Teviot, playing, on all manner of instruments, '*Turn the Blue Bonnets wha can, wha can,*' with such a tremendous din that one would have thought every stone in the walls of Roxburgh was singing out the bravado.

CHAPTER EIGHT

Quhat weywerde elfin thynge is thaten boie,
That hyngethe still upon myne gaire, as doeth
My synne of harte? And quhome rychte loth, I lofe
With not les hanckerynge. His locent eyne,
And his tungis maiter comethe on myne sense
Lyke a remembourance; or lyke ane dreime
That had delytis in it. Quhen I wolde say
'Begone;' lo then my tung mistakethe quyte,
Or fanceyinge not the terme, it sayethe 'Come hidder,
Come hidder, crabbed boie, unto myne syde.'

Old Play

THAT EVENING, AFTER the departure of the noble
and distressed Musgrave, Douglas was sitting all alone
musing in a secret apartment of the pavilion, when he
heard a gentle tap at the door. 'Who's there?' inquired
he surlily: 'It is I, my lor',' said a petulant treble voice
without. 'Aha! my excellent nondescript little fellow,
Colin Roy, is it you? Why, you may come in.' Colin
entered dressed in a most elegant and whimsical livery,
and, forgetting himself, made the Douglas two or three
graceful courtesies instead of bows.

'Aye, hem,' said he, 'that's very well for the page of
a princess. I suppose you have been studying the graces
from your accomplished mistress? But where have you
been all this while? I have felt the loss of you from my
hand grievously.'

'I have been waiting on my royal mistress, my lor','
informing her of all that is going on at the siege, and of your
good fortune in the late captures you have made, wherein
she rejoices exceedingly, and wishes you all good fortune
and forward success; and, in token of kind remembrance,

she sends you this heart of ruby set in gold and diamonds – a gem that befits your lordship well to wear. And many more matters she has given me in charge, my lor'.'

Douglas kissed the locket, and put it in his bosom, and then uttered abundance of the extravagant bombast peculiar to that age. He called her his guardian angel, his altar of incense, and the saint of his devotion, the buckler of his arm, the sword in his hand, and the jewel of his heart. 'Do you think, Colin,' added he, 'that ever there was a maiden born like this royal lady of my love?'

'Why, my lor', I am not much skilled in these matters, but I believe the wench, my mistress, is well enough; – that is, she is well formed. And yet she is but so so.'

'How dare you, you piece of unparalleled impudence, talk of your royal mistress in that strain? Or where did you ever see a form or features so elegant, and so bewitchingly lovely?'

'Do you think so? – Well, I'm glad of it. I think she is coarse and masculine. Where did I ever see such a form, indeed! Yes I have seen a much finer limb, and an arm, and a hand too! What think you of that for a hand, my lor'?' – (and with that the urchin clapped his hand on the green table, first turning up the one side of it and then the other.) – 'I say if that hand were as well kept, and that arm as well loaden with bracelets, and the fingers with diamond rings, it would be as handsome as your princess's, of which you boast so much – aye, and handsomer too.'

'You are a privileged boy, Colin, otherwise I would kick you heartily, and, moreover, cause you to be whipped by the hand of the common executioner. However, you are a confidant – all is well from you; and, to say the truth, yours is a very handsome hand for a boy's hand – so is your arm. But what are they to those of my lovely and royal Margaret? – mere deformity! the husk to the wheat!'

'Indeed, my lor', you have an excellent taste, and a no less gifted discernment!'

'I cannot conceive of any earthly being equalling my beauteous princess, whether in the qualifications of body or mind.'

'I rejoice to hear it. How blind love is! Why, in sober reality, there is the Lady Jane Howard. Is there any comparison between the princess and that lady in beauty?'

'She is, I confess, a most exquisite creature, Colin, even though rival to my adorable lady; in justice it must be acknowledged she is *almost* peerless in beauty. I do not wonder at Musgrave's valour when I see the object of it. But why do you redden as with anger, boy, to hear my commendations of that hapless lady?'

'I, my lord? How should I redden with anger? On my honour, craving my Lord Douglas' pardon, I am highly pleased. I think she is much more beautiful than you have said, and that you should have spoken of her in a more superlative degree, and confessed frankly that you would willingly exchange your betrothed lady for her. I cannot chuse but think her very beautiful; too beautiful, indeed, with her blue eyes, white teeth, and ruddy lips. I don't like such bright blue eyes. I could almost find in my heart to scratch them out, she is so like a wanton. So you don't wonder at Lord Musgrave's valour, after having seen his mistress? Well, I advise your lordship, your captainship, and your besiegership, that there are some who wonder very much at your *want* of valour. I tell you this in confidence. My mistress thinks you hold her charms only at a small avail, that you have not *gone into* that castle long ago, and turned out these Englishmen, or hung them up by the necks if they refused. Musgrave went in and took it at once, for the favour of his mistress; because, forsooth, he deemed her worthy of the honour of such a bold emprize. Why, then, do not you do the same? My mistress, to be sure, is a woman – a very woman; but she says this, that it is superabundantly ungallant of you not to have *gone in* and taken possession of the castle long ago. Do you know that (poor kind creature!) she has retired to a convent, where she continues in a state of sufferance, using daily invocations at the shrines of saints for your success. And she has, moreover, made a vow not to braid her hair, nor dress herself in princely apparel until the day of your final success. Surely, my lor', you ought *to take that castle*, and relieve my dear mistress from this durance. I almost weep when I think of her, and must say with her that she has been shabbily used, and that she has reason to envy Lady Jane Howard even in her captivity.'

'Colin, you are abundantly impertinent: but there is no stopping of your tongue once it is set a-going. As to the taking of castles, these things come not under the cognizance of boys or women. But indeed I knew not that my sovereign lady the princess had absconded from the courtly circle of her father's palace, and betaken herself to a convent on my account. Every thing that I hear of that jewel endears her to me the more.'

'What? even her orders for you *to go into the castle*, and put out the English? I assure you, my lor', she insists upon it. Whether it is her impatience to be your bride, I know not, but she positively will not be satisfied unless you very soon *go into that castle*, and put the Englishmen all to the outside of it, where you are now; or hang them, and bury them out of sight before she visits the place to congratulate you.'

'Boy, I have no patience with you. Cease your prating, and inform me where my beloved mistress is, that I may instantly visit her.'

'No; not for the Douglas' estate, which is now in the fire, and may soon be brought to the anvil, will I inform you of that. But, my lor', you know I must execute my commission. And I tell you again, unless you take this castle very soon, you will not only lose the favour of my mistress, but you will absolutely break her heart. Nothing less will satisfy her. I told her, there was a great moat, more than a hundred feet deep, and as many wide, that surrounded the castle, and flowed up to the base of its walls; that there was a large river on each side of it, and that they were both dammed and appeared like two standing seas – but all availed nought. 'There is a moat,' said I; 'But let him go over that,' said she; 'let him swim it, or put a float on it. What is it to cross a pool a hundred feet wide? How did Lord Musgrave pass over it?' 'There are strong walls on the other side,' said I: 'But let him go over these,' said she, 'or break a hole through them and go in. Men built the walls, why may not men pull them down? How did Musgrave get over them?' 'There are armed men within,' said I: 'But they are only Englishmen,' said she; 'Let Douglas' men put their swords into them, and make them stand back. How did Musgrave get in when it was defended by gallant Scots? Douglas is either no lover, or else no warrior,' added she; 'or perhaps he is neither the one nor the other."'

'Peace, sapling,' said Douglas, frowning and stamping with his foot, 'Peace, and leave the pavilion instantly.' Colin went away visibly repressing a laugh, which irritated Douglas still the more; and as the urchin went, he muttered in a crying whine, 'My mistress is very shabbily used! – very shabbily! To have promised herself to a knight if he will but take a castle for her, and to have fasted, and prayed, and vowed vows for him, and yet he dares not go in and take it. And I am shabbily used too; and that I'll tell her! Turned out before I get half her message delivered! But I must inform you, my lor', before I go, that since you are making no better use of the advantage given you, I demand the prisoners back that I lodged in your hand in my lady mistress' name, and by her orders.'

'I will do no such thing to the whim of a teasing impertinent stripling, without my lady princess's hand and seal for it,' said Douglas.

'You shall not long want that,' said Colin; and pulling a letter out from below his sash, he gave it to him. It was the princess's hand and seal – it being an easy matter for Colin to get what letters he listed. Douglas opened it, and read as follows:

> 'LORD DOUGLAS – In token of my best wishes for your success, I send you these, with greeting. I hope you will take immediate advantage of the high superiority afforded you in this contest, by putting some indelible mark, or public stain, on the lusty dame I put into your hands. If Musgrave be a knight of any gallantry he will never permit it, but yield. As I cannot attend personally, I request that the mode and degree of punishment you inflict may be left to my page Colin. That you have not been successful by such means already, hath much surprised
>
> MARGARET.'

'This is not a requisition to give you up the prisoners,' said Douglas, 'but merely a request that the punishment inflicted may be left to you, a request which must not be denied to the lady of my heart. Now, pray, Master Colin Roy MacAlpin, what punishment do you decree for the

Lady Jane Howard? For my part, though I intended to threaten the most obnoxious treatment, to induce my opponent to yield, I could not for my dearest interests injure the person of that exquisite lady.'

'You could not, in good troth? I suppose my mistress has good reason to be jealous of you two. But since the power is left with me I shall prevent that; I shall see her punished as she deserves: I'll have no shameful exposures of a woman, even were she the meanest plebeian, but I'll mar her beauty that she thinks so much of, and that *you* think so much of. I'll have her nose cut off; and two of her fore teeth drawn; and her cheeks and brow scolloped. I'll spoil the indecent brightness of her gloss! She shall not sparkle with such brilliance again, nor shall the men gloat, feasting their intolerable eyes on her, as they do at present.'

'Saint Duthoc buckler me!' exclaimed the Douglas – 'what an unnatural tyger cat it is! I have heard that such feelings were sometimes entertained by one sovereign beauty toward another of the same sex; but that a sprightly youth, of an amorous complexion, with bright blushing features and carroty locks, should so depreciate female beauty, and thirst to deface it, surpasses any thing I have witnessed in the nature of man. Go to, you are a perverse boy, but shall be humoured as far as my honour and character as a captain and warrior will admit.'

Colin paced lightly away, making a slight and graceful courtesy to the Douglas as he glided out. 'What an extraordinary, wayward, and accomplished youth that is!' said the chief to himself: 'Is it not strange that I should converse so long with a page, as if he were my equal? There is something in his manner and voice that overcomes me; and though he teazes me beyond endurance, there is a sort of enchantment about him, that I cannot give him the check. Ah me! all who submit themselves to women, to be swayed by them or their delegates, will find themselves crossed in every action of importance. I am resolved that no woman shall sway me. I can love, but have not learned to submit.'

Colin retired to his little apartment in the pavilion; it was close to the apartment that Douglas occupied while he remained there, and not much longer or broader than the beautiful and romantic inhabitant. Yet there he constantly abode when not employed about his lord, and never mixed or conversed with the other pages. Douglas retired down to the tower, or King's House, as it was called (from king Edward having occupied it,) at even tide – but Colin Roy remained in his apartment at the pavilion. Alas! that Douglas did not know the value of the life he left exposed in such a place!

On the return of Musgrave into the castle, a council of all the gentlemen in the fortress was called, and with eager readiness they attended in the hall of the great western tower. The governor related to them the heart-rending intelligence of his mistress being in the hands of their enemies, and of the horried fate that awaited her, as well as his only brother, provided the garrison stood out. Every one present perceived that Musgrave inclined to capitulate; and, as they all admired him, they pitied his woeful plight. But no one ventured a remark. There they sat, a silent circle, in bitter and obstinate rumination. Their brows were plaited down, so as almost to cover their eyes; their under lips were bent upward, and every mouth shaped like a curve, and their arms were crossed on their breasts, while every man's right hand instinctively rested on the hilt of his sword.

Musgrave had taken his measures, whichever way the tide should run. In consequence of this he appeared more calm and collected at this meeting than he had done for many a day. 'I do not, my friends, and soldiers, propose any alternative,' said he – 'I merely state to you the circumstances in which we are placed; and according to your sentiments I mean to conduct myself.'

'It is nobly said, brave captain,' said Collingwood: 'Our case is indeed a hard one, but not desperate. The Scots cannot take the castle from us, and shall any one life, or any fifty lives, induce us to yield them the triumph, and all our skill, our bravery, and our sufferings go for nought?'

'We have nothing to eat,' said Musgrave.

'I'll eat the one arm, and defend the draw-bridge with the other, before the Scots shall set a foot in the castle,' said a young man, named Henry Clavering. 'So will I,' said another. 'So will I; so will we all!' echoed through

the hall, while a wild gleam of ferocity fired every haggard
countence. It was evident that the demon of animosity and
revenge was now conjured up, which to lay was not in the
power of man.

'What then do you propose as our mode of action in
this grievous dilemma?' said Musgrave.

'I, for my part, would propose decision and ample
retaliation.' said Clavering. 'Do you not perceive that
there has been a great storm in the uplands last night and
this morning, and that the Tweed and Teviot are roaring
like two whirlpools of the ocean, so that neither man nor
beast can cross them? There is no communication between
the two great divisions of the Scottish army tonight, save
by that narrow passage betwixt the moat and the river.
Let us issue forth at the deepest hour of midnight, secure
that narrow neck of land by a strong guard, while the rest
proceed sword in hand to the eastern camp, surround the
pavilion of Douglas, and take him and all his associates
prisoners, and then see who is most forward in using
the rope!'

'It is gallantly proposed, my brave young friend,' said
Musgrave; 'I will lead the onset myself. I do not only
ween the scheme practicable, but highly promising; and
if we can make good that narrow neck of land against our
enemies on the first alarm, I see not why we may not cut
off every man in the eastern division of their army; and
haply, from the camp and city, secure to ourselves a good
supply of provisions before the break of the day.'

These were inducements not to be withstood, and there
was not one dissenting voice. A gloomy satisfaction rested
on every brow, and pervaded every look, taking place of
dark and hideous incertitude. Like a winter day that has
threatened a tempest from the break of the morning, but
becomes at last no longer doubtful, as the storm descends
on the mountain tops, so was the scene at the breaking
up of that meeting – and all was activity and preparation
within the castle during the remainder of the day.

The evening at last came; but it was no ordinary
evening. The storm had increased in a tenfold degree. The
north-west wind roared like thunder. The sleet descended
in torrents, and was driven with an impetuosity that no
living creature could withstand. The rivers foamed from

bank to brae; and the darkness was such as if the heavens had been sealed up. The sound of the great abbey bell, that rung for vespers, was borne away on the tempest; so that nothing was heard, save once or twice a solemn melancholy sound, apparently at a great distance, as if a spirit had been moaning in the eastern sky.

Animal nature cowered beneath the blast. The hind left not her den in the wood, nor broke her fast, until the dawning. The flocks crowded together for shelter in the small hollows of the mountains, and the cattle lowed and bellowed in the shade. The Scottish soldiers dozed under their plaids, or rested on their arms within the shelter of their tents and trenches. Even the outer sentinels, on whose vigilance all depended, crept into some retreat or other that was next to hand, to shield them from the violence of the storm. The army was quite secure – for they had the garrison so entirely cooped up within their walls, that no attempt had been made to sally forth for a whole month. Indeed, ever since the English were fairly dislodged from the city, the Bush-law, and all the other outworks, the attempt was no more dreaded; for the heaving up of the portcullis, and the letting down of the draw-bridge, made such a noise as at once alarmed the Scottish watchers, and all were instantly on the alert. Besides, the gates and draw-bridges (for there were two gates and one draw-bridge at each end) were so narrow, that it took a long time for an enemy to pass in any force; and thus it proved an easy matter to prevent them. But, that night, the storm howling in such majesty, and the constant jangling of chains and pullies swinging to its force, with the roaring of the two rivers over the dams, formed altogether such a hellish concert, that fifty portcullises might have been raised, and as many draw-bridges let down, and the prostrate shivering sentinels of the Scottish army have distinguished no additional chord or octave in the infernal bravura.

At midnight the English issued forth with all possible silence. Two hundred, under the command of Grey and Collingwood, were posted on the castle-green, that is, the narrow valley between the moat and the river Tweed, to prevent the junction of the two armies on the first alarm being given. The rest were parted into two divisions; and, under the command of Musgrave and Henry Clavering, went down the side of each river so as to avoid the strongest part of the Scottish lines, and the ramparts raised on the height. Clavering led his division down by the side of the Teviot, along the bottom of the great precipice, and, owing to the mingled din of the flood and the storm, was never perceived till fairly in the rear of the Scottish lines. Musgrave was not so fortunate, as the main trench ran close to the Tweed. He was obliged to force it with his first column, which he did with a rapidity which nothing could equal. The Englishmen threw themselves over the mound of the great trench, hurling in above their enemies sword in hand, and overpowering them with great ease; then over one breastwork after another, spreading consternation before them and carnage behind. Clavering heard nothing of this turmoil, so intemperate was the night. He stood with impatience, his men drawn up in order, within half a bow-shot of Douglas's pavilion, waiting for the signal agreed on; for their whole energy was to be bent against the tent of the commander, in hopes, not only to capture the Douglas himself, and all his near kinsmen, but likewise their own prisoners. At length, among other sounds that began to swell around, Clavering heard the welcome cry of 'DUDDOE'S AWAY!' which was a readily answered with 'DUDDOE'S HERE!' and at one moment the main camp was attacked on both sides. The flyers from the lines had spread the alarm. The captain's tent was surrounded by a triple circle of lesser tents, all full of armed men, who instantly grasped their weapons, and stood on the defensive. Many rough blows were exchanged at the first onset, and many of the first ranks of the assailants met their death. But though those within fought with valour, they fought without system; whereas the English had arranged every thing previously; and each of them had a white linen belt, of which the Scots knew nothing. And in the hurry and terror that ensued, some parties attacked each other, and fell by the hands of their brethren. Finding soon that the battle raged before and behind them, they fled with precipitation toward the city; but there they were waylaid by a strong party, and many of them captured and slain. The English would have slain every man that fell into their power, had it not been for the hopes of taking Douglas, or some of his near kinsmen, and by that means redeeming the precious pledges that the Scots held, so much to their detriment, and by which all their motions were paralyzed. Clavering, with a part of the troops under his command, pursued the flyers that escaped as far as the head of the Market-street, and put the great Douglas himself into no little dismay; for he found it next to impossible to rally his men amid the storm and darkness, such a panic had seized them by this forth-breaking of their enemies. Clavering would, doubtless, have rifled a part of the city, if not totally ruined that division of the Scottish army, had he not been suddenly called back to oppose a more dangerous inroad behind.

When Musgrave first broke through the right wing of the Scottish lines, the noise and uproar spread amain, as may well be conceived. The warders on the heights then sounded the alarm incessantly: and a most incongrous thing it was to hear them sounding the alarm with such vigour at their posts, after the enemy had passed quietly by them, and at that time were working havoc in the middle of their camp. They knew not what was astir, but they made plenty of din with their cowhorns, leaving those that they alarmed to find out the cause the best way they could.

The Scottish army that beleaguered the castle to the westward caught the alarm, and rushed to the support of their brethren and commander. The infantry being first in readiness, were first put in motion, but, on the narrowest part of the castle green, they fell in with the firm set phalanx of the English, who received them on the point of their lances, and, in a few seconds, made them give way. The English could not however pursue, their orders being to keep by the spot where they were, and stand firm; so that the Scots had nothing ado but to rally at the head of the green, and return to the charge. Still it was with no better success than before. The English stood their ground, and again made them reel and retreat. But, by this time, the horsemen were got ready, and descended to the charge at a sharp trot. They were clad in armour, and had heavy swords by their sides, and long spears like halberds in their hands. The English lines could not withstand the shock given by these, for the men were famishing with hunger and benumbed with cold, the wind blowing with all its fury straight in their faces. They gave way; but they were neither broken nor dispersed. Reduced as they were, they were all veterans, and retreated fighting till they came to the barriers before the draw-bridge; and there, having the advantage of situation, they stood their ground.

The horsemen passed on to the scene of confusion in the camp, and came upon the rear of the English host, encumbered with prisoners and spoil.

When Clavering was called back, Douglas, who had now rallied about one hundred and forty men around him, wheeled about, and followed Clavering in the rear; so that the English found themselves in the same predicament that the Scots were in about an hour before – beset before and behind – and that principally by horsemen, which placed them under a manifest disadvantage.

It is impossible to give any adequate idea of the uproar and desperate affray that now ensued. The English formed on both sides to defend themselves; but the prisoners being numerous detained a great part of the men from the combat. A cry arose to kill the prisoners; from whom it first issued no one knew, but it no sooner past than the men began to put it into execution. The order was easier to give than perform: in half a minute every one of the guards had a prisoner at his throat – the battle became general – every one being particularly engaged through all the interior of the host, many of them struggling in pairs on the earth, who to get uppermost, and have the mastery. It was all for life, and no exertion was withheld; but, whenever these single combats ended in close gripes, the Scots had the mastery, their bodies being in so much better condition. They made a great noise, both individually and in their files, but the English scarcely opened their mouths; like bred mastiffs, when desperately engaged, they only aimed at the vital parts of their opponents, without letting their voices be heard.

It is vain at this period to attempt giving a better description of the scenes of that night, for the men that were present in the affray could give no account of it next day. But, after a hard encounter and heavy loss, the English fought their way up to their friends before the ramparts, who had all the while been engaged in skirmishing with

the foot of the western division, whom they had kept at
bay, and thus preserved the entrance clear to themselves
and brethren; but ere the rear had got over the half-moon
before the bridge, it was heaped full of slain.

There were more of the Scots slain during the conflict
of that hideous night than of the English; but by far the
greater number of prisoners remained with the former,
and several of them were men of note; but such care
was taken to conceal rank and titles, after falling into the
hands of their enemies, that they could only be guessed at.
De Gray was slain, and Collingwood was wounded and
taken; so that on taking a muster next day, the English
found themselves losers by their heroic sally.

They had, however, taken one prize, of which, had they
known the value, it would have proved a counterbalance
for all their losses, and all the distinguished prisoners that
formerly told against them. This was no other than the
pretended page, Colin Roy, of whose sex and quality
the reader has been formerly apprised, and whom they
found concealed among some baggage in the Douglas'
tent. Grievous was that page's plight when he found
himself thrust into a vault below the castle of Roxburgh,
among forty rude soldiers, many of them wounded, and
others half-naked, and nothing given them to subsist on.
Concealment of his true sex for any length of time was
now impossible, and to divulge the secret certain ruin to
himself and the cause of Douglas.

Next day he pleaded hard for an audience of Musgrave,
on pretence of giving him some information that deeply
concerned himself; and he pleaded with such eloquence
that the guards listened to him, and informed the commander, who ordered the stripling to be brought before
him. The next day following was that appointed for the
execution of Sir Richard Musgrave. Colin informed the
governor that, if he would give him his liberty, he would
procure a reprieve for his brother, at least until the day
of the Conception, during which period something might
occur that would save the life of so brave a youth; that he
was the only man on earth who had the power to alter the
purpose of Douglas in that instance; and that he would
answer with his head for the success – only the charm
required immediate application.

Musgrave said it was a coward's trick to preserve his own life – for how could he answer to him for his success when he was at liberty? But that no chance might be lost for saving his brother's life, he would cause him to be conducted to Douglas under a strong guard, allow him what time he required to proffer his suit, and have him brought back to prison till the day of the Conception was over, and if he succeeded he should then have his liberty. This was not exactly what Colin wanted: However, he was obliged to accept of the terms, and proceeded to the gate under a guard of ten men. The Scots officer of the advanced guard refused to let any Englishman pass, but answered with his honour to conduct the stripling in safety to his commander, and in two hours return him back to the English at the draw-bridge. No more was required; and he was conducted accordingly to the door of Douglas' tent, which, as he desired, he was suffered to enter, the men keeping guard at the door.

In the confusion of that morning, Douglas never had missed the page, nor knew he that he was taken prisoner; and when the boy entered from his own little apartment, he judged him to be in attendance as usual. He had a bundle below his arm tied up in a lady's scarf, and a look that manifested great hurry and alarm. The Douglas, who was busily engaged with two knights, could not help noting his appearance, at which he smiled.

'My lord,' said the boy, 'I have an engagement of great importance to-day, and the time is at hand. I cannot get out at the door by reason of the crowd, who must not see this. Will it please you to let me pass by your own private door into the city?'

Douglas cursed him for a troublesome imp, and forthwith opened the door into the concealed way; and as all who came from the door passed unquestioned, the page quickly vanished in the suburbs of the city.

The officer and his guard waited and waited until the time was on the point of expiring, and at last grew quite impatient, wondering what the boy could be doing so long with the commander. But at length, to their mortal astonishment, they beheld the stripling coming swaggering up from the high street of the city behind them, putting a number of new and ridiculous airs in practice, and quite unlike one going to be delivered up to enemies to be thrown into a dungeon, or perhaps hanged like a dog in a day or two.

The officer knew nothing of the concealed door and passage, and was lost in amazement how the page should have escaped from them all without being visible; but he wondered still more how the elf, being once at liberty, should have thought of coming strutting back to deliver himself up again.

'Where the devil have you been, master, an it be your will?' said the officer.

'Eh? What d'ye say, mun?' said the unaccountable puppy. 'What do I say mun!' replied the officer, quite unable to account either for the behaviour of the prisoner or his address; 'I say I trow ye hae seen sic a man as Michael Scott some time in your days? Ye hae gi'en me the glaiks aince by turning invisible; but be ye deil, be ye fairy, I sal secure ye now. Ye hae nearly gart me brik my pledge o' honour, whilk I wadna hae done for ten sic necks as yours.'

'Your pledge o' honour? What's that, mun? Is that your bit sword? Stand back out o' my gate.'

'Shakel my knackers,' said the officer laughing, 'if I do not crack thy fool's pate! What does the green-kail-worm mean? You, sir, I suppose are presuming to transact a character? You are playing a part in order to get off, but your silly stratagem will fail you. Pray, my young master, what character do you at present appear in?'

'Character me no characters!' said the page – 'it is not with you that I transact – nor such as you! Do not you see who I am, and what commission I bear? Bide a great way back out o' my gate an ye please; and show me where I am to deliver this.'

'And who is that bald epistle for, master Quipes? Please to open your sweet mouth, and read me the inscription.'

'Do you not see, saucy axe-man? Cannot you spell it? "To James, Earl of Douglas and Mar, with greeting, These." Herald me to your commander, nadkin; but keep your distance – due proportioned distance, if you please.'

'No, no, my little crab cherry; you cheated me by escaping from the tent invisible before, but shall not do it again. We'll get your message done for you; your time is expired, and some more to boot, I fear; come along with us.' – And forthwith one of their number waited on the chief with the letter, while the rest hauled off the unfortunate page, and delivered him back to the English.

CHAPTER NINE

His doublet was sae trim and neat,
  Wi' reid goud to the chin,
Ye wad hae sworn, had ye been there,
  That a maiden stood within.
The tears they trickled to his chin,
  And fell down on his knee;
O had he wist before he kissed,
  That the boy was a fair ladye.
Song of May Marley

Who's she, this dame that comes in such a guise,
Such face of import, and unwonted speech?
Tell me, Cornaro. For methinks I see
Some traits of hell about her.
Trag. of the Prioress

IN THIS PERILOUS situation were placed the two most beautiful ladies of England and Scotland, at the close of that memorable year; and in this situation stood the two chiefs with relation to those they valued dearest in life; the one quite unconscious of the misery that awaited him, but the other prepared to stand the severest of trials. Success had for some time past made a show of favouring the Scots, but she had not yet declared herself, and matters with them soon began to look worse. As a commencement of their misfortunes, on that very night the battle took place, the English received a supply of thirty horse-loads of provisions, with assurances that Sir Thomas Musgrave, the governor of Berwick, was setting out with a strong army to their succour.

  The supply was received in this way. There was a bridge over the Teviot, which communicated only with the castle, the north end of it being within the draw-bridge, and that bridge the English kept possession of all the time of the seige. It being of no avail to the Scots, they contented themselves by keeping a guard at the convent of Maisondieu, to prevent any communication between the fortress and the Border. But the English barons to the eastward, whose castles lay contiguous to the Tweed, taking advantage of the great flood, came with a strong body of men, and attacking this post by surprise, they beat them, and, chasing them a considerable way up the river, got the convoy along the bridge into the castle.

This temporary relief raised the spirits of the English, or rather cheered their prospects, for higher in inveterate opposition their spirits could not be raised. On the day following, likewise, a flying party of Sir Thomas Musgrave's horse made their appearance on the height above Hume castle, and blew their horns, and tossed their banners abroad on the wind, that the besieged might see them, and understand that their friends were astir to make a diversion in their favour.

On the same day a new gibbet was erected on the top of the Bush law, with a shifting wooden battery, to protect the executioners; and all within the castle feared that the stern and unyielding Douglas was going to put his threat respecting the life of Sir Richard Musgrave into execution. Therefore, to prevent their captain from seeing the scene, and, if possible, his mind from recurring to it, they contrived to get a council of war called, at which they intentionally argued and contended about matters of importance, in order to detain him until the sufferings of his brother were past.

The Bush-law, on which the Scots had a strong fortification, rises abruptly over against the western tower of the castle of Roxburgh; they were separated only by the moat, and, though at a great height, were so near each other, that men could with ease converse across, and see distinctly what was done. On the top of this battery was the new gibbet erected, the more to gall the English by witnessing the death of their friends.

At noon, the Scots, to the number of two hundred, came in procession up from the city, with their prisoner dressed in his knightly robes; and, as they went by, they flouted the English that looked on from the walls – but the latter answered them not, either good or bad. By a circular rout to the westward they reached the height, where they exposed the prisoner to the view of the garrison on a semicircular platform, for a few minutes, until a herald made proclamation, that unless the keys of the castle were instantly delivered at the draw-bridge, the life of the noble prisoner was forfeited, and the sentence would momently be put in execution; and then he concluded by calling, in a louder voice, 'Answer, Yes or no – once – twice.' He paused for the space of twenty seconds, and then repeated slowly, and apparently with reluctance, 'Once – twice – *thrice*,' – and the platform folding down, the victim was launched into eternity.

The English returned no answer to the herald, as no command or order had been given. In moody silence they stood till they witnessed the fatal catastrophe, and then a loud groan, or rather growl of abhorrence and vengeance, burst from the troops on the wall, which was answered by the exulting shouts of the Scots. At that fatal moment Musgrave stepped on the battlement, to witness the last dying throes of his loved brother. By some casualty, the day of the week and month happening to be mentioned in the council hall, in the midst of his confused and abstracted ideas, that brought to his remembrance the fate with which his brother had been threatened. Still he had hopes that it would have been postponed; for, as a drowning man will catch violently at floating stubble, so had he trusted to the page's mediation. He had examined the stripling on his return to the dungeon, but the imp proved froward and incommunicative, attaching to himself an importance of which the captain could not perceive the propriety; yet, though he had nothing to depend on the tender mercies of Douglas, as indeed he had no right, he nevertheless trusted to his policy for the saving of his brother alive; knowing that, in his life, he held a bond round his heart which it was not his interest to snap.

As he left the hall of council, which was in the great western tower, and in the immediate vicinity of the scene then transacting, the murmurs of the one host and the shouts of the other drew him to the battlement, whence his eye momently embraced the heart-rending cause of the tumult. He started, and contracted every muscle of his whole frame, shrinking downward, and looking madly on each hand of him. He seemed in act to make a spring over the wall; and the soldiers around him perceiving this, and haply misjudging the intent of his motion, seized on him to restrain him by main force. But scarcely did he seem to feel that he was held; he stretched out his hands toward his brother, and uttered a loud cry of furious despair, and then in a softer tone cried, 'Oh! my brother! my brother! – So you would not warn me, you dog? – Nor you? – Nor you? – No, you are all combined against me. That was a sight to gratify you, was it not? My curse on you, and all that have combined against the life of that matchless youth!' and with that he struggled to shake them from him. 'My lord! my lord!' was all that the soldiers uttered, as they restrained him.

At that instant Clavering rushed on the battlement. 'Unhand the captain!' cried he: 'Dare you, for the lives that are not your own, presume to lay violent restraint on him, and that in the full view of your enemies?'

'I will have vengeance, Clavering!' cried Musgrave – 'ample and uncontrolled vengeance! Where is the deceitful and impertinent stripling that promised so solemnly to gain a reprieve for my brother, and proffered the forfeit of his life if he failed?'

'In the dungeon, my lord, fast and secure.'

'He is a favourite parasite of the Douglas; bring him forth that I may see vengeance executed on him the first of them all. I will hang every Scot in our custody; but go and bring him the first. It is a base deceitful cub, and shall dangle opposite to that noble and now lifeless form. It is a poor revenge indeed – but I will sacrifice every Scot of them. Why don't you go and bring the gilded moth, you kennel knaves? Know you to whom you thus scruple obedience?'

Clavering was silent, and the soldiers durst not disobey, though they obeyed with reluctance, knowing the advantages that the Scots possessed over them, both in the numbers and rank of their prisoners. They went into the vaults, and, without ceremony or intimation of their intent, lifted the gaudy page in their arms, and carried him to the battlement of the western tower, from whence, sans farther ceremony, he was suspended from a beam's end.

Douglas could not believe the testimony of his own senses when he saw what had occurred. Till that moment he never knew that his page was a prisoner. Indeed, how could he conceive he was, when he had seen him in his tent the day after the night engagement? His grief was of a cutting and sharp kind, but went not to the heart; for though the boy had maintained a sort of influence over him, even more than he could account to himself for, yet still he was teasing and impertinent, and it was not the sort of influence he desired.

'I wish it been our blessed Lady's will to have averted this,' said he to himself; 'But the mischances of war often light upon those least concerned in the event. Poor Colin! thy beauty, playfulness, and flippancy of speech deserved a better guerdon. How shall I account to my royal mistress for the cruel fate of her favourite?'

With all this partial regret, Douglas felt that, by the loss of this officious page of the princess, he would be freed from the controul of petticoat-government. He perceived that the princess lived in concealment somewhere in the neighbourhood – kept an eye over all his actions and movements – and, by this her agent, checked or upbraided him according to her whimsical inexperience. Douglas was ambitious of having the beautiful princess for his spouse – of being son-in-law to his sovereign – and the first man in the realm; but he liked not to have his counsels impeded, or his arms checked, by a froward and romantic girl, however high her lineage or her endowments might soar. So that, upon the whole, though he regretted the death of Colin Roy MacAlpin, he felt like one released from a slight bondage. Alas, noble chief! little didst thou know of the pang that was awaiting thee!

It will be recollected that, when the Lady Margaret first arrived in the camp in the character of Colin her own page, she lodged her maid in the city of Roxburgh, disguised likewise as a boy. With her she communicated every day, and contrived to forward such letters to the Court as satisfied her royal mother with regard to the motives of her absence – though these letters were, like many others of the sex, any thing but the direct truth. The king was at this period living in retirement at his castle of Logie in Athol, on pretence of ill health.

The name of the maiden of honour thus disguised was Mary Kirkmichael, the daughter of a knight in the shire of Fife. She was a lady of great beauty, and elegant address – shrewd, sly, and enterprising.

Two days after the rueful catastrophe above related, word was brought to Douglas, while engaged in his pavilion, that a lady at the door begged earnestly to see him. 'Some petitioner for the life of a prisoner,' said he: 'What other lady can have business with me? Tell her I have neither leisure nor inclination at present to listen to the complaints and petitions of women.'

'I have told her so already,' said the knight in waiting; 'but she refuses to go away till she speak with you in private; and says that she has something to communicate that deeply concerns your welfare. She is veiled; but seems a beautiful, accomplished, and courtly dame.'

At these words the Douglas started to his feet. He had no doubt that it was the princess, emerged from her concealment in the priory or convent, and come to make inquiries after her favourite, and perhaps establish some other mode of communication with himself. He laid his account with complaints and upbraidings, and, upon the whole, boded no great good from this domiciliary visit. However, he determined to receive his royal mistress with some appearance of form; and, in a few seconds, at a given word, squires, yeomen, and grooms, to the amount of seventy, were arranged in due order, everyone in his proper place; and up a lane formed of these was the lady conducted to the captain, who received her standing and uncovered; but, after exchanging courtesies with her, and perceiving that it was not the princess, jealous of his dignity, he put on his plumed bonnet, and waited with stately mien the development of her rank and errand.

It was Mary Kirkmichael.

'My noble lord,' said she. 'I have a word for your private ear, and deeply doth it concern you and all this realm.'

Douglas beckoned to his friends and attendants, who withdrew and left him alone with the dame, who began thus with great earnestness of manner: 'My lord of Douglas, I have but one question to ask, and, if satisfied with the answer, will not detain you a moment. What is become of the page Colin that attended your hand of late?' Douglas hesitated, deeming the lady to be some agent of the princess Margaret's. 'Where is he?' continued she, raising her voice, and advancing a step nearer to the captain. 'Tell me, as you would wish your soul to thrive. Is he well? Is he safe?'

'He is sped on a long journey, lady, and you may not expect to meet him again for a season.'

'Sped on a long journey! Not see him again for a season! What does this answer mean? Captain, on that youth's well-being hang the safety, the nobility, and the honour of your house. Say but to me he is well, and not exposed to any danger in the message on which he is gone.'

'Of his well-being I have no doubt; and the message on which he is gone is a safe one. He is under protection from all danger, commotion, or strife.'

'It is well you can say so, else wo would have fallen to your lot, to mine, and to that of our nation.'

'I know he was a page of court, and in the confidence of my sovereign and adored Lady Margaret. But how could any misfortune attending a page prove of such overwhelming import?'

'*Was* a page of court, my lord? What do you infer by that *was*? Pray what is he now? I entreat of you to be more explicit.'

'The plain truth of the matter is shortly this: The boy fell into the hands of our enemies that night of the late fierce engagement.'

At this the lady uttered a scream; and Douglas, dreading she would fall into hysterics, stretched out his arms to support her. 'I pity you, gentle maiden,' said he, 'for I perceive you two have been lovers.'

She withdrew herself, shunning his profered support, and, looking him wildly in the face, said in a passionate voice, 'In the hands of the English? O Douglas, haste to redeem him! Give up all the prisoners you have for that page's ransom; and if these will not suffice, give up all the lands of Douglas and Mar; and if all these are still judged inadequate, give up yourself. But, by your fealty, your honour, your nobility, I charge you, and, in the name of the Blessed Virgin, I conjure you to lose no time in redeeming that youth.'

Douglas could scarcely contain his gravity at this rhap-sody, weening it the frantic remonstrance of a love-sick maid; but she, perceiving the bent and tenor of his disposition, held up her hand as a check to his ill-timed levity. 'Unhappy chief!' exclaimed she, 'Little art thou aware what a gulf of misery and despair thou art suspended over, and that by a single thread within reach of the flame, and liable every moment to snap, and hurl thee into inevitable ruin. Know, and to thyself alone be it known, that that page was no other than the princess of Scotland herself; who, impelled by romantic affection, came in that disguise to attend thee in all thy perils, undertaken for her sake. It was she herself who seized her rival, and placed her in your hands, thus giving you an advantage which force could not bestow. And from time to time has she laid such injunctions on you, written and delivered by her own hand, as she judged conducive to your honour or advantage. If you suffer that inestimable lady to lye in durance, or one hair of her head to fall to the ground, after so many marks of affection and concern for you, you are unworthy of lady's esteem, of the titles you bear, or the honour of knighthood.'

When the lady first came out with the fatal secret, and mentioned the princess's name, Douglas strode hastily across the floor of the pavilion, as if he would have run out at the door, or rather fallen against it; but the motion was involuntary; he stopped short, and again turned round to the speaker, gazing on her as if only half comprehending what she said. The truth of the assertion opened to him by degrees; and, it may well be supposed, the intelligence acted upon his mind and frame like a shock of electricity. He would fain have disbelieved it, had he been able to lay hold of a plausible pretext to doubt it; but every recollected circumstance coincided in the establishment of the unwelcome fact. All that he could say to the lady, as he stood like a statue gazing her in the face, was, 'Who art thou?'

'I am Mary Kirkmichael of Balmedie,' said she, 'and I came with the princess, disguised as her attendant. I am her friend and confidant, and we held communication every day, till of late that my dear mistress discontinued her visits. O captain, tell me if it is in your power to save her!'

Douglas flung himself on a form in the corner of the tent, and hid his face with his hand, and at the same time groaned as if every throb would have burst his heart's casement. He had seen his royal, his affectionate, and adored mistress swung from the enemy's battlements, without one effort to save her, and without a tear wetting his cheek; and his agony of mind became so extreme that he paid no more regard to the lady, who was still standing over him, adding the bitterest censure to lamentation. Yet he told her not of her mistress's melancholy fate – he could not tell her; but the ejaculatory words that he uttered from time to time too plainly informed Mary Kirkmichael that the life of her royal mistress was either in jeopardy or irretrievably lost.

The Douglas saw the lady no more, nor regarded her. He rushed from the tent, and gave such orders as quite confounded his warriors, one part being quite incompatible with another; and, in the confusion, Mary glided quietly away from the scene without farther notice. All the motions of Douglas, for two days subsequent to this piece of information, were like those of a drunken man; he was enraged without cause, and acted without consistency; but the only point towards which all these jarring and discordant passions constantly turned was revenge on the English – deadly and insatiable revenge. When he looked towards the ramparts of the castle, his dark eye would change its colour, and sink deeper under his brow, while his brown cheeks would appear as if furrowed across, and his teeth ground and jarred against one another. His counsels, however, were not, at this time, of a nature suited to accomplish any thing material against his rivals. He meditated the most deadly retaliation, but was prevented before he could put it in practice.

On the following evening, when the disturbance of his mind had somewhat subsided, and appeared to be settling into a sullen depression of spirit, or rather a softened melancholy, he was accosted by a monk, who had craved and obtained admittance – for a deference to all that these people said or did was a leading feature of that age. Douglas scarcely regarded him on his first entrance, and to his address only deigned to answer by a slight motion of his head; for the monk's whole appearance augured little beyond contempt. He was of a diminutive stature, had a slight, starved make, and a weak treble voice.

His conversation, nevertheless, proved of that sort that soon drew the attention of the chief.

'May the blessed Virgin, the mother of God, bless and shield you, captain!'

'Humph!' returned the Douglas, nodding his head.

'May Saint Withold be your helmet and buckler in the day of battle—'

'Amen!' said the Douglas, interrupting him, and taking a searching look of the tiny being that spoke, as if there were something in the tones of his voice that struck him with emotion.

—'And withhold your weapon from the blood of the good,' added the monk, 'from the breast of the professor of our holy religion, and dispose your heart to peace and amity, that the land may have rest, and the humble servants of the Cross protection. Why don't you say "Amen" to this, knight? Is your profession of Christianity a mere form? and are the blessed tenets which it enjoins, strangers to thy turbulent bosom?'

'Humph!' said Douglas: 'With reverence be it spoken, monk, but you holy brethren have got a way of chattering about things that you do not understand. Adhere to your books and your beads. I am a soldier, and must stick by my profession, bearing arms for my king and country.'

'I am a soldier too,' rejoined the monk, 'and bear arms and suffer in a better cause. But enough of this. I have a strange message for you, captain. You must know that, a few weeks ago, a beautiful youth came to our monastery seeking supply of writing materials, which he could not otherwise procure. He was a kind and ingenious youth. I supplied him, for I loved him; and I have since seen him sundry times in my cell. But last night, as I was sitting alone, a little before midnight – I am afraid you will not believe me, captain, for the matter of my message is so strange – I had gone over my breviary, and was sitting with the cross pressed to my lips, when behold the youth entered. I arose to receive him; but he beckoned me to keep away from his person, and glided backward. I then recollected that he must be a spirit, else he could not have got in; and, though I do not recollect all that he said, the purport of his message was to the following effect:

'"Benjamin," said he, "arise and go to the captain of the

Scottish army, whom you will find in great perplexity of mind, and meditating schemes of cruelty and retaliation, which would be disgraceful to himself and to his country. But let him beware; for there be some at his hand that he does not see; and if he dare in the slightest instance disobey the injunctions which you shall from time to time lay on him, his sight shall be withered by a visitant from another world, whose face he shall too well recognize ever again to find rest under a consciousness of her presence. Monk Benjamin, I was not what I seemed. A few days ago I was a lady in the prime of youth and hope. I loved that captain, and was betrothed to him. For his sake I ventured my life, and lost it without a single effort on his part to save me. But his fate is in my hand, and I will use the power. It is given to me to control or further his efforts as I see meet – to turn his sword in the day of battle – or to redouble the strength of his and his warriors' arms. My behests shall be made known to him; and if he would avoid distraction of mind, as well as utter ruin, let him tremble to disobey. In the first place, then, you will find him pondering on a scheme for the recovery of my lifeless body – a scheme of madness which cannot and may not succeed; therefore, charge him from me to desist. You will find him farther preparing an embassy to my father and mother to inform them of the circumstances of my death, and that not in the words of truth. But let him take care to keep that a secret, as he would take care of his life and honour, for on that depends his ultimate success. Tell him farther, from me, to revenge my death, but not on the helpless beings that are already in his power; to pursue with steady aim his primary object – and his reward shall be greater than he can conceive."'

'Strange as this story may appear, captain, it is strictly according to truth. You yourself may judge whether it was a true or lying spirit that spoke to me.'

'Are you not some demon or spirit yourself,' said the Douglas, 'who know such things as these? Tell me, are you a thing of flesh and blood, that you can thus tell me the thoughts and purposes of my heart?'

'I am a being such as yourself,' said the monk – 'a poor brother of the Cistertian order, and of the cloister adjoining to this; and I only speak what I was enjoined to speak, without knowing whether it is true or false. I was threatened with trouble and dismay if I declined the commission; and I advise you, captain, for your own peace of mind, to attend to this warning.'

Douglas promised that he would, at least for a time; and the monk, taking his leave, left the earl in the utmost consternation. The monk's tale was so simple and unmasked, there was no doubting the truth of it – for without such a communication it was impossible he could have known the things he uttered; and the assurance that a disembodied being should have such a power over him, though it somewhat staggered the Douglas' faith, created an unwonted sensation within his breast – a sensation of wonder and awe; for none of that age were exempt from the sway of an overpowering superstition.

CHAPTER TEN

What a brave group we have! That fellow there,
He with the cushion, would outprate the cricket;
The babble of the brook is not more constant,
Or syllabled with such monotony,
Than the eternal tingle of his tongue.

Cor. I'll bid him silence, master;
Or do him so, which likes you.

The Prioress

WE MUST NOW leave the two commanders in plights more dismal than ever commanders were before, and return to our warden, the bold baron of Mountcomyn, whose feats form a more pleasant and diverting subject. His warfare all this while was of a predatory nature – for that his warriors were peculiarly fitted, and at this time they did not fail to avail themselves well of the troubles on the border, and the prevailing power of the Scots alongst its line. The warden pretended still to be acting in concert with Douglas, but his operations were all according to the purposes of his own heart. He cared nothing for the success or the aggrandisement of Douglas; but he had a particular eye to the advancement of his own house, and the honour of his kinsmen. It was therefore a matter of daily consulation with him and his friends, how they should act in conformity with this ruling principle. The probability was against Douglas, that he would ultimately fail in his undertaking, and be stripped of all his dominions. Viewing the matter in that light, it was high time for the Redhough to be providing for himself. On the other hand, should Douglas succeed in his enterprize, and become the king's son-in-law, there was no other way by which the warden could hold his own, save by a certain species of subordination, a submission in effect, though not by acknowledgment. Such matters were perfectly understood by the chiefs in these times, and all who proved refractory were taught in silence to feel the grounds on which they stood. This was, therefore, a most critical period for Sir Ringan. The future advancement of his house depended on every turn of his hand. During all the former part of the siege he had conducted himself with an eye to Douglas' failure, to which he was partly incited by the prophecies of Thomas the Rhymer, and those of his kinsman, Master Michael Scott of Oakwood, whom he believed the most powerful wizard, and the greatest prophet, that ever had arisen since the Rhymer's days.

But, on the return of Charlie of Yardbire and Dan Chisholm from the beleaguering army, the warden got the extraordinary intelligence, that the Lady Jane Howard had fallen into the hands of the Douglas, as well as Musgrave's only brother. These things changed Sir Ringan's prospects of the future in a very material degree, and he pondered on changing his mode of operations. Before doing so, however, he called a council of his kinsmen, and brought the matter again before them. Most of them counselled the continuance of the predatory warfare in which they had been engaged; it had served to enrich them, and had proved, as they reasoned, of more service to the Douglas than if they had joined his host. That it proved of more service to himself and his kinsmen than if they had joined the host, the warden was well aware; but he was not satisfied that the Douglas viewed their mountain warfare as of great consequence to him; and he farther knew, that services were always repaid, not according to the toil and exertion undergone, but according as they were estimated, while that estimation was ever and anon modelled by the apparent motives of the performer.

After much slow and inanimate reasoning on the matter, Sir Ringan chanced, after a minute's deep thought, to say, 'What would I not give to know the events that are to happen at Roxburgh between this time and the end of the Christmas holidays?'

'Auld Michael Scott will ken brawly,' said Charlie of Yardbire.

'Then, what for shoudna we ken too?' said the knight.

'Aye, what for shoudna we ken too?' said Dickie o' Dryhope.

'They might get a kittle cast that meddled wi' him, an' nae the wiser after a',' said Robert of Howpasley.

'When he was at pains to come a' the way to the castle of Mountcomyn,' said Simon Longspeare, 'a matter o' five Scots miles ower the moor, to warn our captain, the warden, how to row his bowls, he surely winna refuse to tell him what's to be the final issue o' this daft contest.'

'Ane wad think he wadna spare a cantrip or twa,' said Sir Ringan; 'him that has spirits at his ca', an' canna get them hadden i' wark. It wad be an easy matter for him; an' blood's aye thicker than water.'

'Ay, that's a true tale,' said Dickie o' Dryhope; 'It wad be an easy matter for him, we a' ken that; an' blood's aye thicker than water!'

'If I were to gang wi' a gallant retinue,' said Sir Ringan, 'he surely wadna refuse to gie me some answer.'

'He wad refuse the king o' France,' said Robert of Howpasley, 'if he warna i' the key for human conversation, an' maybe gar his familiar spirits carry you away, and thraw ye into the sea, or set you down i' some faraway land, for a piece o' employment to them, and amusement to himsel'. He has served mony ane that gate afore now.'

'Od I'll defy him,' said muckle Charlie of Yardbire. 'If my master, the warden, likes to tak me wi' him for his elbowman, I'll answer for him against a' the monkey spirits that auld Michael has.'

'Spoke like yourself, honest Charlie!' said the baron; 'and if it is judged meet by my friends that I should go, you shall be one that shall attend me. Certes, it would be of incalculable benefit to me, for all your sakes, to know even by a small hint what is to be the upshot of this business – But should I be taken away or detained—'

'Ay, should he be taken away or detained, gentlemen: think of that, gentlemen,' said Dickie o' Dryhope.

'I approve highly of the mission,' said Simon Longspeare; 'for I believe there is nothing too hard for that old wizard to do, and no event so closely sealed up in futurity, but that he can calculate with a good deal of certainty on the issue. I see that our all depends on our knowledge of the event; but I disapprove of our chief attending on the wizard in person – for in his absence who is to be our commander? And, should any sudden rising of our foes take place, of which we are every hour uncertain, we may lose more by the want of him one hour than we could ever regain.'

'Ay, think of that, gentlemen,' said Dickie: 'My cousin Longspeare speaks good sense. What could we do wanting Sir Ringan? We're all children to him, and little better without him.'

'And old children are the worst of all children,' said the warden; 'I would rather be deaved with the teething yammer than the toothless chatter. Prithee, peace, and let us hear out our cousin Simon's proposal.'

The circle of the gallant kinsmen did not like ill to hear this snub on old Dickie. They could not account for the chief's partiality to him; and they were even afraid that, being the oldest man, he should be nominated to the command in the knight's absence. It was however noted by all, that Dickie was not half so great a man in field or foray as he was at board in the castle of Mountcomyn. Only a very few men of experience discerned the bottom of this. The truth was, that Sir Ringan did not care a doit either for Dickie's counsels or his arm, but he saw that his lady abhorred him, and therefore he would not yield to cast him off. His lady was of a high spirit and proud unyielding temper, and the knight could not stand his own with her at all times and seasons; but before his kinsmen warriors he was particularly jealous of his dignity, and would not yield to the encroachment on it of a single item. It was by this kind of elemental opposition, if it may be so termed, that Dickie maintained his consequence at the warden's castle. In the field he was nothing more than a foolish vain old kinsman.

'I propose,' said Longspeare, 'that we send a deputation of our *notable men* to the warlock, of whom we have some of the first that perhaps ever the world produced. As a bard, or minstrel, we can send Colley Carol, a man that is fit to charm the spirits out of the heart of the earth, or the bowels of the cloud, without the aid of old Michael. As a man of crabbed wit and endless absurdity, we can send the Deil's Tam: As a true natural and moral philosopher, the Laird o' the Peatstacknowe: As one versed in all the mysteries of religion, and many mysteries beside, or some tell lies, we can send the gospel friar. All these are men of spirit, and can handle the sword and the bow either less or more. And as a man of unequalled strength and courage, and a guard and captain over all the rest, we can send Charlie o' Yardbire – and I will defy all the kingdoms of Europe to send out sic another quorum either to emperor, Turk, wizard, or the devil himself.'

Everyone applauded Simon Longspeare's motion, and declared the deputation worthy of being sent out, if it were for nothing but its own unrivalled excellence. Never, they said, since the mind of man was framed, was there such a combination of rare talent in so small a circle. There was none of those nominated for the mission present excepting muckle Charlie Scott. Charlie scratched his head, and said: – 'Gude faith, callans, I hae a queer bike to gang wi! he-he-he! I fear we'll get mae to laugh at us than gie us ought: The Deil's Tam an' the metre poet! the fat gospel friar, and the laird o' the Peatstacknowe! I never gaed out on sic a foray as this afore, an' little do I wot how we'll come on. He-he-he! A wheen queer chaps, faith!'

The jocund kinsmen then shouted to Gibby Jordan of the Peatstacknowe to come into the circle, that they might hear what he had to say about going on this celebrated embassy. This gentleman's name had erst been Gordon: By some mistake, either in spelling, or falling into some foul tub by night, for some grounded it both ways, it had been changed on him to Jordan, and, as he had no resource, he was obliged to admit it as legitimate. He was a man of education, and could read, write, and cast up accounts. But his figure, features, and the nasal twine with which he pronounced every word that he spoke, rendered his discourse irresistibly ludicrous. Every one was so ready to give Jordan the information, that he was chosen as one to go on a deputation to Master Michael Scott the warlock, that the laird for a long time could not get a word said; but stood and looked about him, turning always round his long nose to the speaker that was loudest, or him that was poking him most forcibly to obtain attention.

'Gentlemen,' said Gibby Jordan, 'you mind me of a story that I have heard about a paddock that was lying on the plowed land, an' by comes the harrows, an' they gangs out ower the tap o' the poor paddock, an' every tooth gae her a tite an' a turn ower. "What's the matter wi' you the day, Mrs Paddock?" says the goodman: "Naething ava, but rather ower mony masters this morning," quo' the paddock; "I wish I were safe i' my hole again, an' let them ring on." Sae master's, I'll tak the paddock's hint, an' wish ye a' a good morning.'

There was no such escape for the honest laird; they surrounded him, and insisted on hearing his sentiments at full length, teasing him till he began to lose his temper, a thing in which they delighted, for the more mischief the better sport for these wild border moss-troopers. But muckle Charlie perceiving this, came up to his side. 'Callants, I'm appointit Gibby's guard,' said he, 'an' his guard I'll be. What the deil has ony o' you to say to him?'

'Only to hear what he thinks o' the journey,' was repeated on all sides.

'Gentlemen,' said Gibby, 'the hale affair brings me a-mind of a story that I hae heard about a wife that had a batch o' chickens. But then, ye maun mind, gentlemen, she had a very great deal o' chickens, I daresay nae fewer than a hunner, for she had sax great cleckings; an' she was unco feared that the gled wad tak them away; sae she wales out a wheen o' the fattest an' the best, an' she sends them out to the cock, that he might herd an' tak care o' them. "The cock will fleg away the gleds," quo she, "an' gar them keep their distance, an' I'll get my braw birds a' saved." But by comes the greedy gled; an' when the cock saw him he croups an' he currs; an' blithe to keep his ain skin hale, he staps his head in a hole, an' the gled carried off the hale o' his bit charge. Weel, the gled, he fand them sae fat an' sae gusty, that he never linned till he had taen away every chicken that the wife had.'

'Where is the moral of that story, laird?' cried they: 'We see no coincidence.'

'Because ye're blind,' said Jordan: 'Dinna ye see that Michael's the cock, the deil's the gled, an' ye're the birds. He'll get us first; an' he'll find out that we're sic a wheen rare chaps, that he'll never blin' till he hae ye ilk ane, an' that will be the end o' your daft embassy.'

All the rest of the nominated members being sent for expressly from their different posts, they soon arrived, but they seemed every one to be adverse to the mission, except

Colley the minstrel, who was elevated with the idea of being introduced to the celebrated Master, anticipating something highly romantic, and precisely in his own way. As for Thomas Craik, better known by the singular appellation of the Deil's Tam, he cared not much about any thing, provided he got plenty of drink, mischief, and breaking of heads.

They got all that day to prepare themselves, while Sir Ringan and his friends were considering what they should send as a present to the illustrious necromancer. They weened he despised riches, believing that he could turn small slates to gold by touching them; and, after much consultation, it was resolved to send him a captive maiden and boy, as they had two in the camp, of exquisite loveliness. The maid was the reputed daughter of Sir Anthony Hall, an inveterate enemy to the baron of Mountcomyn, who had burned his castles and plundered his lands; but the warden at length engaging with him hand to hand at the battle of Blaikhope, slew him, and having discomfited his army, he plundered and harried all that pertained to him, at which time he took this beautiful maiden prisoner, whom he treated kindly, and kept as an handmaiden. Her name was Delany; and so lovely was she become in person, and so amiable in her manners, that several of the knight's kinsmen had asked her in marriage. These applications he had uniformly put off, on pretence of his friends degrading themselves by marrying a captive Englishwoman, a term that never sounded in a Scot's ear but with disgust. But, in fact, the warden did not choose that any of them should be so closely connected with an old respectable Northumberland family.

The boy was called Elias, and was the property of Jock o' Gilmanscleuch, having been taken by him in a night foray at Rothbury. When the warden applied to Jock for him, bidding him name his ransom, he answered, that if he wist 'Michael wad either mak a warlock o' him, or tak out his harigalds to be a sacrifice to the deil, he wadna gie him up for a' the lands o' Newburgh an' Birkendely.' Being pacified on these points as well as matters would bear, the two captives were dressed in elegant robes, and delivered to the embassy; Charlie was deputed their captain and leader; the rest were all to be equals, on the same footing, and to choose their own speakers.

After getting every direction regarding the purport of their mission, the caution and respect which they were to use toward the Master, and the questions they were to get answered, they departed; every one well mounted on an English horse, the friar on his own substantial mule, and such provision with them as they judged necessary. Carol, the bard, had a lyre and a flute. Gibby Jordan, ycleped of the Peatstacknowe, had nothing beside a rusty sword; the friar had an immense wallet below him, judged to be all implements of enchantment; the others had deer or goatskin wallets, stuffed with such things as they deemed necessary; and all of them wore arms, in case of meeting with any unknown interruption. Several of the gallant kinsmen shed tears on taking leave of Delany; who, contrary to what they all expected, seemed full of gaiety, and rather fond of the change than disheartened at it.

Well, away they rode; and, as soon as they were fairly out of sight of the army, every one began to attach himself to Delany more closely than his neighbour. The friar talked to her of penances, and the sins of youth, and the unlimited confidence due to the professors of religion. The bard chanted his wildest and most amorous ditties. Tam punned and quibbled on the words of the rest; and Gibby continued to narrate his long-winded parables, sometimes to one, sometimes to another, as he found them disposed to listen, and sometimes to none at all. As for Charlie, he contented himself with laughing at them all alternately, and occasionally exchanging a word or sentiment with a valued friend of his.

'Corby, what's a' this cocking o' your lugs, an' casting up o' your head for, lad? Ye're gaun the wrang road for a battle e'en now. An let you but see the sword an' pree the spur, ye dog, ye wad carry your master to the deil: an' troth, for ought he kens, ye may be carrying him born-head to his honour just now, ye unconscionable tike that ye are.'

Corby first laid back one ear and then the other, which Charlie took for a kind answer; and, patting his mane, he continued: 'Na, na, Corby; I ken ye hae nae ill designs; but only ye ken ye like a little mischief, an' a bit splutter now an' than.'

'That minds me o' the story o' Janet Sandilands an' her son Jock,' said Gibby Jordan the philosopher, 'when he ruggit her hair, an' raive her bussing. "That callant sude hae his hide threshed for lifting his hand to his mother," said one: "Na, na," quo Janet, "he maunna be threshed; Jock has nae ill in his mind, only he likes a tulzie." She that wad hae a close cog sude keep a hale laiggen, Yardbire; for as the auld saying rins, "Lippen to a Corby, an' he'll pike out your een."'

'Shame fa' me gin I see the drift o' your philosophy, Peatstacknowe; but as I'm sure it is weel meant, it sanna be ill ta'en. Corby an' me's twa auld friends, an' we hae a great deal to lippen to ane another. But I wish we had this unsonsy job owner, laird – we're gaun on kittle ground.'

'It minds me something o' the fisher that ran away after the Willy-an'-the-wisp,' said Jordan: 'It's a lang story, but it's weel wordy the hearing.'

'If it be a *very* lang story, we might as well crack about something else,' said Charlie. 'My heart's unco muckle turned on this daft job o' prying into the time that's to come, an' on what we're to say to the warlock. Gude saif us, laird, wha's to be the speaker? I wish that fleysome job maunna light on you? For you see, gin we set the deil's Tam to address him, he'll put him mad at the very first. The poet can bring out naething but rhames o' high flown nonsense; an' for mysel, I'm an unco plain matter-o'-fact man, an' better at good straiks than good words. Sae that the matter maun lie atween you an' the friar. What say you to this, Peatstacknowe?'

'Gude troth, Yardbire, an the task light on either of us, it may weel bring me in mind o' the laird o' Glencarthon, when he stack i' the midden at Saint Johnston, an' tint himsel i' the dark entry. The laird, you see, he comes to the door of a sowhouse, an' calls out, "Good people within there, can you tell me the way to the Queen's hostlery?" "Oogh?" cried the auld sow. The laird repeated his question quite distinctly, which disturbing some o' the pigs, they came to the back o' the door an' fell a murmuring an' squeaking. "What do you say?" said the laird in his turn: "I'll thank you if you will not just speak so vehemently." The pigs went on. "Oh, I hear you speak Erse in this house," said the laird; "but no matter: thank you for your information, I will try to work my way." Now you see, Yardbire, like draws aye to like; an' for the friar, wi' his auld warld says, or me, to address the great Master, it wad be a reversing o' nature an' the very order of things. I hae nae hope o' our good success at a', an it warna for that bonnie Delany. If he's a man, an' no just an incarnate deil, he will be delightit wi' her.'

'I wish we had her safely at him, laird,' said Charlie; 'for, troth, do ye see, thae chaps hing about her, an' look at her as gin they wadna care to eat her.'

'She brings me amind o' a weelfaurd dink gimmer that wench,' said Jordan, 'that I aince saw gaun up Sowerhopeburn. There was a tichel o' wallidraggle tup hoggs rinning after her, an' plaguing her, till I was just grieved for the poor beast. At length down there comes a wheel-horned ram, the king o' the flock, an' he taks up his station by the side o' the bonny thing, an' than a' the young ranigalds slinkit away as their noses had been blooding. Then the bonny she thing got peace, for whenever ony o' the rascallions began to jee up his lug, an' draw near her, ae glent o' the auld fellow's ee stoppit him short. Now, Yardbire, I trow it is a shame to see a pretty maid jaumphed an' jurmummled in that gate: if you will just ride close up to the tae side o' her, I'll tak up the tither, an' we'll gar them keep a due distance. There's nane o' them dares shoulder you aside.'

'I doubt, laird, there is something selfish in that plan o' yours,' said Charlie; 'ye hae a hankering yonder yourself, but ye darena try to make your ain way without ye get me to back ye. Fight dog, fight bane, Peatstacknowe; gin I be to tulzie for a bonny may, I tulzie for my ain hand.'

'It wad be sae weel done to chap them back,' said Jordan: 'See to the metre poet how he's capering an' turning up his mou': Yon fat hypocrite, the warlock friar, is blinking out frae aneath his sanctified eebrees like a Barbary ape: An' there's the deil's Tam; od I think he'll hae his lang coulter nose stappit into her lug.'

'Ride up, neighbour,' quoth Charlie, 'an' tell them that face to face. I like nae yethering ahint backs. Ane may ward a blow at the breast, but a prod at the back's no fair. A man wears neither ee nor armour there. Ride up, ride up, neighbour, gin you winna tell them a' you have said, I'll e'en tell them mysel.'

'Yardbire, I hope ye're no gaen gyte, to breed despite amang the warden's ambassadors to the deil. Stop till I tell you a queer joke that's come into my mind by your speaking about armour ahint. Last year, when the dalesmen were cried out in sic a hurry for the Durham raide, there was ane o' Fairniehirst's troopers got strong breastplates o' steel made to defend his heart. There was ane Brogg Paterson in Hawick, a wag that I kenned weel, was employed to fit the harnessing to the clothes; and learning that the raide was to be early in the morning, an' nae leisure for shifting, an' seeing the trooper so intent on protecting his heart, instead o' putting the steel plates in the inside o' his doublet, Paterson fastened them in the seat of his trews. After passing the Tine, the Scots encamped within a half moon of an impervious brake, and sent out a party of foragers, among whom was this trooper Turnbull. The party were pursued by a body of English horse, and several of them slain; but Turnbull reaching the brake, plunged into it, horse and man. The horse stuck fast, and just as poor Turnbull was trying to extricate himself, by scrambling over the horse's head, an Englishman came riding fiercely up, and struck him such a blow with his lance behind as would have spitted him to the neck – but hitting right on the steel plate, he made him fly heels-o'er-head over the brake, and into a place of safety. A comrade perceiving, came to assist him, and found Turnbull lying on the ground, repeating to himself these words with the utmost devotion: – "God bless Brogg Paterson in Hawick! God bless Brogg Paterson in Hawick!" "Wherefore that?" said the other. "Because," said Turnbull, "he kend better where my heart lay than I did."

Charlie laughed so heartily at this jocular tale, that he did not expose Gibby Jordan of the Peatstacknowe to his associates at that time; but keeping behind with him he held him in conversation, though he saw that his teeth were watering to be near the fair Delany.

They came that night to a place called Trows, on the English side of the border, but adjoining to the very ridge of the fells. The name of the hind who sojourned there was Jock Robson. He had a good stock both of cows and sheep, being so thoroughly a neutral man that both sides spared him, and both sides trusted him. He gave a night's grass to the driven cattle and sheep from each side, and a night's lodging to the drivers; and for this he exacted kane sheep, or a small cow, which none ever grudged him, because they found themselves so much at home in his house. He would assist either party in catching a prey, and either party in recovering it again, taking rewards from both; and, though both the English and the Scots knew of this, they never trusted him the less, for they knew that what he undertook he would fulfil, but no farther; out of your sight, out of your pay and out of your service with Jock Robson.

At this yeoman's habitation our notable embassy arrived at a late hour, for, though scarcely five o' clock afternoon, it was pitch dark. They called at the door, and out came Jock with a light. The first man that he beheld was the friar.

'Saint Mary's jerkin be about us!' cried Jock Robson, half in sport, half in earnest, 'and defend us from our auld black minny's delegates. What seeks Lucky Church amang the hills o' Cheviot, wi' her creeds an' her croons, her trumpery, an' her lang tythes o' sheep an' kye, wild deer, and weathershaker, barndoor an' blackhag fowls? Nought for Minny Church an' her bike here, Sir Monk – naething o' our ain breeding – a' comers an' gangers, like John Nisbet's fat sheep. Howsomever, honest bedesman, I speir ye the auld question,

'Come ye as friend, or come ye as fae?
For sic as ye bring, sic sal ye hae!'

'As thy friends do we come, uncourteous hind,' said the monk; 'and ask only a little of thy bread, and thy strong drink, for the refreshment of our bodies, that are like the grass on the tops of thy mountains, fading ere it be full grown, and require as thou knowest a supply of earthly refreshment as these do the showers of heaven; and also we ask of thee beds whereon we may lie down and rest: and these things thou must not refuse, for we would not that thou shouldst be to us as the children of Amalek and Moab, and those of Mount Seir.'

'Ye speak like a rational man, Sir Monk; but wait till I tell ye the truth, that I lurde see the cross on the handle of sword or spear ony time afore that hanging at the paunch of priest. There's mair honour an' generosity ahint the tane than the tither. But yet it shall never be said o' John Robson o' the

Trows that he refused a friend quarters on a dark night. He kens ower weel that the king may come in the beggar's way. Gin ye be joking, he can stand a joke wi' ony man; but gin ye be really gaun to haud him as an Amalekite, he wad like to ken what that is, an' what lengths ye mean to gang.'

'Thinkest thou that we will come into thy house to take of thy spoil for a prey, and thy maid servants for bond-women, and also thy little ones?' said the friar.

'The deil be there then,' cried Jock Robson. 'I wadna grudge ye meal an' maut, but or ye lay a hand on ane o' my lasses, or kidnap away my bits o' bairnies frae me, ye sal gang owner my breast, an' that wi' a braid arrow through ilk ane o' you. Be at your shift, bauld priest, here's for ye.'

On saying so, he turned hastily about, and the friar that moment clapping the spurs to his mule, gallopped round the corner, leaving the rest to make good their quarters in the best way they could. The mention of the broad arrow made him think it was high time for him to change his ground.

'There rides gospel, guts an' a',' cried Tam Craik, laughing aloud.

The laugh was well known to Robson; for the warden's troopers had been so often there that year, that almost all of them were John Robson's personal acquaintances.

'What?' cried he, turning back his head, 'Isna that the deil's Tam that I hear?'

'Ay, what for shoudna it, lad? an' how dare ye fright away our chaplain wi' your bows an' your braid arrows? Gin we had Jock's Marion, the sow-killer's wife o' Jeddart, at ye, wha wad be crousest then, trow ye?'

'Tam, it is weel kend your tongue is nae scandal; but dinna ye lippen ower muckle to your privilege; gin ye be come to quarter wi' me, dinna let me hear sic a hard jibe as that the night again. Come away, however, the warden's men are welcome, as weel they may be this year. Mony a fat mart they hae left i' my bire. I hope ye hae brought a bonny kane the night.'

'Ay, by my certie, lad, an' that we hae; here's nae less a kane than Jock's Marion hersel.'

'Ye scawed like bog-stalker! skrinkit, skraeshankit skebeld! dare ye to speak that gate to me at my ain door stane? I shall lend you a clout an ye were the king's cousin, an' see if ye dare return the compliment. Wife, bring the buet an' my piked rung here.'

'Peace, in the king's name!' cried Charlie Scott.

'And in the name of St. David!' cried the friar, returning to the charge on hearing Charlie's voice.

'And in my name!' cried Tam Craik; 'an' Gibby Jordan o' the Peatstacknowe's name; and the name o' Jock's Marion, the sow-sticker's wife o' Jeddart. I say unto thee, look here. Here is the kane will please a brave yeoman. Look if this be nae Marion hersel' – and with that he led Delany's palfrey up to the light.

Robson lifted his eyes and saw her, and was so much struck with her dazzling beauty, that he had not power to address even his beloved friend Charlie Scott, far less any other of his guests, but lifting the maiden down in his arms, he led her in to his dame, and said to one of his lads, 'Rin out wi' a light, callant, an' help the troopers to put up their horses.'

The horses were soon put up, for every one seemed more anxious than another to get first in to the cheek of Jock Robson's ingle, and have his seat placed next to that of Delany; but the poet being the most agile, and not the least amorous of the group, effected this greatly to his satisfaction.

CHAPTER ELEVEN

The youngest turned him in a path,
 And drew a buirdly brande,
And fifteen of the foremost slewe,
 Till back the lave couthe stande.

Then he spurred the grey unto the path,
 Till baith her sides they bledde;
'Now, grey, if thou carry nae me away
 My life it lies in wedde.'
                    Ballad of Auld Maitland

WE MUST PASS over a great part of the conversation that evening, in order to get forward to the more momentous part of the history of our embassy. Suffice it to say, that the poet was in high glory, and not only delivered himself in pure iambics, but sung several love ditties, and one song of a foray, that pleased Charlie Scott mightily. But Isaac, the curate, has only given a fragment of it, which runs thus:

If you will meet me on the Dirdam waste,
 Merry man mint to follow;
I'll start you the deer, and lead you the chace,
 With a whoop, and a whoo, and a hollo!
The deer that you'll see, has horns enow, &c.
Marked wi'red and merled wi' blue, &c.
And that deer he will not turn his tail
For the stoutest hinds that range the dale.
Come then, driver, in gear bedight;
Come bold yeoman, and squire, and knight;
The wind soughs loud on craig and heuch,
And the linn rowts loud in the Crookside cleuch;
Nor tramp of steed, nor jingle of spear,
Will ever be heard by the southern deer:

The streamer is out, and the moon away,
And the morning starn will rise or day.
Then mount to the stirrup, and scour the fell,
    Merry man mint to follow;
And over the muir, and the dean, and the dell,
    With a whoop, and a whoo, and a hollo!

'Thy words and thy song, young man,' said the friar,
'are like sounding brass and a tinkling cymbal; if laid in
the balance, they are lighter than vanity.'

'Yours will not prove so,' said the poet, 'provided you
are laid in with them; for, as the old song says—

"His wit is but weak, father;
    His gifts they are but sma';
But the bouk that's under his breast bane,
    It grieves me warst of a."'

'If thou singest this nonsense of me,' said the friar, 'lo, I
will smite thee upon the mouth; yea, upon the cheek-bone
will I smite thee, till thine eyes shall gush out like two
fountains of waters.' And so saying, he began to look
about him for some missile weapon to throw at the bard's
face, his breast burning with indignation – for he loved not
the tenor of the poet's conversation to the maid.

Tam and Jordan encouraged the friar to make the
assault, in hopes that the poet might be dislodged or
affronted; but Yardbire restrained the warmth of the friar,
not being aware of his real sentiments, and ordered peace
and good fellowship.

Dame Robson covered the hearth with a huge fire; and
her husband bringing in a leg of beef, set it upon the table,
and bade every one help himself.

'The words of thy mouth are exceeding good, and sweet
unto the ear,' said the friar, 'as doubtless thy food is to the
taste.' With that he rose and helped himself to three nice
and extensive slices of raw beef, and these he roasted on
the tongs which he had just lifted to smite the poet on
the head.

In good truth, though every one cooked his own supper,
as was the fashion of that iron time, there was none did it
half so nicely as the friar, nor so bunglingly as Jordan, whose
supper, though long behind the others in being ready, was
so unshapely a piece, and so raw on the one side, that

the friar observed, 'it was like Ephraim of old, as a cake unturned.' Some roasted their meat on old swords, some on spindles, for their hosts took no heed how they were fitted, or in what manner they shifted in these respects; seemingly satisfied that they had plenty for the cooking, and leaving them to cook it or eat it raw, as they chose. The poet made haste, and, first of all, cooked two or three nice slices for the maiden, giving her what she would take before he would taste a morsel himself. Some commended him for this, and others jeered him; but the friar, in his grave moral style, said the severest things of all. From the very commencement of the journey, a jealousy or misunderstanding began to subsist between these two, which never again subsided till they came to blows.

The poet answered him again with a song:

'Keep ye to your books and your beads, goodman,
Your Ave Marias and creeds, goodman;
    For gin ye end as ye're begun,
There will be some crack of your deeds, goodman.'

At length the party retired to rest, all save Jordan and their worthy host. The latter never slept in the night; he had always some watching, walking, or work in hand that suited that season best: and as for Gibby, he determined to sit up all night to watch that the poet made no encroachments on the place of Delany's repose. Robson encouraged his purpose, joined him heartily in conversation, listened to his longwinded stories with apparent delight, and, when all the rest were asleep, wormed the whole business of the embassy out of the shallow laird, who unfortunately testified his fears that they were carrying the lovely maiden and boy to the old warlock to be a sacrifice to the devil. Robson appeared terribly confounded at this piece of intelligence – for from the time that he heard it he conversed no more with Jordan. About one in the morning he began to put on his snow-boots, as if preparing for a journey.

'Where are ye going at this time of night?' enquired the laird.

'I maun gang out an' see how the night wears,' said Robson; 'I hae sax score o' Scots queys that are outlyers. If I let the king's ellwand ower the hill, I'll hae them to seek frae the kips o' Kale.'

Gibby accompanied him to the door, hoping the king's ellwand would not be over the hill, for he had no good will to part with his companion. But as soon as Robson turned his eye to the sky, 'Ha, gude faith, I maun post away!' said he, 'Yonder's the king's ellwand already begun to bore the hill; ay, there's ane o' the goud knobs out o' sight already, an' I hear the queys rowting ower the waterfa' o' the height. Gude morrow t'ye, laird, I'm ower lang here.'

Gibby returned in to the blazing fire; and hearing so many persons all snoring in sleep, he caught the infection, stretched himself upon a divot seat, and joined the chorus with as much zeal as any of them.

Morning came, and our embassy made ready for proceeding on their journey; but Robson still was wanting, at which both his dame and household lads seemed to wonder, otherwise the rest would have taken no notice of it. Gibby told her about the queys that were outlyers, but she only answered him with a hem! and a slight shake of the head. Charlie, who knew his man well, began to smell a rat; and, calling Gibby to the door, he inquired if he had hinted ought of their business to their host. The laird at first denied; but Charlie questioned him till he confessed the whole, at which Charlie was exceedingly angry; and hearing that he had informed him all about the maiden, and of what family she was sprung, he called Gibby a worthless inconsiderate being, and said he had ruined their expedition, for that he knew Robson kept up a correspondence with the Halls, who were broken men, and many of them skulking about the border; that Delany had uncles, cousins, and a brother living, if she was the man's daughter she was supposed to be, and that these would without fail waylay them, and kill them every man, for the sake of rescuing her. 'Robson,' said he, 'is altogether selfish, and has some end to serve; perhaps to get the maid into his own hands, for he seemed mightily taken with her beauty; and I calculate widely amiss if we are not watched from this house, and whether we return or proceed we shall be attacked in the first strait or lonely place that we come at.' Jordan looked exceedingly out of countenance, and every feature of his face altered. 'What had I ado to tell the rascal?' exclaimed he, 'or wha wad hae thought o' him playing us sic a trick? Twa-faced dog that he is! It wad be weel done to let his liver pree the taste o' steel!'

Charlie made him promise that he would not mention the circumstance to one of the party, as it was only a surmise, and might impede their progress to no purpose; and forthwith they mounted, armed with such armour as they had, and all, save Gibby Jordan, as cheerful and as jealous of one another as they were on the preceeding day. That worthy kept close by the side of muckle Charlie, and looked so sharp about him, that he perceived every shepherd, traveller, and cairn that appeared on the border fells, always testifying his alarm to his friend that perhaps yon was one of the Halls watching.

Charlie had resolved to go by Jedburgh straight for Oakwood castle; but his suspicions of Robson made him resolve to hold more to the eastward, in order to keep the open road. He knew that if they were watching him, it would be at the fords of Kale or Oxnam, on the Jedburgh road; and by taking the east path, he would not only elude them, but, in case of a pursuit, be near the outposts of the Scottish army.

For a good way they saw nothing, and began to think themselves in safety; but, in coming down Sowerhope-Middle, a little from the point of the debated land, three horsemen appeared to the westward of them. 'His presence be about us,' said Gibby – 'yonder *are* the Halls now!' Charlie said nothing, but kept watch. One of the yeomen vanished in a twinkling at full speed, the other two came at a brisk canter to our notable embassy.

'What do they mean?' said Jordan: 'Do these two fellows propose to conquer us all?'

'It wad appear that they do,' said Charlie, 'for they come on us without halt or hesitation.'

'I hardly think they'll succeed,' added Gibby, 'although they're twa dangerous looking chaps. For Godsake, Yardbire, tak care o' their back strokes; if they bring you down, our chance will be the waur.'

Charlie then called to the rest of his cavalcade, 'Friends, here are some strangers come to join us. Tell them nothing either good or bad, but keep on at a round trot. See, we are not far from the towers of Roxburgh. Whatever these men may say to you, make them nothing the wiser.'

'I will not so much as say unto them, whence cometh thou, or whither art thou going?' said the friar.

> 'I'll sing them a ditty of beauty and love,
> Of the wing of the raven, the eye of the dove,
> And beings all purer than angels above.'

said the poet.

'Sic a rhame o' nonsense is there!' said Tam Craik: 'If ony o' the dogs say an impertinent thing to me I'll gar his teeth gang down his throat like bristled beans.'

It was not long before the two mosstroopers joined the party. They were tall athletic men, armed at all points, and their manner had a dash of insulting impertinence in it.

'A good morning, and fair pace to you, noble and worthy gentlemen!' said the foremost: 'May we presume to be of the party?'

'You may *presume*,' said the deil's Tam, 'for that is what befits you; if you are willing to put up with the presumer's reward.'

'You are witty, sir, I suppose,' said the trooper; 'and pray what may that reward be?'

'Yes, I am witty,' said Tam; 'and my wit is sharp when it is not in its sheath. Do you understand me? As for the reward of presumption, it is in Scotland to be crankit before and kicked behind.'

'The road is at least as free to us as it is to you,' said the mosstrooper; 'and of that we intend to avail ourselves for the present. We go to join the army before Roxburgh, whither are you bound?'

'We follow our noses,' said Tam; 'but they guide us not to the army before Roxburgh, and into your rearward they caution us not to enter. Raw hides and rank bacon, keep your distance.'

While Tam Craik and the trooper were thus jangling on before, Charlie said to Jordan, 'Laird, what do you think o' yoursel' now? Ye hae played us a fine pliskie wi' your ill-tackit tongue! It is my thought that ere we ride a mile and a half we'll be attacked by a hale troop o' horse. That chap that disna speak is ane o' the wale o' the Ha's: I ken him weel for a' his half visor. The other horseman that left them on the height is ower to the fords of Kale, and, if I guess right, he'll appear at yon scroggy bush wi' sae mony

at his back that we wad hardly be a mouthfu' to them, an'
that in less time than ane wad gang a mile.'

'It is an ill business this,' said Gibby: 'It brings me in
mind o' – o' mair than I's name. But, gudesake, Yardbire,
an ye be sure he is ane o' the Halls, what for do nae ye rin
your sword in at the tae side o' him an' out at the tither?
The sooner a knave like that is put down the better.'

'Fair occasion, an' face to face, Peatstacknowe, an' ye
sanna see Charlie Scott slack; but ye wadna hae me stick
a man, or cleave him down ahint his back, an' that without
fair warning and fair arming?'

'Ay, honour an' generosity are braw things, but life's a
brawer thing an' a better thing than ony o' the twa. For
my part, I wad never stop. My very heart flighters when
I look at him, an' I amaist think I find his steel quivering
at my midriff. I wish I had a drive at him, wi' a chance o'
a hale head.' – And from that time Gibby leaned himself
forward on his saddle, and fixed his large grey eyes on the
mosstrooper like a pointer going to fly on his game; and,
in that attitude, he rode several times close up to his side,
or very nearly opposite to him, laying his hand now and
then on his hilt; but Charlie observed that he never looked
his foe in the face with threatening aspect, and, perplexed
as he was, could not help laughing at Gibby.

Yardbire now putting the spurs to Corby, galloped aslant
the brae to a rising ground, whence he could see if any
enemy was approaching by the swire from the fords of
Kale, as he suspected. He had not well gained the height
before he saw a dozen horsemen coming at the light gallop,
but one part of the cavalcade considerably behind the
others, owing to their being either worse mounted or worse
horsemen.

By this time Charlie's own friends were coming round
the bottom of the hill below him, quarrelling with the strangers so loudly, that Charlie heard their voices ascending
on the gale in most discordant notes. The deil's Tam and
the English trooper had never since their meeting ceased
the jibe and the keen retort; but Tam's words were so
provokingly severe, that the mossman was driven beyond
all further forbearance. Just when they were at the hottest,
the helmets of the front men of the Northumberland
cavalcade began to appear in the swire; a circumstance

that was well noted by their offended kinsman, but of which Tam was perfectly unconscious.

'Well, now, thou jaundiced looking thief,' said the moss-trooper, turning his horse's head towards Tam's left hand, and making him amble and curvette with his side foremost; 'thou lean, nerveless, and soul-less jabberer, all tongue and nothing else – I say, what hast thou to say more?'

The alteration in the man's key of voice somewhat astounded Tam; but his perverse nature would not let him soften his reply, although he liked as well to see others fall into a mischief as himself. 'Eh? what do I say?' said he; and with that he turned his horse's head to that of the other, making their two noses to meet; and caricaturing the Englishman's capers, he laughed sneeringly and triumphantly in his face. 'What do I say? Eh? what do I say? I say I thought I heard wind, and smelled it a wee too. Hagg-hiding fox that thou art! Wild tike of the moors, dost thou think Tam Craik fears thy prancing and thy carrion breath, or ony o' the bur-throated litter of which thou art the outwale? Nay, an capering and prancing show ought of a spirit, I can caper and prance as well as thou. Out on thee, thou bog-thumper, thou base-born heather-blooter, what do *you* say? Or what *dare* you say?'

Tam had by this time drawn his sword completely to cow the Englishman, and put him to silence; – but he saw what Tam did not see, and knew more than he.

'I dare both say and do, and that thou shalt find,' said the trooper; and forthwith he attacked Tam with all his prowess, who, not quite expecting such a thing gave way, and had very nearly been unhorsed; he, however, fought stoutly, defending himself, though manifestly at the disadvantage. The brave frair, at the first clash of the swords, wheeled about his mule, and drawing out a good sword from under his frock, (for he wore the sword on the one side and the cross on the other,) he stretched it forth, pointing it as if to thrust it between them. But, addressing himself to the Englishman, he cried with a loud voice, 'Put up *thy* sword again into its place, or verily I will smite thee with the edge of *my* sword.'

The other Englishman, who had never yet opened his mouth, and who had always kept apart, as if anxious to conceal who he was, now rode briskly up to the fray; and

perceiving the quick approach of his friends, and judging
his party quite secure of victory, he struck up the friar's
sword in apparent derision. But the inveterate laird of the
Peatstacknowe had been watching him all this time, as
one colley dog watches another of which he is afraid, in
order to take him at an advantage, and the moment that
his arm was stretched, so that his sword came in contact
with the friar's, Gibby struck him behind, and that with
such violence that the sword ran through his body. The
wounded trooper reined up his steed furiously, in order to
turn on his adversary; Gibby reined his up as quickly to
make his escape, but the convulsive force of the Englishman
threw his horse over, and in its fall it tumbled against the
legs of Gibby's horse with such force that it struck them
all four from under him, and both he and his rider fell in a
reverse direction, rolling plump over the wounded warrior
and his forlorn encumbered steed, that was pawing the air
at a furious rate. The two horses falling thus on different
sides, their iron-shod hoofs were intermixed, and clashing
and rattling away in a tremendous manner, tremendous at
least to poor Gibby, whose leg and thigh being below his
charger, he was unable to extricate himself. 'Happ, Davie,
happ!' cried he to the steed: 'Up you stupid, awkward
floundering thief! Happ, Davie, happ!' Davie could neither
happ nor weynd, but there he lay groaning and kicking
above his master, who was in a most deplorable plight.

Charlie perceiving the commencement of the fray, was
all this while galloping furiously toward the combatants.
But the battle was of short duration; for the English
trooper, seeing his comrade fall he wist not how, and the
friar and Tam having both their swords pointed at him,
broke furiously through between them and fled towards
his companions, Tam being only enabled to inflict a deep
wound on the hinder part of the horse as he passed by.

'I have made him to pass away as the stubble that
is driven by the whirlwind,' said the friar; 'yea, as the
chaff before the great wind, so is he fled from the arm
of the mighty. Brother, I say unto thee, that thou hadst
better arise!' continued he, looking upon the disconsolate
Jordan; and passing by on the other side with great *sang
froid*, he rode up to Delany, the boy Elias, and the
poet, the latter of whom had not been engaged, but,

drawing his sword manfully, had stood as a guard to the other two.

Tam Craik pursued his enemy, although apparently not with a fixed design of overtaking him; and Gibby, being thus left all alone with the two inverted horses and the incensed moss-trooper, extended his voice to an amazing pitch, for he knew not what state of health and strength his opponent retained. This was a horrid consideration; for if he should disengage himself and get up first, there was an end of him of the Peatstacknowe. His nasal twine was increased by his dread, and he cried so vehemently, that his cries grew like the cries of a peacock.

Charlie Scott rode up to the main group, who continued to advance at a quiet pace, for they knew nothing as yet of the approaching danger. He also called and made signs to Tam Craik to return; and as soon as he came up to them he pointed out their pursuers, and charged them to ride for their lives. 'We are betrayed,' said he; 'but the horses of our enemies are jaded, ours are fresh; therefore, brave lads, in our master's name, spare neither spur, nor horse-flesh. Haud on your way, an' never look ower your shoulders: you will find Corby an' me twa gude back friends.'

The friar bent himself forward over the mane of his mule, and opening his eyes wide abroad, he put the spurs to his steed, and set off 'with the swiftness of the roebuck or the hart,' as he termed it.

The boy pursued hard after him; and the bard, taking hold of Delany's bridle by both reins below the neck, for fear her steed should stumble and throw his lovely rider, bade her whip on and fear nothing, and in this friendly guise they also made good speed. Charlie then galloped back to see if any life remained in his friend Gibby – for he only saw him at a distance go down in the encounter, without being exactly versed in the circumstances of his overthrow; but he thought he heard one loud squeak arise from the field after the rest had left it, something like that sent forth by the small drone of the bagpipe; and, guessing that the laird was yet alive, he galloped back to see. By the way he met the deil's Tam, who returned with him, and when they came in view of the spot where the two prostrate heroes had been left, they saw a very curious scene, the more curious because it was transacted by our worthy laird in the presiding belief that he was not seen, for he was too much concerned in his own affairs to perceive the approach of his friends. The Englishman's horse making an exertion, by pressing his feet against the ribs of the laird's Davie, by that means pushed himself forward, and Gibby perceived plainly that his enemy was to be first released. The struggles that Gibby then made were enormous. 'Happ, Davie, happ!' cried he: 'O mother of God, what shall become of me! Happ, Davie, happ, my man; happ, happ, happ!' and, as a last resource, he reared up his body and struck at the Englishman's limb that was above his horse, crying out to Davie to happ, in bitterness of soul. Davie was not long; for the next moment after the Englishman's horse rose, he got up also, his feet then getting to the ground; but the stirrup that had been under him was crushed together, and there his master's foot remained fixed. Gibby was worse than ever. 'Wo, Davie, wo! Tproo, ye thief!' cried he. Davie, finding the weight at his side, wheeled about, and dragged the unfortunate laird round across the breast of the trooper Hall, who seized him by the neck. 'Was there ever a man guidit this gate!' cried Gibby. 'Honest man, an ye please, let gae; it wasna me that hurt ye.' The man answered him not; but Davie being scared by the struggle sprung aside, and the Englishman keeping his hold, Gilbert's foot was released by the loss of his boot. He was not long in making a bold effort to rise, and though Hall hung by his neck a little, it had been in the last agony of receding life that he had seized him, and he dropped dead on the green, having both fists clenched on his breast, in the act of still holding his rival.

When Gibby saw how matters stood, he began to value himself on his courage. 'I's gar ye! I's gar ye!' cried he, lifting up his sword, and giving the dead man several desperate gashes, and always between every stroke repeating, 'H'm! I's gar ye!' His two friends being now hard beside him, the sound of their horses' feet made him start; but lifting his eye, and perceiving who they were, he again repeated his blows, and continued his threats in a louder key—. 'H'm! I's gar ye! I's gar ye, billy! I's learn you to throttle me!'

'Fy, lay on, laird!' cried Tam; 'dinna ye see that the man's no half dead yet?'

'I think I hae done for him;' said Gibby: 'He brings me a-mind o' a wife that had to kill her cat thrice ower. I's learn the best o' the haggies-headed Ha's to meddle wi' me!'

'I think he'll do that ane, however, Gibby; if he had e'en the nine lives o' the wife's cat,' said Charlie: 'therefore, an ye please, put up your sword, an' mount your horse. It's no a time now to examine whether ye hae behaved in a sodger-like manner wi' that bold trooper. If I wist ye had not, it should be the last hour I should ride in your company – but mount quick an' ride; for see whar the rest o' the Ha's are coming across us. Ilk horse an' man do what he can, or dear will be our raide, an' yours, friend, the dearest of a'.'

One look filled Gilbert's eye. He mounted Davie, with the one boot off and the other on, and there was little occasion to bid him ride. Before they turned the corner of the hill, their pursuers came so close on them, that they looked very like cutting off their retreat; but a bog, around which the English were forced to cast a wide circuit, saved our three heroes, and gave them the start, by fully a half mile, of their foes, who still came in a straggling way as their horses could keep up. After a hard chace of two Scottish miles they came up with the friar, whose mule being too heavy loaden had begun to fag. When he saw them gaining on him so hard, he judged that all was over with him, and spurred on his jaded beast in vain. 'O that my flesh were as my armour or my clothing,' cried he, 'that I might put it off at will, and escape from the face of mine enemies, Lo! I shall be left all alone, and surrounded and taken and slain.' As he divined, so it fell out; the others were soon by him, and he was left the hindermost. Then they heard him lamenting to himself in his own sublime eastern stile, that he had not the wings of the eagle or the dove, that he might bear away to the mountains and the cliffs of the rocky hills, to elude the dreadful weapons of death, so often reared over his head, and so often warded by the arm of heaven.

'Poor devil!' said muckle Charlie, the tear standing in his eye: 'Od I canna leave him after a'. Come what will, I for ane shall stand or fa' wi' him. I whiles think there's mair in that body than we moorland men wot of – I canna leave him to be cut in pieces.'

'O fy, let him tak his chance,' said Tam; 'let him bide his weird; he deserves it a'. What signifies the creature? He's just a thing made up o' hypocritical rant, empty words, and stuffed paunches. Let him bide the buffet that fa's to his share.'

'Ay, what signifies sic a corpulation?' said Jordan. 'It will be lang or *he* bring down man an' horse in an encounter. He brings me in mind o' a capon that claps his wings, but craws nane. Let him tak his chance.'

'Na, but callans, troth my heart winna let me,' said Charlie: 'For his good deeds, or his ill anes he's answerable to heaven, an' neither to you nor me. But he's a fellow creature, an' has nane to look to for help but us at this time. Life's sweet to us a', an' it's unco hard to leave our master's bedesman just to be sacrificed. Therefore, come what will, I'll turn an' lend the friar a hand. As for you twa, ride on; the young couple that are committed to our charge may escape.' With that he wheeled Corby's head about, and rode back to meet the gospel friar.

When he met him, the foremost of the riders had advanced within a bow shot, and was fast gaining ground. The friar still continued to spur on, and though his mule likewise continued the motion of one that gallops, the progress that he made was hardly discernible. He had a sort of up and down hobble that was right laughable to behold in one riding for his life. When he saw the dauntless Yardbire return to meet him, with his large seven feet sword drawn, and heaved over his right shoulder, he lifted up his voice and wept, and he said unto him; – 'Blessed be thou, my son! The blessing of a man ready to perish light upon thee! And now, lo, I will draw forth my sword and return with thee to the charge, and thou shalt see what a poor bedesman can do.'

'It is brawly said, good friar – but gin ye wad save yoursel' an' me, ride. An we could but mak the end o' the Thief-gate, they should buy our twa lives dear. If thou wilt but exert man an' beast, father, you an' I shall fight, flee, or fa' thegither. But see, we are already overtaken, and in the enemy's hands.'

The foremost of the riders was now hard behind them; but, perceiving Charlie, he reined up his horse and looked back for his comrades. The frair gave a glance back, and he said, 'Lo, thou art a mighty man of valour, and behold there is but one; do thou fall upon him and smite him; why should one pursue two?'

'I hae heard waur advices frae mair warlike men,' said Charlie; 'Ride ye on, father, an' lose nae time. Gude faith! I sal gie this ane his breakfast.'

Charlie as he said this put the spurs to Corby, and rode full speed against the pursuer. The trooper set himself firm in his stirrups and assumed his defence, for he saw from the prowess of Corby that it was vain to fly. Just as Charlie's mighty sword was descending on his casque, a check that he gave his horse in the hurry of the moment made him rear on end, and Charlie's stroke coming down between his ears, clove his head almost into two halves. The horse reeled and fell; but how it fared with his rider, Charlie never knew; for before he got his horse turned, there were other three of the Halls close at hand. Charlie fled amain. He was nothing afraid of himself, for he knew Corby could outstrip them by one half of the way; but his heart bled for the poor friar, whom he saw he would either be obliged to leave, or fight for him against such odds as it would be madness to withstand. The frair had, however gained the height, and having now a long sloping descent all the way to the Thief-gate-end, he was posting on at an improved pace. Charlie had one sole hope remaining of saving the friar, and that was the gaining the above-mentioned point before they were overtaken. The warriors carried no whips in those days, depending altogether on the ample spur – therefore Charlie, as a last resource, pulled down a large branch from a hazel tree, and attacked the hinder parts of the father's mule with such a torrent of highsounding strokes, that the animal, perhaps more sullen than exhausted, seemed to recover new life and vigour, and fled from the assault like a deer, in the utmost terror and dismay. Little wonder was it! He heard the sound of every descending stroke coming on like the gathering tempest; and, clapping his tail close down between his hips, pricking up his long ears, and looking back first with the one eye and then with the other, he went at such a rate that Corby could do little more than keep up with him.

'My swiftness is greater than I can bear,' cried the friar, pronouncing the sentence all in syllables for want of breath;

'verily I shall fall among the cliffs of the rocks by the side of the highway.'

His danger increased with his fears; for the mule perceiving that exertion availed not, and that there was no escaping from the fierceness of his pursuer's wrath, began to throw up his heels violently at every stroke, nevertheless continuing to exert himself between these evolutions. The frair's riding-gear began to get into disorder, and with great difficulty he retained his seat; therefore he cried out with a loud voice, 'I pray of thee, my son, to desist, for it is better for me to perish by an enemy's hand than thine; seest thou not my confusion and despair – verily I shall be dashed in pieces against the stones.'

The friar saw nought of Charlie's intent, else he would not have besought him so earnestly to desist. The Thief-gate-end was now hard at hand. It is still well known as a long narrow path alongst the verge of a precipice, and all the bank above it was then a thicket of brushwood and gorse, so close that the wild beast of the desert could not pass through it. It was, moreover, shagged with rocks, and bedded with small stones, and the path itself was so narrow, that two horsemen could scarcely ride abreast. By such a strenuous manoeuvre on the parts of Charlie and the mule, the two flyers got into this path, without having lost any ground of their pursuers. When Charlie saw this, he began to breathe more freely, and, flinging away his hazel branch, he again seized his mighty weapon in his right hand.

'Let the chields come as close on us now, an they dare,' said he.

The mule still continued to eye him with a great deal of jealousy, and, perceiving the brandish that he gave his long sword when he said this, he set off again full speed; so that it was a good while before the friar got time to reply. As soon as he got leisure to speak, he opened his mouth and said – 'My son, wilt thou lift up thine arm against a multitude? or canst thou contend with the torrent of the mighty waters?'

'Well, well, they may perhaps lead that winna drive,' said Charlie; and he went by the friar at a light gallop, leaving him behind, who prayed to the other not to leave him nor forsake him; but it was a device of Yardbire's, and a well conceived one. He saw that as long as he kept the rear guard, and rode behind the friar, the men that pursued them would not separate on that long narrow path; therefore he vanished among the bushes, keeping, however, always within hearing of the mule's feet. Accordingly, at the first turn of the road, the foremost of the English troopers, seeing the jolly bedesman posting away by himself, put the spurs to his steed, and made a furious dash at him. The friar cried out with a loud voice; and, seeing that he would be overtaken, he turned round and drew his sword to stand on the defensive; and actually not only bore the first charge of his opponent with considerable firmness, but had 'very nigh smitten him between the joints of the harness,' as he termed it. It happened, moreover, very singularly, from the perversity of the mule, that in the charge the combatants changed sides, at the imminent peril of the Englishman; for the mule brushed by his horse with such violence, and leaned so sore to the one side, that both the horse and his rider were within an inch of the verge of the precipice.

The friar had no sooner made his way by, than he saw another rider coming like lightning to meet him in the face; but at the same time he heard the voice of Charlie Scott behind him, and the rending crash of his weapon. This cheered the drooping spirits of the brave friar, who had been on the very point of crying for quarter. 'They beset me before and behind,' cried he, 'yet shall my hand be avenged. Come on, thou froward and perverse one.' So saying he assumed his guard, and met his foe face to face, seeing he had no alternative. The Englishman drew a stroke, but got not time to lay it on; for just as the mule and his tall horse met, the former, in the bitterness of his ire, rushed between his opponent and the upper bank, and pressed against his fore counters with such energy, that he made the leg next him to slacken, and the horse reared from the other. The intention of the irritated mule was to crush his master's leg, or, if possible, to rub him from off his back; and therefore, in spite of the rein he closed with the Englishman's tall steed in a moment, and almost as swift as lightning. The English moss-trooper had raised his arm to strike, but seeing his horse shoved and rearing in that perilous place, he seized the rein with his sword hand. The mule finding the substance to which he leaned give way, pressed to it the harder. It was all one to him whether it had been a tree, a horse, or a rock; he shouldered against it with his side foremost so strenuously, that in spite of all the trooper could do, the fore feet of his horse on rearing, alighted within the verge of the precipice. The noble animal made a spring from his hinder legs, in order to leap by the obstreperous mongrel; but the latter still coming the closer, instead of springing by he leaped into the open void, aiming at the branches of an oak that grew in a horizontal direction from the cliff. It was an old and stubborn tree, the child of a thousand years; and when the horse and his rider fell upon its hoary branches, it yielded far to the weight. But its roots being entwined in the rifted rock as far as the stomach of the mountain, it sprung upward again with a prodigious force to regain its primitive position, and tossed the intruding weight afar into the unfathomed deep. Horse and rider went down in a rolling motion till they lessened to the eye, and fell on the rocks and water below with such a shock, that the clash sounded among the echoes of the linn like the first burst of the artillery of heaven, or the roar of an earthquake from the depths of the earth.

Charlie Scott gazed on the scene with horror; every feature of his countenance was changed, and every hair on his great burly head stood on end. He gave a look to heaven, crossed himself, and said a short prayer, if a prayer it may be called that consisted only of four syllables. It consisted merely in the pronunciation of a name, too sacred to be set down in an idle tale; but he pronounced it with an emphasis that made it doubly affecting. The friar, on the contrary, astonished at his own prowess, or rather at that of his mule, beheld the scene with wonder, it is true, but also with a shade of ostentation. 'I have overthrown the horse and his rider,' said he, 'and they are sunk down as a stone into the mighty waters.' Corby manifested the fright that he was in, by loud and reiterated snortings; the mule also was astonied, and, that he might witness the horrific scene in more perfection, he kept his tail close to the precipice, and looked back.

'Now, by my honour as a man and a warrior, father,' said Charlie, 'you are a man amang ten thousand. I never knew of a bedesman who behaved so gallantly, nor have I seen a knight behave better. How durst you close so instantaneously and furiously with both these valiant troopers?'

'Thou hadst better put that question to my mule,' said the friar – 'for it is a truth that he hath that in him that is the ruin of many people, viz. obstinacy of heart. When he smelleth the battle he disdaineth all parley or courtesy, as thou beholdest, but rusheth upon his adversary like one of the bulls of Bashan.'

At that moment the friar's eye caught a glance of several horsemen close upon them, but as they could only come one man rank, they paused at seeing their enemies in quiet possession of the way, and standing in peaceful colloquy, apparently about something else.

'By the life of Pharaoh,' said the friar, gazing all around, 'I had forgot the man whom I first engaged and smote as he passed by.'

'You will see nae mair o' him, father,' said Charlie; 'I gae him a deadly wound, but the saddle was locked to the horse, and the man to the saddle, and the furious animal has escaped away to the forest with the dead man on its back.'

'Thou art indeed a man of valour,' said the friar; 'and here will we keep our ground. I will do more in our defence than thou hast yet witnessed; therefore, be not afraid, my son, for that sword of thine is a good sword.'

'It is a good sword at a straik,' returned Charlie; 'but it's no very handy at making a defence. But an I get the first yerk of a chield, I'm no unco feared for his return. However, father, this sword, sic as it is, shall be raised in your defence as lang as my arm can wag it. I like the man that will stand a brush when a pinch comes – see, thae chaps darena come on us. But, ill luck to the coward! gin they winna come to us, we'll gang to them.'

'I will certainly go with thee,' said the friar; 'but I know the nature of the beast that I bestride, and that it will at the first onset bear me into the thickest of the battle; therefore, be not thou far from me in my need, for, though nothing afraid, yet I know it will carry me into peril. Come, let us go and smite these men with the edge of the sword.'

'Gallant friar,' said Charlie, 'the Thief-road is lang an' narrow, an' there's hardly a bit o't that they can come on us twa in a breast; stand ye still; or be chopping on

your way, an' I'll let you see yon lads get a surprise
for aince.'

'Nay, I will certainly stand with thee in battle,' said the
friar; 'thinkest thou I will stand and be a looker on, when
my preserver is in jeopardy? Lo, my heart is as thy heart,
my arm as thy arm, and – but I cannot say my horse is as
thy horse, for the beast is indeed froward in his ways, and
perverse in all his doings.

Charlie hardly smiled at the phrase of the worthy friar –
for he meditated an attack on their pursuers, and his eye
kindled with his heart toward the battle. He heaved up his
sword-arm twice at its full stretch, to feel if it was nowise
encumbered in the armour, and putting Corby in motion,
he rode deliberately up to the face of his enemies. The
foremost man spoke to him, demanding what he wanted;
but he only answered by heaving his sword a little higher,
and making his horse mend his pace. In one second after
that he was engaged with the first man, and in two seconds
the horse and his rider had fallen in the middle of the path.
Charlie listed not coming to close quarter; his sword was
so long and heavy, that it was quite unhandy in warding
the blows of a short and light weapon. His aim, therefore,
was always to get the first stroke, which was as apt to light
on the horse as the man, and thus down both of them
went. Springing by the prostrate warrior, he attacked the
second and the third in the same manner, and with the
same success, always either cutting down the trooper or
cleaving the head of his horse at the first stroke. The path
was now in the utmost confusion. Owing to the pause that
had taken place, all the riders had come up and crowded
each other behind, some crying, 'He is a devil!' and others
at a greater distance shouting out, 'Down with the Scot!
down with him!' Charlie regarded not their cries, but laid
about him with all his might, till, after striking down three
of the foremost and one horse, those next to him were glad
to turn in order to effect their escape; but the hindermost
on the path refusing for a while to give way, many of their
friends fell a sacrifice to Charlie's wrath. He pursued them
for a space, and might have cut them off every man, had
he been sure that all was safe behind – but he had rushed
by some wounded men and wounded horses, and knew not
how matters stood with the friar.

As he dreaded, so it fell out. Two of the Englishmen who had fallen perhaps under their horses, had scrambled up the bosky precipice, and, as he returned, assailed him with large stones, a mode of attack against which he was unable to make the least resistance. Therefore, it was at the utmost peril of his life that he made his way back through the encumbered path to his friend the friar. This latter worthy had found it impossible to lend his friend any assistance. The beast that he bestrode was fonder of rubbing shoulders with a living brute, than a mangled or dead one; so he refused to come nearer the first that fell than about twice his own length, where he stood firm, turning his tail to the scene of battle, and looking back. Our two heroes now set off at full speed after the rest of their party, whom they expected to overtake before reaching the outposts of the beleaguering army.

CHAPTER TWELVE

Lord Duffus: I saw the appearance of a mounted warrior.
　　Whence did it come, or whither did it go?
　　Or whom did it seek here?
　　　Hush thee, my lord;
　　The apparition spoke not, but passed on,
　　'Tis something dreadful; and, I fear me much,
　　Betokens evil to this fair array.
　　　　　　　　　　　　　　　Trag. of the Prioress

THE REST OF our cavalcade continued to advance at a
quick pace, not without anxiety. They were not afraid of
their enemies coming behind them, for they had strong
faith in the prowess of their friend, as well as his horse
Corby. But when they came to the end of the narrow path,
called the Thief-gate, there were two roads, and they knew
not which of these to follow. As bad luck would have it,
they took the most easterly, which led towards Yetholm,
and left the Scottish army to the westward. In that path
they continued to jog on, turning many a long look behind
them for the approach of Charlie; and, at one time, they
thought they got a view of him coming at a furious pace
all alone; but the rider being at a great space behind them,
he was shortly hid from their view in an intervening hollow,
and it was long before they saw him any more. They judged
that the friar was taken or slain, and began to talk of his loss
in a very indifferent manner.

'Alas, how frigid and ungenial must be the hearts of you
men in Scotland,' said Delany. 'Now, of all the men I have
met with since I was brought from my own country, there
is only one whose death I would more regret than that of
the worthy and kind friar. He may have his whims and his
peculiarities, but his manner is pleasing, and his speech has

a strain of grandeur which I love. Where did he acquire that speech?'

'He gets it frae some auld-fashioned beuk,' said Tam, 'that he has pored on a' his days, an' translatit out o' other tongues, till he was nearly hanged for it; and it's weel kend that he is now in hiding wi' our warden for fear o' his life, and has been these half dozen o' years; and though he pretends to be only a friar, he was aince a monk o' the first order of St Benedict, and president of a grand college in France.'

'I would like to converse with him,' said Delany, 'for I have always thought that he feigned to be something a degree lower than he is.'

'You said there was *but one* you would lament the loss of more,' said the poet: 'Pray, who may that *one* be?'

'Could you not guess?' returned she.

'How can I?' said he; 'but this I know, that to be the favoured one I would dive into the depths of the ocean—'

'It wad be for fear then,' said Tam.

'Or traverse the regions of ice,' continued the bard, 'or wander barefoot over burning sands, or—'

'O, alak for your poor feet!' said Delany, interrupting him; 'but rest satisfied you shall not be put to the test: it is not you.'

With such kind of chat did they beguile the way, till Elias, looking back, exclaimed, 'Mercy! see what a guise Yardbire is coming in!'

'St Mary protect us!' said the maid; 'he must be grievously wounded. See how he rides!'

Every one turned round his horse and looked at the approaching warrior; but it was wearing late, and they could not see with distinctness. The horse was coming rapidly, and with apparent impatience, but Charlie appeared as if he were riding in his sleep. When the horse came down hill he bent forward, and on climbing an ascent he bent back, riding with that sort of motion as if his back or neck were out of joint. The whole group showed manifest signs of fear at the approach of such a hideous apparition; and, quite in earnest, though in a pretended frolic, they wheeled about again, and gallopped away. The ground being uneven, and the night-fall coming on, they soon lost sight of him; and, continuing their career as fast as the road would permit, they seemed inclined to escape from their friend altogether. The maid had just begun to remonstrate on their unfriendly procedure, when they beheld the same unaccountable figure coming at the full gallop close behind them. Seeing that he was determined to be of the party, they suffered him to overtake them quietly. He came driving furiously up till he was in the middle of them, and then paused. No one had the courage to speak to him, for he looked not up, nor regarded any of them. His helmed head nodded on his breast, and his arms hung loosely down by his side, the steel armlets rattling on the cuishes. At one time his horse came so near to that on which Delany rode, that she weened she saw the rider all covered with blood, and screamed out; yet in the twilight she could not be certain. The poet, who was never far from her side, and on whom her voice always acted like electricity, immediately demanded the cause of her alarm.

'O Carol!' said she, in an agitated whisper, 'we are haunted. That is a dead man that rides in our company.'

If the maid was alarmed, the poet was ten times more so. If she had said that a lion or a bear was in the company, it could not have struck such a chillness to the poor bard's heart; and, after all, it was no wonder, for there is something exceedingly appalling in the idea of having a dead man riding in one's company. The poet felt this in its fullest measure. He held in his horse and attempted a reply, but a dryness pervaded his mouth so much that he could not make himself intelligible. A damp had fallen on the whole party, and a breathless silence prevailed. Tam put the question, so natural, to him as he passed, 'Charlie, is this you?' – but none answered or regarded. They were riding up a slanting hill when the bard was first apprised of the nature of their guest, and shortly after the figure coming between him and the evening sky, its motions were altogether so hideous, that he roared out in perfect terror as loud as he could bray, scarce letting one bellow await another. This was still worse than the dumb appalling uncertainty in which they were before involved; till at last Tam, losing all patience, let loose his rage against the poet, calling him a bellowing beast, and many other opprobrious names. This encouraging Gibbie, who had the bard at no good will on account of the damsel, he said he brought him 'amind of a story that the fo'k o' Annandale tauld about Andrew Jardine's bull, that was better at booing than breeding.' The boy Elias now coming in behind them, and having heard what Delany said, cried softly, 'Hush! yeomen! hush! we are haunted; it is a ghost that rides in our company.'

They all turned their eyes to the mysterious figure, which they still thought resembled their champion Yardbire, as well as the horse did that which he rode, the redoubted Corby. The horse had started a little forward at the cries of the poet, but when the rest paused the figure seemed to wheel his horse around, and made a dead pause also, standing still with his face toward them, and straight on the path before. Not one durst proceed. The figure neither moved nor threatened, but stood nodding its head on the height at every motion of the steed; yet our party were arrested on their way, nor knew they exactly in what place they were: But from the length of the way they had come, they were sure they were near the Scottish army on one side or other, and free from any danger of the foes they had left behind them on the Border. None of them were good guides in any case, and a man in fear is neither a fit guide for himself nor others. Fear had the sway, and fear gave the word of command without being disputed. The poet was the first to strike from the beaten path, and it was at no easy pace that he rode. He turned westward, and the rest all followed with main speed. Their progress was soon interrupted by a strong cattle fence made of stakes and the branches of trees interwoven, bespeaking the vicinity of some village, or place of human habitation. They soon broke through the fence, but by bad luck did not take time to make up the breach, which they left open, and posting forward came to a large house amid a number of smaller ones. The poet called for admittance in a moving and earnest stile, and at once resolved to take no denial. Before ever he paused, he told them he and his party had lost their way, and that they had seen a ghost.

'Then you must be some murderers,' said the men of the house – 'and here you remain not to-night.'

'We belong to the warden of the marches, the brave baron of Mountcomyn,' said the poet, 'and go on an errand of great import to the army. In that case we might demand what we only ask as a boon, namely, such lodging as the house affords.'

'You had better keep that part to yourself,' said the men of the house: 'Though Sir Ringan is supreme in the middle marches, he is no favourite here. Our master's name is Ker. He is with the Douglas, but may be home to-night. Calm sough and kitchen fare, or ride on.'

'It brings me in mind o' an auld proverb,' said Gibbie, 'that beggars should nae be choisers; sae, honest lads, bring us a light, for our horses are sair tired an' maun be weel put up.'

The party, it will be remembered, consisted only of five, exclusive of Charlie and the friar. They had drawn up their horses close to the hall door, and were still on horseback when the men turned into the house for a light. The poet, whose eager eyes were still on the watch, chancing to look at the heads of his associates between him and the sky, thought he discovered one too many.

'Surely there are six of us,' said he in a hurried tremulous voice. 'Six of us!' said Tam, as doubting the statement.

'Six of us? No, surely?' said Delany.

At that instant a lad came out with a lanthorn, and held it up to look at the party. The poet was nearest the door, and the light shone full on him and the rider that was next him. He cast his eyes on that rider – but one glance was enough to bedim his eye-sight, if not to scare away his reason. It had the appearance of a warrior sheathed in steel, but all encrusted in a sheet of blood. His mouth was wide open, and his jaws hanging down upon his breast, while his head seemed to be cleft asunder. The poet uttered a loud yell of horror, and flinging himself from his horse on the side opposite to that on which the phantom stood, he fell among the mud and stones at the door, yet ceased not to reiterate his loud cries like one in distraction. Every one jumped from his horse, and hurried in at the door; the man with the lanthorn also fled, and with the noise and uproar the horses galloped off, saddled and bridled as they were. As the guests ran into the hall, every one asked at all the rest what it was? 'What is it?' was all that could be heard; all asking the question, but none answering it. Even the people of the house joined in the query, and came all

round the strangers, crying, 'What is it? – What is it?' –
'I do not know – I do not know, Sir – I do not know upon
my word.'

'The people are all delirious,' said the housekeeper:
'—Can no one tell us what it was that affrighted you? –
St Magdalene be with us! whom have we here?'

This was no other than the poor bard coming toward
the light, creeping slowly on all-four, and still groaning as
he came.

'Here's the chap that began the fray,' said Tam, 'you
may speer at him. He rather looks as he were at ane mae
wi't. For my part, I just did as the rest did – ran an' cried
as loud as I could. When a dust is fairly begun, I think aye
the mair stour that is raised the better. I'll try wha will cry
loudest again, an ye like – or rin round the fire wi' ony o'
you, or out through the mids o't either, at a pinch.'

Tam turned round his long nose to see if his jest had
taken, for he always fixed his eyes stedfastly on one object
when he spoke; but he found that his jargon had been
ill-timed, for no one laughed at it but himself. The rest
were gathered round the bard; some pitying, but more like
to burst with laughter at his forlorn state. He fetched two
or three long-drawn moans, and then raising himself up on
his knees, with his eyes fixed on the light, he rolled over,
and fainted.

Delany first stooped to support his head, and was soon
assisted by every female in the house, while the men only
stood and looked on. By bathing his hands and temples
with cold water, they soon brought him out of his faint,
but not to his right senses. His looks continued wild and
unstable, and ever and anon they were turned to the
door, as if he expected some other guest to enter. A
sober conference at last ensued; and as no one had seen
or heard any thing at this last encounter, save the man
that was taken ill, who a few moments before had been
heard to say *there were six of them*, all began to agree that
he had been seized with some sudden frenzy or delirium;
till the lad, who had carried out the light, thrust in his pale
face among the rest, and said – 'Na, na, my masters, it is
nae for naething that the honest man's gane away in a kink;
for, when I held up the bouet, I saw a dead man riding on
a horse close at his side. He was berkened wi' blood off at

the taes; and his mouth was open, and I saw his tongue
hinging out.'

It may well be conceived what an icy chillness these
words distilled round the heart of every one present. The
effect on our travellers was particularly appalling, from the
idea that they were haunted by a phantom from which they
could not escape. The whole group closed around the fire,
and the strangers recounted to the family the singular
occurrence of their having lost two of their number by
the way, and been pursued and overtaken by a phantom
resembling one of them, and that the hideous spectre was,
as it seemed, haunting them still. As they all agreed in
the same story, it was not of a nature to be disregarded
at a period when superstition swayed the hearts of men
with irresistible power. The stoutest heart among them
was daunted, and no one durst go out to the vaults to
look after his master's cattle, nor to take in our travellers'
horses, that were left to shift for themselves during the long
winter night.

The next morning, between day-light and the sun-rising,
the men began to peep abroad, and the first things they
observed were some of the horses of our travellers going
about in a careless, easy manner. This they looked on
as a good omen, knowing that horses were terrified for
spirits; and the men joining in a body, they sallied out to
reconnoitre. The horses had fared well, for they had fed at
the laird's stacks of hay and corn all night; but as the men
were going round to see how matters stood, they perceived
a phenomenon, that, if it had not been open day-light,
would have scared them from the habitation. This was
the identical phantom-warrior still sitting unmoved on
his horse, that was helping itself full liberally out of one
of the laird's corn-ricks. The eye of day expels the films
of superstition from the human eye. The men, after a
short consulation, ventured to surround the phantom –
to seize his horse – (who had given full proof that he at
least was flesh and blood;) – and, after a good deal of
trembling astonishment, they found that he was actually
rode by a dead warrior, whose head was cleft asunder,
and his whole body, both within and without the harness,
encrusted in blood.

The mystery was soon cleared up; but none then knew

who he was. It had become customary in that age for
warriors, who went to engage others, on horseback, to lock
themselves to the saddle, for fear of being borne out of their
seats by the spears of their opponents in the encounter.
This was the individual trooper who had come foremost
in the pursuit of our party, he whom the friar jostled, and
whom Charlie, encountering the moment after, had slain;
but his suit of armour having kept him nearly upright in
his saddle, his horse had run off with him, and followed
after those of our travellers, as every horse will do that is
let go on a highway and gets his will.

Glad were our travellers at an eclaircissement so fairly
within the bounds of their comprehension, and when the
poet saw the gash made in the helmet, he shook his head,
and exclaimed, 'Ha! well I wot the mighty hand of Charlie
has been here!'

Gibbie remarked that he himself had 'killed one very like
him, only he was sure his wad never mount horse again.'
But seeing Tam's ill-set eye fixed on him, he was afraid of
something coming out relating to that encounter which he
did not wish to hear blabbed; so he changed his tone, and,
looking wise, said, 'The hale business brings me a-mind of
a very good story that happened aince at Allergrain; an' if
it be nae true it is behadden to the maker, for the sin o'
the lie lyes nae at my door. The story, you see, is this—.
There was a man, an' he had a wife; an' they had a son,
an' they ca'ed him Jock—'

'Now, d—n your particularity!' said Tam Craik: 'think
you we have nought else to do but stand beside the bloody
man and listen to a long-winded talk like that?'

The poet muttered over some old rhyme in unison with
what he heard. If one word spoken chanced to occur in any
old rhyme or song that he knew, he went over the sentence
to himself, though it had no farther connection with it,
or resemblance to it, than merely that word. This made
his conversation altogether incomprehensible to those not
acquainted with him, but it was always delightful to
himself; a chance old rhyme brought to his remembrance,
would have pleased him almost in any circumstances, while
his words chimed naturally into measure.

Leaving the dead warrior at the house where they lodged
for the people to bury as they liked, they proceeded to the

army, in hopes of finding Charlie and the friar there; for without them they did not know how to accomplish their mission. These two heroes finding, on asking at a hamlet, that their friends had not passed on the road to Roxburgh, suspected what way they had gone, and turning to the southeast they followed them on the track to Yetholm, but missed them at the house into which they had been chased by the dead man, and rode searching for them the greater part of the night. Next morning they again went in search of them, and came up behind them at the convent of Maisondieu near to the Teviot, where a detachment of the army was stationed; and, after conversing two or three hours on the state of the army and garrison, they proceeded on their journey, and reached the abbey of Melrose that night. There they were welcomed by the brethren, and lodged comfortably. There also they got many strange stories told to them about Master Michael Scott, which made the very hairs of their heads stand on end, and the hearts of the boldest to palpitate. When the friar heard them, he seemed wrapt in deep thought; and he opened his mouth, and said: 'If the things that thou hast spoken be according to the light that is in thee, and the truth that is told among men, then this man is not as other men, for the spirit of the immortals is in him, and he communeth with the prince of the power of the air. Nevertheless, I will go unto him, and I will speak to him face to face, as a man speaketh to his friend. Peradventure I shall tell him that which he knoweth not.'

When it was told to the abbot Lawrence, that the servants of the warden were come, and that they were accompanied by his chaplain and bedesman, a learned man in all holy things, the father came to bestow upon them his benediction – for the baron of Mountcomyn had conferred many rich benefices on the abbey. At the first sound of the friar's voice, the abbot started, as if recollecting him; but on looking at the man his hope seemed to die away. Every time, however, that he spoke in his eastern style, the abbot fixed a look on him, as if he would fain have claimed acquaintance, which the friar perceiving, urged their departure with all the interest he had; and accordingly, about mid-day, they set out for Aikwood-castle, the seat of the renowned magician Master Michael Scott.

Ever since the stern encounter with the English moss-troopers on the Thief-road, Charlie had attached himself close to the friar, imagining that he saw his character in a new light, and that he was one who might either be roused to desperate courage, or impressed with notorious dread; and when he heard him say that he would speak to the enchanter face to face, he admired him still the more; for the business of addressing the Master was that which stuck sorest on the stomach of the doughty Yardbire. As for the poet, he scarcely seemed himself all that day. He looked at the mountains, and the wild romantic rivers branching among them in every direction, with looks of which it was hard to say whether they were looks of vacancy or affection, for he looked sometimes as at objects which he was never to see again. His tongue muttered long rhymes in which his heart had little share; so that Delany was obliged to detach herself from his society, and make up to the friar, whom she now addressed with much affection, and some degree of coquetry:—

'Dearest father, why have you neglected me so much on our journey? Ever since our first stage was got over, you have not deigned to take any notice of me. What have you seen in my conduct that you have thus shunned me? It is in sincerity that I assure you there is no man in whose conversation I so much delight.'

'Fairest among maidens!' said the friar, putting his arm gently around her neck, as her palfrey came close up by his side, 'say not so, but come near me, I will kiss thee with the kisses of my mouth, for thy love is sweeter to me than the vintage. Behold thou art even like a tower of alabaster shining from among the cedars of Lebanon. Thy bosom resembleth two young roes that are twins, and feed among the lilies of the valley.'

'Hold, dear father!' said she, 'and do not let your gallantry run away with your good common sense. Yet would I love to hear that language spoken to another, for though it be nonsense it is still beautiful. Tell me, for I long to hear, where, or in what country, you learned to speak in that stile.'

'Daughter of my people,' said he, 'I have learned that language at home and in a far country. In youth and in age hath it been my delight. At noon-tide when the sun shone in his strength, and in the silent watches of the night hath it been my meditation. In adversity hath it been my comfort, and in prosperity my joy; so that now it hath become unto me as my mother tongue, and other language have I none.'

'Is it the language of the convent and the priory alone?' said the maid.

'No, thou rose of the desart,' said the friar; – 'it is not the language indeed, but the stile of language over one half of the habitable world. It is the language of all the kingdoms and countries of the east, from India even unto Ethiopia; and all the way as thou goest down towards the rising of the sun, yea from the river to the ends of the earth it prevaileth. But, O thou fairest among the daughters of women! that language did I not learn in the lands that are watered by the great river, even the river Euphrates. In Ur of the Chaldees have I not sojourned; nor on the mountains of Palestine have I lifted up my eyes. But I learned it from one little book; a book that is of more value to the children of men than all the gold of Ophir. O maiden, could I but make known unto thee the treasures of that book, the majesty of its stile, and the excellency of its precepts, it would make thine heart to sing for joy. If all the writings of this world, yea, if the world itself were to be laid in the balance with that book, they would be found wanting. The mountains may depart, and the seas may pass away, the stars, and the heavens in which they shine, may be removed, but the words of that book shall remain for ever and ever! And this language that I now speak to thee resembleth the words written therein; and I speak them unto thee that thou mayest hear and love them.'

'Dear friar, teach me to read and understand that book, for my breast yearneth to know more about it. I am, it is true, not my own at present to give, but I have some forebodings here that tell me I soon shall; and, father, I will serve thee, and be thy handmaid, if thou wilt teach me the words and the mysteries of that little book.'

'Alas! and wo is me, for the ignorance of my people!' said he, with the tears streaming over his grim cheek; 'they are troubled about that which availeth them nothing, while the way of life is hid from their eyes. Their leaders have caused them to err; and I, even I, have been a dweller in

the tabernacles of sin! But the day-star hath shone upon
my soul and my spirit: For that have I been persecuted,
and hunted as a partridge upon the mountains, chased
from the habitations of my brethren, and forced to dwell
among a strange and savage people. Yet there are among
them whom I love; and could I be the mean of opening
thine eyes, and turning thee from darkness unto light, then
would I know for what purpose the finger of heaven had
pointed out my way to this barren wilderness. Thou can'st
not be a servant or a handmaiden unto one who is little
better than an outcast and a vagabond on the earth. But
better days may come to us both: I am not what I seem; but,
maiden, thou mayest trust me. My love for thee surpasseth
the love of women, for it is with more than an earthly love
that I behold and delight in thee. Come unto me this night,
and I will tell thee things that shall make thine ears tingle.
The book of wonders is here with me, and thou mayest
look thereon and be glad.'

The poet and his associates listened to this rhapsody
apart.

'What book does he mean?' said the poet: 'If it is not
True Thomas's book, or the book of Sir Gawin, he must
be speaking absolute nonsense. I could recite these to lovely
Delany, word for word; and must this clumsy old friar wile
her from me by any better book than these?'

'You are clean mista'en, maister poeter,' said Tam; 'I
ken mair about auld Roger than you do, or than ony that's
here. It is a book o' black art that he carries about wi' him,
and studies on it night and day. He gat it at a place they
ca' Oxford, where they study nought else but sic cantrips.
They hae tried to hang him, and they hae tried to cut off
his head, and they hae tried to burn him at the stake; but
tow wadna hang, water wadna drown, steel wadna nick,
and a' the fire o' the land wadna singe ae hair o' the auld
loun's head.'

'Gude forgie me!' said Charlie: 'An that be true, Corby,
you and I had maybe mair pith than our ain yon time. I
wondered that he rade sae furiously on the drawn swords o'
men and armour, the auld warlock. He-he-he! we'll aiblins
try auld Michael at his ain weapons, an that be the gate.'

'Ye maunna lippen ower muckle to a' this,' said he of
the Peatstacknowe; 'else ye may play like Marion's Jock,

when he gaed away to douk in Commonside loch. "It is
a hard matter," says Jock to himself, "that a' the lave o'
Commonside's men can swatter and swim in the loch like
sae mony drakes but me. I am fain either to poutter about
the side, or down I gang. I can neither sink nor swim; for
when I try to get to the bottom to creep, there I stick like a
woundit paddock, wagging my arms and my legs, and can
neither get to the top nor the bottom. Just half way, there
stick I. But I's be even hands wi' them an' mair, an' then
I'll laugh at the leishest o' them; for I'll stand, and wade,
and gang ower the waves afore them a', aye, and that wi'
my head boonmost." Jock, after this grand contrivance,
coudna rest, but off he sets to Hawick, and gets four big
blawn bladders; and the next day, when a' the lave went to
bathe, Jock he went to bathe amang the rest; and he gangs
slyly into a bush by himsel', and ties twa o' the bladders to
every foot. "Now," thinks Jock, "I'll let them see a trick."
Sae he slips into the loch, and wades into the deep, but the
bladders they aye gart him hobble and bob up and down,
till, faith, he loses the balance, and ower he coups. Nane
o' them kend o' Jock's great plan, and they were a' like to
burst their sides wi' laughing when they saw Jock diving.
But when they saw he wasna like to come up again, they
swattered away to the place, and there was Jock swimming
wi' his head straight to the bottom, and his feet and the four
bladders walking a minuay aboon. Now, let me tell ye, an
ye lippen to the friar's warlockry, and his enchantments,
and divinations, ye trust to as mony bladders fu' o' wind,
and down gae a' your heads, and your heels uppermost.
Na, na; nane maun try to cope wi' auld Michael.'

'I hae heard, indeed, that he coudna brook ony rivalry,'
said Charlie; 'and I hae heard waur instances, and waur
stories too, than that o' yours, laird. But let us draw slyly
near to the twasome, and make lang lugs, to try if we can
learn ony mair about that same beuk. If the friar hae ony
power o' enchantment, it is my opinion the first glamour
he'll thraw will be ower that bonny wench.'

'We ought to keep them asunder by force,' said the poet;
'it would be a shame and a disgrace to us, if we were to let
the auld rogue seduce either her person or her morals.'

'Morals?' said Charlie; 'I dinna ken about them, for I
watna weel what they are; but as to seducing hersel', I think

I could answer for auld Roger the friar. I see there's nae man can help liking a bonny lass; but the better a good man likes ane he'll be the mair sweer to do her ony skaith.'

'Aye; but then how can an enchanter be a good man?' said the poet.

'That's the thing that puzzles me,' said Charlie: 'Let us hear what they are on about sae briskly now.'

They then drew near, and heard the following words, while the remarks that they made were said aside among themselves.

'My fate, you see, has been a strange one, father. I was separated from my parents so young that I scarcely remember them. But the Scots have been kind to me, and I have loved them. I have never been unhappy, except when long confined to a place, which I dislike exceedingly; and as I have hopes that this change will add somewhat to my freedom, I rejoice in it, without weighing circumstances. If those fond hopes should be realised, I promise to you, father, that the first use I will make of my liberty, shall be to sit at your feet, and learn that wonderful and mysterious book.'

'Do you hear that?' said the poet with great emphasis, but in a half whisper; 'he has gotten her broken already to learn the book of the black art. Then the deil's bargain and witchcraft comes next; then the harassing of the whole country side, dancing in kirkyards, and riding on the wind; and then, mayhap, the stake and the faggot end the matter that is but just beginning. Alak, and wo is me! I say, in the king's name, and in the warden's let them be separated.'

'Gude sauf us!' exclaimed Charlie: 'There's nae man sure o' his life an a' this be true! But a' fair play. Nae self amang us. Hist, and let us hear what he is saying in answer.'

'Daughter,' said the friar, half crying with joy, 'doth not my heart yearn over thee, even as a mother yearneth over the child of her bosom? Lo, I will be unto thee as a father, and thou shalt be unto me as a daughter.'

'Hear what the old rascal is saying!' said the poet.

'And behold the fruits of our labours shall spring up into life—;'

'Oh, this is past all sufferance!' said the poet.

'—For, O thou fair one, whose beauty is as the beauty of

the morning, and whose innocence surpasseth that of the kid, or the lamb, or the young roe, when they are playing upon the mountains—'

'Gude faith, Mr Carol,' said Charlie aside, 'it's that auld chap that's the poet, an' no you.'

'Humph! mere fustian!' said the poet.

The friar still went on:—

'—That beauty will decay, as the rose fadeth on the brows of Shinar or Hermon; and that innocence shall be perverted by the sinful and regardless people among whom thou sojournest, and shall become, as it were, betrothed to sin and corruption; yea, and that eye, that shineth like the dews of the morning, shall be darkened. But, O beloved maiden! there is that in this little book, yea, I say unto thee, even in this old, neglected, and despised book, that, unto those who learn it, shall prove the savour of life unto life; and if thou dost learn and cherish the things contained in this book thou shalt never die!'

'Ay, billy, that is a yanker!' said Tam aside: 'When ane is gaun to tell a lie, there's naething like telling a plumper at aince, and being done wi't.'

'Now, but hear to the deceitful old rogue,' said the poet: 'All the books of black art in the world cannot accomplish that. In the name of Saint Barnabas, I say let them be separated!'

'It wad be weel done,' said Tam, 'if ane durst—;' for he wanted to blow up the poet's wrath, for the sake of a little sport.

'Durst!' said the poet, 'durst! – If none other dare, I shall, in spite of all his hellish arts. Durst! that is a good one – to be dursted with an old sackbut!'

They did not hear what answer Delany made to the extraordinary information, as they took it, that, by learning the little black book, she was to be redeemed from death; for the fierce jealousy of the enamoured bard prevented them. But when they listened again so as to hear distinctly, the friar was still increasing in fervency. All that he said was in raptures of divine ecstacy; while his associates, who knew nothing, and cared as little about these things, understood it in another way.

'For I say unto thee, if thou wilt suffer me to instil these truths into thee, thou shalt both blossom and bring forth fruit abundantly; yea, thou shalt shine as the stars in the firmament of heaven. Seest thou yon sun that walketh above the clouds in majesty and brightness? Beyond yon sun shall thine habitation be fixed; and the blue arch that encircles the regions of the air, which thou hast so often seen studded over with diamonds, shall be unto thee a pavement whereon thou shalt tread. All this and more shalt thou possess, if thou wilt learn and obey the things that are written in this book, where it is said by one that cannot err, 'Lo, I will be always with you, and my arms shall be underneath and around you, and when you are faint and weary I will hide you in my bosom.'

'For the blood that is in your body dare to attempt such a thing!' cried the enraged poet. 'Down with hypocrisy and sensuality together! Hurray for the combat, and God defend the right!'

So, crying as loud as he could yell, he pulled out his sword, and rode furiously up between Delany and the friar, shoving the latter rudely as he passed. The maiden's palfrey sprung away, but the friar's mule only leaned with all his might to the poet's steed as he pressed against him in passing; and feeling his prop give way, he leaned round in the same direction, till his tail was exactly where his head was before; and then, dreading some abhorred exertion, he set his feet asunder, and stood immovable. The poet drew up, and wheeled about, and seeing still the hinder parts of the friar and his beast, he cried, exultingly, 'Ay, you are more ready to seduce an innocent and lovely maiden, than to answer for the crime! Vile lump of sin and hypocrisy! turn round and meet me face to face, that I may chastise thee for thy graceless attempt!'

The friar spurred most furiously, but the mule only dashed his head downward and his heels in a contrary direction, and kept his position. All the rest were like to burst with laughter, which still increasing the bard's insolence, he fumed about enchantments and the black art, and dared the friar to turn and look him in the face.

What with one provocation, what with another, the friar's angry passions were roused; and, not being able to make his mule turn round, he drew out his sword, saying at the same time in a voice of great vehemence, 'God do so to me and more also, if I make not—'

He got no farther with his speech, for the mule interrupted him. Obstinate as the brute was, the sight of the
sword, and the sound of his master's angry voice operated
on him like magic. Perhaps he understood that all further
opposition was vain – for in one moment he wheeled
around, his eyes gleaming with rage; and pricking up his
ears to see where the storm of his and his master's wrath was
to alight, he perceived the poet on his tall steed, brandishing
his dazzling sword, and forthwith darted at them with the
swiftness of an arrow, and a fury not to be checked. There
were no more words nor threatenings passed between the
enraged combatants; for more space of time there was none
before the mule had his shoulder to that of the poet's steed,
his teeth fixed in his flank, and was pushing with the fury
of an enraged bull.

On the closing of the two steeds the riders likewise
engaged, the poet coming on with a downward stroke,
which the friar received with great indifference on his sword
crossed above his cowl. But knowing well the nature of his
beast, he kept up the poet's sword and arm both, until the
sides of the two animals were jammed together, as the rider
of the mule well knew they would be. By that time the
poet's arm was pressed up straight by his ear, and his sword
pointed to heaven; and in endeavouring to free his elbow
from the hilt of the friar's sword, he lost his balance. At the
same instant their feet encountering in the stirrups, and
the friar's being below that of his opponent, he gave him
such a ketch with his right foot and sword-arm together,
that he made him fly from his horse to a great distance,
in a sort of arching direction; and the unfortunate poet,
falling on his shoulder and head, was wofully bruised, and
utterly discomfited.

But the combat ended not here. The mule still struggled
with his adversary, which not only kept his ground, but
rather began to force the mule to give way. But the
inveterate mongrel was not to be vanquished in that
way. He pressed, struggled, and wrought himself round,
till he got his tail to the horse's shoulder, and then he
attacked him furiously with his iron-heels. The horse being
a horse of spirit, and scorning to yield to his long-eared
adversary, applied the same offensive weapons with very
little ceremony, wincing and screaming all the while, and

sometimes making his feet to fly as high as the friar's elbows. The mule fought with desperate energy, but in profound silence. Not so the rider; he spurred, struck with his sword, and cried with a loud voice, 'Soh! tproo! thou beast of the pit! sure the spirit of the evil one is in thee! Lo, I shall be beaten to pieces, for the heels of the horses are lifted up against me. By the life of Pharaoh, I will smite thee until thy blood shall be poured out like water – thou perverse and abominable beast! I say unto thee go forward!'

The voice of the friar, during this passionate declamation, had arisen gradually until the last sentence, which was pronounced in his utmost stile of vehemence. The mule heard this, and saw the uplifted sword; and not awaiting its descent, he sprang forward with main force, but no man will guess the issue.

It may well be conceived, that during this desperate combat between the horse and mule, the onlookers were convulsed with laughter. Charlie Scott, in particular, laughed with a 'Ha-ha-ha!' so loud that he made all the woods around to ring, and at every breath exclaimed, 'Gude faith, I never saw ought half so grand! Na, never!' Gibbie was advanced a little before the rest, so as to be near the scene of action, which, without doubt, was bringing him in mind of some excellent story, for his mouth was formed like a seam from the one ear to the other. But it is dangerous putting one's self too forward in life, and that the poor laird of the Peatstacknowe soon found. It is well known that between parties so closely connected as the horse and his rider, passion begets passion. The mule, driven altogether furious by the broil, and the rage and spurs of his master, either wished to rub himself rid of him, or deemed that it was to be a battle general; for he no sooner rushed from one fray than he flew to another, quite open-mouthed on Gibbie, and, seizing him by the thigh, he separated one limb of his buffskin breeches and a mouthful of the laird's own skin from their places, in one moment, and the next had his teeth fixed in the flank of the laird's horse. Gibbie cried out against the friar, irritated by pain, as well as the awkward and dangerous situation in which he was thus momently placed. His horse flung – the mule returned the compliment with hearty good will, and glad was Gibbie to escape, which he did with great celerity as soon as he got leisure to use the spurs. The mule ran straight at the next horse, and then at the next again, but all of them scampered off at his approach, and left him master of the field; on which he turned two or three times sullenly round, throwing himself up behind and down before. The friar's wrath was somewhat diverted by the shouts of laughter from his scattered compeers, and he only smiled grimly as he said to his contumacious beast – 'Thou art even a perverse and an evil one; nevertheless thou hast been to me a beast for these many years, and hast borne me in distant pilgrimages, through many perils and dangers; and I will not act the part of the son of Bosor: peradventure thou mayest amend thy ways and do some credit to old age.'

The laird in his escape galloped by the forlorn poet; who, raising up his head, and perceiving the plight of the dismayed and unoffensive wight, scouring off with the one thigh naked and bleeding, burst out into a hysteric giggle between laughing and crying, and repeated some scraps of old rhyme no way connected with the incident. The attention of the party was now turned to him, and the friar's as much as any, who enquired with great simplicity, 'My brother, why was thine arm lifted up against me?'

The bard was dreadfully abashed, and out of countenance; and he only answered in rhymes, of which none of them could make any thing:

> 'His arm was strong, and his heart was stout,
> And he broke the tower and he got out;
> Then the king he was an angry man,
>   And an angry man was he,
> And he said, 'Go, lock him in prison strong,
>   And hunger him till he dee.'

'That was a hard weird, was it not? Ha-ha! there be many such; for

> 'He had his wale of seven sisters,
>   Of lith, and lire, and limb so fair
> But the loathly dame of the Hazelrig,
>   She ruined his peace for evermair.'

'Lo, my son,' answered the friar, 'thy thoughts are wandering in a wilderness. I only ask thee wherein I have offended thee. For as mine hand is, so is mine heart; and, as my soul liveth, I know not in what respect I have done thee wrong.'

> 'I have not done thee wrong, fair May,
>   I have not done thee wrong,
> But the cup of death has passed my lips,
>   And my life will not be long.'

'No, no; dame Delany, you need not bathe my temples. I am not raving. I am not even hurt. The mischievous beast made my horse throw me, but I am nothing the worse.'

The friar, not being able to make any thing of the poet himself, applied to the rest, and was soon informed by Tam, that 'he was overheard trying to gar the lassie learn the black art, and courting her to nae good; and the poet grew jealous, and was for being revenged.'

The friar uttered a loud groan for the ignorance of his associates; but, hopeless of making any thing of them at such a period, he only began to moralise in a general manner. The poet was again gotten to mount; and shortly after they reached the ancient town of Selkirk, where they halted and refreshed themselves at the monastery of the Cistertians. There the laird got his wound dressed, and his dilapidated robes refitted; and that same evening the party reached the castle of Aikwood, the residence of the celebrated wizard Master Michael Scott.

CHAPTER THIRTEEN

He was a base and a cruel knight,
  As ever my two eyes did see;
And all that he did, and all that he said,
  It was by the might of glamourye.

But yet his gear was o' the goude
  As it waved and wampished in the wind;
And the coal-black steed he rode upon,
  It was fleeter than the bonny hind.
                    Ballad of Sir Colin Brand

THE DISTANCE FROM Melrose to the castle of Aikwood being only about nine English miles, our party came in view of it before sun-set. It was one of those dead calm winter evenings, not uncommon at that season, when the slightest noise is heard at a distance, and the echoes are all abroad.

As they drew near to the huge dark-looking pile, silence prevailed among them more and more. All was so still that even that beautiful valley seemed a waste. There was no hind whistling at the plough; no cattle nor sheep grazing on the holms of Aikwood; no bustle of servants, kinsmen, or their grooms, as at the castles of other knights. It seemed as if the breath of the enchanter, or his eye, had been infectious, and had withered all within its influence, whether of vegetable, animal, or human life. The castle itself scarcely seemed to be the abode of man; the massy gates were all locked; no porter was in attendance; and there was only one small piping smoke issuing from one of the turrets.

'Gude faith! callans,' said Charlie, 'that's a douth and an awsome looking bigging. I wish we were fairly in, and safely out again.'

'Is that now to be my residence, Yardbire?' said the beautiful Delany. 'Will you go away, and leave Elias and me in that frightsome and desolate looking mansion?'

'If the great Master gie us a civil answer,' said Charlie, not well wotting what to say – 'and desire to have you for his handmaiden, or rather the mistress of his castle, to overlook the other maids, and the spinning and weaving concerns like, then we have orders to leave you. But, if he should be cross, and crabbit, and paughty wi' us, ye're in gude hands, and we'll no quat wi' you sae easily.'

'Thou art in good hands indeed,' said the friar: 'But, alas! what is man! a flower of the field that the hand of the mower cutteth down and leaveth to decay: A shadow; a sound that passeth away and is not. But, maiden, thou art in better hands than ours; in hands that will not leave the innocent and guiltless to perish. There is an arm around thee that thou seest not: there is a guardian with a sword behind thee and before thee, of whom thou art not aware. Therefore have thou no fear, for no evil shall befal thee.'

'Methinks I could live any where, and be void of fear, if but suffered to be in your presence,' said Delany: 'There is something in what you have told me that goes to my heart, and on it I think I can rely.'

'Blessed be thou, my daughter!' said he; 'yea, and blessed shalt thou be in thy generation—'

'Hear to that!' said the poet aside: 'Still on one subject! It is all over with some body!'

'—But thou art perhaps going into a place of danger, and evil things may await thee. Here, take thou this, and keep it in thy bosom; and, by the blessing of the Holy Virgin, it shall shield thee from all malevolent spirits, all enchantments, and all dangers of the wicked one; the time may come when thou shalt more thoroughly understand the great things contained in this book.'

As he said this, he put into her hand a small gilded copy of the Four Evangelists, which she kissed and put into her bosom. All the rest saw this, and took it for a book of the Black Art.

By this time they were drawing near to the gate at Aikwood, where all continued silent and still as formerly. Notwithstanding of this, Charlie's horse, Corby, began to cock his ears and snort in a terrible manner. Stout-hearted as Charlie was, his countenance began to alter; but he uttered not a word farther than coaxing Corby to proceed. The mule leading the way altogether regardless, the horses jogged on after him, example going farther than precept, whether with man or beast. All the horses were, however, become restive, though none of them was half so fierce as Corby. He continued to force down his head, as if smelling the ground; anon capering and snuffing the air, snorting aloud, and moving with an elasticity rather like a thing of spirit than of joints and bones. 'Gude faith, Corby, my man,' said Charlie, as he patted his mane, 'a' isna right here! Wend on, ye camstairy thief: what the deil ails ye? But, gude sauf us! ane should take care wha they name here. They say, an speak o' the deil he'll appear.'

The old proverb had scarcely left Charlie's lips, when, all at once, they beheld three pages in black livery standing ranged before the gate, although the moment before there was no living creature there. They seemed to have arisen out of the ground, and as they rose they bowed their heads in a sarcastic way to the embassy. The appearance of the pages, and the motion that they made were both accomplished in the same moment of time, and at the motion every one of the horses broke away, like so many scared wildfowl, some one way, and some another. Charlie tried to restrain Corby with the whole might of his capacious arm; but the impatient animal plunged and bounded into the air with such violence, that his rider was obliged to give him head, and away he sprung like a roe over field and river, straining every nerve to be out of sight of Aikwood, while Charlie's warrior cloak, that hung only by the shoulder clasp, flapped so far behind him that he appeared like a black cloud skimming the valley. Though none of the other horses made equal speed with Corby, every one ran as fast as it could, and all to the eastward, though far asunder.

The mule, on the contrary, never moved nor concerned himself about the matter. He indeed held forward his long ears, and took a serious look of the pages, as of some sort of beings he did not more than generally understand. Nevertheless he despised them, and looked about with apparent astonishment and derision at the madness and folly of his associates. The friar, finding himself left with his mule and the three pages thus unaccountably, began to address the latter; but they only imitated his motions, and made wry faces, without returning him any answer. The mule had by this time taken another serious look at them, and disliking them exceedingly, he sidled towards them with all his mettle, and tried to hit them with his heels. The urchins then raised such an eldritch laugh that they made the arches of the castle to ring, and, skipping about and about, provoked the mule to farther violence. He, on his part, was nothing loth to attack; he ran open-mouthed at one, kicked at another, and tried to crush another up against the gate, all to the great annoyance of the friar, who, with the utmost difficulty kept his seat for a good while, in spite of the mad evolutions of his provoked and provoking beast. But the game once begun was not suffered to subside. The giggling elves, with the swiftness of lightning, skipped about, and, in whatever direction the mule darted, one of them was always pricking him behind. The worthy friar waxed very wroth, and swore by the life of Pharaoh that he would execute vengeance on them. But the noise of mirth and mischief waxed louder and louder, until the austere inmates of the castle heard; and the great Master said to his only attendant, 'Gourlay, what is the meaning of all this uproar?'

'It is only Prig, Prim, and Pricker,' said he, 'making sport with a mendicant friar and his ass.'

'Are they killing him?' enquired his Master, with the greatest composure, and without lifting his eyes from a large book that lay before him.

'I wot not, sire,' said Gourlay, with the same indifference.

'Ay, it is no matter,' returned the Master; 'It will keep them in employment a little while.'

'Perhaps,' said Gourlay – and retired back to the casement with sullen step.

By this time the mule had become so outrageous, that he wheeled, kicked, and plunged, like one of the furies; and, at the last, in spite of all the friar could do, laid him fairly on his back, amid the frantic shrieks and gibberish of his tormentors. Gourlay beheld the incident from the crevice of the turret, and, not daring to discompose the great Master, he walked down to the gate to witness the sport at a shorter distance; though with a callous indifference about the matter, and without the least hope to enjoy it.

When he came nigh to the scene of action, he looked as if he expected the friar to have been dead, and was rather astonished when he saw him raise his head, and utter a solemn anathema against the pages, who fled back as if awed and overcome. The seneschal not comprehending this, turned his pale glazed cheek toward the friar, elevated his brow as if looking at the verge of the high hill beyond the river, and stood motionless, stealing a side glance, now and then, of the stranger.

The latter raised up his gruff face, inflamed with passion, and, seeing the tall ungainly figure of Gourlay standing like a statue, with a red turban on his head, and a grey frock or mantle, that in ample folds covered him from the neck to the sandals, took him at once for the mighty enchanter, and addressed him with as little respect as might be.

'If thou art the lord of this mansion, draw near unto me, that I may tell thee of the deeds of thy servants, which eat thy bread, and stand at thy gate. Lo, have they not lifted up the hand against my life, who am a stranger, and a servant of him against whom thou hast rebelled and lifted up the heel? Go to; thou art a churl, and a derision, and a byeword among thy kindred and people, and not worthy to be called by their name. I came unto thy gate in peace, on a message of peace, and the words of peace were in my mouth; and why hast thou suffered these children of the wicked one to maltreat and abuse me? Why dost thou not open thy mouth?'

The pages chattered with a malicious laugh at a distance, and the seneschal came stalking near, in a sort of confused astonishment, to take a nearer view of this talking phenomenon. He came and looked over him without altering a muscle of his face; and the friar, irritated by pain and the contempt shewn toward his sufferings, went on. At any other time he would haply have been chilled by the pale frigid countenance, shagged beard, and glazed unearthly eye that were now bent over him; but in the present state of his feelings he disregarded them; and, though convinced that he spoke to the mighty enchanter himself, continued his harangue:—

'Come thou near unto me that I may curse thee. Thou

child of all unrighteousness, art thou not already cursed
among the children of men? Where are the wealth and the
cheerfulness, where are the welcome, and the faces of joy
and mirth, that are to be met with at the houses of thy
kinsmen whose bread I eat? Where the full basket and the
welcome store? the wine that giveth its colour in the glass?
the sounds of mirth and gladness? the sounds of the song,
the viol, and the harp? And where is thy tongue, that thou
canst not speak?' cried the friar, elevating his voice to its
highest and most impatient tones.

'Humph,' said Gourlay.

'Humph!' returned the friar; 'What dost thou mean by
humph? Tell me, in one word, Art thou the lord of this
castle?'

'No; but his seneschal,' said Gourlay. 'What hast thou
to say?'

'Then lead me to thy master, that I may see him face to
face, and tell him the words of him that sent me. I will not
be afraid of these dogs of thine and thy master's. What is
become of thy tongue that thou dost not speak? Tell me,
I say, can I see thy master?'

'Perhaps,' said Gourlay; and, seizing the friar by the
shoulder with a rude but powerful grasp, he dragged him
in at the gate.

'With-hold thine hand, and thy unmannerly grasp,' said
the friar – 'else I will smite thee with the sword.'

The seneschal regarded this threat only with a grim
unmeaning smile; and as he held the friar by the right
arm so firmly that he even lost the power of it, it was
impossible for him to draw his sword.

'Nay but hearken unto me,' continued he; 'surely it is
better for thee to live than to die. Therefore bring in my
beast that he may have provender; and let me also bring my
goods and my changes of raiment along with me in peace,
else how shall I set up my face before thy master?'

The seneschal then paused, and motioned with his hand
to the pages to bring the panniers; they ran to obey, but as
soon as any of them touched the huge wallet, he hastened
back and fell to the ground.

'Vermin! cannot you bring the furniture?' cried Gourlay.

They shook their heads, and stood at a distance.

'Humph!' said he, 'I do not comprehend this,' and

leading the friar back, still holding him fast by the arm, he suffered him to lift the panniers himself, which he did with good will, and then allowed himself to be led away by the uncourteous seneschal, who said to the pages as he departed, 'See to the vile animal!'

Without more ado he led the friar in, and pushing him rudely into a small vaulted apartment, he locked first a ponderous iron door, and then a massy wooden one, full of nails, upon him; and, without regarding his complaints or anathemas, or deigning a word in reply to his queries, he left him to his own bitter reflections.

The apartment at first appeared to be dark, but on looking about he found that there were two grated loop-holes in it, and by the light from these he soon perceived that there was nothing in the place save the skeleton of a man of uncommon stature and dimensions. The bones were lying flat on the floor, every one in its place exactly as the man had died, and the flesh wasted away from them. No disarrangement had taken place, nor was the smallest joint wanting. This was a petrifying sight to the poor friar, who, crossing himself, and turning from the horrible spectacle, set his nose through the grating and looked out on the fields.

The first thing be beheld confounded him more than all he had ever seen in his life. The three devilish pages were tampering with his mule to bring him within the outer gate; but he, in his usual manner, proved as refractory as ever, and laid about him with all his might. On this, the boys in one moment whipped him up in their arms, and ere the friar could draw his breath, far less utter a Pater-Noster, they set him down in the middle of the court, straight before the friar's grating, and tied him to the shaft of a well with a strong rope. The friar said a Benedicite; and, ere he had done, the devilish and provoking imps began to torment the poor mule beyond all sufferance, whipping him round and round the post, and making him fling and jump till the blood and sweat were pouring together from his branded sides, and he was no more able to resent the injuries committed on him. The friar fumed, and threatened, and cursed them in the name of the blessed saints; but they only laughed him to scorn: And when the mule could no longer resent the lash, they brought red-hot spindles and pushed them between his hind-legs, which made him fling and rear till he fell down at the post, and lay groaning, unable any more to move.

The thing that provoked the friar worst of all was the sight of the tall seneschal standing looking on, and seeming, by his motions, to be directing the game. Never was such a flood of eastern eloquence heard at Aikwood, as was poured from the small crevice in the bottom of the eastern turret that evening. No one, however, regarded it, or, if they did, it was only to mock or mimic the sublime deprecator.

To all that he said, the seneschal grinned a smile of grim disdain, and motioned to the pages to redouble their sport, which they did, till, as said, the poor animal could furnish them with no more.

The friar now beheld a joyful sight through the twilight, the rest of his companions coming on foot towards the gate. They had gathered together at the mill, about a mile to the eastward of the castle, and made another attempt to approach it on horseback; but their efforts were vain; not a steed would come one step farther than just in view of it; so they agreed to put their horses up at the mill, leaving them in charge of the miller and his two sons, and to proceed on foot to the castle, to join their mysterious associate the friar, whose magical might some of them began to dread, and others to trust.

Gourlay beheld them approaching as well as did the friar, and again waited on the great Master with awe and trembling.

'I pray thee, mighty Master, to forgive me,' said he, 'but too true is it that the wretched pedagogue has said – for here come a body of the warden's friends, with swords in their hands, and one beautiful human thing in their company.'

'And what then?' said Michael, in a stern, hollow voice.

The seneschal trembled. 'I – I – only want to know how they are to be received,' said he.

'Received?' cried the Master, raising his voice to a pitch that made the old wretch shrink as it were within himself. 'Received? As spies should, to be sure. Begone!'

Gourlay ran cowering toward the door.

'Stop—. Come back here. What forces are in the castle?'

'What forces? Hem! Great Master, you only know.'

'Any things of flesh, I inquire?'

'No, not one; if you except the old witch Henbane. Oh! I beg your pardon, great and honoured master! I meant your worthy and respectable housekeeper.'

Michael gave three gentle tramps with his heel, and in one moment the three pages in black livery, Prig, Prim, and Pricker, were at his knee.

'Work, Master, work. What work now?' said they all in one breath.

'Give your master there a toasting for his insolence,' said Michael.

The pages giggled for joy; the seneschal kneeled and roared out for mercy, and, as a motive for granting it to him, said the strangers were at the gate. The pages had already laid their fangs on him; but the Master, on the arrival of the strangers being brought to his mind, ordered the imps to desist. This they did on the instant; but, without delay, rushed on Michael himself, as if they would tear him to pieces. He threatened, cursed, and dared them to touch him; but they seemed nothing daunted by all he said, but danced around him with demoniac gestures, crying still out with one voice:–

> 'Work, Master, work; work we need;
> Work for the living, or for the dead:
> Since we are called, work we will have,
> For the master, or for the slave.
> Work, Master, work. What work now?'

'Miserable wight that I am!' cried the mighty Master. 'Then, d—d dwarfs, since it must be so, bring the slave back, and let him have three varieties, and no more.'

Gourlay had made his escape with all expedition, but it was not long ere they overtook him, and brought him back, leading him in the most grotesque manner that can well be conceived. They then began to twirl him about, first with his face one way and then another; and, latest adventures making the strongest impressions on their wicked imaginations, by some devilish slight they transformed him into the shape of a mule, and practised on him all the wanton cruelties they had so lately done on the friar's, seeming to enjoy the sport all the while with redoubled zest. They next changed him into a dog; and, tying a cannister, containing some small stones to his tail, they pursued him round and round the room, and finally out into the yard, with long whips, every one breaking at him, and giving him a lash as he came by. This caused him always now and then to exert himself with such speed that the cannister was sometimes hitting him on the head with a loud rattling yerk, sometimes on the back, and all over the body, while the poor steward was running, yelping in the uttermost desperation. The friar beheld part of the sport from his grate, but little wist that it was the hated seneschal that was suffering, else he would have doubtless enjoyed the scene in no ordinary degree. The rest of the embassy also saw it from the outer gate, where they now stood rapping and calling without being regarded, the pages being too intent on their game to pay the least attention to such as they.

'Let alane the poor tike, like good lads,' cried muckle Charlie, 'and come and open the yett. What ill has the silly beast done to you?'

'They bring me in mind o' Jock Harper's terriers,' said Gibbie, 'that wad rather do ill for the sake o' doing it, than do ought that was good or right for a' the warld.'

'I hate to see a colley-shangie,' said the poet; 'there is nothing sublime or romantic in it.'

'They're nae canny couts thae three chaps,' said Charlie; 'Corby wadna look at them, and he kens things gayan weel. We maun just hae a wee patience till they be done wi' their chace. It's a queer kind o' place this.'

The poor metamorphosed steward, finding no rest for the sole of his foot, betook him again to the staircase, and crept down at his master's feet, deeming the chastisement to have been over. But he was no sooner there than the pages were after him, and by the time they had whirled him three times about, he started up a hare, and the three pages, turning themselves into colley dogs set all upon him.

With the form of every quadruped into the shape of which he was turned, he seemed to acquire its nature and antipathies, and in none was it so striking as in the hare. When the collies began to snap at him, his terror is not to be imagined; he darted round and round the hall like lightning, breaking out and in to Michael's study, to the great disarrangement of his conjuring apparatus, books, and papers; while every time that a colley sprung with open mouth at him, he uttered a desperate scream.

This was the only one of their frolics that appeared to amuse the great Master, his partiality for the sports of the chase being proverbial to this day. When he saw the old seneschal laying back his long ears, and exerting his powers of speed in such manifest terror, and the malignant collies whinking after him, and waylaying him in every strait, making him often spring aloft, he could not help laughing outright, and baiting the dogs on him. The tears stood in the old hare's eyes when he heard this, nevertheless his fright made him agile; he bolted from the halls and alleys of the castle into the extensive yard; and there was such a hunt! Michael and the friar both ran to their respective windows to see the sport, and our party at the outer gate shouted and hallooed with great energy. Many a time did the dogs get a snap at the steward, and make him scream out, while all the onlookers laughed aloud. At length, thinking he would actually be worried, he cleared the wall, and made a bold effort to gain the wood. But these were a trio of dogs from which there was no possibility of escape. Ran he fast or ran he slow, there were they after him, snatching at his hips and panting sides, and yelping so keenly all the while that the seneschal had no doubt of being torn in pieces should they fairly seize him. They turned him, and made him trace many an acute angle on the hill, while our party were running after him, throwing always sticks or stones at the steward, as he hasted by them, and baiting the dogs on him. Finding, as formerly, no other resource, he returned with main speed to the castle, and crept down at the Master's feet, who, with one touch of his divining rod, changed him into his own native forbidding form.

He started up in great wrath; and, though panting so that he could scarcely speak, swore a horrible oath, that he would no longer be kept in bondage and maltreated in that manner; and that, since it was impossible for him to escape in any other way, he would cut his own throat, and ruin his chance of an after life.

'Poor dastardly braggart!' said Michael; 'not for the soul

that inhabits that old malicious frame, dare you do such a thing. I would seize on it, and make sport of it for ages. I have you wholly in my power, and, dead or alive, it is the same thing to me. Were you to do as you say, and take away your life by a ghastly wound, I could even make one of these fiendish spirits enter into your body, reanimate it, and cause you to go about with your gaping wound, unclosed and unpurified, as when death entered thereat. Think of what an existence that would be, and then go and put your miserable threat into execution.'

'Hah! There it is!' said Gourlay: 'Turn me as I will, I see nothing but wretchedness. Cursed be the day that I saw you, and ten times cursed the confession I made, that has thus subjected me to your tyranny! However, use me another day as you have used me on this, and you do it at your peril, if you were the devil himself. I have warned you.'

Michael only smiled contemptuously at the threat; and again asked what living creatures were in the castle, as he wanted a retinue to receive the message of his kinsmen.

'I have told you already,' said Gourlay, in the same passionate and irritated mood; 'and I again repeat it, that there is no mortal thing in the castle, but the old witch, and perhaps two or three hundred rats.'

'Take that in the first place then,' said Michael, 'for your impertinence' – at the same time laying him flat on the floor by a tremendous blow, although he only moved his hand toward the steward; 'and in the next place go call out these three hundred rats you talk of, marshal them up in the court, and receive the mighty warden's people with all manner of pomp and respect, and use them according to their demerits.'

The steward roared out with pain; and gnashing his teeth with rage, he arose growling, and was hasting away, when the Master asked him if he was going to accomplish what he had bidden him do.

'Without doubt;' said he, 'Is it not very likely that I shall be able?'

'Take that then,' said the Master, 'and put it above the lock-hole of the door; it shall serve you as a summons, and Prig, Prim, and Pricker shall marshal your array.' With that he gave him a small piece of parchment written in red characters, which the steward snatched angrily out of his hand, and going down the stair did as the Master had ordered him.

The charm was effective, and its effects momentary. The bustling and the screaming of rats were heard in every corner of the castle, and forthwith a whole column of men marched out into the court in three files, led by the three pages, and headed by the incensed seneschal in his grey mantle and cap.

Our messengers looked mightily astonished when they beheld such a retinue, and Charlie observed that 'it was a confounded shame for Mr Michael no to join the warden, and had sae mony idle men lying tholing starvation beside him.' But then looking wildly around on both sides to his friends, he added, 'God's grace be about us! wha kens but a' thae may be spirits or elves in the shapes o' men? I think they hae unco queer musty-like looks. An I had Corby here he wad soon tell me wi' a vengeance.'

Old Gourlay, now at the head of his corps, demanded what the strangers wanted; and on being informed who they were, and that they came on a special commission to the Master, they were admitted, and walked up a lane between two ranks of armed men in full caparison.

The Master beheld them from his casement, and was mightily diverted by the whimsical appearance of the various individuals that formed the group, two of whom he conceived to be the most beautiful creatures he had ever seen. Whoever reads this will at once guess who these two lovely beings were; but if he does, he will at once guess wrong. It would seem that a wizard sees every thing in this fair and beautiful creation through an inverted medium, and that all the common and fine feelings of nature are in him changed and distorted. The beauty of the two young captives appeared, in Michael's eyes, hateful, and even affected him with loathing; but two more lovely and engaging creatures than Jordan and the Deil's Tam he had never seen on earth. The hooked nose, wrinkled face, and mouth from ear to ear of the laird, he thought exquisite; but Tam's long coulter nose, turned up in front, his small grey eyes, and shapeless physiognomy, were beyond all expression engaging. So, from the time that the Master got the first look of them, he determined, contrary to his usual custom, to see and converse with his guests.

They were soon conducted to the door of the vault, in which their friend the friar was immured; and, as soon as the door opened, he exclaimed, with a loud voice, 'I charge you, O my brethren, and my companions, that ye come not into this place, nor set a foot within its boundaries; for the place is a place of death, and the bones of the dead men are in it.'

There is no deciding what these words might have produced, had they been pronounced in time; but as soon as Charlie and the laird, who were foremost, heard the friar's voice, they rushed towards him without thought or fear of the consequences, and, ere he had done, the hindmost were pushed in by the relentless arm of the seneschal, and the iron door closed behind them. Perceiving how matters stood, the friar straight lifted up his hands, and continued to declaim in a still more fervent stile.

'Hout! Gude Lord, friar man, haud your tongue,' said Charlie interrupting him: 'What signifies making sic a frase as a' this? or what good will it do? I hae run mysel into mony a priminary in my life, but I never fand that mony words did muckle good. I trowed that ye had mair art about ye than to be feared for a stane an' lime wa,' an' twa or three airn staincheons. Pith can do muckle, but art can do mair.'

Charlie meant the black art; but the friar taking him up in another meaning, shook him by the hand and blessed him.

It may not have occurred to the reader and it is not likely it should, that this same friar was an English monk, the most celebrated man of that age, then exiled from his country, and obliged to skulk in disguise, for fear of being apprehended and burnt as a wizard and necromancer. He was the greatest philosopher and chemist of the age, the real inventor of gun-powder, and many other wonderful discoveries, and, withal, a pious and good man – although one whose character was tinctured with peculiarities so striking, that some took him for a man crazed in his mind, but far more for a powerful necromancer. His name is familiar to every man in the least acquainted with the literature or the science of that age; but while he remained in Scotland being always denominated the gospel friar, we have judged it best to call him by that name. If the reader has not discovered this, it is time he should know it; and whether the friar was a necromancer or not, will appear in the sequel.

When the party got leisure to converse together, their first words were expressive of the astonishment they laboured under at sight of the warlike force kept up by the Master. Charlie only testified his regret that there was not a right and mutual understanding between him and the warden; but the maid Delany was the first to remark that she did not think they were right men, because their faces were all alike, and their eyes were not like the eyes of any human being she had ever before looked on. In this every one present acquiesced, and great was their wonder how or whence that mighty armed force had sprung; but they agreed that there was no contending with such numbers, of whatsoever nature they might be, and that there was nothing for it but submitting to the Master's will.

The day light was by this time quite extinguished, but the moon was up; and it being a hard frost, with a slight covering of snow, or rime, it was nearly as light as some winter days. Their damp, mouldy vault with the grisly skeleton lying at the one side of it, shewed horridly dismal in the wan and shadowy light, and threw a chillness over their hearts. They hoped and looked long for dinner, and then for supper, but neither of them came; nor did they hear or see any living thing all that night, save the friar's mule, that had again got to his feet, and stood at the post groaning and trembling of cold. This was a grievous sight to the friar, for his heart was moved for the sufferings of his poor beast; and in the bitterness of his spirit he vented some anathemas against the unconscionable seneschal, saying – 'Verily if ever that son of Belial fall into my hands, I will be unto him as Adramelech and as Sharezer, and do unto him as they did to the father that begat them.'

Every time that Charlie looked out at the mule, he testified a sort of inward satisfaction that his own trusty steed was not brought into the same scrape, and sundry times said, 'Gude faith, Corby kend better sense than coming into sic a place as this is. He's as weel off down wi' the auld miller; He'll get some pluffins o' seeds or dust, poor fallow. An they gie him but water, I'm no feared for him, for there's plenty o' meat yonder – but he'll never do if they let him want water.'

About two o'clock in the morning the seneschal entered with a light, but had the precaution to lock the wooden door before he opened the iron one. The prisoners had sat down on the floor, and were leaning on one another; and, dismal as their lodging was, some of them had fallen sound asleep. Delany was leaning on the friar's breast, and the poet had laid himself down behind her, and covered her with his mantle. The rest were huddled together, so that they appeared to be lying above one another; but all, or most of them, set up their heads at the entrance of the steward.

Tam was the first to address him. 'What's come o' our supper, goodman, that you are coming toom-handed? Do you no think it is time your guests had something to eat, or hae ye naething either to eat or drink in this great gousty castle? I dinna care what ye may think, or what you may say; but in my opinion you and your master baith are naething but twa ill-bred unmannerly niggards.'

The seneschal grinned disdain, and clenched his teeth in wrath. He was about to reply, but all their tongues were loosed on him at once, some complaining of one thing some of another, and the friar more particularly of the treatment of his beast. All, however, ended with a request for meat.

'No,' said Gourlay; 'we have no meat for spies and forayers. A halter is the only guerdon we bestow on such dogs. I want this fair maiden, and for the rest of you' – He finished the sentence with a sneer and a point with his finger to the bones; and seizing the maid by the shoulder, he dragged her toward the door.

'Softly sir, and if you please,' said the poet, speaking in pure iambics, and seizing the bars of the iron door before the steward and his prize. 'We have indeed this maiden brought, from distant camp and knight renowned, unto the master of this house; and to none else we give her up: No, not to thee, nor arm of flesh.'

As the poet said these words, he bristled up, and faced the steward at the door, to keep him back; but the carl gave him such a blow on the temples that he staggered and fell. The friar then interposed, and though he was a strong and powerful man, the irascible steward plied his blows so fast and so hard about his bare pate, that he was also overthrown. The maiden screamed; and the old incendiary was within a hairbreadth of having her outside of the iron door, when she would have been wholly out of the power of her friends and protectors. But at that critical instant Charlie Scott seized the steward by the arm, never doubting but that he would twist him like a willow; but he was mistaken. The churl seized him by the throat with his left hand, with such prodigious force that Charlie deemed him to have the strength of six common men, and lending him a blow on the face, he made his mouth and nose to gush blood. Charlie returned the salute with interest, yet the steward stood his ground, and a most desperate struggle ensued, in which victory appeared doubtful. Gibby perceiving his friend and champion's jeopardy, drew out his sword, and was going deliberately to stick the old ragamuffin behind, had not Charlie called out furiously to him to forbear.

'Keep back your whittle, you cowardly dog,' cried he, 'else I'll cut you into a thousand pieces. I never yet took odds against a man, nor shall I now, unless I am fighting wi' the devil. In that case I may measure my backbreadth on the floor. But be he the devil, be he dicken, I shall gie him ae squeeze.'

Charlie with that closed with his dangerous opponent, and gave him such a squeeze that he made his back and ribs to crash. The steward twisted his face into the most hideous contortions, and exerted his whole force to extricate himself, but Charlie brought him to the ground, falling upon him with all his ponderous weight. It was among the bones of the gigantic skeleton that the two combatants fell; and Charlie, deeming that he had given his foe enough for once, and a little startled to find himself among the rattling bones, began to unloose his grasp, and said in a hurried way, 'Billy, I'll learn you how to strike fo'k on the gab and the brigg o' the nose sae rashly!' and was getting up as fast as he could, when the steward gave him such a blow with the thigh-bone of the dead man, that he had very nigh brought him down again. If Charlie's bonnet had not had a bar or two of steel, that blow would have shattered his skull. As it was it stunned

him a little, and made the water start into his eyes; and he
had just recollection and strength sufficient to secure his
adversary's arms, by holding them down, so that he might
not repeat the blow. Yet, with all this Charlie's temper was
not to be ruffled. He cared not how often or how much he
fought, but he never fought in wrath.

'Gude faith, my man,' said he, 'but ye're no nice o' your
chapping sticks! and foul fa' me gin ye dinna lay them gayan
freely on. But I dinna blame ye. A wight man never wants
a weapon; only come that gate again an ye dare.'

The steward growled and cursed, trying all that he could
to throw Charlie from above him, and master him by sheer
strength. He had no idea of being overpowered by a single
arm, nor was he wont to fear half a dozen, but he had
never met with the like of Charlie Scott before. He might
as well have tried to remove the hill of Aikwood; so he
was obliged to succumb, which he did with a very bad
grace; nor would he either abate one inch in his demand
of having the damsel unconditionally, or grant one request
that they desired of him.

'Why, then, there's nae help for it, honest man,' said
Charlie; 'I hae ye firm and fast, and what ye winna gie
us we maun e'en tak at our ain hand. Honest friar,
come you here, and tak' a' the keys o' the castle aff
this camstary hallanshaker, and we'll e'en help oursels
to sic as we can get. I sal tak care that he sanna move
a spauld against you, and as for his tongue we maun just
let it wag.'

The rage of the seneschal, when he saw himself robbed
of the keys of the castle, is not to be described: he
cursed and raged in such a manner, that, even after
the friar had both doors fairly open, Charlie durst not
move from off him, or let him go, for fear of some
deadly scaith.

'I dinna ken what I'm to do wi' this deil's buckie,' said
he; 'he's like the tod's whelps, that grow aye the langer
the waur.'

'I wad gie him a settler,' said Tam.

'He brings me in mind o' a barrel o' beer, fuming and
fuffing. He'll no settle till he be pierced,' said Gibbie.

The friar then took up his bulky baggage, and walked
out with that and the light, meaning to bring his mule's

halter wherewith to bind the seneschal; but Charlie, making his escape from him, locked him in – and thus were our messengers left in the full and free possession of the castle of Aikwood.

CHAPTER FOURTEEN

The lady looked o'er the castle wa',
  She looked both pale and wan;
For the door was locked, and the lord within,
  He was no Christian man.
                    Song of May Marley

WHEN THE STEWARD saw that he was fairly mastered, and that neither strength nor words could avail him ought, he remained where he was in sullen silence. He had got no orders from the Master to bring him the maid, but it had come into his head to go and take her to himself, and he had nearly effected his purpose. What might have been the consequence of his success, it is painful even to calculate; but he was thus prevented, though not without blood and wounds.

The guests now traversed all the lower apartments of the castle, there being neither bolt nor bar to interrupt them; but for all the retinue that they had seen at their arrival, there was neither the appearance of man nor beast remaining. The large hall did not seem to have been occupied for a long period. The shelves were empty, and there were neither dishes nor fragments of meat of any description; and every thing within as well as without the castle had the appearance of desolation.

At length they came to a door, from the bottom of which they perceived some light issuing, of which they were glad, as they were afraid the steward's lamp would fail them and leave them in darkness. Deeming themselves on ticklish ground, they consulted in a whisper before venturing in. Charlie Scott was quite a fearless man among his fellow creatures, but all kinds of supernatural agency pressed heavily on his conscience. Therefore, in the present instance, he dissuaded his comrades from entering, with all his eloquence.

'Gude faith, callans, keep back off that place. It is maybe the warlock's room; and gin he should be in the mids o' some o' his cantrips at this eiry time o' the morning, gude sauf us! it is a question what might be the upshot. Na, na, friar; I tell ye, bide back, it is best to let sleeping dogs lye, for fear they get up and bite you.'

But the friar's creed differed from that of Charlie, and he went dauntlessly forward, putting him aside with his hand, and saying at the same time, that he would 'surely go in unto him as with a front of brass or of iron;' that sooner or later the time and the season of their meeting must come, and why should he be dismayed?

The friar then opened the door with caution, and entered, followed by all his associates, Charlie Scott bringing up the rear, and whispering to those next him in a tremulous voice – 'Od that body's mad! He'll lead us into some ill-faur'd snapper. Dinna be ower rash, callans. Just look afore ye.'

Instead of the great enchanter, however, they found only an old woman, so busily engaged with something on the fire, that she scarcely deigned to regard them as they entered. She had a wooden tube, like the barrel of a gun, with which she blew up her fire; and she kept blowing at it till the flame came above the lip of her caldron, and let her see into it; for she had no lamp, nor any other light save that which came from the fire.

When she had made it blaze thus high, she spoke to herself, and without taking her mouth from the tube; saying some words to the following purport:–

> 'Sotter, sotter, my wee pan,
> To the spirit gin ye can;
> When the scum turns blue,
> And the blood bells through,
> There's something aneath that will change the man.'

When Charlie saw her unchristian-like face, and heard her mumbling these horrid words through her long hollow tube, he turned his back and fled, taking shelter in a void entrance, to which he was led by some light that fell into it from the rays of the moon. Full hardly was he then

bested, for he still deemed that he heard the witch's rites at
a distance; and the faint ray of the moon through a narrow
aperture made the rest of the space appear so shadowy and
dim, that Charlie saw he was in a dangerous situation, and
actually began to fancy he beheld a face in the dark staring
at him, and still coming nearer. It was no time to stand
there; so he fled with all his might. But in his dismay he
lost every kind of aim, or consideration whither he was
going, and at once stumbled on the undermost step of a
stone stair. Thinking the apparition he had seen was by
that time hard upon him, and no other way that he knew
of open for flight, he rose and pursued his course straight
up stairs, in a state of perturbation hardly to be accounted
for. The first landing place that he came to he ran himself
against a door, and not finding farther entrance he faced
about, and, leaning over the balluster, he set up such a
yell as never was before breathed from lungs. It is true he
neither heard nor saw aught of the apparition; but Charlie
was a sensible man, and he was certain it might be there
for any thing that he knew; so he set up the same kind of
cry that he was wont to do when he lost his neighbours
in a mist, or in a night foray, only about ten times or so
louder.

'Hilloa! Tam Craik! friar! hilloa! d—n ye a'; what for
winna ye come wi' a light?'

Charlie was now at such a distance from his comrades,
who were still in the witch's small apartment, and the
echoes of the huge void castle so confused the sounds,
that they took the cries of their captain for the rushing of
a whirlwind roaring through the crannies of the castle, and
paid no regard to them. No state could be more deplorable
than that in which muckle Charlie Scott was now placed.
To have returned down the stair would have been meeting
the devil face to face; or, as Charlie much better expressed
it, 'to hae dabbed nebs wi' the deil.'

He had therefore no other resource than to bellow out for
assistance; and seeing none approach, he said aloud in great
agony of spirit, 'Lord, gin I were but on Corby's back again!
ay, though it were in the wildest glen o' a' the Cheviots, and
the Eskdale souple o'er my shoulder,' (that was the cant
name of Charlie's tremendous sword;) 'I might then work
my way: But sic a place as this I saw never! Od, an there

be lugs within the wa's o' the house I shall either gar them hear or crack them – Hilloa!'

Not satisfied with giving yelloch after yelloch, as he termed his loud cries, he flew to every door on the landing place, laid on it with his fists, and kicked it with his foot, calling at each of them in the same key as before, 'Is there ony body here?' He at last prevailed: one door was opened, and he was admitted inside. But, alas for our gallant yeoman! he only by this transition got out of one exceedingly bad scrape into a worse.

These casual separations of *dramatis personae* are exceedingly unfortunate for the story-teller who aims at conciseness and brevity; because it is impracticable to bring them all on at the same time. A story is like a waggoner and his horses travelling out the king's highway, his machine loaden with various bales of rich merchandise. He goes smoothly and regularly on, till he comes to the bottom of a steep ascent, where he is obliged to leave a great proportion of his loading, and first carry one part of it to the top of the hill, then another, and then another, which retards him grievously on his way. So it is with the writer of a true history such as this; and the separation of parties is as a hill on his onward path.

It is otherwise with dramatic representations, and in these the authors have a great advantage. Let their characters separate as they will, or be engaged as they will, they can at any time, with the greatest ease, be brought together on the stage. The one enters from the one side, and the other from the other, and we do not much concern ourselves how or whence they come, taking it for granted that they are there, and that is enough. It is rather delightful to see a hero, in whom one had begun to take some interest, and whom he supposed to be far distant, exposed to dangers abroad and perfidy at home, all at once stalk majestically in from the side scene, and take his place before our eyes. It gives the heart a great deal of relief to see and know that he is there in person to stand up for his own injured rights. But in our own case there is no such expedient. Like the waggoner, we must return from the top of the hill, and bring up those of our characters that are left behind. At present we must return from the top of the great stair-case in Aikwood castle, into the housekeeper's cell on the ground floor.

Charlie had made his escape almost unobserved; those next to him weening that he had only drawn a little back to keep a due distance between the witch and him, so that they pressed forward to the scene without regarding him.

The crone continued her orgies, blowing her fire one while, and again stirring the liquid in the caldron; then making it run from the end of a stick, that she might note its state of gelidity. The friar addressed her in his usual stile of sonorous eastern eloquence; but she only regarded him by a slight stare, and a motion with her hand, as if she wished him and his group to disappear. She had taken them for spirits that she had conjured up, and perhaps thought they were come before the time; for in mumbling to herself, they at one time heard her saying, 'So you are all there, are you? Well, I shall find you work. Sotter, sotter my wee pan.'

This scene went on for a considerable time without any variety, the witch attending solely to her caldron and her fire; the friar standing before the flame, and Tam and Gibbie, with their long kipper noses, peeping over his shoulder. The other three were behind these; the poet with his arm round Delany's waist, and the beautiful face of the boy Elias, the very picture of amazement personified, appeared below the friar's right arm. Scarcely could such another group be formed for the painter's eye. Here sat the witch, haggard and wild, close at the one cheek of the fire, watching over her caldron and infernal morsel with the utmost eagerness. There stood the gruff friar, with the keys of the castle in his right hand, and the dim lamp in his left, raised above his head; so that, from the two groups of light, the marked features of amazement could be distinctly traced; which, with the faint and yellowish hue of their complexions, made the whole highly picturesque.

The witch continued her occupation; till, at length holding up her stick to note the consistence of her jelly, that appeared like boiling blood and water mixed, there was something in its appearance that confounded her. She dropt both her tube and her stirring stick among the ashes, and turned about staring wildly at our group. She appeared as if examining their features one by one in search of some one whose presence she missed; and perceiving the boy's face below the friar's arm, she fixed her eyes on that, cowering down at the same time like a cat that is about to spring on its prey. Then, rising half up, she moved toward him in a stooping posture, turning always her face first to the one side and then to the other, until her nose came almost in contact with the boy's, on which he slipped his face out of her sight behind the friar's back. Observing next the two droll faces over the friar's two shoulders, she appeared delighted with the view; and letting her jaws fall down, she smiled at it, but it was rather a gape than a smile. She then tottered again towards the fire, rocking her body and wagging her head as before, repeating the while this unmeaning phrase:

> 'Niddy, noddy, niddy, noddy,
> Three heads on ae body.'

Haply she deemed all the three faces she had seen belonged to the friar, and was happy at witnessing such a monstrous appearance.

Sitting down on her hams as before, she seized on her two implements, and began to blow and stir for about the space of a minute, testifying great impatience to see how her spell proceeded. But the moment that she held up a part of her morsel on the stick, and let it drip off, she perceived that all was wrong, and that her guests were the reverse of those she expected. As soon as she looked at the liquor, she uttered a horrible scream, while every joint of her body shook with fury; and, lifting a wooden ladle that lay by her side with devilish nimbleness, she splashed the boiling liquid on the faces and bodies of our amazed compeers.

'Deil be in the auld jaud's fingers!' cried Tam: 'Gin she hasna jaupit out baith my een!'

'I have indeed given my cheek to the firebrand!' said the friar; 'and the skin of my forehead hath departed from me!'

'She brings me a-mind o' my mither,' said Gibbie – but he got not time to proceed; for after she had exhausted the contents of her caldron on the intruders, she attacked them with burning coals and pieces of wood. These she dashed among them with such desperate force, that part of them sought refuge in retreat. Not so our redoubted friar. He gave the lamp out of his hand to the laird, bidding him take care of it, and turning his back towards her, and running backward for fear of farther injury to his face and eyes, he seized the witch by the frock, and putting his arm round both hers to restrain them, he held her fast to his side. In doing so, he uncovered the cross that hung at his girdle. When she saw this, and that her body was pressed against it, she uttered the most horrified howlings, and appeared to be falling into convulsions. Nevertheless, the friar kept his hold. He let her scream on, and, dragging her toward the door, said unto her, 'Thou wicked one! as thy works have been, so shall be thy reward; and as thou hast sown, so also shalt thou reap. Come with me, and I will put thee into a place where thou shalt cease from troubling.'

Without more ado, he bore her away to the vault where lay her surly and unyielding associate, beside his mass of dry human bones; and forcing her in, he locked them up together, saying, as he turned the massy bolt, 'Lo, the gates of iron and of brass close upon thee! the bolts of steel are drawn around thy dwelling! There shalt thou remain, and there shall thy flesh be consumed, unless thou repentest thee of the evil that thou hast done.'

There was a shrewd smile on the friar's face as he said this, as of one who either did not mean to put his threat in execution, or marvelled how it was that he should thus be lording it in the castle of Aikwood, and imprisoning whom he would.

Never till that instant did any of the party miss their friend and champion, Charlie Scott; but when they turned from the door of the prison to consult what was to be done next, behold he was wanting. This caused them great dismay, but the friar most of all.

'Wo is me!' cried he: 'How is the mighty departed, and the pillar of our strength moved out of its place! As well may they take my head from my body, and say unto me live, as bid us go on and prosper without that mighty man.'

The poor waggoner must again return from the top of the hill, and bring up the most important and weighty part of his cargo; no less a load than muckle Charlie Scott, laird of Yardbire, and the far famed warlock and necromancer, Master Michael Scott.

★   ★   ★

The mighty uproar that Charlie made at the head of the stair, when he believed the devil to be on the steps, aroused the great necromancer from his nocturnal experiments, all of which were of an infernal kind. At such hours as these his capacious mind was abstracted from all worldly concerns, such as other mortals busy themselves about. If any thing sublunary engaged his studies and calculations, it was how to make the living die and the dead to live – how to remove mountains out of their places, to turn the sea into dry land, and the fields into a billowy and briny ocean – or in any way counteract nature in her goings on. In some of these great enterprises was he doubtlessly engaged that morning, when the voice of Charlie Scott astounded his ears.

Often had hosts of demons mustered at his call in the castle of Aikwood, and the yelling sounds of the infernals were no strangers to his ears; but never had he heard such a potent voice before as that sent forth by Charlie, when he conceived himself cooped up between the devil and a bolted door. Conceived did I say? No: Charlie saw distinctly, by this time, an indefinable being coming slowly up to him. Saint Peter! as he did thresh the warlock's door. 'Is there any body here? Hilloa! Open the door I say.' Thump, thump, thump!

The bolt inside was drawn, and, owing to the strong pressure without, the door flew wide open at once. Charlie perceiving the light, and fearless of ought but the figure behind him, rushed into the room, and made toward the fire. The door was instantly shut behind him with a loud and furious clash; and Charlie then turning around, got the first look of the inmate. He was a boardly muscular man, somewhat emaciated in his appearance, with a strong bushy beard that flowed to his girdle, of a hue that had once been jet black, but was now slightly tinted with grey. His eyes were uncommonly bright and piercing, but they had some resemblance to the eyes of a serpent. He wore on his head a turban of crimson velvet, ornamented with mystic figures in gold, and on the front of it was a star of many dazzling colours. The rest of his body was wrapped in a mantle or gown, striped with all the hues of the rainbow, and many more.

Charlie's eye had lately been lighted up with terror, but as it fell on the majestic figure of Master Michael Scott, its wild gleam softened into respect, and he saluted him with his quick, abrupt, border bow, which rather resembled the motion made by a raven beckoning from his rock as he wakes the surrounding echoes, than the slow and graceful courtesy then so well understood among the great. Michael still kept his erect posture at the back of the door, fixing on our yeoman an indignant and angry glance. That look conjured up a little more of Charlie's breeding; he doffed his steel bonnet with the one hand, stroked down the hair of his forehead with the other, and gave the master another bow, or rather a nod.

'Gude e'en t' ye, Sir; I fancy you're the lord o' this castle?' said Charlie.

'You fancy so, do you?' said the Master with a sneer; and giving three tramps with his heel on the floor, in one moment the three pages, Prig, Prim, and Pricker, stood beside him.

'Work, Master, work – what work now?'

'Take that burly thief and housebreaker, bind him, and put him to the test.'

'Stop short there, my good masters, till I speak t' ye,' said Charlie, 'I'm neither a housebreaker nor a thief, but a leel man, our warden's kinsman, and your ain, Master Michael Scott. I came here on fair and honourable service, and I have been guidit waur than a tike; and I'll just tell you plainly, for I'm rather an e'en-down chap, that if ane o' thae brats dare but to touch me, I'll tak my hand aff his haffet in sic a way that he sanna grene to lay foul finger on a gentleman again.'

The three pages fell a giggling at this speech, and one of them brushed forward and seized Charlie with a force of which he had no conception. But he was one that never suffered any personal attack with impunity. He drew a stroke with his clenched fist, and aimed such a blow at the page's head, that, if he had had a head like other pages, would have smashed it to pieces. Charlie hit no head at all. He struck a thing of nought. But the force of his arm was such, that, about two yards farther on, he hit an apparatus of curious construction, which he called 'a machine for setting the wind on fire,' and which he made to fly all in flinders against the wall. The Master's eye kindled with rage; but the three urchins, who delighted in nothing but mischief, laughed still the louder, and pressed all forward on Charlie. He had been a little astounded at missing the page's head; but, being somewhat flustered, he had not leisure to reflect, and his conceptions were naturally none of the most acute; so, for the present, he took it for a miss. But seeing they purposed to lay violent hands on him, he sprung back into the middle of the room, in order to command weapon space; and drawing out the Eskdale souple, he stood on the defensive in a most determined posture.

The pertinacious elves wheeled also backward, taking a circle round behind the Master, and advanced on him all abreast. Good Lord, with what might Charlie struck at them! He came on them with a hew that he meant should cut them all three through the middle at once. But he, a second time, struck on vacancy. The sword whistled through the void, taking Charlie round with it, and demolishing almost every thing that was in the room. The pages screamed with delight, but Michael foamed with fury. Charlie paid no regard either to him or the devastation he had made among his utensils; but, springing round the board to the other side of the room, said, in a loud perturbed voice: 'Tell me just this ae thing, Michael – are thae three creatures deils? Because an they be deils, I hae nae mair chance wi' them than a cat. But as for yoursel, goodman, I ken ye are flesh and blood, and o' my ain kith and kin,' (and with that he seized Michael by the throat,) 'therefore, either gar thae hellicats gang about their business, or by Him that made us, I'll thraw your neck about.'

Whether it was the might of the enchanter himself, or that of his bond spirits, Charlie wist not; but in one moment after that his feet were tripped from beneath him, and he was laid on his back on the floor. There he was held by a might against which his great strength could not prevail, bound with cords, and stretched on the board. The Master and his familiars then conversed in Latin, a language of which Charlie knew but little, having never been at court; but he heard they were conversing about his baptism. Charlie had not got much time in his life to think about these sacred rites, yet he had always held them in proper respect and veneration; and at that time he blessed the hour he had been presented in holy church, having strong hopes that on that account the powers of hell would not prevail against him. The elves loosed his buff-belt, and unclasped his steel-doublet, laying his manly bosom quite bare. The Master gave them directions in Latin, and each of them went and brought a long knife with two edges, sharp as a razor, and having a point like a lance.

'I didna trow that there had been ought sae misleared in nature as this,' said Charlie. 'It's no that I'm ony feared for death. I hae looked him ower often i' the face to blench at his ca': but I wad just hae liket to hae fa'en i' the field wi' my sword i' my hand, and no to be cut up like a Christmas pye, and carved a' into collops by a wheen damned deils.'

One of them prepared to cut open his breast, and another his belly; but a moment's dispute taking place between them in some unknown tongue, about the mode, as Charlie believed, he crossed himself as well as he could with his bound hands, and pronounced a sacred name into himself. That instant he perceived the pages fall a-trembling, and stand back; their faces blenched with dread, and the weapons fell from their hands. The Master was wroth, and ordered them to proceed, as Charlie weened by his motions; but, instead of that, they retired trembling into a corner. He snatched a knife from one of them, as if determined to do the deed himself. Charlie then deemed himself gone; for he had a sort of confused idea, that, by certain laws of nature, and the use of holy rites, wicked spirits were restrained, else mankind would be destroyed: 'But what law of nature, or what holy word or sign,' thought he, 'can restrain the arm of a wicked man? It is my duty to try, however,' thought he again; and with that he whispered a prayer to the Son of the Virgin, that He would save a warrior from a death like this.

Charlie's prayer was heard, short as it was; for at that very moment, while yet the syllables hung on his lips, entered the gruff figure of the friar, with the keys of the castle over his arm, and followed by his associates.

'What seek you here, you dogs?' cried the Master, turning about with the great knife in his hand: 'Am I thus to have my privacy disturbed, and my abode ravaged by a pack of carrion hounds from the hills? Brave pages mine, bind them all, and cut me them into a thousand pieces.'

Scarcely was the order given ere they had the poet on the floor, and bound with strong cords. The rest prepared to escape; but the great enchanter placed his back to the door, brandished his great knife, and dared them to approach him. The mettledness of these pages cannot be conceived, far less described; they seemed but to will a thing and it was done. Ere ever one of the intruders had time to rally his thoughts, or almost to think at all, three of them and the boy were all lying bound in fetters. But when the imps came to seize on the friar, they could not. They skipped about and about him, but they had not power even to touch his frock. The virgin stood behind him trembling; and on their feeling their want of power over the friar, they turned to lay hold on her. But the moment they touched her robe, they retired back in dismay.

Michael looked as if he dreaded there was something about these two that boded him no good; but he wist not what it was, for he had never seen the prowess of his bond spirits counteracted before; therefore he awaited the event for a space, when he perceived them vanquished.

The friar had time to rally his thoughts, and remembered that the maid had the blessed gospel concealed in her bosom; and judging that these were perhaps fiends with whom they had to do, who durst not stand against the word of truth, he drew his cross from below his frock – that cross which had been consecrated at the shrine of Saint Peter, bathed in holy water, and blessed with many blessings from the mouths of ancient martyrs – had done wonderous miracles in the hands of saints of former days – and lifting that reverendly up on high, he pronounced the words from holy writ against which no demon or false spirit's power could prevail. In one moment all the three imps fled yelling from the apartment. The countenance of the enchanter fell, and he quaked where he stood; but the eye of the friar was kindled up with exultation and joy.

'There worketh the hand of my master!' exclaimed he: 'There have I trusted, and I am not, like thee, ashamed of my trust. I have a strong-hold of hope, and it is founded on a rock, but thy habitation trembleth beneath thee; and dost thou know, or hast thou considered, what is underneath?'

The friar then went up and loosed the bonds of his friend Charlie, and of all the rest, one by one, exulting in his creed, and pouring forth such sentences of sublime adoration as are not suited for an idle tale.

The Master at length took courage and rebuked him, saying, 'It is vain for thee, foolish dupe of a foolish creed, to multiply such great swelling words of vanity. What though thy might hath, for once, prevailed above my might, and thy spell proved more powerful than mine? I will engage, nevertheless, that in nine times out of ten, mine, on fair trial, shall prevail over thine. And at all events I can at this time call in the arm of flesh to my assistance, and do with you whatever seemeth to me good.'

'Ay, gude faith, and that's very true, Master Michael Scott,' said Charlie: 'and that we saw wi' our ain een. It is great nonsense to quarrel with the lord of a castle aneath his ain roof, although, I confess, I was the first to do it mysel'. But there's an auld saying, wha wad sit i' Rome and strive wi' the pope? or misca' a Macdonald in the raws o' Lochaber? We came wi' nae sic intent, but in fair friendship, and on courteous errand. And now when we are a' rather on equal footing again, let me beg o' you, great and powerful Master, to be a reasonable man for aince. Answer the warden's request, and let us gae; for really, great Sir, our master canna well want us; and mair not that, I'm feared you chaps at the mill dinna gie Corby ony water.'

Though the Master did not understand the latter part of this speech, yet the honest simplicity of Charlie somewhat interested him. His stern and sullen brow cleared to something like a smile; and on looking at the singular and original group before him, he half resolved within himself to have some intercourse with humanity once more. 'If it were but for a day, or even an hour,' thought he, 'would it not form some variety in a life thus dedicated to searching after hidden mysteries – a life of turmoil and distraction, in which there is no allay?'

Such were some of the thoughts that glanced on the dark mind of the necromancer, as he turned his eye on the broad weather-beaten face of honest Yardbire. 'And what may your master's request be, yeoman?' said he.

Charlie had great hopes that he would now bring matters to a bearing at once; and, coming a step nearer to the Master, he laid the one fore-finger across the other, and answered him thus: – 'Why, gude faith, Sir, it is neither mair nor less than just this: – Ye ken the last time ye war at the castle o' Mountcomyn, ye gae our master, your kinsman, the warden, some little insight anent things that were to come about:– of some bits o' glebes, and hopes, and glens, ye ken, that war to fa' to his house. Now, Sir Knight, or Master, as I should say, he's a man that, aboon a' ithers that ever war born, looks to the honour and the advantage o' his house. He's as loyal as the day's light, as generous as a corn mill, and as brave as a blast o' snaw or a floody river. Od, you will turn either the ane or the ither sooner than you will turn him wi' his muirland callans at his back—. Ay, I hae seen him—. But it's needless to tell what he'll do for his ain. So you see, Sir Master, that was the preceese thing he sent us for.'

'To send troops to his assistance, I perceive?' said the Master.

'Why, Sir Master, to say the truth, we hadna that in charge; though it wad be far mair mack like, and far mair feasible, and far mair honourable into the bargain, to send yon great clan o' rattennosed chaps to help our master, than to hae them lying idle, eating you out o' house and hauld here. Ye wad aye be getting part o' the spulzie. Half a dozen o' kye at a time now and then disna do amiss. Sae, if you will come to terms, I will engage for ane to see you get fair share, to the hoof and the horn, the barn an' the beef boat, the barrel and the bed blanket. But, ye ken, Sir, in matters like this, we maun do ae thing afore another, like business men; and ye maun be sae good, and sae kind, and sae obliging, as to answer our first request first.'

'As far as I can recollect,' said Michael, 'I never heard any request made.'

'Why, gude faith, Sir, ye ken, I believe I forgot that part o't,' said Charlie: 'But ye see, that's neither here nor there; for the thing requires some explanation. Do you ken a' this mad story about the seige o' Roxburgh?'

'I trouble myself about no worldly things,' said the Master, 'nor do I wish to hear about them. Is there no one present who can tell me this great business at one breath?'

Charlie stepped back. 'There's nae garring him hae patience – and good troth my tongue I fear has outrun my logic,' said he: 'Friar, speak you.'

'Great and magnificent Master of Arts,' said the friar. stepping forward, 'whom I have longed to see above all men! Lo, thou seest, and thou hearest, that this man, although he be a man of might, and a warrior from his youth, is yet uncouth of speech, and altogether diffuse; therefore listen thou diligently unto the voice of thy servant. Behold we are come to thee from the man that ruleth over the borders of the land, and leadeth forth his troops to battle. He sendeth unto thee greeting, and beseecheth to know of thee what shall befal unto his people, and to his house, in the latter days. It is thy counsel alone that he asketh, for thou art renowned for wisdom and foresight to the farthest corners of the earth. The two nations are engaged in great and bloody contest, and high are the stakes for which they play. The man who sent us intreateth of thee to disclose unto thy servants who shall finally prevail, and whether it behoveth him to join himself to the captain of his people. He hath, moreover, sent unto thee, by our hand, these two beautiful captives, the one to be thine handmaiden, and the other to be thy servant and run at thy bidding; and whatsoever thou requirest of our captain, that will he do, even to the half of all that he hath.'

There was but one thing on earth by which the wizard could be flattered, and that was a deference to his profound art. He therefore listened with patience to the friar, and answered, that the request his kinsman had made would take many days to consider of: 'For,' said he, 'I have those to deal with that are more capricious than the changing seasons, and more perverse than opposing tides and winds; therefore remain with me a few days, that I may prove you.'

'Od bless ye! Sir Master, the thing is impossible!' said Charlie: 'I coudna bide frae my captain and chief, and him in jeopardy; neither could I endure to think that my poor beast should want water sae lang. A man's life often depends on his beast.'

'Thou givest us no meat,' said the friar, 'nor wine nor strong drink givest thou unto us. How, therefore, can we remain in thine house? Nevertheless would I love to abide a short time with thee, to witness thy great might, before which the masters of divinations in other lands have trembled. Verily, I would also show unto thee what thy servant can do.'

'If I were to cope with such as thee, it would only be to show thee thy littleness!' said Michael. 'But thy creed is an abomination to me, and I abhor it. In the meantime call up my steward, and I will order him to provide you with meat and drink.'

The poet now, for the first time, spoke up in the Master's hearing; and, indignant at the steward's design on Delany, he delivered himself with great vehemence.

'Nay, say not so, great Master. The devil hath possession of that man, sure as the stars burn on the morning's brow. He give us meat or drink! Sooner he will draw forth the crimson current from our veins, and lay us with the dead: Sooner he will rob beauty of her treasure, and deface the image of his Maker. Let us go forth to hill, or dale, or wood, strive with the crow for carrion, or contend with owlets for a mouse; but to be bearded by that same surly beast, the heart of man not brooks it. As for me, I lift my voice, my absolute protest, against the degradation and effect.'

'He is indeed a son of Belial,' said the friar; 'but I have put him in ward, that he trouble us not. Lo, here be the keys of thy castle, which I intend to keep as our surety. Therefore show me the place where thy good things are disposed, and I myself will be steward for a time; for indeed that man of thine is such a son of Belial that a man cannot speak to him.'

The Master's brow lowered with dissatisfaction. His subordinate spirits in whom he trusted had no power over the friar, and other man had he none within the castle, save Gourlay, who was almost as much fiend as man. He therefore intreated the friar to set his steward at liberty, and restore to him the keys, else no meat or drink could be had; and, at the same time, he gave them all warrandice that they should be kindly used.

'My seneschal,' said he, 'is as stubborn and froward as any demon of the pit, nor will he do one kind or fair action save by compulsion. But he dares not disobey me. If he should presume to dispute my orders in the slightest instance, one word from you shall be sufficient, and I will shew you how he shall be requited.'

It was forthwith agreed that the Master should accompany them down to the dungeon, in order to restrain the fury and violence of his servant. Matters were therefore arranged, and the two prisoners set at liberty. The steward was sullen and intractable, lying still on the dungeon floor, disregardful of the words spoken to him by the friar; but when he heard the Master's threatening accents he sprung to his feet and came forth, looking at Charlie in such a manner as plainly said, 'I shall be revenged on you.'

The Master then took him to task, demanding by whose orders he had shut up his kinsman's friends in the vault. But he only snarled and gnashed his teeth in reply.

'And then to suffer yourself to be mured up there!' said the Master.

'Ay,' said Gourlay; 'some have won a tilt on the king of the field who never saw the day to win it on another.'

'For the viper blood that venoms thy heart do thou ought amiss to these gentlemen,' said the Master, 'or to this obnoxious thing that is their ward! Wherefore, let me ask, were they compelled to shut you up there?'

The steward only grunted in reply; but the poet came again boldly forward, having been exasperated beyond measure at the steward for his attempt on Delany; and he said – 'Sir knight, in that I'll truly counsel you. At dead hour of night, when all was still, save the snell piping of the frosty wind; even we were all at peace, and quiet lay as did the dead man's bones, but that, between, the friar at equal intervals sent forth his nasal roar, so vehement that the mice, yea, and the starveling rats, ceased from their prowling, listened the dire sound from fleshy trumpet of our mother church, then sought, with stretched forth tail, and nimble foot, the depth profound! There quaking did they lie, like fiends driven from the height to the abyss – lank make, chilled heart, and grievous length of tail. At that ill hour, in comes this boding owl, this ill-starred man of sin, and straight demands that peerless maiden for your honour's couch. Him we refused – the maiden shrieked for help – he dragged her forth, and on this laurelled head, crowned by the muses with celestial bays, inflicted ruthless wound. The bedesman also fell; but he our friend, the Hector of the hills, wrought his o'erthrow, and circum-mured him. Thus my say is ended.'

The Master, as the poet spoke, seemed several times so much amused, that they expected he would have burst into laughter. But one look of his eye spoke sentences. When he heard that Gourlay had demanded the maid for him, he gave him such a glance as made the wretch almost cower to the earth; and when the poet ended he turned his eyes on Charlie, measuring him from head to foot, and seeming as if he doubted the fact that he or any man could master his redoubted seneschal. However, the Master had seen so much of the group, that he determined, contrary to his custom, to have some amusement with them. He therefore ordered his seneschal forthwith to provide all good things for their entertainment.

The stubborn wight made no movement betokening obedience. He stood upright with his dull white face a little elevated, and his eyes turned up below his brows, while those who were next him heard him saying to himself, in accents that creaked in his throat, 'Hell must be moved for this repast!' The Master heard not this sentence, but noting his steward's indecision, he stamped with his foot, and pointing with his finger, the latter led the way into an antichamber of the same cold and naked appearance with the rest of the apartments of the castle, where, leaving them with a light, the two went away into the great Master's dormitory, 'To cast their cantrips, and bring up the deil.'

'He keeps an unco cauld house this carl,' said Tam, when they were left by themselves: 'I fancy he'll ken brawly he'll hae ane bien eneugh at the hinderend, and downa bide to see fire in this!'

'He brings me a-mind o' daft Jock Amos i' the Goosegreen,' said Gibbie – 'wha never durst lie down on a bed because his mother died on ane. Whenever he saw a bed wi' white sheets on it he fell atrembling, and ran to the gate.'

CHAPTER FIFTEEN

Goe fetche mee lofe of your wheitan breide
  And ane other coppe of wyne;
For drynke I quhile myne doublet ryve,
  For drynke I moste repine.
I fele not corauge in myne herte,
  Nor mychte into myne honde,
If there is nott wytchrafte forth abrode,
  There neuir was crafte in londe.
                    Ballade of 'Prince Henrie'

THE MORNING HAD by this time dawned on the gray
hills of the forest, and that with an aspect gloomy and
foreboding. The white snowy clouds had crept down into
the bosoms of the hills; and above these clouds were here
and there to be seen the top of a mountain crested with its
dark cairn, so that the heavens and the earth seemed to be
mingled together.

'Gude sauf us!' cried Charlie, as he peeped out at his small
crannied window, 'but this is a grim, gousty-looking morning!
I wish the prince o' the air be nae fa'cn a brewing some o' his
hellish storms and hairikens on us. If there be spirits moving
about on thae hills today, they can be nae good anes, ye may
see by their look out. Sant Mary be with us! see their drumly
heads appear to be raised to double their ordinary height.'

'Be not thou afraid, my son, of the prince of the power
of the air, for there is one that is greater than he,' said the
friar; 'and though the fiends may for a while muster their
fogs, and foment the air with storms, yet will he send forth
his angels and scatter them; yea, he will send them forth
riding on the whirlwind, and the clouds of heaven shall
be their chariots, and the powers of darkness shall fly in
dismay before them.'

199

The friar stepped forward to the window, and gazed for a minute in breathless astonishment; then turning away, he added in a solemn tone, 'Verily, my children, I am afraid to look at the face of the sky, or to behold the hues that are abroad on the firmament this day, though my strength be the munition of rocks.'

The steward now appeared with his rod of office in his hand, and, with all due ceremony, marshalled his guests up the great stair, and finally up a small winding stair, to an apartment at the very top of the upmost tower, above all the turrets and paved battlements. This room was in a blaze of light with flaming torches all around; and (joyful sight to our precious embassy!) the table was covered with rich viands in great abundance. The friar, having got short of breath in his ascent, lagged considerably behind, while the foremost rushing in, every one began to help himself with the greatest avidity; so that, when the friar at length came puffing into the apartment, all the rest had begun without grace. The seat at the foot of the table was still unoccupied; and before that there stood a beautiful smoking sirloin of beef, with a gentle brown crust around it, and half swimming in gravy. Never was there a more delicious sight presented to a hungry man.

The worthy friar, seeing all the rest engaged, would not risk a trespass on good manners by interrupting them, although it was an established custom with him to bless every meal before tasting it. In conformity with this venerable custom among Christians, he lifted up his spread hands, closed his eyes, and leaning forward above the beef so closely that he actually breathed upon it, and felt the flavour of health and joy ascending by his nostrils, in that fervent and respectful attitude he blessed the beef in the name of Jesus. Never had blessing a more dolorous effect. When the friar opened his eyes, the beef was gone. There was nothing left on the great wooden plate before him but a small insignificant thing resembling the joint of a frog's leg, or that of a rat; and perhaps two or three drops of gravy.

The friar's associates were all busily engaged. The steward was moving about behind them, and at that time happened to be passing by near where the friar sat; of course, this latter worthy had no doubt whatever but that the malicious old rascal had stolen the roast slyly from under his nose the moment that his eyes were closed, whereas the steward was as much astounded as he. It was a fine picture. The friar had placed himself hastily to begin; but, missing his beef, and seeing nothing of it on the board, he was moved with great anger and indignation. There he sat, biting his lip, and having his deep dark eye fixed on the seneschal; and there stood the tall seneschal, with his mouth wide open, his face half raised toward the cornice of the chamber, and his dull heavy eye fixed on the friar's plate. He was in utter dismay; for he dreaded that, on such a blessing being pronounced openly, the whole of his provisions would in like manner vanish away; and he was a blithe man when, instead of blessing, the friar, on opening his mouth, was rather inclined to curse.

'Cursed be thy malice, for it is great,' cried he: 'Thou Nabal! thou Rabshakeh! thou Shimei, the son of Bichri! thou Er! thou Onan! thou vile Judas, the son of Simon! Magormissabub be thy name; and may it be blotted out after thee, and become a bye-word, and a proverb, and a hissing among people and children. Restore that which thou hast unjustly taken away, before I thrust my sword into thee, and take away thy life. Give unto me the precious morsel thou hast taken away, or, lo! thou art in the jaws of destruction, and the pit openeth her mouth wide upon thee.'

The steward answered neither good nor bad; for he was afraid of the vengeance of his master, and the evil spirits that wrought at his bidding, and delighted in nothing so much as in tormenting him, else had he not taken the friar's curses without repaying them sevenfold. He therefore shut his mouth, and closed his eyes, putting on a countenance of the utmost derision. But the friar's heart had been set upon the beef, his soul had rejoiced over it, and he could not with patience give way to the idea of losing it; therefore, instead of joining the rest, who were devouring their various fare with great eagerness, he continued his anathemas on the steward.

'Blethering gouk!' cried Charlie: 'Can nae ye tak part o' what's gaun, and haud your jaw? What signify a' thae strings o' gospel phrases at sic a time as this? Will they fill a hungry stamock, or mak the worthy seneschal either better or waur than he is? Come pledge me in a cup o' wine to the health of our great landlord, Master Michael Scott.'

They handed the stoup down to the friar, who filled for himself, and took the pledge, though still with a gloomy and a discontented brow. He then left his seat, and went up one side of the board, close to Gibbie Jordan, where he began a-helping himself to a slice, from a mangled shoulder of venison apparently. But it relished not – for still the lost beef was uppermost in his mind, and his eye glanced hot displeasure at the steward.

'Surely he is of all men the most accursed,' added he: 'He drinketh up malice as the ox drinketh up water; and as his name is so is he. Whereunto he hath conveyed the morsel that I loved, is a matter too high for me to comprehend. I see it not in any corner of the habitation, nor doth the smell of it reach my nostrils. But I will visit it upon his head; and mine eyes shall see my desire on him.'

The dishes of meat were, however, of good quality, and well mixed with fat and lean; yet none of them knew exactly what they were, neither would the sullen steward deign to give them the least information on that head. There was even one large shapeless piece, of a savour and consistence so peculiar that no one of them could tell whether it was flesh or fish. Still they continued their perseverance, devouring one dish after another, and drinking off one stoup of wine after another, without any abatement of appetite on the one side or any exhiliration of spirits on the other, the steward always bringing in a supply with the most perfect equanimity. At length our yeomen began to look at one another. Their hands had waxed weary with cutting, and their jaws would scarcely any more perform their office.

'What is the meaning of this, my brethren,' said the friar: 'Surely it is better for us to desist, lest our table prove a snare unto us. Lo, my hands are weary, and my cheek-bones are pained even to their utmost extremities. Verily, it is all vanity, for my body is only filled as with the east wind.'

'Na, na; ply away. It's good sport. I dinna see how we can be better employed,' said the deil's Tam.

'I think, my brethren, that we should from eating straight refrain,' said the poet; 'for eating is but weariness, and

drinking is but pain. There is no strength into our bread,
nor spirit in our wine: some warlock wight has ta'en the
might out of this food of mine.'

The steward had all this time never spoken word good or
bad; but had served them with the utmost obsequiousness;
and when they had at length ceased from feeding, he went
and gave the Master an account of the repast, which proved
a source of great divertisement to him.

'I have not,' said he, 'for these many years, had any desire
to trifle with the beings to whose species I once belonged;
but this group surpasses all of their kind. I will, therefore,
lay aside my profound studies, and be with them as one of
themselves. If it were but to torment them, I will indulge in
this idle and vain humour. I have almost forgot how human
passions work.'

'I pray of thee, Master,' said Gourlay, 'that thou wilt
suffer me to slay yon grim and snarling dog in the grey
frock. I loathe, hate, and abhor him. He is, moreover, a bit
of a necromancer himself; and has the insolence to suppose
that he can rival you in power.'

'It is there I long to try him,' said the Master. 'In power I
brook no rival in this or any other land, as thou thyself, and
thy wretched companion in bondage, can witness. There
is only one thing in this weak man in shape of a friar that
I fear, and that thing shall be nameless. Perhaps I may
commission thee to take him away. In the mean time,
remove the remainder of their wretched viands, and bring
me in a vessel full of the strong wine of Palestine, mixed
up with the essence of many spirits. It is a beverage fit
for gods. In it will I pledge these deranged mortals; and
thou shalt see some sport for once, if aught on earth can
divert thee.'

'Certes I shall be diverted, great Master of arts. I hope
you will favour them with a touch of *the varieties*, by way
of example?'

'By and by, Gourlay – all in good time. In the mean
while, let us deal with them as men and as gentlemen;
and, before I metamorphose them into quadrupeds, let us
see what kind of beings they will make of themselves.'

The Master accordingly entered the room, where his
guests still sat round the board. All of them rose, and
made obeisance; but, without returning the courtesy, he

took his seat at the end of the table next to the door, and was just about to address them, when he was interrupted by Charlie Scott. There were two great individuals always uppermost in Charlie's mind – these were his master the warden, and his horse Corby; and finding himself again in the Master's presence, and thinking he rather looked better pleased than he was wont, he judged it prudent not to let the opportunity slip: so, after scratching his head violently with both hands, he thus preferred his solicitation:

'Gude faith, Master Scott, I'm glad I hae seen you again; and, nae disparagement either to you or your house, Sir Knight, but the truth is, we canna bide here. For, in the first place, you see, our skins will gang to the bauks in a jiffey; and, in the next place, our captain, the warden, canna want us. It is far mair than our lives are worth for us to stay here; for, troth, Sir Master, the lives o' others depend on it. Now, I wadna like that we were trowed to be corbie messengers. And that brings me a-mind, Sir Knight, how muckle need I hae to be at the mill down by there. I hae a friend at it that I fear is in nae good plight.'

'Content you, gallant squire, for a space,' said the Master; 'I do intend to answer the request of my noble kinsman with all expedition; but such things cannot be done in a moment. I must read the face of the heavens, and listen to the voices from the deep below. I have likewise a master to consult; he has another; and both are as perverse as hell itself. Be content, therefore, and enjoy yourselves for the remainder of this day. Give me all your names that I may register them, and give me them truly.'

Every one gave his name and designation, save that the poet gave the name of the lovely Delany with an encomium on her beauty and virtue. But Michael cared for none of those things. What appeared beautiful in the eyes of other men, to his were loathsomeness and deformity. Far different was the case when the friar announced his own name.

Michael started to his feet, and, with spread hands, and every feature of his countenance dilated with joy, he exclaimed, 'What? Primate of Douay in France, and author of the Book of Arts?'

'The same, great Sir,' said the friar: 'I confide it to you: But haply thou dost not know, in this thy retired habitation, that men thirst for my blood; that I am a persecuted man, and have suffered imprisonments, bonds, wounds, yea, and tortures; that I have been hunted from nation to nation, and from land to land, until I found shelter and protection among these wild and reckless Borderers, a people that neither fear God nor regard man. With them have I taken up my abode. I am become a father to them, and they are as children unto me. I love them. But, if they should be induced to give me up, wo would be unto me!'

'What d'ye say, man?' said Charlie, grasping his hand. 'D' ye think a Scot amang us wad gie you up? If there be sic a man in the Border array, he ought to be d—ned. But I trow I ken a bit o' the warden's mind there; and I can tell you, a' the pens and a' the rapiers in England wadna gar him gie up the gospel friar. Na, na; if ever he's gien up, he maun gie up himsel, and mak his ain conditions too.'

'Great and notable Primate, you are welcome to this castle,' said the Master; 'whether by the title of monk, prior, primate, or friar, I say you are welcome here. I have ridden a thousand miles to meet with you. But that is long agone. I had heard of your great skill in the sublime arts, that surpass the comprehension of ordinary men, and I determined to stake my life on the trial of skill between us. I was disappointed in meeting with you, for you were not to be found, dead or alive. The days of my ambition are fled. My power has been acknowledged so long, none daring to contend with me, that indifference hath ensued; after that came disgust, and with it misery. Thou art the man of all the earth whose fame I have envied; and, if thou darest, I will contend with thee, for freedom or for life, which thou wilt. If thou art overcome, thou shalt be my bondsman and slave, and if thou conquerest I will submit to be thine.'

'Lo, I will contend with thee even for name and being,' said the friar. 'Of the strong-holds of sin and Satan am I not afraid. I have put the ministers of thy vengeance to flight already, and I will chase, yea, I will overcome and pursue them away; as chaff is driven before the wind, will I scatter them. Dare not to contend with me; for, if I judge aright, my Master holdeth thine in chains, and if I interfere thou canst do nothing. I judge it therefore best to contend as brothers contend. To admire what is truly great, and deride that which is insignificant. Mine are the arts of peace, truth, and righteousness, and I hoped thine were the same.'

'Why, art thou not a monk, a follower of the wretched maniac, Benedict of Padua? that driveller in hidden mysteries?' said the Master. 'I do not rightly comprehend thee, or by what power thou didst thwart my servants. Tell me in one word – Art thou not in combination with the potent elemental spirits that rule and controul the earth, the air, the fire, and the waters? If not, thy arts are superficial and worthless.'

'Thou shalt see, and thou shalt judge,' said the friar: 'I am not ashamed of that I can do.' And with that he went and brought up his huge portmanteau, in which he always carried many a small and curious apparatus; but these he kept carefully concealed, having suffered so much from the superstitions of bigotted and illiterate men, in the course of his profound researches. He was the greatest chemist that had ever appeared on the stage of existence; yet that curious and refined art was he obliged carefully to conceal, having been persecuted as a necromancer over every kingdom of southern Europe.

When he went away Charlie Scott was terribly in the fidgets. He expected instantly to witness the raising of the devil, and other infernal spirits, against whom he cherished the most inveterate dislike. His eyes began to set in his head, and the roof of his mouth became so dry that he could not pronounce words distinctly.

'Gude faith, Sir Master,' said he, 'I dinna appruve of a man setting up his birse, and braving a gentleman in his ain house. And, wi' your permission, I hae something o' great importance to do at the mill; sae I'll e'en step down that length, and I shall come up again' the morning by day-light.'

'Please to remain with your friends, good yeoman,' said the Master: 'You shall witness something worth your while. What can you possibly have to do at the mill?'

'Muckle, muckle to do at the mill, Sir Knight; I'll just refer it to yoursel – can either man or beast leeve wanting drink?'

'I beg your pardon,' said the Master: 'I had almost forgot my principal errand. Gourlay, fill me a glass of the wine of Palestine.'

The steward did as he was ordered; and the Master, taking the cup, drank to the health of his kinsman, the warden, and all his friends. Every one of his guests did the same, save the maiden and boy; and every eye was cleared, and every heart warmed, for the liquor was as strong as brandy.

'Weel, Sir Knight,' said Charlie, 'that is what ane wad ca' rather stiff sturdy drink; I hae nae tasted ought as weel worth the drinking: And if ye will just gar auld Crossgrains come ower us again, I think I could even prevail on mysel' to face the deil, and let Corby tak his chance.'

The request was instantly complied with. Each of them got another cup; and the friar having tarried a while to put his affairs in order, when he came back the tongues of all his companions were going at once, and he was apprehensive that they were bewitched. He, however, took the pledge in one full cup, and was greatly revived by it; but refused taking another at that time.

The room in which they sat was lighted by four windows: those to the east and west were small circular ones, having a pane of bright glass in each: those to the north and south were merely long slits in the wall, without any glass; and the first thing the friar did, before producing the specimens of his art, was to close up all these windows, so as to exclude the light of day, and the glass of the western one he either contrived to remove, substituting another in its place, or else he put another piece of magnifying glass over it.

When he began a-closing up the last, Charlie entered a vehement protest against it, on the ground that no body would see what he did, or what he raised, and any one might be seized by the neck ere ever he was aware, by some o' his infernal deils.

'I hate a' surprises,' added he; 'It's best keeping the crown o' the fell, and seeing weel about ane. Room to fight and room to flee, an ye like, Maister Gospel-friar. Wha do you think's gaun to play at hide-and-seek wi' the deil in sic a place as this?'

The Master, in a sneering manner, requested that the great enchanter might have his own way: and Charlie, whose tongue was a little loosed by the wine of Palestine, was at last restrained, though not without a good deal of grumbling and fidgetting. The room was darkened; the friar went into a small alcove, and, by the help of a magic lanthorn, a thing never before seen in Scotland, he raised up a tremendous and horried figure on the wall. It was of gigantic size; its eyes, lips, and paws moved; and its body was thrown into various contortions.

All were in breathless silence on the appearance of this extraordinary shade; but among the darkling group there was distinctly heard one whose breathing was frequently cut short, as if something had been choking him, or seizing him by the throat.

After the apparition had gone through its various evolutions, all apparently at the further end of the apartment, it fixed its eyes, clenched its teeth, and, stretching forth its claws, it appeared to make a spring forward at the party. 'Aih! L—d be here!' cried Charlie in a trumpet voice, and threw himself flat down behind the rest. Hearing that some of them laughed at the fright he had got, he ventured to speak and expostulate a little; but no curiosity could induce him to raise his face from the floor, or open his eyes again while the friar's exhibition continued. 'Lair him, lair him, friar!' cried he – 'or, od I's be about your lugs some day for this. Lair him, lair him, in the name of St Michael! and if that winna do, try him wi' Peter – he'll send him ower the battlements like a shot. O good friar, whatever ye do, lair him!'

The friar went on with his phantasmagoria. The figure, after giving a shiver or two, was parted into three, all of the same form and size, but all making different motions, and different contortions of feature. The three were afterwards parted into six, which, among other grotesque feats, danced a reel, and, on running thro' it, every one threw itself heels-over-head. The group of onlookers laughed outright at this, notwithstanding their astonishment, and called to Charlie to look. But he would not move his face from the earth, and only asked, in a half-suffocated voice, 'Is he no laired yet? Od I shall be about wi' that cursed body for his tricks.'

When the friar had concluded this feat, he put out his small lanthorn, took the machinery out of it, concealing it beneath his ample frock, and again opened all the windows.

Charlie got up, and running to one of the loop-holes,

'Gude be thankit, I'll get a cooke o' the air o' heaven again!' said he, 'for I hae been breathing fire and brimstone this while byegane. Foul befa' me gin ever I saw the like o' yon; I was sair dumfoundered – but wha could stand afore the face of a fiery giant?'

The friar's associates looked at the lanthorn, examining it with curious eyes, but perceived nothing about it which could in any way account for the apparition they had seen. Master Michael Scott did not deign to ask a sight of it, but paced over the floor in sullen and thoughtful mood. The seneschal stood fixed to the spot on which he had witnessed the phenomenon, with his heavy unmoving eyes turned towards his master. He seemed dubious whether he was vanquished or not. The Master at length spoke, addressing the friar: –

'I hope, right worshipful Primate, this is not the extent of your knowledge and power in the sublime art of divination? The whole is only a delusion – a shadow – a phantom, calculated to astonish women or children. I acknowledge it to be ingenious; still it is nothing. You multiplied your shadows, turning three into six; now, if I turn three men into six living, breathing, substantial beings, will you acknowledge yourself outdone?'

'Certes, I will,' said the friar.

'Away, then, with deception,' said the Master: 'What I do, I do in the open eye of day—. Stand forth three of you.'

'Master Michael Scott, I'll tell you what it is,' said Charlie, 'I solemnly protest against being parted into twa.'

'You shall neither suffer nor feel the least inconvenience by the change, brave yeoman,' said the Master; 'therefore be not afraid, but stand forth.'

Charlie hung his head to one side in a deep reverie, till at length his countenance lightened up by degrees, his features opening into a broad smile.

'I'll tell you what it is, Sir Knight,' said he, 'if you will assure me that baith o' us shall be as stout and as wight chaps as I am mysel e'en now, gude faith, I dinna care though ye mak me into twa, for my master the warden's sake. If you could double an army that gate, it wad be a great matter. I doubt sair I'll cast out wi' my tither half

about something that I ken o', and that's Corby; but I'll
run the risk. Nane o' your cutting and cleaving, however,
Sir Knight. Nane o' your imps wi' their lang-kail gully
knives again.'

Charlie stepped up the floor, and took his stand with
his back at the wall, to await doggedly this multiplication
of himself. Tam soon joined him: but there was a hard
contest between Gibbie and the poet, both of whom were
rather personal cowards, and both alike averse to such
experiments. The former was at length obliged to yield,
for Carol clung so close to the maid, that nothing could
induce him to part from her; and, ever since the friar gave
him the grievous overthrow, he had lost all confidence in
his personal prowess.

Michael stamped thrice with his heel, and spoke some
words in an unknown tongue, in a low muttering tone; but
some of them heard the sounds of Prig, Prim, and Pricker.
There was a momentary confusion in the apartment. A
darkening haze flashed over it, and blinded the eyes of
men for a short space; the floor gave a shake, as if it had
sunk down a little – and there stood two of each of the
three friends, so completely alike that no one knew who
was who.

No scene could be more truly ludicrous than the one
which now ensued; each man turned to his prototype, and
the looks of confusion and astonishment in both being
the same, the beholders were seized with irrepressible
laughter.

Charlie felt his legs, thighs, and ribs, if they remained the
same as before. The other boardly personage in the same
shape followed his example, and added, 'Gude faith, the
like o' this I saw never!'

'You may weel say't,' said the other; 'But let me see if
you can draw that lang sword as weel an' as cleverly as I
can do.'

'Gude Lord, hear til him!' said the first: 'He's speaking
as he were the true Charlie Scott himsel! Speak ye, friend:
Were you me before this! That is, did you ride with the
warden over the border?'

'I am sure if you were there, I never saw you before,' said
the second speaker; 'But I dinna ken what I am saying; for
the truth is I dinna comprehend this.'

With that they again gazed at each other, and looked over their shoulders, as if they would not have cared to have fled from one another's presence.

With every pair the scene was much the same. Tam was so much astonished that he turned to his second self, cowered down, leaning his hands upon his knees, and made a staunch point at him. The other took precisely the same posture, so that their long noses almost met. The maid, the poet, and the boy screamed with laughter. Both of the Tams laughed too, so that they very much resembled an idiot looking at himself in a glass.

'Friend, I canna say but ye're very like me,' said Gibbie to his partner; 'But, though nane o' us be great beauties, ye look rather the warst o' the twae.'

'It brings me a-mind o' a story I hae heard my mother tell,' said the other, 'of a lady and her twa Blackamores—'

'What the deil man!' exclaimed the first; 'Did your mother tell that story too?'

'Ay; wha else but she tauld it? I say my mother, auld Effy Blakely of the Peatstacknowe.'

'Eh – ? She your mother? It is gayan queer if we be baith ane after a'! for I never had a billy.'

The two Gibbies then both began to tell stories, which each claimed as originally his, so that the perplexity still increased. Nor was it better when the parties began to mix and address each other. All spoke of themselves as the right and proper persons, and of the others as beings in their likenesses, and the most complete uncertainty prevailed. But, just as the novelty and interest of the drama began to subside, Michael, by a wave of his hand annihilated the three additional personages, and all remained as it was before the grand exhibition commenced, save that our group had got a new topic of conversation and merriment.

'Primate of Douay, so celebrated for thy mighty enchantments, how thinkest thou of this?' said the Master.

'That thou hast done what no man could have done beside,' said the friar; 'and that thy power even surpasseth that of the magicians of Egypt, and of those of the countries in the lands of the east. But in one thing my power is even as thy power. Dost thou know that I could have prevented thy charm, and put a period to thy enchantment at my will and pleasure?'

'It is not the power of prevention that we are trying,' said the Master. 'Suffer my servants to do their work, as I shall suffer thine, and we shall then see who are most punctually obeyed, and who shall perform the greatest works. Only, if I prevail in all things, you will surely have the generosity to acknowledge that my master is greater than thine?'

'Wo be unto me if such a confession proceed out of my lips!' said the friar: 'Who can be greater than he who builded the stories of heaven, and laid the foundations of this earth below; who lighted up the sun, sending him abroad in brightness and in glory, and placed the moon and the stars in the firmament on high? Who is greater than he who hath made the mountains to stand, the seas to roll, and the winds to blow? who hath not only made the souls of men, but all the spirits of the upper and nether world—'

'Peace, thou maniac!' cried the Master, interrupting the friar, in a voice that made him leap from the floor: 'Comest thou here to babble treason against the master whom I serve, and the mighty spirits with whom I am in league? Do what thou canst do, and cease from speaking evil of dignities. What knowest thou of the principalities and powers that inhabit and rule over the various regions of the universe? No more than the mole that grovelleth beneath the sward—. What further canst thou do in proof of thy profound art?'

'Behold with thine eyes, O thou who accountest thyself the greatest among the children of men!' said the friar, with a waggish air; 'that I will but speak the word, and the mountains shall be rent asunder, and the tops of the everlasting hills stand in opposition. Knowest thou the proper name, figure, and dimensions of that peaked mountain over against the castle, to the west?'

'Well may I know it,' said the Master, 'for I have looked out on it these fifty years, and many a hundred times have I followed the chase around it. It is named Cope-Law, and the mountain is my own.'

'Mountain of Cope-Law, hear my voice,' cried the friar in the same waggish tone, in which there was an affectation of sublime command: 'Thou hast borne the footsteps of thy great master and his black horse Beelzebub, yet hast thou neither been scorched nor rent. Yea, though he hath cursed thee in the bitterness of ire, yet hath thy grey head never been shaken—. But, behold, a greater than thy master is here. Mountain of Cope-Law, hear my voice: – Be thou rent asunder and divided into three, that thy owner may look on thee and be astonied. If it please thee, mighty magician, look out on thy mountain of Cope-Law now.'

Many a thousand times had the Master looked out at that circular window; every bush and grey stone on the hill were familiar to him; and, all unsuspicious of the simple deceit that had been practised on him, he went and looked forth from the window, when, in the place where one round peaked mountain was wont to be, he actually saw three, all of the same dimensions; and, as he weened, each of them more steep, tall, and romantic than the original one had been. He looked, and looked again – the optical delusion was complete. He paced the floor in sullen mood; muttered some sentences to himself in an under tone, and once more looked forth on the singular phenomenon. The mountains remained the same. They could not be seen from any other window, and no one thought of descending to the great balcony; so that in the eyes of all the friar remained triumphant.

The Master could not brook this. He strode the floor in gloomy indignation; and at length they heard him saying, 'If I should venture to demand it – But is it then to be my last great work? The demand is dreadful! – I will – I'll demand it. Never shall it be said that Michael Scott was out-done in his own art, and that by a poor peddling friar. Come all of you hither,' added he in a louder tone. 'Look at that mountain to the east. It is known to you all – the great hill of Eildon. You see and know that it is one round, smooth, and unbroken cone.'

'We all know it, and have known it from infancy,' was the general answer.

The Master gave three strokes with his heel, and called the names of his three elfin pages, who in an instant stood before him—. 'Work, Master, work – what work now?'

'Look at that mountain to the east,' said he, 'ycleped the hill of Eildon. Go and twist me it into three.'

The pages grinned, looking at him with eyes of a devilish gleam, as a ravenous creature eyes its prey.

'The hill is a granite rock,' said one – 'and five arrow-flights high,' said another – 'and seventy round the base,' said the first.

'All the powers of earth, and hell to boot, are unmeet to the task,' added the third.

'Thou art a proud and impertinent liar, perverse imp of the regions of flame,' said the Master: 'Note this, The thing must, and shall be done; even though a body and soul should both be given up as the guerdon. I know my conditions; they are sealed, and subscribed, and I am not to be disobeyed. Get to your work without more hesitation.'

The three pages then fell to reeling about and about, singing a wild and uncouth trio, in words of the following import:

> 'Pick and spade
> To our aid!
> Flaught and flail,
> Fire and hail!
> Winds arise, and tempests brattle,
> And if you will the thunders rattle.
> Come away
> Elfin grey,
> Much to do ere break of day!
> Come with spade, and sieve, and shovel;
> Come with roar, and rout, and revel;
> Come with crow, and come with crane,
> Strength of steed, and weight of wain,
> Crash of rock, and roar of river;
> And, if you will, with thunders shiver!
> Come away,
> Elfin grey;
> Much to do ere break of day!'

As they sung these last lines they reeled out at the door in a circular motion, so rapid that the eye dazzled which looked on them. The poet, drawn involuntarily by the ears after that wild fairy lay, hasted out after them. He looked east, and west, and all around, but he only saw three crows winging their flight toward the hill of Eildon.

From the time of their departure the temper of the great Master became extremely variable. At one time his visage would be clouded with the gloom of despair, and at another lighted up with a sort of horrid exultation; but he spake not, save to himself.

The friar, therefore, in order to divert his host, and gratify his own vanity, proposed to show off some more wonders of his art. Accordingly he closed up all the windows once more, making the apartment as dark as pitch, and exercised many curious chemical devices, lighted Roman candles, and made them dance about the chamber in every colour of the rainbow.

He was still busily employed playing off his little ingenious tricks, when the party were disturbed by a bustle in one of the corners. It chanced to be so dark at the moment that no one could see what was going on; but they heard a noise as of two people struggling; then a blow, and one falling down with a groan.

The friar paused, calling out and enquiring what it was. Charlie, never behind in a fray, bustled over the forms toward the scene of action; but falling by the way, the noise was quickly removed to another corner, a door was opened and shut, and all was again quiet.

Every one ran about groping his way in the dark, and coming full drive against others, till the friar had the presence of mind to pull the stuffing out of some of the windows. The first thing they then saw was the poet lying on the floor, void of sense and motion; and then it quickly appeared that the steward and Delany were a-wanting. The whole party, save the Master, set out on the pursuit, headed by the friar and Charlie, and came just in time to rescue the maid as the wretch was dragging her into his abominable cell. It seemed that he had determined on seizing her as his prey, and now that the three infernal pages, his tormentors, were dispatched elsewhere, he feared neither the Master nor his guests; and, taking advantage of the utter darkness, and of the poet and her being in a corner by themselves, he stole up to them, gagged the maid, silenced the poet, who resisted, with one blow, and then bore off the helpless lady with all expedition.

When he saw that he was overtaken and overpowered by numbers, he only laughed at them; and assured them that, in spite of all they could do, he would have possession of her, and that they should see. The girl wept and complained of being hurt; but then he only laughed and mocked the louder. Some of them proposed that they should hew him all to pieces, but the friar had resolved on his measures, and, at his request, they took the culprit up before the Master, and there lodged their accusation against him. But the Master either durst not, or would not say a word against him; for, in fact, it appeared that this great man, without his familiar spirits, shrunk into nothing, and was not only afraid of his own bondsman, but of every thing around him, deeming himself altogether without help.

The friar's eye burned with indignation and rage, at witnessing such arrogance on the one hand, and imbecility on the other; but his bootless wrath only delighted the steward the more; and it was evident that, had it not been for fear of Charlie Scott's long sword and heavy hand, he would have taken his prey from the midst of them.

Delany still wept and sobbed till her bosom was like to rend, and begged to be taken away from the castle, or to be killed and put in her grave. The friar tried, with all the fair and kind speeches he was master of, to comfort her; but when she saw the poet pale, bleeding, and sitting still unable to rise, she only waxed worse, and hid herself from the eye of the wretch behind the friar's frock.

'Daughter of my love, and child of many misfortunes, be thou comforted,' said the friar; 'for though the wicked triumph for a space in their iniquity, yet shall they not thrive. They who refuse to do justice to the innocent and upright in heart shall perish in their sin, and pass away as the smoke that is driven by the wind. Therefore, my daughter, be thou comforted; and that thy heart may be cheered, I will show thee a wonder of my art – a wonder so great that whosoever seeth it his heart shall melt within him; and whosoever heareth of it his ears shall tingle. Come, whoso listeth, forth into the open air, and I will do it in the sight of heaven and of man.'

The friar then lifting up his huge portmanteau, went forth to the large paved gateway that surrounded the whole of the uppermost arches of the castle. It was so ample as to be like a small field, for it covered all the castle, save four small pointed turrets, and the square apartment which the party now left, that rose like a shapeless dome above all. In one corner of this level battlement there stood a leaden vessel that had once been used as a cistern. To that the friar went; and, laying down his huge walise, he took from thence a handful of blackish sand, and strinkled it all around the battlement on the one side to the opposite corner. He then stood and looked awfully around him. He looked to the heavens, but they were shrouded in a dark hideous cloud that now covered the mountains, and hung lowering over the uppermost spire of the castle. Neither the Cope-Law nor the hill of Eildon could be seen, nor could aught be seen save the dark and troubled cloud. The scene was truly impressive; and when the rest saw the friar looking on it with such apparent dread, all of them looked abroad with him, and whispered to one another, 'He's gaun to be about some awesome enchantment now.'

The friar covered up his portmanteau with the leaden vessel, and then desired the Master to bring any weight he chose, and heap it on its bottom, which he had now turned uppermost, and, at one word or sign, he would make his goat-skin wallet carry the vessel, and all such weight, round the battlements of the castle.

The Master, and every one present, pronounced the thing to be impossible – the steward grinned in derision – and, after mocking and taunting the friar on his art in the most gross and provoking terms, he proffered to hold down the leaden tub, wallet and altogether, or to forfeit his head if he failed. Then laying himself over it, in the attitude of holding it down, he called on the friar to proceed, and give him the promised canter round the walls, which he well deserved, he said, not only for his kindness to them all, and to their Miss in particular, but also for his kind intentions. Then he scoffed aloud, crying out, 'Now thou poor vain fool and liar, be as good as thy word, and give me, an it were, but one hobble.'

'God do so to me, and more also,' said the friar, 'if I do not give thee such a hobble as eye hath not seen!'

With that he struck a spark of fire among the black sand, as the rest supposed it to be, that lay among his feet. The sand caught fire – the flame ran sputtering around the western battlement – and the next moment the steward and his tub bolted away into the firmament in a tremendous flash of fire, and with a sound so loud that it shook the castle to its foundations. Some averred that they saw, through the fire and smoke, a momentary glance of him and the cistern both, as they pierced the cloud towards the north; but nothing further was heard or seen – and, in a second of time, all was quiet and gloomy above and around as it had been before.

CHAPTER SIXTEEN

> The wind blew as 'twould blawn its last,
> The thickening showers rose on the blast;
> The speedy gleam the darkness swallowed,
> Loud, deep, and lang the thunder bellowed;
> That night a child might understand
> The deil had business on his hand!
>
> *Tam o' Shanter*

LONG WAS IT before any of the astonished spectators opened their lips. The shock had almost deprived them of sense, sight, and motion; and when they began to articulate, it was only to utter short exclamations, and names of saints. Tam Craik was the first who ventured a remark, which was in the following words: – 'By the Lord Robin!' (meaning, it was supposed, the king,) 'The deil has flown away wi' him bodily in a flash o' fire!'

The great Master stood mute with astonishment; he even trembled with dread; and appeared once as if he would have fallen at the friar's feet: But he never said, Where is my seneschal gone? Whither hast thou sent him? seeming rather to succumb to his guests for the time, being as a man utterly at their mercy. His powerful and malevolent spirits had left him by his command; his steward, and only human attendant, had been blown into the air; and as for the miserable night-hag, they had seen no more of her since her escape from the prison vault, and they wist not whether she remained in the castle, or had fled from it out of dread of the symbols of the Christian religion, which she had seen about the friar, and the effects of which she had felt in frustrating her potent spells. The wizard had therefore none to execute his commands, and appeared a being quite forlorn, as well as greatly troubled in his mind.

No one ever knew to this day by what means the wicked seneschal was borne away among the clouds in a column of fire and smoke; and those who witnessed it spread the word over the country, that the devil took him away with a great roar amid fire and brimstone; and that, after having him up among the dark clouds, he tore him all to pieces. It was a fact that one of the steward's mangled limbs was found hanging on a tree, among some thick branches, in the wood of Sheil's Heuch, over against the castle, which gave some countenance to the report; and no farther remnants of him were ever discovered.

The friar, however, knew well enough by what means he was taken away; and though he never explained it as long as he remained in Scotland, it is meet that the readers of this tale should know the truth. It can be told in a few words. The friar had brought his huge wallet full of the strongest gunpowder he had been able to make, to shew off his wonderful feats, and astonish the great Master. The exigency of the moment induced him to part with it all at once; and, in all probability, he could not have caused so much astonishment by any experiment he could have put in practice.

He was guilty, however, of a manifest oversight; one that had well nigh proved fatal to the whole party in its consequences. When they found themselves freed from their vile persecutor, and the great Master rather their prisoner than they his, their first thought was of departing from that unhallowed place, and awaiting, in the neighbourhood, the wizard's final answer, without which they durst not well return to the warden.

Charlie jumped on the battlement with very joy that he would now get down to the mill to see what was become of Corby, and how he fared; and he was the first man to proceed down the narrow staircase, leading the way to the fair fields. But, alas, how transient are all sublunary joys and hopes! In the middle of this confined and difficult stair, just at its darkest and most acute turn, there was a massive iron door, which Charlie ran his nose against in his descent, and soon found, to his mortification and disappointment, that it was locked and double locked. He returned to those above with the dismal information. The friar's countenance fell, and he became pale as ashes, when it was thus brought to his recollection that he had not only blown the brutal seneschal to the devil, but that he had blown the keys of the castle along with him; and there were they left on the roof to perish with hunger.

After many ineffectual attempts to break open that door, having no other resource, they agreed to go to the topmost tower, and there unite their voices, in order to raise the country to their assistance; for, without ropes and ladders, they saw no means of escape. Accordingly they ascended, and uttered many a prolonged and tremendous shout, for the space of a whole hour. But these unwonted cries only drove the hinds to a greater distance from the castle. Many of them had witnessed the mighty explosion at the exit of the seneschal, which, in the middle of the lurid gloom, had a hideous effect; and when they heard such long and loud howls proceeding from the battlements of that gloomy and desolate pile, they weened that a whole host of demons had assembled about it, and kept far aloof.

In these and other fruitless exertions, our hapless prisoners spent the evening of that eventful day. The sun, or the blue sky, had not once appeared since the break of morn. For a little while, about noon, the hills of the Forest were visible, and, on their back-ground of pale shadowy clouds, formed a scene of dark sublimity. Still, as it approached toward evening, these clouds came lower and lower down upon the hills, and became more dark and dense in their appearance; and precisely at the close of day the storm burst forth in all its fury, sweeping over hill and dale with increasing majesty every minute. The woods roared and crashed before the blast. The snow descended so thick that in a short time every ravine and sheltered dell was heaped. After that came sleet and snow mingled; and, finally, a driving rain dashed with such violence on the earth, that it seemed as if a thousand cataracts poured from the western heaven to mix with the tempest below. Needless is it to describe that night farther. It was that on which the great battle was fought in the camp of Douglas, and formerly mentioned in this momentous history—. It is therefore apparent that Issac the curate is now drawing near to the same period of time when he broke off at a tangent and left the camp, and that every thing will, of course, go on to the catastrophe without further interruption.

*   *   *

Kind hearted and gentle reader, be not too sanguine. Who can tell what is to fall out between the cup and the lip? Incidents seem to have multiplied intentionally to interrupt poor Isaac's narrative. Besides, let any one consider how he is to liberate and get free of this group of interesting individuals, locked up, as they were, to perish on the top of the castle of Aikwood. It was no difficulty to Isaac. He was one of those wise and downright men who know that truth tells always the best, and to that maxim he adhered. But the worst of it was, there were so many truths, that any body may see it was scarcely possible to get them all narrated in their proper places; and that, without the help of the waggoner, the task could never have been effected.

'Gude sauf us, but it is gaun to be an awsome night!' said Charlie Scott, as he stepped the last up into the dark apartment in which the party had spent the greater part of the day, and into which the storm had now driven them once more.

'Gaun to be?' said Tam, taking up Charlie's words; 'I wot nae what it is gaun to be, but it is an awsome night already.'

'It brings me in mind of a story,' said Gibbie, 'that I hae often heard about a friar Gabriel o' St Martin's that raised the deil—'

'Od, Sir, an ye dare, for the blood of you, speak another word about raising the deil the night,' cried Charlie, interrupting him, 'may I be chased by an Englishman, if I dinna thraw you ower the castle wa'. We little ken wha may be near, or wha may be amang us. Gin ane may judge by appearances, that same chap ye hae named (gude keep me frae repeating it) isna in his ain hett hame the night. Heaven defend us, hear how the wind howls and sobs! I wish yon auld houses o' the mill may be safe aneuch; they stand sair exposed. Hech-ho! hear til't! There will be mony cauld quarters on Otterdale the night, but there is some a-wanting there that wad be blithe to share them.'

The friar now set himself to strike a light, which at last he effected; and collecting the oil which remained in the lamps into one, they found, to Charlie's great satisfaction, that they had as much as would burn over-night, besides some remnants of waxen torches. Of all the huge remains of their morning feast that they had seen removed from the table, they could not find one vestige, even though the trenchers remained in the chamber as it was termed; but, to their great joy, they found an article as precious to the eyes, for about two-thirds of the huge flagon of the wine of Palestine were still left. This, in the total absence of fuel, was a discovery of some consequence; and the friar, in the like absence of a steward, took that office voluntarily on himself.

When the lamp was kindled, the first thing that Delany did was to dress the poor poet's hurt head, and bind it up with a napkin. This attention and kindness so thrilled his heart that he could not refrain from tears, and seemed to rejoice in his wound; and as both he and his adored maiden had seen the ruffian steward transported up to heaven in a flame of fire, they were freed from all terror on his account; and, notwithstanding all the perils with which they were surrounded, they appeared composed, and, if not happy, were at least quite resigned to their fate.

The great Master sat muffled up in his cloak, and apart by himself, his brows screwed down into deep curved wrinkles, and his sunken eye fixed on the ground. The friar filled a cup of wine, and, bowing, presented it to him the first. He took the cup, and drank if off, but he spoke not a word: his piercing eyes glimmered round the chamber; he uttered a loud groan, and, apparently, sunk again into his deep reverie. The transportation of his steward, while in the very act of braving the friar's might, made a terrible impression on his mind, and he weened that he now sat before his master – before one that might send him on a voyage of the same nature whenever he chose; and therefore he judged, with great reason, that for a space it behoved him to keep on good terms with so dangerous an opponent.

When each had taken a cup of the elevating beverage, the effect was delightful; all their cares, dangers, and wants faded; the terrors of the storm, that was still increasing, only startled them now and then, as it rattled on the tower, or yelled thro' the crevices below. They chatted, laughed, and broke jokes on each other, till even the sublime Master was diverted from his profound and brooding ideas, and smiled at the rustic simplicity of the characters around him. The laird of the Peatstacknowe told a great number of his long stories, of which something that was seen, said, or done, always reminded him; Charlie told confused stories about battles and forays; and the poet came in always between with his rythmatic descriptions and allusions; until at one time the associations of ideas followed one another in a manner so truly ludicrous, that the enchanter actually laughed till he had almost fallen into a fit, a thing that had not for twenty years been witnessed of him.

The tempest still continued to rage, and the loquacity of the party beginning to flag, they became drowsy as midnight approached. The friar then looking gravely around him, and, laying aside his hood, took a small psalter book from his bosom; which volume also contained the four books of the Apocalypse; and, opening it reverendly, he proposed that they should all join in performing the evening service to the Virgin, and the hymn to the Redeemer. Delany rose from off the lap of the poet's cloak, where she had sat nestling all the evening, and came and kneeled down at the friar's knee. The Master started up with a look of indignation, stamped on the floor, and ordered the friar to put up his vain book, and refrain from such flummery in his presence. The friar looked at him with a steady countenance.

'It is not meet that I should obey man rather than God,' said he. 'I have taken a vow in the face of Heaven, and I will pay that vow in spite of men and devils. I will sing my holy hymns with these my friends and children, and he that listeth not to join, let him be accursed, and translated from the presence.'

This last sentence sounded rather equivocally in the Master's ears. He liked not such a translation as he had lately witnessed; for, with all his power and mysterious art, the terrors of death still encompassed him about. He held his peace, therefore, although he growled like a lion at bay at being bearded thus in his own castle.

The friar proceeded as he had said, and all the rest joined him with becoming devotion, save the poet, whose orisons that night were somewhat cold. He could not brook the charm that drew Delany from his own side to his rival's knee. The Master sat aloof, biting his lip, and grinning in derision; but, at one part of the service, although the curate does not say what part, he was insensibly overcome,

and fell into a painful oblivious dream. The strains of the
sacred music, simple as they were, stole over his soul, as
some remembrance of early life sometimes steals into the
heart of enfeebled age, reminding the decaying and dying
worm of joys he can no more see, and of feelings of delight
that have perished for ever—. If a son of the mountains
of the north were transported to some far foreign clime,
and there doomed to remain for life: After sojourning in
that land for half an age, until grey and bowed down, if
by chance, on some still evening, or mayhap through the
eddies of the storm, one of the strains of his native land
were poured on his ear, think of the recollections it would
awaken in his mind: How painfully thrilling the sensations!
Would it not be like the last sweet beam of a hope he was
never more to cherish, a last look of all that was dear on
earth? – Such were the feelings that crept unbidden over
the soul of the enchanter, on hearing the sweet sounds, that
reminded him of a religion he had for ever renounced, and
in which he had never firmly believed till he had believed
to tremble.

In this troubled trance he sat leaning against the wall,
until the worshippers had reached the middle of the hymn
to the Saviour. He then was seized with strong convulsions,
and, rising up, with staggering steps, he fled from the
chamber, crying as he went – 'Cruel and improvident
things! reptiles! cursed, whining sycophants! that would
send me to my doom before my time!' He rushed out to
the battlements, and, groping his way through the storm,
took shelter in the narrow staircase, that he might hear no
more of the sounds that thus troubled and distracted his
soul. What dread had seized him, or what he had seen
or heard, his guests knew not; but they had scarcely well
ended their hymn, when he rushed again in among them,
with wildered looks, and his hair standing on end, seeming
glad to take shelter among those from whom he had so
lately fled with abhorrence. No one enquired the cause,
for all were so weary and overcome with slumber; and
every one then composed himself to sleep in the manner
that best suited his convenience.

The storm continued to rage with unabated violence,
and, after they had laid themselves down, they found
that the castle was all tottering and quaking before it.

The firmest heart was appalled; for the rocking of the castle was not all; every now and then they heard eldritch shrieks arising, as of some wretch perishing, or rather, as some of them thought, like the voices of angry spirits yelling through the tempest. When one of these howling sounds came on the blast, every one of our prostrate friends breathed a deep sigh, or uttered some exclamatory sound. Charlie had always one, which he uttered even after he was asleep. 'Hech! Gude sauf us, sirs! what will be the upshot o' a' this?' The Master sat muffled up in the corner close behind them, and after he judged them all to be asleep he fell a-crooning a sort of hymn in an under key. The poet was, however, more than half awake, and gathered up some broken fragments of it. Poets are never to trust when they give quotations from memory out of the works of others; and perhaps honest Carol might add some bombastic lines of his own, but he always averred that the following lines formed a part of the warlock's hymn.

> 'Pother, pother,
> My master and brother!
> Who may endure thee,
> Thus failing in fury?
> King of the tempest that travels the plain;
> King of the snow, and the hail, and the rain,
> Lend to thy lever yet seven times seven,
> Blow up the blue flame for bolt and for levin,
> The red forge of hell with the bellows of heaven!
> With hoop, and with hammer!
> With yell, and with yammer;
> Hold them at play,
> Till the dawn of the day!
> Pother! pother!
> My sovereign and brother!
>
> 'O strain to thy lever,
> This world to sever
> In two or in three—
> What joy it would be!
> What toiling, and moiling, and mighty commotions!
> What rending of hills, and what roaring of oceans!
> Ay, that is thy voice, I know it full well;
> And that is thy whistle's majestic swell;

But why wilt thou ride thy furious race,
Along the bounds of vacant space,
While there is tongue of flesh to scream,
And life to start, and blood to stream?
    Yet, pother, pother!
    My sovereign and brother!
And men shall see, ere the rising sun,
What deeds thy mighty arm hath done.'

If it was true that the Master sung these ridiculous lines, which is not very likely, his 'sovereign and brother' had not accepted of his sacrifice, nor paid due deference to his incense of praise. For, a little before the break of day, our group were aroused from their profound slumbers by loud and reiterated cries. The lamp was still burning feebly and blue. Charlie, whose ear was well trained to catch any alarm, was the first to start up; but the sight that he saw soon laid him again flat on the floor, though not before he had leaped clear over a narrow oak-table and two forms. There was a black being, that appeared to be half-man and half-beast, dragging Master Michael Scott along the room toward the door; yet he dragged him with difficulty, and at some times the wizard seemed rather to prevail. Horrible as this phantom was, all those who saw it agreed that there was something about it that instantly reminded them of the late seneschal; and, as they raised their heads and beheld it, every heart was chilled with terror. Charlie pronounced his short, loud prayer, which has already been recorded in this history, and which consisted merely of one vehement sentence of three syllables; yea, he pronounced it as he flew; and then squatting in a corner, and covering his head with his cloak, that, whatever dreadful thing happened, he might not see it, there he lay repeating his little prayer as fast as human breath could utter it.

The demon struggled hard with the Master; and the latter, as may well be supposed, exerted his utmost power – so that his adversary only got him toward the door as it were by inches. When he found himself losing ground, he always made a certain writhing motion, which cannot be described, and which every time extricated him somewhat from his adversary's clutches. Then the apparition laid hold of him again by the left side with his lobster claws, and that gripe uniformly caused the wizard to utter a loud and piercing cry. At such times Charlie's little prayer might be heard waxing still louder as the strife increased; and, though he lifted not his face from the earth, he continued a kind of spurning motion with his feet, as if he would fain have burrowed under the wall like a mole.

For a long time no one durst move to the Master's assistance. The scene so far surpassed ought they had ever conceived in horror, that their senses remained altogether benumbed. The combat continued with unabated ardour. The Master foamed at the mouth, his hair stood all on end, and his bloodshot eyes stared wildly, as if they would have started from their sockets. At length the fiend so far prevailed as to drag the Master close to the door, where he threw him down, and made a motion as if he would have dashed him through below it. But Michael was flesh and blood, and could not enter nor depart by the key-hole, or the foot of the door, like the beings with whom he had to do. The demon therefore tried to open the door; but the enchanter's muscular frame being jammed against it, it could not be opened at once. Michael's efforts were now directed to that object alone, namely, the keeping of the door shut, and he exerted himself till his remaining strength was exhausted, but at last suffered himself to be dragged back from the door, repeating these words as he lay flat on his back: – ''Tis done! 'Tis done! 'Tis over! 'Tis over!'

The lookers on sat and trembled, all save the friar, who had by that time somewhat rallied his scattered senses, and stood on his feet. The fiend had dragged the Master back from the door by the feet, and holding him down by the grey hair with one hand, he opened the door with the other; then, stooping down, he twisted the one hand, armed with red crooked claws, in his hair, and the other in his long grizzled beard. The friar had stepped forward, and, at that moment, laying the rood on the Master's forehead with the one hand, and the open Book of the Gospels on his breast with the other, he pronounced a sacred Name, and in that name commanded the demon to depart. Swift as the javelin leaves the hand of the warrior, or the winged shaft flies from the bow-string, did the monster fly from the symbols of a creed by which he and his confederate powers were all controlled, and from a name and authority at which the depths of hell trembled. He rushed out at the door with a yell of dismay, and threw himself from the battlement on the yielding wind. The friar peeped forth after him, but he only heard a booming sound, which died on the gale, and beheld like a dragon of blue livid fire flying toward the east, in the direction of the hill of Eildon.

The friar returned into the chamber with a countenance beaming with joy. No conqueror ever returned from the field of battle with an exultation of mind so sublime as that which now lighted up his uncourtly mien. His victory had been so sudden and so complete, that all present were astounded at the greatness and extent of his power, and none of his friends doubted that his might was as far above that of their host as the sun or the stars are above the earth. They had in this instance seen it exemplified in a manner not to be disputed; and there was the Master himself still sitting on the floor, and gazing on his deliverer with astonishment.

'Man, may I not thank thee for this?' said he.

'No,' said the friar, 'think not of a poor mortal thing like me, overcome with sins, faults, and follies: You are freed for this time; but thank One who is greater than I.'

'True; I am freed for the present,' said the Master; 'but it is by a mode, and by a power, that I dare not, for my existence, acknowledge or acquiesce in.'

When Charlie heard by what was passing that the devil had been vanquished and was fled, he called out with a voice that seemed to come from under ground – for he was so muffled up in his cloak that the sounds could scarcely be heard – 'Friar, steek the door.' The good man obeyed, and as soon as Charlie heard the welcome sound, he raised his face, which was much of the same colour as a living lobster, and, standing on one knee, viewed all the faces and corners with that eloquence of eye which is quite indescribable. How superior was it to his blunt address: – 'Gude sauf us, callans, is a' safe? – Is the coutribat ower? Sic a fie-gae-to as yon I saw never! Hech! but it is an unsonsy place this! I wadna live here an there warna another place to be had aneath the shoulder o' heaven.'

A long discussion now commenced between the friar and the Master, on the principles which each of them professed. That colloquy is too serious, and too tedious, to be copied

at full length in this place; but it amounted simply to this
– That the one considered the Christian Revelation as the
source of all that is good, wise, or great among men. The
other had disbelieved it from his youth upward; and, not
being able to come to any conclusion from ought he could
learn among men, he had besought communion with the
potent spirits of the elements; and, after seven years of
unparalleled suffering, such as cannot be named, had
attained what he sought. These had confirmed him in
his infidelity. He had entered into a league with them,
renouncing, for ever and ever, all right in a Redeemer, and
signing the covenant with his own blood. That afterwards
he had rejoiced in this fellowship, which had enabled him
to do deeds such as no other man could perform, till by
degrees he discovered that the meanest professor of the
religion of Jesus, if influenced by faith and sincerity, had
the power of counteracting these mighty spirits, and of
frustrating their highest intents. That then his eyes were
opened when it was too late, and he only believed in time
to tremble and despair. The friar urged the inexhaustible
riches of heavenly mercy; but the Master spurned at it,
declaring his resolution to abide by his covenant, whatever
his fate might be. He despised the very name and nature
of repentance, and would rather suffer with the colleagues
he had chosen, he said, than whine and cringe to another
master—. 'Though I now feel to my sorrow that they are
subordinate,' added he, 'yet are they mighty and powerful,
beyond what thou canst comprehend; and why may not I
be a sharer in their energies in a future existence as well
as in this?'

The friar gazed and trembled when he heard the wild
and erratic ideas of this extraordinary man; and, ceasing
to reason further with him, he enquired how it came that
some of these mighty associates of his were his enemies,
and seemed but to watch an opportunity of tearing him
in pieces.

'They are jealous of their rights, and capricious beyond
all conception,' said he. 'The utmost circumspection is not
fit to keep on fair and equal terms with them. Even yet I do
not know but that this is to be my last night here. If I have
gone beyond my commission in the orders I have given,
then am I doomed to be their bond slave for ages: but if

I am within my limited bounds, and the work is effected, then shall I still be obeyed for a time and a season. Would that it were morning that I might know the worst!'

'Scarcely dost thou need to express thy wish again,' said the friar; 'for, lo, the day dawneth in the east, and the shadows flee away before it; the winds have gone to their chambers to sleep, and the rains are over and gone. Let us walk forth and see how the darkness fadeth before the face of the day, and all that is stirring abroad on the fair face of the creation.'

The Master did not move, for it was yet but twilight, and nothing could be seen distinctly; but the friar stepped down to the battlements, and Charlie, who looked on him as their only safeguard, followed. The poet would doubtless have followed also to have seen the dawn of the morning after a storm; but, like all the rhyming race to this day, he was enslaved by the eyes of a maid, languished in chains, and could not move but as she moved. Alas for the poor amorous poet! The others lay in a sluggish and restless slumber.

The friar and the bold yeoman strode together along the paved way, and looked abroad; but they could see only the clouds whitening in the eastern horizon, without being able to distinguish wood from waste, or land from water.

'Let us kneel down and pray, my son,' said the friar, 'even in this quiet place, where we shall be freed from the interruptions of the wicked one; for great and manifold are the dangers that surround us. I see not what remains for us, but either to throw ourselves from the walls and perish, or remain where we are and feed upon one another.'

'It is an awsome eternitive, man,' answered Charlie; 'I'm sure an ye think praying will do ony good, I shall take off my bonnet and kneel down on my knees, and hearken weel; but what mair can I do?'

'You can join with me in spirit, my son,' said the friar, and pray with your heart.'

'I am sure, gin I but kend the process, I am very willing,' said Charlie. With that he took off his steel belted bonnet, and kneeled reverendly beside the friar, who prayed so fervently and sublimely for deliverance, that Charlie looked about every minute, not only then, but all that morning, to see by what means they were to be delivered; for he had no doubt but they would be set free to a certainty, and that in a very short time.

When they arose, the first word that the friar said was the following fervent exclamation – 'Blessed Virgin! What do I see?'

Charlie looked all about for some approaching miracle; he had even some hopes of seeing a detachment from the warden's army; but his eye ranged the dusky fields in vain.

'What a strange world we live in!' rejoined the friar: 'Yea surely there are things in heaven and in the earth, and in the waters – yea many things, of which man knoweth nothing! Why art thou gazing abroad on all nature, my son? Turn thine eyes toward the east, and tell me what thou seest.'

Charlie did so; and, on the instant, the two friends were standing fixed in amazement like two statues. They moved not, save, now and then, to steal a momentary glance at each other. The great mountain of Eildon was actually rent in pieces from the top to its very foundations, and piled up in three towering spiral mountains, as they remain to this day. Only at that time they were taller, darker, and more uniform.

It was a scene of wonder not to be understood, and awfully impressive. The two rivers flowed down their respective vallies, and met below the castle like two branching seas, and every little streamlct roared and foamed like a river. The hills had a wan, bleached appearance, many of the trees of the forest were shivered; and, towering up against the eastern sky, there stood the three romantic hills of Eildon, where before there was but one.

The friar was the first to move from his trance, stepping away in deep meditation. Charlie was by this time likewise released from the spell, and he ran to the door of the high chamber, calling aloud, 'Come a' out, sirs, come a' out. The like o' this was never seen sin the warld stood up!'

They came forth accordingly, and their consternation was correspondent to the extraordinary event. But when the Master came out, and saw what was done, he shouted, and leaped on the battlement like one frantic, boasting, and uttering words of terrible blasphemy. He looked on the mountain of Cope-Law, and he could scarcely believe his eyes when he beheld it standing in one unskaithed unbroken cone, as it had done for ages. He looked again to the three mountains of Eildon, and his exultation and blasphemous boasting was redoubled.

'So, all that you and your master can effect,' cried he, 'is to throw a little glamour on the sight – is to practise a little deception! I never weened the monkish art or profession to consist of more. See what my sovereign and master can do!'

'Hold there,' said the friar. 'Who was it that made these mountains at the first? Was that deception?'

'It was not thou,' said the Master.

'But who was it, then, that sent up your wicked seneschal into the stormy clouds in a flame of fire?' added the friar. 'And who was it that saved your life, but this morning, from a fiend that would have devoured you? Were these both deceptions?'

The Master's countenance fell. The friar said this, because, in their present perilous situation, he wished to keep a little awe over the wizard, and likewise to put a stop to the torrent of blasphemy that proceeded from his lips.

The morning advanced, the sun arose, but no assistance, no relief appeared to our hapless prisoners. They had tasted nothing for a day and night, save one cup of wine each, and they had not above as much more remaining. For all this the Master was so much elated, that his behaviour was rather like that of a person frantic with joy, than that of one shut up among others to perish of hunger. His companions in misfortune noted likewise that he was again disposed to be peremptory and tyrannical with them, and they dreaded that his familiars were again at his command.

The men wrought all the forenoon endeavouring to break up the iron door; but they neither had mattocks nor room to work in, and they made no more impression on it than as many mice would have done. They were now quite disconsolate; and, being unable to do aught else, they puzzled themselves in accounting for the late steward's motives for having locked it. They remembered that it was standing wide open when they brought him up a prisoner before the Master; and they likewise remembered of having seen him step into that stair for a minute or two, immediately before he began to brave the friar. Therefore, all that they could guess was, that it had been locked with some fatal intent.

The friar, perceiving that their efforts were vain, entreated them to come in from the open air, and keep themselves quiet and cheerful, that they might wear the longer. He trusted in Heaven, he said, that they would be delivered, but in the mean time it was absolutely necessary to use every precaution; and for that purpose, he added, if one of them would keep watch at each of the four windows, lest any passengers or countrymen should come near, he would tell them a story, which would at least have the good effect of keeping them quiet. The Master was quite delighted with this proposal; and, taking the flagon of wine, he proposed that they should share it among them; but the rest opposed it, and contented themselves with half a cup each.

Charlie was most of all cast down. He had heard a word from the friar that morning that sunk deep on his heart. It was something about eating one another! And not being able to get rid of the thought, he brought it again overhead. The rest were all struck dumb; for they perceived that it was but too apparent it might come to that. The Master grinned darkly, and said it was well. But Gibbie said he hoped, 'if things came that length, they wad draw cuts, that ilka ane might get a fair chance for his life.' The poet begged, with tears in his eyes, that, out of respect to the tender sex, they would leave Delany the last, or at least that, when the lot fell on her they would take him in her place. To this they all agreed with one voice: but an extraordinary thought striking on the Master's mind at that instant, he made a motion, and proposed to settle if off hand by a vote.

'This maid, whom you term beautiful, is mine on one condition,' said he; 'and as I can now in a very short time comply with that condition, I claim her as my own. I will therefore give her to the man among you who tells me the best tale. She shall be his, fully and freely, to do with her as seemeth him good. And the man among you who tells the worst shall, if need require it, be blooded and flayed in this same chamber for food to his associates.'

Charlie's blood ran cold within him at this proposal. He almost thought he felt the flaying knife and the teeth of the ravenous half-famished eaters; and when the Master called out, 'Approve, or not approve?' Charlie was the first to call out, 'O! Not! not, not!' He was seconded by Tam Craik, but all the rest voted on the other side; so that they were left in the minority, and the matter was finally decided to be precisely as the Master had proposed. The poet stretched himself, so eager was he to begin; for his heart yearned within him to win the beautiful Delany. Gibbie was also uplifted, and sure of victory; but Tam and Charlie were both quite hopeless and cast down.

CHAPTER SEVENTEEN

And I said unto him, Can'st thou tell unto thy servant what is the meaning of this?

Esdras

THE FRIAR HAVING volunteered a tale, the priority was unanimously awarded to him: So, after the watches were set and all quiet, he began the following singular narrative, without further ceremony:

The Friar's Tale

CHAPTER I

1. In the days of the years of my pilgrimage, it chanced to me that I sojourned in the great kingdom that is toward the south.
2. And I passed through the city that lieth on the river of the hills, unto the house of Galli the scribe, who was a good man and a just.
3. And he had one only daughter, who was unto him as a treasure and an heritage, for her mother had been led unto her people before the maid could distinguish between her right hand and her left.
4. And the maiden was fair to look upon;
5. For her neck was as polished ivory, and her chin like the ripened peach basking on a wall that looketh toward the south.
6. Her lips also were like the honeycomb; her teeth were rows of pearl, and her breath was as sweet smelling incense, and myrrh, and cassia.
7. Her eyes were brighter than the dew of heaven, and her

hair was like the beams of the moon streaming through the white clouds that are in the firmament of air.

8. And I loved the maiden exceedingly; and my heart burned within me; and I became as a dead man.

9. And I wist not what to do, or what would become of me; for the vows of the Lord were on me that I could not wed; and I said, Woe is me, for I am undone!

10. And I went in unto her, and communed with her of my great love; and when she had hearkened to my voice, she laughed me to scorn.

11. And I said, Why dost thou laugh me to scorn? Knowest thou not that I would lay down my life for thee? For I love thee so much above all things that are on earth, that I would even lick the dust from off thy feet.

12. And she said, What wouldst thou have me to do?

13. And I looked on my right hand, and on my left, and I communed with my heart.

14. And I perceived that the maid had asked aright, for I knew not what I would have her to do; and lo my countenance became abashed.

15. And she laughed at me exceedingly; yea she laughed at my calamity till the tears streamed from her eyes.

16. I said therefore unto myself that I would die, and be gathered unto my fathers; for how could I live to be a scorn and a derision, and to be burnt up as with a devouring flame? and I had many thoughts of unrighteousness dwelling in me.

17. And she told her father of these matters; and Galli the scribe was wroth with me, and said unto me, Why wouldst thou betray my daughter, the child of my age, and the hope of my grey hairs?

18. Is it not better for thee to depart unto thine own country, and to thy kindred, than commit this great wickedness?

19. And my spirit was grieved within me; nevertheless I could not depart, for my heart clove to the maid, and I loved her as my own soul.

CHAPTER II

1. And it came to pass that the army of the prince of the land encamped in that place;

2. For he was a great prince, and had increased his army; and he had captains over hundreds, and captains over fifties, and captains over tens.

3. And these were clothed in gorgeous apparel, in brocade of gold, and in brocade of silver; and they were vain men, for they had the plumage of birds upon their heads, and gems of silver, and of gold, and of precious stones, on their breasts; and swords girded on their thighs.

4. And the damsel beheld them, and her heart danced with joy; yea, her eyes followed them whithersoever they went.

5. And I was more grieved than ever; therefore I counselled her, and said all manner of evil of the men.

6. But she would not hearken to my reproof, but cast all my counsel behind her back; and she derided me.

7. And it came to pass, in the process of time, that one of the captains of fifty came to her, and spoke kind words unto her, even great swelling words of vanity.

8. And she hearkened unto him, and her ears drunk in his burning speeches, even as the ox drinketh in water; and she delighted therein; and he looked into her eye, and behold he saw his own image impressed in it, as in a glass.

9. And he looked into it many times, and it grew brighter; and every time that he looked into it he saw his own image the more deeply and strongly reflected, until he knew that he lived in her heart.

10. But her image was not in his eye.

11. And I knew this, and was grieved. Therefore I withstood him to his face, and rebuked him; yea, and I also cursed him.

12. But the captain of fifty mocked me; he also told the maid, and she became wroth with me, so that, the two being combined against me, I could do nothing but sit down and weep.

13. And she gave unto him all that she had; yea she gave him until she had no more to give, for she gave unto him herself.

14. And her countenance was changed; her bright eyes retained not their wonted brightness; her voice was broken, and her tongue faltered in her mouth.

15. But the captain of fifty regarded it not; for he left her and went his way, and he did eat and drink, and made himself merry with wine.

16. And he said, What is a maiden that I should regard her? or for what were the daughters of women formed but for my pleasure?

17. And the prince of the kingdoms of the land sent unto his army, that they should go into a far country to fight against the enemies of their lord the king. And the men purposed to go; and the captain of fifty purposed to go also.

18. And when the maiden heard of it her heart failed within her, and she fell sick, and I feared it would be to death.

19. And I tried to comfort her; and I watched with her day and night, and prayed many prayers for her; but she became worse, for her spirit was wounded and cast down.

20. And Galli the scribe was also sorely afflicted, and he mourned exceedingly, saying, Alas! what shall I do for my daughter! she who was the hope of my age, and my only comfort here below. Wo is me, for she is dying of a lingering disease, and I shall be left childless! Now Galli the scribe knew not what the captain of fifty had done unto her, nor of all that she had given unto him.

21. So I went forth unto the host to seek this betrayer of women, and to speak peaceably with him, and to reason with him.

22. But he knew me afar off, and said to his brethren, Lo, here cometh that man of a strange country, let us make him our sport.

23. And they combined against me, and treated me with great indignity; for they bound my hands and put me into the river, and the flood carried me away, so that I said in mine heart, lo, I shall be drowned, for there is not one to pity or save me.

24. But they took me forth before my breath departed clean away; and they stripped me naked, and tied me to a stake, and scourged me.

25. And afterwards they stoned me out of the camp.

26. And I was very wroth, and went unto the captain

of the host, and made my complaint known unto him.

27. And I said, O my lord, hearken unto the voice of thy servant. Behold one of your captains of fifty came unto the house of Galli the scribe.

28. And the man intreated him kindly, yet hath he betrayed his daughter, and refuseth to do her justice; and the maid will die, and her father, who is a good man, will go down to the grave with her.

29. And he answered and said unto me, What have I to do with this matter, or with thee? As a maid treadeth the wine press, so let her drink. It is not meet that I should be troubled with these things.

30. And I went away and wept bitterly, for I could find neither consolation nor redress; and I saw that the wickedness of the men was very great.

31. Then I went and trimmed my beard, and borrowed me a suit of armour; and I put an helmet of steel upon mine head, and a breast-plate upon my breast, and I girded on a sword.

32. And I went forth and challenged the captain of fifty to fight with me.

33. And I said in mine heart, Lo, I will fight this wicked man, and overcome him. And I will take his sword from him, and rend his armour from off his loins.

34. And then will I compel him to do justice to those whom he hath wronged, else will I smite off his head.

35. And we met by the side of the river; and he discerned me not through my disguise, for he said unto me, Who art thou, or what have I to say to thee?

36. And I said, For the wrong that thou hast done to the house of Galli the scribe have I called thee out to battle.

37. And he said, Thou hast done well. I will chastise thee as thou deservest, that thou mayest learn how to lift up thy hand against the servants of our lord the king.

38. So we fought; and his hand was sore against me.

39. For he drove me out of my place, and wounded me, and my hope had nearly perished.

40. But I prayed to the Lord for strength. And we fought again; and the combat was very sore that day, and he prevailed not against me.

41. And after the combat had lasted until my breath was spent, and my arm weary, by the help of the Lord I wounded him in the loins, so that my sword found a passage through his body, and he fell.

42. And I was sore afraid; and fled away, and hid myself; for I trembled at the thing I had done, because I perceived that the last case was worse than the first.

43. And when the soldiers came to him, he said that Galli the scribe had sent out ruffians to slay him.

44. And when these things were told to the captain of the host, he was exceedingly wroth, and he sent forth men to destroy the house of Galli the scribe, and to slay him, and take his substance for a prey.

45. And the captain of fifty died that night; and they buried him with great lamentation, for they wept over him, saying, Alas! our brother! for he hath been cut off before his time.

CHAPTER III

1. And it came to pass, that after I had laid aside my armour, and put on my pilgrim weeds, that I went forth into the plain, and into the city.

2. And when I heard the words of the captain of the host, and the command that he had given, I hasted to the house of Galli the scribe, and said unto him, Go to, put up all thy money, and thy jewels, and fly for thy life, for behold evil is determined concerning thee.

3. But he would not hearken to my voice; for he said, I have done no man wrong.

4. And I intreated him, but prevailed not.

5. Therefore I went unto his daughter, and told her of what I had heard; and I said, Rise up, make haste and escape, for the soldiers will abuse thee.

6. And she was afraid, and said unto me, Take me, and hide me for a short time, for thy words have never deceived me.

7. And I hid her in a palm tree, and remained with her.

8. And the men who belonged to the captain of fifty, even to him whom I slew in battle, came as they were commanded; and they entered into the possessions of

Galli the scribe, and they took all that he had for a prey, and burned his house with fire.

9. And we beheld all from our hiding-place, and were greatly astonished; for we saw Galli the scribe flying through the garden, and the soldiers pursuing hard after him, with their swords drawn.

10. And when his daughter saw it she shrieked and fainted away; and when the men heard her voice they looked about, and some of them ran into the arbour, but they found her not, therefore they pursued after Galli the scribe.

11. And I trembled sore, for I knew not if we were discovered, neither could I support the maiden in her seat.

12. For she beheld whose men they were that pursued after her father to slay him, and she deemed that her captain of fifty had sent out his fifty to devour them, yea to destroy, and to slay, and to ravage; and there was no more spirit in her.

13. And I prayed to the Lord my God out from among the branches of the palm tree, and he heard my voice.

14. For the spoilers came, and they sought, but they found us not.

15. For their eyes were blinded that they could not see. We beheld their eyes, and heard the threatenings that proceeded out of their mouths, yet could they not perceive us.

16. And their threatenings were filled with the abominations of iniquity, for the men were very wicked.

17. And I took her out of the palm tree by night; and I covered her with my sackcloth gown, and we tried to fly and make our escape, but she could not; therefore my distress was very great.

18. And I carried her to the house of a poor widow in the suburbs of the city, and I concealed her there till her strength should recover.

19. And I went about making many inquiries; and I heard that the soldiers had taken Galli the scribe, and had given him up to be persecuted, and tormented, and slain; also that the whole army were abroad searching to recover his daughter, to execute vengeance on her.

20. And I was grieved for that I had done, and for bringing

evil on those I loved; for I knew that the men of the host spoiled the people, and did according to their will.

21. So I borrowed me a pilgrim's robes, and in these I equipped the maiden; and when she was clothed in her flowing sackcloth gown, with her cross, scallop, and shell, behold I myself could not discern her.

22. And we escaped from the city by night, and journeyed toward the north, and at break of day we came to the fords of the great river, where we were encountered by three of the soldiers of the guard, who waylaid us.

23. And I said unto them, Whom seek ye? And they said, We be sent out to seek the daughter of Galli the scribe, for she hath betrayed one of the captains into her nets, and hath robbed him, and also caused him to be cut off from his men; therefore are we sent out to take her, that she may be delivered into the hands of his men, that they may do to her as seemeth good in their eyes.

24. And the maiden trembled, so that the men beheld it; and I turned and said unto her, Said I not that it was so?

25. And I said furthermore, Sit thee down, my brother, until we converse with these men, for they are good men, and filled with wisdom; and lo, have not I strange things to relate unto them?

26. And the men sat down, and we sat down beside them.

27. And I said, We are pilgrims and strangers, and come from a far country. And they said, Peace be unto you.

28. And I said, moreover, that it was given unto me to dream dreams, and to see visions, and that I had a vision of my head upon my bed, which was of this Galli the scribe of whom they spake.

29. For I saw and beheld that he had put forth his hand on a captain of the servants of my lord the king, and had sent forth his bravadoes, who had wounded him until the sword passed through him, even from the left side unto the right. And the men said, Is not this wonderful?

30. And behold I saw the servants of my lord the king enter the dwelling of the man, even of the scribe, and take his goods, and him they pursued with the edge of the

sword, and took by the vineyard as thou goest down towards a river.

31. And they burned his house with fire, so that the flames ascended up on high; and his daughter who was sick, and concealed in an inner chamber, her also did they burn until she was quite consumed.

32. And the men wondered exceedingly; and they bowed down their heads and said, Thou hast told unto us strange things. It is even as thou hast said. Go on your way.

33. And I blessed them; and they returned to tell unto their captains the wonderful things which they had heard.

34. And I fled with the damsel until I came to the sea; and when we had found a ship we went into it, and I brought her to my own country, but not to my kindred, for I placed her in the holy isle near the river of the north.

35. And she mourned night and day for her father, and also for the captain of fifty, whom she called her husband; for she dreaded that some evil had befallen unto him.

36. For, on the day that he had sworn to her, he had given her a graven image, which she kept hid in her bosom, and she wept over it and kissed it.

37. And I was grieved, and rebuked her, but she refused to be comforted; and I went and came and brought her of the good things of the land, for I loved her as the breath of my nostrils.

38. And when the days of her months were fulfilled, behold she brought forth a daughter.

39. And the babe was also beautiful to look upon. And the bosom of the mother yearned over her child, and she called her by her father's name, even by the name of the captain of fifty.

40. And she kissed her child, and wept over it day and night; but the frame and substance of her body were wasted away with perpetual grief, and I saw that the child would die.

41. And when I saw the countenance that was once beautiful as the morning bathed in tears, as her babe lay at a breast in which there was no nourishment, I was exceedingly sorry even unto death.

42. And lo, I took the child and nourished it; yea I fed it with bread and with wine, with butter also, and with honey and milk from the beasts of the field; and the child was restored.

43. But the mother decayed like a flower that is cut down; for the winds of grief had passed over her, and her spirit was consumed. The summer came, and all the herbs of the field were renewed, but the fairest flower of the land was bending down to meet the clay.

CHAPTER IV

1. And it came also to pass that as soon as I found myself in a land of safety, I wrote many letters to Galli the scribe; for I said, Peradventure he may escape out of their hands.

2. I wrote also to the chief of our order, giving account of the whole matter, and attesting the innocence of Galli the scribe.

3. But no answer came to me, therefore was I sore distressed; for I said, If the mother and babe both perish, what shall become of me?

4. And one day as I sat with the babe on my knee, I beheld, and, lo, the eyes of the mother were fixed mournfully on her babe, and she lifted them to my face, and looked at her babe again.

5. And I could not contain myself; so I lifted up my voice and wept bitterly.

6. But she smiled, and said, Wherefore shouldst thou weep? Behold, am not I in the hand of the Lord? And my child, the daughter of my youth, and of my love, thou also art in the hands of thy Maker.

7. May he lead thee, and guide thee, and keep thee from the snares in which thy mother hath fallen.

8. Though thou hast lost thy father, as I also have lost mine, yet hast thou a Father in Heaven who will not forsake thee. Neither shalt thou altogether lack a father's care here below.

9. And she said to me, Is it not even so?

10. And I could not answer her, for I wept aloud; yea, I even wept until the child grew affrighted, and wept also.

11. And the mother took the graven image from her neck, and from her bosom; and she kissed it, and hung it round the neck of her babe.

12. And she said, It is the image and likeness of thy father, wear it, my child, till the day of thy death.

13. Peradventure thou mayest fall among his people, and among his kindred, for they were men of honour and renown.

14. And she kissed her child, and said, Now shall I be taken from thee, and go to my grave, and they will bury me, my babe, among strangers, and there is none of my people to shed a tear over me.

15. And we all wept abundantly, and shed many tears.

16. And while we yet cried aloud, lifting up our voices, behold one entered in, and said, Peace be with you!

17. And I discerned him not, for mine eyes flowed like two fountains of water.

18. But the woman cried out, and sprang from her couch, and she clasped her arms around his neck, and said, My father! my father!

19. And behold it was Galli the scribe.

20. And the woman said, Now hath my child found a father indeed.

21. And he said, Blessed and happy mayest thou be, my daughter, for I bring thee joyful tidings, and blessed be this man who hath befriended and saved thee. His intercession hath also saved the life of thy father; all that was mine hath been restored to me, yea, and more also.

22. And I will give all unto thee and to thy child after thee, and thou shalt have riches and honours in thy own country, and among thy own people.

23. But his daughter answered him not, for the words died on her tongue; but she looked in his face and smiled, and then she looked at her babe as it lay on my knee.

24. And Galli the scribe was sore amazed, and said, What aileth thee, my daughter? and why answerest thou not to the words of thy father?

25. And he held her in his arms, and her hands were clasped around his neck that they would not be loosed.

26. And behold there was a sound like a small voice issued from her mouth, and the light of her eyes became dim, and her head fell back over the arm of her father.

27. And her gentle spirit departed away unto him that gave it; for she spoke no more, neither breathed she any more.

28. And we buried her in the isle of the holy place, and mourned for her many days.

29. And I besought of Galli the scribe that he would leave the child with me, that I might bring her up in our convent, and breed her in the ways of purity and truth.

30. But he refused, and said, I cannot part with the child of my only daughter; she shall go with me and be the heiress of all that I possess.

31. And after I had blessed him, he departed with the little maid to go to his own land, and I saw them no more.

32. For after many years had elapsed, I went again into the country beyond the river, and I visited the house of Galli the scribe.

33. But behold he had never returned to that place; and the people of the land reported unto me, that he fell among thieves, and was slain, and the babe was slain with him, or led into captivity.

34. The ways of heaven are unsearchable, and the hand of man often worketh out its decrees. But for the misfortunes that befel the house of Galli the scribe will I go mourning till the day of my death.

CHAPTER EIGHTEEN

Beef steaks and bacon hams
I can eat as lang's I'm able,
Cutlets, chops, and mutton pies;
Pork's the king o' a' the table!
Fragment of an old Bacchanalian Song

'IT HAS MADE my heart very sair that tale,' said Charlie;
'I wish you hadna tauld it.'

'I think it is nae tale ata',' said Tam Craik: 'If I coudna
hae tauld a better tale than that, I wad never hae begun. I
could now wager sax merks, and sax brass mowdiworts to
boot, that the Gospel-friar is the man that shall be the first
to thole the knife. And what for should he no? He'll make
the best mart amang us.'

'I differ widely from you,' said the poet, 'with regard to
the merits of the tale. I love the friar for telling it; and I love
him ten times better for the part he took in the transaction.
How I do admire the love that has no selfish flaw, no moiety
of sense to prompt its aberrations! Should I ever get free
from this vile pinnacle – this grave in altitude – I'll search
the world for that dear child, and find her too, if in the
world she be.'

'Alas! I have searched, and searched in vain,' answered
the friar. 'It was so long before I knew of the mishap of
my friend, and my darling child, that all memory of the
transaction was lost. I would travel from sea to sea, and
from the river to the ends of the earth, to find out that
dear, that beloved maiden; and could I find her I would
yet put her in possession of the inheritance of her father.
For I have instructed the heads of our order, and they are
preserving it in their own hands as the patrimony of the
orphan and the fatherless.'

During the time of the friar's narrative, Delany had been sitting close by his knee in fixed and earnest attention; and at this time there chancing to be a pause in the conversation, she looked wistfully about, as if afraid she was going to commit herself by telling a lie. But there was such a beam of intelligence playing over her lovely countenance, that all the party fixed their eyes on her, as if watching with the deepest interest what she was going to say.

'I have a confused dream of having heard something of this story before,' said she: 'but subsequent events had quite obliterated the traces of it from my memory, till this narrative renewed them: I think I can give you some intelligence of this lost maiden. You said she was called by her father's name. Do you recollect what that father of hers was called?'

'Ay, that I will never forget while memory retains her seat in this repentant bosom,' said the friar. 'His name was Captain Jacques De-la-Veny.'

'The very same,' said the maid. 'Then do you know ought of this? Or did you ever see it before?' – and she took a small miniature from her bosom, holding it near to the friar's eye.

'By the blessed stars of heaven, and the Holy Virgin that rules above them!' exclaimed the friar; 'it is the graven image of the captain of fifty whom I slew in battle. I saw it placed in thy bosom, yea I held thee on my knee till that chain of gold was locked about thy neck never to be removed. Thou art indeed the daughter of the fairest and the comeliest among women – of her whom I loved far above my own life, and for whom I travailled in pain; yea, thou art the child that I nursed and held on my knee, and all the inheritance of thy fathers is thine. Blessed be thou, my daughter! and blessed be they who have preserved thee! Come to my bosom my child, my beloved, my fair one, that I may fall on thy neck, and bless thee, and weep over thee; for my soul rejoiceth that I have found thee.'

The poet could stand it no longer; he threw himself at the maiden's feet, and embraced them, and wept aloud. Charlie was busied in drawing pictures of swords and cross-bows on the floor with the brazen end of his sheathe,

and always giving a loud sob as if his heart would burst.
Even Master Michael Scott once drew the back of his hand
across his eyes, though no one believed it was ought of
sympathy that affected him.

'The abbreviation of the name was so natural in the
mouths of the people of this land,' said the friar, 'that I
wonder I should never have recognised it, nor yet on the
face of my dear child the features of her mother. Hard has
been thy lot, and the lot of thy fathers, but blessings may
yet remain in store for thee.'

'I dinna see where they're to come frae,' said Charlie,
sighing louder than ever. 'It wad be the hardest thing I
ever kend, if ane sae young, sae bonnie, and sae good,
after a' that she has borne, should be prickit up atween
the yird and the heaven here, to be hungered to dead, and
then eaten wi' the corbies.'

'Life's sweet to us a',' said Gibbie: 'She wad be as little
missed as ony that's here, if she *should* be starved to death
wi' hunger.'

'She shall *not* be starved to death wi' hunger;' cried
Charlie, in a tone of valiant desperation. 'Na, na; afore
she die o' hunger after a' she has come through, I'll
rather cut a limb off my ain body and feed her wi't. An
Corbie be spared, I can e'en ride by the warden's side wi'
a timmer ane.'

'God bless you, for a kind heart,' cried the poet.

'Gin I thought I were to win her mysel,' said Tam, 'and
win away wi' life out o' this luckless place, I wad do a good
deal for her; but if I trowed ony o' you were to get her frae
me – I'll no tell you how I feel.'

'Just as a hungry man should feel,' said Gibbie; 'and as
ane wha has starvation afore his een maun feel. It is e'en
a sair trial, and often brings me a-mind o' the story of
Marion Gib's callant.'

Master Michael Scott, thinking that, in right of seniority,
the Laird was now about to begin his trial story for life
or death, made a signal with his hand for his guests to
compose themselves, which they did with one consent;
while Gibbie, pleased with the mark of deference shown
to him, went on: –

There wad aiblins nane o' you ken Marion. She lived i' the Dod-Shiel; and had a callant to the lang piper, him that Squire Ridley's man beat at the Peel-hill meeting. Weel, you see, he was a gilliegaupy of a callant, gayan like the dad o' him; for Marion said he wad hae eaten a horse ahint the saddle; and as her shieling wasna unco weel stored o' meat, she had ill getting him mainteened; till at the lang and the last it just came to this pass, that whenever Jock was i' the house, it was a constant battle atween Marion and him. Jock fought to be at meat, and Marion to keep him frae it, and mony hard clouts and claws there past. They wad hae foughten about a haggis, or a new kirning o' butter, for a hale hour, and the battle generally endit in Jock's getting a', or a good share o' ilka thing. (I wish we had sic things here, even though we had to fight for them!) When he had fairly gained the possession, by whatever means, he feasted with the greatest satisfaction, licking his large ruddy lips, and looking all about him with eyes of the utmost benevolence. Marion railed all the while that the poor lad was enjoying himself, without any mercy and restraint, and there wasna a vile name under the sun that had ony signification of a glutton in it, that she didna ca' him by. Jock took the bite wi' the buffet; – he heard a' the ill names, and munched away. Oh, how his heart did rejoice o'er a fat lunch o' beef, a good haggis, or even a cog o' milk brose! Poor fellow! such things were his joy and delight. So he snapped them up, and in two or three hours after he was as ready for another battle as ever.

This was a terrible life to lead. Times grew aye the langer the waur; and Marion was obliged to hire poor Jock to Goodman Niddery, to herd his kye and his pet sheep. Jock had nae thoughts at a' o' ganging to sic a job at first; but Marion tauld him ilka day o' the fat beef, the huge kebbucks, and the parridge sae thick that a horn-spoon wadna delve into them, till he grew impatient for the term day. That day came at length, and Marion went away hame wi' her son to introduce him. The road was gayan lang, and Jock's crappin began to craw. He speered a hunder times about the meat at Goodman Niddery's house, and every answer that Marion gae was better than the last, till

Jock believed he was gaun hame to a continual feast. It was a delightful thought, for the craving appetite within him was come to a great height. They reached the place, and went into the kitchen. Jock's een were instantly on the look-out; but they didna need to range far. Above the fire there hung two sides of bacon more than three inches deep of fat, besides many other meaner objects: The hind legs of bullocks, sheep, and deer, were also there; but these were withered, black, and sapless in appearance. Jock thought the very substance was dried out o' them. But the bacon! How it did make Jock smack his lips! It was so juicy that even the brown bristly skin on the outside of it was all standing thick o' eenbright beaming drops like morning dew. Jock was established at Goodman Niddery's; he would not have flitted again and left these two sides of bacon hanging there for an estate. Marion perceived well where the sum of his desires was fixed, and trembled for fear of an instant attack: Well might she; for Jock had a large dirk or sheathed knife (a very useful weapon) that he wore, and that he took twice out of its place, looked at its edge, and then at the enormous bacon ham, which was more than three inches deep of solid fat, with the rich drops of juice standing upon the skin. Jock drew his knife on his sandal, then on the edge of a wooden table that stood beside him, examined the weapon's edge again, and again fixed his green eyes on the bacon. 'What do the people mean,' thought he to himself, 'that they do not instantly slice down a portion of that glorious meat, and fry it on the coals? Would they but give me orders to do it – would they even give me the least hint, how slashingly I would obey!'

None of them had the good sense to give Jock ony sic orders. He was two or three times on the very point of helping himself, and at last got up on his feet, it was believed, for the sole purpose of making an attack on the bacon ham, when, behold, in came Goodman Niddery.

'There's your master, sirrah!' whispered Marion, 'haste ye and whup aff your bonnet.'

Jock looked at him. There was something very severe and forbidding in his countenance; so Jock's courage failed him, and he even took aff his bonnet, and sat down with that in his one hand and the drawn knife in the other. Marion's heart was greatly relieved, and she now ventured on a little conversation:

'I hae brought you hame my lad, Goodman, and I hope he'll be a good servant to you.'

'I coudna say, Marion: Gin he be as gude as you ca'ed him, he'll do. I think he looks like ane that winna be behind at his bicker.'

'Ay, weel I wat, Goodman, and that's true; and I wadna wish it were otherwise. Slaw at the meat, slaw at the wark, ye ken.'

'That *is* a good hint o' my mother's!' thinks Jock to himsel: 'What though I should show the auld niggard a sample? The folk o' this house surely hae nae common sense.'

The dinner was now, however, set down on the kitchen-table. The goodman sat at the head, the servants in a row on each side, and Jock and his mother at the foot. The goodwife stood behind her servants, and gave all their portions. The dinner that day consisted of broad bannocks, as hard as horn, a pail of thin sour milk, called whig, and a portion of a large kebbuck positively as dry as wood. Jock was exceedingly dissatisfied, and could not but admire the utter stupidity of the people, and their total want of all proper distinction. He thought it wonderful that rational creatures should not know what was good for them. He munched, and munched, and gnawed at the hard bread and cheese, till his jaws were sore; but he never once looked at the food before him; but leaning his cheek on his hand to rest his wearied grinders somewhat at every bite he took, and every splash of the sour shilpy milk that he lapped in, he lifted his eyes to the fat bacon ham with the juice standing on it in clear bells.

Marion wished herself fairly out of the house, for she perceived there would be an outbreak; and to prepare the good people for whatever might happen, she said before going away – 'Now, good-wife, my callant's banes are green, and he's a fast growing twig; I want to ken if he will get plenty o' meat here.'

'I winna answer for that, Marion; – he shall fare as the lave fare; but he's maybe no very easily served. There are some misleared servants wha think they never get enough.'

'Tell me this thing, then, goodwife; will he see enough?'
'Ay; I shall answer for that part o't.'
'Then I shall answer for the rest, goodwife.'

Jock had by this time given up contending with the
timber cheese, and the blue sour milk, and, taking a lug
of a bannock in his hand, the size of a shoe sole, he went
away and sat down at the fireside, where he had a full view
of the bacon ham, three inches thick of fat, with the dew
standing on its brown skin.

The withered bread swallowed rather the better of this
delicious sight; so Jock chewed and looked, and looked and
chewed, till his mother entered into the security mentioned.
'That is a capital hint,' thought Jock; 'I shall verify my good
mother's cautionry, for I can stand this nae langer.' He
sprang up on a seat, sliced off a large flitch of bacon, and
had it on the coals before one had time to pronounce a
word; and then turning his back to it, and his face to the
company, he stood with his drawn dirk quite determined
to defend his prey.

The goodwife spoke first up. 'Gudeness have a care o' us!
see to the menseless tike!' cried she; 'I declare the creature
has na the breeding o' a whalp!'

Jock was well used to such kind of epithets; so he bore
this and some more with the utmost suavity, still, however,
keeping his ground.

Goodman Niddery grinned, and his hands shook with
anger, as if struck with a palsy; but for some reason or
other he did not interfere. The servants were like to burst
with laughter; and Jock kept the goodwife at bay with his
drawn knife, till his slice was roasted; and then, laying it
flat on his dry piece of bread, he walked out to the field to
enjoy it more at leisure. Marion went away home; and the
goodman and goodwife both determined to be revenged
on Jock, and to make him pay dear for his audacity.

Jock gave several long looks after Marion as she vanished
on Kettlemoor, but he had left no kind of meat in
her shieling when he came away, else it was likely he
would have followed his mother home again. He was
still smacking his lips after his rich repast, and he had
seen too much good stuff about the house of his new
master to leave it at once; so he was even fain to bid
Marion good-b'ye in his heart, wipe the filial tear from

his eye, poor man, and try to reconcile himself to his new situation.

'Do you carry aye that lang gully knife about wi' you, master cowherd, or how do they ca' ye?' said his master, when they next met after the adventure of the bacon.

'I hae aye carried it yet,' said Jock, with great innocence; 'and a gay gude whittle it is.'

'Ye maun gie that up,' said Niddery; 'we dinna suffer chaps like you to carry sic weapons about our house.'

Jock fixed his green eyes on his master's face. He could hardly believe him to be serious; still there was something in his look he did not like; so he put his knife deeper into his pocket, drew one step back, and, putting his under row of teeth in front of those above, waited the issue of such an unreasonable demand.

'Come, come; give it up I say. Give it to me; I'll dispose of it for you.'

'I'll see you at the bottom o' the place my mother speaks about whiles,' thought Jock to himself, 'afore I gi'e my gully either to you or ony that belangs to you.' He still kept his former position, however, and the same kind of look at his master's face, only his een grew rather greener.

'Won't you give it up, you stubborn thief? Then I will take it, and give you a good drubbing into the bargain.'

When Jock heard this, he pulled out his knife. 'That is a good lad to do as you are bidden,' said his master. But Jock, instead of delivering up his knife, drew it from the sheathe, which he returned to his pocket. 'Now I sal only say this,' said he; 'the first man that tries to take my ain knife frae me – he may do it – but he shall get the length o't in his monyplies first.' So saying, he drew back his hand with a sudden jerk.

Goodman Niddery gave such a start that he actually leaped off the ground, and holding up both his hands, exclaimed, 'What a savage we have got here! what a satan!' And without speaking another word he ran away to the house, and left Jock standing with his drawn knife in his hand.

The goodman's stomach burned with revenge against Jock; so that night he sent him supperless to bed, out of requital for the affair of the fat bacon; and next day the poor boy was set down to a very scanty breakfast, which was not fair. His eye turning invariably to one delicious object, the goodman perceived well what was passing in his heart; and, on some pretence, first sent away all the servants and then the goodwife. He next rose up himself, with his staff in his hand, and, going slowly away into the little parlour, said, as he went through the kitchen, 'What can be become o' a' the fo'k?' and with that entered the dark door that opened in a corner. He made as though he had shut the door, but he turned about within it and peeped back.

The moment that he vanished was the watch-word for Jock; he sprang from his seat at the bottom of the table, and, mounting a form, began to whang away at the bacon ham. Some invidious bone, or hard object of some sort, coming unfortunately in contact with the edge of his knife, his progress was greatly obstructed; and though he cut and sawed with all his might, before he succeeded in separating a piece of about two pounds weight from the main body, his master had rushed on him from his concealment, and, by one blow of his staff, laid him flat on the floor. The stroke was a sore one, for it was given with extreme good will, and deprived Jock of sensibility for the time being. He and his form both came down with a great rumble, but the knife remained buried in the fat bacon ham; and the inveterate goodman was not satisfied with felling the poor lad, but kicked him, and laid on him with his stick after he was down. The goodwife at length came running, and put a stop to this cruelty; and fearing the boy was murdered, and that they would be hanged for it, she got assistance, and soon brought Jock again to himself.

Jock had been accustomed to fight for his meat, and, in some measure laid his account with it, so that, on the whole, he took his broken head as little to heart as could have been expected – certainly less than any other boy of the same age would have done. It was only a little more rough than he had been prepared to look for; but had he succeeded in his enterprise, he would not have been ill content. The goodwife and her maids had laid him on a kitchen bed and bathed his temples; and on recovering from stupefaction, the first thing he did was to examine his pockets to see if he had his gully. Alak! there was nothing but the empty sheathe. Then he *did* lose the field, and fell a blubbering and crying. The goodwife thought he was ill, and tried to sooth him by giving him some meat. He took the meat of course, but his heart was inconsolable; till, just when busy with his morsel, his eye chanced to travel to the old place as if by instinct, and there he beheld the haft of his valued knife sticking in the bacon ham, its blade being buried deep in sappy treasures. He sprang over the bed, and traversing the floor with staggering steps, mounted a form, and stretched forth his hand to possess himself again of his gully.

'Aih! Gudeness have a care o' us,' cried the goodwife; 'saw ever ony body the like o' that? The creature's bacon mad! Goodman! goodman, come here!'

Jock, however, extricated his knife and fled, though he could scarcely well walk. Some of the maids averred that he at the same time slid a corner of the ham into his pocket; but it is probable they belied him, for Jock had been munching in the bed but the moment before.

He then went out to his cows, weak as he was. He had six cows, some mischievous calves, and ten sheep to herd; and he determined to take good care of these, as also, now that he had got his knife again, not to want his share of the good things about the house, of which he saw there was abundance. However, several days came and went, and Jock was so closely watched by his master and mistress all the time he was in the house, that he could get nothing but his own scanty portion. What was more, Jock was obliged every day to drive his charge far a-field, and remain with them from morn till evening. He got a few porridge in the morning, and a hard bannock and a bottle of sour milk to carry along with him for his dinner. This miserable meal was often despatched before eleven o'clock, so that poor Jock had to spend the rest of the day in fasting, and contriving grand methods of obtaining some good meat in future.

There was one thing very teasing: He had a small shieling, which some former herd had built, and plenty of sticks to burn for the gathering or cutting. He had thus a fire every day, without any thing to roast on it. Jock sat over it often in the most profound contemplation, thinking how delightfully a slice of bacon would fry on it – how he would lay the slice on his hard bannock, and how the juice would ooze out of it! Never was there a man who had richer prospects than Jock had: still his happiness lay only in perspective. But experience teaches man wisdom, and wisdom points out to him many expedients.

Among Jock's fat sheep there was one fat ewe lamb, the flower of the flock, which the goodwife and the goodman both loved and valued above all the rest. She was as beautiful and playful as innocence itself, and, withal, *as fat as she could lie in her skin*. There was one rueful day, and a hungry one, that Jock had sat long over his little fire of sticks, pondering on the joys of fat flesh. He went out to turn his mischievous calves, whose nebs were never out of an ill deed, and at that time they had strayed into the middle of a corn field. As bad luck would have it, by the way he perceived this dawted ewe lamb lying asleep in the sun; and, out of mere frolic, as any other boy would have done, he flew on above her and tried if he could hold her down. After hard struggling he mastered her, took her between his feet, stroked her snowy fleece and soft downy cheek, and ever, as he patted her, repeated these words, 'O but ye be a bonny beast!'

The lamb, however, was not much at her ease; she struggled a little now and then, but finding that it availed not, she gave it over; and seeing her comrades feeding near her, she uttered some piteous bleats. They could afford her no assistance, but they answered her in the same tremulous key. After patting her a good while, Jock began to handle her breast and ribs, and found that she was in good earnest *as fat as pork*. This was a ticklish experiment for the innocent lamb. Jock was seized with certain inward longings and yearnings that would not be repressed. He hesitated long, long, and sometimes his pity awoke – but there was another natural feeling that proved the stronger of the two; so Jock at length took out his long knife and unsheathed it. Next he opened the fleece on the lamb's throat till its bonny white skin was laid bare, and not a hair of wool to intervene between it and the point of his knife. He was again seized with deep remorse, as he contemplated the lamb's harmless and helpless look; so he wept aloud, and tried to put his knife again into its sheathe, but he could not.

To make a long tale short, Jock took away the lamb's

life, and that not in the most gentle or experienced way. She made no resistance, and only uttered one bleat. 'Poor beast!' said Jock; 'I daresay ye like this very ill, but I canna help it. Ye are suffering for a' your bits o' ill done deeds now.'

The day of full fruition and happiness for Jock was now arrived. Before evening he had roasted and eaten the kidneys, and almost the whole of the draught or pluck. His heart rejoiced within him, for never was there more delicious food. But the worst of it was, that the devils of calves were going all the while in the middle of a corn field, which his master saw from the house, and sent one running all the way to turn them. The man had also orders to 'waken the dirty blackguard callant if he was sleeping, and gie him his licks.'

Jock was otherwise employed; but, as luck would have it, the man did not come into his hut, nor discover his heinous crime; for Jock met him among the corn, and took a drubbing with all proper decorum.

But dangers and suspicions encompassed poor Jock now on every side. He sat down to supper at the bottom of the board with the rest of the servants, but he could not eat a single morsel. His eyes were not fixed on the bacon ham as usual, and moreover they had quite lost that sharp green gleam for which they were so remarkable. These were circumstances not to be overlooked by the sharp eyes of his master and mistress.

'What's the matter wi' the bit dirty callant the night?' said the latter. 'What ails you, sirrah, that you hae nae ta'en your supper? Are you weel eneugh?'

Jock wasna ill, he said; but he could not enter into particulars about the matter any farther. The goodman said, he feared the blade had been stealing, for he did not kythe like ane that had been fasting a' day; but after the goodwife and he had examined the hams, kebbucks, beef barrel, meal girnel, and every place about the house, they could discern nothing amissing, and gave up farther search, but nót suspicion.

Jock trembled lest the fat lamb might be missed in the morning when he drove out his flock, but it was never remarked that the lamb was a-wanting. He took very little breakfast, but drove his kine and sheep, and the devils of calves, away to the far field, and hasted to his wee housie. He borrowed a coal every day from a poor woman, who lived in a cot at the road side, to kindle his fire, and that day she noticed, what none else had done, that his coat was all sparked over with blood, and asked him of the reason. Jock was rather startled by the query, and gave her a very suspicious look, but no other answer.

'I fear ye hae been battling wi' some o' your neighbours,' said she.

This was a great relief for Jock's heart. 'Ay, just that,' said he, and went away with his coal.

What a day of feasting Jock had! He sliced and roasted, and roasted and ate till he could hardly walk. Once when the calves were going into a mischief, which they were never out of, he tried to run, but he could not run a foot; so he was obliged to lie down and roll himself on the ground, take a sleep, and then proceed to work again.

There was nutrition in the very steams that issued from Jock's hut; the winds that blew over it carried health and savoury delight over a great extent of country. A poor hungry boy that herded a few lean cows on an adjoining farm, chancing to come into the track of this delicious breeze, became at once like a statue. He durst not move a step for fear of losing the delicious scent; and there he stood with his one foot before the other, his chin on his right shoulder, his eyes shut and his mouth open, his nose being pointed straight to Jock's wee housie. The breeze still grew richer, till at last it led him as straight as there had been a hook in his nose to Jock's shieling; so he popped in, and found Jock at the sublime employment of cooking and eating. The boy gaped and stared at the mangled body of the lamb, and at the rich repast that was going on; but he was a very ignorant and stupid boy, and could not comprehend any thing; so Jock fed him with a good fat piece well roasted, and let him go again to his lean cows.

Jock looked very plump and thriving-like that night; his appearance was quite sleek, somewhat resembling that of a young voluptuary; and, to lull suspicion, he tried to take some supper, but not one bite or soap was he able to swallow. The goodwife, having by that time satisfied herself that nothing was stolen, became concerned about

Jock, and wanted him to swallow some physic, which he peremptorily refused to do.

'How can the puir thing tak ony meat?' said she. 'He's a' swalled i' the belly. Indeed I rather suspect that he's swalled o'er the hale body.'

The next morning, as Jock took out his drove, the goodman was standing at the road side to look at them. Jock's heart grew cold, as well it might, when the goodman called out to him, 'Callant, what hae you made o' the gude lamb?'

'Is she no there?' said Jock, after a long pause, for he was so much astounded that he could not speak at the first.

'Is she no there!' cried the goodman again in great wrath, imitating Jock's voice; 'If ye binna blind, ye may see that. But I can tell you, my man, gin ye hae letten ought happen to that lamb, ye had better never hae been born.'

'What can be comed o' the beast?' said Jock; 'I had better look the house, she's may be stayed in by herself.'

Jock didna wait for an order, but, glad to be a little farther off from his master, he ran back and looked the fold and sheephouse, and every nettle bush around them, as he had been looking for a lost knife.

'I can see naething o' her,' said he, as he came slounging back, hanging his head, and keeping aloof from the goodman, who still carried his long pike staff in his hand.

'But I'll mak you see her, and find her baith, hang-dog,' said he; 'or deil be in my fingers an I dinna twist your neck about. Are you sure you had her yestreen?'

O yes! Jock was sure he had her yestreen. The women were examined if they had observed her as they milked the cows. They could not tell. None of them had seen her; but they could not say she was not there. All was in commotion about the steading, for the loss of the dawted pet lamb, which was a favourite with every one of the family.

Jock drove his cattle and nine sheep to the field – roasted a good collop or two of his concealed treasure, and snapped them up, but found that they did not relish so well as formerly; for now that his strong appetite for fat flesh was somewhat allayed, yea even fed to loathing, he wished the lamb alive again: He began, moreover, to be in great bodily fear; and to provide against the probability of any discovery being made, he lifted the mangled remains of his prey, and conveyed them into an adjoining wood, where he covered them carefully up with withered leaves, and laid thorns above them, 'Now!' said Jock, as he left the thicket, 'let them find that out wha can.'

The goodman went to all the herds around enquiring after his lamb, but could hear no intelligence of her till he came to the cottage of poor Bessie, the old woman that had furnished Jock with a coal every day. When he put the question to her, the rock and the lint fell out of Bessie's hand, and she sat a while quite motionless.

'What war ye saying, goodman? War ye saying ye had lost your bonnie pet lamb?'

'Even sae, Bessie.'

'Then, goodman, I fear you will never see her living again. What kind o' callant is that ye hae gotten? He's rather a suspicious looking chap. I tentit his claes a' spairged wi' blude the tither day, and baith this and some days bygane he has brought in his dinner to me, saying that he dought nae eat it.'

Goodman Niddery could make no answer to this, but sat for a while grumphing and groaning as some late events passed over his mind; particularly how Jock's belly was swollen, and how he could not take any supper. But yet the idea that the boy had killed his favourite, and eaten her, was hardly admissible: the deed was so atrocious he could not conceive any human being capable of it, strong as circumstances were against his carnivorous herd. He went away with hurried and impatient steps to Jock's wee house, his old colley dog trotting before him, and his long pike-staff in his hand. Jock eyed him at a distance, and kept out of his path, pretended to be engaged in turning the calves to a right pasture, and running and threshing them with a long goad; for though they were not in any mischief then, he knew that they would soon be in some.

The goodman no sooner set his nose within Jock's shieling than he was convinced some horrid deed had been done. It smelled like a cook's larder; and, moreover, his old dog, who had a very good scent, was scraping among the ashes, and picking up fragments of something which he seemed very much to enjoy. Jock did not know what to do when he saw how matters stood, yet he still had hopes that nothing would appear to criminate him. The worst thing that he saw was the stupid hungered boy on the adjoining farm coming wading through the corn. He had left his dirty lean kine picking up the very roots of the grass, and had come snouking away in hopes of getting another fat bit for his impoverished stomach. But, when he saw Goodman Niddery come out of the cot with impassioned strides, he turned and ran through the strong corn with his whole might, always jumping up as he proceeded.

The goodman called angrily on his old dog to come after him, but he would not come, for he was working with his nose and fore feet among Jock's perfumed ashes with great industry; so the goodman turned back into the house, and hit him over the back with his long pike-staff, which made him glad to give over, and come out about his business; and away the two went to reconnoitre further.

As soon as the old dog was fairly a-field again, he took up the very track by which Jock had carried the carcase that morning, and went as straight as a line to the hidden treasure in the thicket. The goodman took off the thorns, and removed the leaves, and there found all that remained of his favourite and beautiful pet lamb. Her throat was all cut and mangled, her mouth open, and her tongue hanging out, and about one half of her whole body a-wanting. The goodman shed tears of grief, and wept and growled with rage over the mangled form, and forthwith resolved (which was hardly commendable) to seize Jock, and bring him to that very spot and cut his throat.

Jock might have escaped with perfect safety had he had the sense or foresight to have run off as soon as he saw his master enter the wood; but there seems to be an infatuation that directs the actions of some men. Jock did not fly, but went about and about, turning his kine one while, his nine sheep another, and always between hands winning a pelt at one of the ill-conditioned calves, till his incensed master returned from the fatal discovery, and came up to him. There was one excuse for him, he was not sure if the carcase had been found, for he could not see for the wood whether or not his master went to the very place, and he never thought of the sagacity of the dog.

When Goodman Niddery first left the wood, he was half running, and his knees were plaiting under him with the anticipation of horrid revenge. Jock did not much like his gait; so he kept always the herd of cows, and the sheep too, betwixt himself and this half-running master of his. But the goodman was too cunning for poor Jock; he changed his step into a very slow careless walk, and went into the middle of the herd of cows, pretending to be whistling a tune, although it was in fact no tune, but merely a concatenation of tremulous notes on C sharp, without the least fall of harmony. He turned about this cow and the other cow, watching Jock all the while with the tail of his eye, and trilling his hateful whistle. Jock still kept a due distance. At length the goodman called to him, 'Callant, come hither, like a man, and help me to wear this cow against the ditch. I want to get haud o' her.'

Jock hesitated. He did not like to come within stroke of his master's long stick, neither did he know on what pretence absolutely to refuse his bidding; so he stood still, and it was impossible to know by his looks whether he was going to comply or run off altogether. His master dreaded the latter, and called to him in a still kinder manner, until Jock at last unfortunately yielded. The two wore the cow, and wore the cow, up against the ditch, until the one was close upon her one side, and the other upon her other. 'Chproo! hawkie! chproo, my bonnie cow!' cried the goodman, spreading out his arms, with his pike-staff clenched fast in his right hand; then springing by the cow in a moment, he flew upon Jock, crying out, with the voice of a demon, 'D—n you, rascal! but I'll do for you now!'

Jock wheeled about to make his escape, and would have beat his master hollow, had he been fairly started, or timeously apprised of his dreadful danger; but ere he had run four or five steps the pike-staff came over the links of his neck such a blow that it laid him flat on his face in a mire. The goodman then seized him by the cuff of the neck with the one hand, and by the hair of his head with the other, and said, with a triumphant and malicious laugh, 'Now, get up, and come away wi' me, my braw lad, and I'll let you see sic a sight as you never saw. I'll let you see a wallydy sight! Get up, like a good cannie lad!'

As he said this he pulled Jock by the hair, and kicked him with his foot, until he obliged him to rise, and in that guise he led him away to the wood. He had a hold of his rough weatherbeaten hair with the one hand, and with the other he heaved the cudgel over him; and as they went the following was some of the discourse that passed between them.

'Come away, now, my fine lad. Are nae ye a braw, honest, good callant? Do nae ye think ye deserve something that's unco good frae me? Eh? Ay, ye surely deserve something better nor ordinar': And ye shall hae it too——.' (Then a kick on the posteriors, or a lounder with the staff——.) 'Come your ways like a sonsy, brave callant, and I'll let you see a bonny thing and a braw thing in yon brake o' the wood, ye ken.'

Jock cried so piteously that, if his master had not had a heart of stone, he would have relented, and not continued in his fatal purpose; but he only grew the longer the more furious.

'O let me gang! let me gang! let me gang!' cried Jock. 'Let me gang! let me gang! for it wasna me. I dinna ken naething about it ata'!'

'Ye dinna ken naething about what, my puir man?'

'About yon bit sheep i' the wood, ye ken.'

'You rascal! you rogue! you villain! you have confessed that you kend about it, when I wasna speiring ony sic question at you. You hound! you dog! you savage wolf that you are! Mother of God! but I will do for you! You whelp! you dog! you scoundrel! come along here.' (Another hard blow.) 'Tell me now, my precious lad, an ye war gaun to be killed, as ye ken something about killing, whether would you choose to have your throat cut, or to have your feet tied and be skinned alive?'

'O dinna kill me! dinna kill me!' cried poor Jock. 'My dear master, dinna kill me, for I canna brook it. Oh, oh! an ye kill me I'll tell my mother, that will I; and what will Marion say t'ye, when she has nane but me? Oh master dinna kill me, and I'll never do the like o't again!'

'Nay, I shall take warrant for that: you shall never do the like o't again!'

In this melancholy and heart-breaking manner he dragged him on all the way by the rough towsy head, kicking him one while, and beating him another, till he brought him to the very spot where the mangled remains of the pet lamb were lying. It was a blasting sight for poor Jock, especially as it doubled his master's rage and stern revenge, and these were, in all conscience, high enough wrought before. He twined the hapless culprit round by the hair, and knocked him with his fist, for he had dropped the staff to enable him to force Jock to the place of sacrifice; and he swore by many an awful oath, that if it should cost him his life, he would do to Jock as he had done to that innocent lamb.

With that he threw him on the ground, and got above him with his knees; and Jock having by that time lost all hope of moving his ruthless master by tears or prayers, began a struggling with the force which desperation sometimes gives, and fought with such success that it was with difficulty his master could manage him.

It was very much like a battle between an inveterate terrier and a bull dog; but, in spite of all that Jock could do, the goodman got out his knife. It was not, however, one like Jock's, for it had a folding blade, and was very hard to open, and the effecting of this was no easy task, for he could not get both his hands to it. In this last desperate struggle, Jock got hold of his master's cheek with his left hand, and his nails being very long, he held it so strait that he was like to tear it off. His master capered up with his head, holding it back the full length of Jock's arm; yet still being unable to extricate his cheek from Jock's hold, he raised up his knife in his right hand in order to open it with his teeth, and, in the first place, to cut off Jock's hand, and his head afterwards. He was holding down Jock with his right knee and his left hand; and while in the awkward capering attitude of opening his knife, his face was turned nearly straight up, and his eyes had quite lost sight of his victim. Jock held up his master's cheek, and squeezed it still the more, which considerably impeded his progress in getting the knife open; and, at that important moment, Jock whipped out his own knife, his old dangerous friend, and struck it into the goodman's belly to the haft. The moment he received the wound he sprang up as if he had been going to fly into the air, uttered a loud roar, and fell back above his dead pet lamb.

Lord, how Jock ran! He was all bespattered with blood, some of it his own, and some of it his master's; wanted the bonnet, and had the bloody knife in his hand; and was, without all doubt, a wild frightsome-looking boy. As he sped through the wood, he heard the groans and howls of

his master in the agonies of death behind him. Every one
of them added to Jock's swiftness, till it actually became
beyond the speed of mortal man. If it be true that love lends
a pair of wings, fear, mortal fear, lends two pair. There is
nought in life I regret so much as that I did not see Jock
in this flight; it must have been such an extraordinary one.
There was poor Jock flying with the speed of a fox from
all the world, and yet still flying into the world. He had no
home, no kindred to whom he durst now retreat, no hold
of any thing in nature, save of his own life and his good
whittle; and he was alike unwilling to part with either of
these. The last time he was seen was by two women on
Kirtle-common. He appeared sore bespent, but was still
running on with all his might.

The goodman was found before the evening, but only
lived to tell how he had come by his end. All his friends
and servants were raised, and sent in pursuit of Jock. How
he eluded them no man knows; but from that day Marion's
Jock has never been more seen or heard of in this land.

CHAPTER NINETEEN

> *Cher.* That story of our captain's is rather an odd story.
> Is it not, Mark? *Mark.* Rather of the wonderful.
>
> *Ford*

'I DINNA KEN but I could maybe tell ye something about him an I liket,' said Tam Craik, 'but I wad maybe be as wise to haud my tongue.'

'I wad like very weel to hear mair about him,' said Charlie; 'for his life has had such a queer beginning, it maun surely hae had a queer end.'

'But what an it shouldna be endit yet, Yardbire,' said Tam: 'Marion's Jock is perhaps living, and life-like, to tell his ain tale. However, we'll say nae mair about that just now, till you tell us what you think o' Gibbie Jordan's tale. For my part, I never heard a tale I was sae muckle interested in a' my life.'

'It is ane o' the best tales *o' the kind* that ever I heard,' said Charlie.

'It is a most abominable tale,' said the poet.

'In what way, Master Poet?' said Charlie: 'I dinna like to hear ony body condemned without reason.'

'It is for the badness of the moral that I do it dislike,' said the poet: 'The moral is so truly bad, all mankind it must shock; it is to kill this harmless lamb, the flower of all the flock – to feed upon her lovely form that's fairer than the snow – to eat her flesh and drink her blood! It makes mine eyes to flow!'

'Gude faith, an I thought that war his drift, I wad brain him,' said Charlie; 'and I confess it looks rather like it.'

'There can be no doubt of it,' said Master Michael Scott: 'The maid Delany is the favourite lamb, whom he wishes you to kill and feast on in the same delicious manner as did the hero of his tale; and I am the goodman whom you are to stick afterwards, and fairly make your escape.'

'It is a shocking tale I really doubt,' said Charlie; 'and throws a disgrace and an imputation o' something unseemly on my chief and a' his friends, and I winna put up wi' it.'

'I do propose that from the walls the caitiff we do throw,' said the poet; 'or kill and eat for dainty meat the laird of Peatstacknowe.'

'I fear if the votes were to be ta'en just now he wad hae an ill chance,' said Charlie: 'But it's fair in ha' where beards wag a'. Let ilk ane o' us hae a fair chance. There may be mae bad morals amang us. Wha's turn is't next?'

Charlie himself, being next in point of seniority, was called on for his tale.

'I hae been thinking hard what tale I should tell you,' said Charlie; 'but I find I can tell nought but the thing I hae seen, and I'll be pinched sair eneuch to make sense o' that. Therefore, gin ye like, I'll tell ye my first adventure in war – for I aye mind it the best, and will do as lang as I live.'

Charlie Scott's Tale

It was under the command of Hab Elliot that I made my first raide; a gay rough spun cout he was, and nae cannie hand for a southland valley. Well, you see, there was a chap came to my father's house at Yardbire ae morning, and he says to my father, 'Wat,' says he, (that was my father's name, what he ca'ed me Charlie for I dinna ken, for I never spier'd,) 'Wat,' says the chiel, 'ye maun raise your lads, and tie on your wallets, and meet the warden the morn at the Hawk-Hass, there's gaun to be a stoure on the east border.'

'An there be a stoure on the east border I's be there for ane,' said my father; 'but the de'il ae man hae I left but auld Will Nicol and the callant Charlie. There hae seven men o' Moodlaw and Yardbire fa'en sin Beltan. I canna mak men, but I shall fight wi' them I have. As for Charlie, he disna want spirit, but he's unco young and supple, and will mak but a weak stand in a strong blast: Auld Will he kens brawly how to take care o' himsel; and, atween

the twa, I may be ill bestedde. But, gae as it will, I'll
be there.'

I was a massy blade that day when I gaed o'er Craik-
Corse riding at my father's side. I was sae upliftit I could
hardly sit on my yaud; and I saw my father was proud o'
his callant, as he ca'ed me – that made me ten times waur.
The first men we came at were the lang-shankit Laidlaws
o' Craik; and then the Grahams o' Drife they came up wi'
us; and when we came to Howpasley, my father got the
laird's right hand, and we gaed ower Skelfhill-swire seven
score and ten, but there were only fifty o' us had horse,
and mine was ane o' the best.'

'Wha's this stripling that rides the good dun mare?' said
the laird o' Howpasley.

'That's my bit niff-naff of a callant,' says my father:
'That's my Charlie, cousin John.'

'He's a twig of a good tree,' said Howpasley: 'I like the
spark gayan weel, if he wad ride a little evener up, an' no
haud forrit his head like a woodcock. But, my word, he
has a lang arm!'

'Ay, a pair o' them, cousin,' said my father; and the twa
carles hotched and leuch at my father's joke.

The warden was lying at the Hawk-Hass wi' twal score
o' good men; but there were nane o' them had horses but
the Elliots, and some gentlemen of the Scotts. When Sir
Ringan saw us coming, he came out on foot to meet us;
and when the gentlemen of our party saw that, they lighted
off their horses, gae them to their henchmen, and walked
out before the men. Howpasley walked on the right hand,
my father next, and, as he desired me, I came slounging
up next him. I lookit best on foot, for my legs were sic a
length; I was higher in fact by half a foot than either John
of Howpasley or my father, but a perfect tripe for sma'ness.
When our captain, the brave Redhough, came near to us, I
thought I should hae swarfed; my heart dunt-duntit like a
man humblin bear, and I was maist gasping for breath. I
had heard sae muckle o' his bravery that I expectit an auld,
gruff, austere carle, as proud as Lucifer, to meet us. But,
instead o' that, I sees a boardly knight in the very prime
o' manly beauty: his cheeks were ruddy, his eyes dark, and
the black beard on his booner lip was just beginning to curl
upward. My heart was a' his ain at the first look; and I said

to mysel, 'Ye're the man that I'll risk my neck wi' ony day.'
I likit him sae weel that I mind I thought I could just hae lain
down in a gutter, and letten him tramp on the tap o' me.

He first shook Howpasley by the hand, and then my
father; and then he gave a broad look to my beardless face,
turning his eye back to my father's.

'That's my Charlie, Sir Ringan; my only son now,' said
my father.

'You are welcome, cousin Charlie, to our camp,' said
he: 'If ye be as brave a man as your father, I shall never
want a hero at my side.'

I should hae said something in return, but the deil a
word I could say, for I was like to fa' to the fuffing and
greeting. He spake to a' the gentlemen in the same kind
hamely manner; and then lookit at a' the men, and spiered
how mony belonged to every ane.

'And how many are with you, cousin Yardbire?' said
he.

'They are a' here that I hae, noble chief,' said my father:
'Last year at this time I brought forty to the field, and now
I hae nae ane but my auld henchman and that lad. We hae
somehow been ower rash, and I now get a' the wyte. They
ca' me Wat the Waster – and not a man will haud land
under me.'

'Ay, ay, Yardbire,' said he; 'you and your men hae stood
the brunt o' the battle ower often for me and mine. But
you are grown auld, and ye maunna claim the post of
honour ony mair till Charlie come to his strength. I'll
make you captain this day o' the best troop you ever led.
You shall hae the hard-headed Olivers, the grimy Potts,
and the skrae-shankit Laidlaws; and you shall form my
flying party—'

My father here interrupted him with 'Na, na, my master,
deil a flying troop I'll lead! if it binna a fighting ane, it winna
follow me lang.'

The warden smiled; and calling out all the men of the
families he had named, he put such of them as had horses
under the command of my father. Of these there were
forty-seven, so that our troop consisted of fifty men in all.
We were joined with the Elliots; but Habby having ninety
men of his own name, the command of the horse devolved
on him, and my father was only looked on as the second.

I didna like this unco weel; but it coudna be helped, and I was glad to be in the field ony way.

The first sight we got o' the English was frae the top o' Penchrist; but a' that day we could only ken where they were by the reek they were raising. My blood boiled when I saw them burning the houses o' Scotsmen, and fain wad I hae had a hand-shaking wi' them.

There was ae message came after another a' that day. The Kers had been beat and chased across the river, and the English host had over-run their territory. Our chief didna seem to care for that sae muckle as I thought, nor wad he stir his foot till they crossed the Rule. There war mae men came in every hour, for the beacons were a' bleezing; and as soon as the English set foot on the territory of the middle marches, away we rade straight to meet them.

It was on the hill of Hawthornside where I first saw the face o' an enemy; and I'll never forget sic queer strummings as I had within me. Oh, I wad fain hae been at them! There was a kind o' yeuk, a kind o' kittling, a sort o' prinkling in my blood like, that I fand wadna be cured but by the slap o' a sword or the point o' a spear. Instead o' being feared for a wound, I wad hae gi'en my horse and light armour baith to have had a good prodd frae an Englishman – but I wad hae liket that the warden had seen me.

We kept the hills between them and the border wi' our horse, but the foot kept the straits to the westward. Forbye the Elliots, and my father's troop o' Potts, and Olivers, and skrae-shankit Laidlaws, the warden had three hundred Scotts on horseback; so that in all he had short o' five hundred horse, and about eight hundred foot. At the head o' his horse he rade straight up to the faces o' the English, and challenged them in our king's name to tell their business in that place. Up came an English knight, Sir Robert Neville of Ravensworth, and he crackit baith proudly and saucily, but I didna ken weel what he said. He threatened no to leave a beast or a body atween Borthwick and the Border. Our captain was as crouse as the other, sae there was nothing but ill blude atween them; but the thing that we likit warst of a' was the certainty that he had eight thousand men, being just sax for our ane.

The warden then held a council o' friends upon the top of the hill, and in view of the English host. Some said ae thing and some said another to him; but at length he turned to my father, and he says, 'What says our cousin Walter o' Eskdale to a' this? But I needna speer that – he never gae me aught but ae advice a' his life.'

'I'll tell you what I wad do, captain,' says my father: 'Afore yon sun were twa cock-strides down the west I wad fight them.'

'I kend what it wad be,' said the warden. 'But, my brave Yardbire, are you considering the disproportion o' force?'

'What's that to think about?' said he, 'the greater the better!'

The warden claspit him in his arms, and the tears came hopping down my muckle soft flobby cheeks.

'Yes, captain,' continued my father, 'I hae been thinking o' the odds against us, and I am thinking o't just now. But ye ken art may do muckle.'

'Now, to hear him speaking about art!' said the warden, pushing him playfully around by the shoulder – 'To hear a man speaking sagely about art, that never thought of ony other art in his life but hard hand nevel! Pray now, my dear cousin, will ye let us hear this deep profound art o' yours, that will enable ae man to beat half a dozen?'

'I wad form our little army into the shape o' a wedge,' said my father; 'and I wad yerk that little wedge into the heart of their great log of an army, and split it a' to shivers.'

'G—d a mercy, hear to him!' cried the warden. 'And pray what is to form the point o' this wedge, Yardbire?'

'Just my grey naig's head, captain.'

'I kend weel what it wad come to, cousin. Your grey naig's head wad soon be cracked; but an ought were to happen yours, what wad come o' me?'

I thought sae muckle o' my auld father, that I couldna haud my tongue nae langer, and that was the first word I ever spake to the warden in my life. 'Never fear, my master,' quo' I; 'it winna be ilka ane that sal crack his grey crown the day.'

'Weel said, Charlie!' cried the auld hero; and he waved his cap round his head. 'Weel said, little Charlie! Now, captain, for the wedge!'

The warden lookit a good while at us without speaking, and I gart mysel trow there was a blink o' admiration in his dark eye; 'Ah, Wat, Wat!' said he; 'weel do you ken I'm ower ready to follow your mad schemes! But they have sae often proved successfu', though wi' very hard wark, that I'll e'en take the risk, and sey your skill aince mair.'

He then drew his horse from the height into the glen behind, and formed them precisely on my father's plan, with a troop of horse in front, and one on each wing, the foot being arranged in close column in the middle; and as my father claimed the post of honour as his right, he rode the front man: Will Nicol and I were next him, and behind us there were four of the Laidlaws. I saw no farther, but was informed after that when the horse made the charge, the foot had orders to run and keep up with them.

We took a sweep down the water to the north, and appeared all of a sudden in the rear of the English army. Their scouts had seen us, but could not guess our intent; for as to a thought of our attacking them, that never entered their heads, so that their host was not new-modelled farther than their columns facing about toward us. They deemed we were going to retreat toward the north, and were making ready to pursue us, when all at once the point of the wedge turned at a right angle, and rushed with all haste on the centre of their line.

Then there was such a hubbub, and calling, and noise of armour rattling throughout their army as I had never heard! My father spurred on, and, after some few hard blows, opened the line. He had the least to do of any, for the ranks opened naturally before him as he heaved his heavy sword. But ever as their wedge grew thicker, their columns being pressed together, lay the heavier on our flanks, and several gallant men of the Scots fell. I saw naething o' this, but soon fand the effects of it; for my father drove faster on than the flankers could bear up after him, and our point lengthened out and grew thinner at every step. I had been unco keen o' fighting, but I got my fill o't then. I trow I gae some o' them some gay good yerks on the chafts.

Ravensworth by this time perceiving the danger in which his army stood of being divided, brought up his side columns and closed around our front. I heard him saying in a loud exasperated voice, 'For shame, countrymen! for shame! will ye suffer a landward Scots laird, an auld crabbit

loun like that, to ride in through your ranks and out through
your ranks, as they were files o' thistles? Down with the
moorland thief! down with him!'

'Aha, Robin o' Ravensworth, is that you?' cried my
father: 'An I win within sword's length o' you I shall settle
your crack.'

As he said this he raised himself up in his stirrups. Auld
Will Nicol roared out, 'For Christ's sake, master, stop!'
But, in place of that, he spurred up to the captain with
all his might, challenging him to come forward. Neville
kept his ground, and prepared for the attack, but refused
to come forward; and just as my father and he began to
measure swords, my father was struck by six or seven spears
all at once on his left side. Some of these he received on his
buckler, but others of them pierced his side, and, before any
of us could lend him the least assistance, he was unhorsed.
Ravensworth also gave him a wound as he was falling. I,
who was close behind him, and ahead of all the rest, was
now hard bested. I clove the head of the first spearman
on my left; and ere I had recovered my sword from the
stroke, Ravensworth's sword was at my breast; and I have
no doubt that stroke would have slain me, had it not been
for a plunge made by my father's horse, that came between
us and marred it. By this time the Laidlaws had come up
on my right – a wheen as hardy, determined louns as ever
brak warld's bread – and they were laying about them like
incarnate devils. The horse kept the lancers from reaching
me on the left, so that Ravensworth and I met fairly hand
to hand. Sure am I that I never gae sic a straik sinsyne, nor
ane wi' sic good will. I dinna think I clave his helmet, but
I gae him sic a devil o' a knab on the temple, that he was
stoundit, and fell as dead as a stane at my horse's feet. My
father was at that time on his knee, and I saw him trying
to raise himself up by the stirrup-leather, for he had never
yet quitted the bridle of his horse. He saw me bring down
Neville, who fell almost at his very side; and he looked to
me, and cried, 'Weel done, little Charlie! weel done, my
brave man!'

That was the last word I ever heard him say. My brave,
worthy, auld father! He was sae used to ca' me little Charlie
when I was young, that he coudna gie it ower when I grew
bigger than him; and he cried to me, 'Weel done, little

Charlie! Weel done, my brave man!' I'll never forget that moment. My honest, kind-hearted father! Ye maun forgie me, sirs, for taking a hearty greet at this part o' my tale. Mony a ane hae I ta'en at the same bit—. Ay – he often ca'ed me little Charlie, and he cried, 'Weel done, my brave man!' That was the hindmost word, and I hae good right to mind it.

The battle thickened, and thickened round us, and we were borne back; for there was sic a rush made by the English to the rescue, that, an their captain had been living, they wad hae tramped him to pieces. I was driven clean stupid, and cared nae ae preen for my life, after I saw the ranks rush over my father; but the skrae-shankit Laidlaws defendit me, and did most excellent work. I never saw ony men that thought less about fleeing or retreating than the Laidlaws. Pell-mell, swap for swap, was a' that they countit on. I heard Davie o' Craik saying to his brother, 'Take care o' that lang swabble Charlie, and keep by his side. Deil hae him, gin he be nae better than he looks like.' The grim Potts were mair cunning than rash; and the hard-headed Olivers could be led but never driven. The Laidlaws were the men for me. Pell-mell, yank for yank. 'Thresh on, Will!' 'Ay, here's w'ye, Davie; deil tak the hindmost!' I hae stood mony a stoure wi' the Laidlaws, and never wished for better lads – lang-shanks and a' thegither.

But I'm forgetting my tale; for aince I get into the mids o' a battle, it's no easy getting me out again. I canna tell you a' the feats that were done that day, especially by the warden. When he saw the great brulzie in front, he came up with the Scotts, and the Johnstons, and the Grahams o' Drife – and hearing that my father had fallen, and that the English captain was also slain, he took the front himself, and scattered the English commoners like crows.

When we had thus fairly broke through the centre, we turned to the right, and drove that division of the army before us till they took shelter in Jed forest; but seeing the rest, who formed the strongest wing, marshalling up behind us, we drew off to the hills, and encamped that night at the Brae of Rule.

There was heavy morning for the loss of my father, and we buried him next day at Hassendean. The English were as much exasperated. Dick Neville, the brother of Sir

Robert, took the command, and up Teviot they came, laying all waste behind them. We durst not engage them again in close battle, for they were by far too numerous; but we kept hovering around them, and harrassing them whenever we could get a chance. In spite of all we could do, they took the town of Hawick, plundered it, and burnt it to ashes. The warden was neither to haud nor to bind wi' anger then; and, as he durst not leave the country, nor tine sight o' them for an hour himself, he sent off Hab Elliot and me, wi' our hunder and fifty horse, to plunder the castle and lands of Ravensworth, by way of retaliation.

'Now, Charlie,' said he to me at parting, 'Mind what the Nevilles hae done baith to you and me, and neither leave them cow nor ewe, man, woman, nor bairn, blanket nor sheet, dish nor spoon.'

Aweel, aff Habby and I set; he wi' his Elliots, and me wi' my hard-headed Olivers, my grimy Potts, my skrae-shankit Laidlaws, and auld Will Nicol – that was my army, and a gay queer ane it was: I hadna a man o' my ain name but mysel; for the warden kept them a' about him: He wadna part wi' the Scotts at no rate. It was clear moonlight, sae we set off before sun-set and rade a' the night, keeping aye the height between Tyne and Reid; and at daylight we fand oursels at the place where the twa Tynes meet. We were terrified for raising the country, and were obliged to ride out to a little hollow place in a wild moor, and hide oursels a' the day, where our horses got nothing but a rive o' heather, but they had plenty o' water, puir things! Habby kept watch himsel, and let us a' sleep; and there was ae camstary English chap that wad be up to the tap o' the hill reason or nane, Habby chappit aff his head – he wasna very sticking that way.

The next morning after that, we gae the castle o' Ravensworth and the rich domains o' the Nevilles an unco surprise. Habby gaed up by himsel to the gate, and asked a word o' the porter. The man came snooving out half sleeping. Habby had him dead, and the keys in his ain hand, in half a minute. It was a shamefu' morning that; for we killed, and harried, and burnt a' that came afore us; and Lady Ravensworth was burnt, and her bairn was trowed to be burnt. That sat sair on my conscience, for she came to me and beggit her life. I had nae thought o' taking her life;

but I was sae intent on the spulzie, that I lost her again, and never saw mair o' her. It was rather cruel o' Habby to lock every door when he set fire to the castle. I saved ae little chap that morning, though I wasna muckle the better. We were flinging blankets, and sheets, and thousands o' things out at a large window, when I hears a bairnie greeting most bitterlie, and aye crying out, 'Daddy, daddy! O daddy, daddy!' 'Poor little English brat,' says I to mysel, 'there's nae daddy near you.' Sae I could nae help rinning into the room to see what kind o' creature it was; and there lay a fine bonnie callant on the bare bedstrae, for they had pu'ed the down bed, and blankets, and sheets, and a' off him; and when he saw me, he held out baith his hands, and cried, 'O daddy, daddy!' I could nae think to leave him to be burnt, sae I rowed him in some blankets and tossed him out at the window; and when I lookit out after him to see if he wasna killed, I heard him crying louder than ever, 'Daddy's boy fa'en! Take ye up, take ye up! O daddy, daddy! take ye up, take ye up!'

When we came to pack up our goods he was still lying sprawling amang the blankets, and insisting on his daddy taking him up as fervently as before. I was wae for the poor thing, and didna ken what to do, for I didna like to be nursing a bairn afore my new warriors. But as luck wad hae had it, up comes Will Laidlaw o' Craik. Will cared nae what ony body thought.

'What, lad?' says he to the boy: 'What's the matter, billy? What are ye lying yammering there for? Eh?'

'Daddy's good boy fa'en,' says the child; 'O take ye up! take ye up!'

'Poor deevil!' says Will, wi' his muckle een wauling till they were like to come put; 'Poor deevil! Indeed and I will take ye up, though I should get nae mair o' the spoil for my share but yoursel.'

Will fauldit a blankit, and rowed the callant carefully up in't like a web. He didna come weel behand at rowing up a bairn; but he did as he could, and had the sense to leave the head out, which was a main concern. Just at that very moment, when Will was at the thrangest, by comes ane o' the Olivers in a great haste wi' his sword drawn, and it was a' bloody. Now, thinks I to mysel', the puir bairn's gane; for I saw what kind o' chap he was that Oliver. Will unluckily had the boy's head out o' the blanket, and was busy speaking to him without regarding ony thing else; and ere ever he was aware Oliver heaved his bloody sword, and was just coming down wi' a swap on the boy's neck, and he wad hae cuttit it through like a kail castock. Will's e'e caught a glimpse o' the sword as it was coming down, and with a dash of his elbow he drove it aside. 'Eh? What are ye about, min?' said Will, speaking over his shoulder, and keeping his body between Oliver's sword and the child.

'Ooh? What are ye about min?' returned the other, mimicking Will's voice and manner: 'Hae ye nought ado but to work on a dirty English paddock like that? Cut the neck o't.'

'Will I, min?' says Laidlaw: 'I'll see you d – d first, and a' the Olivers atween Jed head and Tyot stane – humph? A bonnie trick to come and meddle wi' me and my bit bairn!'

Oliver went away laughing at Laidlaw, leaving him to manage his nursing concern as he could.

I had witnessed Will's undaunted bravery, and yet I canna say but I was as weel pleased wi' this bit kind turn as ought I had seen him do. I think I see him yet wi' the child in his arms foussomly rowed up in a blanket, like a web – the head o' the boy out, a great neuk o' the blanket hinging down to the ground, and Will glowring back at Oliver's face: 'Eh? What are ye about, min? A bonnie story, to come and meddle wi' me and my bit bairn!' Ha! ha! ha! Honest Laidlaw! I can never forget him and his bairn. 'Cut the neck o't,' says the other. 'Will I, min? I'll see you d – d first,' says Will. Ha! ha! ha! ha! – But then his look! that was the best sport ava; wi' his bendit face and muckle great wulcat een turned o'er his shoulder. 'Cut the neck o't,' says Oliver. They that had seen Laidlaw then! ha! ha! ha! 'Will I, min?' Ha! ha! ha!

'My son, is there not a time for every thing?' said the friar. 'If thou thinkest at all on our condition and thine own, surely thou wilt refrain from such a torrent of vain jesting. Remember that the words of thy mouth are for death or life; for the possession of maiden beauty, and love, and pleasure; or for the most dismal, and miserable, and wretched of all fates – to be killed and eaten up of thy brethren, the companions of thy journey.'

'Gude faith, the thing's hardly to be thought of, let be spoken about,' said Charlie. 'But I beg your pardon, callants, I maun get on wi' my tale; for if I stick it in the middle, ye ken it is a' ower wi' me.'

'I wish you would get on with it then,' said Tam; 'for if ye maun aye stop to laugh at your ain jests, we'll be a' dead o' hunger or ever the votes be ta'en. Nane but fools laugh at their ain sports.'

'Whisht, whist, Tam,' returned Charlie – 'I hae a gay wide wizen when I am amang friends, but there are some things that I canna swallow for a' that – Where was I at? Aye at the sacking o' Ravensworth.'

We drave the richest prey that morning that I ever yet saw liftit, if we had gotten it a' hame. We had thirty horses laden wi' stuff, and other thirty led anes, besides thirteen score o' good cattle; and we gae the banks o' the Teme and the Blackburn an unco singe afore we left them. I was rather against the burning, but Habby wadna be stayed; 'Na, na; tit for tat, Charlie. That will stand for Hawick and Abbotrule.'

We drave on, and drave on, as fast as the cattle could gang, and some o' the heavy soft anes we were obliged to leave behind sair against our wills. We were terrified for raising the country, for we had sic a far drive: but luckily the Nevilles had ta'en amaist every man with them in their expedition into Scotland; and the first time that we hovered was on Tersit-moor in Northumberland, a little before the break o' day. At that place there was the strangest thing happened to us that ever happened to men – and it was for that that I began my tale.

My heart had been unco sair a' the night wi' thinking about the bonnie Lady Neville o' Ravensworth; and I had often been sae grieved about her death, and her bairn's death, that I hardly kend what I was doing. I thought I saw her kneeling on her knee, and begging of me to spare her life, and the life o' her child; and then how cruel it was in me to rin away rummaging up the stair, and lose the opportunity of preserving her. These thoughts had made my heart wholly inclined to pity, and, as soon as we lighted,

I sought out Will Laidlaw o' Craik, to see if he had still been able, amang a' the confusion, to preserve the life of the child. Will had had a great deal o' trouble wi' him, chiefly from his associates, but he had him still safe an' sound. He had stuffed him in a horse's pack o' blankets and sheets, *wi' his head out*, and had kept beside him a' the gate; and now when I found him he had laid the boy down on the heather to sleep, and had him weel happit up, and Will himsel was lying streekit beside him. He thought that I was gibe him about the business, and tried to waive the subject; but when I told him how much I was pleased wi' what he had done, he grew rather crouser, and could speak about naething else but the boy and his little sayings to him by the way. 'Poor little dear soul!' said Will; 'I think some body had flung him o'er the castle wa' in an armfu' claes, and never kend; and wha kens, but he may be the heir o' Ravensworth himsel. He has been sae miraculously saved that he will surely come to something. But do ye ken, Charlie, my heart is already sae closely knitted to that bit helpless bairn, that I wadna see ony ill come ower him for a' the kye on the Crib-Law.'

'Laidlaw, you shall never rue your kindness o' heart and attentions to that puir misfortunate bairn,' quo' I: 'The moment that I saw you take him up, and row him in a blanket, *wi' his head out*, as ye had been rowing up a wab, I resolved to reward you wi' my hale share o' the spulzie.'

'Never speak about that, Charlie; if we get safe hame wi' every thing we'll no differ about the spulzie.'

'Ha, but Will, your rowing up o' the bairn was a rare scene! ony other body but you, ye ken, wad hae taken the creature up in their arms and rowed a blanket about it: but instead o' that you doubled a pair o' blankets their hale length on the green, laid the bairn across the one end o' them, and rowed it ower the body, and ower the body, and ower the body, till ye came to the far end; and it was but ill rowed up after a' – ha! ha! ha!'

'Hout, Charlie! deil a bit but ye're ower muckle ta'en up about trifles. I wish ye wad think mair about the perilous situation we are in. Watch a wee while, and let me get a sleep.'

Will then laid his arm over the boy and the hott o' claes, and fell sound asleep. Our men were a' placed two and three around the hale muir to guard the cattle, and all were resting on their arms, to be ready to rush together on any alarm. I was sitting and keeping a good look out a' round about, and Will he was swuffing and sleeping. Every thing was quiet, except now and then that the hum of an ox was to be heard which missed his neighbour, or the eiry whistle o' the moss-plover. It was a while before the day-sky, and I was just beginning to turn drowsy, when I thought I saw something white on the muir, about two hundred strides from me. 'St Mary be my buckler!' said I to mysel: 'What can you be? It is surely a flight o' white mist risen out o' the earth, for I see it moving. If it be a mist fawn, as I dare say it can be naething else, it has drawn itself up into a form the likest that of a woman of ought ever I saw.' As I was mumbling and speaking this to mysel, I perceived that it still drew nearer, and that it wasna ane o' the fairy fawns o' mist whiles to be seen stealing about i' the night-time, but a lady a' clad in white. It glided athort the moor, and athort the moor, as if it had been looking for something it had lost; and at last I saw it spring away from one point to another at a considerable distance, as swift as a flash o' fire, as if something had startled or offended it. I learned after that the point from which it fled was the very spot where Habby Elliot lay, and who at that time was lying in a sound and troubled sleep. When it again stopped, its motions were very extraordinary – for though the morning was dark, there was such a pale and a pure whiteness about it, that I saw it the better. It was like a streamer o' light, or the reflection of a starn in the water, that aye in the darkest nights appears brightest. When it paused at the place I mentioned, it bent its body backward, its arms were crossed on its breast, and I saw like its hair streaming in the air behind it. Then it spread both its hands toward heaven, as in the act of making fervent supplication. From that point it came straight toward me, after giving a shiver that made all my een dazzle.

'Will Laidlaw!' cried I, but in a violent whisper below my breath; 'Will Laidlaw o' Craik! for God's sake waken up, and see what this is.'

I was sitting, but Will sprang to his feet, and seized his sword. 'Where? where? where? Where is it, Charlie? Where is it, callant?' whispered he. I pointed to it, but durst not speak. Will rubbed his een and rubbed his een, and at length perceived it. 'I do believe, lad, that is some hizzy – and a weel dressed ane she is,' said he; still speaking in a whisper, and sitting down close beside me. 'What on God's earth can she be seeking on this waste at sic an untimely hour?' I durst hardly draw my breath, let be to answer him; and sae he continued, 'I think it wad hae been as decent-like an she had lain still in her bed rather as comed raiking out amang a wheen wild men on sic a wild height. Oho! I'll wager my neck it is some spy in disguise.'

She was by this time within ten paces o'us, and we both sat still in breathless suspense till she came close to us. I thought I had seen the face before, but couldna tell where, till she kneeled on one knee at my feet, crossed her hands, and looked me in the face with the most piteous expression of countenance. Then I saw it was the lady o' Ravensworth, and in the very posture that I had seen her for the first and last time. Yet there was no anger in her face; it seemed merely a look of supplication; and at length she touched her lips three times, as an intimation that she wished to speak and could not. As for me, my mouth was sealed; and that I might see nae mair than I had seen, I threw mysel agroof, wi' my face to the ground, and held by the heather firmly wi' baith my hands.

Honest Will had nae suspicions o' ony thing beyond nature; and at length he says, 'What are you wanting wi' us, Madam, that ye're making a' thae murgeons?'

'You do not know me,' returned she, 'but that young warrior beside you does. He has been guilty of a neglect that he will rue till the day of his death. But, for another deed of mercy that you and he have done, your fates are averted, and your heads shall be covered in the hour of danger, which is fast approaching. You have saved a child from the devouring flames; – if you dare to wrong a hair of that child's head, how dreadful will be your doom! There is a terrible hour approaching; – look at his breast that you may know him again, for I cannot see the fate of the day. But if you would thrive on earth and be admitted into heaven, guard and preserve that dear child – That child is mine—'

'Say nae mair, honest woman,' says Will, perfectly undismayed, 'an the child be yours you're perfectly welcome to him. It was to save his bit innocent life that I brought him away, and no for ony greed o' other folks bairns. I kendna wha was aught him, but sin he be yours I'll deliver him safe into your hands. Take care an' no let him get cauld, for the morning air is no gude for a bairn.'

So saying, Will howked the boy out o' the mids o' a great heap o' claes, rowed him up as weel as he could, and then said, after two or three sobs, 'I like ill to part wi' him, but a mother's aye a mother.' Then he kissed him, and added, 'Fare-ye weel, my wee man! You and I will maybe never meet again; but, whether or no, you will be nae the waur o' a trooper's blessing. An ye be spared ye'll be a man when auld Will Laidlaw's head is laid i' the grave. Hae, honest woman, there's your son, and God bless you baith!'

She bent her body over him in the most affectionate way, and stretched her arms as if to embrace him, but she neither touched him nor any part of Laidlaw's claes. The boy had awakened, and when Will held him out to give him up to his mother, he cried out, 'No-no-no-no. No go ty'e, no go t'ye. Daddy's boy feared, daddy's boy feared.'

'Gude faith, sae ye may, my man!' thinks I to myself, 'an ye kend about a' this as weel as I do!'

I saw naething that was passing, for I was lying close on my face, and hinging by the heather; but I heard a that was said, and Will tauld me the rest afterwards. He said, she made the sign of the cross above her child's breast, then over his own head, as he stooped forward with him in his arms. Then she glided aside, and made the cross over my head and shoulders, and it was heaven's grace that I didna ken, else I wad hae swarfed away. Last of all, she again bent herself over her child, and stretched out her arms on each side of him; then, leaning herself back on the air, she arose gently from the ground, and sailed away through the dim shades of the morning toward the verge of the heaven.

I wondered what was asteer then, for I heard Will crying on the Virgin Mary to preserve him, and rhaming o' er the names o' a' the saints he had ever heard of; and at length he gae a great gluther, like a man drowning, and fell down wi' sic a dunt he gart a' the moss shake again. The bairn screamed and grat; and I didna ken what to do, for I durstna look up for fear o' seeing the ghost; till at length I heard that the rest of the sentinels had caught the alarm, and were passing the watchword frae ane to another, and then I ventured to set up my head. But, gude and gracious, sic a grip as I did haud by the heather!

I took up the child, covered him with my cloak, and soothed him; and the poor little harassed thing hid his face in my bosom. Will lay quivering and struggling like ane in a dream, or under the influence of the night-mare; and, after I had rolled him three times over, he awoke in the most horrid consternation. 'Charlie, where are ye? Speak to me, Charlie, and tell me where I am.' Then a whole string o' saints and angels were a' invoked, one after another, ower and ower again. 'Mercy on us, Charlie! I hae had sic a dream as never mortal man had; and a' sae plain and sae particular, I could amaist swear it was real. What do ye think, Charlie? Didna this bairn's mother come to me in my sleep? and she says to me, "That bairn's mine—." Na, that wasna what she said first. "Ye dinna ken me," says she.' And then Will began and told me all that I had heard pass between them before, and all that I had seen, and some part that I had not seen; but a' that I could do, I couldna persuade him that it wasna a dream. And it was better it was sae; for if he had kend and believed that he had conversed with a spirit, it wad hae put him daft. It pat me clean out o' my judgment; and for that day, and mony a day and night after, I kend nae mair what I was doing than ane dreaming, and remembered nae mair what I had been doing than if I had been asleep all the time. I can therefore gie but a puir and a lame account o' what followed, for it is maistly from hearsay, although I was tauld that I bure a principal hand in the fray.

We started at the scraigh o' day, and drove on. There were always four or five light horsemen, well mounted, who rode before our array to see if the coast was clear; and as we went round the head of the Gowan Burn, about mid-day, ane o' these came galloping back, and told us that the English were awaiting us at the fords of Keilder, with an army of a thousand horse.

'Aha!' quo' Habby Elliot! 'I thought we warna to get hame this way. We hae just twa choices, callants, either to fight or flee.'

There was not a man in all our little army that could

think of scampering off for bare life, and leaving such a prey behind him; so, with one assent, we rode forward in a body to the brow of the hill that overlooks the fords of Keilder. The English were stationed on a rising ground to the west of the river, and that being passable only by one ford, which was very rough, we could not attack them without the certainty of being cut to pieces; so we kept our station on the steep brae over against them, and sent some few of our oldest and weakliest men to be moving the prey out toward Keilder-head.

We calculated the English to be about five hundred; but neither durst they cross the ford to come to us. They sent a few flights of arrows among our men, which we regarded very little, and determined, if possible, to keep them at bay there till our rich prey had crossed the border fell. But just at the fall of the evening, to our great surprise, the English rushed at once into the ford, with loud and reiterated shouts; and scarcely had we begun to advance down the steep to meet them, when we were attacked by another body of horsemen behind.

These men were led by a great priest whose name was Bishop Boldone, but who was always called Bloody-Sark; and at the very first encounter Hab Elliot rushed among the English ranks and slew the Bishop with his own hand at the first blow. But it cost Habby dear, for he was cut down in endeavouring to retreat, and fell under a dozen of spears. In short, our small band, being inclosed between two stronger bodies, was literally hewed in pieces, but not before they had slain a great number of our enemies. Will Laidlaw and I fought side by side; and though enclosed in the very middle of our foes, we cut our way through, and escaped without a wound, and with short pursuit.

Our prey was gone. We saw a great part of them scattered on the hills, and heard them lowing, as they returned toward their native pastures. Our drivers, having watched the fate of the day, made their escape when they saw us surrounded, abandoning the spoil. We two fled in silence toward the north-east, and could not even get time to look for the child, in whom we were both so much interested. We had lost our well earned prey; we had lost our friends and companions in arms, and we had lost our honour by suffering ourselves to be surprised by the ambush behind;

yet we both felt as if the loss of the child sat heavier on our
hearts than all. There was something so mysterious in our
connection with him, that it could not fail making a deep
impression on our minds. The vision that we had seen, and
the promise that had been made to us – that 'for what we
had done our heads should be shielded in the day of battle'
– soon recurred to us, and we both agreed that our escape
was miraculous, and perfectly unaccountable to ourselves.
There were not two in the battle who exposed themselves
more, and Laidlaw averred that he sometimes saw twenty
weapons raised against us at once, and that still, as we
approached, the bearers of them seemed to lose the power
of striking. It was no wonder that we were impressed with
deep awe, nor that we both wished it had been in our power
to have preserved the boy, over whose life there seemed to
be some good guardian spirit permitted or appointed to
watch. Our conversation was all about him. There had
been a nest made for him in a pack of clothes. Laidlaw had
led the horse himself all the way, and the child had chatted
to him, till the alarm was given that we were waylaid, and
he had then given the horse in charge to one of the drivers,
with particular injunctions to take care of the child; but he
could not even remember who that driver was. I came up
immediately after, and charged the lad to take care of the
child; and, in the hearing of several of my followers, said
that I would rather they lost the whole drove than that
ought should happen to him. But now we had lost him;
we had lost all but our horses and our swords.

We jogged on all the night in melancholy mood, crossed
the Border, and then turned westward toward the Cowd-
Peel, which we reached about sun-rise. A little after the
break of day, as we were coming through a hollow of the
height, called the Spretty-Grain, we perceived something
before us that appeared to be moving, and of a prodigious
bulk, which, after some hesitation we made up to, and
found that the phenomenon consisted of eight horses, all
well loaden, and every one with its head yerked to the tail
of the one before him; and all these were driven by one
yeoman on horseback, who rode beside them with a long
goad in his hand.

We soon overtook and examined him; and never was I
so much astonished in my life as when I found it was my

own henchman auld Will Nicol. He was very dour and shy of communication at first.

'Will Nicol! Is it you?' said I. 'How in the name of wonder did you escape?'

'Humph! I think I may as weel speir that question at you: Humph!' says Will.

'I thought you had fallen with the rest in the battle,' said I.

'Humph! but I'm here,' says Will. 'And I think there's mae here nor me: humph! and I rather think I hae brought mair wi' me nor some fock: humph! I'm comed as fu' handit as some fock, I think. Humph!'

'But, Will, were you in the engagement?'

'What need ye speir that? humph! Where was I else but in the engagement?'

'And did you stay till it was over?'

'Humph! I stayed lang aneuch, I think! humph! It is needless to wait ower lang on a seen bad job. Humph!'

But the real truth of the story was, that instead of staying till the battle was ower, Will didna stay till it began, nor near that time. He was an auld-farrant chap Will, and had a great deal o' foresight; and when he saw us begin to stop, and the English standing peaceably before us, *herding us*, as he ca'ed it, he was sure there were more enemies coming up behind.

'Will, if I were sure that ye deserted our cause, and came off before the engagement began,' said I, 'although I have not a man left that I ken o', but Will o' Craik and yoursel, may I be a coward and a traitor if I wadna cut you down i' the place where you stand.'

Will had nothing to say for himself but 'Humph! humph!' and he scratched his head and grumbled. I was quite indignant at the old fellow, and was getting into a greater rage than ever I hae been in at a friend sinsyne, when all at once I heard a weak tremulous voice say, 'Daddy's boy cold.'

'Aih-hay-hay!' shouted Will Laidlaw, as loud as he could yell: 'Hilloa, hilloa, hilloa!' – and he sprang first on the back of his own horse with his feet, and from that he darted upon one of those that carried the packs. When I rode up he was sitting on the rumple o' the beast, hugging the child, that he had deemed lost, in his bosom, kissing him, and exclaiming – 'Aih, my man! my dear man! are ye safe? are ye safe? God bless auld Will Nicol! God bless auld Will Nicol!'

It was impossible for two down-cast and broken-hearted warriors to be more uplifted at any incident than Will Laidlaw and I were, at discovering that the boy was safe; and even auld Will Nicol began to recover some confidence—. 'I heard you giving a chap some charges about him, that I kend weel caredna if his head were off – od, he was ane o' the hard-headed Olivers. What cares an Oliver for a man's life, or a bairn's either? – Sae I thinks, sin my young master has ta'en a liking for the bairn, I's e'en gang and look after him. It is a good sign of a young warrior to like to save women and bairns. Sae I gangs, and sae I thinks sin I is bringing away this wee chap out o' danger, I may as weel bring something wi' me as naething; sae I brings aught o' the best horses, and the best laden anes that I could wale, and bound for the Border. A fashous job I hae had wi' them a' night.'

It is needless to tell how frankly auld Will was forgiven.

The Cowd-Peel being a rallying point on all Border raides, we stayed there a whole day and a night, in hopes that some part of our men wad come up; but out of all my fifty men there were none appeared but three of the Potts. The hard-headed Olivers had been slain to a man, and all the Laidlaws save my brave companion. Out of ninety valiant Elliots there were only twelve remaining, and some of these were of the drivers.

There were fifty-seven Scots, and nearly as many English, with Bloody-Sark at their head, buried in one cairn; and, for the sake of the Bishop, the English raised a heap of stones above them as huge as an abbey church, which will be seen on the height above the ford of Keilder for ever.

Laidlaw slept that night in a good bed with the boy in his arms, for we had no lack of the finest blankets and sheets; and that night the white lady appeared to him again, claiming her child, yet still declining to accept of him, and promising Will protection on earth and a reward in heaven if he continued to guard and protect that boy. Whether this was in a dream or not, Laidlaw could not be positive; but he rather inclined to think he was wide awake, for he remembered of speaking to her audibly. Among other things, she asked him if he knew it was the

child that had slept by him on the waste the night before
the battle. Will said he was sure. She asked him how. He
answered, that 'unless the fairies had changed him it could
nae be ony other.'

'But the fairies or some one else may change him,' said
she. 'You may be separated amid the confusion and uproar
now on the Border; and when you meet again, you may not
be able to prove the identity of my child. I bade you the
other night examine his bosom, but you neglected to do
so. If you had, you would there have found the spur of
Ravensworth, testifying his lineage and descent to all the
world.'

Will came to me in a great ferment the next day, and
told me of all this. I had heard the same words the night
before the battle, but had quite forgot them among other
matters, and wist as little what they meant as Will did.

'I hae lookit a' his bits o' claes, and graepit them a','
said he; 'but I can find nae spur. How could there be a spur
about a nakit bairn? It is may be in amang the blankets.'

'It is perhaps some private mark,' said I. 'Let us examine
the child's body very narrowly.'

On doing so we found a slight mark on his breast, that
seemed to have been made by applying a hot iron at some
time previous, and it was exactly in the form of a V with
the wrang end uppermost. So we both concluded that this
was a private mark of some family, that neither fairies nor
men kend o', and that it was perhaps a stamp that keepit
them a' away.

'It is the stamp of the heirs lineal of the house of Neville,'
said the friar; 'I have impressed it with my own hand, after
many masses and Ave Marias said. What became of that
child? or whither is he gone? I pray thee to inform us in
the words of truth not lengthened out.'

Alas, I cannot tell! He was visited by the white lady of
Ravensworth every night, and when the gloaming came she
would be seen hovering on the skirts of the wood near to
him. I grew that I durstna sleep a night within ten miles
o' him, and Will Laidlaw turned clean bumbazed about
the thing; sae we were obliged to send him to board wi'
auld Lady Lawder, her that was put out o' the convent for
witchery and the ill arts. She cared nought about spirits,

and conversed wi' the white lady as she had been her door neighbour; and it was said there were strange mysterious sayings past between them. She book-learned the boy, pen-learned the boy, and learned him mony other things foreby that were thought to be nae better than they should hae been. She chauntit sangs til him, and tauld him tales, and, there was little doubt, meant to breed him up to be a terrible enchanter; but afore that could be effeckit, the white lady came and took him away a' thegither.

From that day he was never been seen or heard of in this world, neither as boy nor man. And now, sirs, I find that my story's worn to a head hair, and that I maun cut it short. So it is done, and that's an end til't.

CHAPTER TWENTY

I have been a skipper in my time,
And something more. Anon, I'll tell it you.
Ogilvie

'IT IS NAE worth the name of a story that,' said Tam
Craik; 'for, in the first place, it is a lang story; in the second
place, it is a confused story; and, in the third place, it ends
ower abruptly, and rather looks like half a dozen o' stories
linkit to ane anither's tails.'

The poet was by this time on his feet, and, coming
forward to Charlie, he looked him sublimely in the face,
stretched out his hand, and spoke as follows: 'There is some
being, wheresoe'er he dwells, that watches o'er the fates of
mortal men: now do I know it. Yea, and that same being
has spirits of all casts at his command, that run, and fly,
and trim, and trim, and trim about this world. And it is
even true that I have seen of these, yet knew them not. Look
here, brave hero, man of heart and hand! and see if thou
canst note thy mark once seen? Thy spur; thy A without
the crossing stroke; thy V with the wrong end upmost – is
it here?'

The poet bowed his breast, and exposed it to Charlie's
eye, which, at the first scrutinizing look, discerned the mark
he had formerly seen – the mark of the spur of Ravensworth.
Charlie's visage altered into lengthened amazement. It
could scarcely have been more strongly marked when he
was visited by the white lady on Tersit moor, even when
he was glad to hide his face in the moss, and hold by the
heather with both his hands.

'And are you really the chap that I threw out at the
window in the castle of Ravensworth,' said he, 'and
boarded wi' auld lady Lawder? The creature that had

292

a ghaist for its guardian, and a witch for its nurse? But what need I spier? My ain een convinces me. Gude faith but we are a queer set that are prickit up on the top o' this tower thegither! I am amaist terrified to enquire where you have been since the white lady took you away; for ye must have been in the fairy land, or the country o' the gruesome ghaists, or perhaps in a waur place than either.'

'We are a queerer set than you are thinking of,' said Tam; 'for here am I standing, Tam Craik, liege man and true to the brave Scottish Warden, and I carena wha kens it now; but I am neither less nor mair a man than just Marion's Jock o' the Dod-Shiel, that sliced the fat bacon, ate the pet lamb, and killed the auld miser, Goodman Niddery. Here's the same whittle yet, and ready at the service of ony ane that requires it for the same end. Od, we seem to ken mair about ane anither than ony ane o' us kens about ourselves.'

'The day wears on apace,' said the Master; 'and I foresee that there is relief approaching from more quarters than one.' (This made all the party spring to the windows to look—.) 'It is not yet visible to your eyes, but it will come time enough. In the meanwhile, it would be as well to get through with the stories, that we may know and fix on our victim, for, perhaps, we may need a mart this night. And, it being now your turn, liegeman Thomas, or John, by right of seniority, if you know of nothing better, I should like much to hear the adventures of such a promising youth, from the day that you made away with the farmer to this present time.'

'Better, Master Michael Scott?' said Tam. 'Better, does your honour say? Nay, by my sooth I ken o' naething half sae good. I hae been an ill-guided chap a' my life; but, as you will hear, I hae guided others at times but in a middling way.'

Tam Craik's Tale

My friend, the laird, has given you my early history, perhaps better than I could hae done myself, but that is to judge of. He hath added and diminished – but yet he told his story wi' some life, and a' the better that he didna ken wha heard him. In one thing he was wrong informed, for

I was not seen on Kirtle-common that night I fled from the slaughter of the old inveterate wretch. I ran in a contrary direction, and slept that night in a moss-hagg, at the head of a water called Lanshaw Burn. Many a hard night I have had, but that was one of the bitterest of them all. I did not rue having killed the goodman, for I rejoiced at having let out his dirty miserable life and saved my own – but then I was sure to be taken up and hanged for a murderer; and I was chased away from my mother and my country, and durst not face a human being. I saw some goats and some sheep, and would gladly have killed one to have eaten, for I saw hunger staring me in the face; but they would not let me come near them. I likewise saw a shepherd's or forester's house, but kept aloof; and going up into a wild bushy glen, I cried myself asleep, half naked as I was, and slept till about the break of day. When I awakened, starving with hunger and cold, I had no shift but to pull rashes and eat the white ends of them, which I continued to do all that day whenever I came to a rash bush. The next night I came to a solitary house, where I ventured to go in, and there I first gave myself the name of Tam Craik, telling abundance of lies as to my origin. The master of the house was a wealthy vassal, and had great numbers of fat oxen, with cows and calves, besides a few sheep, and he kept me to help him to herd these, promising me a grey coat if I attended to his satisfaction. He was a most extraordinary man, and none of the best – for his words and actions were at variance: Though he conversed with me, or any one, with the utmost familiarity, I never found out that he had told me one word of truth. The first friend that came to visit him after my arrival, he overloaded so with kindness, professions of friendship, and respect, that I believed he loved him as his own soul; and, after he was gone, as my master and I went out to the fields, I observed what a treasure it was to have so good and so valued a friend as he had in that neighbour of his. What was my astonishment to hear from the same tongue that had lauded him to the skies, that he was a cheat, a liar, and a scoundrel; – a greedy sordid wretch that robbed his own hinds, and such wandering pedlars as came by that road, not daring to venture on higher game; one who seduced men's wives and daughters indiscriminately; and was, in short, a perfect demon, and a pest to the whole neighbourhood. 'But, master, why did you caress and commend him so much to his face?' 'O! that is all very well; that goes all for nothing. He is to be sure a vile scoundrel!' 'There are queer people in this world,' thought I: 'There is nothing for it, I see, but, *Tam, mind yoursel.*'

The farmer continued very kind to me in his own deceitful way; but the meat that we got was very bad. It consisted of lean beef, and venison as black as soot, with plenty of milk; but as for bread we had none of any description. So, from the day that I entered to his service, I determined to kill a lamb, or a sheep of any sort, the first time I could get one; but I never could get the least chance, and might as well have tried to get hold of a deer. I could not help thinking of the delicious feasting that I had in my little shieling, dear as it had like to have cost me; and every day my appetite for fat flesh became more insufferable, till at last, by a grand expedient, I got satisfaction of it. I had thirty fat stots in my herd, and I observed that, in hurrying them through a bog, they sunk, and stuck quite fast: so, having no other resource, I drove a few of them one day, when I was very hungry, into a mire in a wood, and rushing forward on them while they were struggling, I sticked the fattest among them to the heart, so that he floundered and bled to death in the slough. 'Well done again, Marion's Jock!' said I to myself. 'Here is feasting for you now! Here is a feast that will last you a twelve month at odd times, if you can but preserve it.' I declare when I began to cut up that huge animal, I almost trembled at my atrocity; but these kind of feelings soon wear off. I was obliged to eat some collops that day without any cooking, and never relished ought better; I wish we saw such a meal again! My thin yellow beard was a little discoloured to be sure, but that was nothing; I washed it, and went home as boldly among the rest as if nothing wrong had been done.

When I returned to my prey, I found to my great grief that the foxes, dogs, ravens, and every savage beast and hind on these mountains, were determined to share with me; they had actually eaten more in that one night than would have served me a week; – so the next day I employed myself in cutting off all the good, fat, and savoury pieces, and secreted them in well-springs, covering them up with stones; this I did to preserve them from the beasts and from putrefaction; and that day I am sure I had at least ten stones weight of excellent beef – the white and red were so beautifully mixed, it did one's heart good to look at it.

Pleasures are of short date, and the greatest pleasures have the shortest! My master went over the lake next day to look at my herd, and I knew the ox would be missed. Had it not been for my beloved beef I would have made my escape forthwith; but my heart was knit to it, and for my life I could not leave it. I went home at night in great terror, but to my joy I never saw my master half so kind. He told me I had suffered one of my stots to be stolen, but what could the like of me help it: he had a rough guess who had taken him, and would perhaps make him repent it. I was perfectly overjoyed at this construction, and resolved to revel in feasting and gladness; but next day when I went back to my ox, the hide was neatly taken off him, so also was the head, and both were taken away. This was perfectly unaccountable to me; and I saw the marks of men's feet in the mire, confirming the fact that some body had been there stealing the head and the skin of my ox, which were in my eyes not worth half the labour of taking them off. I knew not what to make of this, but it was evident that my prey had been discovered by some one; and all that I could calculate farther on was, that the hide had been stolen by some body who stood in need of it for shoes, and the head by one who wanted bugle-horns. It was all one to me, as I grew more and more a favourite with my master, who now began to caress me more than his own sons. No young lad in the land could be more thrifty about meat than I was. Being anxious to have the remainder of my bullock out of sight, I stole salt and a small barrel, and salted my stuff in a hole below ground; then, when no very good meat was going by day at my master's house, I often fasted the greater part of it, and then taking a coal by night, I stole away into the wood, and roasted, and boiled, and feasted the whole night. The beef was delicious, and it was amazing what great quantities I sometimes snapped up at once; for even after I thought I could eat no more, there was a part of white marrowy substance about the joints, and the sides of the bones, that I could not give over – no man could give it over. Marry, how delicious it was! I account that

fine meat mixed with white, that lies wedged in along the
doublings and shelves of the bones, as the most glorious
species of man's food; – round the broad shoulder-bone,
for instance, the spoolbone – that through which we look
for the storms. Think but of the layers of the red and the
white that lie bedded around that. Peatstacknowe, let me
feel your shoulder. I suppose a man has no spool-bone – ah
no! – none! Blessed Virgin! when shall I again shire the long
crooked slices of the red meat, mixed with white, from the
flats and the hollows of a broad spool-bone!

'He is hungering and yearning to pick my bones, the
cannibal dog,' said Gibby. 'But it brings me in mind of
a good saying and a true: The swine that is most eager to
feed itself is the first slaughtered to feed others.'

'The horse-leach hath drawn thee aside from thy onward
relation, thou froward and voracious one,' said the friar:
'Verily, it is better for thee that thou return to thy tale,
before thy strength be consumed within thee.'

The loss of this sturdy ox of my master's gave rise to strange
matters; matters which quite confounded my judgment,
and which to this day I do not comprehend. My master
went away to the sheriff, and the lord of the manor, and
made a complaint that his neighbour before-mentioned
had stolen one of his cattle, the best that he had on his
farm. This was the man that he caressed so much, yet knew
to be a scoundrel. The complaint was attended to, and the
injury deeply resented. My master returned with a strong
body of men, and orders to seize Glendairg, and search all
his premises; and if evidence appeared against him, he was
to be carried before Lord William, called the Severe, and
there imprisoned in the dungeon till time should be given
him to clear himself, which, if he failed to do in a certain
period, he was to be swung. All my master's servants, men
and women, were ordered to proceed with the party; I went
among the rest, and certainly never witnessed so curious a
scene. Glendairg came out and met the party with all the
consciousness of innocence; and even when he was seized
and bound, he still appeared to doubt of the sincerity of the
men, especially when they told him it was at the instance
of my master.

'If that is all, it is well,' said he; 'I am sure my kind friend and neighbour can mean me no ill by it.'

My master took him aside, and said to him in the kindest and most soothing manner, 'Do not be the least disheartened, my dear friend: You know how far I would be from injuring you. I would not do it for all the cows in my byre. I ken weel wha has the ox. There is little doubt but he is in our neighbour Bauldy's beef stand. I have long suspected him, and many is the good beast I have lost. You little know how many good beasts I have lost, and was still so loth to make it public. But I can suffer it no longer. Let the skaith fall upon the skaither. In the mean time I know you are quite innocent, but I instituted this search as a blind to him: You must just submit and never mind it.'

'O, very well, neighbour, very well,' said Glendairg; 'I knew you could not intend me any ill – search all out and in, and welcome.'

They did so; they searched all out and in, and at last, when about to give up, they found the individual ox's hide that I slew in the bog, lying hid deep below some hay and corn in the corner of a barn. In another place still more unfeasible, they found the ox's head. They were both laid upon the green, and my master and all his servants, myself included, swore to their identity, as we could not do otherwise. Glendairg looked like one bewildered, and said there was a plot laid against his life, which he neither understood, suspected, nor merited. The shrieve's officers laughed him to scorn, and proposed to hang him up on the nearest tree; and I believed they would have done it, had it not been for the kindness of my master, who came forward with tears in his eyes, and addressed them somewhat thus:

'Alas, my masters, this is a heavy and a sorrowful sight for me! This is the bitterest day of my life! I have lost many and many good cattle, and yet I would not – I could not, let myself suspect my intimate friend. Think how I am grieved to see these proofs. Yet perhaps he may be innocent, and this may be some vile plot laid against his life. I beg, therefore, that he may be set at liberty, and the whole business hushed up.'

'You are a good man and a kind,' said the men; 'but this thing must not be. With our lord and master, justice must have sway; but we will report your goodness and generosity to him, and be sure it will not go unrewarded. We can assure you, that this man has not only forfeited his life, but all his farms, as well as his stock of cattle and sheep to yourself.'

For all this my master refused to be comforted, but wept and followed after the men, pleading for the life and the freedom of his friend, but he pleaded in vain; the men bound him on a horse, and carried him away with them to the dungeon of the castle of Coombe. I marvelled greatly at the great kindness and generosity of my master, knowing, as he did, that the man was a scoundrel; but I wondered far more what could induce the man to steal the hide and the head from off my ox.

My master was a married man, and had four children; and though he was apparently a kind husband, his wife seemed quite unhappy and discontented, which I thought highly unreasonable on her part. She knew more, however, than I did; and there are some small matters that women never patiently put up with. He had a number of servant-maids for the purpose of milking cows, making hay, and cheeses, and such things; and among them there was a very pretty one named Kelly, with whom he had fallen in love; and, after long toying and courting, he had seduced her. I knew nothing about these sorts of concerns; but I thought Kell, as we called her, the most beautiful, sprightly, and innocent being that lived, and I liked to look at her and hear her speak; and whenever she came near me, I was like to fall atrembling. She slept with a little child in a large open loft, above the room where my master and mistress slept; and it so happened that something came by night and frightened her, and she refused to sleep there any longer without some one beside her. I slept by myself in one of the outhouses; and it was immediately proposed by my master that my bed should be removed, and put up in the loft beside Kell's. I was drunken with delight at hearing this intelligence; yet I pretended to be very averse to the plan, hanging my head, and turning about my back, when any one spoke of it, nor would I answer a word to one of them but 'Tutt,' or 'tutts.'

'Tam Nosey, it seems ye're gaun to be bedded wi' bonny Kell the night?'

'Tutt!'

'Ye're gaun up to sleep beside her, and do ye think ye'll never brik lair?'

'Tutt!'

'She's a bonny burd yon, Tam, ye maun tak care.'

'Tutts!'

Well, up I went the next night to sleep in a bed that stood side by side, or rather end by end, with that of Kell. Oh I was so terrified for her, or for having any communication with her, that I would not speak a word even when she spoke to me, but covered myself over the head with the bed-clothes, and lay puffing till I was like to choak for want of breath. I did not sleep well at all. I could not sleep, for she was always yawning, and then saying, 'Heigh-ho!' and then hushing the child to sleep. The next night I ventured to lye with my head out from beneath the clothes, unless when she spoke, which alarmed me exceedingly; and so I did the next night again, behaving myself with great magnanimity. At length I came to that pass, that when she spake to me I did not creep down beneath the bed-clothes, but only made a great bustle and flinging as if I *had been* hiding myself. This practice of deception I continued for several nights, always making more and more pouncing and scraping every time she addressed me. She laughed at me, and seemed highly amused, which made me still the worse. At length she said one night, 'Pray do not creep through the house for fright; what makes you so afraid of me? what ill do you think I will do to you? Heigh-ho, Nosey! I wish the bogle may not come to-night. I am afraid it will come, for I thought I heard it. Look that it do not rise at the back of your bed, for that is a very dangerous place. If it come, Nosey, I must either come in beside you, or you must come in beside me—.' 'Tutts!' said I, and that was my first word of courting; the first syllable that I spoke to Kell in that luckless loft. I said, 'Tutts!'

I suspected no evil intention on the part of my kind and indulgent master, and far less on that of Kell; indeed, how could I suspect either? One day he said to me in the fields, 'I do not know what to do about you and that wench Kell: for both your sakes I believe I must separate you. She is fallen in love with you, quite over head and ears, and has been complaining to our dame of your unkindness to her. We

have a great regard for the girl, and cannot part with her
– but, out of respect for you both, you must be separated.
I will, however trust you together until next week; and if
she do not complain any more, you may remain where you
are; but I suppose I will be obliged to part with you then,
though against my will.'

This was a terrible stound to my heart, and shewed my
master's masterly policy; for, notwithstanding of all my
pretended aversion to the company of women, and to that
of pretty Kell in particular, I would not have been parted
from her at that time for all the world, not even for all the
beef and bacon that was in it. I did not know well how to
make up matters with her so as to retain my place, but I
thought I would try. So that night I sat down on my own
bed-side with my clothes on, and scratched my head, and
beat with my bare heel against the loft; but she had lost all
hope of gaining me to the measures agreed on between her
and her master, and took no heed of me till I was obliged
to speak first myself, when the following highly interesting
dialogue passed between us:

'I'm unco feared the bogle come the night, Kell.'

'So am I!'

'I wasna sure, but I thought I heard it yestreen!'

'I aince thought that I heard it a wee too!'

'How does it play when it is gaun to rise?'

'It begins a scart, scarting, like a rattan, making holes, I
fancy, to come out and take us away.'

'Aih! then it has just been it that I heard!'

'Oh! I'se warrant it was, and that I heard too!'

'Ay; O it's terrible! we're ill, ill set here! but I'll watch
a' night, and keep it aff you, Kelly.'

With that I came and sat down on the side of her bed,
to keep the invidious scratching bogle away from her; but I
soon became drowsy, and was like to fall down. She begged
me to lay down my head on her pillow, but I would not
hear of that. Oh! no, no, I durst not lie down there; so I
stretched me on the loft at her bed-side, and fell asleep.
Awakening before day, the first thing I heard was the bogle
scratching. Kell had stretched her arm below the bed, on
the side opposite to me, and was scratching slowly and
fearfully; then, pretending to awake, she hid herself among
the bed-clothes, muttered prayers, and cried, 'Heigh-ho!'

I groaned; and, stretching my hand round the corner, scratched on the other side even more solemnly, and at more awful intervals than she had affected; so that we lay in great tribulation till the dawning of the day.

Afraid that I had still been too slightly obliging, and that I run the risk of being separated from her, I studied the whole day on the most becoming way of conducting myself, and entered on several most amorous resolutions; but the higher my resolves were, the more pusillanimous was my behaviour when put to the test. I durst not even touch the side of her bed that night; but the wicked unsonsy bogle still continued its scratchings, sometimes on the one side of the bed, and sometimes on the other, I was therefore obliged once more to sit down on her bed side, to guard her from its inroads. In sitting there I dropt asleep, and my head fell down on her pillow – it was impossible I could help that; and then she kindly laid the uppermost coverlet over me for fear of my catching cold; but I was by far too sound asleep to perceive it. She had to pull the covering from below me, in order that she might lay it above me – for all that I did not awake, which was a great pity, but always as she made the greatest stir, I sniffed the louder. A while after, I turned myself about, and gave my head a ketch toward the back of the bed, till my cheek came in contact with something soft; but it was in my sleep – and I was in one so profound, that I could not possibly know what that thing was. What a fright I got next morning on perceiving my situation! I sprung from the bed, and ran away to the hills to my charge, without speaking a word.

I was, however, quite intoxicated with delight, and endeavoured to ingratiate myself with my master, by paying every possible attention to his behests, lest I should lose so delightful a place both for stolen meat and approaching pleasures, which I perceived would still grow more and more sublime, and was glad when he said to me one day that Kell had given over complaining of my rudeness and incivility, and he would trust me as her companion for a little while longer. In the mean while, I was to take care and do nothing improper; but he had such trust to put in me, he was not afraid of that.

He was informed every day by this subservient beauty how matters proceeded; so he let them go on by degrees till they arrived at such a crisis as he desired, which was no more than a boy lying on a girl's bed-side with his clothes on. He then came up with a light one night at midnight to see how his child was resting, pretending that he thought her ill, and found me lying sound asleep, where perhaps I should not have been, though I was as innocent and as free of his mistress as the child that lay in her bosom. He was in great wrath, and pulled me over the bed, giving me two or three gentle thwacks with his open hand: he also rebuked her very sharply, but said to us before going away: 'Keep your own secret. For both your sakes I will conceal what I have seen, although you have acted so *very* improperly; but let me never catch you in the like fault again. If the church get hold of you, you are both undone.'

I was dreadfully ashamed; and thenceforward felt my heart quite reckless and desperate, disregardful of all danger or propriety; and my master made me still worse by telling me that I was to part from Kell in a few days, but that he did not like to put me away just then, for fear of awakening suspicions against us, for he had a great regard for us both! I laid all these things to heart, and could not then have staid from Kell's bed-side a night, if my head had been to answer for it next day. One night we were informed that some strangers had come to the house and were making merry, and before we went to bed our master sent us something to eat and drink. I thought there was something going on that night, for I heard a great deal of muttering and saying of paternosters till a late hour. However, I took up my old birth, and after a while fell sound asleep. About midnight we were awaked by four or five gruff looking fellows, with long beards, and staves in their hands, who ordered us both to get up and dress ourselves. Our master made a speech to them, lamenting our guilt, and, with tears in his eyes, beseeching their clemency toward us; but at the same time said, that he could not suffer such immoralities under his roof: he had a family of his own coming up, and bad example was pernicious. Then he related what strict injunctions he had given us, yet we had continued to persist in our wicked unlawful courses; that, therefore, he had been obliged to give us up as lawless and irreclaimable delinquents.

All that he could now do was to intreat theirs and the holy

fathers' merciful clemency towards the youthful offenders; for that, although we had both mocked and set at defiance the statutes of holy church, he had hopes of our repentance and amendment: And with that he delivered us over to the officers of the church, whom he had trysted and suborned for that purpose. They said he was a good man, but that the offenders must needs suffer a heavy penance, in order that they might be again rendered pure and without blame, in the eyes of their fostering and protecting parent.

When Kell saw that she was betrayed and abandoned, her grief and despair knew no bounds, and she would doubtless have accused her master to his face had she been able to articulate aught distinctly – but she fell into fits, and they hurried her away. We were confined to cells in different religious houses, but both in the same ward. It is well known what tyranny prevails here, and what vengeance is wreaked against all those guilty of breaches of morality, especially if those possessed of riches or power desire it; but it is nothing to that which predominates over the west country, where I then was. They fed me on bread and water, though I asked for fat flesh, and longed for it every hour of the day: and always when the people assembled to worship, I was put in the juggs; that is, I was chained to the kirk wall with an iron collar about my neck, and every boy brought a rotten egg, or some filth, and threw at me, till I was all over bedaubed and plastered like a rough stone wall. The men gave me a kick, and the old maids spit upon me as they passed, but the young women looked on me with pity; and the old wives, before my time of penance was expired, espoused my cause, and defended me from the rabble. I heard them saying to one another, 'Poor fellow, somebody may be the better o'him yet. What wad the mother that bore him say if she saw him standing in that guise? Surely she wad think the punishment far outwent the crime.'

One day, just when I was about to be set at liberty, I saw my kind master speaking to some of the holy brethren, and was glad when I saw him, thinking I saw the face of the only man on earth that cared for me. But he came with a different intent from what I supposed, namely, with the benevolent one of getting me hanged. He said he had missed some money out of his house ever since I came away; and though he should be sorry indeed to find any part of it on me, for his own satisfaction he requested to search my clothes in their presence, to which I submitted without reluctance, being conscious of my innocence. But he that hides knows best where to seek. It was not long before my kind master took out from between several of the button-holes in the breast of my grey coat, two gold moudiwarts, three silver merks, and several placks and bodles. In vain did I protest that I knew nothing about them; the brethren pronounced me the most incorrigible wretch and vagabond that traversed the face of the earth; and, as their jurisdiction extended not to such crimes as this, they sent me off with the proofs of my guilt to Lord William for judgment and execution. I shall never forget the figure I cut that day when brought before Lord William, and accused. I was in a wretched state as to clothes, having stood so long in the juggs. I had been hungered almost to death, and maltreated in every way, and altogether looked extremely ill. He asked them to go over the charges against me, when one of the brethren came forward and spoke to him as follows:

'My noble Lord and benefactor, a worthy gentleman within our bounds of censure and controul, lodged a complaint with us against two of his servants that had been tempted by the devil to fall into lawless and sinful communication; and notwithstanding of all his admonitions and threatenings of church discipline, they not only continued in their mal-practices, but every day grew worse and more abandoned. He therefore prayed us to take cognizance of the offence, which, for the sake of their souls, and the general benefit of our community, we undertook. Accordingly, my lord, as he suggested, we went disguised as strangers, and at midnight we found this same young gentleman lying snugly in bed beside our friend's principal maid-servant, the very maiden to whom he had entrusted the care of his children, one of whom lay in the bed with them. Think of the atrocity of this my lord, and look at the man!'

The judge did so, and could not help smiling.

'What do you say to that master?' said he, 'Is it truth?'

'Yes,' said I.

This answer made him burst out a laughing. 'Upon my

word,' said he, 'you are a most extraordinary youth! Was the girl pretty, say you, monk?'

'The woman was indeed very beautiful, my lord.'

'She has been blessed, however, with a singular taste. I think the stripling may almost be excused for this crime.'

The monk then related the circumstances of the stolen money having been found on me, at which the judge shook his head, and said, 'Alak, it is all over with him. He is unfit to live. What do you say to this, sirrah? Is it true?'

'Yes,' said I.

'True that you stole your master's money?' said he.

'No, I never stole it, but it is true that it was there.'

'What? you found it I suppose? Tell me the truth, did not you find it?'

'No, I never found it, nor ever saw it till it was taken out of my coat yesterday. I never had either gold or silver in my hand in my life.'

'Your woman took it and sewed it in for you, then, I suppose?'

'I do not know who took it, or how it came there, but there it certainly was.'

'Did you ever part with your coat to your sweetheart? Did you ever lend her it to mend, or leave it at home with her?'

'I have often on warm weather left my coat at home for three or four days rinning.'

'But you declare you did not take the money?'

'I never saw the money, nor heard of it till yesterday.'

When I said this, he looked stedfastly on me as if he had discovered something he saw not before. There was no man on earth could discover truth like Lord William. 'Who is this youth's accuser?' said he. They told him it was sleeky Tam.

'I have observed of late,' said he, 'that that gentleman never searches that he does not find, and never accuses that he does not bring proof. I have caused several to be executed on the evidences raised by him, and have always remarked that he is the only profiter by their being put down. We must move with more caution. Let that wench be brought before me, and stop the execution of Jock's Sandy, whom I ordered to be hanged to-morrow.'

My late benevolent master was watching the course of

these events with punctuality, and was terribly chagrined when he heard that his neighbour Jock's Sandy was reprieved. He was almost beside himself; but, having great influence with the holy brethren, he persuaded them to retain Kell under their jurisdiction, and not give her up to Lord William. In the course of his scrutiny he had likewise discovered some of his gold pieces on her, and had doomed her to destruction with the rest; yet, at the same time, he told the holy fathers to be lenient, and altogether to overlook that fault, which had originated from the first, and that was one to which youth was liable. He conjured them not to give her up to William the Severe, who would infallibly doom her to an ignominious death. If she had deserved that, he said, it was much better that she should die privately, in which case he would pay seventy merks annually to the church for the securing of her soul. He was frightened for the meeting of so many criminals before Lord William, wicked as we were; and so high was the influence of the convent, of which this was a branch, that the brethren refused to give up the offender to Lord William's officers.

After my first examination was over, I was thrust into a dungeon beside Jock's Sandy, who had been cast to die for stealing the ox which I myself slew; and, when we began to converse freely together, what a tissue of deceit was unraveled! He asked me if I knew any thing about that ox for which he was to lose his life! I said I knew very well about the ox, for I had killed him myself: 'And what a great fool you were,' said I, 'to incur so much danger for the sake of a nout's hide and a pair of horns, for these you certainly did steal.'

The man was perfectly amazed when I told him all the truth, and promised to procure me as much fat flesh as I could eat every day, if I would tell the truth of the story to Lord William. I catched at the offer, for I had suffered so much in my stomach of late, that I would have done far more than he required of me for such an advantage. Indeed I would have done any thing, or said any thing in the world, that I might once more enjoy my beloved mess. He proved as good as his word, for before night the keeper brought me a whole apron full of bits and scraps of the fattest meat that I ever saw – beef, mutton, and pork. There were some square pieces of perfect, pure white fat,

that I sliced down like cheese! They were from the flanks
of fat beeves, the briskets of wedders, and the ribs of fatted
hogs; and I could not but admire the want of good taste
among the gentles who had left these savoury bits to their
slaves and prisoners. I was so delighted that I could not
sleep by night, but always awakened from my straw and fell
a-munching. I wish we saw such a feast again; but, indeed
I saw nothing, for our house was in utter darkness; but it
was a good meat house, and I could have been content to
have lived in it all my life.

In a few days I was once more carried above ground for
examination, where I told the whole truth boldly, but was
not believed. No one would give credit to the tale, that I
had slain one of my master's fattest oxen for the sake of
good cheer; such a thing, they said, would never come
into a stripling's head, and I had been suborned to my
evidence by my fellow prisoner. Lord William asked if
there was any proof remaining that I could produce in
support of my assertion? I said I had a part of the beef
remaining, well salted up in a barrel below ground, and
covered with a moss divot; and that I had likewise some
hid for fresh meat in some cold well springs, and I would
shew them these if they liked. I was sent with a guard,
and shewed them the remains of my ox; and when this
was reported to Lord William, he called me a rogue and a
glutton, and caused them to tie a rope about my neck and
lead me through the streets of the town naked, lashing me
with a whip all the way. He then bade me make off with
myself, for if I was found within twenty miles of that place
where I stood, he would cause me to be hewed in pieces.

My late master was taken up, and examined face to face
with those he had accused; but how he contrived to elude
justice I never knew: ten years after, one informed me that
the dame Kelly had accused him before Lord William of
having seduced her, and that in the most disgraceful way,
and then of forcing me into the situation in which I was
caught, for a screen to his own guilt and shame. For all
that, it seems poor Kell was returned to the convent, and
never more heard of, and sleeky Tam possesses both his
own and his neighbour's farm at this day.

I had begun to think that ill deeds throve best; but I now
conceived that I had paid very dearly indeed for my late

pleasures of feasting and love, being almost flayed alive. I cried bitterly as I fled, and cursed Lord William and his raggamuffians that had scourged me, and vowed to myself, if I lived to be a man, that I would be revenged on them. I likewise cursed my deceitful master, but I did not curse poor Kell; indeed I found that it was for her I wept most bitterly, thinking myself the cause of all her shame and suffering.

I fled next into a country called Galloway, a place which some of you may have heard of by chance; but I found it the worst meat country, and the worst country altogether, that I had ever seen. I lived there for a number of years, leading a sort of vagabond life, but quite an honourable one. I learned naturally among them to be a great thief, and an acute liar; but I never stole any thing but fat flesh, nor do I account any thing else worthy of running the risk for – from that no danger ever could, or ever shall debar me. I care not much what sort it be, provided it be juicy, and a layer of white next the bone. I wonder whether men's flesh is likest to beef, or mutton, or venison?

'I wish ye wadna always turn your green een on me that gate when you speak about your fat flesh,' said Gibbie. 'I assure you, mine is neither like beef, nor mutton, nor venison; and, what is more, you shall never taste it. I appeal to you all, masters and friends, if this man has not fairly fallen through his tale.'

'I suppose it must be very like veal, then,' continued Tam; 'and if so, I have seen a joint of cold veal very excellent meat, more especially that adjoining the white gristly part; with a little salt, a man can eat a great deal of that without being any thing the worse.'

'My masters, I do protest against these carnivorous looks of the story-teller,' rejoined Gibbie; 'they make ane feel so queerly. It is as if he were tearing my flesh quick from the banes with his teeth. And I call you to note that he has sticked a story, which, from the beginning, is no story.'

'Stay till it be done, an you please,' said Tam; 'the best of my tale is yet to come; and any man may be allowed a breathing space and a little refreshment.'

At Castle-Fern I fell in with an old man called the Gorb, an itinerant fencer, who travelled the country teaching the art of the sword. To him I attached myself, somewhat against his will; for I saw that, though he was not everywhere a welcome guest, he was nevertheless a privileged one, and always admitted. He was six feet high, with a beard that hung to his middle, and his frame was entirely composed of bones and sinews. The feats that he described to me of warrior prowess first raised in me a desire to learn his noble art; and as soon as I began to manifest a partiality for his profession, he began to attach himself to me, but in a manner so ungracious, that if I had not been a being quite desperate, I never could have borne it. We moved on from place to place; the young men of the country assembled in parties, as we passed, to attend his lessons; and at night we had free-quarters wherever we went; that is, the Gorb was a free man – but many pointed inuendos were thrown out against my introduction as an additional burden. These people had better have let the matter pass over, for he did not fail to pay them back with interest in bitter and sarcastic retorts. On some of these occasions he gave me a terrible character of the country and its inhabitants.

'You are come, poor man, to sojourn in the worst country under the cope of heaven,' said he, 'into a place where there is no faith, no honour, no money, and very little meat.'

'What do they live on in general?' said I.

'On some wretched roots, pulse, and black corn,' said he; 'some lean unhealthy fish, and still more lean and sapless cattle.'

'I like the country a great deal the worse,' said I. 'Is the flesh here so very lean?'

'Why ask?' said he; 'have you not witnessed it?'

'No, I am very sorry I have not,' said I. 'I supposed it had been lent in this country. As for their faith or honour I care not a pin. Their money is of little avail to me; but I hate to stay in a country where there is no meat: and how they can transact business without money is beyond my comprehension.'

'They have none, however,' said he, 'nor was there ever any in this country. They transact all their business on a thing called credit, which commonly attaches itself to a man for a number of years, sometimes for a long, and sometimes a very short term. This enables him to cheat his neighbours for a time, and all his exertions tend only to this, namely, how many he can take in, and to what amount; and when he has gone as far as this ideal quality of his can carry him, he takes to the bent, and leaves them all in the lurch. This is the exact state of this blessed country called Galloway, and will be its state as long as it continues to exist. The only rational hope concerning it is, that, as it is a sort of butt-end of the creation, it will perhaps sink in the ocean, and mankind will be rid of it.'

He then took a hearty fiendish laugh at the conceit of the country being sunk, and went on—.

'After all, I cannot help being amazed at the rascally crew. Do you not see how suspicion and distrust are stamped on every countenance? Every man makes a bargain with apparent reluctance, and with a dread that his neighbour is going to cheat him; and he is never mistaken. Such is the country, and such are the people to whom you have now come, and such must they ever continue to remain. It is in their nature to be so, and they cannot be otherwise. Here am I, their master and benefactor, who have spent my life in teaching them the noblest of all sciences, without which they could not have defended their country. I have taught every chief in the country, and every one of their vassals, and how am I requited? Ill-clothed, worse fed, and not a bodle in my purse. All my recompense is the freedom of living a life of fatigue and wretchedness.'

'I will not stay another night in the country of such a parcel of rogues,' said I.

'You are wrong,' answered he: 'It is the best country you can be in. You have nothing to lose, and you may gain much. Experience is a man's greatest riches; and of that you will gain abundance. You will here learn hourly how to oppose cunning to cunning; and I will teach you the noble art of opposing masterly skill to brutal force, until you may haply be established as my assistant and successor.'

'I would rather dispense with the honour,' said I: 'You are too lean for me to think of being your successor. Were you a fat full-fed man, I would not say what I might do to attain the distinction; but I have made up my mind to one thing, which is, always to have my meat, honestly if I can, but at all events to have it.'

'You are so far right in your principle,' said he: 'For when we consider of it, a man can have very little more than his meat in this world, for all the struggling and strife there is in it. But since you set so high a value on good living, I can, if I please, assist you to it; for, poor and wretched as I appear, and as I am, I have a right to call for and command the best in every house. I could likewise take their clothes, for money they have none; but it would be like tearing the hearts out of the dogs – so I content myself with the meanest fare, rather than humble myself to ask ought of them.'

'You are an extraordinary man,' said I: 'But when I look at you, I cannot conceive this privilege of yours to exist in aught but in theory.'

'You shall see,' said he. 'What sort of meat would you prefer?'

'Fat flesh at all times and all seasons,' said I: 'There is nothing like that. Whether it be the flesh of bullock, hog, or wedder, the fattest is always the best.'

'What a kite! What a raven! What a dog!' exclaimed he: 'Well, you shall have it, if it were but to kill you of a surfeit.'

We were lying in a barn when this discourse occurred, and I could not but wonder what the old fellow would do. It was customary for us to take our breakfast at the place where we lodged, and if I might judge from our supper, the place where we then were gave no prospect of very rich fare.

The breakfast was produced; a quantity of black brochen and lentiles. The master of defence wist not how to break the ice by introducing a refusal of the proffered meal! but he considered himself as pledged to me, and his haughty spirit would not succumb. His looks were particularly embarrassed and amusing, and I saw that he would gladly have been free of his engagement, as he began a long palaver of general remarks. I kept up my good hopes, and gave him always an expecting look now and then, to make him hold to his resolution. The people of the house paid little attention to his harangue, till at length he concluded with these words:

'Such being the case, and such the state of the country, I am obliged now to claim all my rights, privileges, and dues from every vassal of my lord of Galloway, as well as from every subject of our liege lord the king, whose commission I bear. Goodman Latchie, I accept no more of black croudy and lentiles for breakfast: I claim, order, and command the best that is in this house. In place of that hog's meat, let us have a rasher on the coals, if you so please.'

'The muckle fiend be atween your teeth, then, to choak you wi' the first bite!' said the goodwife.

'Farmer Latchie, I contend not with women,' said the man of the sword: 'Are you aware of my rights, or do you know and dispute them?'

'I consider yours as merely a nominal right,' said he, 'which no man is bound to fulfil, because no man does it. All my lord's vassals treat you with common fare. Why should I do more?'

With that a raw-boned young man stepped forward, with a black beard and a ruffian look. He was the farmer's eldest son, and his name was John.

'What is all this din about,' said he: 'Let me speak, will ye, Master Gorb? Either take that which is set before you, or go away without it. I say that.'

'You say that? Do you, sir?' said my master.

'Yes; sure I do,' said he: 'I says that, and I'll say it again too, to be sure I will.'

'Then there is my gage, sir. Do you know to what you have subjected yourself?' said my master, pulling out his sword, and laying it on the board: 'You have given the king's ordained swordsman the denial; you must fight him, or find one on the instant to do it for you. If he kills you, he is entitled to take off your head and send it to the king; and if you kill him, you lose your head, and all the goods and chattels of your house are to be confiscate. Rescue or no rescue? Draw, craven! or yield me up the keys of your pantry, your chest, and your sunken cellar, you dog.'

'I does nae see the sense o' that, Master Gorb,' said John, with a countenance right sorely altered: 'that a man maunna say his awn's his awn, or what's his father's is his father's, but that he maun tak up sword and swordsman. I does nae fear thee. It's no to say that I fears thee; but I winna be bullied intil aught; and I just tells thee, that I'll neither fight thee nor suffer thee to get a scrap o'aught better than is set afore thee; and gang and seek thy mends. Now I says that.'

'Thou art a craven and a nincompoop,' said my master, with the highest indignation; 'and I lift my pledge, and will report thee to thy betters.'

'Do if thou mayest,' cried old Latchie, running to an armour chest, and taking from thence a sword and buckler. 'Disgrace of my house! To give the challenge, and then to flinch. Have with thee, Bellwether! I will give you to know, that old masons are the best barrowmen.'

'I ground my pledge again, and I take thee,' said my master. But now the old woman came running between them, crying out, 'Deil be i'your teeth! deil be i' your teeth! Tak a' that's i' the house an' haud you wi't: there are the keys; there are the keys! deil be i' your teeth, take a' – and let us alane o' your din.' The Gorb waved the keys aside with his arm in high indignation; but the wife clung to her point. 'I take you a' witnesses,' cried she, 'I take you a' witnesses, I have offered him the keys, and he has refused them. Here, young Gorb; young hing-by-the-gut, take ye them, take ye them. Deil be i' your teeth, take a' that's i' the house.'

I took the keys lest they should be forgot in the hurry; the two old fellows took to the field with sword and buckler, while both the old dame and her son John strove to interfere; but the old yeoman silenced them both with a word, and I thought he would have struck his son down with the sword, so much was he enraged at his behaviour.

I had seen much sword play by this time in the way of amusement, or lesson-taking; but I had never seen two men meet in deadly foil, and I trembled for the event; for I judged, that if the old Gorb was killed, it would fare hardly with me, being conscious that I was the moving cause of the combat. My master's demeanour was altogether inimitable. He went through every thing as if it had been a matter of mere ceremony, first slipping gracefully to one side, crossing his hands on his breast, bowing profoundly, and then shaking hands with Latchie: then swimming gracefully to the other side, and repeating the same manoeuvre. Last of all, he wheeled about, cut some wild flourishes with his sword, and took his distance. The yeoman bit his lip, and appeared to be viewing all these things with disdain; but he set himself firm on his legs with his left foot foremost, and setting up his broad bonnet before, waited the onset. The Gorb on the contrary advanced with his right foot foremost; and, instead of availing himself of the buckler as the former did, he came forward bearing it up behind him as high as his head. He seemed to wear it merely because the other did, but he was too proud to make any use of it. Nothing ever did, or ever will exceed the singularity of that combat: the figures of the men, and their manner of fighting, being so different. Latchie was short and squat, the Gorb somewhat like the skeleton of a giant. The art of fighting which the former pursued was to shield himself behind his broad buckler, peep over it, and now and then make dreadful blows around it with the full swing of his body, as if he meant to cut my master through the middle, or shear off both his thighs. On such occasions the Gorb, beside parrying the stroke, made such tremendous springs off at a side, that he rather appeared like a spirit than any thing of bones, sinews, and blood, for as to flesh there was none on him; and at every one of these leaps he uttered a loud 'Hoh!' as if he had been mortally wounded, or in great danger of having been so; yet all the while his face was so sublimely grave and serious as if every movement were to have been his last. He never attempted to hit the yeoman, and had apparently no other aim in fighting, than merely to show his dexterity in fencing, retreating, and advancing. I deemed that all was over with him, and began to be mortally afraid of myself; and any man would have acknowledged what good reason I had, if he had witnessed with what looks the wife and son regarded me. Every one of them thought the Gorb had the worst of it, and that the farmer was sure of the day. Indeed by this time there was little doubt of it. The old wife thrice clapped her hands, and screamed out, 'Weel proven, goodman! that gars him scamper! Weel proven, Daniel Maclatchie! Lie to the breastleather.' At these words I began to look over my shoulder, and meditate a most strenuous flight. But now the most novel scene of all occurred: my master still continued to change his ground, and to skip and fly about, until at length the yeoman, encouraged by his wife's words, came hard upon him, and, heaving up his shield a little, he came with a deadly stroke round below it, ettling to cut off both my master's legs. 'Hoh!' cried the Gorb, as loud as he could vociferate; and as the little squat yeoman stooped to the stroke, he made such a spring into the air that he leaped fairly over his head; and as he passed like a meteor over above him, he gave him such a slap with the broad side of his sword on the hind cants of the head, that it made the farmer run forward and fall with his nose on the ground. He was again on his feet, however, in an instant, and faced about, while his eyes streamed with water from the sharpness of the stroke. This feat astonished the Latchies; but the wife cried out, 'A barley! a barley! foul play! – he's fighting on springs.'

'Emblem true of thy accursed country!' cried the Gorb, and kicking off his sandals at her head, he took his ground on his bare soles. The combatants set to it again; but the yeoman was now on his guard, and fought shy, standing on the defensive. My master soon grew tired of this way of fighting; and, after two or three flying feints at an attack, in a moment he wrenched Latchie's sword from his grasp, and threw it into the air like a sling-stone. The lookers on gazed in amazement – and the astonished yeoman traced the course of his erratic weapon, which, after forming an arch like a rainbow, lighted at the distance of forty yards. John, the farmer's son, was the first who ventured a remark on the phenomenon, which he did with his accustomed shrewdness, and in the Cumberland brogue, which he had learned by living some years in that district.

'Feyther, I thinks thou hast thrown away thee swoard.'

'Ay,' said his father, biting his lip, and looking after it.

By this time the Gorb had his sword at Latchie's throat, crying, 'Rescue, or no rescue, I say? Yield, traitor, or die.'

Latchie paid no regard to him. He only bit his lip, looked after his sword, and stood his ground firm without moving, showing a most unyielding and dauntless spirit.

The Gorb repeated his threat, but the yeoman paid no further attention to it than before.

'What an unlucky accident!' said he. 'Had I not thrown away my sword, I would have humbled you.'

'Do you regret the loss of your sword so much?' said the Gorb. 'Will you promise, on the honour of a good yeoman, not to throw it away in like manner again?'

'Promise?' said the other: 'I will swear on it, and by it, never to part with it in like manner again.'

'Young man,' said my master to me, 'run and bring me this brave yeoman's sword.'

I brought it, and he took it by the point, and delivered it back to the owner with all manner of courtesy. Latchie took it in his hand, and let the point of it slant towards the ground in token of submission.

'Nay, nay, I deliver it,' cried my master. 'I would not see such a man show fear or pusillanimity for any thing. Exchange me three times three, and no more; and God stand by the right. I counsel thee, moreover, to assume thy best defence, as I propose to do thee all manner of injury.'

'So be it. I defy you still,' said Latchie, and took his ground a second time. His wife and son spoke a great deal by way of interference, but were totally disregarded. The combat began again with more fury than ever; but at the second or third time of crossing their weapons, Daniel Maclatchie's sword betook itself again into the firmament, and after tracing nearly the same course as formerly, alighted on the same spot.

'You are the devil and none else,' said Latchie, 'and I yield to my conqueror. I am at your disposal.'

'And I will use my advantage, as in duty and in honour bound,' said the Gorb: 'Rise up my friend and brother; you are a man of true genuine spirit. I honour you, and I estimate your country more this morning, for your sake, than I have hitherto done. I claim your friendship as a brother in arms. You shall not have cause to repent this spirited encounter.'

The farmer was greatly flattered by this speech. I gave up the keys; and there was no end of kindness and endearment between the two old fellows. We had our rasher on the coals; and I think I have scarcely risen from a better diet than I did that day. I got the greater part to myself, for the rest were all so busy talking and drinking cold ale, that they hardly thought of the bacon. It was nicely toasted, and the fat stood on it like small drops of honey. But I must not dwell on the recollection else I shall faint.

At our meal the yeoman offered my master a new war cloak, with belts, bands, and haversack, if he would tell him by what means he disarmed him with such ease, and in so extraordinary a manner; but the other absolutely refused.

'It is allowable in chivalry,' said he, 'to learn and practice any mode of manual defence, and to keep that mode a secret till you prove it on your opponent. That is my secret, and by that mode I would forfiet my life, nay my character itself, to disarm any man that ever pointed a two-edged sword at my breast.'

'I should have liked very much to have known that secret of his,' said Charlie Scott.

I found it out privately with the most perfect certainty, continued Tam; but durst never let him know that I understood aught of the matter. It was owing to his sword's handle, which was made for the purpose. It had an inner shell of steel polished like glass; then an outer one of basket-work, formed with rounded bars in such a manner that, by turning his hand in a slight degree to humour the position of the opponent's sword, and dashing his hilt against the point of it, that entered between those of the cross-bars, and, running up the polished steel within, bent and fixed itself; then by a sudden wrench against his opponent's thumb, of which he was a perfect master, he not only disarmed him to a certainty, but generally left his arm powerless. After I had discovered it, I went by myself to try the experiment, fixed my own sword, and taking my master's in my hand, I pushed the basket of that slightly against the point of the other, and behold it fixed in it so close, that with all my might, and all my art, I could not extricate it without breaking it in two, and, in that case, I saw I would leave the point sticking where it was, which I durst not do for my life. At length it came into my head to do as my master did. This had the effect at once; the vibration in the blade caused by the swing and jerk, made it loosen, and it flew away through the air like a fiery dragon.

'Master Michael Scott,' said Gibbie, 'and my friends, I again appeal to you all if this man has not fallen through his tale. It is turning out no tale at all, but merely an offputting of time, till we shall all perish of hunger.'

'The story of the hapless maiden Kell, and of our hero's first essays in love, I did admire and prize,' said the poet.

'Od help your crazed head,' said Charlie: 'I wadna gie

that duel atween the twa auld chaps for a creelfu' o' love stories.'

'Lo, the tale is good,' said the friar; 'but it goeth here and there, without bound or limit; and wherefore should not a man relate all that befalleth unto him. I suppose it behoveth our friend to go on, without turning aside to the right hand or to the left.'

'My tale is indeed long, but to me it is momentous. I should stop here pleasantly; but life is sweet – and, to give me a fair chance for mine, I beg to be permitted to relate one adventure more.' This, after some demur, was granted, and Tam went on:

After spending several years among the hills of Galloway, and being approved of by the Gorb (as he was called by every body, though his name was Macdougald) for a good swordsman, I tired of the country, being persuaded that the ground did not fatten the cattle properly; and from the moment I began to suspect that, I had no more satisfaction in the place, but utterly despised it. I perceived that their beef was never above an inch thick in the ribs, and what was worse, it was not properly mixed with white layers of fat; even the doubles in the broad bone of the shoulder were nothing but pure red lire. This will never do, thought I. How I despise the people that can put up with such a country as this!

'Master,' says I, one day, 'I am quite tired of this country, and am going to leave it.'

'Wherefore are you going to leave it, Thomas? Have not I been better and kinder to you than to myself?'

'For all that, master, I am resolved not to sojourn another week in it.'

'I warned you that they were a deceitful people before,' said he; 'but we must take them as they are. We cannot make mankind as we would wish to have them.'

'It is not for the men, nor for the women either, that I dislike the country so much,' said I.

'What is it then for?' said he.

'It is,' said I, 'because I suspect that their grass is not of a good quality.'

I will never forget the look that the Gorb turned on me. He was walking somewhat before me, but when he heard my reason for disliking Galloway he wheeled about, and, taking one of his most striking upright positions, with his lean shoulders set up like two pins, he stared at me with his mouth wide open; and then put the following questions to me at long intervals.

'Grass! eh! How do you mean?'

'Look at it,' said I; 'What substance is in that wiry stuff, and on these hills of black heather!'

The Gorb's jaws fell down with dismay. He visibly thought that I was deranged, but he answered me mildly to humour my malady.

'True, the grass is not good; it never was, and never will be so. But I have not observed that you ever eat much of it; nor can I see how a man's happiness any way depends upon the quality of the grass of a country.'

'If that be all the sense that you have,' thought I, 'I will disdain for my part to exchange another word with you on the subject. Since you think that a man's happiness can depend on *any thing else* but good grass, you shall be followed no longer by me.'

'Well,' continued he, after waiting a while for an answer, 'I see you are sulky about this whim, but I will humour it. I have nearly finished my terms among the mountains, and we shall descend upon the shores, where there is as good grass as any in Scotland, and I promise you full liberty to go into every field that you chuse, and take your bellyful of it. I have likewise many things to teach you, which will amuse you in the highest degree, and which belong to the sublime art of legerdemain.'

'What is that?' said I.

'It is the art,' said he 'that enables us to see things and people as they really are. There is scarcely any thing on this earth really what it appears to be; and this art I have yet to teach you.'

From that day forward he began and performed feats that entirely bewildered my senses, but which furnished, wherever we were, a great fund of amusement; all the young people believed him to be in compact with the devil. I have forgot them all but one, which I will remember as long as I live.

We came to a wealthy yeoman's house on the river Urr, where we were to remain several days; and while

he exercised the farmer's sons in fencing, I kept the
young peasants in exercise – and then in the hall in
the evenings he went on with his cantrips. There was a
delicious shoulder of bacon hanging up on the farmer's
brace, among many meaner hams and pieces of wretched
dried flesh. I believe I had fixed my eyes on it, and perhaps
my heart a little too. Whether the Gorb noticed this and
dreaded the consequences or not, I cannot tell, but he
began a speech about things not being what they appeared
to be, and offered to give us a striking instance.

'Take down the choicest and best ham among all these
above the fire,' said he. I did so, taking down the shoulder
of bacon with great alacrity.

'Take down the worst,' said he. I did so; it was one of
venison dried like a crooked stick.

'Which do you account the best?' said he. I told him.
'Well, you are mistaken,' said he; 'and I'll convince you
of it. Roll them both neatly up in straw, or as you will.'

I did so.

'Now, do you know the one from the other?'

'Yes.'

'Very well: heave them up again that you may not be
mistaken in the weight. Now, cross your hands, and
heave them with different hands. Quite sensible they are
the same?'

'Quite sensible.'

'Very well. Take them aside by yourself and look at
them. You will now see them as they really are, not as
they appeared to your eyes.'

I hastened and opened out the shoulder of bacon. It
was nothing but three dried bones, hanging together by
tendons, and stuffed up into the shape of an overgrown
shoulder of bacon with brawn, which was covered round
with a piece of sow's hide. I shed some tears at this blighting
discovery; for though the bacon was not mine, I felt in my
heart that I did not know how matters were to come about.
I hung the two hams up as they were, and was cured of my
itching eye; but no man can tell how things will come round
to the advantage of an acute and clever fellow.

While we were at that house, the country was raised to
follow the Lord of Galloway into Cumberland. It was a
great rising, the utmost quota being demanded of every

yeoman in the country, in terms of his villanage. Our
landlord got a charge to find five, whereas he had none
to send save three, unless he and his eldest son both went,
which would have been grievously against him at that time;
so he applied to my master and me to go on his behoof,
offering large conditions, which were soon accepted. The
principal, if not the sole thing that induced me to go out
on that raide, was the stipulation that I was to have my
choice of all the meat in the house, to the amount of what
I could conveniently carry on my back in a march. After a
great deal of choosing, I fixed on a small beef-ham, because
it was solid, and no bones in it, and blest my master's
ingenuity that had let me into the secret of the deceitful
shoulder of bacon. The next that came after me was a
blade of endless frolic and humour, named Harestanes. He
instantly snapped at the bacon-ham, and popped it into his
goatskin wallet, nodding his head, and twisting his mouth
at me, as much as if he had said, 'What a taste you have! I
am glad you had not the sense to take this.' I could easily
have prevented him, by revealing the secret; but he had
always been trying to make a fool of me, therefore I could
scarcely contain my mirth at his mistake; and resolved
to enjoy his disappointment in full. He was a sprightly
handsome youth, and had such a forward and impertinent
manner that he contrived to make friends in every family
that we passed by, particularly with the women, so that he
lacked nothing that he desired; and tho' I watched him
night and day for fear of losing the sport, he never took
out his bacon to break it up till the fourth day after our
departure. My beef-ham was by that time more than half
done. It was a most wretched piece of meat, being as hard
as wood, and bitter as gall; but I was still comforted with
this, that it was so much better than my comrade's.

It was about eight o'clock on a morning, on the English
side of the Border, that Harestanes first loosed out his
wallet to make a breakfast of his bacon; and he being very
hungry, I sat down beside him to enjoy the sport, taking
out my black beef likewise. All that I could do I could
not retain my gravity while he was loosening the cords,
and taking the straw from his ham, which made him look
wistfully at me, and ask what the fool meant? But when I
saw him look seriously and greedily at it, and then take out

his knife to cut off a great slice, I lost all power, and fell on the ground in a convulsion of laughter, while my voice went away to a perfect wheezle. He could not comprehend me in the least degree, and actually began to cut! yes, he actually began to cut through the bristly skin, while I lay spurring the ground, and screaming with anticipation of the grand joke that was to ensue. Before I could recover my sight from amid the tears of extravagant mirth, the scene was changed; and I shall never forget the position in which the puppy sat, when my eyes cleared. No, it is impossible I ever can forget it! Conceive a wicked impertinent frolicksome whelp of a tailor, for he was nothing better, who had been with Sir Robert Graham's maids all the night, and was so hungry that you might almost have cast a knot on him, sit down to take a hearty luncheon of his bacon ham; and then conceive his looks when he found he had nothing but rubbish and dry bones. If you conceive these, you will conceive the very scene that I saw, at least that I conceived and saw in my mind's eye. How could I but laugh? No! It was impossible I could abstain from laughter; – but yet, for all that, things turned out quite the reverse. He had actually sliced off a rasher of bacon, the fattest, the whitest, and the most beautiful rasher of bacon ever I had seen in my life! There were three distinct layers of lire and fat, curving alternately through it like quarter moons. No man ever beheld such a sight! He sliced out another piece, which was still more perfectly beautiful than the preceeding one. My eyes darkened. I had seen enough to shew me the enormity of my folly, and my irreparable loss! He roasted his rashers on the fire. The fat fried out of them, and flamed among the embers; and when he laid them on his bread, they soaked it all with pure liquid fat. And there was I sitting beside him, gnawing at my piece of infernal beef, the sinewy hip of some hateful Galloway stott that had died of the blackleg, and, having been unfit for ought else, had been dried till the hateful substance was out of it. Yet I had my choice of both, and took this. I shall never wish any friend of mine to suffer such pangs as I did that morning; for all that I had suffered in my dangers and disappointments was nothing to them. I would fain have slain the Gorb privately; but not daring to do that, I resolved never to see his face again, after the vile trick he had played. All my hopes and all my enjoyments of the foray being now ended, I resolved on taking my departure, and that by the time my enemy had the first slice of bacon eaten.

We had orders to halt all that day, for the Johnstons and the Jardines were a day's march before us. Their advanced columns had fallen back; and as the troops were sleeping or straggling about, I prepared for my departure. My comrade having been with the knight's women all the night, a set of creatures madder than himself, he was quite worn out; and as soon as he got his inside lined with the salutary beverage, he fell fast asleep. An inward light now began to dawn on my heart, brighter than the sun at noon day, and lighting my steps forward to future felicity. My breath cut short with ecstatic delight, and my knees trembled as I formed the resolution of changing hams with my hopeful comrade. His wallet was lying open – not so the tailor's eyes: I might have exchanged coats, and shoes too, for him. The great work was done in an instant. I whipped out his shoulder of bacon, and put my piece of black timber in its place. 'Take you that, honest man,' said I to myself: 'Time about is fair play. I have given you something that will exercise your jaws for a while.'

When I found that I had this most delicious of all morsels on my back, I was so light that I scarcely felt my feet touch the ground; and there being no time now to lose, I made straight away into England; for I durst not turn towards Scotland, the sentinels being so very thick on that quarter. Our advanced guard was composed of the Gordons from the Ken – a set of desperate raggamuffins whom I durst not have gone among had it not been fair forenoon. I had my wallet on my back and my sword by my side; and when I saw any of them eying me, I went up to them and asked how far the Johnstons were before us?

'What the devil was I wanting with the Johnstons?'

'O, I was afraid there might be a battle fought before I saw it, which I would not should happen for any thing in the world.'

'Hear to the coulter-nibbit piper,' said one.

'He is as like supping a pint o' fat brose as killing an Englishman,' said another.

'I wadna trust him wi' ought beyond a litter o' English pigs,' said a third.

'Let him gang forrit, and fiend that he get his chafts clawn the first sword that's drawn! I wadna that his name were Gordon for a hunder civis.'

Accordingly I got liberty to pass; but as soon as I got out of sight, I turned to the left, and escaped to the moors of Bewcastle. I had now found out the invaluable art of flint and frizzle, and could kindle a fire whenever I pleased. So I sought out a lonely wild dell, and lighting a fire of birns and strong heather, roasted two slashing slices of my shoulder of bacon. I also took a good shave of bread from my friend the tailor's hearth-bannock; but after all I could not think of adulterating the savoury delicious fare by any unnatural intermixture – so I ate up the dry bread by itself, and then smacked up the bacon afterwards. I cannot describe my sensations of delight, not only in my meal, but in contemplating the beauty of the object. I sat long feasting my eyes on the beauty of the slices before I committed them to the coals. They were curved so beautifully in semi-circles, the fat and the lire time about, that, unless for such an object, the term *beauty* would have no meaning. They lay alternately, as if it were this way, and this way, and this way.

'I protest against your drawing of your pictures on my shoulder,' cried Gibbie; 'and also against the party being any longer mocked with such fulsome trash in place of a story. Do you not perceive, Sir Master, and do you not all perceive, that he is havering and speaking without end or aim? He is sensible that he has failed in his story; and that a dismal fate awaits him, and all that he is now intent on is driving of time.'

'I confess that I am sick of the bacon and other fat things,' said Charlie.

'My soul disdains the abject theme,' said the poet: 'Its tantalizing sight is like the marshfire's vacant gleam to the bewildered wight. 'Tis throwing meat to hungry souls, with fainting sore opprest; or drink unto the parched lips, whereof they may not taste.'

'Let us show some spirit, wretched as we are,' said Gibbie, 'and protest with one assent against being farther sickened, as well as mocked by such loathsome stuff.'

'This is unfair, and using undue influence,' cried Tam.

'None of you were thus interrupted, but got time to finish your stories as you liked. Mine is not done; the best part of it is yet to come, and I say it is unfair. Great Master, you sit as judge; I appeal to you. My life has been varied. Let them chuse what sort of a theme they want, and I will fit them, only suffer me to relate one other exploit.'

The Master, on whom hunger seemed to make no impression, thought the request was reasonable; but in making choice, every one of them, young and old, pitched on a different subject, so that Tam could not get proceeded; neither can this chapter, as an extraordinary incident befel, which naturally brings it to an end.

CHAPTER TWENTY-ONE

And he said unto Satan, whence comest thou?
And he answered, and said, thou knowest it is true,
That I come from wandering on the earth,
And from going to and fro on it,
Like a masterless dog, with my bow-wow-wow.

Zach. Boyd's Bible

AT THE VERY time they were disputing about the right of Tam to proceed with his tale, their ears were astounded by a loud hollo! at the gate. Every man's heart leaped for joy, and every one was instantly on his feet; but Charlie was first on the platform, and answered the hollo! with full stentorian voice. The same voice called again,

'A Bellandine.'

'Where bye?' answered Charlie.

'By the moon,' said the voice.

'And the seven stars!' rejoined Yardbire, clapping his hands, and shouting for joy, 'The Warden for ever! My chief for ever! He is the man that cares for his own! Ah! he is the noble master.'

Charlie well knew the voice that hailed him. It was that of his friend and companion in arms, Dan Chisholm, whom the Warden had indeed despatched all the way from Northumberland to Aikwood, to see what was become of his embassy, with six-and-twenty chosen troopers. Charlie Scott's arm was a bulwark of strength, and his breast a tower of fidelity, the value of which Sir Ringan knew how to estimate, while his acts of kindness and regard made a deep impression on Charlie's honest unsophisticated heart; and before he would say a word about the situation of either himself or his associates, he caused Dan to inform him of the Warden's fortune and success in their absence. Being satisfied concerning these, he called out,

'What ither uncos, Dan? What mair news are come out?'

'O, God shield you!' cried Dan, 'Do nae ye ken that the world's amaist turned up-side-down sin ye left us? The trees hae turned their wrang ends upmost – the waters hae drowned the towns, and the hills hae been rent asunder and riddled up like heaps o' chaff. 'Tis thought that there has been a seige o' hell, and that the citadel has been won, for the deils are a' broken loose and rinning jabbering through the land. They hae been seen, and they hae been heard; and nae man kens what's to be the issue, or what's to fa' out neist.'

'Blaw lown, Dan; ye dinna ken wha may hear ye,' said Charlie. 'We hae had hand in these matters oursels: But for the sake of a' that's dear to you and to us bring gavelocks and ern mells, pinching-bars, and howies, and break open every gate, bar, and door in this castle; for here are we a' imprisoned on the top of it, and famishing to dead wi' hunger and starvation.'

'That I will do wi' a' expedition,' answered Dan. 'It is a shame for the master of the castle to imprison his kinsmen's friends, who came to him in peace and good fellowship. What strength of opposition holds he?'

'Nane, good Chisholm, but these gates. The great Master is himself a prisoner, and suffering with us.'

'That dings a'!' said Dan; 'I canna understand it! But it's a' ane for that; ye maunna stay there. I shall gar his gates flee a' into as mony flinders as there are hairs on his grey beard.'

'If you demolish one bar of these gates, young man,' cried the Master fiercely, 'You do it at your peril.'

'So I do, and so I will,' answered Dan: 'Either bring down my friends and companions to me this instant, or – I have orders – and here goes.'

'Man of mystery and of misery, what dost thou mean?' said the friar. 'Lo I have saved thy life; and if thou refusest to let us escape from the face of death, I will even throw thee from the top of thy tower, and they blood shall be sprinkled on the wall.'

The Master gave him a fierce look, but made no reply. As

he strode the battlement, however, he muttered to himself with great violence, 'Does the Christian dog dare to beard me thus? To what am I fallen? I am fallen low, but not to this. And not to know what I am! nor what power remains with me? Would that I were in the midst of my arcana and of the spirits once more! Young warrior, use your liberty. Break up and demolish. Set us all free, and see who is the profiter.'

Dan scarcely needed such permission. He and twenty others had each a stone of at least half his own weight heaved on his shoulder, which, at a given signal, they all dashed on the gate at once. The bars bent, but nothing gave way; and it was not before the twentieth broadside, in the same irresistible style, that the cross bars became like a bow and the lock slipped. As for the large bolt, one of the men had climbed over the counterguard on the shoulders of the rest and drawn it. When they came to the gate of the castle, entrance seemed hopeless. It was stedfast and immoveable, the door being double. Dan bellowed for the porter, and asked those on the top what was become of him; but none made answer to his rash question. After waiting a while for it, with his face placed horizontally, he muttered to himself, 'Aha! mum there! He has gane nae gude gate, I'll warrant him. It's a queer place this, an' as queer folk about it.'

'What's queer about it, lad?' said a strange voice through the key hole, whence it would not speak again.

They had nothing for it but to begin with such awkward mattocks as they had, namely, a score of huge stones; but, to their excessive joy, the doors gave both way at the first assault. This was owing to a most fortunate blunder of the friar, who, during the time he was in possession of the keys, had gone forth to provide for his mule, which he did in an ample manner, but, on returning, had either been unable or unwilling to turn the tremendous locks again into their sockets; and open flew the gates with a jarring sound. Of course, it was not long till our yeomen were thundering at the iron door on the small stair. It was a double door of strong iron bars, and the lock was inclosed between them, so that all attempts to open it appeared fruitless, one man only being able to get to it at once, (that is, one on each side,) and these had no footing. After tugging at it in vain for a space, Dan swore that, to open it, it would be necessary either to begin at the top of the tower and demolish downward, or at the bottom and demolish upward. This appeared a job so tedious to starving people, that it was agreed to feed them with meat and drink through the bars. Every man readily proffered the contents of his wallet; but the getting of these through the bars required ingenuity. They poured the meal through in tubes made of leather, and water and strong drink in the same way; but the flesh could only be got through in long small pieces; and Tam Craik having taken his station at the back of the door, in order to hand up the provisions to his companions, none of the butcher-meat (as it is now called) found its way farther. By the time they had got a supply of meal, water, and distilled liquor, some of Dan's party, by the direction of the Master, went to bring mattocks for raising the stair, and forcing a passage through below the door; others had gone to the brook for more water; so that none remained in the narrow stair save Dan Chisholm and another person.

By this time there was one who had been silently watching the progress of affairs at Aikwood castle, where he had long been accustomed to reckon on every thing as his own; but now there were some things passed under his potent eye, the true motives for which he could not comprehend, and these actions were still growing more and more equivocal; so he resolved on trusting his sworn vassals no more to their own guardianship, but to take an active management in guiding the events that so deeply concerned his honour and power. Who this august personage was the reader will scarcely guess. He may perhaps discover it in the detail.

It was wearing toward evening, the sun being either set or hid behind dark clouds; for, short as these tales may appear as here related by Isaac the curate, they had taken a day in telling by the wights themselves. The individuals who had been shut up were all light of heart and rejoicing. Delany had fainted in ecstacy, or partly, perhaps, by exhaustion, but was soon recovered by a cup of cold water. They had got plenty of stores laid in for a night and more; so that they were freed from the dread of perishing by starvation, or saving their lives by a resource of all others the most repulsive to humanity. Such was the state of affairs, when the most appalling noise was heard somewhere about the castle – a noise which neither could be described nor the cause of it discovered. The people below ran out to the court or to the tops of the outer walls, and those above to the battlements – but they saw nothing save the troopers' horses scowering off in all directions, every one of them snorting aloud, and cocking their heads and their tails. Tam Craik and Dan Chisholm were still standing with their noses close to the iron door, and conversing through it. Another trooper stood close at Dan's back; and, when the rushing sound arose, the one said to the other,

'What the devil is that?'

'Take care wha ye speak about here, friend, or wi' reverence be it spoken,' said Tam. Then turning round, he called out, 'Yardbire, what hurly-burly is that?'

'I cannot tell,' answered Charlie; 'only I think the devil be entered into the horses.'

Tam, who did not hear distinctly from the top, answered Dan thus: 'He says it's only the devil entered into the horses.' Dan was just about to reply, when the trooper tapped him on the shoulder, and said in a whisper, 'Hush, squire! Good Lord! look what is behind us.' He looked about, and saw a terrific being standing on the landing-place, beckoning him to come down. From an irresistible impulse, he lost no time in obeying; and, pushing the trooper down before him, he descended the steps. When he came to the bottom he got a full view of the figure, that stood upright between two pilasters, with its face straight to the aperture that lighted the place. One may judge of our yeomen's feelings when they gazed on a being which they always described as follows:

It appeared about double the human size, both in might and proportion, its whole body being of the colour of bronze, as well as the crown upon its head. The skin appeared shrivelled, as if seared with fire, but over that there was a polish that glittered and shone. Its eyes had no pupil nor circle of white; they appeared like burning lamps deep in their sockets; and when it gazed, they rolled round with a circular motion. There was a hairy mantle hung down and covered its feet that they could not be seen; but Dan saw its right hand, as it pointed to them to retire, every finger of which terminated in a long crooked talon that seemed of the colour of molten gold. It once opened its mouth, not as if to speak but to breathe, and as it stooped forward at the time, both of them saw it within. It had neither teeth, tongue, nor throat, its whole inside being hollow, and of the colour of burning glass.

It pointed with its right hand across its bosom for them to be gone, and, as they passed by with hurried strides, it drew a stroke with its paw which threatened to send them heels over head down the stair; but it withheld the blow in a moment, as if moved to some higher revenge; and all the way down the great winding stair, it followed and showered on them such a torrent of burning sulphur that they were almost overwhelmed, all the while vomiting it from its burning bosom, with a noise that resembled the hissing of a thousand great serpents. Besides this, on every landing-place there were a pair of monsters placed as guards, immense snakes, bears, tigers, and lions, all with eyes like burning candles. For all these, our two yeomen still kept their feet, which was a wonder, and escaped fairly into the court of the castle.

When they arrived there, every one of their companions had taken leg-bail, and were running as if for death or life; and after what our two champions had seen, there was no occasion to bid them run after the others. Those above heard only the rushing noise, which still increased as long as there was one of those below within the gate, but they saw nothing further – and wondered not a little when they saw first the horses run away, and then the men after them. When Charlie saw that they *were* gone, and his brother-in-arms Dan leaving the outer-gate the last, he called after him to go *by the mill, and see that Corbie got plenty of water.*

What our prisoners had witnessed was, like every thing else about that castle, quite incomprehensible. Even the great Master himself was manifestly at a loss; when he first heard the sound, and saw the beginning of the confusion, his eyes beamed with exultation. He gave three stamps with his foot, and called aloud, as to some invisible being, in an unknown tongue; but on receiving no answer his countenance fell, and he looked on in gloomy mood.

The flyers vanished after their horses on the hill to the eastward of the castle. Once a few of them rallied and faced about; but on the next one coming up they betook them again to their heels; and thus was our hapless embassy left in the same state as before, save that they were rather in higher spirits, their situation being now known, and instant death averted. After they had refreshed themselves, most of them fell into a slumber; but at length, as the evening advanced, the poet claimed his privilege of telling a story. Some of them proposed that the conversation should be general instead, seeing the great stake for which they contended was now, in all likelihood, superseded. The poet, however, was of a different opinion, on the ground that the highest stake, in his estimation, still remained. 'What though my life may not be forfeited,' said he, 'to feed the hungry and carnivorous maw of this outrageous baconist; although my warm and oozing blood may not be sucked up like the stagnant marsh by bittern vile, or by the tawney snipe; yea, though my joints should not be skatched and collared by the steel, or sinews gnawed up by officious grinder: What's that to me? a gem of higher worth, of richer acceptation, still remains. Beauty unsullied! pure simplicity! with high endowments, in affliction nursed, and cramped by bondage! Oh my very heart yearns to call such a pearl of lustre mine! A kindred soul! A bosom friend! A oh – oh – oach.'

Charlie hasted to clap his hand on the poet's mouth, as he burst out a-crying, 'Hout, hout, Colly!' said he, 'I am quite o' your opinion; but truly this is carrying the joke ower far. I wish ye maunna hae been hauddin rather freely to your head o' thae strong liquors; for the singing crew are a' drowthy deils, ilk ane o' them. Whisht, whisht, and ye sal tell your tale, or sing your sang, which you like; and then you are free to take a collop, or gie a collop, wi' the best o' them.'

'I flatter myself that's rather a good thing? Eh?' said the poet.

'What thing?' said the other.

'The song that we overheard just now. Do you know who made that song? Eh?'

'Not I.'

'But you have heard our maidens chaunt it – have you not? God bless them! Sweet, dear, sweet, sweet creatures! Why, Sir, that song happens to be mine; and I think I may say, without vanity, it is as good a thing of the kind as you ever heard? Eh?'

'Faith, I believe it is,' said Charlie – not knowing well what to say, for he had heard no song whatever; and then turning to the rest, while the poet was enlarging on the excellency of his song, he said, in an under voice, 'Gude faith, the poet's either gaen clean daft, or else he's drunk. What shall I say to him?'

The poet tapped him on the shoulder, seeing he was not paying attention.

'It is not for this, I say, that I judge the piece worthy of attention; nor yet what it shows of ability, hability, docility, or any of the terms that end in *ility*; nor for its allegory, category, or any of the terms that end in *ory*. Neither is it for its versification, imagination, nor any of the thousand abominable terms that end in *ation*. No, sir, the properties of all my songs, I am thankful to Saint Martin, end in *icity* and *uity*. You know the song, Yardbire?'

'O yes. Quite weel.'

'What do you think of the eleventh verse? Let me see. No, it is the thirteenth verse.' 'Good Friday! are there so many?' 'Hem – m – m. The tenth is, the Ox-eye, I am sure of that. The eleventh is the Millstone. The twelfth, the Cloudberry and the Shepherd Boy. The thirteenth, is the Gander and Water-Wagtail. It is the fourteenth. What do you think of the fourteenth? Ay, it is the Gowans and the Laverock that you will like best. You remember that, I am sure?'

'O yes; to be sure I do—.' (Aside,) 'Good Lord, the poet's horn mad! Heard ever any body the like o' this?'

'How is this it runs? Ay,

> When the bluart bears a pearl,
>   And the daisy turns a pea,
> And the bonny lucken gowan
>   Has fauldit up his ee,
> Then the laverock frae the blue lift,
>   Doops down and thinks nae shame
> To woo his bonny lassie,
>   When the kye come hame.

'The song is good, and the music of the song also is delectable,' said the friar; 'but the voice of the singer is like a sweet psaltery that hath lost a string, and hath its belly rent by the staff of the beater. Lo, I would even delight to hear the song from beginning to end.' 'Sing it, poet, and let it stand for the tale,' cried two of them at once. 'That I will not,' answered he; 'I will tell my tale in my own style, and my own manner, as the rest have done: nevertheless, if my throat were not so dry, I would sing the song.' 'It is plain what he wants,' said Charlie. ''Tis the gate wi' a' the minstrels – *wet the whistle, or want the spring.*'

Charlie handed him another cup of strong drink, desiring him to take it off and sing. He did the first freely, and attempted the second with equal alacrity; but his voice and memory both failed him by the way, to the great amusement of the whole party – even the captive boy screamed with laughter, and the great Master was twice constrained to smile. But we must describe this scene as Isaac himself gives it.

The poet was sitting on a bench, with Charlie on the one hand, and Delany on the other; and, fixing his eyes on the ceiling, and clasping his hands, which he heaved up at every turn of the tune, he went on thus:

THE SWEETEST THING THE BEST THING

A Song

VERSE FIRST

Come tell me a' you shepherds
　　That love the tarry woo',
And tell me a' you jolly boys
　　That whistle at the plow,
What is the greatest bliss
　　That the tongue of man can name,
'Tis 'To woo a bonny lassie
　　When the kye come hame.'
When the kye come hame,
　　When the kye come hame,
'Tween the gloaming and the mirk,
　　When the kye come hame.

That's the burden, or the quoir, as father Cormack calls it; – the o'erword, like.

VERSE SECOND

'Tis not beneath the burgonet,
  Nor yet beneath the crown,
'Tis not on couch of velvet,
  Nor yet in bed of down;
'Tis beneath the spreading birch
  In the dell without the name,
Wi' a bonny bonny lassie,
  When the kye come hame.
When the kye come hame, &c.

VERSE THIRD

There the blackbird bigs his nest
  For the mate he lo'es to see,
And on the topmost bough,
  Oh a happy bird is he!
There he pours his melting ditty,
  And love 'tis a' the theme;
And he'll woo his bonny lassie
  When the kye come hame.
When the kye come hame, &c.

VERSE FOURTH

When the little wee bit heart
  Rises high in the breast,
And the little wee bit starn
  Rises red in the east,
O there's a joy sae dear,
  That the heart can hardly frame,
Wi' a bonny bonny lassie,
  When the kye come hame.
When the kye come hame, &c.

VERSE FIFTH

Then the eye shines sae bright,
  The hale soul to beguile,
There's love in every whisper,
  And joy in every smile.
O wha wad chuse a crown
  Wi' its perils and its fame,
And miss a bonny lassie

When the kye come hame.
When the kye come hame, &c.

Here the poet warred a long time with recollection, always repeating, 'I made the thing, and it is impossible I can forget it – I can't comprehend—' At length he sung the following verse, which he said was the fifteenth.

VERSE THE FIFTEENTH

See yonder pawky shepherd,
    That lingers on the hill,
His ewes are in the fauld
    And his lambs are lying still;
Yet he downa gang to bed,
    For his heart is in a flame,
To meet his bonnie lassie,
    When the kye come hame.
When the kye come hame, &c.

VERSE SIXTEENTH AND LAST

Away wi' fame and fortune,
    What comfort can they gie?
And a' the arts that prey
    On man's life and libertye;
Gie me the highest joy
    That the heart of man can frame,
My bonny, bonny lassie,
    When the kye come hame.
When the kye come hame,
    When the kye come hame,
'Tween the gloaming and the mirk,
    When the kye come hame.

'I made the thing,' added the poet; 'but God knows how I have forgot it. Since I came to the top of this cursed tower, the wind has blown it out of my head.' With these words he fell into a profound sleep, which they suffered him to enjoy, before he began his competition. In the meantime, Isaac relates an extraordinary story of a certain consultation that took place in the castle in that very interim, but does not say on what authority he had it, none of the parties yet named having apparently heard it.

The castle of Aikwood, says he, being left as before, an ample and perilous void, some old and frequent inmates took undisputed possession. The leader and convoker of this gang was no other than the Master Fiend who ordered our yeomen out of the castle, and chased them forth, with so little ceremony. In the great Master's study was his gigantic and commanding frame placed at the end of the board, while the three pages, Prig, Prim, and Pricker, were waiting his beck.

'Come nigh me, my friends,' said he; 'and read me what is to be done with this king of mighty conjurors now?'

'What thou willest, our Lord and Master,' was the reply: 'Give the command with the power, and thy pleasure shall be done.'

'How canst thou answer for thy negligence in suffering this cowled and canting vagabond to gain admittance here with his saws and parables, his crosiers and his writings?'

'We meant to devour him, but our power extended not to it. Thou hast seen the bones of one whom we suspected.'

'You are indolent and wayward slaves. Either separate our greatest vassal on earth from this captious professor, or you shall be punished with many stripes. Our sway is dishonoured if such a man as he is suffered to take shelter under a crosier, and there hold our power at bay – our control at defiance––.' 'Return to him that power which since his dejection has been withdrawn, and you are sure of him still. Riches and honours he despises: feasting and wine-bibing he abhors: but for power to do what no other man can perform, he would sell twenty souls, were they in his power of disposal.'

'He is a great man, and well suited for our free independent government. By his principle of insubordination to established authorities, I yet hope to bring all mankind to my own mind and my own country. Read me my riddle, you three slaves. What is the most hateful thing in nature?'

'A saint.'

'More ready than right, and more right than ingenious. Show cause.'

'Because he is the greatest coward, and all that he does springs from the detestable passion of terror.'

'Right. Which being is the most noble?'

'The opposer of all established authorities ordained by the tyrant of the universe.'

'Right! Right! These are the men for me, and of these this Master was a great ensample. Therefore, Separate! Separate! Separate! My elemental power is solemnly engaged; but on the morning of the third day, it shall be given to you to work again at your Master's will. Till that time it will be as well to prevent all ingress and egress here; and at that time I will come again. Speed you well, nimble noddies; shape well and shard well, and the day is your own. While I transform my shape, sing me the song that I love. Whenever I hear it, my furtherance is the better.' The imps complied, and the redoubted fiend laughed till the walls of the castle shook, while those on the top took it for the great bittern of the Hartwood, called there the Bogbumper.

HYMN TO THE DEVIL

Speed thee, speed thee!
Liberty lead thee!
Many this night shall hearken and heed thee.
Far abroad,
Demigod!
What shall appal thee?
Javel, or Devil, or how shall we call thee?
Thine the night voices of joy and of weeping,
The whisper awake, and the vision when sleeping:
The bloated kings of the earth shall brood
On princedoms and provinces bought with blood,
Shall slumber, and snore, and to-morrow's breath
Shall order the muster and march of death:
The trumpets shall sound, and the gonfalons flee,
And thousands of souls step home to thee.
Speed thee, speed thee, &c.

The warrior shall dream of battle begun,
Of field-day and foray, and foeman undone;
Of provinces sacked, and warrior store,
Of hurry and havoc, and hampers of ore;
Of captive maidens for joys abundant,
And ransom vast when these grow redundant.

Hurray! for the foray. Fiends ride forth a souling,
For the dogs of havock are yelping and yowling.
  Speed thee, speed thee, &c.

  Make the bedesman's dream
  With treasure to teem;
  To-day and to-morrow
  He has but one aim,
And 'tis still the same, and 'tis still the same.
But well thou knowest the sot's demerit,
His richness of flesh, and his poorness of spirit;
And well thy images thou canst frame,
On canvas of pride, with pencil of flame:
A broad demesne is a view of glory,
For praying a soul from purgatory:
And, O let the dame be fervent and fair,
Amorous, and righteous, and husband beware!
For there's a confession so often repeated,
The eyes are enlightened, the life-blood is heated.
Hish! – Hush! – soft foot and silence,
The sons of the abbot are lords of the Highlands,
Thou canst make lubbard and lighthead agree,
Wallow a while, and come home to thee.
  Speed thee, speed thee, &c.

Where goest thou next, by hamlet or shore,
When kings, when warriors, and priests are o'er?
These for thee have the most to do,
And these are the men must be looked unto.
On courtier deign not to look down,
Who swells at a smile, and faints at a frown.
With noble maid stay not to parle,
But give her one glance of the golden arle.
Then, oh, there's a creature thou needs must see,
Upright, and saintly, and stern is she!
'Tis the old maid, with visage demure,
With cat on her lap, and dogs on the floor,
Master, she'll prove a match for thee,
With her psalter, and crosier, and Ave Mari.
Move her with things above and below,
Tickle her and teaze her from lip to toe;
Should all prove vain, and nothing can move;
If dead to ambition, and cold to love,
One pasion still success will crown,
A glorious energy all thine own!

'Tis envy; a die that never can fail
With children, matron, or maiden stale.
Shew them in dreams from night to day
A happy mother, and offspring gay;
Show them the maiden in youthful prime,
Followed and wooed, improving her time;
And their hearts wil sicken with envy and spleen,
A leperous jaundice of yellow and green:
And though frightened for hell to a boundless degree,
They'll singe their dry perriwigs yet with thee.
    Speed thee, speed thee, &c.

Where goest thou next? Where wilt thou hie thee?
Still there is rubbish enough to try thee.
Whisper the matron of lordly fame,
There's a greater than she in splendor and name;
And her bosom shall swell with the grievous load,
And torrents of slander shall volley abroad,
Imbued with venom and bitter despair:
O sweet are the sounds to the Prince of the Air!
Reach the proud yeoman a bang with a spear,
And the tippling burgess a yerk on the ear;
Put fees in the eye of the poisoning leech,
And give the dull peasant a kick on the breech:
As for the flush maiden, the rosy elf,
You may pass her by, she will dream of herself.
But that all may be gain, and nothing loss,
Keep eye on the men with the cowl and the cross;
Then shall the world go swimming before thee,
In a full tide of liberty, licence, and glory!
    Speed thee, speed thee, &c.

Hail, patriot spirit! thy labours be blest!
For of all great reformers thyself wert the first;
Thou wert the first, with discernment strong,
To perceive that all rights divine were wrong;
And long hast thou spent thy sovereign breath,
In heaven above and in earth beneath,
And roared it from thy burning throne,
The glory of independence alone;
Proclaiming to all, with fervor and irony,
That kingly dominion's all humbug and tyranny;
And whoso listeth may be free,
For freedom, full freedom's the word with thee!
That life has its pleasures – the rest is a sham,

And all that comes after a flim and a flam!
   Speed thee! Speed thee!
   Liberty lead thee!
Many this night shall hearken and heed thee.
    Hie abroad,
    Demigod!
   Who shall defame thee?
King of the Elements! how shall we name thee?

As the imps concluded their song, our prisoners on the top of the castle perceived a large rough watch-dog jogging out at the gate of the castle, and following in the direction of the fugitives. When the brute saw that he was perceived he turned round, set up his snout toward the battlements, and uttered a loud bow-wow-wow, which, when the great Master heard, he started to his feet, and, with wild staring looks, and his hair standing on end, took shelter behind the friar.

'Behold thou, and see with thine eyes, that it is only a watch-dog come from the camp of our captain,' said the friar. 'Lo, thy very nature is changed since first I saw thee.'

'Then would to the gods that I had never seen thee, or that I had seen thee sooner,' said the Master; and strode away to discourage any farther reply. The dog followed the fugitives, and bent his course toward the mill.

That being the next inhabited house to the eastward, Dan Chisholm and his yeomen landed all there; and in full assembly he related, to their terror and astonishment, how he had seen the devil himself and several of his monstrous agents, who had chased him from the castle, spuing fire and brimstone on him like a cataract. The rest said, that though they had not seen the devil, they had seen and heard enough to put any rational being out of his senses, and as much as to teach them never to go there again. Dan swore that they were not to be taught any such thing; for, said he, 'Our captain's friends, and our own brethren in arms, are most unwarrantably, and I must also say unaccountably, confined there – and we will either free them or perish in the attempt. I can find plenty of holy men that, with book and candle, can withstand the devil, and shall make him flee from his stronghold like fire from the flint. If I had the gospel friar on the one side of him, and Father Brand,

or Capuchin Cairnabie, on the other, I shall gar him skip.'
While Dan was in the middle of this speech, in comes the
great rough watchdog; who, after fawning on some of the
warriors as on old acquaintances, took his station in a dark
corner of the miller's thronged hall, and began a licking
his feet, but at the same time taking good heed to all that
passed. It was finally agreed that Dan and a companion
should ride straight to Melrose, and represent their case
to the holy abbot there, who was devoted to the interests of
their captain, and who, it was not doubted, would devise
means of expelling the old demon from his guardship, and
letting free their friends, who were all baptised men and
good Christians. As they formed these sapient devices,
many hard things were said of the devil; and our warriors
seemed rather inclined to make a laughing-stock of him,
till the miller's maid interrupted them with the following
question:

'Wha o' you trooper chaps does this maskis dog belang
to?'

'To nane o' us,' was answered by several at the same
time.

'I wish ye wad tent him, then,' said she, 'for, this wee
while bygane, his een hae been glentin like twa blue burnin
candles. I wish he be nae a mad ane.'

'Sneck doors, and out swords,' cried the miller: 'We'll
hae him proven.'

The doors were shut, and the yeomen surrounded the
dog with their drawn weapons. The poor beast lay as
harmlesslike as a lamb, with his head upon his fore feet so
as to hide them, turning up his eyes from below his shaggy
brows in a beseeching manner, and wagging his tail till it
played thump, thump, on the floor. But this did not hinder
the miller from reconnoitring, though it gave him rather a
favourable opinion of his shaggy guest. 'Poor fellow,' said
the miller, 'wha's dog may ye be?' The dog forgot himself;
he lifted up his head in a kind acknowledging manner to the
miller, who, looking narrowly at him, cried out: 'A marvel!,
a marvel! saw ever ony mortal man the like o' this? Here's
a tyke wi' cloven cloots like a gait, fairney cloots and a'
thegither. The Holy Virgin be wi' us! I believe we hae
gotten the—'

Here the miller was interrupted, without getting the

sentence concluded. The dog sprung to his feet, appearing twice as big as when he entered. 'Bow-wow-wow!' roared he in the miller's face with the voice of an enraged lion; 'Bow-wow-wow!' And as he bayed from side to side on the warrior circle, they all retreated backward till the wall stopped them. Well might they – for they perceived, by his open mouth, the same appearance that Dan had before witnessed, namely, a stomach and chest of burning flame. 'Bow-wow-wow!' reiterated he: 'Youph, youph, youph.' All fled back aghast: but the attack was of short duration. The miller had a huge fire of seeds, above a burning log of wood, which he had heaped on for the comfort of his guests. When the dog reached that, he broke into it, appearing to bury himself in the coil of fiery dust. It flashed upwards in millions of burning atoms, and in the midst of them up flew the dog out at the top of the lum, with a tremendous 'Bow-wow-wow!'

All was silence for a few seconds, while our yeomen stood in a circle, with their weapons drawn, and their backs at the wall, gaping with affright, and staring on one another. 'By Saint Thomas, we are haunted!' cried Dan, breaking silence; 'That is the same chap I forgathered wi' afore in the staircase of the castle, I ken him by his lowin lungs, though he has changed his shape.' He was interrupted by a loud laugh on the top of the house, and a voice that said, in a jeering tone, 'Ha, ha, ha! Andrew Chisholm is that you? I have found out a' your plans – and ride you to Melrose, or ride you to Dryburgh, I'll be there afore you to lend you a lift. Ay, and I'll keep Aikwood castle in spite o' you and a' your master's men.'

Dan could not contain his indignation on hearing this brag. He ran forward to the brace, put his neck under it, and turning his nose up the lum (or rustic chimney) answered, 'Deil o' that ye're fit to do, auld tyke. Ye're but a liar at best and the father o' liars. Gang and toast heathen bacon in your ain het hame. What seek ye here amang leel men?'

'Weel answered, and like yoursel, Dan!' said one of the yeomen, and slapped him on the shoulder, which rousing his spirit still farther, he added, 'Confound you Robin's Geordie o' Feindhope-haugh, what for didna ye strike when the foul thief set up his gousty gab at your nose

wi' his impudent bow-wow-wow; I see nae right ony
o' God's creatures hae to be hurlbarrowed out o' their
standing wi' him.'

As he finished the remark, there was something came to
the door, and gave two or three rude impatient scratches,
exactly in the same manner that a strong dog does that
wants to be in. This instantly changed the cheer of our
sturdy group, that with one involuntary movement closed
round the hearth, at the point the most distant from
the door.

'That's him again,' said the miller's lass.

'The Lord forbid,' said the miller: 'I wonder what
multure he wants frae me. Though I live on the lands of
a Master of Arts, I had nae inkling that I was thirl to hell.
Brave lads, can nane of you rhame a mass, a credo, or a
paternoster? He is but a coward at best; I hae kend a monk,
wi' his crosier and his cowl, chace him like a rabbit.'

'I fear we'll prove but lame hands at that,' said Dan, 'and
think we had better sally out on him sword in hand, and
see what he can either say or do for himself. But, Chryste,
I needna say that, considering that I ken sae weel what his
lining's made of.'

'I hae a cross and chain in the house,' said the miller,
'that was consecrated at the shrine of St Bothan; whoever
will be our leader shall bear that before him, and we'll bang
the auld thief away frae our bigging.'

The scratching was renewed with redoubled fury. Our
yeomen crowded closer around the fire, till all at once their
ears were saluted by a furious 'bow-wow-wow' down the
lum, which, in spite of their utmost resolution, scattered
them like a covey of heath-fowl over which the hawk is
hovering, when every one endeavours to shift for itself,
and hide in its own heather bush.

Their faces were by this time flushed with shame as well
as fear, that they should be thus cuffed about by 'the auld
thief,' as they styled him. Resolved, therefore, to make
one great and strenuous effort, the miller brought out his
consecrated cross, some tied sticks, and others horn spoons
across, till all were armed with the same irresistible symbol,
and then they marshalled up before the fire, uncovered their
heads, and with the ensigns reared before them, waited for
a moment the word of command to march out to the grand

attack. The arch fiend, not choosing to wait the issue, raised such a horse laugh on the top of the lum that their ears were deafened with the noise; and clapping his paws that sounded like the strokes of battering ram's horns, he laughed till the upper and nether millstones chattered against each other, and away he bounded through the clouds of the night, apparently in an agony of laughter.

'Aha! there he goes!' said Dan: 'There's nae guidance to be had o' him, and as little mense in meddling wi' him.'

'Ay, let him e'en gang,' said the miller; 'he's the warst mouse o' the mill. Ane had better tine the blind bitch's litter than hae the mill singed wi' brimstone. I lurd rather deal wi' the thankless maltster, that neither gi'es coup, neivefu', nor lippie, than wi' him. I have no part of the breviary but a glorious preamble; kneel till I repeat it.'

The troopers kneeled round the miller, who, lifting up his hands, said, with great fervour, 'O semper timidum scelus! Obstupui, steteruntque comae et vox faucibus haesit. O Deus; nusquam tuta fides! Amen.' 'Amen!' repeated all the group, and arose greatly strengthened and encouraged by the miller's *preamble*.

They spent that night around the miller's hearth, and had a cog of good brose to their supper. The next morning Dan and two associates rode off for Melrose, to lay their case before the friendly abbot, and to beg assistance; which, notwithstanding the devil's brag, they were not afraid of obtaining. But the important events that followed must be related in course, while we return to those friends in their elevated confinement, to whom that night the poet related the following tale.

CHAPTER TWENTY-TWO

> *Lord Duf.* Did you not wake them, Cornaro?
> *Cor.* Alas! my lord, I could not.
> Their slumber was so deep, it seemed to me
> A sleep eternal. Not a sleep of death,
> But of extatic silence. Such a beam
> Of joy and happiness I ne'er beheld
> Shed from the human face.
> *The Prioress, A Tragedy*

The Poet's Tale

FAIN WOULD I tell my friends and fellow sufferers of my translation hence. Of all the joys and ecstacies of that celestial clime, ycleped the land of faery; were it not that one is here whose sex forbids it, and whose gentle nature from such a tale would shrink, as doth the flower before the nipping gale. You all have heard of that celestial form, the white lady? And of that wan and beatific presence there lives in my remembrance some faint image of saintly beauty. But list to me, my friends, and do not smile, far less break forth with loud uncourteous neigh, like war horse in the charge – vile waste of breath! convulsive, unrestrained. But hear the truth: *It was not she who bore me from this land* – not she, *the white lady*, as all divined. No, it was a form of flesh, and that flesh too of most rare quality. Fair, witching, plump, rosy and amorous; and of unmarred proportions. Sooth, she who lured me from my rustic home no other was than wandering minstreless, queen of the mightiest harper ever born. Sole empress of a tuneful wayward choir, thoughtless and giddy. But their music stole my very soul away. What could I do but follow it, to listen and to sing. In that bright train I sought the Scottish court, the nobles'

347

hall, and every motely scene of loud festivity throughout the land. There have I heard and seen such scenes of love, of dalliance, and of mirth, of deep intrigue and violent cruelty, as eye of minstrel hath not witnessed. Yes, I have seen things not to be expressed, at least not here. Therefore I'll change the rule this night pursued, of saying what myself have seen and done. The fairy land in which I sojourned was fair Caledon; and there I had my living minstrel joys in high abundance. But I grieve to say, a fatal brawl placed all of us within the line to which the sword of vengeance extends its dreadful sway. Our group dispersed. The soul of melody was then no more! The sounds of harmony divine were hushed; all scattered on the winds of other lands, and other climes, to charm with wailing numbers. Southward I came, amid the border clans to trust my life, men lawless as myself. They once had saved me when a helpless orphan. Whom could I better trust? And I have found their generosity alone out-done by their own courage. For my adventures, let this sketch suffice. And though not of the fairyland, I will relate a tale, as pure, as wonderful and full of mystery, as if in other worlds I'd learned it. I had it from a simple peasant's mouth, an old grey hind upon the Sidley hills, who vouched its truth. With faltering tongue, and palpitating heart, for love, for life, and all the soul holds dear, I say my tale. O be my soul rapt to the estimate at which I hold the prize, and the divine and holy narrative.

Once on a time, in that sweet northern land called Otholine, the heathen Hongar landed, and o'er-ran city and dale. The rampart and the flood in vain withstood his might. Even to the base of the unconquered Grampians did he wend with fire and sword; and all who would not kneel, and sacrifice to his strange northern gods, he tortured to the death. Some few renounced the cross, for sordid life, and dread of unheard torments. Men were roasted, matrons impaled; and pure virginity was given up to the rude soldiery to be abused, or humbled as they termed it. Then were they decked with flowers and ornaments, led forth in pairs unto the horrid shrine, and sacrificed to Odin.

At that time there lived three beauteous sisters of the line of mighty kings. They were so passing fair, that all who saw them wondered, and all who wondered loved. Hongar and Hubba, these two heathen brothers, and princes of the Danes, heard of their fame, their beauty, and their excellencies of nature, and sent to seize them in their father's tower, that in the heights of Stormonth stood secure. The castle was surprised, the virgins seized, and carried to the camp. There to their dreadful trial were they brought, and bid to curse the sacred name they feared and worshipped; to renounce the holy cross, and worship Odin, or give up their bodies to shame, to ignominy, and to death on Odin's hideous altar. Marley and Morna both kneeled and intreated, begged a little time to ponder on the dread alternative. But the young sprightly Lena, fairest she of Albyn's virgins, browed the invader's threat with dauntless eye: That eye whose liquid smile in love's sweet converse had been formed to beam.

'Thou savage heathen!' cried she, 'dost thou think to intimidate the royal maids of Caledon to thy most barbarous faith? Tyrant, thou art deceived. I dare thine ire. Thou may'st torment me; for I'm in thine hands, and thy heart ne'er knew pity. Thou may'st tear this tender fragile form with pincing irons. But my soul's purity thou never shall subdue by threat, by engine, or by flame. Thee and thy god I scorn – I curse you both. I lean upon the rock that will not yield; and put my trust in one whose mighty arm can crush thee and thy idol to an atom. I know he'll save me. He will save us all, if we but trust him without sinful dread. Here, underneath his bleeding cross, I kneel, and cast myself and my poor sisters here, upon his mercy. Here I make a vow to stand for him, and for his sacred truth, and for no other. Now, thou ruthless savage, here I defy thee. Do thy worst to us, and thou shalt see if Jesus or if Odin shall prevail, and who can best preserve their worshippers.'

The heathen brothers smiled; and Hongar said, 'How wildly sweet the little Christian looks! I make my choice to humble and prepare her for the base slaves of Odin's warlike halls. Go warriors, lock them up in donjon deep, until the hour of midnight, when the rites of Odin shall begin. Then will we send and bring them to the test; and all shall see whose God is most in might, and who must yield.'

In prison dark the virgins were immured, with sevenfold gates and sevenfold bars shut in. Soon as they were alone, the sisters twain, Marley and Morna, in fond tears embraced their youngest sister, lauded her high soul, and vowed with her to stand, with her to die, unsullied in the faith they had been taught.

Then did they kneel on the cold dungeon floor, and one by one offered their fervent prayers at mercy's footstool. But chiefly were their vows made to the Holy Virgin; for they hoped that she would save their pure virginity from sin's pollution. Never did prayers ascend up to heaven with greater fervency. And as the hour of midnight on them drew, they kneeled; and, side by side, with lifted hands, and eyes turned toward heaven, sang aloud this holy simple hymn to their Redeemer.

HYMN TO THE REDEEMER

Son of the Virgin, hear us! hear us!
Son of the living God, be near us!
Thou who art man in form and feature,
Yet God of glory, and God of nature,
Thou who led'st the star of the East,
Yet helpless lay at a Virgin's breast;
Slept in the manger, and cried on the knee,
Yet rulest o'er Time and Eternity.
Pity thy creatures here kneeling in dust;
Pity the beings in thee that trust!
    Thou who fed'st the hungry with bread,
And raised'st from the grave the mouldering dead;
Who walked'st on the waves of the rolling main,
Who cried'st to thy Father, and cried'st in vain;
Yet wept for the woes and the sins of man,
And prayed'st for them when thy life-blood ran;
With thy last breath who cried'st Forgive!
When bleeding and dying, that man might live!
Over death and the grave hast the victory won,
And now art enthron'd by the stars and the sun,
For thy name's glory, hear us, and come,
And show thy power over idols dumb.
    O leave the abodes of glory and bliss,

The realms of heavenly happiness;
Come swifter than the gale of even
On thy lightning's wing, the chariot of heaven;
By the gates of light and the glowing sphere,
O come on thy errand of mercy here!
But Lord of glory we know not thee,
  We know not what we say;
We cannot from thy presence be,
  Nor from thine eye away:
For though on the right hand of God,
Thou art here in this dark and drear abode:
Beyond the moon and the starry way
Thou holdest thy Almighty sway,
Where spirits in floods of light are swimming,
And angels round thy throne are hymning;
Yet present with all who call on thee
In this world of wo and adversity.
    Then, O, thou Son of the Virgin, hear us!
God of love and of life be near us!
Our hour of trial is at hand,
And without thy aid how shall we stand?
Our stains wash out, our sins forgive;
And before thee may our spirits live.
For thee and thy truth be our bosoms steeled:
O be our help, our stay, our shield:
Show thy dread power for mercy's sake,
For thy name, and thy glory, and all is at stake;
Bow down thy heavens, and rend them asunder,
And come in the cloud, in the flame, or the thunder.

The trumpets now were sounding, while the host arose from wine and wassail, to prepare the baleful sacrifice of Christian souls. The virgins heard, and trembled as they kneeled; and beauteous Lena raised her slender hands, and prayed, with many tears, that the Almighty would stretch out his right hand and close their eyes in everlasting sleep, to save them from self-slaughter, or the fate they dreaded more.

While yet the words were but in utterance, and ere the vow was vowed, they heard the gates unbarred one after one, and saw the lights glance through the lurid gloom. Each youthful heart turned, as it were, to stone; for well they weened the Danish soldiers came to bring them forth to shame and death. They kept their humble posture, with hànds and eyes upraised, for they expected no pity or compassion save from heaven.

The inmost door upon its hinges turned, like thunder out of tune; and, lo! there entered – no heathen soldier – but a radiant form covered with light as with a flowing robe. In his right hand he bore a golden rod, and in his left a lamp that shone as bright as the noon-day sun. A thousand thousand gems, from off his raiment, cast their dazzling lustre. Diamonds and rubies formed alternate stars, while all between was rayed and spangled o'er with ever-varying brightness. Round his head he wore a wreath of emeralds; these were set with never-fading green. They deemed he was the great high priest of Odin come to lead them to the sacrifice. But yet his look, so mild and so benign, raised half a hope within their breasts of pity and regard. They were about to plead; but ere a sound breathed from their lips, the stranger beckoned them to silence. Then, in mild and courteous strain, in their own tongue, he thus accosted them:

'To ONE already have your vows been framed; and would you bow to another? You have pleaded to heaven's high King; and would you plead to man? Rise up, and follow me.' The virgins rose; they had not power to stay – and followed him, alas! they knew not whither. They had no voice to question or complain. Door after door they passed; gate after gate; and still their guide touching them with his golden rod, they closed in jangling fury. Onward still they moved, and met the heathen bands, led by their chiefs, Hongar and Hubba. They were drunk with wine; and loudly did they halloo when they saw their prey escaped, and walking on the street all beauteous and serene. Closing around the fugitives, and jabbering uncouth terms and words obscene, the chiefs opened their arms to seize the helpless three. Just then their guide turned round unmoved, and waving his bright rod, the heathens staggered, uttered mumbling sounds, and, trying vainly to support themselves, reeling they sunk enfeebled to the earth, where all as still and motionless they lay as piles of lifeless corpses. How the virgins wondered at what they saw! and fearless now they followed their bright leader. Next they met the priests of Odin, in their wild attire, marching in grand procession to the scene of mighty sacrifice. Aloft they bore their hideous giant idol; by his sides his loathsome consort and his monster son, Freya and Thor, while all their followers sung this choral hymn in loud and warlike strains:

HYMN TO ODIN

I

He comes! he comes!
Great Odin comes!
Who can rise or stand before him?
The god of the bloody field,
The sword, and the ruddy shield;
The god of the Danes, let all adore him.

II

Wake the glad measure to
The goddess of pleasure too,
Who fills every hero with joy and with love!
And hail to dread Thor,
Great son of great sire,
The quaffer of gore,
And the dweller in fire:
The god of the sun, and the lightnings above.

III

Prepare! prepare!
The feat prepare,
Since mighty Thor our guest shall be:
Three times three,
And three times three,
This day shall bleed for repast to thee!

IV

Strike the light,
Make the flame burn bright,
Since Freya is here who gives delight!
Three times three,
And nine times nine,
This day shall bleed on altar of thine.

V

Shout and sing,
Till the mountains ring!
The father of men, and of gods the king!

> See him advance
> With sword and lance;
> Billows of life-blood, heroes, bring!

VI

> God of Alhallah's dome!
> God of the warrior's home!
> Who can withstand thee in earth or heaven?
> Bring to his altar then,
> Of Christian dames and men,
> Nine times nine, and seven times seven.

VII

> Bend to your place of birth,
> Children of sordid earth;
> The gods of battles your homage disdains.
> Who dare oppose him?
> Christian or Moslem?
> Who is like Odin, the god of the Danes?

The maids and their angelic guide went on following the cross; and as they went, they sung in sweet and humble aspirations the song of the Lamb. They met the gorgeous files. Fair met with fair. The hideous idols sat an hundred cubits high; whereas the cross a maiden's hand upbore. But when they met, the proud and mighty peal, swelling from Odin's worshippers, was hushed as with a sob. The hills rang with the sound; and the o'erburdened air bore the last knell up to the skies. It quavered through the spheres, and died in distance, to be heard no more, while nought but the sweet notes the virgins sung rose on the paths of night. The motely mass of heathens stood amazed, and as they stood they listened and they quaked. The words were these at which they paused, and which the virgins sung:

> Silence the blasphemers thee that defy,
> Strike down the mighty, Son of the Most High;
> Rise in thy power, that the heathen may see,
> What dust are their gods and their glory to thee;
> Raise thy right hand, and in pieces them shiver,
> That to the true God may the praise be for ever.

At every line the bearers and their gods trembled the more, and as the last notes closed, the mighty Odin toppled from his throne, and crashed amid his powerless worshippers. His wooden spouse and son fell with the sire of Gods and men, and in a thousand pieces their gilded frames were dashed. Confusion reigned. The host fled in dismay; but Odin's priests sunk down in low prostration, groaning and howling for the fall of Odin – the shield and glory of the Danish host.

From out this wild confusion the bright guide conducted the three virgins to a cave close by the river's brink, and charged them hide until the wrath of the enraged foe should be abated. 'Here,' said he, 'you are in perfect safety. No one living knows of this retreat. Here sleep and take your rest. May angels watch around your flinty couch. Farewell, I must begone on the employ assigned me by your father and by mine.' He left the lamp and went his way. Forthwith they kneeled in prayer, thanking their Saviour for their great deliverance, then laid them down to rest. They kissed the cross, and folded closely in each other's arms, cheek leaning unto cheek, with holy hymns they sung themselves asleep.

Great was the rage among the Danish chiefs, and wide the search for these presumptuous and bold aggressors. The host was all discouraged and amazed, and nought but terror reigned. Earldoms were offered for the audacious maids, dead or alive. But nor alive nor dead could they be found, either by friend or foe. O dreadful were the execrations uttered by the Danes. They called them demons, witches, and the worst of all incendiaries. Well they might. The terror of their arms was broken. Great was the rejoicing mid the hills and glens of Albyn, but the eastern vallies groaned beneath the fury of the savage Dane, and Christian blood was shed on every cross.

The virgins waked at morn, and still the lamp sent forth its feeble glimmer through the cave. The day-beam through the crevice of the rock streamed in and mixed with it. The virgins strove to rise, to speak – to sing a morning hymn. But all their limbs were cold, and their tongues clove fast to their thirsty palates. Lena, first of all the three, upraised her pallid form, and on the lamp turning her drowsy eye, there did it settle, closed, and oped again, but still with faded and uncertain light, as if the mind were lacking. Long she sat, half raised in this uneasy torpid state – this struggle 'twixt oblivion and life. Oft she assayed her sisters

to awake, by naming them; but still as oft the names died in
a whisper. By degrees her mind dawned into recollection, as
the moon breaks o'er the sullen twilight. Then the wonders,
that she had seen o'ernight, aroused her soul to all its
wonted energy. She kneeled, and thanked her Maker for
the great deliverance to them vouchsafed. And when her
sisters woke, they woke to join her in a heavenly song.

'What ails our sister? Here we are in safety. Why does
our dear beloved not rest in peace? The night is not far
spent: the dawn of morn is yet far distant. O dear Lena
sleep. Sleep on, and take your rest. The morning sun is
yet beneath the deep. Our limbs are cold; our eyes are
heavy; yet we cannot rise, for we are weary and not half
awake.'

'Wake, my beloved sisters. It is time. The noon is at its
height. See how the sun peeps through the granite cliffs,
and on the stream sheds ray of trembling silver. Let us rise
and talk of all the wonders we have seen.'

Long they conversed in tears of gratitude, still peeping
from their cavern, lest the Dane again should find and
drag them to the altar. Sore were they pressed by hunger.
From the stream they drank abundantly with thankful
hearts. But food for many a day and many a night they
scarce had tasted, and they longed for it with more than
ordinary longing. Night approached; and there they sat,
not knowing what to do, a prey to gnawing hunger. At
the last, young Lena said, 'I cannot ween that heaven hath
wrought a miracle for our relief, and for no higher purpose
than that we should be left to die of hunger in this dark
and hideous den. Again I'll put my life into its hand, and
go into the city after twilight in search of bread; and if I
die I die: Heaven's will be done.' Her sisters looked at her,
and blessed her in the holy Virgin's name. They could not
bid her go where danger waited, so great, so imminent; and
yet they felt they could not press her stay. With cautious
eye, and with enfeebled step, trembling she sought the city
gate. But when, afar, she saw by torchlight porters striding
to and fro, with glittering lances of enormous length, and
ponderous battle axes, her heart failed, and she drew back.
But then she thought again of those she left behind, and
all the throes of perishing with hunger, and resolved to risk
all hazards. The huge gate stood open, and strangers went

and came. 'I'll join,' thought she, 'this straggling crew, and enter among them; they speak my native tongue. Ah! they must be a band of traitorous base renegades, that have renounced the cross and joined the Dane; else wherefore free to go and come and trade? I'm all unsafe with such.' The strangers eyed her with most curious and piercing looks, and whispered as they went. They seemed afraid, and shunned her by the way, as they who shun a being infected by the pestilence, or spirit from the dead. No one addressed a word to her, but hurried to the gate.

She came alone, for feeble was her step, and her breast palpitating as with throb of burning fever, hopeless of admission.

The porters stared with wide extended gaze, and eyes protruding; but no word they spoke, nor crossed their lances. Straight she entered in. 'What can this mean?' thought she; 'There is a change since yester-even that it passes thought to comprehend. These keepers are not Danes; I heard them speak in Albyn's ancient tongue; and yet methinks they wear the Danish garb. How's this? that I am free to come and go, as in my childhood, when the land was free?'

She passed the sacred fane, and there beheld crowds entering in; but fast she sped away, weening they went to Odin's cursed rites.

She went to those that sold, and asked for bread. The woman stared at her with silent gaze. She asked again, and straight the huckster fled in floundering haste. Poor Lena stood amazed. 'How's this?' said she, 'where'er I show my face the people shun me. Here I shall remain, for I am faint with hunger, till I taste some of these cakes, which I can well repay.'

She stood not long until she was accosted by holy bedes-man, who, with cautious step, and looks of terror, entered, fast repeating his *Ave Maria*. 'In the Virgin's name,' cried he, 'and under sanction of this cross, I charge thee tell who or from whence thou art.'

The virgin kneeled, and kissed the holy symbol, but waived direct reply. 'I lack some bread to give to those that famish, and I'll pay for that which I receive,' was her reply.

'Then 'tis the bread of life that thou dost lack; man's

natural food I fear thou can'st not use, for thou art not a being of this world, but savour'st of the grave. Thy robes are mouldy, and fall from off thy frame? Thy lips are parched and colourless. These eyes have not the light of human life. Thou ominous visitant, declare from whence thou art, and on what mission thou com'st to this devoted wasted land?'

Lena looked up. The holy father's face to her appeared familiar. But how great the change since last she saw it. 'Father Brand, dost thou not know me?' was her home reply.

With blenching cheek and with unstable eye the father gazed, and, faultering, stammered forth, 'No. Jesu Maria, be thy servant's shield! Yes. Now I know thee. Art thou not the spirit of the hapless Ellamere, who was put down within our convent for a wilful breach of its most sacred law? Avaunt! Begone! Nor come thou here t' accuse those that grieved for thee, while they executed just vengeance on thy life. Injurious ghost! Thy curses have fallen heavy on our heads, and brought the wrath of heaven upon our land in tenfold measure. In the Saviour's name, whose delegate I am, I charge thee hence unto thy resting-place – to that award that heaven's strict justice hath ordained for thee; and come not, with that pale and withering look, more curses and more judgments to pronounce.'

'Reach me thine hand,' said she, and held hers forth, meaning to work conviction on his mind that she was flesh and blood. Her arm was wan as death itself, emaciated and withered, and furred with lines, livid and colourless, as by corrodent vapours of the grave. The monk withdrew his hand within his frock, shook his grey locks, and, with slow palsied step, moved backward till the threshold stone he gained; then turned and fled amain. The household dame fled also from her inner door, from which she peered and listened, and the wondering virgin again was left alone. She waited there in wild and dumb incertitude a space; then took some bread, some fruits, and baken meat, laid some money down as an equivalent, and went away to seek her dark retreat.

But as she passed the fane, with wary step she ventured to the porch, and marvelling, heard the whole assembly, joined in rapt devotion, praising the name of Jesus. Close she stood, and, darkling as it was, joined in the choir so much beloved. But all the wonders she so late had seen yielded to this. In one short night, one strange eventful night, such things were done as human intellect, with all its cunning, could not calculate.

She passed the gate. The gaping sentinels stood, as they did before, immoveable, each casting sidelong glances unto his mate, to note who first should fly or call the word. She beckoned them as with intent to speak; but in one moment porters, spears, and axes scattered and vanished in the darksome shade.

Reaching the cave, she found the lamp gone out that their mysterious deliverer had left them over night. First she regaled her sisters' hearts with the miraculous tidings that all the people worshipped Jesus' name without dismay or molestation, who, but the night before, not for their lives durst have acknowledged him: That all seemed free to go and come, and pray to whom they listed. The tale seemed a romance – a dream of wild delirium. The Danes could not be banished in a night, and all the land cleared of the vile idolatry of Odin. They disbelieved the whole, as well they might, but held their peace, dreading their sister's mind mazed in derangement. Still, as she went on, saying that all whom she had met or seen supposed her one arisen from the dead, or ghost of some departed criminal, strangled for breach of a monastic vow, then did they grasp each other's hands, and weep for their dear sister's sad mishap. They deemed her mad as raving whirlwind, or the music of mountain cataract. Yet she had brought them food of various sorts, which in the dark she gave them; and they fed, or strove to feed – but small indeed the portion they devoured.

'How's this,' cried Morna, 'that my little cake grows ne'er the less? Can it be so that we are truly spirits – ghosts of the three maids that overthrew the Danish god last night? I hunger and I thirst, 'tis true. Tell me, Can spirits drink the element of water? Certes they may. But then, how did we die, or when? for I cannot remember me of passing death's hideous and dreary bourn, though something of a weary painful dream hangs round my heart.'

This vague disjointed speech, the wayward vision of distemperature, struck the two others motionless, and

set them on cogitations wandering and wild as meteors
o'er a dreary wilderness. The thought of being in a new
existence, with all its unknown trials, powers, and limits,
their struggling minds essayed in vain to grasp.

Reason returned, but as a step-mother returns to frenzied
orphan's dying bed. They felt each other's pulses. There
was life – corporeal life; but still there was a change,
which no one chose to mention – yet a change quite
unaccountable for one night's sleep to have effected. From
their cavern's porch they viewed the stars of heaven. They
were the same as they were wont. They saw the golden
wain, the polar plough tilling his ample field with slow
unwearied furrow, and the sisters – the seven lovely sisters
of the sky, arching their gorgeous path. Far to the east they
spied a star beloved, which in their childhood they oft had
watched, and named the 'tiger's eye,' changing its vivid
colours as of yore. And then they wept to think of former
days of innocence and joy. And thus in tears, clasped in
each other's arms, they laid them down their mazed and
oppressed spirits to compose.

While thus they lay, romantic Morna said: 'My sisters,
it is evident to all that some great change has happed to
us last night. We are not what we were. What can it be but
change from one existence to another? A mortal creature
cannot touch or feel a disembodied spirit; but we know
not how spirits feel each other. Sure as life and death hold
opposition in this world, from the one into the other we
have passed. I feel it in my being. So do you, though
unacknowledged. Let us rise and walk as spirits do by
night, and we shall see the change in us, not over a whole
land in one short night. Come, let us roam abroad. I feel
a restlessness – a strong desire to flit from place to place –
perchance to fly between the mountain and the cloud, and
view the abodes of those we love.'

This wild romance waked in the virgins' hearts an energy
between despair and madness. All extremes erratic and
unnatural, on the minds of females, act like the infection
of virulent disease. Up they arose, and, stepping from their
cavern, took their way along the river's brink. Midnight
was past. The tiger's eye had climbed the marble path
that branches through the heaven, and goggled forth, now
red, now blue, now purple and now green, down from his

splendid ceiling far on high. 'Twas like a changeful spirit.
In the east the hues of morning rose in towering streaks,
as if the Almighty had caused light to grow like cedars
from the summits of the hills. It was a scene for spirits!
There were three abroad that morn before the twilight rose
– three creatures spiritual, yet made of flesh! First they
espied an aged fisherman, who passed without regard.
Then did they deem they were invisible, and wilder still
their fancies worked. The suburbs now they gained of the
resplendent ancient Otholine, the emporium of the east,
and hand in hand, with hurried, but enfeebled step, they
trode its lanes and alleys. Those who saw them said their
motions were erratic, like the gait of beings overcome with
wine, or creatures learning to walk for the first time on
earth. The early matron, and the twilight groom, fled with
hysteric cries at their approach. The gates were left a-jar,
the streets a waste: porter and sentinel joined in the flight,
and nought but terror and confusion reigned.

The virgin sisters wist not what to do, or what to dread.
Within the convent's porch, they halted, turned, and gazed
on one another, and wondered what they were, that nature
thus shuddered at their approach, and held aloof. Three
creatures spiritual yet made of flesh, belonging not to
heaven nor earth! but shunned by the inhabitants of both.
Just then, while standing in despondency, they heard the
grey cock crow; the eldritch clarion note chilled every heart,
and twanged on every nerve.

'That is our warning call,' wild Morna said: 'My sisters
now we must hence and begone: that is the roll-call of
the murdering spirits. We shall be missed at matins. To
your homes! your damp and mouldering homes, ye ghastly
shades! The daylight will dissolve you! Does that voice not
say so?'

'Hush thee, gentle Morna! drive us not to distraction.
Here we'll wait until the convent matin; then we'll ask
the holy prioress what things we are. What say you, gentle
sisters? can we live outcasts on earth in such incertitude?
Our father's towers are distant. We can glide, like passing
shades with slow and feeble motion, but nothing more; –
spirits can sail the air in skiff of mist or on the breeze's
wing. Such powers we have not; and to journey there we
lack ability. Here then we stay until we are resolved what

strange events have happened to us, to our native land, and church, of late so grievously oppressed.'

'Yes, here we'll stay. Come, rouse the porteress! For see the sun tips the far hills with gold, and we shall melt before his tepid ray, all gentle as it is at early morn! My frame is like a mildew. The hoar frost of death hath fallen on it. Oh, for the guide – the angelic youth that left us yester-eve. Ho! daughters of the Cross! If any here hath 'scaped the murderous Dane, come forth and welcome the conquerors of Odin. Ho! within! Wake ere the sun upbraids you. He is up, on service to his Maker, yet you sleep. I say, wake.'

'Who calls? What are you there?'

'We know not what we are. For that we come, to see if any here can us resolve. But two short nights ago, we were three maids of royal lineage. Thou stern porteress, come forth and look on us. Canst thou not tell what we are made of? Why stand'st thou aloof?'

'Speak calmly, sister Morna. See she trembles and dares not answer. Gentle dame, we pray admission to your lady prioress, for sake of him who died upon the cross, whose name we worship.' Straight she vanished upon her fearful mission, glad to 'scape from such a colloquy. Soon then arrived the aged prioress, who them approached with dauntless countenance, and, unappalled, asked of their errand. 'Venerable dame, dost thou not know, or hast thou never heard of the three maids of Stormont, who of late, led by a heavenly messenger, o'erthrew the god of Denmark, and upheld the cross triumphant o'er the breasts of prostrate heathens?'

'Ay, I have heard of them; and often joined in prayer and thanksgiving for the deliverance wrought by these royal virgins. That was a conquest that roused the spirit of the Christian to deeds of more than mortal energy, and humbled the proud confidence the Dane placed in his idols. Ay, that was a conquest shall cloud the brow of the idolater while the world stands! But what was it you spoke of yester-eve? Either you are deranged, or shallow poor impostors: for that time hath long gone past, and the three wondrous maids were in the sight, and from the middle of that mighty host translated into heaven. Unless you came from thence on sacred mission, and bringest evidence of identity by further miracle, better you had keep silence and depart.'

'We are those maids, the maids of Stormont, nieces to the king; and we require of you lodging and fair protection, till we prove our lineage. There is something passing strange hath happened to us. But what the circumstance, or how accordant with the works of God, is far beyond the fathom and the height of our capacity. We are the maids of Stormont. To that truth we will make oath upon the holy cross.'

The prioress crossed herself, commended her to heaven, and, with deep awe and dire astonishment, admitted them. She gazed upon them: their fair cheeks were pale, and their benignant eyes looked through a haze that was not earthly; it was like the blue mists of the dawning. All their robes were of the fashion of a former day; and they were damp and mouldy, falling piecemeal from off their bodies with their rottenness.

'I dread to question you, mysterious things. That you are earthly forms, I see and feel. Whence are you? In what dreary unknown clime have you been sojourning? Or are you risen from out your graves? If you have truth in you, and power to tell it, pray resolve me this; for I am lost in wonder.'

'What we are we know not. For that purpose we came hither, that you might tell us. All we know is this: Last night but one we were the maids of Stormont, doomed to a dreadful fate. An heavenly one came to our rescue; led us through the gates of iron and of brass. Still as we went, we conquered. Ranks of proud idolaters fell prostrate in the dust; and the great god, the mighty Odin, was o'erthrown, and dashed into a thousand pieces. Straight our blessed guide conducted us into a lonely cave close by the river's brink, and bade us sleep and take our rest until the day should dawn and shadows fly away. We slept, and yester-morn, when we awoke, the lamp our guide had left still feebly burned. Impelled by hunger, from our cave we ventured. All people fly from us; the Danes are gone; the name of Christ is mentioned. Nought we see and nought we hear is comprehensible.'

'A miracle! a mighty miracle! Within that secret cavern you have slept for days and years, in quiet sweet repose, the lamp of heaven still burning over you, until the day hath dawned – such a day of grace as Scotland hath not seen. The heathen Dane, with all his hideous gods, was vanquished, but days of darkness and contention rose, until this time, when all the glorious rays of mercy and of grace have shed their influence on this benighted persecuted land; and you are waked to enjoy it. Let us go straight to the altar, and beneath the cross join in elated thanksgiving.'

The chancel door opened before the altar. When the three virgins entered in, and saw the figure on the cross, they cried aloud with one combined voice, ''Tis he, 'Tis he! What? Have these heathens dared to lay their impious hands on him? 'Tis he! 'Tis he! Our heavenly guide that saved us from the death. And have they slain him? Has the cursed Dane—'

'Hold, hold, for mercy's sake; you do not know the things you utter. What you look upon, hangs there to represent the death of him who died that man might live.'

'And is it so? Then be our lives sacred unto the service of him who laid his life down for our race, and sent his angel to deliver us, in his own likeness too; for this is he who came to us in great extremity, when we called on the name of our Redeemer in agony of soul.'

'Remain with me till our great festival. This miracle must be made known to all that trust in Jesus' name. Meanwhile I will cherish and comfort the beloved of heaven.'

The day arrived of the great festival, the anniversary of the overthrow of mighty Odin – that sublime event that broke the bands of iron and of steel, and threw the gates of superstition open to Albyn's Christian triumph. On that day the king's whole household, nobles of the realm, high dames and commons, abbots, monks, and mendicants, a motely and a countless multitude, assembled early at the monastery of ancient Otholine, to render thanks for their deliverance. Masses were said; and holy hymns of praise ascended to the skies. With one accord, then all the grateful multitude agreed to canonize the three heroic virgins, who, with the aid of angels, had wrought out the Christian's triumph, the beloved of heaven, translated to the blest beatitude, where souls of saints and blessed martyrs dwell, and whose joint prayers might with the holy Virgin much avail.

A joyful clamour for the ordinance then spread around, so eager were the crowd to kneel and pay their humble adorations to the three maids, translated to the heavens with bodies like their own. Applauses rang; and from behind the altar was given forth a song divine, in which a thousand voices joined, till all were hushed at this ecstatic strain.

> Hail to the happy three!
> Vessels of sanctity!
> Now honoured to stand
> At the Virgin's right hand.
> (Mater Dei!
> Remember me!)
> Remember us all, and send us for good,
> Bone of our bone, and blood of our blood—.
> Song of harp, and voice be dumb!—
> The heaven is oped. They come, they come!

A bustle rose. The abbot on his knees sunk down and leaned upon the altarcloth, and only a few voices whispered round, 'They come, they come!' The congregation turned their eyes into the chancel, and beheld three virgins, all in robes of purest white, stand over against the altar. The loud choir was hushed, and every brow was forward bent in low obeisance: All believing these three beauteous flowers from paradise had come arrayed in robes of heaven, with angel forms that bloomed like winter roses newly oped, in high approval of the festival, and sacred honours to be paid to them.

The virgins beckoned, raised their flowing veils, and their right hands to heaven. 'Stay,' they cried, 'stay the solemnity, ere you profane the name and altar of the God of heaven. Here stand the three unworthy maids of Stormont whom you would deify. Come nigh to us our father and our king, and ye chaste ministers of him we serve: Come nigh, and feel that we are mortal like yourselves, and stop the rite. Pay adoration to that Holy One who pitied us in misery extreme, and you in grievous bonds. There be your vows and worship paid, in which we three shall join. He hath indeed done wondrous things for us, works of amazement, which you all shall hear, and whoso heareth shall rejoice in heart.'

Then came they all unto their father's knee, kneeled and embraced him, while the good old earl shed tears of joy, and rendered thanks to heaven: their soverign next, their former lovers, friends, and all they knew in that mixed multitude, they did embrace, that no remaining doubt might spring and spread to their identity. It was a joyful meeting, such a one as hath not been in any land for happiness and holy ecstacy. They lived beyond the years of women – but their lives were spent in acts of holiness, apart from grandeur's train. In curing of the sick, clothing the naked, ministering to all in want and wretchedness, and speaking peace unto poor wandering and benighted souls. Their evening of life was like the close of summer day, pure, placid, and serene – the twilight long, but when at last it closed, it was with such a heavenly glow, it gave pure prospect of a joyous day to come. Thus ends my legend; and, with all submission, I bow to your awards, and wait my doom.

CHAPTER TWENTY-THREE

Garolde. Prick on good Markham. That galled jade of yours
    Moves with a hedgehog's pace. Is this a time
    To amble like a belle at tournament,
    When life and death hang on our enterprize?
Mark. We've had long stages, Garolde;
    We must take up. What miscreants have we here?

                                       The Prioress

'LO, HAVE NOT I taken great delight in the words of
thy mouth?' said the friar, 'for it is a legend of purity and
holiness which thou hast told, and the words of truth are
contained in it. Peradventure it may be an ancient allegory
of our nation, in which manner of instruction the fathers of
Christianity amongst us took great delight. But, whether it
be truth, or whether it be fiction, the tendency is good; and
behold, is it not so; do not I even thank thee for thy tale?'

'It is the most diffuse, extravagant, and silly legend that
ever was invented by votary of a silly and inconsistent
creed,' said the Master.

'I side wi' you, Master Michael Scott,' said Tam Craik;
'I think the tale is nought but a string of bombastical
nonsense.'

'Excepting ane about fat flesh, I think I never heard the
match o't,' said the laird of the Peatstacknowe; 'It brings
me amind o' our host's dinner, that was a' show but nae
substance.'

'If I foresee aught aright,' said the Master, 'of many a
worse dinner shall I see thee partake, and enjoy the sight.'

'Was not that a beautiful and sublime tale, father?' said
Delany: 'I could sit and listen to such divine legends for
ever.' The poet's eyes shone with tears when he heard
the maid he loved say these words to the friar apart, who

answered and said unto her, 'Lo, there are many more
sublime and more wonderful in thy little book; nevertheless
the tale is good for instruction to those that are faithless and
doubting.'

'Alak! I fear I shall not live to learn and enjoy these.
Do not you think, father, that we shall all perish in this
miserable place,' added Delany – 'this horrible place of
witchcraft and divination?' Charlie Scott stepped forward
when he overheard some of these words. 'Eh? what was the
lassie saying?' said he. 'Eh? I'll tell ye what it is, hinney:
I believe ye see things as they are. There's naething but
witchcraft gaun on here; and it is that, and that alone, that
a' our perils and mischances rise frae. Begging your pardon,
father, I canna help thinking what I think, and seeing what
I see. But, gude faith! we maun blaw lown till we win aff
the tap o' this bigging, if that ever be.'

'My hand hath prevailed against his hand,' said the friar,
'and my master over his master; and had it not been for this
miserable accident we should have had nothing to fear from
his divinations, sublime and mighty as they are. What hath
become of the mighty men of valour from the camp of our
captain?'

'O there's nae mortal can tell,' said Charlie: 'It was not
for naething that Dan and his lads ran off and left us
without ever looking ower their shoulders. A' witchcraft!
a' witchcraft! Ane may stand against muckle, but nae man
can stand against that. I wish we were where sword and
shield could aince mair stand us in stead. But this I'm
sure o' – Now that our situation is kend to our kinsman,
it winna be lang before some aid appear. O if it wad but
come afore we are driven to that last and warst of a' shifts
to keep in life.'

'We canna live another day,' said Tam: 'I therefore
propose that the maid and the boy try ilk ane their hand
at a tale too, and stand their chances with the rest of us.
Their lives are of less value, and their bodies very tender
and delicate.'

Every one protested against Tam's motion with abhorrence; and it was agreed that they would now appeal to
the Master who had told the worst tale. Not that the
unfortunate victim was to be immediately sacrificed, nor
even till the very last extremity; but with that impatience

natural to man, they longed to be put out of pain; every one having hopes that his own merits protected himself from danger. Every one also believed that judgment would be given against Tam, except he himself; and that, at all events, such an award would put an end to his disagreeable and endless exultations of voracious delight. They then went before the renowned wizard, and desired him to give judgment who of them had related the worst and most inefficient tale, laying all prejudice with regard to creeds and testimonies aside.

He asked them if they referred the matter entirely to him, or if they wished to have each one a vote of their own? Tam said it was an understanding at first that each should have a vote, and, as he had made up his mind on the subject, he wished to give his. Charlie said it was a hard matter to vote away the life of a friend; and, for his part, he would rather appeal to the great Master altogether. But if any doubts should remain with any one of their host's impartiality, he thought it fairer that they should cast lots, and hazard all alike. The poet, who had heard the Master's disapprobation given pointedly of his tale, sided with Yardbire, and voted that it should be decided by lot. Gibbie, though quite convinced in his own mind that he had told the best story, yet having heard the *morality* of it doubted, and dreading on that score to have some voices against him, called also for a vote; for he said the referring the matter to the Master brought him in mind of the story of the fox sitting in judgment, and deciding against the lamb. The friar also said, 'Verily, I should give my voice for the judgment of the Master to stand decisive: But, lo! is it not apparent that his thoughts are not like the thoughts of other men? Neither is his mind governed by the motives of the rest of the children of men. I do therefore lift up my voice for the judgment that goeth by lot. I would, notwithstanding of all this, gladly hear what the Master would say.'

'I will be so far just that I shall give you your choice,' said Master Michael Scott: 'Nevertheless I can tell you, if there be any justice in the decision by lot, on whom the lot will fall.' A pause of breathless anxiety occurred, and every eye was fixed on the grim and stern visage of the great necromancer, over whose features there appeared to pass a gleam of wild delight. 'It will fall,' added he, 'on that man of fables and similitudes, who himself bears the similitude of a man, just as the lion's hide stuffed does the resemblance of a real one. How do you call that beautiful and amiable being with the nose that would split a drop of rain without being wet?'

'Most illustrious knight, and master of the arts of mystery,' said the friar – 'as this man is, so is his name; for he is called Jordan, after the great river that is in the east, which overfloweth its banks at certain seasons, and falls into the stagnant lake called the Dead Sea, whose waters are diseased. So doth the matter of this our friend overflow, pass away, and is lost. But what sayest thou of the default of his story? Dost thou remember that it is not for the best story that we cast lots, but the worst?'

'Ay, that's weel said, good friar,' said Charlie; 'for, trifling as the laird's story was, I never heard ought sae queer, or that interested ane mair. If there be ony justice in lots, the laird's safe.'

'Your's was the best tale, gallant yeoman,' said the Master, 'and you may rest assured that you are safe. The dumb judge will not err, and there is one overlooks the judgment by lot, of whom few are aware. I say your's was the best tale.'

'Thank ye kindly, Master Michael Scott,' said Charlie; 'I'm feared ilk ane winna be o' your opinion.'

The friar then took from the side-pockets of his frock a few scraps of parchment, amounting to fifteen. Twelve of these he marked with a red cross, and three with a black one, to prevent all infernal interference; then rolling them closely up, he counted them all into his cowl before his companions, and, shaking them together, he caused every one to do the same. Then putting the cowl into the virgin's hand, they desired her to hold it until they drew forth their scraps one by one. She did so, while her bright eyes were drowned in tears, and each of the candidates put in his hand, selecting his lot.

'Let them be opened, one by one, before all these witnesses,' cried the Master; 'that no suspicions of foul play whatever may remain.'

The friar drew forth his without one muscle of his unyielding features being altered, and turning deliberately about, he opened it before them all. It was red. The friar bowed his head, and made the sign of the cross. Charlie thrust in his hand – pulled out a ticket – and tore it open, all in one moment, and with the same impatience that he fought in a battle. His was likewise red.

'Gude faith I'm aince ower the water,' said Charlie.

Tam put in his hand with a decision that would have done honour to a better man, the form of his mouth only being a little altered.

'Now, who will take me a bet of a three-year-old cout,' cried Gibbie, 'that the next shall turn out a black one?' and he grinned a ghastly smile, in anticipation of the wished event. Tam kept his hand within the cowl for a good while, as if groping which to select. At length he drew one forth; and before he got it opened, Gibbie's long nose and his own had met above it, so eager was each of them to see what it contained. It was opened. Each of them raised up his face, and looked at the face of his opponent; but with what different expressions of countenance! The cross on the lot was red! Grief, dread, and disappointment were all apparent in the features of poor Jordan, while the exulting looks of his provoking neighbour were hardly to be endured.

'What think you o' that now, laird?' cried he. 'What does that bring you in mind o'? Eh? I say, wha's jugular vein swells highest now; or wha's shoulder-blade stands maist need o' clawing?'

This was rather more than Gibbie was disposed at that juncture to bear; and when Tam, as he concluded, put forth his forefinger to ascertain the thickness of fat on the laird's ribs, the latter struck him with such force on the wrist, that he rendered his arm powerless for a space. He put his hand to his sword, but could not grasp it; while Gibbie, seeing the motion, had his out in a twinkling; and if the staunch friar had not turned it aside, he would have had it through the heart of the deil's Tam in a second, which might have prevented the further drawing of lots for that present time, and thereby put an end to a very critical and disagreeable business. Gibbie was far from being a hot or passionate man; but whether his rage was a manoeuvre to put by the decision, or if he really was offended at being handled like a wedder for slaughter, the curate pretends not to guess.

He however raged and fumed exceedingly, and tried again and again to wound Tam, while the rest were remonstrating with him; nor would he be pacified, until Tam's disabled arm by degrees regaining somewhat of its pristine nerve, he retreated back towards the battlement for sword-room, and dared the laird to the combat. Gibbie struggled hard; but finding that they were about to let him go, his wrath subsided a little; he put up his sword, and said the whole business reminded him of a story of the laird of Tweelsdon and his two brothers, which he assured them was a prime story, and begged permission to tell it. This was protested against with one voice until the business of the lots was decided, and then all were willing to hear it. 'Oh, the lots? that is quite true,' said Gibbie: 'I declare that business had gone out of my head. Let us see what casts up next.' There was a relaxation in every muscle of Gibbie's face as he put his hand into the cowl. But Gibbie's was a sort of a cross face. It did not grow long and sallow as most other men's faces do when they are agitated. The jaws did not fall down, they closed up; so that his face grew a great deal shorter and broader. The eye-brows and the cheekbones met, and the nose and chin approached to a close vicinity. He drew forth the momentous scrap, and, with fumbling and paralytic hand, opened it before them. The cross was black. He dared not lift his eyes to any face there save to Delany's, and when he saw it covered with tears his looks again reverted that way. This lot it is true was not decisive, yet it placed Gibbie on ticklish ground; it having been agreed, that whoever should draw the two first black crosses, subjected himself to immolation, if the necessity of the case required it. The great Master and Tam were visibly well pleased with the wicked chance that had fallen to the laird. The motives of the former for this delight were quite a mystery to those who beheld it; as for Tam, he seemed determined to keep no more terms with poor Gibbie.

The poet also drew a red one; and then it was decreed, that the next round Gibbie should have his choice of the time, if he judged it any advantage either to be first or last. He seemed quite passive, and said it was all one to him, he should draw at any time they chose, and desired his friend Yardbire, as he termed him, to choose for him.

Charlie said he deemed the first chance the best, as he had then four chances to be right, for one of being wrong; and it would be singular indeed if his hand fixed on a black cross again for a time or two, when more of them might be on an equal footing.

Gibbie accordingly turned round, and drew out one more of the ominous scraps, opening it under the eyes of all the circle with rather a hopeful look. 'If the deil be nae in the cowl, I shall hae a red ane this time,' said he, as he unrolled it; but as soon as the head of the cross appeared the ticket fell from his hand; and, as the friar expressed it, there was no more strength remaining in him. 'Verily, my son, thy fate is decided,' said the latter worthy; 'and that in a wonderful and arbitrary manner. As the Master said, so hath it come to pass, although to judge of any thing having been done unfairly is impossible.'

'It is absolute nonsense to talk of aught being done fairly in this place,' said Charlie Scott: 'There's naething but witchcraft gaun. I tell ye a' things here are done by witchery an' the black arts; and after what I heard the king of a' warlocks say, that the lot wad fa' in this way, I winna believe that honest Gibbie has gotten fair play for his life.'

'If you would try it an hundred times over,' said the Master, 'you would see it turn out in the same way. Did not I say to you that there was a power presided over the decision by lot, which you neither know nor comprehend. Man of metaphors and old wives' fables, where art thou now?' 'Keep a gude heart, Peatstacknowe,' said Charlie; 'perhaps things may not come to the worst. I have great dependence on Dan Chisholm and the warden's good men. I wonder they have not appeared wi' proper mattocks, or ladders, by this time o' the morning.'

'If they should,' said the Master, 'and if we were all set at liberty this minute, he shall remain my bondsman, in place of these two and him of whom your arts have bereaved me. Remember to what you agreed formerly, of which I now remind you.'

'I think that is but fair,' said the poet.

'I do not know, gentlemen, what you call fair or foul,' said Gibbie: 'I think there is little that is favourable going for somebody. Of the two evils, I judge the last the worst.

I appeal to my captain the Warden.' Gibbie's looks were so rueful and pitiable when he said this, that no one had the heart to remonstrate farther with him on the justice or injustice of his doom. The Master and Tam enjoyed his plight exceedingly; the poet rejoiced in it, as it tended to free Delany from a vile servitude; and the friar also was glad of the release of the darling of his younger years, the grand-daughter of Galli the scribe. Charlie and Delany were the only two that appeared to suffer on account of the laird's dismal prospects, and their feelings were nearly as acute as his own. Stories and all sorts of amusements were now discontinued. A damp was thrown over these by the dismal gloom on the laird's countenance, and the congenial feelings of others on his account. The night had passed over without any more visitants from the infernal regions; the day had arisen in the midst of heaviness and gloom; and every eye was turned towards the mill, in the expectation of seeing the approach of Dan and his companions.

CHAPTER TWENTY-FOUR

Ask me not whence I am;
My vesture speaks mine office.
Female Parliamenters, a MS Com.

AFTER THE FRIGHTSOME encounter at the mill, with 'the masterless dog and his bow-wow-wow,' Dan and his companions spent a sleepless night, not without several alarms and breathless listenings on the occurrence of any noise without. Few were the nightly journies on the banks of the Ettrick in those days, and few the midnight noises that occurred, save from the wild beasts of the forest. There were no wooer lads straying at that still and silent hour, to call up their sweethearts for an hour's kind conversation. Save when the English marauders were abroad, all was quietness by hamlet and steading. The land was the abode of the genii of the woods, the rocks, and the rivers; and of this the inhabitants were well aware, and kept within locked doors, whose lintels were made of the mountain ash, and nightly sprinkled with holy water. Cradle and bed were also fenced with cross, book, and bead; for the inmates knew that in no other way could they be safe, or rest in peace. They knew that their green and solitary glens were the nightly haunts of the fairies, and that they held their sports and amorous revels in the retiring dells by the light of the moon. The mermaid sung her sweet and alluring strains by the shores of the mountain lake, and the kelpie sat moping and dripping by his frightsome pool, or the boiling caldron at the foot of the cataract. The fleeting wraiths hovered round the dwellings of those who were soon to die, and the stalking ghost perambulated the walks of him that was lately living, or took up his nightly stand over the bones of the unhouseholded or murdered

375

dead. In such a country, and among such sojourners, who durst walk by night?

But these were the natural residenters in the wilds of the woodland, the aboriginal inhabitants of the country; and however inimical their ways might be to the ways of men, the latter laid their account with them. There were defences to be had against them from holy church, which was a great comfort. But ever since Master Michael Scott came from the colleges abroad to reside at the castle of Aikwood, the nature of demonology in the forest glades was altogether changed, and a full torrent of necromancy, or, as Charlie Scott better expressed it, of *witchcraft*, deluged the country all over – an art of the most malignant and appalling kind, against which no fence yet discovered could prevail. How different, indeed, became the situation of the lonely hind. Formerly he only heard at a distance on moonlight eves the bridle bells of the fairy troopers, which haply caused him to haste homeward. But when the door was barred and fenced, he sat safe in the middle of his family circle as they closed round the hearth, and talked of the pranks of *the gude neybouris*. When the speats descended, and floods roared and foamed from bank to brae, then would they perceive the malevolent kelpie rolling and tumbling down the torrent like a drowning cow, or mountain stag, to allure the hungry peasant into certain destruction. But, aware of the danger, he only kept the farther aloof, quaking at the tremendous experiment made by the spirit of the waters. It was in vain that the mermaid sung the sweetest strains that ever breathed over the evening lake, or sunk and rose again, spreading her hands for assistance, like a drowning maiden, at the bottom of the abrupt cliff washed by the waves – he *would not* be allured to her embraces.

But what could he do now? His daughters were turned into roes and hares, to be hunted down for sport to the Master. The old wives of the hamlet were saddled and bridled by night, and urged with whip and spur over whole realms. The cows were deprived of their milk – the hinds cast their young, and no domestic cat in the whole district could be kept alive for one year. That infernal system of witchcraft then began, which the stake and the gibbet could scarcely eradicate in a whole century. It had at this time begun to spread all around Aikwood; but of these things our

Border troopers were not altogether aware. They dreaded the spirits of the old school, the devil in particular; but of the new prevailing system of metamorphoses they had no comprehension.

Dan and three chosen companions, mounting their horses by the break of day, rode straight for the abbey of Melrose, to lodge their complaint against the great enemy of mankind, and request assistance from the holy fathers in rescuing their friends out of his hands. They reached Darnick-burn before the rising of the sun; and just as they passed by a small deep-wooded dell, they espied four horsemen approaching them, who, from their robes and riding appurtenances, appeared to belong to the abbey, and to rank high among its dignitaries. They were all mounted on black steeds, clothed in dark flowing robes that were fringed with costly fringes, and they had caps on their heads that were horned like the new moon. The foremost, in particular, had a formidable and majestic mitre on his head, that seemed all glancing with gems, every one of which was either black, or a certain dazzling red of the colour of flame.

Dan doffed his helmet to this dignified and commanding personage, but he deigned not either to return our yeoman's low bow, that brought his face in contact with the mane of his steed, or once to cross his hand on his brow in token of accepting the submission proffered. He, however, reined up his black steed, and sat upright on his saddle, as if in the act of listening what this bold and blunt trooper had to say.

'Begging pardon of your grand and sublime reverence,' said Dan, 'I presume, from your lofty and priest-like demeanour, habiliments, and goodly steed, and also from that twa-horned helmet on your head, that you are the very chap I want. I beg your pardon I canna keep up my style to suit your dignity. But are nae ye Father Lawrence, the great primate, that acts as a kind o' king or captain ower a' the holy men of Scotland, and has haudding in that abbey down by there?'

'Certes I am Father Lawrence. Dost thou doubt it?'

'No, no; what for should I doubt it when your worship has said it? An we dinna find truth aneath the mitre and the gown, where are we to look for it?'

The sublime abbot shook his head as if in scorn and derision of the apothegm, and sat still upright on his steed, with his face turned away. Dan looked round to his companions with a meaning look, as much as to say, 'What does the body mean?' But seeing that he sat still in the act of listening, he proceeded.

'Worthy Sir Priest, ye ken our captain, Sir Ringan Redhough, warden of the Border. He has helpit weel to feather your nest, ye ken.'

'He has. There is no one can dispute it,' said the abbot, nodding assent.

'Then ye'll no be averse, surely, to the lending o' him and his a helping hand in your ain way.'

The priest nodded assent.

'Weel, ye see, Sir Priest, there is a kinsman of our master's lives up by here at Aikwood, a rank warlock, and master o' the arts of witchcraft and divination. He is in compact wi' the deil, and can do things far ayont the power o' mortal man. What do ye think, Sir Priest? he can actually turn a man into a dog, and an auld wife into a hare; a mouse into a man, and a cat into a good glyde-aver. And mair than that, Sir, he can raise storms and tempests in the air; can gar the rivers rin upward, and the trees grow down. He can shake the solid yird; and, look ye, Sir, he can cleave a great mountain into three, and lift the divisions up like as mony gowpens o' sand.'

The stern abbot gave a glance up to the three new hills of Eildon, that towered majestically over their heads; but it seemed rather a look of exultation than one either of wonder or regret.

'Weel, Sir, disna our captain send a few chosen friends, a wheen queer devils to be sure, on a message of good friendship to this auld warlock Master Michael Scott, merely with a request to read him some trivial weird. And what does the auld knave, but pricks them a' up on the top o' his castle, wi' a lockit iron-door aneath them, and there has keepit them in confinement till they are famishing of hunger, and I fear by this time they are feeding on ane another. And the warst o't ava, Sir, is this, I wad break his bolts and his bars to atoms for him, but has nae he the deil standing sentry on the stair, spuing fire and brimstone on a' that come near him in sic torrents that it is like the fa'

o' the Grey-mare's-tail. Now, maist reverend and worthy
Sir, my errand and request to you is, that, for my master's
sake, and for his men's sake, that are a' good Christians,
for ought that I ken to the contrary, you will lend us a lift
wi' book and bead, Ave Marias, and other powerful things,
to drive away this auld sneckdrawing thief, the devil, and
keep him away till I get my friends released; and I promise
you, in my master's name, high bounty and reward.'

'Ha! is it so?' said the abbot, in a hollow, tremulous
voice. 'Are my friend and fellow-soldier's men detained
in that guise? Come, my brethren, let us ride – let us fly
to their release, and we shall see whose power can stand
against our own. For Aikwood, ho!'

'For Aikwood, ho!' shouted Dan and his companions, as
they took the rear of the four sable dignitaries; and striking
the spurs into their steeds all at the same time, they went
off at their horses' utmost speed, but in a short time the
four yeomen were distanced. The black steeds and their
riders went at such a pace as warrior had never before
witnessed. Up by the side of Hindly-burn they sped, with
the most rapid velocity – over mire, over ditch, over ford,
without stay or stumble. Dan and his companions posted
on behind, sparing neither whip nor spur, for they were
affronted that these gownsmen should display more energy
in their master's cause, and the cause of his friends, than
they should do themselves. But their horses floundered,
and blew, and snorted, and puffed, and whisked their tails
with a whistling sound, and still lagged farther and farther
behind.

'Come, come, callants,' cried Dan to his companions,
'let us rein up. These bedesmen's horses are ower weel fed
for our bog-trotting nags. They fly like the wind. Od, we
may as weel try to ride wi' the devil.'

'Whisht, whisht,' said Will Martin; 'I dinna like to mak
ower familiar wi' that name now-a-days. We never ken
wha's hearing us in this country.'

They were nigh to the heights when these words passed,
and the four black horsemen perceiving them to take it
leisurely, they paused and wheeled about, and the majestic
primate taking off his cornuted chaperon, waved it aloft,
and called aloud, 'For shame, sluggish hinds! Why won't
you speed, before the hour of prevention is lost? For

Aikwood, ho, I say!' As he said these words, his black courser plunged and reared at a fearful rate; and, as our troopers thought, at one bolt sprung six or seven yards from the ground. The marks of that black horse's hoofs remain impressed in the sward to this day, and the spot is still called *The Abbot's lee*. At least it had been so called when Isaac the curate wrote this history.

To keep clear of the wood that was full of thickets, they turned a little to the left, and pursued their course; and the ground becoming somewhat firmer, our yeomen pursued hard after them. But on coming over the steep brow of a little hill, the latter perceived a mountain lake of considerable extent that interrupted their path, and, to their utter astonishment, the four black horsemen going straight across it, at about the same rate that the eagle traverses the firmament. 'The loch is frozen and bears over,' said Dan: 'Let us follow them across.'

'The loch is frozen indeed,' said Will Martin, 'but, ony man may see, that ice winna bear a cat.'

'Haud your tongue, you gouk,' said Dan: 'Do ye think the thing that bore them winna bear us?' And as he spurred foremost down the steep, he took the lake at the broad side; but the ice offering no manner of resistance, horse and man were in one moment out of sight. The sable horsemen on the other side shouted with laughter, and called aloud to the troopers, 'to venture on, and haste forward, for the ice was sufficiently strong.'

The bold trooper and his horse were extricated with some difficulty, and the monks testifying the utmost impatience he remounted, dripping as he was, and not being able to find the passage across the lake on the ice, he and his companions gallopped around the head of it. As he rode, the morning being frosty, he chanced to utter these words: 'Heigh-ho, but I be a *cauld cheil!*' Which words, says Isaac, gave the name to that lake and the hill about it to all future ages; and from those perilous days of witchcraft and divination, and the shocking incidents that befel to men, adds he, have a great many of the names of places all over our country had their origin.

The dark horsemen always paused until the troopers were near them, as if to encourage them on, but they never suffered them to join company. When they came over a ridge above old Lindean they were hard upon them, but lost sight of them for a short space on the height; and, coming on full speed, they arrived on the brink of a deep wooded dell, and to their utter astonishment saw the four gownsmen on the other side, riding deliberately along, and beckoning them forward.

'I am sair mista'en,' said Will Marton, 'gin thae chaps hae nae gaen ower the cleugh at ae bound. An it warna for their habits I wad take them for something nouther good nor cannie.'

'Haud your tongue, or else speak feasible things,' said Dan; 'Can the worthy Father Lawrence, and his chief priors and functionaries ever be suspected as warlocks, or men connected wi' the devil and his arts? If sic were to be the case, we hae nae mair trust to put in aught on this earth. The dell maun be but a step across. Here is a good passable road; come, let us follow them.'

Dan led the way, and they dived into the dell by a narrow track, rather like a path for a wild goat than men and horses; however, by leaping, sliding, and pushing one another's horses behind, they got to the bottom of the precipice, and perceiving a path on the other side, they expected to reach the western brink immediately. But in this they were mistaken; abrupt rocks, and impenetrable thickets barred their progress on every side, and they found it impossible to extricate themselves without leaving their horses. They tried every quarter with the same success, and at the last attempted to ascend by the way they came; but that too they found impracticable, and all the while they heard the voices of their fellow travellers chiding their stay from above, and shaming them for their stupidity in taking the wrong path. At one time they heard them calling on them to come this way, here was an excellent outgate; and when the toiled yeomen stuck fairly still in that direction, they instantly heard other voices urging them to ascend by some other quarter. At other times they thought they heard restrained bursts of giggling laughter. After a great deal of exertion to no manner of purpose, they grew they neither knew what to do nor what they were doing, and at last were obliged to abandon their horses, and climb the ascent by hanging by the bushes and roots of trees. When they emerged from the deep hollow, they perceived eight black horsemen awaiting them instead of four; but as the country around Melrose and Dryburgh swarmed with members of the holy brotherhood of every distinction and rank, the troopers took no notice of it, thinking these were some of the head functionaries come to wait on their abbot. The latter chided our yeomen in sharp and resentful language for their utter stupidity in taking the wrong path, and regretted exceedingly the long delay their mistake had occasioned, his time he said being limited, as was also the time that his power prevailed in a more particular way over the powers of darkness. 'For us to go alone,' added he, 'would signify nothing. The manual labour of breaking through the iron gates we cannot perform; therefore, unless you can keep up with us, we may return home by the way we came.'

'I am truly grieved,' said Dan, 'at our misfortune. We have certainly been more forward than wise, and I fear have marred the fairest chance we will ever have for the deliverance of our friends. But I have a few fellow warriors at the mill who will accompany you for a word of your mouth. I beg that you will not think of returning, for the case brooks no delay. We have lost our horses, and can hardly reach the castle on foot before it be evening. I wot not what we shall do.'

'Brethren, I am afraid I must request of you to lend these brave troopers your horses,' said the abbot to the four last comers. 'My esteem for the doughty champion of my domains is such, that I would gladly do him a favour.' 'O thank you, thank you, kind sir; we are mair behadden to you than tongue can tell,' said Dan. The four new come brethren dismounted at their abbot's request; and, without taking a moment to hesitate, the four yeomen mounted their horses. The abbot Lawrence charged them to urge the steeds to their utmost speed. Away went the abbot and his three sable attendants, and away went the four troopers after them; but from the first moment that they started the latter lost sight of the ground, unless it was, as they thought, about a mile below their feet. The road seemed to be all one marble pavement, or sheet of solid alabaster; there was neither height nor hollow in it that they could distinguish; but the fire flew from the heels of the horses, and sparkled across the firmament like thousands of flying stars. The velocity at which they went was such, that the borderers could not draw their breath save by small broken gulps; but as they imagined they rode at such an immense distance from the ground, they kept firm by their seats for bare life, leaning forward with their eyes and their mouths wide open. Having never in all their lives rode on such a path, they were soon convinced that they could not be riding toward Aikwood, around which the roads were very different. They often attempted to speak to one another, but could not utter any thing farther than one short sound, for the swiftness with which they clove the atmosphere cut their voices short. At length Dan, perceiving his comrade, Will Martin, scouring close by his side, forced out the following sentence piecemeal:

'Where – the – devil – are we – gaun – now?'

'Straight – to – hell——. What – need – ye – speer?'

'The – lord – for – for – for – bid – Will Martin,' was the reply, which has since grown to a proverb.

On they flew, over hill, over dale, over rock and river, over town, tower, and steeple, as our yeomen deemed; but they might deem what they pleased, for they saw nothing except now and then the tails of the churchmen's gowns flapping in the air before them. However, they came to their goal sooner than they expected, and that in a way as singular as that by which they reached it.

The miller at Aikwood-mill had a whole hill of kiln-seeds, or shealings of oats, thrown out in a heap adjoining to the mill. Ere ever our yeomen knew what they were doing from the time they mounted, they were all lying in this immense heap of kiln-seeds, perfectly dizzy and dumfoundered, and setting up their heads from among them with the same sort of staring stupid attempt at consideration as the heads of so many frogs which may be seen newly popped up out of a marsh. The bedesmen were a-head of them to the end of the course, and drew up by wheeling their horses round the kiln as if it had been a winning-post; but the yeomen's horses, in making the wheel, threw their riders, one by one, with a jerk over head and ears among the loose heap of seeds, and galloping off around the corner of the hill, they never saw another hair of their tails.

The miller came running out from his mill with his

broad dusty bonnet; the smoky half-roasted kiln-man out from his logie; the mill-maidens came skipping from the meal-trough, as white as lilies; the rest of the warden's men, and the four sable dignitaries of the church came also, and all of them stood in a ring round our dismounted troops, some asking one question, some another, but all in loud fits of laughter. Their wits could not be rallied in an instant; and all that they could do or say was to blow the seeds out of their mouths, with which they were literally filled, and utter some indefinite sentences, such as, 'Rather briskish yauds these same!' 'May the like o' mine never be crossed by man again!' 'Hech! but they are the gear for the lang road!' 'What's become o' them? I wad like to take a right look o' them for aince.' 'Do ye want to look if they have mark o' mouth, Will? You may look at some o' these that came foremost then. Yours are aff wi' their tails on their rigging; there are some cheated if ever you see mair o' them.' Will Martin looked at the abbot's horse; but when he saw the glance of his eye, he would not have taken him by the jaws to have looked his mouth for all Christendom.

The four sable horsemen led the way, and all the yeomen followed on foot, bearing with them such mattocks as they had been able to procure about Selkirk that morning, and away they marched in a body to Aikwood castle. That was a blyth sight to our forlorn and starving prisoners; even Gibbie had some hopes of a release: but whenever Master Michael Scott got a near view of the four sable equestrians, he sunk into profound and gloomy silence, and every now and then his whole frame was observed to give a certain convulsed shake, or shudder, which cannot be described. The rest of the sufferers supposed it to proceed from his rooted aversion to holy and devout men; but they were so intent on regaining their own liberty that they paid little attention to the manner in which he was affected. Father Lawrence bade the men proceed to work, and he would retire into an inner chamber and exercise himself so as to keep from them all sorts of interruption from spirits of whatever denomination, and he pledged himself for their protection. They thanked him, and hasted to execute their design; nor were they long in accomplishing it. By the help of huge scaling hammers they broke down a part of the narrow staircase, and actually set their friends at liberty. But the abbot enjoined them in nowise to depart, or to do any thing contrary to the desire of the mighty Master, while they remained in his premises, else he could not answer for the consequences. This our yeomen readily assented to, and undertook to prevail with their friends to acquiesce in the same measure.

As soon as the iron-door was forced, the abbot Lawrence sent one of his officers to desire Master Michael Scott to come and speak to him privately in the secret chamber. The wizard looked at the messenger as a sovereign does to a minister of whom he is afraid, or a master to a slave, who, he knows, would assassinate him if he could; nevertheless he rose and followed him to his superior. What passed between these two dignified characters it is needless here to relate, as the substance of the matter will appear in the sequel. But the Master returned into the great hall, where the warden's men were by that time all assembled, an altered man indeed. His countenance glanced with a sublime but infernal exultation. His eye shone with ten times the vigour of youthful animation. It was like a dying flame relumined, that flashes with more than pristine brightness; and the tones of his voice were like those of a conqueror on the field of battle. With this voice, and with this mien, he ordered the friar and his ward Delany instantly to quit the castle; and if an hour hence they were found on his domains, he would cause them to be hewed into so many pieces as there were hairs on their heads.

'Lo thy threats are unto me as the east wind,' said the friar: 'Yea as the wind that cometh from the desert, and puffeth up the vapours on the stagnant pools of water. If my companions in adversity go, then will I also go along with them. But if they remain, by the life of Pharaoh, so likewise will thy servant; and what hast thou more to say, thou man of Belial?'

The Master shook his grey locks and his dark silvery beard in derision; and Charlie Scott, whose confidence in his friend the friar was now unbounded, stepped up to back what he had said, and to protest against parting company. Dan, however, interfered hastily, and told them he was bound by a promise to the holy father, who had wrought their liberty, to do nothing adverse to the will of the Master, while they remained in his castle and on his domains; and therefore he begged they would comply without more words, and without delay. The friar then consented, much against Charlie's inclination; and taking Delany by the hand, he said: 'Lo I will even depart; but I will remain at the ford of Howden-burn until my friends arrive, for then am I from off the territory of this blasphemer and worker of all manner of iniquity. See that you tarry not at the wine, neither let your eyes behold strange women, that it may be well with you.' So the two went away, and did as they had said. The friar found his mule in good keeping, and he remained with the maid in a cottage at the fords of Howden-burn, to await the issue of this singular and unfortunate embassy.

'Now shall I have my will, and do that which seems meet to me,' said the Master, as he strode the hall with unrestrained energy. 'Did the dolt imagine he could, with his tricks of legerdemain, outdo me in the powers and mysteries of my art? No, that man is unborn! Let him go with his crosiers and his breviaries; I am Michael Scott once again!'

'It is needless to say ought here,' said Charlie Scott aside to his companions: 'Fock should ken weel what they say, and where they are saying it. But the truth is, that the friar was the greatest man o' the twa; and that auld birkie was right sair cowed in his presence. It is sair against my will that we hae been obliged, by your promise, Dan, to part wi' the gospel friar; for, d'ye ken, I feel amaist as the buckler were ta'en aff my arm, to want him as lang as I am here. What do you think the carl did, Dan? Come here, you and Will, and I'll tell you. When we came here, ye see, the master had a steward, a perfect hound o' hell, wha thought to guide us waur than dogs; and he crossed the friar unco sair, till at length he lost a' patience wi' him, and, lord sauf us! sent him up through the clouds in a flash o' fire; and there has never been mair o' him seen, but some wee bits o' fragments. I can tell you the loss o' sic a man as the friar, out o' sic a place as this, is a loss no easily made up.'

'Have a little patience, brave Yardbire,' said Dan: 'We have the great and the grave abbot Lawrence in his place. He is our firm friend and our captain's friend, and every thing will now be settled in the most amicable manner—.'

'That holy father and his assistants are the only hope I hae,'
returned Charlie: 'An it warna for their presence, I wadna
stay another half hour in sic a place as this. Ye little ken
what scenes we ha'e witnessed during the days and nights
that we ha'e been here. However, as I had the charge of
the embassage, I will gang and speak to the auld billy. He
seems to be in a high key. Master Michael Scott; ye ken
that yoursel' and our auld friar, by your trials o' skill in
your terrible arts o' witchcraft, brought about an accident
that has kept us ower lang here, to the great trouble and
inconveniency of our captain, your own brave kinsman.
Now, since we are a' at liberty again, we beseech you to
give us our answer; and if you canna read the weird that
he desires of you, why tell us sae at aince, and let us gang
about our business.'

'Gallant yeoman, your request shall be granted without
loss of time,' said the Master. 'But it is the venerable
father's request that I should regale my kinsman's people
before dismissing them, to make some small return for the
privations they have suffered. Be satisfied then to remain
for a few hours, till you taste of my cheer; and in the
meanwhile I will look into the book of fate, and not only
tell you what your captain, Sir Ringan, ought to do, but
I will show you demonstratively what he *must* do, if he
would succeed in raising his name and his house above
that of every Scottish baron.' 'Thank ye, noble sir,' said
Charlie: 'There shall never be another word about it. If
we gain our errand sae satisfactorily at last, I'll count a'
that we ha'e bidden weel wared.'

'Noble and worthy Sir, you never yet have said who told
the most efficient tale, and unto whom the maiden should
belong,' said the poet.

''Twas he, your captain there, who said the tale I most
approved, and to him I award my right in the toy, the
trifle you call maiden,' returned the Master. 'And it is well
remembered, squire; amongst you, you deprived me of my
steward, a man that could have accomplished a great deal
– I therefore claim this worthy in his stead, as agreed; and
glad may he be that he escapes so well.'

'I fear I will be a bad cook, and an awkward valet,' said
Gibbie. 'I was never very handy at ought that way. Tam
wad answer a great deal better, an it were your will.'

'We will have you taught practically, and to profit,' said the Master: 'The three brethren, attendants on father Lawrence, shall take you to task this instant. They will act as your assistants and masters to-day, and to their hands I recommend you. Be expert, and spare no cost.' So saying, he gave three tramps with his heel, as he was wont to do in time past, and instantly the three sable monks stood before him. 'Take that comely youth,' said he, 'and bestow on him a few cogent lessons in the mysteries of the culinary art. You may teach him a few *varieties*.' As he said this, there was a malignant smile rather darkened than lighted up his stern features, and on the instant the three monks had Gibbie from the ground; and one holding by each arm and another by both his feet, they rushed out of the hall with him, in the same way that one drives a wheelbarrow. When the men of the embassy heard the three tramps, and the words about the varieties, they looked at one another with rather uneasy sensations. But the presence of father Lawrence, and the other three holy brethren, encouraged them still to acquiesce in the Master's request.

A short time after this, as they were sauntering about the castle, they heard some loud giggling laughter, intermixed with squeaking cries of despair; which last they could well distinguish as proceeding from the lungs of poor Gibbie Jordan; and immediately after that there came among them a huge red capon, fluttering and screaming in a most desperate and deplorable manner, and all the three monks pursuing him with shouts of delight. The feathers were half plucked off him, and his breath quite spent, so that they easily laid hold of him, and carried him away by the neck to have him spitted living, as they said. Our yeomen saw nothing but an overgrown bird, but they heard well that the voice was the voice of Jordan. 'These monks are trifling and amusing themselves,' said Tam; 'we shall get no dinner before night.'

The words were hardly well said when the castle bell rung, and in they all rushed to the great hall where stood a plentiful dinner smoking along the board, and the abbot and the Master both seated at the upper end, side by side. Our yeomen thought it extraordinary to see the great warlock and the reverend father in such close compact, but they held their peace. The abbot rose and pronounced a blessing on the food, but it was in an unknown tongue, and little did they wot of its purport. There was great variety on the table of every kind of food, yet there was not one of our yeomen knew of what the greater part of the dishes consisted. But the huge capon stood at the head of the table, and though he had been killed and cooked in a few minutes, the bird looked exceedingly well. The abbot and the Master devoured him with so much zest, that no one liked to call for a piece of him, save Tam Craik, who eat a wing of him; but there was no broad bone in his shoulder, yet Tam declared him the first meat he had ever tasted, save once, in his life. Charlie was placed next the Master, and Dan next the abbot Lawrence. The three monks, attendants on the latter, served the table, but nothing of the new steward made his appearance. The wine and other strong liquors were served round in great abundance, and the quality was so excellent, that, notwithstanding of the friar's charge, every one drank liberally, and soon got into high glee. Whenever the supreme and haughty abbot swallowed a cup of wine, Dan, who sat next him, heard always a hissing sound within his breast, as if one had been pouring water on red hot iron. This startled the trooper terribly for two or three times at first, but his surprise lessened and wore off by degrees as the liquor continued to exalt his spirits. The feast went on, and the wine flowed; but, as on a former occasion, the men ate without being satisfied. The wines and liquor were all however real, and had their due effect, so that the spirit of hilarity rose to a great height.

It was observed that father Lawrence conversed with no one but the Master, and the dialogue they held was all in an unknown tongue, in which tongue also, they sometimes conferred with the servitors. The Master left the table three several times, for he had a charm going on in another part of the castle, and at the third time returned with the black book of fate, the book of the dynasties of men, below his arm, and laid it closed on the table before him.

'Now, my brave and warlike guests,' said he, 'Before I open this awful book, it is meet that every one of you be blindfolded. I ask this for your own sakes. If any one of you were to look but on one character of this book, his brain would be seared to a cinder, his eyes would fly out of their sockets, and perhaps his whole frame might be changed into something unspeakable and monstrous.'

'Gude faith, sir Master, I'll haud my een as close as they were sewed up wi' an elshin and a lingel,' said Charlie. So said they all, but they were not trusted; the monks were ordered to go round the table and tie every one's eyes closely up; and when this was done, they were desired to lay all their heads down upon their hands on the board, and to sit without moving, whatever they might hear. He then proceeded to open the massy iron clasps, and as soon as they were unloosed, three spirits burst from the book with loud shrieks, and escaped through the barbican. The yells were so piercing that some of our yeomen started from their seats, but dared not lift their heads. 'Ah! They are gone,' said the Master: 'This weird will cost me dear!'

'Fear nothing, but proceed,' said father Lawrence.

He opened the book, and three peals of thunder ensued that shook the castle to its foundations, every one of them louder than the last; and though our yeomen sat trembling in utter darkness, they heard voices around them as if the hall had been crowded full of people; among others, they deemed that they could distinguish the voices of the warden and his lady. They, however, sat still as if chained to their places, awaiting the issue; and, after much noise and apparent interruptions, the great Master read out as follows:

'He for whom this weird is read,
Be he son of battle bred,
Be he baron born to peril,
Be he lord, or be he earl,
Let him trust his gallant kin,
And the sword below the skin.
When the red buck quits the cover,
When the midnight watch is over,
Then, whatever may betide,
Trust the horn, and trust the hide,
He that drives shall feel the gin,
But he that's driven shall get in.
All for whom this weird is read,
For the living, for the dead,

From the chief with corslet shorn,
To the babe that is unborn,
Let them to the sceptre lean,
Till the place where they have been
See their sway expand untroubled,
Doubled, doubled, nine times doubled;
First to rise and rule the rings,
Mixed with blood of mighty kings.
This is read for princes, peers,
And children of a thousand years;
Now begins their puissant story;
Strike the blow and gain the glory.
Rise not against feudal union,
No advance but in communion,
Though through battle, broil, and murther—.
Shut the book, and read no further.'

The book was closed, and loud shouts of applause, as
from a great multitude, were heard at a distance; as that
died away, a peal of thunder burst forth over their heads,
which rolled away with an undulating sound, till lost in
the regions of the western heavens.

Our yeomen's eyes were then unbound, and when they
looked up the book of fate was removed, and the Master
was fallen back on his seat, with his countenance mightily
distorted; but the abbot and his attendants would not suffer
any to touch him till he recovered of himself. He again rose
into high and unwonted spirits; but his elevation was rather
like the delirium of a man driven to desperation, than that
flow of delightful hilarity, the offspring of a temperate and
well regulated mind. The borderers persevered in their
libations, and the mirth and noise increased till near the fall
of the evening, when Charlie again proposed to go; but the
Master protested against it for a short space, adding, that he
had to give them a practical lesson how their captain ought
to proceed, if he would be the greatest man in Scotland.
This was quite sufficient to prevail on Yardbire, and none
of the rest appeared much disposed to move.

About this time some of our yeomen, sitting with their
faces toward the casement, beheld a novel scene, which
they called up the rest to witness. This was the Master's
new steward, the late laird of the Peatstacknowe, making
his escape from the castle with all possible speed. He was

stripped half naked, and bareheaded; had thrown himself over the outer wall, lest he should be seen going by the gate, and was running up the hollow of Aikwood burn, among the trees, to elude discovery. Presently afterwards they beheld two of the monks stretching after him with a swiftness not to be outrun. Poor Gibbie was soon overhied and brought back, not in the most gentle manner; and, instead of carrying him round by the gate, which, having been broken up, stood wide open, they took him by the heels, and threw him over the wall, at the place he had leaped before. Gibbie gave a loud squeak in the air, as he came over the wall with a wheeling motion; and falling on the other side, every one believed that there would not be a whole bone left in his body. Instead of that he sprung to his feet, and ran across the court, saying to himself, 'I'll tell you what – It minds me o' hell this place – if ever there was ane upon earth.' He got not time to finish the sentence till he was again seized, and hauled into the castle.

'Master Michael Scott, I protest in my master's name against this usage of a leal vassal and tiend laird,' said Charlie.

'The comely youth is mine by your own agreement,' said the Master: 'He shall be well seen to. Perhaps I shall only keep him for a season, until better supplied. Be content; the matter is now beyond disputation. In the meantime I will proceed to give you a specimen of my profound art, of which you have now seen many instances; and also of my esteem for your captain, to whom you will be so good as repeat this.'

He then went away to his arcana, and brought a bason of liquor, resembling wine, which he sprinkled on all his guests in small proportions, and taking his seat beside the supercilious abbot, the two sat apparently waiting for some grand metamorphosis. The spell, powerful as it was, had not the effect that was surmised. These rude warriors of a former age had principles of virtue and honour in their natures that withstood the charms of necromancy – those charms before which noble dames, cruel laymen, and selfish clergy sunk down confounded and overpowered. The countenances of a few of the troopers were somewhat changed by the spell, assuming thereby a sort of resemblance to beasts, but this their associates only laughed at, deeming it occasioned by the drunkenness of the individuals affected. The two great personages at the head of the table viewed the matter in a different light, and that with evident symptoms of disappointment. They comprehended the reason, for they knew there was but one against which the powers of darkness could not prevail; and, after holding a conversation about it in their own mysterious language, they set about the accomplishment of their desires, for, though a matter of no great avail, the Master could not brook to be baulked in any of his works of divination. The purport of this conversation was, what the Master had once proposed before, that the men must be made accessory to their own transformation; and in this project he forthwith engaged with all manner of earnestness.

CHAPTER TWENTY-FIVE

He can turn a man into a boy;
  A boy into an ass;
He can change your gold into white moneye;
  Your white moneye into brass;
He can turn our goodman to a beast
  With hoof, but, an' with horn,
And chap the goodwife in her cheer,
  This little John Barleycorn.

Old Song

THE PLAN OF our great necromancer was no other than that of pushing round the wine, and other strong intoxicating liquors, to the utmost extremity; and it is well known that these stimulating beverages have charms that no warrior, or other person accustomed to violent exertions, can withstand, after indulging in them to a certain extent. The mirth and argument, or rather the bragg of weir, grew first obstreperous, afterwards boisterous and unruly, and several of the men got up and strode the hall with drawn swords, without being able to tell with whom they were offended or going to fight. Neither the Master nor the abbot discouraged this turmoil, but pushed round the liquor, till some of the most intimate friends and associates of the party, in the extravagance of intoxication, actually wounded one another, and afterwards blubbered, like children, for vexation. While they were all in this state of unnatural elevation, father Lawrence got up, and addressed himself to the party, for the first time. He represented to them, by striking metaphors, the uncertainty and toil of the warrior's life; and requested all such of them as loved ease, freedom, and independence, to become inmates of his habitation; and during the time of their noviciates, he promised them every good thing. Several of them pretended to snap at the proffer, some on one condition, some on another; but when he presented a scroll of parchment, written in red characters, for their marks or signatures, no one would sign and seal, save Tam Craik, who put his mark to it three times with uncommon avidity, on the positive condition that he was to have as much fat flesh as he could eat for the first three years, at all times that he chose, by day or by night.

When matters were at this pass, and our brave yeomen could with difficulty rise to their feet, they heard a chorus of sweet and melodious music approaching, which still drew nearer and nearer. This was a treat they little expected in such an habitation; but how much greater was their surp.ise, when the hall-door was thrown open, and there were ushered in thirty of the most lovely maidens that the eyes of men had ever beheld. They seemed, too, to be all of noble lineage, for they were dressed like eastern princesses, rustling in their silks, and covered over with dazzling gems. The Master welcomed them with stately courtesy, apologizing for the state of his castle, and the necessity they would be under of sitting down and sharing the feast with warriors, who, however, he assured them were all gallant gentlemen, of his own kin, and some of them of his own name. The splendid dames answered, that nothing on earth would give them so much delight as to share the feast with gentlemen and warriors, the natural protectors of their helpless sex, to whom it should be their principal aim to pay all manner of deference.

As soon as the door was opened, our brave yeomen, with the profound respect that men of their boisterous occupation always pay to female beauty and rare accomplishments, started all to their feet, and made their obeisance. But the worst concern for them was, that they could not stand on their feet. Some of them propped themselves on the hilts of their sheathed swords, leaning the points backward against the wall. Others kept a sly hold of the buff-belt of the comrade next to him; and a few, of whom the poet was one, and Tam another, lost their balance, and fell back over the benches, showing the noble dames the soles of their sandals. All was silence and restraint, and a view of no group could be more amusing; for though our heroes were hardly able to behave themselves with the utmost propriety, yet they were all endeavouring to do it; some keeping their mouths close shut, that no misbecoming word might possibly escape from their lips; some turning up their white faces, manifesting evident symptoms of sickness, and some unable to refrain their joy at this grand addition to their party.

The first breaking up of the conversation was likewise extremely curious; but it was begun in so many corners about the same time, it is impossible to detail it all. Will Martin, with a lisping unbowsome tongue, addressed the one next to him to the following effect.

'Fine evening this, noble dame.'

'Do you account this so very fine an evening, gallant knight?'

'Hem, hem; glorious roads too; most noble lady – paced all with – marble, you know. Hem! Came you by the marble path, fair lady? Hem! hem!'

'Not by the marble path, most courteous knight, but on one of alabaster, bordered with emeralds, rubies, and diamonds you know. Hem! hem!'

'May all the powers – Hem – powers of beauty, you know – Ay – hem! and love. Hem! What was I about to say?'

'Could not guess, knight.'

'That smile is so sweet. Will such an – hem! – such an angelic creature – really con – descend to converse familiarly with a plain homely warrior?'

'Your notice does me far too much honour, worthy knight.' And so saying she put the tip of her palm gently on the warrior's rough hand. Intoxicated as Will was with wine, he was petrified with astonishment and delight, and could not find terms to express his gratitude and adoration. Many others were likewise by the same time testifying, by their bright and exulting looks, the joy and delight they were experiencing in the conversation of those most beautiful and refined of all earthly objects. Tam Craik beheld, or thought he beheld, his lovely Kell among them, blooming in tenfold loveliness. He was so drunk that he could not articulate one syllable; but he fixed his long coulter-nose and grey eyes steadily in the direction of her face, and put his hand below the table and scratched.

Still the cup and the cates circulated without any respite.

The Master and the abbot both called them round and round; and though the lovely and high-born dames tasted sparingly, nevertheless the circumstances of their having touched the cup with their lips was sufficient to induce the enamoured warriors to drink to them in healths deep and dangerous. Reason had long been tottering on her throne with the best of them, but these amorous draughts of homage overthrew her completely, and laid her grovelling in the dust. The heroes fell from their seats first by ones, but ere the last in threes and fours. Still the courteous and sympathetic beauties tried to administer comfort and assistance to their *natural protectors*, by holding up their heads, and chafing their temples; but, in spite of all they could do, total oblivion of passing events ensued to the whole of our incautious troopers.

The next morning presented a scene in the great hall of Aikwood, which, if it cannot be described, neither can it ever be conceived. There lay our troop of gallant yeomen, as good as ever heaved buckler, scattered over the floor; some in corners, some below benches, every one of their eyes sealed in profound slumber though the day was well advanced, and every one having an inamorata in his arms, or clinging close to him of her own accord. At a given signal, the great bell of the castle was rung with a knell that might have wakened the dead. The sleepers raised their drowsy and aching heads all at the same time; and, as was natural, every one turned his eyes first toward the partner of his slumbers. Their sensations may be in some measure conceived, when, instead of the youthful, blooming, angelic beings, whom they had seen over-night, there lay a group of the most horrible hags that ever opened eyes on the light of day. Instead of the light, flowing, and curled hair, there hung portions of grey dishevelled locks. Instead of the virgin bloom of the cheek, and the brilliant enamel of the eye, all was rheum, haggardness, and deformity. Some had two or three long pitted teeth, of the colour of amber; some had none. Their lovely mouths were adorned with curled and silvery mustachios; and their fair necks were shrivelled and seriated like the bark of a pinetree. Instead of the rustling silks and dazzling jewels, they were all clothed in noisome rags; and, to crown the horror of our benumbed and degraded Bacchanalians, every one of the witches had her eyes fixed on her partner, gleaming with hellish delight at the state to which they had reduced themselves, and the horrors of their feelings. The poet, and two or three others, fell into convulsions; and all of them turned away groaning, and hid their faces from these objects of abhorrence.

The Master came with his enchanted liquor once more, and sprinkled it over the prostrate and humbled group, who were now in that state of mental agony that rendered them indifferent to aught that could occur; and, as he sprinkled them, he said to himself, 'I now have the power over you, though you had been seven times anointed in holy church.'

'Aye, seven times seven,' said a tremendous voice; and the words were followed by a laugh that shook the vault of the hall, which laugh was echoed by three or four accordant voices, and afterwards by all the witches in the apartment. The astounded warriors again raised their heads, and beheld their friend, the abbot, stalking along and along the hall in the midst of them in majesty sublime. He wore the same sable and flowing robes, and the same mitre, that he did on the preceding day; but he was now striding openly in his own character, with his legs shagged and hairy, shaped like those of a goat, and his feet cloven into two distinct and horny hoofs. The three attendants were there also, but they were no more three monks, but the identical Prig, Prim, and Pricker, the infernal pages of Master Michael Scott. In short, our yeomen discovered, to their utter despair, that they had been riding, eating, and drinking, hand to fist, with the devil in *propria persona*.

Before giving any of them time to recover their senses, he strode up to Dan Chisholm, and stooping over him with exultation, he said, 'Did not I tell you, Christian droich, when I bayed you at the mill, that I would be before hand with you at Melrose, and have not I kept my word?' As he said these words, Dan once more saw down his throat, and beheld the burning flame within. Half-dead with fright, he threw himself back on the floor, and held up one foot and one hand, as his last inefficient defence, on which his infernal Majesty vomited such a torrent of sparkling flame out upon him and his forlorn partners, that they lost all hope of ever again moving from the place where they were.

'Take heart, my brave fellows,' said the Master. 'This great primate, you see, is no other than the prince of the power of the air, the great controller of the mighty elements, who has honoured us with his company. You are now in his power, and lie at his mercy; but he is more of a gentleman than he is generally represented to be, and will scorn to take advantage of a few poor insignificant creatures, who call themselves Christians, of whose company he is sure before he wants it. He knows you will fume, and bully, and fight for a few short years, sending one another home to his ample mansions in myriads before your time. Both he and I would scorn to take farther advantage of beings so blind ignorant, and inconsistent, than suits our own amusement. We only love to mock you, show you your own littleness, and how easy a prey you would be, were there a being in the universe that watched for ever over your destruction. Cheer up, gallant soldiers! and now for the long-waited development of mighty moment. I will show you the manner, and very mode, by which your captain must only hope to succeed in his great enterprise.'

He then touched every one of them with the divining-rod that was in his hand, pronouncing at the same time some mystic words, which none of them comprehended. While he was thus occupied, the witches rushed from the hall, and as soon as he had touched the hindmost, he himself also made his escape, and looked from a crevice of an inner wall. The enchantment began immediately to take effect; the warriors rolled about on the floor in strong convulsions, bellowing and flouncing, trying always to run on all-four, and then tumbling over again. At length their noses and chins began to grow forward in hideous disproportion, till their heads began to assume something of the forms of the heads of beasts, and liker to those of calves than any things else. The laughter that pealed from loop-hole, crevice, and barbican, was, at this eventual period, excessive. The devil, the three wicked spirits, the great enchanter, and his conventicle of witches, seemed all to be in convulsions at witnessing how the metamorphosed champions shook their long heads, looked at one another, and tried to speak. How their language changed from long-drawn words, half pronounced, to downright confused bellowings; and how their forms, in the space of a few minutes, gradually assumed those of as many mighty and ferocious bulls.

'I have now given you your own proper shapes, and showed you in frames suited to your natures,' cried the Master, from a crevice.

'Pass forth, and be gone; and carry my respects to your captain.'

Then there was a combined bellow of rage arose in the hall that would have rent any castle to the top but that of Aikwood; and benches, boards, and couches, flew about in flinders on the horns of the furious monsters. Forthwith they rushed out into the great court, and from that to the side of the hill, bellowing, and tearing up the ground with hoof and horn, till the country was alarmed for many miles round; and, believing that all hell was broke loose from the castle of Aikwood that day, they betook them to their heels, and fled away out of sight and out of hearing.

The outrageous drove looked back as they ascended the brae to the eastward of the castle, and saw the devil and the great warlock, standing on the topmost tower, laughing at them; the former appearing of a size and dimensions equal to those of another castle. The grand mitre that he wore on his head, shaped like a crescent to conceal his horns, now moved like a cornuted black cloud amid the firmament; his eyes glimmered like two of the reddest of the stars of heaven; and the sceptre that he waved in his right hand was like a tremendous pine all in flame, or rather like a burning aerial meteor. Our transformed warriors galloped away in terror as fast as cloven hoofs could carry them, with one mighty bison, that had once been Charlie Scott, far a-head of all the rest; for, notwithstanding of all that Charlie had seen and heard in favours of the devil, he felt as much affrighted for him as ever, degraded as he was in form. No wonder was it that our tumultuous group was terrified and galloped off; for at the same time that they saw Satan stretching out his sceptre in his right hand, he held out Tam Craik by the nape of the neck in his left, while the poor fellow was seen sprawling and spurning the air over an unfathomed void. When the arch-fiend made his retreat from among the warriors that morning, in the midst of the confusion he carried Tam off with him, according to compact – fed him for some time on animal food of the richest quality, which, never once satisfying him, the devil grew weary of such a voracious cur, and twisted his neck about.

The drove was no sooner out of sight, than the Master said to one of his pages, 'Pricker, assume thou the habit that thou hadst yester-eve; mount, and ride after these wild cattle, and deliver them over to the charge of their dolt of a confessor. He will try to rescue them from their present degraded and brutal forms, but he will not be able. Spirit, thou sawest a part of the charms performed. Give him the proper directions how to find it out before leaving him. It boots nothing offending my kinsman, the Warden.'

Pricker mounted his horse, and rode straight for the fords of Howden-burn, where he knew the friar was awaiting his companions, and meant to have driven them all up before him to the cottage door, where the friar and his fair ward sojourned, and there delivered them over to the care of these two, as a present of fine beeves from the great Master to Sir Ringan Redhough. But before the infernal page overtook them they were all at the door of the cottage, bellowing and kneeling, and trying in vain to make their hard case known to the friar.

Pricker came up, and saluted the friar, who, observing his clerical habit, returned the compliment in a hurried and careless manner – for he was confounded by the arrival of so many mad bulls.

'Reverend brother mine,' said the page, 'I deliver over into thy charge this herd of beautiful cattle, the best breed that ever roamed the forests of Caledon. They are a present from Master Michael Scott to his cousin the Warden of the middle marches. See that you deliver them safe and sound.'

'Lo, thou seest with thine eyes, and thou also hearest with the hearing of the ear,' said the friar, 'that the creatures are outrageous, and not to be governed by the hand of a single man. And thinkest thou a brother of the holy order of Benedict would take a goad in his hand, and ride forth after these bulls of Bashan? Lo, would they not even run headlong upon my mule, and thrust their horns into his side? Thy servant also, and this maiden, would they tread under their feet? Go to! Thou speakest as one lacking understanding.'

'I give them in charge to thee, as desired by one with whom it is dangerous to contend,' said the page; 'and alongst with them this request, that your captain will make away with them as quickly as possible for food to his army.'

At these words of the apparent sacristan there was such a roaring and bellowing commenced among the herd, that, for the first time, the friar began to suspect some horrid enchantment, but wist not what to dread. The drove turned round their heads to the speaker – shook them in disapproval of what he had said, and joined in such a ferocious roar against him, that it was not like ought the friar had ever witnessed among the brute creation before. The metamorphosed troopers, however, knew too well now who Pricker was to attack him, but, turning again round, they came in a row, and kneeled around the friar, looking at him with the most supplicating expressions of countenance that ever cattle put on.

'Lo, methinks I have looked upon these wild beasts of the forest in some of the days that are past,' said the friar, 'and that their countenances are not entirely unknown to me; though when, or in what place, in that thing my memory upholdeth me not. I pray thee, brother, to declare unto thy servant where thou camest by these beasts of mine acquaintance. If thou art a follower of the worthy Father Lawrence, thou must speak the truth—. Tell me, art thou a Christian?'

The bulls gave not the infernal page time to reply. They turned about, shook their heads, and tossed the earth at him with their horns, raising at the same time such an outcry of rage against him that the friar himself was afraid, and retreated within the door of the cottage; and he thought that, amid their confused bellowings, he could distinguish as it were these words pronounced, 'He a Christian! Away with him! Away with him!'

'Lo, what am I to understand by all this?' said the friar.

'Come near unto me, thou man of mystery, that comest like one of the children of Esau, with thy cattle and thy herds, and tell unto thy servant what are these?'

Pricker would not, however, come nigh the friar, but still kept his distance; for against the friar's spiritual armour he durst not engage; but he called out to him, in mockery,

'I then declare unto thee, O thou great magician, who camest to cope with the prince of all magicians, Master Michael Scott, that these are thy master's yeomen whom thou leftest with him yesterday. Now, what sayest thou? Hast thou ever witnessed power like this?'

The friar lifted up his eyes to heaven, and tears fell down on his dark beard. 'O wretched man that I am!' cried he, 'why did I leave my children in the lion's den? yea, even in the den of the great lion. Wo is me, that this breach hath been made among the followers of my Master! But there is One that can yet controul all the powers of darkness, and to Him alone must I apply without delay.'

The friar went instantly to his devotions, and performed many rites of a nature too sacred to be here minutely described; yet, after all his exorcisms, the men could not regain their natural shapes, but lay and rolled about on the valley in awful convulsions. The hellish page, who had kept far aloof during the time of the friar's sacred appeal, now came galloping near to enjoy the convulsions of the herd, and the grief and astonishment of the friar; and after mocking for some time, in obedience to the great wizard's command, he called to the friar, and said, 'I see he that brought about this wonderful metamorphosis – for which you shall one day be grateful – can only effect the counter-charm. Look into the manes on their foreheads, and look narrowly;' and having said these words, he darted off towards Aikwood with the speed of lightning.

The friar did as this flying horseman had directed, and searching the long curled mane between the horns of the first monster that came to his hand, he there found stitched a small scroll of parchment, neatly rolled up, and written in blood. Then he caused them to bring him fire, in which he burnt it, and presently there stood up at his hand one of Sir Ringan Redhough's warriors, in all his arms and accoutrements as he first arrived at the castle of Aikwood. 'By the life of Pharaoh!' cried the friar, 'surely this excelleth all that I beheld heretofore!'

The spell was now quickly dissolved; but no pen can do any justice to the feelings of our amazed troopers, as they again strode the green in their own forms and vigour, embracing the friar, and thanking him as their deliverer. They returned back over the ridge, not without some dreadful apprehensions, to the mill of Aikwood for their horses, but went no more in view of the portentous castle. They found their horses at good feed; and whenever Charlie saw Corby's skin, that glittered like the plumes of the raven, he cried, 'Aha, Corby lad, ye haena wantit either meat or drink, ye rascal! Od ye hae fared better than your master, ye cock-luggit glooming thief; stall up, ye dog, till I caparison you, and then let us bound for the border.'

But the most curious and least suspected of all the circumstances attending the horses was, that Dan Chisholm's horse and those of his three companions, that they left stabled in the deep dell above Lindean, were all found standing at the mill among the rest. The miller could give no farther account about them, than that a lad brought them all tied to one another's tails, and said they belonged to four of the baron of Mountcomyn's men that were gone to Aikwood. 'By the Lord Soules,' cried Dan, 'then it is true that Master Michael Scott said of the devil being more of a gentleman than he had been generally represented. For all the pranks he has played us, I'll think the better of him for this the longest day I have to live. What say you to this, friend Yardbire?'

'I shall be twenty miles off Aikwood at least afore I speak another sentence about either him or some others that I ken o'. Mercy on us! poor Tam Craik! What an end he has made wi' his fat bacon! Hech, but it be a dcspisable thing to rin open mouth to the – I'll no mention whae – for their greed o' meat. Some may hae gotten nae mair than what they deserved; but as for sachless Gibbie Jordan, he has been right hardly dealt wi'. My heart's unco wae for the poor laird, and I think something should be done to recover him.'

'Something *shall* be done for him,' said the friar, 'and that of such momentous consequence, that, if his own iniquities keep him not in bondage, all the powers of the evil one shall be unequal to the task.'

After all these horrid perils of weird women and witchcraft thus miraculously overcome, our troop rode straight on to the camp of the Warden, and found him in the vicinity of Wooller, having come into those parts to counteract the rising about Berwick in behalf of the English garrison. And the time being at hand on which he must either do or not do, either join with heart and hand in the cause of the Douglas, or leave him to stand or fall by himself, and abide by the consequences – his impatience for the return of his men from Aikwood castle had been commensurate with the importance that he attached to their mission. But when they informed him of all the wonders they had witnessed, and the transmutations they had seen and undergone – how the warlock and his spirits had raised the tempests, deluged the plains, levelled the forests, and cleft asunder the everlasting mountains, the baron was like one in a trance. It was long before they could make themselves accredited, or impress him with any other idea than that it was a story made up to astonish him. With the feats performed by the friar, he was particularly pleased, and from that time forth paid him more honour than he had ever been seen pay to man. But the precise meaning of the destiny, read for him out of the book of fate, puzzled and interested him most of all. It was dark and full of intricacies; and it was not till after long consultation with wise men, as well as women, that any thing like a guess could be formed of its tendency. By making words and actions to coalesce, a mode of procedure was at the last pitched on as the only one reconcileable with the predictions. This mode will eventually appear without giving the detail at present, and the reader will then be better able to judge whether or not the Redhough and his sages understood the Master's signs and injunctions properly.

CHAPTER TWENTY-SIX

Here away, there away, wandering Willie,
Here away, there away, haud away hame.
Old Song

WE HAVE NOW performed the waggoner's difficult and tedious task with great patience, and scarcely less discretion, having brought all the various groups of our *dramatis personae*, up to the same period of time. It now behoves us (that is, Isaac the curate and me,) to return again to the leading event, namely, the siege of Roxburgh.

The state of mind to which the two commanders were now reduced was truly pitiable. Within the castle of Roxburgh, all was sullen gloom and discontent. In one thing, and that only, were they unanimous, which was in a frantic inveteracy against the Scots; and though Musgrave, with the feelings of a man, would gladly have saved those dearest to him in life, yet he found that to have proposed such a thing as yielding to the garrison, would have been but adding fuel to flame in order to extinguish it. Their small supply soon began again to wear short; and, moreover, the privations to which they were subjected, had brought on an infectious distemper among them, of which some died every day; but every item added to their sufferings, fell into the scale against the Scots, and all the cruelties exercised by the latter, in order to break the spirits of their opponents, only militated against themselves. Opposition to the last man was a sentiment nursed in every English bosom within the garrison, with a brooding enthusiasm of delight. There can be no doubt that they felt intensely for their gallant captain, considering the dismal situation in which he stood with respect to their enemies, and the strong hold they had been enabled to keep over his heart. It was probably the burning intensity of these feelings that was the great source of their unhappiness, and gave rise to the fierce spirit of dissension that daily manifested itself. Although they detested the deed the Scots had committed in executing Sir Richard, yet they felt his death a sort of relief, as by it one-half of the cord which their hated adversaries held round the breast of their commander was broken, and there is little doubt that they wished themselves free of Lady Jane Howard, by fair and gentle means if possible, but at all events to be rid of that remaining tie, which almost maddened them to think of.

There was one circumstance which of late was to all of them wholly unaccountable. As the day of the Conception of the blessed Virgin approached, the mind of Lord Musgrave, instead of becoming altogether deranged as they had foreboded, became more and more steady and collected. He watched over every part of the economy within that huge fortress, and gave his orders with punctuality and decision, although with a degree of sterness that had not previously been observed.

The dreaded day of the Conception at length arrived; and, before noon, crowds of the citizens, and people from the surrounding country, began to assemble around the Scottish camp. These were forcibly kept beyond the line of circumvallation, while the regular troops were drawn up in columns both to the east and west of the fortress, and particularly round the gibbet on the Bush-Law. At eleven o'clock the Scottish trumpets sounded; the English soldiers crowded to the battlements around the western tower of the citadel, and Lord Musgrave came up among the rest, arrayed in a splendid suit of light armour, and gallantly attended.

These battlements and the new gibbet were, as before stated, right opposite to one another, and separated only by the breadth of the moat and a very small slope on the western ascent; so that every object could be distinctly seen from the one place to the other, and, by raising the voice somewhat, a conversation could be carried on across. At the very time that Lord Musgrave thus appeared on the wall, the Lady Jane Howard and Sir *Richard* Musgrave were introduced on the boards of the gibbet. Yes – read it over again. I say Sir Richard Musgrave, for it was truly he.

The Douglas, seeing that he could not prevail, and that the gallant youth was given up by his brother and the English to his fate, could not brook the idea of losing by his death the one-half of the influence he held over Musgrave. But that he might try it by stretching it to the very last, he clothed another culprit in Sir Richard's habiliments, tied a white cloth over his face, let him stand a proclaimed space on the boards with the cord about his neck, and, at the last moment of the given time, there being no parley sounded for the delivering up of the keys of the fortress, the board sunk, and the man died; but Sir Richard was safe in hold.

He was again produced that day, being the eighth of December, along with Lady Jane. He was dressed in the suit of armour in which he fought on the day he was taken prisoner, and Lady Jane in pure snow-white robes, betokening her spotless virginity. Sir Richard's eye beamed with manly courage, but the fresh hues of the rose on the cheeks of Lady Jane had blenched, and given place to the most deadly paleness. Both hosts were deeply affected with the sight, and on this occasion both felt alike. There was not a heart amongst them that did not overflow with pity at the unhappy fate of the two youthful prisoners, whose dismal doom could now no longer be averted, unless by a sacrifice on the part of the English, with which even the most sanguine of the beleaguering army doubted their compliance.

The Douglas then caused a herald to make proclamation in a stentorian voice; first stating the cause why he had put off the execution of Sir Richard Musgrave until that day, namely, his anxious desire to save the life of the noble youth, on the ground that the purposed holding out of the garrison till the twenty-fourth was a chimera; and, secondly, declaring that, unless the keys of the castle were previously delivered up to him, precisely at the hour of noon, the noble and gallant Sir Richard, the flower of English chivalry, should be put down; and the beautiful and accomplished Lady Jane Howard, the betrothed bride and devoted lover of Lord Musgrave, subjected to a fate the most humiliating, and the most deplorable, that ever noble maiden suffered, and that in full view of both armies. A loud murmur of detestation sounded from the walls of the castle, but the columns of the Scottish army stood and looked on in mute and tender sorrow. Lord Musgrave placed himself right opposite the prisoners, turned his face straight toward them, and gazed with an unmoved and undaunted air. Sir Richard addressed him in the same sentiments he had formerly expressed, the purport of which was, it will be remembered, the madness and folly of holding out the castle, now when the bright and unequalled prize for which he contended was lost. For his own life, he said, he accounted it as nothing in the scale; but the fate that awaited the lady of his love, who had shewn such devotion to his person and interests, was not to be endured or permitted by any knight of honour. Lady Jane cried out to him to save her from a doom before which her whole soul shrunk; adding, that she had done much, and suffered much, for him, and would he not make one effort, one sacrifice, to save her?

'Lord Douglas,' cried Musgrave, 'Will not a formal consignment of all my lands, titles, and privileges in the dominions of England, ransom the lives of these two?'

'Not if they were ten times doubled,' returned the Douglas: 'Nor shall any earthly thing ransom them, save the full and free possession of the castle of Roxburgh. I have myself suffered a loss at your hands, of which you are not aware; and I long and thirst to revenge it on you and your house.'

'Then my resolution is fixed!' cried Musgrave: 'Though all England should deprecate the deed, and though I know my brethren in arms disapprove of it, I must and will redeem the lives of these two. Yes, I will save them, and that without abating one iota from the honour of the house of Musgrave. Not make one effort, Lady Jane? Not one sacrifice to save your honour and life? Effort, indeed, I will make none. But, *without* an effort, I will make a sacrifice of as high estimation for you as ever knight offered up for the lady of his love. Perhaps it may not be in my power to save you; but in the sight of these rival armies – in yours my only brother and betrothed bride – and in the sight of heaven – I offer the last ransom that can be offered by man.' As he said these words, he flung himself headlong from the battlement of the western tower, struck on the mural parapet around the lower platform, then on the rampart, from which he flew with a rolling bound, and flashed with prodigious force into the ample moat. There, by the weight of his armour, he sunk forthwith to rise no more. The troops of the rival nations stood aghast, with uplifted hands, gazing on the scene; but no more was to be seen of the gallant Musgrave! A gurgling boil of bloody water arose above him as he sank to the bottom – and that was the last movement caused in this world by one whose life had been spent in deeds of high chivalry and restless commotion.

Excepting one shriek uttered by Lady Jane, the Douglas was the first to break the awful silence, which he did by these words: 'There fell a hero indeed! Noble and resolute Musgrave! I cannot but envy you such a chivalrous fate as this!' Many such expressions of enthusiastic admiration burst from both armies, not in shouts of applause, for these were suppressed by sorrow, but in a low and melting pathos that bespoke the soul's regret as well as approval.

When these first expressions of feeling were over, the dark and manly countenance of Douglas sunk into more than usual gloom and dejection. All the advantages given him, and which he had deemed insurmountable by his opponents, were by this desperate act of Musgrave's extinguished. He had now no more power over the English garrison than what he could make good with his sword and his bow. To have executed his threats on Sir Richard, and the lovely and romantic Lady Jane, would only have been an act of poor and despicable revenge, which would have disgusted his own followers, and could in no degree have furthered his cause; so he ordered them back to confinement, with directions that they should be attended according to their rank.

What was next to be done? That was the great question. Douglas never once conceived the idea of giving up the enterprise; for though the princess for whom he had undertaken it was now no more, his broad domains were all engaged. The very existence of the house of Douglas depended on his success; and, besides, the king had more daughters, though none like his beloved and accomplished Margaret. Therefore Douglas had no hesitation regarding the necessity of taking the castle. He was determined to have it. But what to do next, in order to accomplish this determination, was the question. Circumstances were grievously changed with him. The garrison had got a supply across the Teviot-bridge during the time of the flood and the tempest, but the Scots could not ascertain to what amount. Sir Thomas Musgrave had been joined by some troops from the shores of Northumberland, and had issued forth with these and the greater part of the garrison of Berwick, to the amount of 5000 men, in order to make a diversion in favour of the garrison of Roxburgh. This movement by the governor of Berwick disconcerted the Douglas most of all. A party of these marauders had shewed themselves on the height about Hume castle, with trumpets sounding and colours waving in the air. From thence they marched on, keeping the backs of the hills, until they came into the lower parts of Leaderdale, which they harried, burning in their way the town and castle of Ercildon. They next made a movement towards Melrose, meaning to establish themselves in the rear of Douglas, and either to cut off his supplies, or force him to abandon the siege, in order to preserve his own country behind him. But when they came to the river Tweed they were opposed by the brave abbot Lawrence, not the feigned and infernal abbot that our yeomen left at Aikwood, but the real worthy and apostolic Lawrence himself. He had raised all the abbey vassals and retainers, and shewed fairly disposed to dispute the passage of the English over the river. In the meantime he posted message after message to Douglas, to come, or send to his assitance, before the abbey of the holy Virgin, with all its sacred stores, should fall into the hands of their ruthless enemies.

Douglas was hardly put to it. If he drew off from a close blockade, the English were sure to take advantage of his absence, make a sally, and procure plenty of more provisions; and, in that case, his only probable hope of success was cut off. On the other hand, if he suffered himself to be inclosed between two armies, his situation would become every day more precarious, and perhaps in the issue quite untenable. He was, therefore, in a manner forced to the resolution of making an effort to join father Lawrence, and of giving the captain of Berwick battle before he attained possession of the rich monastry of Melrose.

The time was now arrived when the support of Sir Ringan Redhough and his borderers was become absolutely necessary. Without their co-operation in a more close and decisive manner than that in which they had hitherto conducted themselves, he could not now proceed one foot, and his great cause was ruined. He therefore dispatched a pressing message to the chief, conjuring him as his friend and fellow-soldier, either to come and supply his place in the blockade of Roxburgh, or march with all expedition to Melrose, and give battle to the governor of Berwick. The dogged and unyielding Warden returned for answer, that it had always been his chief and undivided aim to act in concert with his noble and gallant friend, and lord superior, the Earl of Douglas and Mar. But that he had a peculiar charge from his Sovereign, of the English marches, which it was his bounden duty to attend to, prior to all other considerations. Whatever he could do conformable with this first duty, should not be wanting. Finally, he sent him word, as he had done formerly, 'that if he coudna take the castle, and confessed that he coudna take it, he might send word to him, and he wad take it for him.'

'What does the crabbed carle always mean by that answer?' said the Douglas, when it was reported to him: 'Perhaps he has some means of communication with those within the fortress, some secret friend in disguise among our enemies. Perhaps he knows of some weak or accessible point among these extensive bulwarks, or perhaps he reckons on some plausible means of surmounting them; for the devil's head is not more fruitful in expedients than his. This is a matter of such importance to me at present, that I must try to probe it to the bottom. Were I sure that he could accomplish his boasted feat, I had better engage him to it with one-third of my dominions; and at all events, I must procure the active assistance of his energetic force at present, whatever may be the equivalent required. Let my white stead Beaver be caparisoned, and my attendants in readiness; I must have an interview with this man of the mountains before I sleep.'

The Warden had drawn his force down to Wooller, with the intention of co-operating more effectively with the Douglas. He had heard of the advantages that lord held over his adversaries, but nothing of the late catastrophe by which they were all removed. Deeming therefore that the chances were mainly on the side of the Douglas, he judged it his safest course to act in complete concert with him. Above all, the words out of the black book of fate had been conveyed to him as read by the greatest magician in the world. From all that could be made out of that mystic rhyme, after long consultation, it appeared that it behoved the Warden and his friends to go hand in hand with Douglas. 'Rise not against feudal union – No advance but in communion,' were words hardly to be misinterpreted. The words of the prophecy, and the ludicrous metamorphosis were all taken into account, compared, computed, and over again computed – and the sequel was a decisive resolution to support the Douglas and join issues with him. But, in the meantime, *still to make the most of a bad bargain.*

This resolution had been taken, and so far acted upon, that trusty agents had been despatched all over the country in disguise, to execute a portion of the great concerted plan, when the Douglas, at a late hour in the evening, arrived in the Warden's camp. He then had proofs experimentally of the Warden's caution and vigilance. He came upon his outposts at a great distance from the main body of his army. These withstood his passage, but seeing his retinue so small, for he was attended only by two knights, a squire, and a guide, they conducted him from one post to another, till at length they brought him completely guarded to the Warden's head-quarters; which was nothing more than a lowly cottage at Wooller haugh-head.

The doughty chief and his kinsmen were still sitting in earnest conversation round a rustic table, with a tremendous torch in the middle of it. This was nothing less than a huge broken jar full of refined ox's tallow, and a slow peat stuck to the head in the middle, which being kindled emitted a blaze like a fish light. The gallant kinsmen were in deep consultation anent their grand plan of warlike operations, and the more they conversed about it the more eligible did it still appear to them, and the more deeply did they get interested in it; so that when the knight in waiting announced a stranger who requested an interview with Sir Ringan, every one seemed disposed to refuse him admission.

'Tell him I am engaged,' said the Warden.

'O yes. By all means. Tell him we are engaged,' said Dickie o' Dryhope.

'If it is another message from the Douglas, I have had enough of him,' said the Warden.

'Ay, faith, we have had enough of him,' said Dickie.

'It is perhaps from Master Michael Scott' said Yardbire: 'Or maybe himsel, wha kens. Lord sauff us!' 'D'ye think sae?' said the Warden, starting to his feet: 'That would indeed alter the case!'

'Ay, that would alter the case indeed!' said Dickie, starting to his.

'Who is he? or what is he like?' enquired the Warden.

'Ay, that is the principal thing to be attended to,' said Dickie; 'What is he like?'

'He is delivered as a knight of most noble bearing and courtly deportment,' answered the knight in waiting. 'I suppose we must admit him, and hear what he has to say,' said the Warden, again taking his seat.

'O yes. By all means. Let us hear what he has to say,' said Dickie, sitting down likewise.

As the courtly and athletic form of the Lord Douglas came up the hovel, the Border gentlemen stood all up to receive him, save Sir Ringan, who throwing himself back on his seat, leaned his chin on his hand, and in that indifferent posture awaited till the quality of his guest was made manifest. But no sooner did the voice of Douglas reach his ear, than he rose up to salute and receive him with as much ease as if he had been his daily visitor.

'You are hard of admission, noble Sir Ringan,' said he, 'thus to let your friends wait at the door of your pavilion, after riding so far in the dark to see you.'

'I am chafed with visitors from both countries every hour of the day, Lord Douglas; many of them coming with complaints which it is out of my power to rectify. I have therefore a sly inquisition established around me, that might haply give your Lordship some interruption. But it was your own blame. Had you announced the name of Douglas, that would have opened a lane for you from my farthest outpost to this chair, which I request you to occupy, while I take my place here at your right hand. You are welcome, noble Earl of Douglas and Mar, to our rude habitation. There is no man more so, beneath our sovereign lord the King. I give you and your attendants all kind welcome and greeting.'

'You are become as much an accomplished courtier among these wild wastes as you were before an accomplished warrior, Sir Ringan,' said Douglas.

'I always make points of speaking as I am spoken to, drinking as I am drunk to, and going to a battle when sent for,' said the Warden. 'H'm h'm h'm,' neighed Dickie o' Dryhope, screwing up his mouth on one side like a shrew: 'It is all true our Captain tells you, Lord Douglas. That's his rule. Mh? mh? Mh? H'm h'm h'm.' The Douglas cast at Dickie a curious searching glance from his dark eye that was half hid by a shaggy eyebrow; and then turning to Sir Ringan, replied, 'I am heartily glad of it, noble Baron of Mountcomyn, it having been for that very purpose I sought this interview with you. Sir Ringan Redhough, you must to battle with me to-morrow.'

'With all my heart, my lord,' was the reply.

'Come, that is as it should be. We'll no more of it. We *can* have no more of it,' said Douglas: 'Let us have a flaggon of your best wine to drink success to our arms.'

The wine was soon produced, with plenty of other good cheer, with which the Warden's camp was then abundantly stored; and the two chiefs conversed together with as much freedom, and as little apparent jealousy with regard to rank or fame, as if they had been two brothers. The Douglas delineated his affairs as in that posture in which success could not fail him; at the same time he admitted the ticklish situation in which he stood, owing to the diversion made by the captain of Berwick, and that without an instant effort he would be inclosed between two fires. Sir Ringan answered, that he had heard of the incursion, and therefore he had drawn his troops down from the dales of Northumberland to support his friend and firm ally in any case of necessity; and he concluded by boldly proffering either to supply the Douglas's place in the blockade, or march to the west, and hold Sir Thomas Musgrave in check. Douglas was delighted to find the crabbed, cross-grained Warden, as he was wont to call him, in such a complaisant humour; and testified that delight by many well-turned compliments and encomiums on his vigilance and gallant support. He got introduced to all the gentlemen of the party, with whom he exchanged civilities, desiring them all to regard him as their friend, and one ready to do them a kindness whenever it lay in his power. 'And now, Sir Ringan, since you hold the taking of the castle of Roxburgh so light,' said he, 'I think it is meet that my men and I should march and give battle to Musgrave. Probably you may have taken possession of that troublesome garrison before we return.'

'If I do, my Lord of Douglas, I take it for myself,' replied Sir Ringan; 'and claim all the privileges, rights, and immunities that were to devolve on you as the reducer of it. Now, if I should take the castle of Roxburgh before your return, I suspect you would find it as hard work to expel me, and these Border warriors of mine, as the half-starved English that you have there already. I have all these brave fellows to hold in beef and malt, my Lord of Douglas; and for their sakes I have laid down a golden rule to walk by, which is, *To do nothing for nothing*. If I take the castle of Roxburgh, I take it for myself and them.'

Douglas, who knew nothing of the prophecy and injunctions from the book of the destinies of men, became more convinced than ever, that the Warden knew of some flaw or some tangible point in the garrison; and if there existed a knowledge of such a thing, he resolved to avail himself of it by any means. He knew Sir Ringan too well to suppose he would confide his secret to him, without a certainty of reaping due advantage; and that, therefore, it behoved to give him a prevailing interest in it. With this view, he answered him, jocularly: 'Though you were to receive all that was promised to me, in the event of my success, you would probably find yourself only a loser by the guerdon.'

'Why, are you not to be made the king's son-in-law?' replied Sir Ringan 'and thereby the first subject, or rather the first man of the realm; for, by the indolence and retired habits of our sovereign, you would have the whole kingdom at your beck. Call you this nothing, my Lord? Or would it be fair and reasonable – supposing the thing possible, which I do not pretend to say it is – that if my warriors and I should put you in possession of all this power, riches, and honours, would it be fair, I say, that we should be again turned out to these Border wastes, to live by our shifts, without reaping any thing of the benefit?'

'Should you take the castle for me, in my absence, noble Sir Ringan, your reward shall be of your own naming.'

'Would it not be better, Lord Douglas, that the reward were settled before-hand; and, then, I lose or gain at my own risk and peril. If I deliver you no produce, I ask no pay.'

'And what is the reward Sir Ringan would ask for such a piece of incalculable service?'

'My choice of seven baronies on the West Border, to divide amongst these gentlemen commoners, to whose support I owe every thing.'

'You are a master worth serving, brave Sir Ringan. But such a grant would break my power on the Border for ever.'

'It is that your power on the Border *may not* be broken for ever, Lord Douglas, that I make the proffer. I am safer without the venture. But you are a day's march nearer to the English army – draw off your men silently before the break of day, and march against it. I shall supply your place at the blockade, to the west of the castle, without loss of time, and answer to you at your return for all ingress or egress that takes place in that division. If Sir Thomas proves hard for you, you have only to keep your men together, and fall back toward the entrenchments. You shall find you have some good back-friends there.'

Douglas had determined on no account to let this proffer of the Warden's ingenious head and powerful arm in the taking of the fortress pass without trial; so, without more ado, he called for the friar's tablets, and made out a grant to Sir Ringan, in free present, of the barony and lands of Gilterscleuch, and his choice of seven of the best baronies belonging to the house of Douglas in the districts adjoining to the West Border, in the event of his putting James, Lord of Douglas and Mar, in full possession of the castle of Roxburgh. This grant signed and sealed, the Douglas departed, after pledging the Warden and his friends in a hearty stirrup cup, both chiefs being alike well pleased with the agreement they had entered into. The Douglas posted back to Roxburgh, and reached it just in time to put the western division of his army in motion at break of day; while Sir Ringan made his musters by the light of the moon, and marched off to the siege of Roxburgh.

CHAPTER TWENTY-SEVEN

Aboon his skins he sat and rockit,
And fiercely up his bonnet cockit;
Then at ha' doors he crousely knockit
    Withouten dread,
Till wives and bairns around him flockit,
    But now he's dead.

Then he wad claw, and he wad hustle,
Till all the skins played rap and rustle;
While up his thighs, wi' devilish bustle,
    Ran mony a ked;
Now they hae lost their gume and gustle,
    Sin' Robin's dead.

De'il on the yaud, that I should ban!
That brak the neck of sic ane man;
Now wha will wucked dames traupan
    Wi' siccan speed?
Or drive the hides to them wha tan,
    Sin' Robin's dead?
          Rob Paterson's Elegy

ON THE SAME day that Douglas marched his men up
the Tweed towards Melrose, and the Warden his troopers
across the Border to the siege of Roxburgh, a band of
twelve men and thirty horses came up out of Eskdale
towards Craik-Cross, the most motely group that had
ever been seen traversing that wild country. The men
were dressed as English peasants of the lowest order,
with broad unshapely hats, made of a rude felt of wool
and hair mixed; wide coarse jockeycoats that came below
their knees; and, instead of loops or buttons, these were
bound round the middle with a broad buff-belt; the rest

of their dress was all conformable, save that each of them
had a noble broad-sword girded by his side. Some of their
horses were loaden, some of them half-loaden, and a few
had scarcely any thing on their backs at all. But no man
will guess what that loading consisted of. Not to keep the
reader in suspense, it was of *nolt-hides*; that is, of cow-hides,
oxen-hides, bull-hides, and all sorts of hides that ever came
from the backs of cattle. There were raw hides and dried
hides, black hides and white hides, hides with horns, and
hides without horns; and of these consisted their loading,
and nothing else.

The men alighted at Craik-Cross to bait their horses, and
the following conversation ensued, which will let the reader
into the secret who these skin-dealers were, thus strangely
accoutred.

'Will Laidlaw o' Craik, ye're a gayan auld-farrant chield.
Come near me, and sit down, and tell me gin ye can hae
ony guess what our master the Warden can be wanting wi'
a' thir confoundit ill-smelled hides?'

'I hae puzzled my brain to nae purpose about it, Dan
Chisholm; but am convinced it is some way connected
wi' the siege of that unlucky castle; and the maist part o'
us trows that they are for making raip-ladders, or rather
whing-ladders, for climbing ower the wa's; an gin that be
the case, Dan, there will mony ane o' us throw away our
lives to little purpose.'

'Now to hear you talk about fock throwing away their
lives! You that wad risk your life for naething but a broken
crown every day o' the year. Why, Will Laidlaw, I hae
foughten often in the same field wi' you afore this time,
and I never saw you set your life at a cow's horn, let be
the hide o' ane (for whilk we wad gie a good deal the
day.) I hae seen ye ride from your ain party, when that
wing wasna hotly enough engaged, and blatter into the very
thickest and hettest part o' the field, just girning and laying
on like some lang-nosed deil come out o' the pit. But let me
tell ye, Will o' Craik, it is a sair fault o' your's, and it is a
clagg o' the hale clan – the deil be your landlord, (as he
has already been mine, quietly,) gin the hale tott o' ye be
nae ill for saying ae thing an' thinking another. If ane hear
a Laidlaw complaining o' pinching and poverty, ye may
amaist be sure that he has the best stockit mailings, and

the best filled beef-barrels in the country. If ye hear him complaining, that the English are herrying the Scots up, stoop and roop, ye may rely on it the Scots hae been getting the upper hand and enriching themsels; and if ye hear a Laidlaw pretending to be averse to a foray or a battle, ye may depend on it that his very knuckles are itching, and his teeth watering, to be at it—. Na, ye needna waul wi' your muckle een, Will, for ye canna deny the thing; and it is a d—n'd provoking gate ye hae.'

'Hout, dear Dan! we just hae it by kind to try what fock thinks on the subject a wee; to sound them like, afore we tell our hale minds. But a' comes aye freely out ere the hinder-end. But the truth is, about this that we were cracking; ye ken I dinna mind a bodle what the Warden be gaun to do wi' the skins, provided he keep his promise, and gie me a living English cow for the hides of every three dead anes that I bring him.'

'There it goes now! There you go again! Weel I ken ye carena ae doit about the kye. Ye hae plenty o' baith kye and ewes already, and, on the contrary, ye wad *gi'e them a'* to ken what our chief is gaun to be about wi' thir hides. But it is needless to fight w'ye! Ye canna help that cross gate o' expressing yoursel. Gin ever ye be drowned we may seek you up the water. There's ae thing, Will – ye may see the Warden means some general good to us a' by this project, whatever it is, for he has sent ae man o' every name to gather up the skins o' his native district. Ae Oliver, ae Armstrong, ae Laidlaw, ae Chisholm, and twa o' the Redhoughs; for ye ken he is always maist behadden to his ain name. But what can be the meaning o' this ugly disguise, I canna form a single conjecture; and he is sae strick about it too, that if ane o' us let oursels be found out, we lose a' chance of reward or advantage. Sae, Will, ye're unco weel kend about Craik and Howpasley, and a' the links o' Borthwick, and so am I about Castle-Wearie and Chisholm, and thereabouts. Gang ye into my father's house a'night, and I'll gang to Craik; gather ye up the hides o' Teviot, and I shall take Borthwick in my road. My father will maybe be a wee sweer to take ye in, but ye maun make your way on him the best gate ye can; he has the best stockit pantry on Teviot head, but a bit of a Laidlaw's fault, complaining aye maist when he has least reason. He has a capital stock o' hides, but seeing that English disguise he may deny them; therefore try him first, and if he winna produce them, gang up the burn about half a mile, and in a lown crook, weel hidden frae a' the world, ye'll find a bit housie wi' a dozen o' good hides in it. If he winna gi'e you them at a fair price, ye maun e'en take them for naething, as it is a' for his ain advantage.'

'Na, na, Dan. Weel I wat I'll do nae sic thing! I wadna dispute wi' the auld man, nor anger him for a' the hides in the hale barony.'

'There again! Aye the auld man! Now, the Lord forgi'e ye; for ye never met wi' him a' your life but ye baith angered him and disputed wi' him. But nae mair about it. Take ye Sandy Pot o' the Burnfit, the queer hairum skairum devil, Tam Oliver, Bauldy Elliot, and Bauldy Armstrong wi' you; and I'll take Jamie Telfer o' the Dodhead, Jock o' the Delorrin, Jock Anderson o' nae place, and Geordie Bryden o' every place, wi' me – and good luck to the skin trade!'

It was one of those sort of winter days that often occur in January, when the weather is what the shepherds call 'in the deadthraw,' that is, in a struggle between frost and thaw. There was a dark cloud of rime resting on the tops of the hills, which shrouded them in a veil impervious to vision beyond the space of a few yards, and within that cloud the whole height appeared to be covered with millions of razors, every pile of bent and heath being loaded with ice on the one side, so that each had the exact resemblance to a razor blade, all of which appeared to be cast in the same mould, and of the same beautiful metal. The feet of the horses as they travelled through this made a jingling noise, as if they had been wading among crystal. As they came lower down on the hills the air became softer, and the ground was free of those ice-candles; but an uncommon gloom hung over holm and dale.

Old Peter Chisholm was walking on the green to the westward of his house, looking at his ewes coming bleating down from among the dark foldings of the rime, and saying to himself, 'I wonder what can be word o' thae dirty herd callants the day, that they are letting the sheep come a' stringing in lang raws, and rairing and bleating, into the how o' the water that gate. The country's in a loose state e'now, for the strength is a' out o't; a raid o' thirty stout English thieves wad herry the hale water. An sic were to come this gate the day, my stock wad be a' gane.'

Peter was proud of his ewes for all that, and, giving them a whistle, he threw the plaid over his shoulder, set his broad bonnet up before, and turned about to go home to look after the shepherd lads. As he turned his face to the north, he naturally cast his eye up toward the Limycleuch hills, where it instantly embraced the appalling sight of Will Laidlaw o' Craik, and his disguised compeers, with their fifteen horses, coming stretching down the ridge, right opposite to Pate Chisholm's hirsel of bonny wheel-horned ewes. The old man's eyes were dazzled in his head, and a paralytic affection seized his whole frame. 'Lord pity us! Now see what's coming yonder,' said Peter: 'I tauld them aye what wad happen! but no ane wad heed me! O dool to the day! A man may soon hae muckle, and soon hae naething in this wearifu' country. O Dan, Simon, and Jock, the strength o' my house! wherefore are ye a' gane and left your gear to gang as it came! Dear bought! far sought! and little for the haudding.'

By the time Peter got thus far with his soliloquy he was quite out of breath; for he was not only walking fast, but he was absolutely running towards home, with a sore stoop, and knees bent much forward. Still as he hobbled he continued to apostrophise in short sentences, as he could gather a little breath now and then to utter a small portion of the concatenation of repulsive ideas that presented themselves one after another – 'Naething but trash left – Heh-heh – Rob-in-Laid-law! – I hae seen – Heh-heh the – day, but – Heh – that's – gane – Lasses, too! – Hoh – oh! – O ay! – Half – breed – bring – up – Oh – Dan – Dan, &c. &c. Daughter! Bessy Chisholm – Heh! Are ye therein? May Chisholm – where's your titty? Poor tafferel ruined tawpies! What are ye gaun gaindering about that gate for, as ye didna ken whilk end o' ye were uppermost?' 'That's easily kend, father. What has come ower ye? Hae ye seen a warlock that ye are gaping and glowring at sic a dismal rate?' 'War than ony warlock, ye twa glaikit idle hizzies. Off wi' jerkin and wilycoat, and on wi' doublet, breeks, and buskins instantly. Belt on bow, buckler, and brand, and stand for life, limb, gear, and maidhood, or a's gane in ae kink. O dool be to the day! dool be to the day! What are ye standing glinting, and looking at ane anither there for? Cast your een up to the Carlin-rigg, and see what's coming. A'harried! ravaged! and murdered! Come, come: Don your billies' claes; let us make some show; it will maybe save something. Warn the herd callants; let the stoutest of them arm, and the weakest rin and drive sheep and cattle an' a' out o' sight amang the clouds. O dool to the day! Na, na; for a' the houses that are in the country here they come straight! Nae winning by this place.'

The lasses seeing their father in such a querulous mood, and the motely troop fast approaching, acquiesced in his mandate, and without delay mounted themselves each in a suit of their younger brother's clothes, while old Peter stood over them to see that they put all to rights, always giving such directions as these: 'Come, come, come! strap, clasp, belt and buckle; and gude-sake fauld up your cuffs. Your arms hing at your shoulder blades as they were off joint. Hout fie! hout fie! Wha ever saw young chields hae sic luchts o' yellow hair hingin fleeing in the wind? Come, come, strap and string down; swaddle it round wi' sax dizzen o' wheelbands, and fasten a steel-belted fur cap ower aboon a'. Yare, yare! Lord sauff us! Here they come! What's to be our fate? Keep close for a wee while.'

'Hilloa! Wha hauds the house!' was vollied from the door by the deep-toned voice of Will Laidlaw.

'There's nae body in but me, and I downa come to the door. Ye had better ride on,' cried old Peter, in a weak tremulous voice.

'Wilt thou answer to thy name, or hast thou a name to answer to?' said Will, feigning to speak the broad Northumberland dialect, which sorted very ill with his tongue: 'An thou be'st leel man and true, coome and bid thee guests wailcome. It is God speed, or spulzie wi' thee in three handclaps.'

'Spulzie, quo the man!' exclaimed Peter: 'The muckle fiend spulzie the unmannerly gab that spake it!' – and with that he came stooping over his staff, and coughing to the door, speaking in a quavering treble key. 'A bonny like purpose! What wad ye spulzie frae a poor auld man that hasna as muckle atween him and the grave as will pay for howking it, and buy a hagabag winding sheet? Spulzie,

quo he! That is a good joke! – he – he – he, (cough) hoh
– hoh – hoh. I'm sae ill wi' that host! Eh? wha hae we a'
here? Strangers, I think!'

'Goodman, we were directed to your house for a night's
entertainment or two, if you are the old rich yeoman
ycleped Patrick Chisholm of Castle-Weary.'

'Na, na! I'm nae rich yeoman! I'm naething but a poor
herried, forsaken, reduced auld man! I hae nae up-putting
for ought better than a flea. Ye had better ride on down
to Commonside. There's plenty there baith for man and
horse. Come away. I'll set you down the length o' the ford,
and let ye see the right gate.'

'Come neighbours, let us go away as he says. We'll never
make our quarters good on this auld carle,' said Sandy Pot,
in a whisper to his companions: 'And troth do ye ken I wad
rather lie at the back of the dike, before I imposed myself on
ony body. Od my heart's wae for the poor auld niggard.'

'Come away, lads, come away,' cried Peter. 'The days
are unco short e'now; ye haena time to put off.'

'Stop short there, my good fellow,' cried Laidlaw, 'We
have some other fish to fry with you before we go. I am
informed you have a large stock in hand of the goods in
which we deal. You have had lucky lifts this year. Plenty
of good hides with you?'

'Rank misprision, and base rascally jests on a poor auld
man. Not a single hide about the hale town, foreby the ane
on my back,' cried old Peter.

'My orders are, worthy old yeoman, to give fair prices to
such as produce their hides,' said Laidlaw. 'But whoever
refuses, I am obliged to search for them; and if I find any
I take them at my own price.'

'O dear, honest gentleman, I downa joke wi' ye: hoh,
hoh,' coughed Peter. 'Gin ye be for a place to stay in a'
night, come away as lang as it is daylight.'

'Why, with your leave my good fellow, we must lodge
with you tonight. Hearth-room and ha'-room, steed-room
and sta'-room, is the friendly stranger's right here. Small
things will serve: a stone of English beef or so, and two or
three pecks of oats.'

'Beef, quoth the man? Ye may as weel look for a white
corby as beef in my pantry, or aits in my barn. Will ye no
come away?'

'Not till I make a search for your nolt hides, honest yeoman. To that am I bound.'

The four skin-dealers next the door alighted and went in, leaving their horses with the other two, who went and put them up in a good large stable with plenty of stalls. Peter ran back to the house in perfect agony, speaking to himself all the way. 'They are very misleared chaps thae. They maun surely either be Low Dutch, or else sutors o' Selkirk, that they are sae mad about skins. I little wat how I am to get rid o' them.'

The two lasses appeared armed cap-a-pee like two young men; and though Bess was Will Laidlaw's own sweetheart, he did not recognize her through the disguise, neither did she once suspect him. The two made a little swaggering about the *pelt-dealers* as they called them entering the pantry, but not choosing to measure arms with them, the weak suffered the strong to pass; and Will having his cue, soon discovered the huge barrels of beef below the ground, with empty ones above them. Old Peter shed tears of vexation when he saw this huge and highly-valued store was all discovered, but had not a word to say for himself, save now and then 'A' fairly come by, and hardly won; and there is nae right nor law that says honest men should be eaten up wi' sorners. May ane speir where ye come frae, or by wha's right ye do this!'

'Why man dost thou no hear and dost thou no see that we're coome joost from Nworthoomberland!'

'Aha!' thought Peter to himself; 'English thieves after a'! I had some hopes that I could distinguish Scots tongues in their heads. But a's gane, a's gane!'

'Now auld yeoman, if thou hast a word of trooth in thee, tell us where the hides are, and we will pay thee for them.'

'No ae hide about the town. No ane, either little or muckle.'

'Why soore am I them coos doodnae coome to thee withoot heydes, did they? That I can answer for, they had a' heydes and bonns baith when they came from hwome.'

'Waur than ever! Waur than ever!' exclaimed Pate Chisholm to himself as he sought another apartment: 'The very men that the kye were reaved frae come to take revenge! Callant, come here and speak wi' me. Haste to a neighbour's house, and raise the fray. We shall never be a' quietly put down wi' half a dozen.'

'Dearest father,' said May, 'I dinna think the men mean ony ill, if ye wad be but civil.'

'Civil or no civil, wench, it is as good to have half a dozen armed men lying concealed near us,' said Peter: 'An we dinna need them, the better. Rin your ways, and gar raise a' the auld men and the young lads in the two neist towns, for there is nae ither left. Pith's good in a' play.'

The maid did as she was ordered, and Peter, seeing that no better would be, tried to compel himself to a sort of civility, which, however, sat on him with a very bad grace. But, hides! hides! – nothing but hides was the burden of their enquiries; while Peter durst not for his life produce the hides, deeming that every man would know the hides of his own kine, and wreak tenfold vengeance on himself and household. He knew not, he said, what his son Dan, who took care of all these matters, had made of them – sold them he supposed to the curriers and sutors of Selkirk – and more than this Pate would not acknowledge. There was no other thing for it, nor perhaps did Laidlaw want any thing else, than for him and his companions to walk up the burn and make a seizure of the whole of Peter's excellent hides, with which they returned loaden to his dwelling. His confusion and distress of mind were most appalling when Laidlaw spread them all out before him, and asked in a very particular manner to be informed where he had got them. O! Peter knew nothing about them. They were not his at all. He did not know to whom they belonged. But he would not stand to speak, turning his back always on the men, and hasting away, coughing and speaking to himself. He could have seen these presumptuous skin-men roasted on a brander, for they had now put him out of all patience, and all hope!

'Pray thee now, mine good friend, inform me this,' said Laidlaw; 'Did'st thou nwot get this seame fleckered one, and this brwoad one here, on the third of the last mwonth; and here's wother three, did'st thou nwo get them on the twentieth of the seame mwonth? Now tell me this I say? Why where is thou gwoing groombling inte theesel? Turn about thee feace to the heydes, and answer to the pwoint.'

'Aff hands is fair play,' said old Pate: 'I winna be forced wi' ony unmannerly English lown that ever I saw atween the een;' and with that he heaved his staff and struck Laidlaw across the shoulders, and over the steel bonnet repeatedly, who was like to burst with repressed laughter, but still persisted in his queries.

'What ails the owld catwiddied carle,' said he, 'that he winno answer a ceevil question? I's jwost wanting to tauk to thee aboot boosiness, and thou flees out in a reage and breaks me head. Come tourn again, and tell me when and where thou got'st this one, see, this wheyte one here! What's 't moombling at? Wolt thou tell me the price of them, then?'

'I want to hae naething to do wi' you, and as little to say to you; therefore, gang about your business, and dinna plague a poor auld unfeiroch man. The gate is afore ye, and your company's wanted elsewhere.'

Will would take none of those hints; he followed his uncourteous host about and about, till at last he fairly holded him beyond the fire; and then he took his seat over against him and conversed on, while his companions dropped in one by one and joined in it. For a while they got it all to themselves, but at length Pate, not being able to make better of it, suffered himself to be drawn in by degrees to join them, still preserving the same strain of disingeniousness. They asked who the two handsome striplings were that attended him, and spread the board with provisions? He answered that they were two sons of his own. 'Sons of thine?' said Laidlaw, 'Whoy, what are their neames?' 'Simon and John,' answered he; 'or rather Sim and Jock, for that's how we ca' them.'

'Whoy, mon, that is the queerest thing I ever heard,' said Laidlaw: 'Then thou hast two swons of the neame of Jock, and other two of the neame of Sim, for I saw two of that neame, strapping youths, in the Warden's camp.'

Peter wist not well what answer to make; and, therefore, only added, 'Ay, Ay! Were you in the Warden's camp? Then tell me, is their ony word frae my son Dan?'

'Ay man, I can tell thee sic news of Dan as thou never heard'st; he has sitten at his supper hand and neive wi' the deil.' At these words one of the young men behind them (May Chisholm to wit,) uttered a suppressed scream, and from that moment Will Laidlaw smelled a rat, and soon discovered his own beloved Bess Chisholm standing gazing at him as he related the wonderful story of her brother's adventures with the devil, the warlock, and the three evil spirits; of his race with those infernals along the marble pavement of the air; his transformation into a horned beast; and of his eating and drinking with the prince of darkness. But the two striplings were most of all shocked at hearing of the devil's burning stomach, and how the wine *fizzed* as it went down.

After listening and wondering while all these things were in relation, Bess said to the skin-dealer next to her, who chanced to be Sandy Pot, 'Pray, Sir, when you were in the camp of Sir Ringan Redhough, did you note a brave trooper, a friend of ours, named Laidlaw?'

'Oh, yes, that I did,' said Sandy: 'I know him well.' This was a glorious joke for Pot, and his comrades were afraid he would persevere in it till he put their secret out altogether.

'How is he reported in the army?' said she: 'Is it still alleged that he is the bravest and most successful battler in the baron's array?'

'*Bottler*, I suppose you mean,' said Sandy, 'for as to his battling, God mend that. He is not noted for ought that I ever heard of, except for keeping a flunkey, or a wall-i'-the-chamber, as the Frenchmen ca' it; and it is reported thro' all the army, that that *wally* o' his is an English girl. I can tell you that your neighbour, Will Laidlaw, is notorious for nothing else beside this.'

'It is false as thyself, and thy perjured ungenerous nation,' said the disguised maiden. 'I know my friend to be honour's self, and of a house whose courage and integrity were never called in question. The man that dares to slander him had better do it somewhere else than in my presence, and under my father's roof. But I degraded him myself, by putting his name into the mouth of such a mean forager as thou art! The man whose actions are base, always accuses the brave and generous of deeds such as his own.'

'Bless me, what ails the chiel?' said Sandy, laughing good humouredly: – What's the great ill o' keeping *a wally*? I aince keepit ane mysel, there's nae doubt o't, till my uncle,

Gideon Scott, set up his birse, and gart me part wi' the creature.'

The rest laughed at Sandy being put out of countenance by the indignant stripling; but Bessy Chisholm turned on her heel, and walked out at the door, muttering expressions about vulgarity, raw hides, and maggots; and Will Laidlaw, not able to contain himself, rose and walked out after her, in a visible state of mental agitation. As he approached the stable door quietly, into which she had turned, he heard her saying to herself. 'Laidlaw keep an English mistress in disguise! No, the fellow is a poltroon, and a liar, and I will not believe it.' Will entering at that moment, seized her hand between both his, and kissed it, saying, in a passionate style, 'My own dear and high-spirited Bess Chisholm still!'

Never was there seen such a statue of amazement! The tones of the voice, now uttered in its natural key, were familiar to her. But the figure that uttered them! To be addressed in that style by a great burly thief of an English skin-buyer, outwent all comprehension. She was in a man's dress, be it remembered – and there she stood, with her face half raised, her ruddy lips wide apart, and her set eyes of lucent blue showing a mixture of astonishment and disdain. 'What? what? Sir,' was all that she could say, until the ragamuffin figure reminded her of the weaponshaw at Mountcomyn, and some love-tokens and vows, of which none knew save one. But, with a woman's natural caprice, she now was angry at him in turn having discovered her true sentiments, and refused to acknowledge him as her lover in that hateful disguise, unless the meaning of it was explained to her. He told her, that the meaning of it was unknown to himself; that he took it at his captain's command; but that his fortune depended on the secret being kept.

'There you are safe, at all events,' said she; 'and it is well you have disclosed yourself in time, for my father has raised the country, and it is not improbable that, before to-morrow, you should have been all dead men.'

'I think we have been in greater jeopardies,' said he: 'But in the mean time keep up your disguise, that my comrades may not discover your sex; – and we two must have some private discourse during the night, for I have much to say to you.'

'Not I, master, I winna court ae word wi' a man in the dress of a vulgar English boor; for it is sae hatefu' to me, I can like nought that's within it. Ah me! I wot ill how it is; but I think I hardly detest it sae sair already.'

'My bonny, haughty, pawkie, sweet Elizabeth!' cried Laidlaw—. But Isaac the curate says, that, being himself a married man, he could not go on with all the overcharged outrageous stuff that passed between these two fond lovers; so he passes it over, as well as the conversation at their evening meal, which Bess took care to make a plentiful and savoury one; and in the mean time, she was in such high spirits herself, that the troopers, who did not know her, took the young man for the most swaggering puppy they had ever seen. She challenged Sandy Pot to fight her with single rapier, knowing well that Laidlaw would find some means of preventing it; but it was evident that old Peter thought her entirely out of her senses, for he tried to get her away from about the house to the residence of one of the neighbouring gentlemen yeomen for the night, but the experiment was vain.

When he saw such a goodly supper, or dinner, (for they were both in one) set down to these uncouth, and, to him, unwelcome guests, he could not contain his chagrin, and at first refused to turn out to the board, or partake with the rest. But when he saw that the good fare would all go, he grew as restless as if he had been sitting on pins, till Bess, who knew his way, took him by the arm, and pretended to force him jocularly out to the table. But Peter was not ill to force; for in place of receding, he made all the haste into the head of the board that he could, though at the same time always repeating, 'I tell ye, callant, it is downright wastery.' He, however, plied as good a knife and as good a horn-spoon as any of them all.

While they were yet busily engaged at their meal, the tramp of horses was heard approaching the door in a cautious and uncertain manner, and by a circuitous way. The two disguised maids, (whom, by-the-by, we should distinguish by the names of Sim and Jock, as they sustained these that night,) were standing eating at the hall-dresser, behind the backs of the troopers; and when the trampling was first heard, Jock grew as pale as death, but Sim, who knew what guests were within, which the other did not know, shewed a courage so undaunted, that it appeared wonderful to all present, save one, but to Jock in particular: 'O ho! The nearer night the mae beggars,' cried Sim. 'Who have we next?'

'That beats ought I ever heard in my life!' exclaimed Pate: 'I think the fock be gane distractedly mad! What brings them a' here? Is there no another ha' house and pantry in the hale country but mine? It is hard to be eaten out o' house and hald wi' sorners and stravaegers this gate. May Liberton's luck befa' the hale o' them. Callant Jock, set by that meat out o' sight.' 'Stop for a wee bit, an ye like, goodman,' said Bauldy Armstrong: 'It is best aye to do ae thing afore another.'

By this time the dialogue had commenced in the court; Simmy went briskly to the door by himself, and demanded of the strangers who they were, and what they wanted? They answered, with hesitation, that they supposed they had lost their way, and requested to know who held the house, and how it was called? 'The house is held by my father, a leel Scottish yeoman,' said the youth; 'and already full of strangers to the door, as well as every stall of his stable with their horses. Pass on your way, and peace be with you.' 'Did I not tell you we had *lost* our way,' said the first speaker, riding up to the door. 'Pray, who are the strangers within? We have lost a party of our friends.'

'The men are from the south, master: free-traders, they may be called. Men of horns, hides, and hair, Sir. You, I suppose, are of the same profession?' 'Precisely of the same,' said the stranger, alighting from his horse, and entering the house.

He was followed by other two, for there were but four in all, and the fourth was a boy whom they left holding their horses. When they came in upon Peter and his jolly hide-merchants, they were visibly disappointed, and viewed the grotesque-looking group with marked curiosity. These were not the men they expected to have found, that was evident; but perceiving their English habits, they ventured to address them. They were answered in blunt cutting terms; for our troopers knew them, although the disguise prevented their being known again. Having learned the name of the house and its owner, they began forthwith to inquire if any thing of a young nobleman had been seen at that place, with such and such attendants; for they had traced them to that very house, they said, and if the possessors could give no account of them they would be held as responsible. Old Peter said, there were so many people came to that house, that it was impossible he could tell a tale of one of them distinct from another; but the intrepid Sim, knowing his back friends, told him the whole story in a few words, and then asked them in turn what they had to say concerning it.

'Whoy, I has joost to say this, young chap, that I am to boond thee and all the faymilie, and carry you all to answer before a meeting of the wardens.'

'Ay, and it is prwoper reyght and prwoper reason too, that they should, friend,' said Laidlaw, pretending to take his part, to see what he would say. Will knew the three men to be three notorious English thieves, of the set of the Halls and Reids, and that they could not, in fact, be sent in search of the Lady Jane Howard; but he could not divine their motive for coming there, or making the inquiry; therefore he took the Northumberland tongue as well as he could, and encouraged them in conversation till a late hour. Yet he could learn nothing; only he was sure they were come about no good end. As for old Peter, when he saw two parties of Englishmen come upon him, and heard that they laid their heads together, he gave himself and all that he had up for lost; and hoping to conciliate their favour in some measure, he actually intreated these last comers to sit down and share of the remnants of their supper, which they did in a right liberal manner, while Peter went out and in to learn the news. He found by this time nine men, well armed, assembled in the barn, that had gathered from the neighbouring houses, whose inhabitants were all bound to rise and assist one another on any emergency. These were mostly old men or very young ones, the flower of the Border districts being all in the Warden's camp. Will likewise informed his sweetheart privately of his suspicions; and perceiving that the strangers were extremely well mounted, and heavily armed, he desired her, if possible, to find means of concealing their horses. This the supposed Sim soon effected. The boy still held them at forage by the side of the old castle-wall; and he being brought in, and set down to supper, some of those in the barn were warned to take the horses quietly to the concealed house up in the hollow burn. They were soon secured there; and the thieves perceiving that no one left the house, never had the smallest suspicion of any trick, the boy being fast asleep behind the board. At length all of them grew drowsy, and began to compose themselves to rest as they best could, save two fond lovers, that were whispering their vows and their secrets to each other in the little chamber mentioned in a former part of this history.

About midnight, when all was quiet, these two heard the cry of *Welhee! Welhee!* from a neighbouring mountain, which in a short time was returned from two different places in the valley.

'Now, I will lay my neck in wad,' whispered Will to his sweetheart, 'that there is a thief-raid to-night; and that these three have either come here to watch you, or to cut your throats in case of resistance; or perhaps they may have indeed lost their party in the mist. But this I ken, neither a Reid nor a Hall ever came thus far into Scotland for good. If the fray rise, take you the command, and fear nothing. My friends and I will defend you, and clear your way.'

'But what shall we do, dear Laidlaw, with these three mosstroopers and the boy?'

'We must either slay or bind them the first thing we do, or perhaps leave them to waddle to the hills in their armour on foot the best way they can.'

The maiden's heart trembled at the thoughts of what lay before her; as for old Pate, he kept going out and in like a restless spirit; and if he had not lost his daughter, and knew not where she was, he proposed to have fastened doors and windows, and burnt all the nine English-men where they lay, for he had no faith in any of them, and weened them all come for the purpose of ruining him. As he was going about preparing matters for this laudable purpose, one of the shepherd lads came with the fray, and related a dismal tale. He said, that he and his companions had driven out all the sheep and cattle to the heights among the mist, as they had been commanded; that in the course of the evening they heard many calls and whistles around them; and just as the moon rose, a band of English thieves came round them, and drove them all off towards Bilhope-head. Peter's assembled friends advised him to take the skin-men's fifteen horses, and what remained at home of his own, and ride off and try to recover the prey, without alarming his dangerous guests; but Peter was bent on fastening the doors, and burning them skin and bone, for, he said, they would never get so easily quit of them. The two anxious lovers hearing a bustle without, opened the casement, and overheard a part of these perplexed words and reasonings. Then hastening out to join counsel, they raised the fray openly. The heroic Sim flew to horse, and desired all that were friends to the Scots to follow, while Laidlaw addressed his compeers, saying, 'Up, lads, and let us ride; our host must not be herried while we are under his roof.'

'No, no!' exclaimed the thieves, all in a breath; 'he must not be herried and we under his roof;' and no one appeared in half such hurry as they were to mount and be gone.

'Stop short, my good fellows, till I speak with you for a minute,' said Laidlaw: 'Make me sure which side you will take before you go, else one foot you stir not from that fire-side. I know you for Anthony Reid of Whickhope, and those for two of your cousins of Tersithead, and shrewdly suspect you to be at the head of the foray.'

Anthony drew his sword: so did Laidlaw. But the English troopers were bold and desperate fellows; and before Laidlaw's friends could gather round him to his assistance, the three having covered themselves with their bucklers, forced their way out, back to back, and ran Sandy Pot through the left shoulder, who pressed on them too rashly. When they missed their horses, and saw that they were clean gone, they foamed like as many furies, and, setting their backs to the wall, swore they would fight it out. The combat might have been attended with much bloodshed, had not all the people rushed from the barn, and overpowered them. They were then taken into the house and bound, while Pot and May Chisholm, alias Jock, were left as guards on them, with orders to kill the first that should offer to loose either himself or any of his companions. This whole scene was quite beyond Peter Chisholm's capacity. He could in nowise conceive how the one party of Englishmen assisted with such energy in detecting and binding the others. Still he was any thing but satisfied; the matter having outgone his comprehension, as well as that of all his associates, save one.

They now mounted without delay, and rode with all manner of speed toward the Pass of the Hermitage, by which path they supposed the droves must necessarily proceed; and just as they went down the Redcleuch, leading their horses, they saw the cattle passing at the foot of it. The party amounted scarcely to their own number; but the sheep-drivers were not come in view; so they mounted their horses, and instantly mixed with the men behind the drove, without offering to stop the cattle. At the same time they placed a guard of two farther behind, to prevent all intelligence from passing between the two parties. When this was effected, Simmy challenged the cattle as his father's, and desired the drivers to give them up; but to this the captain of the gang, whose name was Gabriel Reid, the younger brother of Anthony, and captain in his absence, only mocked, imitating the sharp treble notes of the petulant younker, and telling him that he would not give them up for three score such men as *he* was, else he was better than he looked. As he said this, however, he kept a curious eye on the rough exterior of the tall athletic English peasants by whom the youth was surrounded, which Laidlaw perceiving, accosted him in his feigned tone.

'Whoy, friend, we are countrymen of thee own, and know thee full weel. Thou's Gabriel Reid of Trochend. But thee billy Anty is taken prisoner this seame mworning, and if thou disna gie up the kie, his head will be chappit off, as weel as these of thee twa coosins the Ha's. Sae thou hast ney choice left but to yield up thee ill gotten gain.'

'And what dog art thou, that takest part against thee own countrymen?' said Reid.

'Oo, I's a dealer in the leather line, as weel as all my friends there. We have our free passages and warranty for the good of both countries; but we are honest men, and by chance were lodged in the house of the owner of these coos, and must see joostice doone to him. I boond thee brwother with mee own hands.'

'Then the devil bind thee, thou traitor knave! and for thee reward, this to thy harnpan!' said Gabriel, drawing out his sword, and attacking Laidlaw without more ado. Will, who was never backward at a brulzie, received the encounter without flinching, and, calling for fair play and elbow-room, both proceeded to decide the day by single combat, while the rest drew aloof and looked on, encouraging them only with cheers and applausive words. Laidlaw was mounted on Anthony Reid's gallant steed, which Gabriel remarked, and that added to his rancour against the skin-man at least ten degrees. The ground was exceedingly bad, so that they could not wheel for weapon-space without a parley; but neither would ask it. They fought close together, first with their sword-blades, and afterwards, as their horses came in contact, they dashed each other with their hilts. Both were slightly wounded, but Laidlaw rather had the worst of it. 'Beshrew thine heart, if thou hast been a skin-merchant all thy life,' said Gabriel, as he turned his horse in the path for another encounter. They had now changed sides, and this encounter was longer and more inveterate than the first. Laidlaw not being quite master of his mighty and furious steed, was twice in imminent danger, losing his broad slouched hat in the struggle, the crown of which was cross-barred with steel.

Poor Sim had changed colours ten times since the combat began; and, on seeing this last struggle, he lost all command of himself, and rushed with his sword drawn to Laidlaw's rescue. *Himself*, did I say? alas, no one knew the true sex, save her lover, and no one interfered till she was met by an English trooper half-way, who unhorsed and wounded her with as much ease, of course, as she had been a child. Will's eye caught the first glance of her, as she was falling, and galloping up to the rescue, bare-headed as he was, he clove the trooper's burgonet, and slew him at the first stroke. Reid followed him up; but Laidlaw's spirit, now fully proportioned to the high mettle of his steed, was a match for any thing. He rode against his antagonist with all his fury, and having the advantage of the brae, overthrew horse and man, and galloped over them. Then throwing himself from his horse, and seizing the forlorn warrior by the throat, called out with a voice of fury – 'Rescue or no rescue?' 'No rescue! Redsdale to the fray!' was the resolute and fatal reply. Will could not stand to reason any more at that time, so, without more ado, he ran him through the body, and flew to the rescue of his beloved and heroic Elizabeth, for there the combat began to thicken. She was on her feet ere he arrived, and well guarded, and, mounting her palfrey, she bade her lover head the fray, and pay no regard to her, for she was nothing the worse. He, however, saw the blood upon her bassonet, and was roused to perfect fury. The battle now became general; but it was no regular engagement, being scattered here and there through all the drove – some fought before the cattle, some behind them, and some in the middle. It was reported, that at one time there were fifteen single combats all going on at the same instant. Therefore, to have been an engagement on a small scale, it proved a very bloody one, many being slain and wounded on both sides. But the tremendous skin-merchants bore down all before them wherever they went. These were inured to battle, while the thieving moss-troopers, as well as the hinds on the Scottish side, were only used to desultory warfare. The bare-headed leather-merchant, in particular, was a dismal sight to the forayers, for having soon rid himself of his first antagonists, he continued galloping about the field wherever he saw two engaged, and cut down all of the adverse party as he went, or rode them down, giving, with every stroke, a hard grin and a grunt. The men thought the devil was come among them, or else that he had fairly taken possession of a skinmerchant; and, giving up the contest, a few of them tried to escape by flight, which they did by quitting their horses, and gaining some inaccessible ground. The drivers of the sheep likewise made their escape, for they found the droves deserted in the Hope. The weakest of the men having been left behind with them, they had come in view of the field of combat, and, marking how it terminated, had sped them away out of danger.

Chisholm's party brought home five prisoners with them, twelve English horses well caparisoned, and all the prey, save one ox that Will Laidlaw had ridden over and slain in the plenitude of his wrath. The Scots had no fewer than nine killed and grievously wounded out of their small party, of whom one of the latter was the brave and lovely Bess Chisholm, who was so faint, that Will was obliged to carry her all the way home on his horse before him, clasped to his bosom, he not failing to kiss her pallid cheek many a time by the way, while all the rest wondered at Laidlaw's great concern about the youth. When Peter saw his child borne

into the house pale and wounded, he lost all recollection
of the secret of her sex, and cried out 'O my poor Bess!
my dear daughter! What had I ado making a man of thee!
Thy blood is on thy old father's head. Alas, for my beloved
daughter!'

'Daughter!' exclaimed they all again and again, 'Daughter!' reechoed Will Laidlaw, as if he had not known well
before. 'Daughter?' cried the skin-men: 'Have we then been
led to the field by a maid? Shame on our heads that suffered
the overthrow! against the rules of chivalry as her attempt
was! Alas, for the gallant and high spirited young dame!'

They put her to bed, and dressed her wounds, and from
all appearances had high hopes that she was more afraid
and fatigued than hurt. She soon fell into a quiet slumber,
in which they left her, and retired to take some refreshment,
and talk over their morning's adventure. It turned out as
suggested, that their three prisoners were the three chief
men of the gang, who had completely lost themselves and
all traces of their companions among the mist; and having
heard a report of the seizure formerly made at that place,
they cunningly tried to pass themselves off as messengers
sent in search of the lost travellers. If they had been with
their own party, that would have proved an overmatch for
the Chisholms. The Reids and Halls had been herried
of their whole live stock by the Warden's people, and
learning that the greater part of it was driven up into
these mountains, they naturally wanted to make some
reprisals and recover their own again. Had it not been
for their misfortune in separating, and the exertions of the
gallant hide-men, they would have effected their purpose
with the utmost ease. It proved a luckless raid for them,
for they lost all their horses, the greater part of their men,
and the chief, squire Anthony, and six of his friends, were
sent prisoners to the castle of Mountcomyn.

The country people at Chisholm's board were loud in
praise of the skin-men, and of their trusty and gallant
behaviour; in particular, they averred that Laidlaw had
killed the half of the thieves with his own hand, for that
he rode about the field like a resistless angel, destroying all
before him. When Peter heard that he fought so valiantly
for the recovery of his stock, and regained his darling
daughter's life, his heart warmed toward him, and he bid

him ask any thing he chose that was in his power to give,
and he should not be said nay. Will at once asked the maid
whose life he had saved for his wife. Peter hesitated, and
said it was hard to bestow the flower of all the Chisholms
on a English skin-merchant, a man who seemed to have
neither house nor name, or was ashamed to own them.
However, as he had proved himself a warrior and a hero,
Peter consented, provided the maid grew better, and was
herself satisfied with the match. Will said he asked her on
no other terms, and went ben to see her before he departed.
She was still sound asleep, or pretended to be so; therefore,
unwilling to disturb her, he breathed a blessing over her,
and impressed two or three warm affectionate kisses on
her lips. As he came away he felt a slight pressure of her
arms around his neck.

When Sandy Pot learned that the lovely youth with
whom he had watched the prisoners all the night and
morning of the battle was a maid, and the younger sister
of his gallant friend Dan, Sandy's wound grew so ill that
he could not be removed, so he remained where he was,
and the other four went off with their uncouth loading.
They found Dan Chisholm at Hawick waiting for them
in the utmost impatience, having collected no fewer than
twenty horse-loads of hides, every one of them in size like
a hay-stack; and away the motely train marched and joined
the Warden on the night after his arrival before the walls of
Roxburgh.

CHAPTER TWENTY-EIGHT

So they shot out and they shot in,
  Till the morn that it was day,
When mony o' the Englishmen
  About the draw-brigg lay;
When they hae yoket carts and wains,
  To ca' their dead away,
And shot auld dikes aboon the lave,
  In gutters where they lay.
                    Ball. of Old Mettlin

THE EXPEDITION OF the Douglas against Musgrave
is, like the innumerable Border battles of that reign,
only shortly mentioned by historians; and although it
was a notable encounter, and is detailed by Isaac at
great length, it lies out of our way here. Let it suffice
that they skirmished cautiously for two days with various
success, and at last came to an engagement on a field right
opposite to the junction of the Tweed and Gala. After a
hard fought battle, Douglas' left wing was discomfited;
and just as he was arranging his force so as to cover the
retreat, an unaccountable confusion was noted among the
English ranks, which seemed to be engaged anew, and with
one another, there being no other army nigh. Douglas,
recalling his routed squadrons, faced about, but advanced
with caution, till he saw Musgrave's army broken and flying
in all directions. This gallant feat was accomplished by a
Sir John Gordon, who was on his way with seven hundred
fresh men to the assistance of Douglas; and as he came on
the English ranks behind at that important crisis, he broke
them at the first onset, and took Sir Thomas Musgrave
prisoner with his own hand.

  Thus far the affairs of Douglas wore the aspect of

prosperity – but a settled gloom hung over his mind; an oppression of spirits was apparent in every sentence that he uttered and every plan he suggested, and these were far from being traits of his wonted disposition. But the monk Benjamin had been with him again and again! – had been harrassing his soul with commissions and messages from the mansions of the dead; and one night he heard the voice of his lost and dearly regretted princess, speaking to him in his tent, as it were out of the canvas. Still the most solemn injunctions of secrecy were imposed on him, insomuch that he deemed himself not at liberty to open his mind to any one. Besides all this, the disconsolate Mary Kirkmichael had been constantly lingering nigh to him, and always presenting herself in the utmost agony of mind, to make enquiries about her royal mistress. That lady's appearance became so terrible to him that he was unable to bear it, and gave strict charges that she should not be suffered to come within the limits of his camp. But for all that, availing herself of her rank and her sex's privilege, she forced her way to him several times, and at every visit filled his soul with the most racking torments; so that, harrassed with *war* as he was, he found this his first intercourse with *women*, attended with ten times more distracting and grievous perils than the former. While, on the other hand, the heroes that visited the castle of Aikwood, even those who escaped, not including the wretched victims who remained behind, discovered, to their dear bought experience, that there were perils in nature infinitely superior to both.

It is now absolutely necessary to shorten the curate's narrative, to prevent this work running to an inordinate length; and though two of his tales have been left out already, the great events that follow must also be related in a style abbreviated, though not mangled by indistinctness.

After the intrepid Lord Musgrave had sacrificed his own life in order to save those of his only brother and the lady of his love, Clavering was unanimously chosen captain in his room, and every soldier took a new oath to him to die in defence of the fortress. The commission of which he accepted was a dismal one; but he entered into all the feelings of the famishing inmates in their hatred of the Scots, and implacable enmity against them – therefore, he was the very man for their purpose.

Every attempt of the besiegers to scale the walls of the castle, or to gain an entrance by fraud or force, had hitherto proved utterly abortive; the determined sons of England laughed at them, regarding them in no other light than as freaks of mere insanity, or the gambols of children. The fortress was impregnable with such heroes within, had they been supplied with sufficient stores of food and of arrows, both of which had long been exhausted; and though a small and welcome supply of the former had been obtained during the tempest and the flood which followed, for which they were obliged to the devil and Master Michael Scott, yet, like all the benefits derived from that quarter, it proved rather more hurtful than advantageous, for they devoured it with such avidity that the distemper, with which they had formerly been visited, broke out among them with greater violence than ever. Yet disregarding all these privations, which a looker-on would suppose might naturally tend to break the human heart and daunt the resolution of the boldest – with famine and pestilence both staring them in the face – they bound themselves by a new and fearful oath never to yield the fortress to the Scots while a man of them remained alive. Every new calamity acted but as a new spur to their resolution; and their food being again on the very eve of exhaustion, their whole concern was how to procure a new supply. Not that they valued their own lives or their own sufferings – these had for a good while been only a secondary consideration – but from the excruciating dread that they should die out, and the Scots attain possession of the fortress before Christmas.

The warders soon noted the alteration that had taken place in the beleaguering army. They perceived the ground that had formerly been occupied by the Angus men, and the Mar Highlanders, now taken up by the tall, athletic, and careless looking borderers, against whom they found their antipathy was not so mortal: and they had some surmisings of what really was the case, that a strong diversion had been made in their favours, that had drawn off their inveterate and hateful enemy Douglas from the siege. Every hour convinced them farther of the truth of this suggestion; for they perceived a laxness in the manner of conducting the blockade which they had not witnessed for many days, and all their conversation turned on the manner in which they ought to avail themselves of it. The carelessness of the besiegers themselves, or something subordinate thereto, soon furnished an opportunity to them of putting their policy once more to the test, and that by an adventure the most ardently desired. On the second day after the departure of Douglas the warder on the topmost tower perceived, on a rising ground two miles to the southward, about thirty head of cattle, that came gradually in view as a wing of a large drove might be supposed to do; and after they had fed for some time there, two men came before them and chased them back out of sight of the castle, as if a great oversight had been committed by letting them come in view of it. Notice of this important discovery was instantly given to the captain, and the news spreading among the garrison, many a long and longing look was cast from the battlements and loopholes of the high western tower that day. They were not cast in vain. Just toward the fall of evening they perceived a part of the drove appear again only a very short space from the castle, and they likewise perceived by their colours that they were a drove of English beasts which had been brought from their native pastures by the strong hand of rapine, for the supply of this new come border army. They perceived likewise that they approached the army by a concealed way, that the two glances they got of them were merely casual, and that they were very slightly guarded.

A council of war was immediately called, in which it was agreed, without one dissentient voice, that the garrison should make a sham sally at the eastern drawbridge, as if with intent to gain the city, in order that they might draw the attention of the besiegers to that point; and in the meantime the captain, with the choicest of the men were to march out by Teviot-bridge, of which the garrison had necessarily the sole possession, and endeavour to seize the prey. Thence they were to proceed westward, and try to elude the enemy's posts, or give them battle, if the former were found to be impracticable; but at all events, either to die or succeed in attaining that valuable supply, or a part of it. The success of the contest now turned on that single point as on a pivot; the balance was against them, but, that turned in their favours by an exertion of warrior prowess, they could then reckon on a complete triumph over their unappeasable foes.

Besides, every thing seemed to concur in support of their gallant expedition. The nights were dark even beyond their usual darkness at that gloomy season, and the moon did not arise till two in the morning. Both these circumstances were in their favour – the one in attaining possession of the prey unperceived, and the other in enabling them to fight their way home; for they knew that though they themselves might pass the strong Scottish posts favoured by the deep darkness, still it was impossible to bring the drove through them, and along the bridge, without a hard skirmish. The captain, therefore, gave command to the division left behind, that the more noise they heard of an engagement about the bridge of Teviot, and the gate toward the west, the more they should press their battle eastward, to divert the strength of the army to that quarter. Because on that side the Scots could make no impression, and the English could lose nothing there save a few lives, which they accounted of small avail; but if the expedition to the west failed, their cause was finally ruined.

That was a busy evening within the walls of Roxburgh, while all was quietness and indifference without. Within there was arming and disarming, for the suits of armour that once fitted these emaciated warriors would not now hang on their frames. There was grinding of swords, pointing of spears and ox-goads, and even the houses of the fort were cleared, with a provident concern seldom overlooked by Englishmen; and at eleven o'clock at night, by the convent matin bell, Clavering, with five hundred chosen men, well armed, issued silently from the garrison, creeping along the Teviot-bridge on their hands and knees. From that they proceeded westward in the most profound silence, and so close by the Scottish posts, that they heard them breathing and conversing together. One party crept up all the way within the water-brae, and the other, led by Clavering himself, past through between two Scottish posts, drawing themselves along the ground close on their breasts, and once or twice were obliged to squat close down, and lie silent for a considerable space, while the following dialogue passed between the sentinels.

'Od, Sandie Scott, think ye it can be true that the English are eating ane another?'

'There's nae doubt o't. I hear that they're snapping up five o' the fattest o' their number every day. They will eat themsels out bit by bit that gate.'

'Aih wow, man! I wad rather die o' hunger than pick the banes of ane acquaintance. Bursten devils, that they are!'

'Aha, Sandie, billie, ye dinna ken till ye be tried. A man will do ought or he die o' hunger. An do you ken, Sandie Scott, I think our captain has done wrang in bringing sae mony fat bullocks a' sae near the castle at ae time. Thae hungered louns will hae a haud o' some o' them, and maybe cut a wheen o' our throats into the bargain, some o' thir dark nights.'

'Now, ye see neighbour, I ken sae weel that our master never does the sma'est thing without some design, that I think he wants to wile out the English, and then kill them; and that he has brought a' thir braw stots o'er the border, just on the same principle that a fisher throws a bait into the water.'

'Na, na, Sandie, that canna be the case, for he has gi'en strict orders that no ane o' them be suffered to come within sight o' the castle. He just thinks the beasts canna be sae safe ony where else as beside himsel' and his lads. But hunger has sharp een, and I wadna wonder if this drove should lead to some hard tulzie.'

'Whisht! Godsake, haud your tongue! What's that I hear?'

'The English, I'll warrant you. If hunger hae clear een, fear has unco lang lugs. What was it that Sandie heard?'

'I heard a kind o' rubbing and thristing, as a fox or a foumart had been drawing himsel through a hole aneath the ground. Hilloa! What guard?'

'Howpasley and Gemelscleugh.'

'Watch weel. There's something stirring.'

'Not a mouse.'

'So say the sleeping foresters; but I can tell you, men o' Gemelscleuch and Howpasley, an there be nought stirring aboon the ground, the moudies are very busy aneath it the night. Clap close, and keep an ee on the withergloom. I had a heavy dream at nightfa', and I'm resolved no to close an ee. Come, neighbour, tell a tale, or say a rhame to keep us wauking.'

'Have ye heard the new ballant made by the rhiming dominie o' Selchrit, the queerest thing ever was heard? It begins this gate:

> The Devil he sat in Dornock tower,
>   And out at a slip-hole keekit he,
> And he saw three craws come yont the lift,
>   And they winged their flight to the Eildon tree.
> O whow, O whow, quo the muckle deil,
>   But yon's a sight that glads my ee,
> For I'll lay the steel-brander o' hell
>   There's a storm a-brewing in the west countrye.'

'Whisht, for heaven's sake! I heard the tod again, Hilloa! Gemelscleuch to the glaive! Have lug and hawk e'e, or there'll be news afore the morn that's unheard tell o' yet.'

'And that there will! Saint David be with us! and the blessed Saint Mary, the mother of God, be with us! Hist havering, say Benedicite.'

At that instant a sharp breeze arose which drowned the noise, and Clavering and his men passed fairly by on their perilous expedition. Beyond the next hollow they found the cattle all lying puffing and dozing on a round hill. An immense drove of them there seemed to be, for the hill appeared to be literally covered, but the night was as dark as pitch, and they could see nothing distinctly. Clavering gave his commands in a whisper to his chief men, to surround the whole drove, and drive them furiously, that by these means they might throw the enemy's lines into confusion. 'We have the advantage of the ground,' said he; 'the bridge is clear, and the gates open. Let us play the men for once, and our difficulties are all over. Providence has favoured us beyond what could have been calculated on. Our force is superior to that of our enemies on this side the river. On whatever side our column is attacked, let us keep a running fight, so as to push on and preserve the prey, and the day is our own: And now, Saint Anthony for the right!'

The men then formed themselves into a crescent behind the cattle six-line deep, and with club, goad, and spear pushed them on. There were a few dour lazy driving runts behind that bore all the thumps, but the bulk were high-spirited, and galloped off on the path toward Roxburgh with the utmost fury, insomuch that the delighted drivers never got a sight of them. They broke through the Scottish lines without either stop or stay. The alarm was instantly given, but a night muster is always attended with some delay. So the English thought – so they said; and to their great joy they found their suggestions realized; for not till the last cow was past the strong line of posts on the height were they attacked by the Scots. But then, indeed the Gemelscleuch and Howpasley men set upon them with unparallelled fury, and being every five minutes joined by more of their companions, they pressed hard upon the English, who, being obliged to keep up a retreating battle, fell thick on the brae beyond the bridge. The brave and judicious Longspeare himself led the attack, and behaved like a lion; for though wounded in three different places of the body, he fought in the front of the main battle all that night.

The Scots, to the utter amazement of their enemies, never once offered to stop the cattle, but merely attacking the English crescent behind, drove them and cattle and all towards the bridge. This Clavering and his chief men attributed wholly to the surprise by which the Scots were taken; and when the former saw the dark column of cattle take the bridge, he thanked the God of heaven, the blessed Virgin, and all the saints whose names were known to him, for such a wonderful success and merciful deliverance. The English host then raised such a shout of triumph that the echoes called from the castled towers to the forest, and from the forest to the distant rocks. The Scots soon joined in it with equal enthusiasm; and the two main armies then engaged at the eastern gate, also joined their voices to the general chorus. They gray friars of Roxburgh, and the Benedictine monks of Kelso, raised their heads from their flinty pillows, committed themselves to heaven, and deplored the madness and folly of the men of the world. The city dames wept and prayed, and the men ran to head-quarters to learn the cause of the uproar. The sounds were actually heard in the camp of Douglas, at the distance of sixteen miles; and when this was reported to him next morning, he said, 'There was the Redhough on the ramparts of Roxburgh!'

But man's thoughts are vanity! He cannot judge of events so as to calculate on what is to happen from one moment to another: incidents of the slightest moment so often having the effect of overturning the greatest and most momentous enterprizes. Never was there one so nearly overturned as this, although it was not once thought of till afterwards – and it was on this wise: There was a strong guard of English placed at the south end of the bridge, to guide the foremost of the drove on to it, or help to cut a way for the cattle through such troops as might interpose. The cattle, as was said, came galloping furiously without intervention, and, as if led by an unseen providence, took the bridge with all their vigour, the battle being then raging behind them, and the shouts beginning to rend the sky. This guard had nothing to do, of course, but to open into two lines, and give them head. But at the end of the bridge there was a deep puddle, and among the men there chanced to be a little boy, who was running about and thrashing the cattle as they went through this puddle, which made them spring up the arch with redoubled velocity, which the urchin thought good sport. But in the midst of this frolic he bolted away at once with such velocity that he had almost overthrown one of the men in the file, and as he ran he cried out, 'Lord, saw ever ony mortal the like o' that?' 'What was it, rash idiot?' said the man. 'Grace and mercy, man, did you not see how yon great black stott stood straight up on his hind legs and waded the pool?' said the boy. 'Take that to clear your eyes, impertinent brat,' said the man, and gave him a blow with his fist that made him run away howling and crying, always repeating as he went, 'I'll tell your captain – now! 'at will I that – now!'

The combat behind the cattle thickened apace. The English were sore borne down on the hill, but when they came to the little plain at the bridge-end they stood firm, and gave as hard blows as they got. They had fairly gained their aim, and their spirits, so long depressed, mounted to an unusual height. The last lingering hoof of the whole countless drove was now on the arch, and they could calculate on holding out the fortress against their hated foes not only till Christmas, but till that time twelvemonth.

Their shouts of joy were redoubled. So also were those of the Scots. 'The people are mad!' said they, 'thus to shout for their own loss and their own defeat. It is a small trait of the cursed perversity of the whole nation!'

The English narrowed their front and narrowed their front still as their files found room on the arch of the bridge, which was long and narrow, and very steep at the south end, that rose directly from the plain. But the road up to the castle by the two tremendous iron gates was likewise exceedingly steep, and went by a winding ascent, so that the latter end of the drove, those dull driving ones that bore all the strokes, got very slowly up, and with great difficulty. There was a guard of considerable strength left in this gateway by Clavering, lest any attempt should be made by the enemy to enter in his absence. But these men had strict charges to clear the way for the cattle, and help to drive the foremost ones up the steep. The fore part of the drove however came up the steep with such main fury, that the men were glad to clear a way for them, by flying out of the path, up to the citadel. There was not a man left in the gateway, save two at each of the iron portcullises, and these stood in deep niches of the wall, out of all danger. Each of these men held the end of a chain that was twisted round an immense bolt in the wall – and these bolts, Isaac says, are to be seen sticking to this day. On untwisting this chain the portcullises fell down, and when they were to raise up it was done with levers. Well, as the two outermost men stood in their niches, holding by the ends of their chains, they observed, that two of the oxen that first came in, nay the very first two that came in, turned round their ugly heads, leaned their sides to the wall, and kept in their places, the one on the one side and the other on the other, till the whole drove passed them. The men could not move from their posts to drive them on with the rest, but they wondered at the beasts; and the one cried to the other, 'What can ail them two chaps?' 'O them are two tired ones,' said the other: 'Dom them for two ugly monsters! they look as them hod been dead and roosen again.'

At length, by dint of sore driving and beating, the last hoof of the Warden's choice drove passed inward through the castle gate of Roxburgh, for the maintenance of his irascible enemies. Could any thing be so unfortunate? or how was he to set up his face, and answer to the Douglas now? But the Redhough was determined that he would set up his face and answer to the Douglas and his country too, as well as to his kinsmen and followers, whom he valued highest of all. Just as the last lazy cow crossed the gate, and when the triumphant shouts of the English were at the loudest, the two great lubberly oxen that stood shaking their ugly heads, and leaning against the wall, ripped up their own bellies; and out of two stuffed hides two most ingenious cases, started up two no less men than Sir Ringan Redhough and his doughty friend Charlie Scott of Yardbire. Off went the heads of the two porters in one moment, and down came the portcullis with a thundering rattle, and a clank that made the foundations of the gate shake. 'Now, southron lads, haud ye there!' cried the Redhough: 'Time about is fair play. Keep ye the outside o' the door threshold as lang as ye hae gart us keep it.'

They next went up and seized the other two porters, whom they saved alive, to teach them how to bolt, bar, open, and shut the gates; but the men had taken the oaths with the rest, and remained obstinate. No threatening could make them move either finger or tongue except in mockery, which provoked the Redhough so that he despatched them likewise. On reaching the great square the Warden found his men in peaceable possession. Six score brave chosen men had entered among the cattle, each in a stuffed ox or cow hide, and had now like their captain cast their sloughs, and stood armed at all points to execute his commands. They found nothing to do, save a prodigious difficulty in working their way from the western to the eastern gate. There were so many turnings and windings; so many doors and wickets; so many ascents and descents – that an army might have gained possession of the one end and yet have been kept out of the other for years. But the surprise here was so complete, that the Borderers had in fact nothing to do but to keep the possession, thus obtained in so easy and at the same time so gallant a style. The shouts that arose from the western battle had so much encouraged those at the eastern gate, that they had sallied out, and attacking the besiegers sword in hand, had driven them back within their strong line of defence. This retreat was a part of the plan of the Scots, to draw off the remaining force from the gate, and while they were in the hottest of the skirmish, down came Redhough and his lads from the interior of the castle behind them, cut down the few guards about the entrance and the draw-bridge with ease, and having raised that, and shut the double gates on that quarter likewise, he placed the Armstrongs there as a guard, and returned into the interior, still uncertain what enemies he had to combat within.

This mighty fortress was, from the one drawbridge to the other, a full quarter of a mile in length, walled and moated round, and contained seven distinct square or castles, every one of which was a fortress of itself. But the strongest of all was the division on the western part, which was denominated the citadel, and had gates and bars of its own, and towers that rose far above the rest. Into this strong place the sole remnant of the English soldiers had retreated, which consisted merely of the guard that kept the western porch and made way for the cattle, a few stragglers beside, and some official people that kept always within. Through every other part of the castle the Scots found free passage; and by the time the moon had been risen for an hour, the shouts of 'A Douglas! a Douglas! a Redhough! a Redhough!' were heard from every part of the walls, excepting the western tower. There indeed a faint and subdued shout announced at intervals the name of the King of England, for it was now no more a Musgrave! and as for Clavering they wist not whether he was dead or alive, taken or at liberty.

When the first ranks of the Englishmen that came up behind the cattle saw the gates shut against them, they took it for some accident, or some mistake that the porters had fallen into, on listening to the shouts of the adverse parties: but after calling and remonstrating to no purpose, they began to suspect that there was treason at the bottom of it, and the whisper of treason spread among that part of the forces which was now forced against the gate. They could do nothing; for they neither had room to fight nor fly, and they knew not whom to suspect, or what had befallen them. As for those at the farther end of the bridge, they were so hotly engaged with their opponents, that they had little time to consider any thing; but finding themselves fixed to the spot, and no movement making toward the gate, they conceived that something there was wrong, which retarded the regular entrance of the troops for so long a time. They now fought only three to three abreast on the steep arch of the bridge, down which the English drove the Scots six or seven times, the latter always returning to the charge with that vigour which a certainty of success inspires. Clavering fought them in the rear, and in the hottest of the battle still encouraging his men to deeds of desperate valour, little weening how matters went within. But when the names of the Scottish chiefs were resounded from the walls, every heart among the English was chilled, and every arm unnerved in one instant. They had no conception how the thing could have happened; it appeared so far beyond all human power to have effected it, that it was several hours before it gained general credit among them. They had kept the fortress so long, with so little dread of its being wrested from them, and withal suffered so much in it, that they could not believe the evidence of their senses, that by a course of events entirely of their own planning, they should be all without the walls, and the Scots within. It was like a work of enchantment. Like some of the last inconceivable works of the spirits of divination.

The Scots could make no impression on them upon that long narrow bridge; but they could not long stand cooped up there; and when they saw that all hope was lost of regaining entrance, they threw themselves over a high parapet, and took possession of the steep bank between the bottom of the southern wall and the river Teviot. The river being dammed below, it stood like a frith round the bottom of this bank, which was so steep that they could not stand on it, but were obliged to clamber alongst it on their hands and feet. Escape being impracticable, the Scots suffered them to take possession of that bank undisputed, and to keep it, supposing they must surrender next day; but a great number were slain before the latter end of the train was disentangled of the bridge.

The Scots had now free access to the gate, into which Gemelscleuch and Howpasley were admitted. The Warden embraced them, and thanked them for their wise counsel, as well as their great bravery; and they again set about traversing and surveying the fortress, concerning which Charlie Scott said, 'It wad tak a man a year and a day to find out a' the turnings and windings about it.'

The battle at the eastern draw-bridge had continued from midnight without intermission; and after the break of day our chiefs witnessed a scene from the walls that was without a parallel. That division of the Scots army was composed of Douglas' men, being the same troops that were there before, and they were commanded by Sir James Douglas of Dalkeith. That knight got private intelligence of the Warden's intention to storm the castle, by what means he knew not, but resolved to hold himself in readiness; and, as he was desired, when the sortie was made, he retreated at first, drawing them off from the gate. When the cry arose that the castle was taken, his men became frantic with joy, and resolute on taking ample vengeance on their enemies, they burst upon them without regularity, making great havock, and at the same time throwing away many of their own lives. Sir James with great difficulty restrained them, called a parley, and offered the expelled garrison quarter; but they returned for answer, that they weened he had called the parley to ask quarter of them, and they had determined to refuse it. They concluded by telling him to see to himself, and insult them no more by such messages, for as yet he knew not with whom he was warring. The battle was then renewed by the light of the moon with greater fury than ever; they fought like baited bears, with recklessness of life and the silence of death. Deadly hate was in every thrust, and the last words of every falling warrior were, 'Have at them yet.'

When the day light arose, the English fought within a semicircular wall of mangled carcasses; for, grievous to relate, they were not corpses; yet were they piled in a heap higher than a man's height, which was moving with agonized life from top to bottom, and from the one end to the other; for the men having all fallen by sword wounds, few of them were quite dead. The English were now reduced to a small number, yet, in the strife, their ardour seemed to prevail over that of their opponents. The Border chiefs, inured as they were to war, stood amazed, and even shocked, at the scene presented to their view. Yardbire was the first to deprecate it in these words: 'Gude faith, Sirs, it strikes me, that this is rather carrying war to an extremity.'

'Rescue! rescue!' shouted the Warden: 'Give quarter to these men for my sake. I will pay their ransom myself.'

When the Douglas' vassals heard this, they lowered the points of their swords, and drew back from the slaughter, commanding the English to ground their weapons. The latter consulted together for a few minutes, and void of all dread, save that of being obliged to submit to the Scots, they broke with one consent over the pile of human bodies, and, carrying destruction before them, opened a way into the middle of the Scottish columns; nor ceased they fighting until every man of them was cut down. The rest of the English army were in a fold. Escape was impossible. Ten men could have prevented it on all sides, yet for a whole day and night did they hold their tenure of that perpendicular bank, although before the evening many were losing their holds, and rolling into the river from exhaustion. Then the sudden immersion arousing them somewhat from their torpor, scores of them might be seen at a time crawling to the side of the water, and endeavouring to clamber once more up the bank; but at last they sunk back into the deep, and their last breath arose to the surface in small chains of fetid air bubbles. No one knew what became of the young and intrepid Clavering – at what time, or in what place he fell; and without a head as these men were, it was not till the second morning, when the breath of revenge had cooled, and after much expostulation on the part of the conquerors, that the wretched remnant yielded themselves prisoners of war, and were all suffered to depart on their parole, with high encomiums on their valour. But these commendations were received with the gall of bitterness; and none of them could tell, when they went home, how or by what means they were expelled.

The Warden and his men now set themselves with all their endeavour to take the citadel; and, feebly as it was defended, it cost them no little trouble. It is probable that it might have held out a few days longer, but when Douglas and his army were seen approaching on their return from the battle, the impatience of the Borderers could be no longer restrained; and Yardbire, with a remnant of his Olivers, Potts, and Laidlaws, scaled the wall in the faces of the enemy, who had scarcely power left to cleave a head without a helmet, and throwing themselves into the square, became masters of the gate in a few minutes; so that before Douglas reached the top of the hill of Barns, his colours were placed on the topmost tower of the citadel.

It may easily be conceived with what joy, wonder, and admiration he gazed on this phenomenon. Joy that his broad lands and possessions were thus insured to him, of which for some time past he scarcely retained a hope; and admiration how that indefatigable chief had accomplished, in a few days, that which he had exerted himself in vain to accomplish for the space of as many months. The idea of being so far outdone in policy was without doubt somewhat bitter to the palate of a Douglas, for never till this day can they brook a competitor in the field; but, considering how matters stood, it would have been the worst of policy to have let such a feeling appear. Douglas therefore testified the highest satisfaction, extolling the Warden's head to conceive and hand to accomplish, in terms such as he had never been heard to utter. 'Glorious Redhough! unparallelled Redhough!' exclaimed he again and again: 'Thou and thy lads are the men to trust.'

The chief received him at the castle gate, welcoming him in jocular terms of high chivalry to the castle of Roxburgh, which he took care always to denominate 'my castle.' This was soon noted by the Douglas; and as soon as they entered the governor's house in the citadel, Douglas made over to him, by regular deeds and instruments, the seven first baronies he chose to name. This document, together with the royal charters confirming it, is extant, and in the possession of one of the Warden's lineal descendants at this day. On receiving this grant, signed, sealed, and witnessed, Sir Ringan delivered over the keys of the castle to the Earl of Douglas and Mar, and the two exchanged seats at the table. Douglas also conferred the honours of knighthood on Charlie Scott, Simon Longspeare, and John of Howpasley; while Sir Ringan bestowed one of his new baronies on each of these brave gentlemen in support of their new dignities, burdened only with a few additional servitudes. On his right hand hero, the hereditary claimant of the post of honour, he conferred the barony of Raeburn and Craik, that he might thenceforward be the natural head of his hard-headed Olivers and skrae-shankit Laidlaws. To Long-speare he gave Temadale; and to Howpasley, Phingland and Langshaw. When Charlie first rose from his knee, and was saluted as Sir Charles Scott of Raeburn and Yardbire, he appeared quite cast down, and could not answer a word. It was supposed that his grateful heart was overcome with the thought that the reward bestowed on him by his generous chief had been far above his merits.

The news of the capture were transmitted to court with all expedition; on which King Robert returned word, that he would, with his queen, visit the Douglas in the castle of Roxburgh, and there, in the presence of the royal family, and the nobles of the court, confer on him his daughter's hand in marriage, along with such other royal grants and privileges as his high gallantry and chivalrous spirit deserved. He added, that he had just been apprized by his consort, that his daughter, the princess Margaret, had been for some time living in close concealment in the vicinity of Roxburgh, watching the progress of her lover with a devotion peculiar to her ardent and affectionate nature. If the Douglas was aware of this, which the King had some reasons for supposing, he requested that he would defer seeing her until in the presence of her royal parents. There was a thrust indeed! An eclaircissement was approaching too much for man to bear—. But that heart-rending catastrophe must be left to the next chapter. In the meantime, for perspicuity's sake, we must relate how this grand device of the Warden's originated, by which the castle was won, and himself and followers honoured and enriched.

It was wholly owing to the weird read by the great enchanter Master Michael Scott. So that though the reader must have felt (as the editor did in a very peculiar manner,) that Isaac kept his guests too long in that horrible place the castle of Aikwood, it will now appear that not one iota of that long interlude of his could have been omitted; for till the weird was read, and the transformation consummated, the embassy could not depart – and unless these had been effected, the castle could not have been taken. The editor, for brevity's sake left out both the youth's and maiden's characteristic tales, which shall appear by and by, but more he durst not cancel.

When the passage out of the book of fate was repeated to Sir Ringan, he never for a moment doubted either its truth or fulfilment, provided he and his friends could discover its true meaning. But the words were wrapt in mystery; and, when conjoined with the enchantment practised on his men, were for a long time so completely unintelligible, that all save Sir Ringan himself, and his echo Dickie of Dryhope, gave up the hope of reconciling the given destiny with reason or common sense. As for the friar, he entered his protest against paying any regard to it from the beginning, on the principle that all the Master's powers and foreknowledge were deputed to him by subordinate and malevolent spirits, and that good could not arise out of evil. The Warden's philosophy, on the other hand, taught him to estimate facts and knowledge as he found them developed among mankind, without enquiring too nicely into the spirit of their origin; for the more deeply that was wrapt in mystery, the more powerful was its sway over his imagination. Charlie Scott felt much disposed to coincide with his master in these principles, but in all deep matters he was diffident in offering his advice or sentiments. He, however, hit upon the right cue in this instance, and that by the most natural combination of ideas that ever presented themselves to mortal man. The right understanding of the prophecy was about to be given up in despair. The intervals of silence during the discussion were becoming longer and longer each time. It was in order to break one of these, rather than to impose his advice on his chief, that Charlie ventured to deliver himself as follows: 'Gude faith, my masters, I see nothing for it, but that we get Master Michael Scott to turn us into fat owsen again, or bulls, or stotts, or what ye like. Then the English will drive us a' gladly into the castle for marts to their beef barrels. But when we are fairly in, we wad need the gospel friar to change us to men again, or, gude faith, we wad be in a bad predicament. But I hae some faith to put in auld Michael's power, (as I hae good right,) and gin that could be done as he seemed to hint, by the blood of Bruce! but we wad dowss their doublets for them.'

'Might we not rather disguise ourselves as cattle, cousin?' said Howpasley.

'I have seen our jugglers and mountebank players,' said

Long-speare, 'disguise themselves as a lion, a tiger, a bear, a wolf, and even as a great serpent, and dragon, so that I myself took them for these animals.'

'Why then may not we disguise ourselves as oxen, so that we may pass for them in a dark night?' said the Warden.

'Ay, in a dark night,' said Dickie; 'what is to hinder us? If we but walk on all four we will pass with hungry men for oxen in a dark night.'

Thus was the hint given, which was improved on as above related, till it effected the desire and important event, the taking of Roxburgh castle, and that in the most masterly and prudent style ever conceived by man. They had a small drove of cattle collected, as well as hides; but the disguised ones took care to keep in the front or the middle of these, in short on the side farthest from an Englishman. The one who walked through the dub in an upright posture, had not perceived the shabby boy so near him.

Abundance of all the good things that the kingdom could produce were now poured into the castle with all expedition; and every preparation made for the reception of the King and Queen of Scotland. The carnage had been so great at the two gates that night the fortress was taken, that the citizens of Roxburgh, as well as the three establishments of monks and friars in the vicinity, besought of Douglas that the slain might not be buried nigh to the city, for fear of infection; and if this was granted, they proffered to be at the sole charge of removing and burying them with all holy observances. This was readily granted, and they were removed to a little plain behind the present village, where thousands of their bones have lately been dug up. The burying continued for three days.

CHAPTER TWENTY-NINE

O I hae seen the gude auld day,
    The day o' pride and chieftain glory,
When royal Stuarts bore the sway,
    And ne'er heard tell o' Whig nor Tory.
Though lyart be my locks and gray,
    And eild has crook'd me down – what matter?
I'll dance and sing ae ither day,
    That day our King comes o'er the water.

Jacobite Song

FROM THE TIME of the taking of the castle until the arrival of King Robert, was an interval of high festivity. The Border chiefs and yeomen went home to their respective places of abode with abundant spoil, having been loaded with rich presents from the Douglas, as well as their share of Sir Ringan's numberless booties, which he always divided among them with great liberality; and it was computed that, in the course of that predatory warfare, he drove thirty thousand domestic animals out of the English territory. The Scottish Border districts were never so well stocked before. For a century previous to that, they had lain waste, having been entirely depopulated, and left no better than a hunting forest. That reign enriched them, and its happy effects have never since been obliterated.

Among other things that happened in this joyful interval, old Peter Chisholm received a message one day, informing him that the stranger to whom he had betrothed his daughter would appear next day to claim the fulfilment of his promise.

'They'll eat up every thing that's within the house,' said Peter: 'If he will have her, it wad suit better for us to meet them at Hawick. The half o' the expences there wad lye to him at ony rate; and if he made weel through wi' his hides, mayhap he wad pay the halewort. He's a brave chield enough, it wad appear; but I wish he had fawn aff the tap o' his humphed ill-smelled hides, and broken the bane o' his neck; for it will be a wae sight to me to see the flower of a' the Chisholms gang away wi' an English cadger. Oh, wae be to the day!'

'What is a man but his word, father?' said Dan. 'I think the gallant way in which the stranger behaved entitles him well, not only to the flower o' the Chisholms, but to the best in the house beside.'

'Ay, ay, that's aye the gate! fling away! fling away! till ye'll soon fling away every plack your auld father has gathered for ye. But, hark ye, callant Dan: Gin ye will stand by me, I'll gainsay the fellow yet, and refuse to gie him my Bess.'

'Hear what Bess says hersel,' said Dan, 'and then I'll gie my answer.'

Bess was sent for, who declared not only her willing-ness, but her resolution to abide by her father's agree-ment; but, added, that if a better came before him, and made her an offer, she would not wait a minute on her leather-merchant.

'Heard ever ony body the like o' that?' said Peter: 'What trow ye is the chance for that? How lang hae ye hung on the tree wi' a red cheek an' a ripe lip, and never man to streek out the hand to pu' ye? There was aince a neighbour I had some hopes o'; an' he has a good heart too, for a' his jibes, an ane durst but tell him!'

Peter said these last words to himself, as he was turning about to leave the apartment – for he was at that time forming in his mind one of those superlative schemes which strike dotage as plans of the mightiest and most acute device, but which youth and energy laugh at. This was no other than to be early astir next morning, and, before any of his family was aware, gallop over to Craik, a matter of seven miles, and beg of Will Laidlaw to come and run off with his daughter before she fell into the hands of an English skinman. This grand scheme he actually put in practice, but met Laidlaw and his jovial party by the way, who wondered not a little when they saw old Pate coming gallopping up the Fanesh ridge, having his great pike staff heaved over his shoulder, with which he was every now and then saluting the far loin of his mare, and that with an energy that made all his accoutrements wallop. He never perceived the bridal party till close on them, and till he was asked by half a score voices at once, 'What's the great haste, Castleweary! Where are ye gawn at sic a rate sae early in the morning? Are your ha's burnt? Are your cattle driven? Have the Ha's and the Reids been o'er the fells aince mair?' And many other such questions were put, before Peter got a word spoken or a thought thought. He only bit his lip, and looked very angry, at being caught in such a plight. But seeing Will Laidlaw at the head of his kinsmen, he took him aside, and imparted his grand secret. Will's sides were like to burst with laughter. He, however, contained himself, while Peter went on 'But ye had better turn a' that clan again, wha hae nought ado at a' wi' us but put things to waste. The less din about the thing the better.'

'But how are we to answer the skin-merchant when he comes then, Castleweary? That tremendous buyer of hides will hew us all to pieces.'

'Ay, ye maun just take a' the blame on yoursels, you and Bess. He'll no mak muckle at the Laidlaw's hands, or he'll do what never ony did afore him.'

'I certainly have the greatest respect for your daughter; but times are hard and dangerous, and I have nae great opinion o' marriage.'

'Come, now, I like to hear that; for ye ken fock maun ay read a Laidlaw backward; and if the times are hard, I shall be satisfied with a very small dowry. Perhaps the matter o' ten tup hogs aff the Criblaw, sax owsen aff Hosecot, and—

'Hold there, my old friend; and I will run all risks, and take away your daughter Elizabeth; let the skin-man look to himself.'

'Weel, God bless ye wi' her. Ye'll get the flower of a' the Chisholms, and the best bairn o' the bike.'

Bess was a winsome and a blithe bride that day, and though the wounds she received in the engagement with the marauders were not quite whole, she danced the best at the wedding, and was the first that lighted on Craik-green. Dan entertained his fellow-soldiers nobly; but old Peter was terribly in the fidgets, not only at the huge waste of meat and drink that he now saw going on, but for the fear of the arrival of the outrageous and ill-used hide-merchant, and never till his dying day could he be brought to identify his son-in-law with the stranger to whom he first promised his daughter. But for many a day, when the dogs barked, he hasted out in great agitation, lest the dealer in skins and his associates should come upon him unawares. Sandie Pott having found a very kind, attentive, and, withal, a very indulgent nurse, in the younger daughter, May Chisholm, there chanced two weddings at Castleweary on the same day.

Among other matters of that eventful period, Isaac the curate mentions also a petition of the friar to Sir Ringan, that he would use his interest to get the youthful bard, who had come an adventurer into his army, replaced in his rights of the lordship of Ravensworth; and likewise that he would grant him the captive maid, Delany, for his bride. These important connections had never before come to the Warden's ears; and when he heard the extraordinary adventures, and early misfortunes of the twain, he manifested the greatest concern for their welfare. But the maid, by the laws of those days, was the right and property of Sir Charles Scott, who seemed unwilling to part with her, and she not less so to be divided from him, now that his late honours became him so well. This was a distressing consideration to the poet, and he would in nowise leave her, to lay claim to his paternal estate, till he saw how matters would turn in his favour. But the friar still encouraged him, assuring him, 'that he should be restored to the house and to the inheritance of his fathers; and that the fairest among the daughters of women, even the sole remaining stem of the house of Galli the scribe, should be unto him as a spouse and a comforter.'

But among all the festivities at Roxburgh, and all the mighty preparations for the reception of royalty, and the spending of the Christmas holidays in such company, the countenance of Douglas was manifestly overcast. He affected mirth and gaiety, but a hideous and terrific gloom frequently settled on his dark manly countenance. The princess's shameful and untimely death hung heavy on his mind, and the secret of it still heavier. His conscience upbraided him, not with any blame in the matter, for he was alike ignorant of the rank and sex of his fantastical page: But her devotion to his cause and person; the manner in which she had exerted herself by putting her rival into his hands; the love-tokens slily given to him by her own dear self; her admonitory letters; and all her whimsical and teazing inuendos, came over his mind, and combined in rendering her memory ten times dearer to him than ever he conceived that of human being could have been. And then, how was all this requited? By bad humour, disrespect, and a total disregard of her danger and sufferings. The most enthusiastic, affectionate, and accomplished lady of the age in which she lived, was suffered to be put down as a common criminal, without one effort being made to save her; and that delicate and beautiful form thrust down into a common charnel-house among the vulgar dead. Knowing all these things as he did, how could he again behold her royal parents? and knowing all these things as he did, why had he not related the lamentable facts as they had happened, and conducted himself accordingly? There was fixed the acme of his dilemma. The detail of that lady's love and fate rose before his mind's eye, like a dark unseemly arch, of which this was the keystone; and there was a power stood above it that held his soul in controul, and beyond that he could not pass. Was it indeed true, that the spirit of his royal and beloved mistress walked the earth, and from day to day laid her stern behests upon him? And could it be that such a spirit attended upon him in his most secret retirements; and, though unseen, watched over all his motions, words, and actions? Or how else could the very thoughts and purposes of his heart, together with his most secret transactions, be repeated to him by this holy monk? Nay, though he had never actually seen this apparition, he had heard his mistress's voice one night speaking to him as from behind the hangings, and charging him, as he respected his own and her soul's welfare, to keep her fate concealed from all flesh.

Whenever the Douglas got leisure to think at all, amid the hurry of his military duties, these cogitations preyed on his mind; and one night when they had thrown him into a deep reverie, the monk Benjamin was announced.

'I cannot see him to-night: Tell him to come and speak with me tomorrow,' said Douglas.

'He craves only a few moments audience, Lord of Douglas; and he says, that, unless he is admitted, a visitor of another nature will wait on you forthwith.'

'What is the meaning of this?' said Douglas: 'Must my privacy be broken in upon, and my mind placed on the rack, at the pleasure of every fanatical devotee? Tell him that I will not be disturbed to-night. But – I think not what I am saying. Admit him. Well, reverend and holy father – madman rather! What is your important business with me?'

'That saintly vision has again been with me.'

'Out upon thee, maniac and liar! There has been no such thing with thee; and thou hast trumped up a story in order to keep the power of the Douglas under thy ghostly and interested controul.'

'If I am a visionary, Lord, it is for thyself to judge. I speak nothing as of myself, but the words of one that has sent me. If thou darest say they are the visions of a maniac, in future I keep them to myself, and do you abide by the consequences.'

'Thinkest thou that I will not, or that I dare not abide by any consequences? Hence! Begone!'

'Rash precipitate man! thou shalt repent this! What interest can I possibly have in whispering these truths in thine ear? Did I ever ask or hint at a favour from thee? Or was aught ever, save thy own welfare, the purport of my messages? Adieu, my lord! There must another commissioner wait on you presently, and one who will elude the most vigilant of your sentinels.'

'Stay, Benjamin: Thou art, indeed, blameless. If thou hast ought to warn me of, say it and have done, for I am not in a mood to be trifled with.'

'I have been bid to caution you to look to yourself, for that there is treason within the walls of this castle. Will you answer me one or two queries truly and seriously, that I may know whether the being that commissioned me be a true spirit or a false one?'

'I will.'

'Have you got a private offer to a prodigious amount for the ransom of Lady Jane Howard?'

'Monk, thou hast had this from hell—. I have.'

'Which thou hast rejected, with the secret intent of asking

her in marriage yourself, should circumstances concur to favour the device?'

'It is false! – false as the source whence thou hadst it.'

'Ah! Then have I done! my informant is a false one.'

'Or, if I had, it was some passing thought, which no man can gainsay, and for which none are accountable.'

'Neither is it true that you visited her in disguise last night?'

The Douglas gazed upon the monk in silence, with an eye in which there was an unnatural gleam of madness. He drew his breath three times, as if he would have spoken, but made no answer. The monk continued: 'If these are truths, then list to the following behest – if they are false thou needest not regard it: There is a conspiracy among thy people for the rescue of Lady Jane. They have been bribed by unheard-of rewards. Thy guards are of course to be cut down, otherwise the rescue cannot be effected; and if thy own head is added to the convoy, the guerdons are all to be doubled.'

The Douglas started to his feet, and held up both his hands: 'By the blessed Virgin it is true!' exclaimed he – 'True every word of it! There have been petitions made to me for the use of certain keys already. Ay, and I have granted some of them too. I see through a part of the conspiracy. But I'll sift the traitors! I'll make carrion of them.'

'If I am rightly informed, it may yet be prevented without being made manifest, which would be greatly preferable. Beware of Kinlossie. And list, for my time is expired: If you value your own name, see not the face of Lady Jane again, till you present her to your sovereign.'

The monk retired with precipitation, and left the Douglas overwhelmed with tumultuary and adverse passions. 'Still the Lady Jane Howard!' said he to himself: 'Nothing but the Lady Jane Howard! Is it possible this can be an agent of hers? But the inference contradicts the whole scope and tendency of his missions. I must investigate this matter without delay.' He raised his small bugle to his mouth, for in those days that answered all the purposes of a house bell, and many more. Every officer in castle or camp knew, by the blast blown, when his personal attendance was required. Douglas lifted his to his mouth

– but before he sounded it, the knight in waiting announced 'a lady.' No bolder heart than that of Douglas beat in a Scottish bosom. Nevertheless it quaked; for he thought of the threatening of the monk, that another commissioner should visit him, whom his guards should not be able to repel. His agitation was now wrought up to the highest pitch, for he attempted to pronounce some words, of which the knight knew not the import – probably it was a command to expel her, or to call in some guards; but before the order could be understood or complied with, the lady herself entered. 'There she is, my lord!' said the knight in a whisper; 'and none of us know whence or how she came hither.'

The lady came slowly by, and the knight retired with all speed. She bore indeed the figure and form of the late princess, but the roses of youth and beauty were gone, and in their room a clayey paleness pervaded the features, which were even whiter than the cambric by which the face was surrounded. The figure held up its right hand as it advanced, and fixed its eyes on the earl; but no man to this day ever knew any thing farther of that conference. The knight in waiting, shortly after he had retired, heard a noise within as of a man choking and endeavouring to cry out; and, bringing two more attendants with him, they all three rushed into the apartment, and found the Douglas fallen back on the embroidered couch in a state of mental abstraction, or rather of total insensibility, and the lady was gone. They immediately applied themselves to the restoration of their lord, which they effected in a short time. Animation soon returned, but reason wavered in a state of instability for several hours. During that period he had for a number of times inquired who admitted that stranger, or who saw her depart? The men assuring him each time, that no one saw her till she was observed standing in the anti-chamber; and that none was either admitted into the citadel or seen depart, save the starveling monk who attended him frequently as his confessor. 'There has been another lady,' they added, begging admission to your presence for a whole day and night, which has always been refused her, in consequence of your peremptory order. She has at the last resorted to the means always at a woman's command, tears and threatenings; and she vows, that if she is not admitted to an audience, you shall dearly repent it.'

'What, another still?' said the Douglas: 'No, I'll see no more women today, nor tomorrow, nor next day. Do you know, Eveldon, what I think of women?'

'No, Lord Douglas, but well what I think of them myself, which is, that they are nature's masterpieces.'

'The pests of society, Eveldon. I deem them subordinate creatures, created solely for man's disquietude. The warrior is naturally surrounded by dangers; but, till he engages with women, he rises superior to them all; it is then that his troubles and perils begin. No, I'll see no more women tonight.'

'Might I advise, my lord, it would be, that you should give her admission. It appears so strange to see a lovely and most courtly dame standing weeping at your gate. The very commonest of the people sympathise with her, and blame your neglect. Beshrew me, if any knight in the realm would refuse such a suit; no, not the King himself.'

'Do you think, Sir John of Eveldon, that I can submit to be ruled by women and their agents? I, who never held them as ought save as beings formed for man's pleasures or his interests. My hands are free of their blood, Sir John – my heart, if ever it was in bonds, is now emancipated; and yet, by their means, has my life of late been held in thraldom.'

'Say that I may admit this dame, my lord.'

'Well, be it so, and let us be quit of her. In the mean time, let the guards be tripled, and stand to your arms. I have had strange intelligence to-night; if true, there will be a dangerous commotion in less than an hour hence.'

'The forces of the two kingdoms cannot disturb you here to-night, Lord Douglas.'

'See to it – there is treason within our walls. Who are on guard?'

'The Gordons, and Lindsay of Kinlossie's men.'

'The Gordons I can trust – let the others be changed without delay, Sir John, and see them consorted to the camp—. Call up the Douglasses of the Dales, and let them look to themselves. Admit that petitioner in whom you are so much interested, and call me on the slightest appearance of insubordination.'

Sir John did as he was commanded, and forthwith introduced Mary Kirkmichael of Balmedie. The impatience and mortification that the Douglas manifested under this trial is not to be described, for he had promised to give her information of her royal mistress as soon as he had it in his power, and yet he neither had the heart nor the resolution, after the charges he had received of secrecy, to tell her of her mistress' woeful fate. At Mary's first entrance into his presence, she rushed forward and kneeled at his feet, crying, in the most passionate manner, 'O, my dear lord, tell me what has become of my mistress. This suspense is dreadful. The castle is now in your hands, and all the prisoners, if such there were; but there are shocking insinuations whispered abroad. Her father and mother are on their way to visit you here; and what shall I say to them for the loss of my dear mistress? O, Lord Douglas, if you know of her, as know of her you must, tell me where I can see her. Dead or alive, let me but see her. Or tell me when I shall see her.'

'Lady, that is more than I can tell you; but if it will give you any heart's ease, as certainly as I speak to you I saw her in this apartment to-night.'

'Blessed are the news to me, my lord! But why, then, won't you admit me to her? Send me instantly to her presence, Lord Douglas, for I know she cannot be in any state of concealment in which my company cannot be welcome. I implore you to send me forthwith to her presence.'

'Send you to her presence? That would be a cruel act! Dame, you and your sex have moved my spirit from its erect and heavenward position. It is like a tree bowed by the wind, and the branch of memory is stripped of its fruit. Did I say I saw the Princess Margaret in this apartment? – You must not credit it. There's an incoherence in the principle, or nature has hasty productions not accounted for. You must not believe it, lady; for till the porter opens the great gate to you, your royal mistress you shall not see again.'

'Are not all the gates opened or shut at your controul, my lord? You speak to me in paradoxes. I comprehend it all well enough, however. I will go in or out at any gate; only, in one word, conduct me to my mistress.'

'Hell has no plague like this! No, there are no other fiends that can torment a man in this manner.' He blew his bugle—. 'Eveldon, conduct this dame to her mistress. She is in the great state prison, you know, the receptacle of royalty and thraldom, and let me not hear another word. I'll throw him over the battlements that next mentions the name of a woman to me.'

The lady curtsied, and thanked the Douglas; and Sir John, mistaking his lord's frantic sarcasm for a serious command, hurried Mary Kirkmichael up stairs to the topmost apartment of the great tower, and ushered her in, without farther ceremony, to Lady Jane Howard and her attendant. Lady Jane rose and came running toward them; but, seeing who approached, she started, and retreated to her place. As the two ascended the narrow staircase, there was a great commotion in the square below, therefore, Sir John turned the key and hastened down again. The noise increased, and he heard there was a stern engagement, in which the name of Lady Jane was given as a rallying word on the one side. At the bottom of the stair the conspirators met him, having broken through the ranks in that direction; for the Gordons flew to guard the apartments of the Douglas, not knowing what the object of the insurrection was. Sir John had just time to shut a doublebarred door in front of them; and, retreating up one storey, he shouted from the balcony to apprize the Douglas, else the Lady Jane Howard was gone. One from the ranks ran to apprize the captain, but losing himself among the intricacies of the entrance, he shouted out, 'Lord Douglas! Lord Douglas!' with the utmost vociferation. The Douglas was sitting in a deep reverie; his drawn sword was lying on the table beside him. He heaved it above his shoulder, and running to the door of the apartment, opened it, and asked the fellow, who was still bawling in the dark, what it was? ''Tis the Lady Jane Howard!' answered he, in the same shouting voice. 'Damnation on the tongue that says it!' exclaimed the Douglas in ire: 'Am I never more to hear aught repeated but the names of women? Do you know the penalty of that word, recreant? I have sworn to throw you from the battlements, but that shall not prevent me from cleaving you to the earth in the first place. Women! women! Nothing but one woman after another! I'll cut down every man that dares name one to me in that manner!' As he said these words, he rushed toward the soldier with his heavy sword heaved, but the man, flying with all expedition, escaped into the court. The Douglas followed him, and was soon in the midst of a confused engagement; and hearing the conspirators shouting the same name, 'Lady Jane Howard!' he took it as in derision and flew on their ranks with such fury, that every man at whom he struck fell to the ground. The Gordons followed him up, crying 'A Douglas!' but the conspirators were the stronger party, and would ultimately have prevailed, had not the Douglasses of the Dales arrived to change guard as formerly ordered; and then, Kinlossie having fallen in an attempt to slay the Douglas, his party surrendered. There was a strong troop of English horsemen waiting on the other side of the Teviot with a raft, to whom she was to have been let down from the wall. But the information lodged by the monk not only frustrated the whole of the desperate expedition of the Howards, but saved the life of Douglas. For the conspirators receiving the unexpected orders to depart to the camp, were driven to make the attempt prematurely, before their measures formerly concoctcd were ripe for execution.

Of all the circumstances that had hitherto occured, the reflection upon this bewildered the mind of Douglas the most. The manner in which these secret combinations had been revealed to him filled his heart both with gratitude and amazement; and as all endeavours at reconciling them with nature or reason only increased the mystery, he resolved to shake the load from his spirits and think no more of them. That he might effect this with greater promptitude, he kept his noble kinsmen constantly about him by night as well as by day. The Redhough also returned from his visit to Mountcomyn, as did all the knights and gentlemen commoners of his party from their respective homes, mounted in their most splendid accoutrements, to greet their Sovereign, render him an account of their services, and proffer him due homage. But, among all these Border chiefs, there was none whose appearance attractcd so much admiration as that of Sir Charles Scott of Raeburn and Yardbire. Before that time, the only attention he had ever paid to his habiliments, was that of procuring the best suits of armour that could possibly be obtained. As the leader of the Warden's vanguard column, and his right-hand files in line, he knew it behoved him to be well armed, and in that article he was never deficient. But now that he had to appear before his Sovereign in full pride of array, as the knight of Raeburn and the Warden's right-hand man, he deemed it requisite to have an equipment becoming his rank; so he rummaged the old oaken wardrobe and armour-chest at Yardbire, and from the knightly spoils of ages got himself fitted out, by a skilful hand, in a style that amazed all his former compeers. Both himself and his horse Corbie were literally covered with burnished gold; while the playful restiveness of the one, and the manly and almost colossal figure of the other, rendered the appearance of our warrior a sight truly worthy of admiration. The activity and elasticity of all his motions, combined with his invincible muscular strength, and urbanity of countenance and manners, rendered Charlie at all times an interesting object; but till once he appeared in his plumes and light armour studded with gold, no one could have believed that he was so comely and graceful a personage. At the same time the very consciousness of his appearance, and the rank that he was obliged to support, raised his personal carriage and address many degrees, as by a charm; so that wherever the Warden and his train presented themselves, strangers always appeared disposed to move their bonnets to Sir Charles, whom they took for a king, or an earl at the very least.

The arrival of these heroes added a great deal to the hilarity, tilting, and other military amusements at Roxburgh; until at last the 24th of December arrived, and with it the word that the King and Queen were on their way to Roxburgh, and approaching by the wild path of Soutra-edge. There was no bustle at the castle or city of Roxburgh, save by the city dames and maidens, for whom the approaching festival appeared a glorious epocha; for since the days of Edward Longshanks, who kept his court there for some weeks, there had not been a crowned head within the precincts of that illustrious city. Consequently, with these fair denizens, and with the merchants who attended that mart once a year from many of the towns on the Continent, it was a time of hurry and preparation; but with the warriors it was far otherwise. They were ready before; every one being alike anxious to fulfil the part entrusted to him – so that they had nothing ado but to mount and ride in the order assigned to them.

First of all rode Sir Ringan Redhough, supported by all the gentlemen of the middle and west marches – the Scotts, the Elliots, the Armstrongs, and the Olivers, were the most powerful of these: And next in order came the Laidlaws, the Brydens, the Glendenyngs, and the Potts. After them rode the copper-nosed Kers, the towzy Turn-bulls, and the red-wudd Ridderfords; for in those days every sept had some additional appellative or by-name. These were also mixed with a number of smaller septs, such as the Robsons, the Dicksons, the hurkle-backed Hendersons, and the rough-riding Riddels; and they were all headed by the doughty Sir Andrew Ker of Aultonburn. Next in order rode Old Willie Wiliecoat, named also *Willie wi' the white doublet*, the ancestor of the Earls of Home – a brave and dauntless character, who for the space of forty years had been a sight of terror to the English, with his white jacket. With him rode the gentlemen of his own name, the hard-rackle Homes, the dorty Dunbars, the straitlaced Somervilles, and the Baillies. Then came the proud Pringles, a powerful sept, mixed with a countless number of dependent families, headed by Pringle of Galashiels; and after them the Gordons, led by Sir John of that ilk.

All these held lands of the Douglas, on conditions of certain services; they were nevertheless all independent chiefs, these services performed; but at this time they attended personally, with their kinsmen, to pay their dutiful respects to their Sovereign. Last of all came the Douglasses, in five separate bodies, every one headed by a lord or knight of the name; and these made up one-third of the whole cavalcade, the Earl himself being with the last party of all, and most gallantly attended.

The two parties met at Earlston, but the royal party was nothing in point of bearing and splendour to that of the Doughlasses. The King and Queen travelled each in a litter borne by two gallant steeds. These carriages were very splendid in their decorations, and constructed in the same way as a sedan chair, and it was truly wonderful with what velocity they were borne along. They were contrived for the King's use, who had a halt, and could not travel on horseback; and they suited the state of the roads in Scotland at that period exceedingly. Two heralds rode before his Majesty, who introduced the various chiefs to him as he passed, and those others of whose names he enquired, among whom Sir Charles Scott was the first. The Queen and her Maries also saluted him along with the Warden. The whole procession then drew up in files until their Majesties passed, after which they fell all into their places, the order of precedency being then reversed, and the Doughlasses next to the Sovereign. There was no time for delay, considering the season, the darkness of the night, and the shortness of the day; so they posted on with all manner of expedition, and yet it was dark before they reached the abbey of Kelso. But all the way, by the cloisters, the bridge, and up the High-street of the city of Roxburgh, there were tiers of torches raised above one another that made it lighter than the noonday. Never was there such a scene of splendour witnessed in that ancient and noble city; to which the darkness of the canopy above, and the glare of torchlight below, added inconceivable grandeur. It seemed as if all the light and beauty of the universe had been confined within that narrow space, for without all was blackness impervious to the eye, but within there was nothing but brilliancy, activity, and joy. Seven score musical instruments, and as many trilling but discordant voices, yelled forth, from the one end of the street to the other, that old song beginning,

> 'The King came to our town;
> Ca' Cuddie, ca' Cuddie!
> The King came to our town,
> Low on the Border.'

The trumpets sounded before, and the bugles behind; and the Border youths and maidens were filled with enthusiastic delight at the novelty of the spectacle. They followed with shouts to the castle gate, and then returned to talk of what they had seen, and what they should see on the morrow.

The royal party was conducted to the citadel, where every thing was in readiness for a grand entertainment; and there the Douglas delivered into the King's hands the keys of the castle of Roxburgh. His Majesty received them most graciously, and thanked him for all the cost, pains, and trouble that he had taken for the good of the realm; and added, that he came prepared in heart and mind to fulfil his engagements to him in return. There was now a manifest embarrassment on the part of the Douglas; his countenance changed; and he looked as he would have asked for the Princess, or, at least, as if some one were wanting that ought to have been there; but after an agitated pause, he could only stammer out, that 'he was much beholden to his Majesty, who might at all times command his utmost services without bounty or reward.'

'I trust that is not as much as to say that you now decline the stipulated reward for this high service,' said the King.

'Sire, I see none either for your Majesty to give, or your servant to receive,' said the Douglas; and at the same time he cast a hasty and perturbed glance at the courtiers and warriors ranged around the hall. The king nodded by way of assent to his hint; and at the same time said to him, aside, 'I understand you, Lord Douglas. You will explain this gallantry of yours, in keeping your sovereign's daughter in concealment from her natural guardians, in private to-morrow. But, pray, can we not see our darling to-night?'

'Alas, my leige lord and sovereign,' said Douglas, passionately, 'sure you jest with your servant, thus to tax him with that of which he is innocent.'

The King smiled, and waving his hand jocularly, by way of intimating that he thought his affected secrecy prudence at that time, left him, and forthwith went halting up among the Borderers, to converse with them about the affairs of the English marches. The stately and commanding figure of Charlie Scott, who was like Saul among the people, again attracted the King's eyes, and he went familiarly up to him, and said at once, 'Well, gallant knight, how have accounts balanced between you and your southern neighbours since last Lammas-tide?'

'Gude faith, my liege lord and king, I can hardly tell you,' said Sir Charles, without hesitation: 'There hae been some hard yerks gaun; but the last quarter stands rather aboon an average wi' us. It is a kittle bauk that hings o'er the Border, my liege; it is often nae sooner down to the yird than it is up to the starns again.'

'Well said, knight! I like your fair wit and free humour,' said the King. 'So, upon the whole, you judge that the balance preponderates on our side just now?'

'I should think sae, Sire, when sic a clod as this castle of Roxburgh is thrown into the bucket. It is nae witherweight this for the end of a weigh-bauk. A' the kye o' the Seven Dales winna carry the swee to the south side again.'

The Queen, hearing her lord conversing so freely and jocularly with this goodly personage, came also up with two of her ladies of honour, in order to put in a word; 'for (says Isaac, with great simplicity) women always like to be striking kemps with a handsome and proper man; and the bigger of bone, and the stronger of muscle, the more is he the object of their admiration.'

When Sir Charles had finished the last remark, therefore, the Queen smiled complacently in his face, and said, 'You must certainly acknowledge, gallant knight, that you have been much indebted to heaven for your singular success in this instance?'

Sir Charles nodded his head. 'Its a' that ye ken about it, my lady queen. But saft be the sough that says it. I trow we were mair indebted to some other place in the first instance.'

The Queen held up her hands: 'Uh! what does the knight mean? Say, my lord, What? What place?' Then turning to Sir Ringan, who was terribly in the fidgets about what had dropped from his kinsman, she added, 'I trust our right traist warden and loving cousin did not practise any of the diabolical arts, so prevalent of late, to accomplish his hard task?' And then, with a woman's natural volubility, when once her tongue is set a-going, she added, turning to Charlie, without waiting the Warden's reply, 'What place does Sir Charles mean? I hope you would not insinuate that you had any dealings with the spirits of darkness?'

'Not with hell directly, madam,' answered Charlie, (for Isaac can never help calling him occasionally by his old title,) 'but I canna say that we didna get a strong hint frae ane or twa of its principal agents. No offence, my lady queen. I ken by report, that your Majesty takes supreme delight in religious devotions; and, to tell the truth, I have always had a strong hankering that gate mysel', and hope I will hae till the day of my death. But there is ae thing in the whilk I am greatly altered. Pray, may I take the liberty to ask what is your Majesty's opinion about the deil?'

'Uh! gracious St Mary be with us! What a question, knight! Why, what can I think but that he is the great enemy of God and man, and the author of universal evil?'

'There I think differently,' said Charlie, bowing very low: 'Always begging my lady queen's gracious pardon, that's the only tenet o' my belief that is altered; – at least an it be nae fairly altered, it is considerably jumbled, and nought like sae steadfast as it was. Always begging your pardon though, madam.'

'I am quite confounded,' said the Queen. 'Pray, warrior, what do you mean?'

'Plainly this, my lady queen; that I think the old gentleman has been sair abused; and that there are some na meikle better than him wha have been a great deal better ca'd. It may sound a little odd in your ears, but I hae now seen him. I hae sat wi' him; I hae eaten, I hae drunken wi' him; and gin it hadna been for the interference of women, we wad hae partit civilly. But whenever they get a finger in a pye, there will be some ane burnt in the opening o't. Always begging your Majesty's pardon, though.'

The Queen crossed herself, and counted her beads; but at the same time bestowed a smile and look of admiration on this extraordinary hero who had accomplished such singular adventures. These encouraging Sir Charles to finish his sentence, he added: 'They hae frightit me wi' him lang; and sair has my neb been hauden at the grindstane wi' the fear o' him. I durst hardly say or think that ane of a' the members of my body was my ain wi' perfect terror. But thae days are a' o'er. An' the bedesmen be gaun to fright me only langer wi' a deil, they maun get a new ane; for the auld ane winna stand his ground to any extent wi' me on that score. He has doubtless some bad qualities; some wicked vagaries about him; but, upon the whole, I hae met wi' waur fellows.'

This introduction, in spite of Sir Ringan's endeavours to waive the subject, led to the whole narrative of the transactions at Aikwood, of which the Queen and her maidens of honour were never wearied, although at the same time many an Ave Maria and Paternoster the subject cost them. When obliged, from the lateness of the hour, to desist listening to the agitating theme, the Queen was never at rest until it was renewed next day; nor even then till she had gone and visited the great hill of Eildon thus miraculously cleft asunder and divided into three; and even after quaking at the scene, she grew still more importunate in her inquiries, so that there was no satisfying her curiosity on the subject of the enchantments of Master Michael Scott all the time she remained in Roxburgh.

When she retired to her chamber that first night she inquired for a confessor, and the knight in waiting introduced the monk Benjamin; intimating, that since the capture of the castle he had been confessor-general to all within its walls. The Queen's devotions that night were prolonged until an early hour next morning; nevertheless she arose from her sleep greatly refreshed, and in high spirits, and at the breakfast-table was more than usually gay. Not so with Douglas, over whose countenance, in spite of all exertions to the contrary, hung a heavy gloom, as well as a manifest abstraction of thought. The King, who was a person of strong discernment, observed this, and, from some indefinite dread of the cause, involuntarily partook of the sensation.

CHAPTER THIRTY

I want none of your gold, Douglas,
  I want none of your fee,
But swear by the faith of thy right hand
  That you'll love only me:
And I'll leave my country and my kin
  And wend along with thee.
                                    May Marley

WHEN THE MASS, and a plentiful morning meal, were over next day, every one began to prepare for such exercises as the season admitted. All lingered about for some time, but seeing that no orders were likely to be given out for any procession or general rendezvous during the day, which every one had expected, some betook them to the chace, others to equestrain exercises with sword and spear, while the Homes and the Gordons joined in an excursion into English ground, keeping along the southern bank of the Tweed. The King observing them all about to disperse, reminded the Douglas that it was a high festal day; on which the latter made a low obeisance, and remarked, that he was only now a guest in the castle of Roxburgh, and that his honoured liege sovereign was host; that his foresters and sumptuary officers had got timeous notice, and nothing would be lacking that his Majesty could desire for the entertainment of his nobles and friends. The King then caused it to be intimated, that he would be happy to meet all his lords and nobles in the banquet-hall at even-tide, where every knight, gentleman, and yeoman, were expected to attend in their several places, and all should be heartily welcome. 'And now, Lord Douglas,' said he, leading the way into an antichamber, 'let us two retire by ourselves, and consult what is to be done next.'

Lord Douglas followed, but ill prepared to answer the inquiries about to be put to him. He had received injunctions of secrecy from one who had in no instance misled him, and to whom he had been of late indebted for the preservation of his life. But how was he now to conduct himself, or how answer his sovereign in any other way than according to the truth as it had been stated unto him? His predicament was a hard one; for he was, in the first place, ashamed of the part he had acted, of never having discovered his royal mistress while attached to his side, notwithstanding of all evidences in confirmation of the fact, which he had never once seen till too late. And then to have suffered even his mistress' page to fall a victim to such a shameful death, without either making an effort to save him, or so much as missing him from his hand, or mentioning his loss – were circumstances not quite consistent with the high spirit of gallantry, as well as chivalry, he had displayed at first by the perilous undertaking. Gladly would he have kept his knowledge of the transaction a secret; but then there was the monk Benjamin, who, by some supernatural agency, had been given to understand the whole scope and tenor of it; and there was dame Mary Kirkmichael knew the whole, except the degarding catastrophe, and had unfolded it all to him when it was too late. He run over all these things in his mind, and was as little, as at any previous period, prepared what part to act, when the King turned round, and, in the most anxious and earnest manner, said, 'Lord Douglas, where is our daughter?'

'My liege lord and sovereign, ought not I rather to have asked that question of you?' said the Douglas: 'And I would have done it at our first meeting, only that I would not trifle with your feelings on such a serious matter, perceiving that you laboured under a grievous misconception regarding my conduct. You have not, it seems, brought the princess Margaret along with you, as was expected by all my friends and followers?'

'Not by yourself, I am certain. I say, Lord Douglas, where is my daughter? I demand a categorical answer.'

'Sire, in what way am I accountable for your daughter?'

'Lord Douglas, I hate all evasion. I request an answer as express as my question. I know my darling child, in admiration of your chivalrous enterprise, resolved, in the true spirit of this romantic age, to take some active part in the perils undertaken solely on her account: I know her ingenuity, which was always boundless, was instrumental in performing some signal services to you; and that finally she attached herself to your side in a disguise which she deemed would ensure her a kind and honourable protection. Thus far I know; and, though the whole was undertaken and transacted without my knowledge, when I was absent in the Highlands, I am certain as to the truth of every circumstance; and I am farther certified that you know all this.'

'Hear me, my liege sovereign. Admitting that your daughter, or any other king's, lord's, or commoner's daughter, should put herself into a page's raiment, and—'

'Silence, lord!' cried the king, furiously, interrupting him: 'Am I to be mocked thus, and answered only with circumlocution, notwithstanding my express command to the contrary? Answer me in one word. My Lord of Douglas, where is my daughter?'

'Where God will, sire,' was the short and emphatic reply. The king eyed Douglas with a keen and stern regard, and the eagle eye of the latter met that of his sovereign without any abashment. But yet this look of the Douglas, unyielding as it was, manifested no daring or offensive pride; it was one rather of stern sorrow and regret; nevertheless he would not withdraw it, but, standing erect, he looked King Robert in the face, until the eyes of the latter were gradually raised from his toward heaven. 'Almighty Father!' cried he, clasping his hands together – 'Where, then, is it thy will that my beloved child should be? O Douglas! Douglas! In the impatience and warmth of temper peculiar to my race, I was offended at your pertinacity; but I dread it was out of respect to a father's feelings. I forgive it, now that I see you are affected, only, in pity to this yearning bosom, relate to me all that you know. Douglas! can you not inform me what has befallen to my daughter?'

'No, my liege, I cannot. I know nothing, or at least little save from report; but the little that I have heard, and the little that I have seen, shall never be reported by my tongue.'

'Then hope is extinct!' cried the King. 'The scene that

can draw tears from the stern eye of the Douglas, even by an after reflection, is one unmeet for a parent's ear. The will of the Almighty be done! He hath given and he hath taken away: blessed be his name! But why have the men of my household, and the friends in whom I trusted, combined against my peace?' The King said this in a querulous mood. 'Why did you not tell me sooner?' cried he, turning to Douglas, his tone altering gradually from one of penitence and deep humiliation to one of high displeasure: 'Why bring me on this fool's errand, when I ought to have been sitting in sackcloth and ashes, and humbling myself for the sins of my house? These must have been grievous indeed, that have drawn down such punishments on me. But the indifference of those in whom we trusted is the worst of all! O, my child! My darling child, Margaret! Never was there a parent so blest in a daughter as I was in thee! The playfulness of the lamb or the kid – the affection of the turtle-dove, were thine. Thy breast was all enthusiasm and benevolence, and every emotion of thy soul as pure as the ray of heaven. I loved thee with more than parental affection, and, if I am bereaved of thee, I will go mourning to my grave. Is there no one in this place that can inform me of my daughter's fate? Her lady confidant, I understand, is still lingering here. Send for her instantly. Send for her confessor also, that I may confront you altogether, and ascertain the hideous and unwelcome truth. If I cannot have it here, I shall have it elsewhere, or wo be to all that have either been instrumental in her fate or lax in warding it off! Do you think, Lord of Douglas, that I can be put off with a hum and a haw, and a shake of the head, and, "it's God's will?" Do you think I should, when I am inquiring about my own daughter, whom I held dearest of all earthly beings? No, I'll scrutinize it to a pin's point. I'll wring every syllable of the truth out of the most secret heart and the most lying tongue. I'll move heaven and hell, but I'll know every circumstance that has befallen to my daughter. Send, I say, for her foster-sister and faithful attendant, dame Mary Kirkmichael. Send also for her confessor, and for all to whom she has but once spoken since she arrived here. Why are they not sent for before this time?'

'My liege lord, restrain your impatience. They are sent

for; but they will tell you nothing that can mitigate your sorrow. If it be all true that has been told to me, and that you yourself have told to me, of the disguise the Princess assumed, then it is also true that you will never again see your daughter in this state of existence.'

'Ah! is it even so! Then is the flower of the realm fallen! then is the solace of my old age departed! But she is happy in the realms of blessedness. While love, joy, and truth are the delight of heaven, there will my Margaret find a place! O, that she had staid by her father's hand! Why was my jewel entrusted to the care and honour of those who care but for themselves, and who have suffered the loveliest flower of the world to be cropped in its early blossom? nay, left it to be sullied and trodden down in forgetfulness. Lord Douglas, did you see my daughter perish?'

'Now, my liege lord, can I act the man no longer. Forgive me; and may the holy Virgin, the mother of God, forgive me; for I indeed saw with these eyes that inestimable treasure cut off, without one effort on my part to save her, and without a tear wetting my cheeks.'

'Then, may all the powers of darkness blast thy soul, thou unfeeling traitor! Thus! thus will I avenge me on the culprit who could give up his sovereign's daughter, and his own betrothed bride, to a violent death, and that without a tear! O thou incarnate fiend! shalt thou not bewail this adown the longest times of eternity? Darest thou not draw against an injured father and king?'

'Put up thy sword, sire. The Douglas draws not but on his equals, and thou art none of them. Thy person is sacred and thy frame debilitated. He holds thee inviolate; but he holds thee also as nothing!'

'Thou shalt know, proud lord, that the King of Scotland fears no single arm, and that he can stand on one limb to avenge the blood of his royal house.'

'My gracious lord, this is the mere raving of a wounded spirit, and I grieve that I should have for one moment regarded it otherwise than with veneration. I had deserved to die an hundred deaths, if I had known who the dear sufferer was; but, alas! I knew not ought of the sex or rank of my page, who was taken prisoner in the great night engagement. But I can tell you no more, Sire; nor is it needful; you now know all. I am guiltless as the babe unborn of my royal mistress's blood; but I will never forgive myself for my negligence and want of perception; nor do I anticipate any more happiness in this world. I have been laid under some mysterious restraints, and have suffered deeply already. And now, my gracious lord, I submit myself to your awards.'

'Alas, Lord Douglas, you are little aware of the treasure you have lost. Your loss is even greater than mine. It behoves us, therefore, to lament and bewail our misfortunes together, rather than indulge in bitter upbraidings.'

Here they were interrupted by the entrance of the Queen, who brought with her the Lady Jane Howard, dressed in a style of eastern magnificence, to introduce her to the King. The King, amid all the grief that overwhelmed his spirit, was struck with her great beauty, and paid that respect and homage to her which high birth and misfortune always command from the truly great; and the Queen, with the newfangledness of her sex, appeared wholly attached to this captive stranger, and had brought her down at that time to intercede with the King and Lord Douglas for her liberty, loading her with commendations and kind attentions. To check the Queen's volatility of spirits, the King informed her shortly of the irreparable loss both of them had suffered, but the effect was manifestly not at all proportionate to the cause. She appeared indeed much moved, and had well nigh fallen into hysterics; but if her grief was not assumed, it bore strong symptoms of being so. She first railed at, and then tried to comfort the Douglas; but finally turned again to Lady Jane, (who wept bitterly, out of true sympathy, for the Princess's cruel and untimely fate,) and caressed her, trying to console her in the most extravagant terms. The King, on the other hand, sobbed from his inmost soul, and bewailed his loss in terms so pathetic and moving, that the firm soul of Douglas was overcome, and he entered into all his Sovereign's feelings with the keenest sensations. It was a scene of sorrow and despair, which was rather increased than mitigated by the arrival of two more who had lately been sent for. These were the monk Benjamin and the lady Mary Kirkmichael, whom the King began anew to examine, dwelling on every circumstance that occurred during the course of his darling child's extravagant adventure with a painful anxiety. But every now and then he became heated with anger, blaming some one for the want of discernment or respect. When he came to examine the monk, who shewed great energy and acuteness of speech, he lost his temper altogether at some part of the colloquy; but the monk was not to be daunted; he repelled every invective with serenity of voice and manner, and at sundry times rather put the monarch to shame.

'Hadst thou ever an opportunity of confessing and shriving my child, previous to the time she fell into the hands of her enemies, reverend brother?'

'No Sire, she never made confession to me, nor asked absolution at my hand.'

'And wherefore didst thou not proffer it, thou shriveled starveling? Were there no grants to bestow? no rich benefices to confer for the well-being of a royal virgin's soul, that caused thee to withold these poor alms of grace? Who was it that bestowed on thy unconscionable order all that they possess in this realm? And yet thou wilt suffer one of their posterity to come into thy cell, to ask thy assistance, without bestowing a mass or benediction for the sake of heaven.'

'Sire, it is only to the ignorant and the simple that we proffer our ghostly rites. Those who are enlightened in the truths and mysteries of religion it behoves to judge for themselves, and to themselves we leave the state of their consciences, in all ordinary cases.' The monk was robed in a very wide flowing grey frock, and cowled over the eyes, while his thin and effeminate-looking beard trembled adown his breast with the fervency of his address. As he said these last words, he stretched his right hand forth toward the King, and raising the left up behind him, his robe was by that means extended and spread forth in a manner that increased the tiny monk to triple the size he was before. 'And for you, King of Scotland,' added he, raising his keen voice that quavered with energy, 'I say such a demeanour is unseemly. Is it becoming the head and guardian of the Christian church in this realm – him that should be a pattern to all in the lower walks of life – thus to threat and fume beneath the chastening of his Maker? You ask me who bestowed these ample bounds on my order? I ask you in return who it was that bestowed them on thy progenitors and thee, and for what purpose? Who gave thee a kingdom, a people, and a family of thy own? Was it not he before whose altar thou hast this day kneeled, and vowed to be for him and not for another? And what he has bestowed has he not a right to require of thee again, in his own time, and in his own way?' The King bowed with submission to the truth of this bold expostulation, and the impetuous and undaunted monk went on: 'It is rather thy duty, most revered monarch, to bow with deep humiliation to the righteous awards of the Almighty, for just and righteous they are, however unequal they may appear to the purblind eyes of mortal men. If he has taken a beloved child from thee, rest assured that he has only snatched her from evil to come, and translated her to a better and a happier home. Why then wilt thou not acknowledge the justice of this dispensation, and rather speak comfort to the weaker vessels than give way to ill-timed and unkingly wrath?'

'As for thee, noble lord, to the eyes of men thine may appear a hard lot indeed. For the love of one thou adventuredst thy life and the very existence of thy house and name. The stake was prodigious, and when thou hadst won it with great labour and perseverance, the prize was snatched from thy grasp. Thy case will to all ages appear a peculiarly hard one; still there is this consolation in it—'

'There is no grain of consolation in it,' said Douglas interrupting him: 'There can be none! The blow on my head, and my hopes of happiness, is irretrievable.'

'Yes lord, there is,' said the monk; 'for has it not been decreed in heaven above, that this union was never to be consummated? Man may propose and scheme and lay out plans for futurity, but it is good for him that the fulfilment is vested in other hands than his. This then is consolation, to know that it was predestinated in the counsels of one who cannot err, that that royal maid never was to be thine; and therefore all manner of repining is not only unmanly and unmeet, but sinful. It behoves now thy sovereign, in reward of thy faithful services, to bestow on thee another spouse with the same dowry he meant to bestow on his daughter. And it behoves you to accept of this as the gift of heaven, proffered to thee in place of the one it snatched from thy grasp. As its agent, therefore, and the promoter of peace, love, and happiness among men, I propose that

King Robert bestow upon thee this noble and high born dame for thy consort. Both of you have been bereaved of those to whom you were betrothed, and it cannot fail to strike every one that this seems a fortune appointed for you two by Providence; nor can I form in my mind the slightest objection that can be urged to it on either side. It is desirable on every account, and may be the means of promoting peace between the two sister kingdoms, wasted by warfare and blood, which every true Christian must deplore. I propose it as a natural consequence, and a thing apparently foreordained by my master; and give my voice for it. King and Queen of Scotland what say you?'

'I hold the matter that this holy and enlightened brother has uttered to be consistent with truth, reason, and religion,' said the King – 'and the union has my hearty and free approval. I farther promise to behave to this lady as a father to a daughter, and to bestow upon our trusty and leal cousin, the Lord Douglas, such honours, power, and distinction as are most due for the great services rendered to this realm. The match has my hearty concurrence.'

'And mine,' said the Queen: 'I not only acquiesce in the reverend brother's proposal, but I lay my commands on my noble kinsman the Lord Douglas to accept of this high boon of heaven.'

'Pause my sovereign lady,' said the Douglas, 'before you proceed too far. In pity to the feelings that rend this bosom, let me hear no more of the subject at present. In pity to that lovely and angelic lady's feelings, that must be acute as my own, I implore that you will not insist farther in this proposal. Do not wound a delicate female breast, pressed down by misfortunes.'

'This is something like affectation, Lord Douglas,' rejoined the Queen: 'If I answer for the lady Jane's consent, what have you then to say against this holy brother's proposal?'

'Ay, if your Queen stand security for the lady's consent, and if *I stand security for it likewise*,' said the monk – 'what have you to say against the union then? Look at her again, lord. Is not she *a lovely* and *angelic* being? Confess the truth now. For I know it to be the truth, that never since you could distinguish beauty from deformity, have your eyes beheld *so lovely* and *so angelic* a lady? Pressed down by misfortunes, too! Does that not add a triple charm to all her excellencies? You know what has been done for her? what has been suffered for her? what a noble and gallant life was laid down for her? Was such a sacrifice ever made for a lady or princes of your own country? No, never, heroic lord! Therefore bless your stars that have paved out a way for your union with such a *lovely, angelic,* and *matchless lady*; and take her! take her to your longing and aching bosom.'

'Moderate your fervour, holy brother,' said the Douglas, 'which appears to me rather to be running to unwarrantable extremes. Granting that the lady Jane Howard is perhaps unequalled in beauty and elegant accomplishments—'

'Is she not so? Is she not so?' cried the monk with a fervour that raised his voice to a scream of passion: 'Did I not say that she was? And now am I not warranted by your own sentiments, *freely expressed* enough. Sure, lord, you cannot deny that I said, that I told you, the lady was *peerless in beauty and accomplishments*? I knew it, and told you before that she was *the queen of beauty*. Why then do you hesitate, and make all this foolish opposition to an union which we all know you are eager to consummate? Yes, you are: And we all know it. You are!'

'Holy brother, what unaccountable phrenzy has seized upon you,' said the Douglas; 'and why all this extravagant waste of declamation? Let me not hear another sentence, nor another word on the subject: only suffer me to finish what I had begun. I say then, granting that the lady Jane were peerless in beauty and accomplishments, still there is an impression engraven on my heart that can never be removed, or give place to another; and there will I cherish it as sacred, till the day of my death. And, that no reckless importunity may ever be wasted on me again, here I kneel before the holy rood, which I kiss, and swear before God and his holy angels, that since I have been bereaved of the sovereign mistress of my heart and all my affections – of her in whom all my hopes of happiness in this world were placed, and who to me was all in all of womankind – that, never shall another of the sex be folded in the arms of Douglas, or call him husband! So help me thou Blessed One, and all thy holy saints and martyrs, in the performance of this vow!'

During the time of this last speech and solemn oath, the sobs of the monk Benjamin became so audible that all eyes were turned to him, for they thought that his delicate frame would burst with its emotions. And, besides, he was all the while fumbling about his throat, so that they dreaded he had purposed some mortal injury to himself. But in place of that, he had been unloosing some clasps or knots about his tunick: for with a motion quicker than thought, he flung at once his cowl, frock, and beard away – and there stood arrayed as a royal bride the Princess Margaret of Scotland! 'Journeyer of earth, where art thou now?'

Yes; there stood, in one moment, disclosed to the eyes of all present, *the princess Margaret Stuart herself*, embellished in all the ornaments of virgin royalty, and blooming in a glow of new born beauties.

'Thank heaven I have been deceived!' cried she, with great emphasis; and when she had said this, she stood up motionless by the side of lady Jane Howard, and cast her eyes on the ground. No pen can do justice to the scene. It must be left wholly to conception, after the fact is told that no one present had the slightest conception of the disguise save the Queen, who had been initiated into the princess's project of trying the real state of the Douglas's affections on the preceding night. It was like a scene of enchantment, such as might have been produced at the castle of Aikwood. But a moment ago all was sorrow and despair; now all was one burst of joyful surprise. And, to make it still more interesting, there stood the two rival beauties of Scotland and England, side by side, as if each were vying with the other for the palm to be bestowed on her native country. But to this day the connoisseurs in female beauty have never decided whether the dark falcon eyes and lofty forehead of the one, or the soft blushing roses and blue liquid eyes of the other, were the most irresistible.

The King was the first to burst from the silence of surprise. He flew to his daughter's arms with more vigour than a cripple could well be supposed to exert, kissed and embraced her, took her on his knee and wept on her neck; then, striking his crutch on the floor, he scolded her most heartily for the poignant and unnecessary pain she had occasioned to him. 'And the worst of it is,' added he, 'that you have caused me show too much interest in an imp that has been the constant plague of my life with her whims and vagaries; an interest, and an intensity of feeling, that I shall be ashamed of the longest day I have to live.'

'Indeed but you shall not, my dear lord and father, for I will now teaze another than you, and teaze him only to deeds of valour and renown; to lead your troops to certain conquest, till you are fully avenged of the oppressors of your people.'

Mary Kirkmichael hung by her seymar and wept. The Douglas kneeled at her feet, and in an ecstacy took her hand and pressed it to his lips. 'I do not know whether or not I shall have reason to bless heaven all my life for this singular restoration,' said he; 'but for the present I do it with all my heart. Tell me, thou lovely cameleon, what am I to think of this? Wert thou indeed, as was related to me, the page Colin Roy Macalpin? He with the carroty locks and the flippant tongue?'

'You need not doubt it, lord Douglas. I was. And I think during our first intimacy that I teazed you sufficiently,'

'Then that delicate neck of yours, for all its taper form and lily hue is a charmed one, and rope proof; for, as sure as I look on you now, I saw you swing from a beam's end on the battlement of this same tower.'

'Oh! no, no, my lord! It was not I. Never trust this head again if it should suffer its neck to be noosed. *You* suffered it though; that you must confess. And I dare say, though a little sorry, felt a dead weight removed from about your neck. You suffered me to be taken prisoner out of your tent, and mured up among rude and desperate men in a dungeon. It cost me all my wits then to obtain my release. But I effected it. Swung from a beam's end, quoth he! Och! what a vulgar idea! No my lord, the page whom you saw swung was *a tailor's apprentice*, whom I hired to carry a packet up to your lordship, with my green suit of clothes, and a promise of a high place of preferment, and I kept my word to the brat! An intolerable ape it was. Many better lives have been lost in this contention; few of less value – I never deemed he was so soon to be strung, and my heart smote me for the part I had acted. But the scheme of turning monk and confessor suited me best of all: I then got my shacles of mystery riveted on you; and, heaven! what secrets I have found out.'

At this part of the narrative, Isaac the curate bestows a whole chapter and a half on the description of the wedding, and all the processions, games, and feasting that ensued; but as none of these things bore the slightest resemblance to ought that has ever been witnessed in the present age, like a judicious editor I have passed them over. Suffice it that the Border never witnessed such splendor of array, such tournaments, such feasting, and such high wassail. For why? because it never witnessed the marriage of a king's daughter before. The streets of the city, and the square of the fortress, that had so lately been dyed with blood, now 'ran red with Rhenish wine.' And be it farther known, that Sir Charles Scott and his horse Corbie bore off every prize in the tilting matches, till at last no knight would enter the lists with him; but the fair dames were all in raptures with the gallantry of his bearing, and the suavity of his manners. As for the Queen, she became so much enamoured of the hero, that she was scarcely to be kept in due bounds, and if she had not been advanced in years he might have deemed she was in love with him. In the lists she drew up her snow-white palfrey by Corbie's side, and in the revel hall the royal dame herself was sure to be at the knight's side, except when at table, on pretence of hearing something more about his perils at Aikwood, and in particular about the scene with the beautiful and splendid witches; at which, as Sir Charles related it with abashed countenance, the Queen and her Maries laughed till the salt tears ran from their eyes. As for the description of their appearance the succeeding morning, and the feelings of the warrior, both then and afterwards when transformed to a huge bull, these never failed to throw the gamesome group into convulsions of mirth. In short, the knight of Raeburn was of all the gallants quite the favourite at that splendid festival in the hall, as well as the hero in the lists, in which he six times received the prize of honour from the hands of the royal bride and those of lady Jane Howard, who, at the Queen's earnest request was made principal bride's-maid, and presiding lady at the sports.

But if Charles was the hero of those engaged in the games, his friend the gospel friar was as completely so among the gay onlookers, and created them more sport often than all in the lists. Ever since the various affrays in which his mule had been engaged, and come off with such decided success, the mongrel had learned to value himself solely as a beast of warfare, and no man who rode near him was sure of keeping his seat a minute, especially if he rode a high mettled and capricious charger. By the side of a horse of modesty that bore himself with candour and humility of countenance, the mule was a beast of sociality and decorum; but whenever he saw a steed begin to cut any unnecessary capers, he deemed himself insulted or put to the challenge, and on the instant began to lay back his long ears and switch with his tail, while his grey sunk eyes emitted a hellish gleam. It was no matter at what distance such a horse made his appearance, if the mule disliked his deportment, he would have flown across a whole field to attack and humble him. He had borne his master headlong into so many unpremeditated and unwarrantable scuffles since his return from Aikwood, that he had bestowed on him the name of Goliah of Gath; and besides giving him that veteran title, he often averred that he believed one of the necromancer's imps of darkness had taken possession of his beast.

The friar had, however, learned to distinguish all his motions, and knew from these the exact points and stages of his irritation; and when his offence began to reach its acme, he had no other resource than that of wheeling his head forcibly around, and turning his tail toward the object of his displeasure. Without this precaution, the friar would have been carried into the lists every day merely to gratify the spleen of Goliah, who could not endure the curvetting and jangling that was going on there. And even this inverse precaution did not at all times prove effectual, as in the following pleasant instance.

It chanced one day that the knight of Kraeland entered the lists alone, no opponent appearing against him, owing to some mistake made in the arrangement by the officers. He was a goodly youth, but uplifted above the earth with vanity, and of his vapouring and airs there were no end. Imagining that he attracted the eyes of all the beholders, and elated because no one had the courage to appear against him, for so he affected to regard the circumstance, he paraded the circle round and round, brandished his lance, and made his horse to curvette, rear, and wheel, accomplishing many grand evolutions. The lookers on were all beginning to get sick of him, and to view his vapourous manoeuvres with disdain, but amongst them all there was none so much moved with spleen as Goliah of Gath. From the first moment that the knight entered the lists that uncircumcised Philistine began to manifest a mortal dislike towards him: the more so it was believed that he was mounted on a milkwhite steed, a colour peculiarly disagreeable to the mule's optics. The judges of the games wist not what to do, and appealed to the King, who gave it as his opinion that this unchallenged appearance should be accounted as a victory, and that the knight should take his course in the next round; and the heralds got directions to make proclamation accordingly.

But long before this period the friar had been compelled to turn away the face of Goliah from this scene of vanity, and, as chance would have had it, he was in the innermost circle, so that retreat outward through the innumerable files was utterly impracticable, and there sat the gruff uncourtly form of the gospel friar, with the tail of his beast where the head should have been, to the great amusement of the spectators. For all this the malevolent eye of Goliah, as well accustomed to look backward as forward, perceived all the outrageous rearings and snortings of that proud and gaudy animal, and became moved with so much indignation that he would no longer be restrained, either by bit or spur, soothing or threatening. Just as the herald had taken his place to make proclamation, the mule fell a running backward; and the more fiercely that the friar spurred, and the more bitterly he threatened, the beast of Belial retrograded the faster, till at last, after two or three intemperate plunges, he got his head straight to the white charger, and then in one moment he was upon him, and had him by the brisket with his teeth. The horse reared furiously, but the mule pressed still closer to him, fixing his long teeth in the horse's shoulder, till on a sudden, in an attempt to clear both Goliah and his rider, or, at least, to leap over the mule's neck, the white steed was overturned, and thrown right on his back, above his overweening rider. All this was transacted in a space of time shorter than the time taken up in reading the relation; and the moment that Goliah of Gath had achieved this overthrow, he wheeled about with a mettledness and inveteracy beyond all description, and attacked the couple with his heels, prostrate as they were, yerk for yerk, indiscriminately. The friar sunk the rowels of his spurs to the head in his sides, and uttered some strong declamatory sentences against him in the style of the nations of the East; but Goliah plied his iron-heels still the faster, although he groaned, as he kicked, in the bitterness of his spirit. The scene was perfectly irresistible, grievous as the consequences threatened to be on the one side. The lists were all in convulsions of laughter, and involuntary shouts of applause shook the storeys of the firmament. The King laughed till he sunk down in his litter, and his attendants had some fears that he would expire in a convulsive fit. The knight of Kraeland was carried out of the lists, maimed, and in a state of insensibility; and the friar, maugre all he could advance in opposition to the award, was proclaimed the victor in that course, and obliged to appear in the next encounter in opposition to the knight who had been the conqueror in the preceding combat.

Had Goliah of Gath restrained his wrath when this conquest was achieved, it would have been all very well, save for Kraeland and his white charger; but the mongrel's wrath once aroused was not easily abated. Therefore, when the friends of the fallen knight and his squire forced the Philistine to forego his attack and battery, his gleaming eyes glanced all around for another proper object whereon to wreak his horrid revenge. Now it so happened, that the Queen and her Maries were all mounted on white palfreys; and as these stood in the inner circles, arching their proud necks, and champing the bits, he was moved with choler against them, and resolved within himself to give them a surprise, and shew them the prowess of a veteran warrior; for, over and above their saucy demeanor, the glaring whiteness of colour that pervaded them and their riders his heart could not endure: And, besides all these, the shouts and laughter of the multitude were thought to have added greatly to his ire. The friar, who knew him well, said so; 'for' added he, 'the shouts of joy and laughter are unto him as a portion of gall and of worm-wood.' Certes, when he was driven from the prostrate champion, by dint of club and lance, he straightway laid back his long ears, and with a swiftness hardly imaginable, scoured the plain to the attack of the dames and their strutting genets. The friar soon perceived the dangerous dilemma into which he was about to be precipitated; and, all unable to restrain this champion of the Philistines, he cried out with a loud voice, 'O wretched man that I am! lo, I shall work destruction among the daughters of women! Will no man come to the assistance of those who have no strength of man at all? Wo is me! will the mighty men stand and look on till the daughters of their people are cut off from the face of the earth?'

Long ere this sentence had proceeded out of the friar's mouth, the work of deray and confusion was begun. The column of white palfreys were routed in one moment, and their gentle and affrighted riders kicked off in pairs, like so many diving swans. Never was there a warrior like Goliah of Gath! for he tore with his teeth, and struck with both hind feet and fore feet, all at the same instant. The Queen of Scotland would in all probability have been laid low with the rest, had it not been for the prowess of her favourite hero, who sprung from Corbie's back, and seized the audacious mule by the bridle. 'Smite him, my son!' cried the friar, with a loud voice: 'Draw thou forth thy sword, and smite him to the earth, for it is better for him to die than to live.'

The mule thought to prove contumacious at the first; but feeling Charlie's powerful grasp, he calmed himself, turned the one ear back, the other forward, and switched his tail, listening with much gratification to the hysterical cries of the discomfited damsels. Not so his master, who was grieved in spirit, and very wroth with his old servant and companion; insomuch that when he alighted from his back, and seized his curb, he exclaimed, 'O thou limb of the wicked one! Thou emblem of the evil principle working in the children of disobedience! What shall I do unto thee? Lo, now, if I had a sword in mine hand, would I not strike thy head from off thy body, and cause thee to be buried with the burial of an ass?' The mule let his ears fall down very wide asunder, like the horns of a Lancashire ox, putting on a face of great humility, as he looked out from beneath his heavy eyebrows, with many a sly demure glance at the friar's face. The good man led him around the lists in search of an opening to get out, for he durst not again

mount him for fear of being instrumental in some farther
outrage among the ranks of the great and the noble. As he
passed by the King, his Majesty caused him to be called
up into his presence, and asked him what sum it would
please him to ask as the price of his mule?

'Verily, my lord, O King,' answered the friar, with great
readiness, 'that beast hath been unto thy servant as a friend
and an inheritance. He hath borne me over the mountains
of Palestine, and hath drunk from the fords of Jordan, as
well as from Abana and Pharpar, the rivers of Damascus.
Yea, bestriding that woful beast, hath thy servant fought
the battles of the cross; and the hooves that have in thy sight
been lifted up against the fair and the lovely, the meek and
the innocent, have been dyed red in the blood of infidels.
Money is of no avail to thy servant; and he cannot part
with his old and trusty companion, even though the spirit
of those that are cursed from the heavens be in him.'

'Then wilt thou come thyself unto me at the Scottish
court?' said the King to him, somewhat in his own style –
'and I will cherish both thee and thy doughty companion,
and thou shalt minister unto me in holy things, and shalt
be unto me as a father, and I and my children will be to
thee as sons and as daughters; for my trusty and well tried
friend, Sir Ringan of Mountcomyn, saith well of thee and
of thy great wisdom, valour, and prudence.'

'Verily, most noble King, I have yet many things to
accomplish in other lands than this, which, by the strength
of the Lord, must be fulfilled; when these are finished, then
shall thy servant come unto thee, and visit thee for good.'

'And thou shalt be a welcome guest,' said the King:
'Wear thou this ring for my sake, which I give thee as
a pledge of friendship, and of protection through my
kingdom. Remain in the lists, for thou hast yet battle to
do against two knights of the lance and the sword.'

'Lo, I will even strike with the sword and the spear, if
my lord the King commandeth it. But I lack armour, and
am not a man of war, save when the lives of the innocent
or the cause of the cross is at stake. And, moreover,
the beast that thou seest is as a beast of the bottomless
pit; he hath antipathies and sympathies of his own; and
instead of bearing me full force against my opponent, he
may carry me to make war against women and children.

Nevertheless, I will do all that it behooveth me to do. Who are my adversaries?' – He was told they were the knights of Gemelscleuch and Raeburn—. 'Then God do so to me, and more also, if I lift up my hand against any of these my brethren, the men of my right hand, and the preservers of my life. Neither will one of them put his spear in rest against me; so that the battle would perish. Thy servant is not afraid to fight, but as a gladiator he is unwilling to exhibit; therefore my lord, O King, suffer him to depart in peace.'

These reasons were cogent, so the King admitted them; and the worthy and heroic friar was suffered to lead off Goliah of Gath, amid thundering shouts of applause.

CHAPTER THIRTY-ONE

> This general doctrine of the text explained, I proceed, in what remains of this discourse, to point out to you three important and material considerations concerning the nature and character of woman. These shall be, 1*stly*, What she was; 2*dly*, What she is; and, 3*dly*, What she will be hereafter. And are not these, my brethren, matters of high importance?
>
> *Dickson's Sermons*

ALL THINGS OF this world wear to an end, saith Isaac; so also did this high Christmas festival within the halls and towers of Roxburgh. The lady Jane had borne a principal share in all the sports, both in and out of doors. In the hall she was led up to every dance, and in the lists she presided as the queen of the games, distributing the prizes with her own fair hands to the Scottish heroes, and, of course, crowning her old friend Charlie with the bays at least once a day. Sir Charles was a most unassuming character, and seldom adventured on addressing his superiors first. But when once they addressed discourse to him, he never failed answering them with perfect ease and unconcern; and often, as is well known ere this time, with more volubility than he himself approved of. Once, and only once during all these days of his triumph and high honours, did the lady Jane remember him of having brought her into captivity, and of the high bribe he had refused for her liberty. 'An' if it be your will, honoured lady, I wish ye wadna say ony mair about that matter,' said Sir Charles; 'for mony queer fidgetty kind o' feelings I hae had about it sinsyne. And if I had kend then what I ken now – if I had kend wha I had in my arms, and what I had in my arms, I had nae borne the honours that I wear the day. My heart had some sair misgiving aince about you, when there were hard news gaun of your great jeopardy; but now that you are in sic high favour, I am e'en glad that I brought you, for troth ye hae a face and a form that does ane good to look at.'

The lady Jane only sighed at this address, and looked down, thinking, without doubt, of the long and dismal *widowhood* which it would behoove her to keep for the dismal end of her betrothed knight, and then a virgin widowhood too, which was the worst of all. There was an obscure glimpse of the same sort of ideas glanced on Charlie's mind as he viewed her downcast blushing countenance; and afraid of giving birth to any painful sensations in such a lovely lady's mind, he desisted from further conversation.

The Queen was still so much interested in that lady as to endeavour by all means to procure her liberty without any ransom, somewhat contrary to her son-in-law's opinion. The Queen reasoned, that she was not a lawful prisoner of war; the Douglas that she was, there being no bond of peace subsisting between the nations, and she entering Scotland with forged credentials, at least signed and sealed in favour of another and non-existing person. She applied to the King, who gave his consent, but, at the same time, professed having nothing to do in the matter. At length she teazed Lord Douglas so much that he resolved to indulge her Majesty before the court took leave of him, but to leave it until the very last day. He, however, reckoned before his host; for now that the abbot of Melrose had conjoined him with royalty, he found that he had at the very least two to please instead of one.

Here, we must, with that regard to veracity which so well becomes every narrator of a true tale, divulge a disagreeable secret; that is, we must delineate truly a trait in the character of our heroine, the lady Douglas, (lately the princess Margaret of Scotland,) which we would rather have concealed, had it been possible to have done so. But she could not conceal it any longer herself – and why should Isaac and I vex ourselves about it; for one day when Mary Kirkmichael waited on her in her chamber, she found her drowned in tears, and with great perplexity, and no less curiosity, set herself to discover the cause.

'What? My dearest and most noble lady in tears?' exclaimed she. 'Now, a plague on these teazing, battling, boisterous, deluding creatures called men, that will not let poor innocent maids alone to live at heart's ease, but hold them thus in constant ferment, married or unmarried! Well did I ween from experience, that the maiden's troubles were the most insufferable to be borne! The neglects – the disappointed hopes – the fears – and, above all, the jealousies! Oh these jealousies! What infernal tormentors they are! But now little wot I what to say, or what to think; for beshrew me if I remember the time when I saw my royal mistress in tears before. Let me recollect. No, not since dame Mary Malcolm's palfrey leaped the ravine before the lords of Huntly and Athol, and yours refused. Then, indeed, you wept; and when I laughed you struck me. Yes, you know you struck me, and that had nearly made matters worse.'

'Pray, madam,' said lady Douglas, 'could you conveniently command yourself so far as to bring a surgeon here on the instant?'

'A surgeon! Sanct Marie's grace! what is your ailment, my dearest lady?'

'It is not for myself, it is for you I want him. You are very ill of a quinsey, dame, and bleeding below the tongue is necessary. Go bring my father's leech to me, without delay, and come with him.'

'You have not forgot your sweet maiden frolics for all that is come and all that is done. Well, I am glad you are still in that whimsical humour. I was afraid you were grievously vexed or disappointed at something in your new state.'

'Step forth, I say, and bring me in a surgeon, for I insist on having you bleeded under the tongue. You are very ill indeed, and the disease is infectious.'

'By my maidhood, and by your own, sweet lady, (the Douglas's I mean,) there shall no leech that ever drew lancet open a vein in my blessed and valuable member. No, not were it to humour a queen, or a *lady Jane Howard*.'

'Now, may all the plagues that prey on the heart of woman seize and torment thee if thou hast not guessed the cause of my uneasiness. There's a latent devil within thee that whispers to thy imagination the thoughts that are passing in my heart. O Kirkmichael, I am ill! I have suffered many distresses in my time! many, many distresses!'

'Yes, indeed you have, my royal mistress! many, many distresses!'

'Bring the surgeon, I say. Cannot you, for the life of you, compose yourself for a little space, when you see me in such distress? Your royal mistress, Mary? I am no royal mistress now! No, I a'nt! Nothing but a plain jog-trot wife of a lord, or earl, or how do you call that beautiful title? While the lady Jane Howard! – Oh Kirkmichael, I cannot tell you the half of what I feel!'

'I know it all. Jealousy! my dear lady, jealousy! Think you I know not what it is to suffer that? Do you remember young Spinola, that came to our court from the places abroad? He loved me the best after all; I had certain demonstrative proofs of it. But do you know what I suffered? Racks, tortures, strangulations! Fiends tearing out my eyes, pouring hellebore into my ears, and boring through my heart with red hot irons! Not know what jealousy is? Was not I telling your royal self the last minute—'

'Mary! stop, and be advised. You are very ill.'

'I humbly ask forgiveness. I was coming to it. Dear lady, I have noted your trouble these nine days past, and that it was still gaining ground. But I can partly account for it, so that, with a little prudence and patience, it may be removed. Ever since the day on which you was a bride, or the one following perhaps, there has been more court and more flattery paid to the southern beauty than to the northern one. It is the course of nature, madam; you are now a married wife, and your charms must be admired at a distance with respect and awe. The maid must still be courted and flattered. Quite natural, madam, I assure you. Think you any knight durst caper and bow, and prate to the lady Douglas, as they do to *the English puppet?*'

'Mary, I will give you all my wedding apparel for these two last words. Is not she a mere puppet, without soul or magnanimity? But – Mary! – How gladly would I change places with her, Mary! She has conquered after all. Yes: She has conquered Margaret Stuart, there is no denying of it to one's own heart.'

'Gramercy, dearest lady, are you not raving? Has not the

noble lord of your adoption proved victorious, and gained you with all honour and approbation?'

'But then the lord of *her* adoption *died* for her, Mary. Think of that. The gallant, faithful, and magnanimous Musgrave *died* for the mistress of his affections. But who died for the poor degraded lady Margaret of Scotland? I am conquered with my own weapons. There is no denying of it! I would rather that one lover had laid down his life for me than have had fifty husbands.'

'Palpably wrong! I'll prove it. Fifty husbands! How delightful – beg pardon, madam.'

'I tried the Douglas hardly for it. But he was too selfish, and would not die for me. Base, cruel knight! No, he *would not* die for me; even though I got him to believe that I was put to death, and my ghost haunting him, yet he *would not* kill himself. What a value those monstrous men set upon their lives! Musgrave died. Lady Jane has conquered, and I am *married!* I wish I were dead, Kirkmichael!'

''Tis a pity but that you were, madam! If ladies are to live on these terms with the world, they had better be out of it. For you know if the man that one loves best will not condescend always to die when the gratification of his mistress' vanity requires it, why there is an end of all endurance. I managed otherwise with young Spinola.'

'Mention the name of your Spinola again to me for the head that stands on your body, since you deprecate the more gentle prescription of bleeding below the tongue; and now find me some anodyne without delay for the distemper that is preying on my vitals. None of your jeers and your jibes, Kirkmichael, for I am not in humour to bear them. The worst thing of all is yet to come. This puppet – this painted doll – this thing of wax! after triumphing over me in my own country and among my own people – after being died for, while I was only lived for – after being courted, and flattered, and smiled on, while I was only bowed to and gazed on – after being caressed by my father, and bedaubed with praises by my newfangled and volatile mother – after all this, I say, there is she going to be set at liberty, and without all question wedded to one of the royal dukes, one of the princes of the blood! How shall the blood of the Bruce and the spirit of the Stuart brook this? Before I heard of that lady's name, I knew not what jealousy was.

Ever since that time has she held me in misery. I thought I had once achieved the greatest conquest that ever was accomplished by heroine. And I *did* seize a noble prize! How has it turned out? – in every instance to her honour, and my disparagement. And there, through the unnatural fondness of my doating mother, will she return home, and be courted for her princely fortune, not for her beauty I am sure! But then, they will hear that the bravest and most chivalorous knight in England *died for her*; and as certainly as I speak to you, will she achieve a higher marriage than Margaret, and how shall she ever show her face again?'

'A higher marriage than you, dearest lady? Then must she be married to some of the kings on the continent, for in all the dominion of England there is not a subject of such power as your lord, the Earl of Douglas and Mar, nor one whose military honours flourish so proudly.'

'My lord and husband is all that I could wish in man, only—'

'Only that he is *not dead*. That's all.'

'You had better! *Only* I say that he is not a *prince of the blood royal*, Mary. Think of that. There are many such in England. And there to a certainty will my great and only rival be wedded to one of these. The Duke of York or Glocester, mayhap; or to Prince Henry, the heir of the house of Mortimer, and then she'll be *a queen!* Yes, Kirkmichael! then she will be *queen of England!* – And I – what will I be? No more than plain *Lady Douglas!* The wife of *the Black Douglas!* – Och! what shall I do, Mary? I'll go and wipe my shoes on her as long as I have it in my power.'

'Marry for a small space; there is time enough for that afterward, my dearest lady. Be staid for a little while, till I tell you a secret. A very important and profound one it is, and it behoves you to know it. There is a certain distemper that young newly married ladies are subjected to, which is entitled PHRENZY, or some such delightful name. Some call it *derangement of intellect*, but that is too long a name, I hate long names, or very long things of any sort. So you must know, madam, that this delightful trouble, for it is delightful in its way, produces a great deal of animation. It is quite proper you should know this grand matrimonial secret, madam. This delicious, spirit-stirring trouble then soon goes off, and when it goes all the giddy vapours of youth fly with it. The mirror of the eye is changed, its convex being thence turned inward, reflecting all nature on the soul in a different light from that in which it had ever appeared before; and, at the same time the whole structure and frame of the character is metamorphosed, and the being that is thus transmuted becomes a more rational and respectable creature than it was previously; and at the same time a more happy one, although it must be acknowledged its happiness is framed on a different model. This is my secret, and it is quite proper that every *young* lady who is married should be initiated into it. As for the old ones, they are too wise to be initiated into any thing, or for any thing to be intiated into them.'

'Now, you imagine you have said a very wise thing; and it is not without shrewdness. But I can add a principal part which you have wholly left out, and it is this: When the patient is labouring under this disease, it is absolutely necessary that she be indulged, and humoured in every one of her caprices, else her convalesence is highly equivocal. Don't you acknowledge this?'

'I grant it. And the first case that comes under my care I promise to abide by this prescription.'

'That is spoken like yourself – like the trusty friend and confidante. What then is to be done? for something must be done, and that suddenly.'

'That is easily decided. She must be kept in confinement. Kept here a prisoner at large, until she turn an old maid and lose a few of her fore-teeth. That will be delightful! Eh! Then make her believe all the time that it is a duty incumbent on her to remain in that widowed state for the sake of Musgrave – Hoh! beg pardon, madam!'

'I charge you never to let that triumph of hers sound in my ears again. It creates the same feeling within me as if you informed me that an adder was laced in my stays. Kirkmichael, you never took any thing in hand that you did not accomplish for me. This lady must be retained for the present, till we can determine on some other course. I gave my lord a lesson about it already, but his reply was not only unsatisfactory but mortifying in the extreme. It has almost put me beside myself, and my pride will not suffer me to apply to him again.

'My dearest love,' said he, 'I pray that you will not shew a sense of any inferiority by a jealousy of that unfortunate lady.' Inferiority! I never had such a sentiment as a feeling of inferiority! What absurd notions these men imbibe. Is it possible, Mary, that I can have a sense of inferiority?'

'No, no! quite impossible! Think no more of such antiquated and absurd apothegms as these. I will manage it for you. I take in hand to keep her as long as I live, if that will satisfy you. But are you sure that your brother will not fall in love with her, and marry her, and then she will be queen of Scotland?'

'Ooh! – Oooh! Give me a drink, Mary. I am going into fits! Ooh! – Yes: as sure as you stand there, he will. The prince is his mother all over, newfangled and volatile in the extreme, and amorous to an intolerable degree. Disgustingly amorous, she is the very sort of food for his passion. Then her princely fortune, and the peace of the two realms! Oh! give me another drink, Mary; and bathe my hands – and my brow – That is kindly done. Queen of Scotland! Then I must pay court to her – perhaps be preferred as lady of the bedchamber. No, no. To the Scottish court she *must not go!*'

'Be calm, my sweet lady! I have it. You shall assume your brother's character once more – pay court to her – seduce her, and have her disgraced.'

'What did you say, Kirkmichael? repeat that again. What did you say about disgracing? I am so very ill.'

'O no! That scheme will not do. It will end ill! it will end ill! You are lady Douglas now, not the maiden princess. Why, I will get her married to one of your footmen for you. That will do.'

'Prithee speak of things possible, and within some bounds of probability. If she were but married to a knight but one step below my lord in dignity, I would be satisfied. Nay, were that step only ideal it would give my heart content.'

'Is that then so much to make such a pother about? I will accomplish it in two days. So difficult to get a maid of her complexion to marry? Difficulty in fattening – a pig! baiting a hook for a bagrel! – a stickleback! – a perch! I'll do it in two days – in one day – in half a day, else never call me Mary Kirkmichael of Balmedie again. Difficulty in marrying a maid with light blue eyes – golden locks and rosy cheeks –

with a languishing smile always on her countenance? and that maid an English one too? Peugh! Goodbye, my lady, Lady Black Douglas. I'm off. (Opening the door again.) It is a shame and a disgrace for any gentleman not to *die* for his mistress! I say it is! Young Spinola would have died for me cheerfully if I would have suffered him – that he would! Goodbye, madam.'

Mary was as busy all the remaining part of that day as ever was a bee in a meadow. She had private business with the Queen, and had art or interest enough to get two private audiences. She had business with the lady Jane Howard; a word to say to the King, and two or three to the lord Douglas – But it is a great loss that these important disclosures cannot be imparted here – for every word that she told to each of them was a profound secret! Not a word of it ever to be repeated till death! What a loss for posterity! It had one quality, there was not a word of truth in all this important disclosure; but an ingenious lie by a woman is much more interesting than one of her true stories. There was, however, one of Mary Kirkmichael's secrets came to light, though none of those above-mentioned; and from the complexion of that, a good guess may be made at the matter of all the rest.

Sir Charles Scott, alias Muckle Charlie of Yardbire, was standing at the head of his hard-headed Olivers, his grimy Potts, and his skraeshankit Laidlaws, in all amounting now to 140 brave and well appointed soldiers. He had them all dressed out in their best light uniform, consisting of deer-skin jackets with the hair outside; buckskin breeches, tanned white as snow, with the hair inside; blue bonnets as broad as the rim of a lady's spinning wheel, and clouted single-soaled shoes. He was training them to some evolutions for a grand parade before the King, and was himself dressed in his splendid battle array, with his plumes and tassels of gold. His bonnet was of the form of a turban, and his tall nodding plumes consisted of three fox tails, two of them dyed black, and the middle one crimson. A goodlier sight than Sir Charles at the head of his borderers, no eye of man (or woman either) ever beheld. As he stood thus giving the word of command, and brandishing the Eskdale souple by way of example, in the great square in the middle of the fortress, a little maid came suddenly to his side and touched him. Charles was extending his voice at the time, and the interruption made him start inordinately, and cut a loud syllable short in the middle. The maid made a low courtesy, while Charles stooped forward and looked at her as a man does who has dropt a curious gem or pin on the ground, and cannot find it. 'Eh? God bless us, what is't hinny? Ye war amaist gart me start.'

'My mistress requests a few minutes private conversation with you, sir knight.'

'Whisht dame! speak laigh,' said Sir Charles, half whispering, and looking raised-like at his warriors: 'Wha's your mistress, my little bonny dow? Eh? Oh you're nodding and smirking, are you? Harkee, It's no the auld Queen, is it? Eh?'

'You will see who it is presently, gallant knight. It is a matter of the greatest import to you, as well as your captain.'

'Ha! Gude faith, then it maunna be neglected. I'll be w'ye even now, lads; saunter about, but dinna quit this great four-nooked fauld till I come back again. Come along, then, my wee bonny hen chicken. Raux up an' gie me a grip o' your finger-ends. Side for side's neighbour like.' So away went Sir Charles, leading his tiny conductor by the hand, and was by her introduced into one of the hundred apartments in the citadel.

'Our captain is gaun aff at the nail now,' said Will Laidlaw; 'Thae new honours o' his are gaun to be his ruin. He's getting far ower muckle in favour wi' the grit fo'k.'

'I wonder to hear ye speak that gate,' said Gideon Pott of Bilhope: 'I think it be true that the country says, that ye maun aye read a Laidlaw backward. What can contribute sae muckle to advance a gentleman and his friends as to be in favour with the great?'

'I am a wee inclined to be of Laidlaw's opinion,' said Peter Oliver of the Langburnsheils, (for these three were the headsmen of the three names marshalled under Sir Charles) – 'Sudden rise, sudden fa'; that was a saying o' my grandfather's, and he was very seldom in the wrong. I wadna wonder a bit to see our new knight get his head choppit off; for I think, if he haud on as he is like to do, he'll soon be ower grit wi' the Queen. Fo'k should bow to the bush they get bield frae, but take care o' lying ower near the laiggens o't. That was a saying o' my grandfather's aince when they wantit him to visit at the castle of Mountcomyn.'

'There is he to the gate now,' said Laidlaw, 'and left his men, his breadwinners, in the very mids o' their lessons; and as sure as we saw it, some o' thae imps will hae his simple honest head into Hoy's net wi' some o' thae braw women. Wha wins at their hands will lose at naething. I never bodit ony good for my part o' the gowden cuishes and the gorget, and the three walloping tod tails. Mere eel-baits for catching herons!'

'Ay weel I wat that's little short of a billyblinder, lad!' said Peter Oliver; 'I trow I may say to you as my grandfather said to the ghost, 'Ay, ay, Billy Baneless, 'an a' tales be true, yours is nae lie,' quo' he; and he was a right auldfarrant man.'

But as this talk was going on among the borderers, Sir Charles, as before said, was introduced into a private chamber, where sat no less a dame than the officious and important lady of all close secrets, Mistress Mary Kirkmichael of Balmedie, who rose and made three low courtesies, and then with an affected faltering tongue and downcast look, addressed Sir Charles as follows: 'Most noble and gallant knight – hem – Pardon a modest and diffident maiden, sir knight! – pink of all chivalry and hero of the Border: I say be so generous as to forgive the zeal of a blushing virgin for thus presuming to interrupt your warrior avocations—. (Sir Charles bowed—.) But, O knight – hem – there is a plot laying, or laid against your freedom. Pray may I take the liberty to ask, Are you free of any love engagement?'

'Perfectly so, madam, at – hem!—'

'At my service. Come – that is so far well. You could not then possibly have any objections to a young lady of twenty-one or thereby, nobly descended, heir to seven ploughgates of land, and five half-davochs, and most violently in love with you.'

'I maun see her first, and hear her speak,' said the knight, 'and ken what blood and what name; and whether she be Scots or English.'

'Suppose that you *have* seen her and heard her speak;' said the dame; 'and suppose she was of Fife blood; and that her name was *lady* Mary Kirkmichael: What would you then say against her?'

'Nothing at all, madam,' said Sir Charles, bowing extremely low.

'Do you then consent to accept of such a one for your lady?'

'How can I possibly tell? Let me see her.'

'O Sir Charles! gallant and generous knight! do not force a young blushing virgin to disclose what she would gladly conceal. You *do* see her, Sir Charles! You *do* see her and hear her speak too. Nay, you see her kneeling at your feet, brave and generous knight! You see her *tears* and you hear her *weep* – and what hero can withstand that? Oh Sir Charles!—'

'Hout, hout, hout!' cried Sir Charles interrupting her, and raising her gently with both hands, 'Hout, hout, hout! for heaven's sake behave yoursel, and dinna flee away wi' the joke athegither, sweet lady. Ye may be very weel, and ye are very weel for ought that I see, but troth ye ken a man maun do ae thing afore another, and a woman too. Ye deserve muckle better than the likes o' me, but I dinna incline marriage; and mair than that, I hae nae time to spare.'

'Ah, Sir Charles, you should not be so cruel. You should think better of the fair sex, Sir Charles! Look at this face. What objections have you to it, Sir Charles?'

'The face is weel enough, but it will maybe change. The last blooming face that took me in turned out a very different article the next day. Ah, lady! Ye little ken what I hae suffered by women and witchcraft, or ye wadna bid me think weel o' them.'

'Well, knight, since I cannot melt your heart, I must tell you that there is a plot against your liberty, and you will be a married man before to morrow's night. It is a grand plot, and I am convinced it is made solely to entrap you to marry an English heiress that is a captive here, who is fallen so deeply in love with you that, if she does not attain you for her lover and husband, her heart will break. She has made her case known to the Queen, and I have come by it: therefore, sir knight, as you value my life, keep this a *profound* secret. I thought it a pity not to keep you out of English connections; therefore I sent for you privily to offer you my own hand, and then you could get off on the score of engagement.'

'Thank you kindly, madam.'

'Well, Sir. On pretence of an appendage to the marriage of the king's favourite daughter with the greatest nobleman of the land, before the festival conclude, it is agreed on that there are to be a number of weddings beside, which are all to be richly endowed. The ladies are to choose among the heroes of the games; and this lady Jane Howard is going to make choice of you, and the law is to be framed in such a manner that there will be no evading it with honour. You have been a mortal enemy to the English; so have they to you. Had not you better then avoid the connection by a previous marriage, or an engagement say?'

'I think I'll rather take chance, with your leave, madam: Always begging your pardon, ye see. But, depend on it, I'll keep your secret, and am indebted to you for your kind intentions. I'll take chance. They winna surely force a wife on ane whether he will or no?'

'Perhaps not. One who does *not incline marriage*, and has not *time to spare* to be married, may be excused. Tell me, seriously; surely you will never think of accepting of her?'

'It is time to decide about that when aince I get the offer. I can hardly trow what ye say is true; but if the King and the Warden will hae it sae, ye ken what can a body do?'

'Ah, there it is! Cruel Sir Charles! But you know you really have not a minute's *time to spare* for marriage, and the want of *inclination* is still worse. I have told you, sir knight, and the plot will be accomplished to-morrow. I would you would break her heart, and absolutely refuse her, for I hate the rosy minx. But three earldoms and nine hundred thousand marks go far! Ah me! Goodbye, noble knight. Be secret for my sake.'

Sir Charles returned to his men in the great square, laughing in his sleeve all the way. He spoke some to himself likewise, but it was only one short sentence, which was this: 'Three earldoms and nine hundred thousand marks! Gudefaith, Corbie will be astonished.'

It was reported afterwards, that this grand story of Mary's to Sir Charles was nothing at all in comparison with what she told to lady Jane, of flames and darts, heroism, royal favour, and distinction; and, finally, of endless captivity

in the event of utter rejection. However that was, when
the troops assembled around the fortress in the evening,
and the leaders in the hall, proclamations were made in
every quarter, setting forth, that all the champions who had
gained prizes since the commencement of the Christmas
games were to meet together, and contend at the same
exercises before the King, for other prizes of higher value;
and, farther, that every successful candidate should have
an opportunity of acquiring his mistress' hand in marriage,
with rich dowries, honours, manors, and privileges, to be
conferred by the King and Queen; who, at the same time
gave forth their peremptory commands, that these gallants
should meet with no denial, and this on pain of forfeiting
the royal favour and protection, not only towards the dame
so refusing, but likewise to her parents, guardians, and
other relations.

Never was there a proclamation issued that made such
a deray among the fair sex as this. All the beauty of
the Lowlands of Scotland was assembled at this royal
festival. The city of Roxburgh and the town of Kelso
were full of visitors; choke full of them! There were
ladies in every house, beside the inmates; and, generally
speaking, three *at an average* for every male, whether in
the city or suburbs. Yet, for all these lovely women of
high rank and accomplishments, none else fled from the
consequences of the mandate but one alone, who dreaded
a rival being preferred – a proof how little averse the ladies
of that age were to the bonds of matrimony. Such a night as
that was in the city! There were running to and fro, rapping
at doors, and calling of names during the whole night. It
was a terrible night for the dressmakers; for there was such
a run upon them, and they had so much ado, that they got
nothing done at all, except the receiving of orders which
there was no time to execute.

Next morning, at eight of the day, by the abbey bell, the
multitude were assembled, when the names of the former
heroes were all called over, but only sixteen appeared,
although twenty-two stood on the list. The candidates
were then all taken into an apartment by themselves, and
treated with viands and wines, with whatever else they
required. There also they were instructed in the laws of
the game. Every one was obliged to contend at every one

of the exercises; and the conqueror in each was to retire into the apartment of the ladies, where they were all placed in a circle, lay his prize at his mistress's feet, and retire again to the sports without uttering a word.

The exercises were held on the large plain south of the Teviot, so that they were beheld by the whole multitude without any inconveniency. The flowers of the land also beheld from their apartment in the castle, although no one saw them in return, save the fortunate contenders in the field. The first trial was a foot race for a chain of gold, given by the lady Douglas, and all the sixteen being obliged to run, the sport afforded by the race was excellent; for the eager desire to be foremost acted not more powerfully to urge the candidates to exertion than the dread of being the last, so that the two hindmost were straining every nerve, and gasping as voraciously for breath as the two foremost. Sir Charles Scott took the lead, leaving the rest quite behind, so far that every one thought he would gain with all manner of ease, and they began to hail him as conqueror. But owing to his great weight he lost breath, and in spite of all he could do the poet made by him and won the prize, which he took with a proud and a joyful heart, and laid at the feet of Delany. 'Bauchling shurf!' exclaimed Sir Charles, laughing when he saw the poet passing his elbow, 'Useless bauchling shurf! an I had kend I wad hae letten ye lie, and been singit to an izle in the low o' Ravensworth.'

'Knight, I think ye hae lost,' cried one.

'I think sae, too,' said Charles. 'I liket aye better to rin ahint an Englishman than afore him a' my life.'

The next game given out was a trial in leaping, for a pair of bracelets, clasped with gold, and set with jewels, given by the Queen. These also the poet won, and laid at Delany's feet. Sir Charles won three; one for tilting on horseback, one for wrestling, and one for pitching the iron bar, and he laid all the three prizes at the feet of lady Jane Howard. Two lords won each of them two prizes, and other two knights won each of them one; and all, unknown to one another, laid them at the feet of lady Jane Howard.

When the sports of the day were finished, the seven conquerors, all crowned with laurel, and gorgeously arrayed, were conducted to the gallery where the ladies still remained; and after walking round the room to the sound of triumphal music, they were desired to kneel one by one in the order in which they had entered before, and each to invoke his mistress's pity in his own terms. It fell to the poet's lot to kneel first, who stretched forth his hands toward a certain point in the room, and expressed himself as follows: 'O lovely darling of my soul! in whom my every hope is centered; at whose feet I laid my honours down. This laurel wreath I also consecrate to thee. By all the love that I have borne for thee, the pains that I have suffered, I conjure you to raise me up, and say thou wilt be mine: – else here I'll kneel till doomsday!'

A pause ensued; the King and his nobles looked on in breathless curiosity, for they knew not where he had bestowed his favours. The dames also gazed in envious silence, and in hopes that the supplicant would be refused. He soon himself began to dread what they hoped; his countenance changed; the wild lustre of his eye faded; and he began to look around to see where he could get a sword on which to fall and kill himself. He cast one other pitiful look to Delany, but she deigned no movement to his relief – still keeping her seat, though visibly in great agitation. But, at length, when hope was extinct in his bosom, there appeared one to his relief. This was no other than his old rival the gospel friar, who had been admitted in an official capacity, in order to join hands and bless unions if any such chanced to be agreed on. He was standing ruminating behind backs; but seeing the first offer about to be rejected, and aware of the force of example, whether good or bad, and how little chance he had of employment that day if the first effort misgave, he stepped briskly up to Delany, and, taking her hand, said, 'Lo, my daughter, have not I travelled for thee in pain, and yearned over thee as a mother yearneth over the son of her youth? Why wilt thou break my heart, and the heart of him that burneth for thy love?' Delany then rose, and with trembling step came toward her lover, led by the grotesque form of the good friar. The tears gushed from the poet's eyes as she lifted the laurel crown from the floor, and replacing it on his head, said, as she raised him up, 'Thou hast adventured and overcome. Hence be thou the lord of my heart and affections.'

The friar gave them no more time to palaver, but joined

their hands, pronounced them a married pair, and blessed their union in the name of the Trinity. Then Sir Charles Scott kneeled, and, casting his eyes gravely toward the floor, said only these words: 'Will the lady whom I serve take pity on her humble slave, or shall he retire from this presence ashamed and disgraced?'

Woman, kind and affectionate woman, is ever more ready to confer an obligation on our sex than accept of one. Lady Jane arose without any hesitation, put the crown on the knight's head, and, with a most winning grace, raised him up, and said, 'Gallant knight, thou wert born to conquer my countrymen and me; I yield my hand and with it my heart.' The friar lost no time in joining their hands; he judged it best and safest to take women at their first words; and short time was it till the two were pronounced husband and wife, 'and whom God hath joined let no man dare to put asunder. Amen!' said the friar, and bestowed on them an earnest blessing. – Isaac the curate expatiates largely on the greatness and goodness of this couple; how they extended their possessions, and were beloved on the Border. Their son, he says, was the famous Sir Robert of Eskdale, the warden of the marches, from whom the families of Thirlstane, Harden, and many other opulent houses are descended. No union could be more happy; and besides, it rendered the Lady Douglas the happiest of women, and Mary Kirkmichael the proudest.

But to return to the scene in the gallery with the knights and their mistresses. The King and his nobles who accompanied the gallants into the apartment of the ladies, knowing nothing of the choices each had made, expected great amusement from compliances and non-compliances; and at all events, after so fair a beginning, a number of weddings to be the result. Every one of the successful knights expected the same thing; for it is a curious fact, which shows the duplicity of our character in a striking light, that, when the champions were all in the apartment together in the morning, some mentioned one lady as the flower of the land and of all present, some mentioned another, and so on. But no one ever mentioned the names either of *Delany* or *Jane Howard*. Sir Charles indeed mentioned no name, but when each had named a pretended favourite with mighty encomiums, he only added, 'I'll no say muckle; but there's ane that I rank aboon a' thae.'

The master of the ceremonies looked round to call the next champion to kneel; but, behold, he was not there! He called the next again. He was gone also! Every one of the knights had vanished, each thinking *himself* slighted by the preference given to Sir Charles Scott, but none knowing that for his sake they were all slighted alike. The noblemen were all in the utmost consternation; the King became highly offended, and said 'What is the meaning of this? Have these knights dared to desert their colours on the very eve of action? This is not only an affront put upon *us*, but upon our fair and noble visitors, of whose honour and feelings we are more jealous than of our own.'

But the friar, who was a man of peace, and disliked all sort of offence, when he saw the King was displeased, took speech to himself, and his speech set all the gallery into a burst of laughter. He was standing in the midst of the floor, with his book in hand, ready and eager to officiate still farther as a knitter and binder; but when he saw the knights all fled, and the King offended, he uplifted both of his hands and one of his feet, standing still on the other, and cried with a loud voice, 'Behold my occupation is ended! Woe is me for the children of my people! For the spirit of man is departed away, and he hath no strength remaining. Oh what shall I do for the honour of my brethren! For, lo, the virgins are come to the altar, and there is none to accept of the offering. The men of might are dismissed, yea they are confounded and fled away, and the daughters of the land are left to bewail the months and years of their virginity. Woe is me, for my hand findeth nothing more to do!'

The ladies laughed immoderately at the cases of the forlorn and discomfited knights; for they had witnessed the proceedings, and saw that all their devotions were paid to one object; and as no lady of Scotland had been chosen, one could not envy another – so they tittered and laughed off the affront as well as they could.

The friar got passports into England, and after much labour and pain got the poet established in his father's possessions, and acknowledged as the lord of Ravensworth. He also regained for him his lady's possessions on the continent, which the Nevilles retained for the space of two hundred years. That amiable couple cultivated the arts of peace, music, and song, as long as they lived. After these things, the friar was preferred to great emoluments in his old age, and he spent them all in acts of charity and benevolence.

From Roxburgh the royal party proceeded to Melrose, where they remained two days, which they spent partly in devotion and thanks-givings, and partly in viewing the magnificent scenes in the neighbourhood, particularly the great hill of Eildon, so lately reft asunder and divided into three by the power of the elemental spirits. To this awful theme the mind of the Queen still reverted; and, on her last visit to these mountains, she passed through the recent chasms, gazing and trembling at the effects produced by that tremendous convulsion of nature; and, at length, she had spoken and dreamed so much about it, that she proposed to go and visit the castle of Aikwood, and if possible to get a sight of the great enchanter himself, before she left the Border counties, where, she said, she might never be again. Every one tried to dissuade her from the attempt, and the King got into a high passion, but still she could not be driven from her purpose. 'As we return to the abbey,' said she, 'we will go by the ford of Dornick-burn at the foot of the deep dell that you told me of, where the devil first made his appearance on horse-back to the four warriors. I should not wonder that we shall see him there again under some disguise.'

'I would not wonder that we should,' said Sir Charles: 'I have been told that he is sometimes seen there in the shape of a clerk; sometimes as a mariner; and sometimes in the form of the King of Scotland. Always begging your pardon, royal madam.'

'There is no offence, Sir Charles, as long as you do not tell me that he appears in the shape of a Queen. I hope he has never yet been known to assume the shape of a woman.'

'He has enow to appear for him in *that* form, which I ken something about to my cost; and which your royal majesty kens mair about than I could have wished. What does your majesty account the greatest peril that man is subject to in this world?'

'Oh war, war, certainly! Nineteen out of twenty of his perils concentrate in that, or are derived from it.'

'Ye may be thankfu' ye ken nae mair about it than that, my lady queen! Aince ye gang near the castle of Aikwood ye'll get a little mair experience perhaps. Now ye are determined on ganging there the morn, and I am determined on accompanying you, since you will go. But troth I would be right wae to see my queen turned into a cow, and a little deil set to drive her; or into a grey mare, and a witch or warlock set to gallop on her; or a doe, or a hare, or a she-fox, and a tichel o' tikes set after her to tear her a' to tareleathers. Always begging your pardon, my liege lady.'

As they were chatting on in this familiar and jocular style, they came to the identical little deep dell, at the meeting of two rivulets, or moorland burns, where the devil and his three attendant imps had appeared to our warriors on their way to Melrose; and, as Dan Chisholm was of the party, the Queen caused him to be called up to describe the whole scene – with the personal appearance of the arch fiend – the words he spoke, and also the extraordinary course that he had with him along the marble pavement of the air. All these matters were detailed to her by the trooper with perfect seriousness and simplicity, which made such an impression on the Queen's romantic and superstitious mind, that her countenance altered in every feature, and she was every now and then gazing around as if expecting Satan's personal appearance before them once more. The party were sitting on horseback conversing together, when the sharp eye of Sir Charles, well accustomed to the discernment of all living or moving objects, whether by night or by day, perceived a miserable looking wight approaching them by the very path on which the infernal cavalcade had formerly proceeded. The Queen was talking to Dan, still pushing her inquiries, when Sir Charles touched her gently on the shoulder, and said, 'Hush, your majesty. See who is this approaching us by the very road that the deils took? It is a question who we have here. Ane is nae sure of ony shape that appears in sic a place and sic a time as this.'

Then there was such crossing and telling of beads, and calling on the names of saints, took place with the Queen and her ladies, every one of them asking the same question in terrified whispers, 'Is it he, think you? Is it he? Oh, is it he?' Then there was a general request made that they should take instant flight, and ride home to the abbey full speed; but an opposition arose to this proposal from a quarter not expected. This was from no other than Sir Charles' English lady, whose education had taught her to despise the superstitions so prevalent in Scotland; and seeing them all about to fly from a poor wo-begone, half-famished wretch, she opposed it with indignation, adding, that she would abide his coming by herself if none else would. Sir Charles was still far from being clear about these matters, hard experience having taught him caution; however, he commended his lady's spirit, and drew up by her side: The rest marshalling behind them, they awaited in a body the coming of this doubtful guest; and every eye being fixed on his motions, so every tongue was busied in giving vent to the spontaneous movements of the mind. 'It is a palmer,' said one. 'It is a warlock,' said another. 'It is the devil,' said a third; 'I ken him by his lang nose!' 'Aha, my royal and noble dames!' cried Sir Charles exultingly: 'If it be nae the deil, it's his man; sae we may expect some important message, either frae his infernal majesty or the great enchanter, for this is no other than his seneschal. My royal liege, this man that you see approaching is no other than Gilbert Jordan, the late laird of the Peatstacknowe, who was drawn by lot to supply the room of the wretch whom our gospel friar sent up through the clouds in a convoy of fire and brimstone. Whether this be Gibbie or his ghaist, it is hard to say; but I ken weel by the coulter nose it is either the one or the other. Your majesty will scrimply believe it, but the last time I saw that carl the deil was hauding him by the cuff o' the neck ower the topmost tower of the castle of Aikwood, and the poor laird was sprawling like a paddock in a gled's claws, when fifty fathom frae the ground. There is nought in nature I expected less to see than that creature again in the land of the living; yet it is actually he himself in flesh and blood, and that is all, for he is worn to skin and bone, and his nose is even longer than it was! Hech, laird, is this you? And are you indeed returned to the Christian world aince mair?'

'Aye troth, Yardbire, it is a' that's to the fore of me. But who have you got all here? Good-e'en to you, gentles. This brings me in mind of a story, man, that I hae heard about the hunting of Stanebires' cat—'

'Whisht, Gibbie, and gie us nane o' your auld stories about cats even now. This is the Queen of Scots and her attendants. Rather tell us, in one word, how you have made your escape from yon infernal gang in the castle of Aikwood?'

'Aha, Yardbire, that is a tale that winna tell in ae word, nor twa neither, it wad take a winter night in telling, and it is the awesomest ane that ever passed frae the lips o' man; but I am ower sair forespent at this time to begin to it.'

'Oh, no!' cried the Queen: 'Honest man, do not begin it at present. It shall serve for our evening's amusement, and you shall tell it before your King and his nobles, after you have had such refreshment as you stand in need of.' She then caused one of her squires to alight, and mounting the wearied and exhausted laird on his horse, they rode off to Melrose, where, after a plentiful meal, the laird was brought into the apartment where the King, the Queen, the abbot, with the nobles and ladies of the court, were all assembled; and then, at the royal request, he related to them the following narrative.

CHAPTER THIRTY-TWO

Commissions and black bills he had,
And a' the land went hey-gae mad,
    The like was never seen, joe:

To dance and caper in the air,
And there's an end of him, joe.
                    Old Jacobite Song

WEEL, YE SEE, my masters and mistresses, this is what I never expected to see. There is something sae grand in being in the presence of a King and Queen and their courtiers, that it brings me in mind of the devil and his agents that I have been in the habit of entertaining for a month bygane. But there is some wee difference in masters for a' that; for, in my late service, if I had been brought in to entertain them, in an instant they would have had me transformed into some paltry animal, and then amused themselves by tormenting that animal to death, by dissecting it while living. But the queerest thing of all was this – there was aye a spark of life that they could not destroy, which, for all their cruelties, remained active and intelligent as before; and the moment they put that spark of life out of one animal, they popped it into another, and there was I obliged to undergo the same dismemberment and pain once more, and so on for ever. The inflicting of torment was their chief delight, and of that delight there was no satiety – it seemed still to increase by gratification.

On the very first day that I entered on my probation they had a feast, as my comrades know, and as I also have good reason to know, for on that day I suffered death nine times; and yet I was Gibbie Jordan again before night. They first turned me into a cock, and after the three pages had chased me round the castle, and thrown stones at me till I was hanging out my tongue, and could not cackle another lilt, they seized me, took me into the scullery, and drew my neck. Ere ever I was aware, they had me transformed into a huge lubberly calf, while one of the hellish pages was dragging me by the neck with a prickly rope made of hurcheon hides, and the two others were belabouring my rumple with cudgels. I suspected their intentions, and being still terrified for death, and inclining rather to suffer any thing, I drew back, shook my head, and bellowed at them, while they still redoubled their blows on my carcase, and cursed me. In spite of all I could do, they dragged me gasping into the slaughter-house, kept the knife an excruciating long time at my throat, and then, after piercing the jugular vein, they laughed immoderately to see me running about, bleeding to death, with my glazed stupid eyes; and when, through faintness, I began to flounder and grovel on the floor, they laughed amain, threshed me to make me plunge a little more, and when I could do nothing farther than give a faint baa! they thought that the best sport of all, and mimicked me.

I had scarcely ceased baaing as a calf, when I found myself a beautiful cappercailzie, winging the winter cloud, and three devils of falcons after me. 'Now,' thinks I to myself, 'If I do not give you the glaiks now, my hellish masters, may I never wap a wing again. By all the powers of swiftness, but I shall try for once if the feathers shall not carry the flesh away.' Sanct Martha, as I did scour the rimy firmament! I took the wind in my tail, but I went with such amazing velocity that I left it behind me, and as I clove it, it seemed to return in my face. I reached the shoulder of a lofty mountain, and then I laid back my wings, and bolted through the air like a flash of lightning. 'O ho! Messrs Hawks, where are you now?' thought I to myself. Good Lord! ere ever I was aware, there was ane o' them gave me a nab on the crown, that dovered me, and gart me tumble heels-o'er-head down frae the shelves of the clouds; and lighting with a dunt on the ground, I had nae shift but to stap my head in a heather bush, and let them pelt at me till I got some breath again. Then I made for a cottage, thinking the inmates could not but pity my condition, and drive the hawks away from me. I took cover among their cabbage, in the sight of both man and wife; but instead of pitying me, the one came with an old spear, and the other with the tongs, to finish my existence – and always when the falcons came down on me with their talons, the two cried out, 'Weel done, little hawkie! Yether him up! puik him weel!' I was forced to take wing again, till at length, through fatigue and want of feathers I dropt close to the castle whence I had set out, and the three falcons, closing with me, first picked out my eyes and then my brains. I was stabbed as a salmon, hunted as a roe-buck, felled as a bull, and had my head chopped off for a drake. The dinner was made up of me. I supplied every dish, and then was forced to cook them all afterward. It was no wonder that I could not partake of the fragments of the meal.

From the moment that the Christian warriors were all dismissed with disgrace from the castle, the devil became contumacious with the Master, and assayed to carry matters with a very high hand. But he had to do with one that would not succumb, no not in the smallest point, but who opposed him with a degree of virulence of which even the master fiend seemed scarcely capable. It was a scene of constant contention and rage, and the little subordinate demons did not always know which to obey. It was, if it please your Majesties, a scene acted in terrible magnificence, of which I have seen several poor and abortive emblems among mortal men. And henceforth I shall always believe and feel, when I see a family or society constantly involved in disputes, wranglings, and angry emotions, that they are children of the wicked one, and moved by the spirit of discord, that bane of the human race.

'The worthy gentleman hath said well,' said the abbot. 'It is a moral truth that can never be too deeply impressed, that *peace and love only lead to happiness*. They are emanations from above, and the contrary passions from beneath. All the fierce and fiery passions of the soul are the offspring of hell fire. But a truce with preaching. Honest friend, go on with your strange relation, and acquaint us in what manner his infernal majesty and the king of mortal magicians spent their time.'

In constant discord and jarring. The devil challenged the Master with impotency in entertaining a poor crazy monk, and submitting to be protected and even cowed by him; at which the Master took high offence, and retorted in the bitterest terms; while the other always hinted that he would make him repent his intercourse with that preposterous and presumptive fool. So he termed our own worthy friar and head chaplain.

In one thing only they agreed, and that was in abusing the witches. Never were there poor deluded creatures guided in such a way as they. The devil says to the Master one day in my hearing, 'Brother Michael,' says he, 'I have an act of justice to perform to all our true and trusty female lieges in this quarter. I gave them my princely word of honour, that on their yielding themselves up souls and bodies to me and to my service, they should all be *married!*, and all to young and goodly husbands too. That having been the principal, and almost the only boon, the good consistent creatures required of me for the sacrifice they made, they must not be disappointed.' The Master acquiesced, but at the same time remarked, with what I judged unreasonable chagrin, that when he was keeping his word so punctually, it betokened nothing good for those to whom he kept it.

Well, we had a witch's wedding every night for nine nights running; but such extreme of wickedness is past all human comprehension, beyond the possibility of description. The marriage ceremony itself, always performed by a demon in the habit of a friar, was a piece of the most horrid blasphemy ever conceived; and every night one of the witches was married to the devil in disguise. Sometimes the bridegroom made his appearance as a gay cavalier, sometimes as a country squire, a foreign merchant, a minstrel, and a moss-trooper. The old wretch of a bride was all painted by some devilish cantrip, and bedecked with false jewels, and though she seemed always aware of the deceit in a certain degree, from former experiences, yet it was wonderful with what avidity each of the old creatures clung to her enamoured and goodly husband! How they mumped and minced in their talking, and ogled with their old grey ropy eyes! And then how they danced! Gracious me, how they flung, and danced among the deils and the warlocks! and capered and snapped their fingers, giving their partners often a jerk on the nose or the temple as they passed and repassed in the reel, as quick as green clocks on a pool. Then the bedding of the brides, these surpassed all description; and as they had me fairly in thrall, I was suffered to witness every thing. The first witch bride was led out at the back door of the castle with much state and ceremony, into a place that had been a bowling green, and in which there was nothing else save a bowling green: Yet, to my amazement, there stood a bower of the most superb magnificence; and there, in a chamber hung with gorgeous tapestry that glittered all with gold and rubies, the loving couple retired to their repose, and to all the delights and joys of so happy an union. Then wishing them the greatest conjugal felicity, all the gallants returned to the castle. But I, being curious to see what would be the end of this grand pavilion in the bowling-green, which I knew must be merely a delusion, a vision, a shadow of something that had no stability of existence, went up to the top of the castle, and from a loop-hole sat and watched what was to be the end of this phenomenon. I waited a good long while, and began to think all was real, and that the splendid witch had met with a happy fortune – for I knew them too well to be all witches from former happy experience. But at length the lusty bridegroom, as I supposed, began to weary of his mate, for I saw the form of the bower beginning to change, and fall flat on the top, and its hue also became of a lurid fiery colour. I cannot tell your Majesties what sort of sensations I felt when I saw the wedded couple sinking gradually down through a bed of red burning fire, and the poor old beldame writhing to death in the arms of a huge and terrible monster, that squeezed her in its embraces, and hugged her, and caressed her till the spark of wretched life was wholly extinguished. I saw distinctly by the light of the flame that surrounded them, and marked every twist of the features, and every quiver of the convulsed limbs; yet these were not more impressive than the joy of the exulting fiend, who continued to caress and kiss his agonized mate to the last, and called her his love, and his darling, and his heart's delight. At length the distortions of the human countenance reached their acme – the shrivelled bosom forgot to throb, and, with the expiry of the mortal spark, the lurid flame that burnt around them also went out, and all was darkness, There was no bower, no chamber, no bridal bed, but a cold winter soil; and I thought that, through the gloom, I perceived the couple still lying on it.

As I could get no rest all that night for thinking of the terrible scene I had witnessed, as soon as the sun rose next morning I went out to the bowling-green, but found nothing there save the strangled body of the wretched woman – a dismal and humbling sight – squeezed almost to a jelly, and every bone broken as if it had been smashed on an anvil. Being curious to examine her robes in which she appeared with such splendour the evening before, and her jewels, part of which I had seen her lay carefully aside, I took every thing up as it lay. Her robes were a small heap of the most wretched rags imaginable: her pearl necklace was a string of dead beetles, and her diamond rings pieces of thread, on which were fastened small knots of clay, and every thing else proportionally mean. While I was standing considering this vile degradation that had taken place, I heard a voice at a little distance that called to me and said, 'Gibbie Jordan! Gibbie Jordan! why standest thou in amazement at a true emblem of all worldly grandeur! It is all equally unreal and unsubstantial as that on which thou lookest, and to that it must all come at last.'

'Hout, friend,' thought I, 'it canna surely be a' sae perfectly unreal as this, else what does it signify?' But a' that I could look and glime about, I could never discover the speaker that said this; and when I thought seriously of the matter, I found that it comes a' to the same thing in the end.

'Honest friend, thou hast again illustrated a momentous moral truth,' said the abbot – 'and I thank thee for it. Thou hast the art, in thy simplicity, of extracting more good out of real evil than any expounder of divine truths throughout the land. Thou art both a moral and a natural philosopher, and I intend conferring on thee some benefice under the church, that thy talents may no longer remain locked up in a helmet. Prithee, go on with thy extraordinary narrative; but these witch weddings are too horrible for mortal ears.'

Then you may consider, my Lord Abbot, what they were for mortal eyes, especially such a run of them, which were every night varied in their horrors, and terminated in something perfectly distinct from all those preceding. On the second night the bridegroom was a foreign merchant, a man of bustle and punctuality, who said he could not remain late with his kind convivial friends, and was under the necessity of carrying his bride off at an early hour, having business of importance to transact on the morrow. It was a speculation, he said, on which he calculated making a good profit, and a man who was coming in to have a wife, and in all probability a small family to maintain, required to look after and attend to these matters. The witch caressed him in ecstasy when he made this speech, and proffered to go with him as soon as he chose. She saluted her cronies, and bade them farewell; and although there is no love among those sort of people, yet there was still so much of human nature remaining, that there seemed to subsist a degree of regret that they should never meet again. My own heart was even sore for the wretched beldame; for I had witnessed a scene the preceding night which had been withheld from her view, and those of the other brides that were to be; and I knew that a fate somewhat similar awaited them all. They mounted this one behind the spruce merchant on a tall gallant charger whose eyes gleamed like lightning, and away they set over the leas of Carterhaugh, at a light gallop; but at every bound the swiftness of the steed increased, till it was quickly beyond the speed of the eagle. The witch held like grim death, and would fain have expostulated with the bridegroom on the madness of risking their necks for a little per centage – but her velocity was such that she could make no farther speech of it, than just a squeak now and then like a short hare. The reckless merchant flew on, still increasing his rapidity, until he came to the very highest rock of the Harehead linn. The witch knew of the dreadful chasm that was before them, and weening that her husband did not know she uttered a piercing shriek; but the void was only thirty yards across and a hundred deep, so the fearless merchant, meaning to take it at one leap, made his charger bound from the top of the precipice. The infernal courser cleared the linn, but the witch's head failing, she toppled off about the middle space. There were two fishermen spearing salmon in the bottom of the gulf, who saw the phenomenon pass over their heads, and the wife lose her hold and fall off; they heard her likewise saying, as she came adown the air, 'Aih, what a fa' I will get!' And as she said, so it fell out; for she alighted on the rocks a short space from the place where they stood, and was literally dashed in pieces; but the steed ran away with the merchant over hill and dale like a thunderbolt, and neither the one nor the other ever looked over his shoulder to see what had befallen the bride.

This continuation of horrors still depriving me of rest, I went into the linn the next morning to look after the corpse; but the three pages, Prig, Prim, and Pricker, were engaged with it, cutting it trimly up, and hanging it on the trees of the linn to be frozen, so that they might thereby be enabled to preserve it for some grand experiment. In the same manner did they serve the remains of all the brides; none of them ever being buried – but there was one ⸱aken away bodily. I shall now, in conformity with your reverence's hint, desist from the description of any more of these weddings, and proceed to the adventure by which I attained my liberty.

I had often attempted this, both by night and by day, but these imps seemed to possess a sort of prescience, for in all my attempts I was seized and maltreated so grossly that I gave up all hopes of escape, otherwise than by some upbreaking of the warlock's establishment, and of all such incidents I had resolved to avail myself, and you all see that at last I have succeeded – which happened on this wise.

Still as Christmas tide drew on, the wranglings between my two chief masters, the devil and the warlock, grew more and more fierce; and as I heard they were obliged to sever before that time, I both hoped and dreaded some terrible convulsion. The fiend, for several successive days, was always hinting to the Master that it now behoved the latter to deliver him up the black book and the divining rod; and he tried to cajole him out of them by fair speeches and boundless promises: but with these requests the Master testified no disposition to comply, and the promises he utterly disregarded, bidding him bestow his promises on those who did not know him. At length the fiend fairly told him, that he must and would have the possession of these invaluable treasures, which ought never to have been put into the hands of mortal man, and that now he would have them if he should tear his heart from his bosom to attain the boon.

I weened that matters were come to that pass now that the Master would be obliged to yield, and that all this show of resistance was only the ebullition of a proud and indignant spirit struggling against the yoke under which it knew it was obliged to bow, like a horse that champs the bit, to the sway of which it knows too well it must submit. In all this, however, I had reckoned before mine host, and knew not the resources of the great magician. Beneath the influence of the cross I found him a child, a novice, a nonentity, unresolved and inconsistent in his actions. But amongst the beings with whom he associated I found him a superior intelligence, a spirit formed to controul the mightiest energies, and not brooking submission to any power unless by compulsion. To my utter astonishment he not only gave the archfiend absolute refusal, but haughty defiance; and then it was apparent, that, except from necessity, all forbearance was at an end.

'Preposterous madman! dost thou know whom thou beardest?' said the fiend, gnashing his teeth with rage and thirst of vengeance: 'Knowest thou with whom thou art contending, thou maniac? – and that I can wring thy soul out of thy body, consigning the one to the dunghill, and the other to elemental slavery, at my will and pleasure?'

'I defy thee,' said the Master: 'Do thy worst. He that imparts a moiety of his power to another, must abide by the consequences. Do I not know with whom I am contending? Yes! I know thee! And thou art so well aware that I do, that at this moment thou tremblest beneath my rod. I know thee for a liar, a deceiver, a backbiter, and a spirit of insatiable malevolence. Who can lay one of these charges to my name? Were I immortal as thou art, how I would hurl thee from thy usurped and tyrannic sway over the mighty energies of nature. Were I freed of the incumbrances of mortality – of blood that may be let out by a bodkin – bones that may be broken by the tip of an oxgoad – and breath that may be stopped by the twang of a bow-string; of vitals, subjected to be torn by disease – preyed on by hunger, thirst, and a thousand casualties beside: – yes, were I rid of these congregated impediments, as I shall soon be, I would thrust thee down into that subordinate sphere of action to which only thy perverse nature is fitted. This black book and this divining-rod are mine. They were consigned to my hands by thyself and the four viceroys of the elements, and part with them shall I never, either in life or in death; and while I possess them I am thy superior. Begone, and let me hear no more of thy brawling at this time, lest I humble thee, and trample on thee before thy day of power be expired.'

This the Master pronounced in loud and furious accents; and as he finished he struck the devil across the gorge with his golden rod. The blow made him spring aloof, and tumble into the air, it had such powerful effect on his frame; and when he stood again on his feet, he roared with rage and indignation, in a voice that resembled thunder. The Master had the black book belted to his bosom, with bands of steel, that were hammered in the forge of hell; and laying his left hand upon that, and brandishing his divining-rod in his right, he dared the fiend to the combat. The latter approached, and poured from his mouth and nostrils such a stream of liquid flame on the magician, that it appeared like a fiery rainbow between them. This greatly incommoded the Master, and made him skip like a mountebank; but it was soon exhausted, and then the fiend threw trees and rocks at him, some of the latter of the weight of five tons. All these the Master eschewed; and though he sought no other weapons but his rod, he brake in upon his antagonist, and chaced him from the field. Then the war of words again commenced, which increased to a tempest of threatening, wrath, and defiance. The arch-demon boasted of his legions, and of their irresistible power; and threatened to bring them all to the contest, and annihilate the Master and his adherents, root and branch.

'I have already said that I fear neither them nor thee,' said the Master. 'What though thou hast the sovereignty over the element of fire, and all the fierce and indurated spirits that sojourn and ply in the sultry regions of flame, as also of the grovelling spirits of the mould? Have not I at my command those of the air and the water? I can muster against thee the storm, the whirlwind, and the raging tempest, the overwhelming wave, and the descending torrent. These shall extinguish thy meteor hosts, and sweep thy moldwarps from the face of the earth. I am in the midst of my elements here. Thou art out of thine, and that thou shalt feel when thou bringest it to trial.'

Thus parted these two once-bound associates, but now jealous and inexorable foes – a good lesson to all those who form combinations inimical to the laws or authority of the land in which they reside. Like those master-spirits, such are likewise conspirators against rightful sovereignty, although on a smaller scale; and like those whom they imitate, and by whom they are moved, their counsels will always be turned either to foolishness or against themselves.

'The sphere that this man hath filled in society,' said the abbot, 'is far below that in which he ought to have moved. If his narrative is true, which I can hardly believe, he turns it to most excellent uses; and if it is an apologue, it is one well conceived for the purposes of instruction. Verily, this gentleman hath never moved in his proper sphere.'

'I think it is not very unlikely that your reverence says,' said Sir Ringan, 'for he made no great figure in it. Tho' I had always a partiality for him, I had no great faith in his valour. He would rather have cut down a warrior behind his back than before his face any time. He has made mare quake this night wi' his tale than ever he did wi' his weapon. I entreat ye to get on, laird, and let us hear how they made up matters.'

Made up matters, does my cheif say? That was a term no more mentioned between them. They separated but to raise their different forces, and meet again with more fury and effect. The Master spoke to his three pages, and asked if they were resolved to stand firm to his interest? They answered, that they would, till the term of their bondage expired.

'Then am I doubly armed!' said the Master, exultingly; 'and I will show your tyrant that I can quell his utmost rage. Speed thee, my trusty and nimble spirits; speed to the western and northern spheres, and rouse the slumbering angels of the winds and the waters. Tell them to muster their array, and bear hitherward – to rear the broad billows of the Atlantic up against the breast of heaven, and to make a bellows of every cloud to gather the winds up behind them. Then bring down the irresistible spirits of the frozen north in ambush – and who shall stand against their fury! How soon will you execute your commissions?'

'Master, I'll ring the surface of the ocean, from the line

to the first field of pickled ice, before the hour-glass is half run.'

'Master, I'll look south on the polar star – call every whale, sea-monster, and ice-shagged spirit by his name, and return to you before the cock-bittern can boomb his vesper.'

> 'And I'll to the moon,
> And the stars aboon,
> And rack my invention
> For the coming contention:
> And the wind and the weet,
> And the snow and the sleet,
> I'll gather and gather,
> And drive them on hither.'

With that the three imps departed on their several missions, but not before they had seized me, and bound me to a ring on a turret of the castle. The Master retired into his apartment for some time, but soon came up to the level space on the top of the castle, our old birth, and strode about in the most violent agitation, but appearing rather to be moved by anger and impatience than by dread. At length, he came up to me, and said, 'How now, droich? What thinkest thou of all this?'

I said nothing, for I durst not answer a word.

'Dost thou think,' continued he, 'that there exists another being, either mortal or immortal, like me, thy master?'

I still durst not answer a word; for if I had said *no*, it would have been blasphemy; and if I had said *yes*, it would have provoked him to do me a mischief; so I looked at my bonds, and held my peace.

'Thou darest not say there is,' continued he; 'but I know what thou thinkest. Sit thou there in peace till this great trial of power be over; and if thou darest for thy life invoke another name than mine, thou shalt never stir from that spot dead or alive. But if thou takest heed to this injunction, and cease from all petitions to, or mention of, a name which thou mayest judge superior to mine, then shalt thou be set at liberty to join thy friends.'

I determined to attend to this – but he waited not for my answer, but strode away, looking now and then on the book of destiny, and at the western heaven alternately. At

length he exclaimed, 'Yonder they come! Yonder they rise
in grand battalia! Noble and potent spirits! How speedily
have you executed your commission. Yonder comes the
muster of my array, and who shall stand against them!'

I looked towards the west when I heard him talking
in such ecstacies, but could see nothing save a phalanx
of towering clouds, rolling up in wreaths from the dun
horizon. I had seen the same scene a hundred times, and
could hardly help smiling at his enthusiasm, especially
when he went over a long muster-roll of the names of
spirits and monsters whom he saw approaching in the
cloud. 'It is a sign that warlocks have clear een,' thinks I,
quietly, 'for I see nothing but a range of rolling and restless
clouds.' However, he was so overjoyed with the sight of this
visionary array, that, having no other to communicate with,
he came rapidly up to me, and said, 'Tell me, droich, didst
thou ever witness any thing so truly grand as the approach
of this host of mine?'

'You must first lend me the use of your eyes that I may
see them,' said I; 'for, on my word, I see nothing save
two or three files of castled clouds, which I have seen an
hundred times.'

With that he lent me a blow with his rod, and said,
though not apparently in wrath, 'Thou hast no brighter
eyes, and no brighter conceptions, than a hedgehog, but
art a mere clod of the valley, a worm; if I knew of aught
lower to liken thee to, I would do it! Dost thou see nothing
like fleets and armies approaching yonder? Dost thou not
see an hundred and seven of the ships of the ocean above,
coming full sail, with colours flying, and canvas spread?
Seest thou not also, to the south of these, two files of
behemoths, with ten thousand warriorspirits beside?'

I looked again, and though I was sensible it must be
a delusion brought on by the stroke of his powerful rod,
yet I did see the appearance of a glorious fleet of ships
coming bounding along the surface of the firmament of
air, while every mainsail was bosomed out like the side
of a Highland mountain. I saw, besides, whole columns
of what I supposed to be crocodiles, sharks, kelpies, and
water-horses, with a thousand monsters never dreamed of
by human being. The Master marked my astonishment,
and exulted still the more; and then he desired me to turn

round, and look toward the north. At first I could see nothing; but on being touched again with the divining-rod, I shall never forget such a sight as opened gradually to my view. The whole northern hemisphere, from the eastern to the western horizon, was covered with marshalled hosts of the shades of gigantic warriors. They were all mailed in white armour, as if it had been sprinkled with hoar-frost; and their beards, which had the appearance of icicles, hung down, swinging in the wind, like so many inverted forests, stripped of their foliage and bark, and encrusted with ice. They were all mounted on the ghosts of crackens, whales, and walruses: and for bows and quivers each had a blown bladder on his back as large as the hill of Ben-Nevis. My heart quaked at the view of these tremendous polar spirits, and I said, 'Great and magnificent Master, are yon terrible chaps all coming hither?'

'Certes they are,' said he: 'Why dost thou ask after having heard my mandate sent forth?'

'Because,' said I, 'If you bearded spirits be a' coming here, I wish I were somewhere alse, for the like of yon was never beheld by man. If your opponents dare face you, they have a spirit beyond what I can conceive.'

'They will be here, and that instantly,' said he, 'And lo! yonder they come! I will go down and meet them on the open field. But, in the meantime, I will loose you with my own hands, for who knows what may be the issue of this day; remain where thou art, for here thou shalt be safe, but no where else.'

I looked; and as far as my eyes could discern, I saw as it were a thousand thousand sparks of fire rising from the east, that came in a straight line toward me, and with great velocity. As they came nearer I perceived that they were all fiery serpents, with faces like men, and small flaming spears issuing from their mouths, which they held between their teeth, or drew in as they listed. These were led on to the combat by the arch-fiend himself, who came at their head in the form of a huge fiery dragon with his iron crown on his head, and wings springing from his shoulders behind, that reached as high as the hill of Blackandro. 'Aih! God guide us!' thinks I to mysel, 'Michael has an awsome adversary to contend with the day!' He was nothing daunted, however, but went boldly down the valley, where he was met by hosts of crawling monsters, such as snakes, lizards, and a thousand others. These I took to be the spirits of the element of earth – but they were lubbards in a field of battle, for, at a brandish of the Master's magical rod, they ran off wagging their tails in such a vengeance of a hurry that they overturned one another.

The van of Michael's western array had by this time gained the middle sky, and hung boiling and wheeling like a troubled ocean straight above his head and above mine. Its colour was as dark as pitch, but there was now and then a shade of a dead white colour rolled out, and as suddenly again swallowed up in the darkness. I never saw ought so awfully sublime. It had now descended so low, that it hid the polar giants entirely from my view, and the Master kept waving his rod towards it, and clapping his left hand always on the black book, till at length, with the motion of a whirlpool, the cloud came and settled all round him. The fiend and his firebrands perceiving this, darted with the utmost fury into the middle of it, and the most tremendous crash of thunder ensued that ever shook heaven and earth. My eyes were dazzled so that I could not see ought distinctly, but I perceived these flaming meteors glancing and quivering round the verges of the darkness, and ever and anon darting again into it. Seven of these peals of thunder succeeded one another, and then I saw the spirits of flame would overcome, for the darkness began to scatter, and I saw the Master hard bested, defending himself with his rod against a multitude. He then cried with a loud voice, and waved his rod toward the north, and that moment the giant warriors of the polar regions loosed all their quivers at once, and with such effect, that they tossed the opposing legions before them like chaff. The hailstones, the snow, and the sleet, poured upon them thicker and faster, and the wind roared louder than their thunders had done before. There was no more power in their foes to stand before them; they were scattered, driven away, and extinguished. When the Master saw this, he shouted aloud for joy, calling out 'Victory!' and leaping from the ground in ecstacy. But when he was in the very paroxysm of exultation, the great dragon came round with a circular motion behind the castle, and approaching behind the wizard's back before he was aware, seized him by the hair with one paw, and by the iron belt with the other, and bore him off into the air straight upward. The Master struggled and writhed very hard, but never opened his lips. At length, after great exertion, he struck the monster a blow with his rod that made him quit his hold, and fly away yelling after his discomfited legions.

The Master fell to the ground from a great height, and lay still, and when I saw no one to come near him, I left the corner where I had hid myself, and ran to his assistance; but he was quite dead. His teeth had severed his tongue in two, and were clenched close together; his eyes were open, and every bone of his body was broken. Having witnessed the unspeakable value of the golden rod, I put out my hand and took hold of it, wanting to bring it away with me, but I might as well have tried to have heaved the castle from its foundations. Besides, when I tugged at it, the dead man turned his eyes toward me with a fierceness that chilled me to the heart, so I fled and came hitherward with all my might. He is lying in a little hidden valley, at the side of the burn, immediately above the castle, with the book of fate locked in his bosom, his rod in his hand, and his eyes open. I have now described to your Majesties this scene exactly as I saw it; but I must also tell you, that when I came to the mill, both the miller and his man, neither of whom knew me, said it had been an awful storm of thunder and lightning. I asked if they perceived nothing about it but a common storm of thunder and lightning? And they said, nothing, save that it was exceedingly violent, and rather uncommon at such a season of the year. I have, therefore, some suspicions that there might be magical delusion operating on my sight; but of this I am certain, that the great enchanter was carried up into the middle space between heaven and earth, fell down, and was killed.'

'I think there can be no doubt,' said the King, 'that what you have told us is the plain and unvarnished truth, though, perhaps, the rod of divination might open your eyes to see the storm in a different light from that seen by the eyes of common men. Of this there can be no doubt, that the greatest man, and the most profound scholar of the age, has perished in this conflict of the elements. He has not only kept the world in awe, but in dreadful agitation for the space of thirty years; let us, therefore, all go to-morrow and see him honourably interred. I ask no rites of sepulture to be performed over his remains, which, if living, he would have deprecated, only let us all go and see his body reverendly deposited in the tomb, lest it be left to consume in the open fields.'

They went, and found him lying as stated, only that his eyes were shut, some of his attendant elves having closed them over night. His book was in his bosom, and his rod in his hand, from either of which no force of man could sever them, although when they lifted the body and these together, there was no difference in weight from the body of another man. The King then caused these dangerous relics to be deposited along with the body in an iron chest, which they buried in a vaulted aisle of the abbey of Melrose; and the castle of Aikwood has never more been inhabited by mortal man.

The Text

THERE ARE TWO forms of the romance: the edition of 1822[1] and *The Siege of Roxburgh*, which appears in volume six of *Tales and Sketches, by the Ettrick Shepherd*, published by Blackie and Son in 1837. Comparison of the two forms, hereafter referred to as 1822 and 1837, shows 1837 to be mainly an awkwardly cut version of 1822, the sections roughly linked, with occasional attempts to bowdlerise and similarly modify the original. 1822 and 1837 are virtually identical to the end of chapter nine of Vol. I 1822. The remaining three chapters of Vol. I, all of the eight chapters of Vol. II, and the first five chapters of Vol. III, are omitted from 1837. Chapter six of Vol. III corresponds to chapter six of 1837; at chapter ten considerable differences begin to appear and 1837 ends at a point in the middle of chapter eleven (ch. XXXI of this edition).

The second version is carelessly printed in respect of spelling, punctuation, even word order. In several places Hogg's spelling has been interfered with. Only rarely does 1837 supply a correction, and then of a simple kind. Not all changes have been noted; those of punctuation are recorded only where another meaning is conveyed. It is hoped, however, that all the more significant differences have been listed, so that the student may observe how Hogg 'improved' his work.

In the textual notes printed here such a notation as 'II 14.5' represents ch. II, p.14, L.5 .

I	1.8 bread o' Binnorie 1837. 9.11 somethink 1837.
II	15.39 a Scot 1822, 1837.
IV	25.21 cauldron 1837. 37.16 choose 1837.
V	44.25 enterprize 1837.
VI	53.19 style 1837.
VII	61.7 feriye 1837. 78.13 the everlasting resources of your cursed nation, *om.* 1837. 79.11 gaurdians 1837. 79.15 assunder 1837.
VIII	85.17 Saint Duthoe 1822; Saint Duthoc 1837.

[1] Some copies of Vol. I lack pp.9–16 (here 'father's vow' 4.30 to 'that can understand' 8.12).

IX   100.9 teazing 1837. 101.32 mein 1837.
XI   130.40 *and froid* 1822.
XII   154.2 Jock to hims 1822.
XV   211.11 an ideot 1822.
XVIII   251.15 a good shareo' 1822.
XIX   275.18 a-head 1822. 285.39 Habby Elliot! 'I thought
            1822.
XX   315.34 gars him scamper? 1822.
XXII   361.39 more spirits; – can sail 1822. 365.3 would be
            fy 1822.
XXIV   389.37 dynasties 1822.
XXVI   406. 4–9 We have now performed . . . siege of Roxburgh,
            om. 1837. 410.30 farthered 1837. 411.11 had shown
            1837. 411.22 –24 not the feigned . . . Lawrence himself,
            om. 1837. 413.4 –16 Above all, the words . . . a bad
            bargain, *om.* 1837. 414.7 –12 It is perhaps . . . Dickie
            starting to his, *om.* 1837. 416.20 –21 who knew nothing
            of the . . . destinies of men, *om.* 1837. 416.21 now more
            convinced 1837. 417.34 Gilkerscleuch 1837.
XXVII   419.11 eume 1822, gume 1837. 421.14 cracking, ye
            ken. I dinna 1822, 1837. 423.30 –33 Heh-heh Rob-
            in-Laid-law! . . . Dan, &c. &c., *om.* 1837. 425.13 as
            he says, We'll 1822, 1837. 426.38 bonns 1822, bones
            1837. 429.3 –12 as he related . . . all these things were
            in relation, *om.* 1837. 432.39 knew them although 1837.
            439.33 the chief, and six 1837.
XXVIII   442.21 –33 so that, harassed . . . mangled by indistinct-
            ness, *om.* 1837. 443.11 for which they were obliged . . .
            Michael Scott, *om.* 1837. 443.12 like all the benefits
            derived from that quarter, *om.* 1837. 443.37 favour
            1837. 449.1 There 1822, Then 1837. 449.28 hin legs
            1837. 450.25 Isaac says, *om.* 1837. 453.23 –24 like some
            . . . spirits of divination, *om.* 1837. 453.27 –28 all hope
            of regaining entrance was lost 1837. 454.18 havoc 1837.
            457.27 –459.17 In the meantime . . . the shabby boy so
            near him, *om.* 1837.
XXIX   463.12 –33 Among other matters . . . comforter' *om.*
            1837. 463.34 But among 1822, Among 1837. 471.38 –
            472.28 . But, among . . . at the very least *om.* 1837.
            473.9 the Glendonyngs, and the Pots 1837. 474.6 –9
            and those others . . . the Warden, *om.* 1837. 475.33 –
            478.24 The stately . . . the sensation, *om* 1837.
XXX   488.14 –20 'Is she not so? . . . queen of beauty, *om.*
            1837. 488.23 Yes; you are . . . You are!', *om.* 1837.
            490.41 shackles 1837. 491.1 –7. At this part . . . Suffice
            it that 1822; The marriage of the princess Margaret of

Scotland and the Earl of Douglas was not now long delayed 1837. 491.8 wassail as what accompanied the wedding 1837. 491.13 Sir Charles Scott of Raeburn and Yardbire 1837. 491.17–32 As for the Queen . . . convulsions of mirth, *om.* 1837. 491.32 In short, Charlie Scott or the knight 1837. 491.39–497.13 But if Charles . . . shouts of applause, *om.* 1837.

XXXI   498.9 saith Isaac, *om.* 1837. 499.27 but to leave it . . . the matter of all the rest 1822; Meanwhile lady Douglas (lately the princess Margaret of Scotland) through the instrumentality of her tirewoman, Mary Carmichael, furthers, in the following manner, a match between Sir Charles Scott, and her former rival, lady Jane Howard 1837. 506.24 One day Sir Charles, alias 1837. 506.32 single-soled 1837. 510.6 festal conclude 1837. 512.10–34 The first trial . . . at Delany's feet, *om.* 1837. 512.34 three 1822; three prizes 1837. 512.38–39 And all . . . Howard 1822; and each laid them at the feet of their lady 1837. 512.40 seven, *om.* 1837. 513.4–514.2 It fell to the poet's lot . . . the Trinity, *om.* 1837. 514.2 Then, *om.* 1837.

Notes

(For place-names the reader is referred to the map on pp. 574–5)

INTRODUCTORY NOTE

Hogg's romance pretends to be based on Border history of the reigns of Robert II of Scotland (1371–1390) and Richard II of England (1377–1390). It introduces as one of its principal heroes James, Earl of Douglas and Mar, who is doubtless the same as the historical personage of that name and title who married a daughter of King Robert and was killed at Otterburn in 1388. Moreover, certain key figures, Sir Thomas Musgrave, Percy, Earl of Northumberland, Sir John Gordon, and many others, all played notable parts in history as well as in Hogg's romance. The work is packed with names, places and other circumstantial material, all of which have some connection with actual Border events. Hogg would appear, from his first scene-setting references to the days of the Stewarts, Randolphs and Douglases, to be following the method of Scott in seeming to give a sound historical background to his tale. It is, of course, only a matter of seeming. That the reign was not one of peace and happiness as Hogg asserts, that Robert II has acquired his lameness from his successor, and his daughter Margaret and son Alexander are wholly imaginary, are matters for comment, hardly for criticism.

The major discrepancy between history and Hogg's version of it relates to the taking of Roxburgh castle. Contrary to Hogg's statement that it had been 'five times taken by the English, and three times by the Scots, in less than seventeen months', in the entire fourteenth century the Scots took the castle only twice: in 1313 Sir James Douglas took it for Robert I, in 1342 Sir Alexander Ramsay recaptured it from the English, but it was lost after the battle of Durham in 1346, and thenceforth not retaken till the siege of 1460 that was fatal to James II. Roxburgh town and district was often the scene of violent and bloody action in the reign of Robert II, but even at the height of Douglas success in recovering Teviotdale and most of its castles in 1384 Roxburgh stood out as the exception. James, second Earl of Douglas, did

540

try, with French help, to recapture it, but abandoned the siege after eight days.

One important event in Hogg's romance demonstrates exactly his treatment of real events. In the closing stages of the tale he has Douglas sore beset by diversionary English troops from Northumberland and the garrison of Berwick, under Sir Thomas Musgrave, who is described by Hogg as governor of Berwick. In the battle that ensues Douglas is aided by a Sir John Gordon, who captures Musgrave. Hogg is in fact conflating two separate events. In 1372 Sir John Gordon captured Musgrave when he was on his way to help Percy of Northumberland, one of the English wardens of the Marches. In 1378, William, first Earl of Douglas, captured Musgrave on his way to Melrose with an advance party from Northumberland. Neither occasion falls within the period of James, second Earl of Douglas (1384–1388), nor was Musgrave governor of Berwick within that period, although he was governor from 1373–1378.

It would appear that Hogg was content to work from a very general awareness of the period. Possibly he drew this from sources like George Ridpath's *Border History of England and Scotland* (1776), and the other eighteenth and early nineteenth-century Scottish histories. I have been unable to find any individual source for the facts of the romance, or any body of material that can be linked to it more closely than Ridpath's. In any case the wealth of folklore and legend that he obtained from his mother and his Border background, relating to the Douglases and the Scotts, would (as we know from his discussion with Walter Scott about their relative treatments of Covenanters in the *Brownie of Bodsbeck* and *Old Mortality*) be of at least equal value in Hogg's estimation, with the accounts of the historians.

Thus his siege of Roxburgh castle draws from many such sieges, of legend and fact, of the fourteenth century. Barbour's tale of how Douglas and his men took Roxburgh castle in 1314 doubtless suggested the final ruse of Hogg's narrative; the advancing Scots were mistaken by the English for straying cattle. But the taking of castles in the period of Robert I was frequently attended with romantic detail which tradition would preserve for Hogg. Often chivalric conditions were agreed on by besiegers and besieged, as in Hogg's romance.

And just as Hogg conflates details from many historical and legendary sources to form the circumstances of his own siege of Roxburgh castle, the same procedure shows in his principal characters. His King Robert owes something to both Robert II and Robert III. His Earl of Douglas seems to be a blend in deed and character of many fourteenth-century Douglases.

The surrounding *dramatis personae* are likenesses or distortions of real figures, or, as in the case of Sir Philip Musgrave, creations suited to the time and Hogg's narrative. With a few exceptions, his use of Border names is shrewd and imparts an air of probability to the tale. The technique is at least as old as Hary's *Wallace*.

Three other points of historical inaccuracy on Hogg's part require brief notice here. The first two concern characters in the romance, namely, the gospel friar who turns out to be Roger Bacon, and the wizard Sir Michael Scott. Their appearance in a tale of the fourteenth century is, of course, anachronistic, since they flourished in the early thirteenth century (see notes). The third concerns the Border family of Scott as presented by Hogg.

His treatment of the clan is fascinating, reflecting as it does Hogg's relations with Walter Scott, and beyond the latter the chief branch of the Scotts, headed by the Duke of Buccleuch. Hogg's original intention was to pay a compliment to both, by creating his own version of the rise to power of the Scotts; and from letters (published and unpublished) to Walter Scott in 1821 it would appear that his original intention was to feature 'the chief Sir Walter Scott the first baron of Rankleburn' as his main Scott. Scott (hearing of this from his Border friend Laidlaw) wrote a 'more than fatherly' letter which struck Hogg as 'containing matter of very serious consideration'. Scott's letter we do not have; but we have Hogg's answer of Nov.16th, 1821 in the Blackwood papers in the National Library of Scotland. Hogg was obviously reproached by Scott for his delineation of this first Sir Walter. He answers:

> I had my suspicions of the thing before, which made me mention it to Laidlaw saying how anxious I was that you should glance over the proofs for I am grown to have no confidence whatever in my own taste or discernment in what is to be well or ill taken by the world or individuals. . . . Laidlaw has however mistaken the character of the chief Sir Walter Scott the first baron of Rankleburn. It is thus toward his own powerfull sept he is as generous as the sun perfectly adored by them all and has no ambitions save the honour and advancement of his house and name. Beyond that he is jealous and selfish loyal to his sovereign but jealous of the Douglases and some other neighbours. In short Lord Douglas draws his whole character in one sentence 'He is cunning as a fox stubborn as an oak and brave as a lion'. I have drawn Sir Walter as I suppose he existed. As a warrior and a chief I am sure of the justice done him and he still rises in estimation till the end. But

then I have made him somewhat blunt and un-courtly
uttering at times strange expressions of broad Scots and
besides he is not a little *superstitious*. The character is a
noble character and in any hands but those of one situated
as I am would have done well and you may be sure I meant
it well. Still I do not know the slightest blot thrown upon
the first of a long line of noble ancestors would be a kittle
cast and that line too terminating in my own master and
benefactor. Not terminating. God forbid that it ever should
terminate but existing and flourishing in him.

Thus stands the case. The first three sheets of proof are in
my hands. The alteration of the name and title throughout
is a trifle; but then he is warden of the marches; has all to
do in that line, and acts a principal part throughout. While
all the subordinate chieftains Gemelscleugh Howpasley
Yardbire (the champion and hero of the tale) Dickie of
Dryhope etc. etc. are all characters likewise so that the
name of the warden can never be concealed under any
title. It is a puzzling concern for me. I do not know this
day what to do. But of this I am satisfied that I must either
make the character of the Warden such a one as will bear
me through at all events with his illustrious house, or alter
the whole of my romance, and it is a hard pill to swallow to
write three volumes over again . . . The surest way would
be for you to look over the proofs however slightly and
make the Baron of Rankleburn *what he should be* . . . As
for Charlie Scott of *Yardbire* . . . you have a son's right to
have the portrait coloured as you please. All that I can do
at present is to stop the press until we shall decide what is
fit and proper to be done . . . for after your letter I neither
will nor dare trust the work as it is.

On Scott's advice Hogg had already drastically cut the part of the
gospel friar. Now Scott was to give a new name to the 'chief Sir
Walter'; he became 'Sir Ringan Redhough' (one remembers the
warrior 'Ringan Red' in Scott's version of the ballad *Lord Soulis*
in his *Minstrelsy*). We can never know if Scott altered more; but
it seems as though he 'gave in' to Hogg's heart-felt plea that
he should not have to write the work again, since Charlie Scott
and indeed the entire early family of Scotts as projected by Hogg
survive.

One can understand a part of Sir Walter's dismay, since
Hogg's entire 'history' of the Scotts is based on little more
than his supposition of what they must have been like, together
with a general awareness of places and names associated with
them. Scotts of Rankleburn are in fact found as early as the
period of Alexander III. For the period of Hogg's romance a

Sir Robert Scott was chief; he died in 1389, and was succeeded by Sir Walter. Only as late as 1415 was Bellandean acquired by exchange. It was during the reign of James II that the Scotts rose high in favour with the king at the expense of the Douglases. And while Hogg rightly associates places like Howpasley, Gemelscleugh, Dryhope, with the family, their respective lairds would not then have been vassals of Sir Ringan.

In view of Hogg's permissibly cavalier treatment of the facts of history, there is little point in attempting to explain every personage or event introduced. The Notes venture into this region only where it is felt that the reader needs further information in order to understand the narrative.

p.1. *Old Song*: this seems to be a version of ballad 10, *The Twa Sisters*, in F. J. Child's collection, *The English and Scottish Popular Ballads* (5 vols. 1882–1898). *The Piercies, the Musgraves, or the Howards*: the first two of these names were famous in the Border wars of the fourteenth and fifteenth centuries. The Howards were not Borderers but one of them, the Earl of Surrey, commanded the English army at Flodden.

p.2. *the manuscript of an old Curate*: devices like this, whereby Hogg seeks to convince the reader of the veracity of his tale by inventing pieces of circumstantial evidence, court records, manuscripts and the like, recur in his work; the most notable example being the entire third section of the *Justified Sinner*. One precedent known to Hogg would be the parson's chronicle cited by Hary as the source of his *Wallace. the richest city of this realm*: Roxburgh. The present village is some two miles away from the site of the castle, of which there are only slight remains on a mound between the rivers Tweed and Teviot. But the former burgh beside the castle ranked with Edinburgh, Stirling and Berwick, as one of the four royal burghs of the thirteenth century; and the castle was a royal residence and place of strength at that time. *Robert the Second*: see Introductory Note. *The strong castle of Roxburgh*: see above. *gallant Lord Musgrave*: see above.

p.3. *Margaret*: see Introductory Note. *the palace of Linlithgow*: although there was some kind of royal residence here at the period of Hogg's romance, the palace as such was begun by James I of Scotland.

p.5. *James, the gallant earl of Douglas and Mar*: the rise of the house of Douglas began with the lands and powers given to the 'good sir James' by Robert I. William, first Earl of Douglas (1358), acquired the earldom of Mar by marrying Margaret of Mar. On his son and heir James see Introductory Note. *the bloody heart*: Sir James Douglas, friend of Robert I, taking the heart of Bruce to the Holy Land, was killed in Spain fighting against the Moors, hence the heart in the Douglas arms. *Sir Ringan Redhough*: see Introductory Note on Hogg's account of the rise of the Scott family.

p.6. *Tell him . . . Cocketfell*: an approximate translation would run as follows: 'tell him [Douglas] to keep their hands busy [the English in the castle], and their jaws empty, and they'll soon need to forget the girl [Lady Jane Howard] because of hunger; and not a single supply will be allowed to cross the Border [between Dirdanhead and Cocketfell] to fill their cooking pots.' The Warden means that Douglas should starve the English out of the castle; and that he himself will intercept all the castle's supplies. The phrase 'gar their pots play brown' means 'cause their cooking pots to be filled with meat and gravy', brown presumably referring to the colour of the contents. *an old man with a cowl*: the identity of this mysterious figure is never established throughout the romance. Sir Ringan presumes him to have been Sir Michael Scott but this hardly seems likely in view of the reception given by that person to Sir Ringan's embassy. And in view of his own words it does not seem that he is Thomas the Rhymer. *the Rhymer's days*: Thomas the Rhymer, also known as Thomas of Erceldoune (Earlston) and Thomas of Learmont. He lived at the latter end of the thirteenth century, and is said to have prophesied the death of Alexander III, the succession of Robert the Bruce, the battle of Bannockburn, and the union of Britain under one of Bruce's blood. The ballad of *Thomas the Rhymer* accounts for his prophetic powers by a seven-years stay in fairyland. See Walter Scott's remarks in the chapters on Thomas the Rhymer in vol. 4 of his *Minstrelsy of The Scottish Border* (ed. T. F. Henderson, 1902).

p.8. *the prophecy of the Hart and the Deer*: Hogg makes up this prophecy. He may have been prompted by the legend which said that Thomas was summoned back to fairy-land by the appearance of a hart and a hind in Earlston. The prophecy bases its symbolism on the heraldry of the Houses of Douglas and Scott. The

Douglas crest has at its centre the heart (see note on the bloody heart, p.5), while the Scott crest has the moon and stars, a deer, and two maidens as supporters. Hogg thus puns on 'heart' and 'hart'; and a translation of the 'prophecy' would run as follows:

Where the hart, in hot blood, moved over hill and dale
There shall the neat deer call for the doe;
Two fleet footed maidens shall tread the green,
And the moon and the stars shall flash between.
Where the proud hold state and bear heavy hand
A crowd shall feed on a father's fair pastures,
In reaching for the stars, the D shall fall down
But the S shall be S when the head S is gone.

The sense is that the Scotts will profit from the downfall of the ambitious Douglases and will even outlast the Stewarts. Hindsight makes a good prophet.

p.9.   *the king's elwand*: Orion's belt. *the Charlie-wain*: Ursa Major, also the Plough. *Master Michael Scott*: a mediaeval scholar said to have been attached to the court of the Emperor Frederick II at the beginning of the thirteenth century, and to have been sent by him to the universities of Europe to communicate versions of Aristotle made by Scott and others. In his note XXVIII, 'the wondrous Michael Scott', to *The Lay of the Last Minstrel* Walter Scott associates him with Balwearie, in Fife, and imagines him to have been the ambassador of the same name who was sent to bring the Maid of Norway to Scotland on the death of Alexander III. His treatises on natural philosophy, judicial astrology, alchemy, chiromancy and the like caused him to be regarded by his contemporaries as a skilful magician. Certainly his fame as a wizard had spread over Europe by the time of Dante, who refers to him in the *Inferno* as such. Hogg changes Scott's period and uses the legend of Michael's magic books, which were dangerous to open, and were supposed to have been buried with him. He also uses the tradition that Scott cleft the Eildon hills in three. But Aikwood or Oakwood castle or tower near Selkirk, given by Hogg as Scott's seat, only dates from the sixteenth century (the 'Jingler's room' there was reputed to be his). Hogg may again have been turning a compliment of sorts to Walter Scott, as Oakwood tower was the property of the Scotts of Harden, and had been so for a very long time; especially as he later refers to him as a relative of Sir Ringan Redhough. *the words of True Thomas*: again Hogg's invention. An approximate translation would run:

When the winged horse shall kick at his master
Let wise men change their methods of self-advancement.

The winged horse is the Douglas family, with its high-flying ambitions; the master, the king; and wise men refers to the Scotts in general and Sir Ringan in particular.

p.10.   *the Ha's*: the Halls, an English Border family.

p.11.   *Old Play*: it is almost certain that Hogg here and elsewhere writes his own epigraphs (after the manner of Scott throughout the Waverley novels). *His batteries . . . trapt palfrey*: the 1822 text has 'butteries and his craboun', where 'craboun' is a variant of 'carbine', so that 'butteries' should be the author's or printer's slip. 'Ploydenist' is unknown, but may be a coinage from 'ploy', which signifies 'frolic', 'trick', 'escapade', so here a sportive or 'tricky' person. The sense may be: 'His batteries and his carbines he discharges abruptly (?on impulse). Is it likely that such a rascal should become a peace-maker', etc.

p.12.   *his short clippit Highland tongue*: this may be a reference to the fact that Robert II, as a Stewart, owned lands in Bute and had a castle at Logierait in Perthshire.

p.13.   *Maxwells . . . Gordons . . . Hendersons*: Scots Border families, as are the Setons, Elliotts and others mentioned on p.14. The term 'up' applied to them refers to their having risen in arms.

p.14.   *Davie's Pate*: Davie's serving man or son.

p.19.   *Sir John Oldcastle*: the original name of Shakespeare's Falstaff; it was retained in some early editions.

p.20.   *the convent of Maisondieu*: really a hospital on the right or east bank of the Teviot. It dated back to before 1140 and survived for many centuries. *Sir Thomas de Somerville of Carnwath*: the surname occurs in the *Wallace* and Hogg may have read *The Memorie of The Somervills*, Edinburgh, 1815. *Sir Comes de Moubray*: a fictitious personage. *Simon of Gemelscleugh . . . John of Howpasley . . . and the Laird of Yardbire* (p.21): see the note on Hogg's account of the rise of the Scotts in the Introductory Note.

p.25.   *Old Rhyme . . . Old Ballad*: the first is probably Hogg's own writing, the only puzzle of interpretation being that Peggy is usually a girl's name. This may be deliberate irony on Hogg's part, as the 'young noblemen' of the chapter are in fact girls. The second may well be part of a ballad.

p.26.   *what hae they't hinging geaving up there for?*: 'why do they have it (the pot) hanging staring up (open)?'

p.29.   *Prince Alexander Stuart*: a fictitious personage.

p.31.   *Lord Jasper Tudor*: fictitious.

p.31.   *'Tis just pe te shance she vantit*: here as elsewhere Hogg attempts to convey dialect by a roughly phonetic spelling. This highlander's statement is followed by that of a Scottish lowlander, then by that of an Aberdonian (his statement, 'fat te teel's . . . a beedle', being translateable as 'what the devil's taken the bits of wee laddies to fly into such a hot temper about their bits of lassies. I wouldn't have my feet in their shoes for three placks and a bodle.') Finally a Scottish borderer speaks, as 'before the Englishman had time to reply' indicates. *What the muckle deil's fa'en a bobbing at your midriffs?'*: 'What the devil's got into you?' (p.36).

p.36.   *Deil's i' e' wee . . . e' sel o't*: 'The devil's in the wee bit stupid laddie,' said Buchan the Aberdonian, 'he thinks they're making him out to be a whore himself!' *Weall, yuoung Scuot . . . lig woth mey*: Hogg attempts here to render with phonetic spelling Northumberland dialect – 'Well, young Scot, are you going to lie with me?' (p.33).

p.41.   *Ballad of Rob Roy*: a version of ballad 225, *Rob Roy*, in Child's *English and Scottish Popular Ballads*. *Ballad called Foul Play*: unidentified.

p.50.   *my master has nae name*: Sir Ringan cannot write and thus cannot sign his name.

p.53.   *Sir Dav. Lindsaye*: from *The Historie of Squyer William Meldrum*. It is a conflation of ll. 13–35. The four verses are the last lines of Lindsay's *The Complaynt and Confession of Bagsche*. In both quotations Hogg differs in several points of spelling and meaning from Douglas Hamer's text (Scottish Text Society 1931).

p.58.   *Edmund Heaton . . . Belsay*: a suitable English Border name. Hogg again attempts to render Heaton's North-of-England accent by a rough system of phonetic spelling.

p.59.   *St Leonard's day*: 6 Nov. but often held on Whitsunday. A crusader, Saint Leonard was miraculously conveyed from Saracen hands to a field in Yorkshire.

p.60.   *The Laird of Johnson*: the lairds of Johnson, north of Lochmaben, figured frequently in Border warfare. *Sir William Fetherstone*: a suitable Border surname. *the Earl of Galloway*: there were no Earls of Galloway at this time, but Hogg would know of Archibald Douglas the Grim, first Lord of Galloway 1369 to 1400, who became Earl of Wigtown in 1371 and third Earl of Douglas on the death of James in 1388.

p.61.   *Old Song*: possibly Hogg's. *Pal. of Hon.:* from verse 13 of the Prologue to Gavin Douglas's poem *The Palace of Honour.* Hogg has either used a faulty source or misquoted, for editions of Douglas's poems from that of Morrison of Perth in 1787 to that of P.J. Bawcutt in 1967 (Scottish Text Society) print *that* for Hogg's *thocht; wirkis* for Hogg's *wirk*; and *me* for Hogg's *him.* In addition Hogg confuses the sense by inserting a comma between *awail* and *until. Berwick was then in the hands of . . . Sir Thomas Musgrave*: see Introductory Note.

p.63.   *He's no to cree legs wi'; I's be quits wi' him*: 'he's not one to meddle with; I'll have nothing to do with him.' *straight on for Aikwood*: that is, to Michael Scott's castle.

p.70.   *the High-town*: Roxburgh. See note under p.2 above. a *tower . . . called the King's house*: Hogg later explains that 'King Edward', presumably Edward I, stayed there.

p.73.   *Cleland and Douglas of Rowlaw*: the Lanarkshire family of Cleland or Kneland is represented in Hary's *Wallace.*

p.77.   *the day of the conception of the Blessed Virgin*: in the Church's calendar this is fixed as 8 December.

p.79.   *Turn the Blue Bonnets*: is song 51 in the second series of Hogg's *Jacobite Relics*, 1821. The term 'blue bonnets' was customary for Scotsmen, especially in their English raids.

p.80.   *Old Play:* probably of Hogg's invention.

p.85.   *St. Duthoc:* St Duthac's body was translated to Tain in Rosshire in the thirteenth century. Several Scottish kings made pilgrimages to his chapel there.

p.88.   *Grey and Collingwood:* convenient since well known names of northern England.

p.89.   *Duddoe's Away:* unexplained.

p.94.   *master Quipes:* probably equivalent to 'Mr Know-all' i.e. full of *quips*, referring to the page's youthful cheekiness.

p.96.   *Song of May Marley:* probably Hogg's own composition. He has a short poem *Meg o' Marley* where only the name is similar. The fact that, like the 'Old Rhyme' noted under p.25, there is play made on ambiguity of the sex of the person in the poem suggests even more that Hogg tailored these to suit the following chapters. *Trag. of The Prioress:* the first of a series of citations of this pretended 'Old Play'.

p.100. *his castle of Logie in Athol:* Logierait, Perthshire, said to have been a royal hunting seat of Robert II.

p.105. *Saint Withold:* a fictitious personage.

p.106. *Cistertian order . . . adjoining to this:* the only Cistercian monastery in the neighbourhood was that at Melrose, some eight miles away, and thus hardly 'adjoining'. The convent that existed in Roxburgh at this time was for Franciscan or 'grey' friars, not monks.

p.108. It is at this point in his later *Siege* that Hogg begins to alter and shorten *The Three Perils of Man*. See textual note.

p.110. *a matter o' five Scots miles:* an old Scots mile was 1984 yards.

p.110. *he wad refuse the king o' France:* Sir Michael Scott was reputed so powerful a wizard that several legends show him refusing his services to potentates like the Pope and the king of France.

p.111. *Colley Carol:* there may be a reason, undiscovered, for this choice of name. Colley Cibber, as a poetaster in the *Dunciad* may have provided the Christian name. *Gibby Jordan:* there seems to be a play on 'jordan', a chamberpot.

p.114. *the battle of Blaikhope:* Blackhope in the Moorfoot hills on the border of the counties of Edinburgh and Peebles. The 'battle' has not been identified.

p.116. *she that wad hae a close cog sude keep a hale laiggen:* she who would have a watertight tub should make sure the bottom hoop is sound.

p.116. *I wish that fleysome job maunna light on you:* lit. 'I hope that fearsome job doesn't fall to you'. But it seems to be a colloquial way of saying exactly the opposite, considering what Charlie then goes on to say. *Erse:* Gaelic.

p.117. *Fight dog, fight bane:* i.e. if a dog fights, it's because he wants the bone for himself. *Fairniehirst's:* the Kerrs of Ferniehirst Castle, vassals of the Douglas; but the castle was not built till 1410.

p.119. *kane sheep:* sheep as payment in kind. *Lucky Church . . . Minny Church:* popular expressions for 'mother church' but with insulting overtones. *her lang tythes:* excessive church dues.

p.119. *the children of Amalek and Moab, and those of Mount Seir:* a partial recollection of 'the children of Ammon and Moab and mount Seir' (2 *Chronicles*, 20.10), whom Jehoshaphat accuses of ingratitude for trying to drive Israel from its rightful possessions. *the king may come in the beggar's way:* there were traditions of James IV and

James V travelling the country disguised as a begger, in order to sound the temper of their subjects, or in search of adventures. A typical legendary account can be found in John M. Wilson's *The Royal Bridal*, in vol. 3 of his *Tales of the Borders*, which began to be published about the time of Hogg's death. It ends with the phrase, 'the king cam' in the cadger's (beggar's) way'.

p.122. *Ballad of Auld Maitland:* the ballad which Scott heard Hogg's mother chant 'with great animation' and which so impressed him that he included it in his *Minstrelsy of the Scottish Border* (with improvements). Later editors have doubted its authenticity. *If you will meet me on the Dirdam waste . . . hollo!*: this and other songs within the narrative, sung by the poet or Michael Scott's familiar spirits, are all Hogg's own or his re-working of traditional material.

p.124. *Ephraim of old:* in *Hosea* 7.8 the tribe of Ephraim, having lost its purity of religion, 'is a cake not turned'. Hogg's Biblical references have little relevance to their application.

p.126. *the debated land:* usually 'the Debateable Land,' a district which extended from the Solway firth eastward for ten miles towards Liddesdale, lying roughly between the rivers Sark and Esk.

p.132. *I's gar ye*: 'I'll fix you!'

p.134. *bide his weird*: accept his fate.

p.142. *the worthy and kind friar*: from this point on the reader is given more and more hints that the mysterious friar is, in fact, Roger Bacon (1214–94). Bacon studied at Oxford and Paris, joined the Franciscan Order but incurred its suspicion on account of his scientific and philosophical enquiries, and was therefore confined for much of his life in Paris under surveillance. Like Michael Scott he came to be reputed a magician. Hogg never actually names the 'gospel friar' but such broad hints as calling him 'auld Roger', frequent references to his persecution and forced exile on account of his studies, and his reputation as a magician, make clear that Hogg intends us partly to identify the friar with Bacon. Note the reference to him as an 'outrageous baconist', ch. XXI, p.333. *some auld-fashioned beuk*: Tam refers to the Bible. The first and only complete translations were those of Wycliffe and his followers, which appeared about 1382 and 1388. Where possible they were suppressed by the authorities. The friar's style of speaking derives partly from the Authorised Version of 1611, partly from pietistic literature and its parodies. *order of St. Benedict*: Bacon was a Franciscan. *president of a grand college in France*: it is not known that Bacon was ever head of a college in France, but Hogg would think of the many Scots of the period who did fill such an office.

p.147. *at ane mae wi't*: made a sheep by it.

p.153. *True Thomas's book*: either the popular collection of Thomas's prophecies, or the balled of *Thomas the Rhymer*, *the book of Sir Gawin*: this must be the romance, *Golagros and Gawain* (c.1476) published by John Pinkerton in his *Scotish Poems*, 1792.

p.160. *the son of Bosor*: another Biblical borrowing, more of language than sense; 'Balaam the son of Bosor' was rebuked by his ass for 'madness' (2 *Peter* 2.15–16).

p.160. The fragments of verse and song here are doubtless of Hogg's composition, perhaps with elements of traditional verse. *the monastery of the Cistertians*: Selkirk Abbey was founded by Prince David (later King David I) in 1113 but it was a Tyronensian (branch of the Benedictines) establishment; not a Cistercian one. Moreover, it was moved to Kelso in 1128.

p.162. *Ballad of Sir Colin Brand*: this would appear to be the work of Hogg.

p.170. *Work, Master, work*: verses written for the occasion by Hogg.

p.175. *this same friar*: Hogg, with his typical love of mystery, develops his hints that the friar is Roger Bacon. Bacon knew that the mixture of sulphur, saltpetre and charcoal would produce explosions, and was sometimes (wrongly, of course) credited with the invention of gunpowder.

p.176. *as Adramelech and as Sharezer*: Adrammelech and Sharezer killed their father, Sennacherib, king of Assyria (2 *Kings* 19.36–7).

p.178. *dicken*: a common substitute for 'devil'.

p.181. *Song of May Marley*: see note under p.96.

p.185. *orgies*: used in the strict, older sense of rites in worship of a heathen god.

p.199. *Ballade of 'Prince Henrie'*: possibly a fragment of the ballad included in Scott's *Minstrelsy* as *King Henry* (and as balled 32 in Child's collection) but may be Hogg's work.

p.204. *our skins will gang to the bauks*: lit. 'our skins will go to the beams', i.e. we will lose our lives.

p.204. *Primate of Douay in France . . . Book of Arts*: the Catholic seminary of Douai became prominent in the sixteenth century.

p.206.   *Benedict of Padua*: the founder of the Benedictine Order is meant, but he was of Nursia, in central Italy.

p.207.   *gar auld Crossgrains come ower us again*: make old crosspatch (i.e. Gourlay) serve us again.

p.211.   *made a staunch point*: stare fixedly, in the manner of a dog pointing.

p.214.   *a wild and uncouth trio*: Hogg's own verses.

p.219.   *Tam o' Shanter*: Hogg may be quoting from memory; he has 't'would blawn' for the accepted 't'wad blawn', 'thickening showers' for 'rattling showers'.

p.226.   *the warlock's hymn*: composed by Hogg.

p.248.   *Fragment of an old Bacchanalian Song*: probably Hogg's.

p.268.   *Ford*: probably an invented attribution.

p.269.   *nae cannie hand for a southland valley*: that is, hardly the kind of person who would act with restraint when raiding in the South. *Beltan*: Beltane, May 1st.

p.270.   *like a man humblin bear*: like a man separating the grains of barley from the beards.

p.272.   *Sir Robert Neville of Ravensworth*: Ravensworth castle in county Durham figures in the *Wallace*. Neville is one of Hogg's names of convenience, since prominent in late medieval history.

p.279.   *bendit face*: it would seem that Hogg transposes the adjective 'bendit' from its more usual association with an animal. Elsewhere he has 'glowering like a bendit wulcat' where 'bendit' means ready to spring.

p.286.   *Bishop Boldone*: possibly an invented name, equivalent to 'bold one', but 'Bolden' is a common enough name and as 'Bowden' is a parish of Roxburghshire.

p.289.   *a heap of stones . . . above the ford of Keilder*: for Keilder in Northumberland see map. 'Gigantic Keeldar's grave', 'the Keeldar Stone' and a supposedly Pictish castle nearby (perhaps the 'Cowd-Peel' mentioned above) all figure in John Leyden's ballad, *The Cout of Keeldar*.

p.290.   *auld Lady Lawder*: perhaps partly suggested by the formidable stepmother of Sir John Lauder, whose ferocity towards Sir John in an action of 1690 concerning the family estates encouraged Robert Chambers to compare her with the Medea of Euripides (*Biographical Dictionary*, vol. 3, 1835). A Margaret Lauder was burned as a witch in 1643.

p.292.   *Ogilvie*: possibly John Ogilby (1600–76), Scottish-born poet and translator of Virgil's *Iliad* and the *Odyssey*. He also wrote plays. Dryden grouped him with Flecknoe; Pope features him in the *Dunciad*.

p.314.   *Bellwether*: probably a version of 'bellwaver', one who constantly changes his ground. The old man is reproaching his vacillating and cowardly son. *old masons are the best barrowmen:* 'old masons are best at carrying bricks and mortar', i.e. the old man is fitter to fight than his son. *hing-by-the-gut:* presumably one whose happiness depends on a well filled stomach, thus an allusion to Jock's great appetite.

p.322.   *villanage:* villeinage.

p.327.   *Zach. Boyd's Bible:* Zachary Boyd (1585–1683) was a learned minister in Glasgow, and rector and vice-chancellor of Glasgow University. He was popularly credited with translating the whole of the Scriptures into verse, but 'Zachary Boyd's Bible' was in fact made up of verse paraphrases of parts of scripture only (e.g. one volume on the Kings of Judah, the next on 'the bookes of Job, Ecclesiastes and the Song of Songs, all in English verse'), as well as many miscellaneous poems of his own on sacred topics. *A Bellandine:* the original home of the Scotts, near the centre of the territory they later acquired, was a small area round Bellenden, near the head of the Ale water in Roxburghshire. This became the rallying ground and the battle cry of the clan. However, the Scotts did not acquire Bellenden till 1415. See also the note on Hogg's account of the rise of the Scotts. The following reference to the moon and the seven stars is, of course, to their coat of arms. See note under p.8 on the prophecy of the Hart and the Deer.

p.334.   *When the bluart bears a pearl:* this appears in collections of Hogg's poetry as '*When the Kye comes Hame*'. Usually two versions are given, this is a blend of the two. Nowhere does Hogg give more than eleven stanzas, although here he claims there are fifteen.

p.345.   *St Bothan:* the cousin and successor of St Columba at Iona. The Cistercian nunnery of St Mary in the Parish of Abbey St Bathans in the Lammermuir district of Berwickshire was commonly known as 'St Bothan's'.

p.346.   *tine the blind bitch's litter:* the 'blind bitch' was a bag illicitly used by millers to cheat their customers of some of their meal. The miller would rather lose his ill-gotten wealth than have his mill burned down. *O semper . . . Amen:* 'O ever fearful evil! I was amazed, and the hair of my head stood up, and my voice stuck in my throat. O God, is there nowhere that faith can be safe? Amen.' A very odd prayer!

p.347.   *The Poet's Tale:* the style here derives much from James MacPherson's supposed translations (1762–3) from the

Gaelic of the poet Ossian. The Tale has obvious affinities
with Hogg's poem *Kilmeny*, and the theme is a favourite
of Hogg's, as is the 'white lady'.

p.348.   *the Sidley Hills:* presumably the Sidlaws, east of Perth
and north of Dundee.

p.353.   *Hymn to Odin:* Hogg's verses. *Alhallah:* Valhalla in
Scandinavian mythology, the hall destined for dead
heroes.

p.361.   *the grey cock crow:* the traditional time for spirits to go
back to their own world; see, for example, *The Wife of
Usher's Well*.

p.375.   *Female Parliamenters, a MS Com.:* a 1754 'entertainment'
(Allardyce Nicoll, *The London Stage*, vol. 3, p. 327). *the
mountain ash*: the Rowan tree, reputed to keep off evil
spirits, thus often grown outside the cottage as well as
being used in the lintel.

p.376.   *the gude neybouris:* the fairies. *a whole century:* 'a long
period of time'. Witch-burning was actually much
less frequent in Scotland than in England. Hogg's
attitude to witches throughout his fiction is strangely
ambiguous; he often appears to comply with the notion
of punishment.

p.377.   *Father Lawrence:* no Lawrence is traceable as Abbot of
Melrose within the period of the romance. Indeed, the
only possible candidate for the office described by Hogg
as 'kind o' king or captain ower a' the holy men of
Scotland' is the notorious Abbot Laurence of Lindores,
who held the office of 'Inquisitor of Heretical Pravity'
in the reign of James I and was indeed (to use Burns's
phrase) 'A burning and a shining light' in the Kirk of
his day.

p.379.   *the Grey-mare's-tail:* a 200-foot waterfall formed by the
Tail burn as it drops from Loch Skene to meet Moffat
water. It lies off the main road from Moffat to St
Mary's Loch.

p.380.   *The Abbot's lee:* presumably Hogg invents the legend to
fit the existing place name, as with the following story
of the origin of Cauldshiels loch (which lies in the hills
between Melrose and Selkirk).

p.384.   *mark o' mouth*: an indication of a horse's age and
condition.

p.390.   *He for whom . . . read no further*: Hogg's own composition
for the occasion. It prophesies the rise of the Scotts and
how this will be achieved.

p.404.   *By the Lord Soules*: the Border family of Soulis was
powerful until William, Lord Soulis was found guilty

of conspiring against the throne of Robert I, when their lands were forfeited. William was remembered in popular tradition as a cruel tyrant and sorcerer, as can be seen in the ballad *Lord Soulis* which Scott included in his *Minstrelsy*.

p.406. *Old Song*: Burns wrote a four-stanza song which included a version of these two lines.

p.417. *grant to Sir Ringan*: this is a totally fictitious account of the rise of the Scotts (see Introductory Note).

p.421. *Gin ever ye be drowned we may seek you up the water*: Laidlaw is of such a contrary nature that his body would drift against the natural flow of the water.

p.427. *Pray thee now*: in Laidlaw's speeches in the pages following this Hogg again tries to convey the English Border dialect.

p.432. *Liberton's luck*: obscure.

p.441. *Ball. of Old Mettlin*: see note under p.122 on *Ballad of Auld Maitland. shot auld dikes*: knocked down old dykes or walls.

p.447. *the rhiming dominie o' Selchrit*: the place-name seems to be a variant of Selkirk. The verses appear to be Hogg's. *The Devil he sat . . . the west countrye*: the verses are Hogg's. *the Eildon tree*: according to some legends Thomas the Rhymer delivered his prophecies under this tree. Others say this is where he met the Queen of Fairyland and entered into the hill to stay for seven years in fairyland. The spot, on the eastern slope of the Eildons, is now marked by a stone, called the Eildon Tree Stone.

p.448. *Longspeare*: an invented name. *gray friars of Roxburgh*: Franciscans had a convent in Roxburgh as early as 1235, but as 'black' friars at that time.

p.454. *Sir James Douglas of Dalkeith*: a branch of the Douglas family had the barony of Dalkeith.

p.456. *This document*: the transaction and the document are, of course, fictitious.

p.460. *Jacobite Song*: song 27, in the first series of Hogg's *Jacobite Relics*, 1819.

p.472. *Edward Longshanks*: a Scots nickname for Edward I of England. *First of all rode Sir Ringan . . . gallantly attended*: while Hogg includes typical Border family names of the period here, many persons are referred to anachronistically, for example, Sir Andrew Ker of Aultonburn belongs to the early fifteenth century.

p.474. *The king . . . who had a halt*: Robert III's lameness is here attributed to Robert II. *The Queen and her*

Maries: 'Maries' was a term for Scottish Maids of Honour, particularly those of Mary, Queen of Scots; cp. the ballad of *Mary Hamilton. Ca' Cuddie:* possibly a variation on 'curcuddie'; 'to dance curcuddie' was a children's game, so that 'curcuddie' could easily be included as a refrain in a popular song.

p.476. *the Seven Dales:* the well-known ones are – Ewesdale, Eskdale, Liddesdale, Tweeddale, Annandale, Teviotdale and Lauderdale.

p.476. *striking kemps:* Jamieson in the Supplement to his *Dictionary of the Scottish Language* claims that this phrase comes from the children's game of the same name, where 'kemps' are stalks of ribgrass and the object of the game is to decapitate the stalk of one's opponent by striking it with one's own. Hogg seems to use the phrase with the same sense of a game, but in this case a game of friendly banter or 'flyting' between the sexes. *saft be the sough that says it:* whisper it.

p.479. *May Marley:* see note under p.96.

p.498. *Dickson's Sermons:* David Dickson (1583–1663), minister of Irvine and Professor of Divinity in Edinburgh from 1650.

p.507. *gaun aff at the nail:* gone mad. *Hoy's net:* probably merely 'hoys', or 'hose net', a small net fixed to a pole.

p.520. *Old Jacobite Song:* unidentified, doubtless Hogg's or Hogg's version.

Further Reading

For a good brief introduction to Hogg's work, see Thomas Crawford's 'James Hogg and the Play of Region and Nation', in Douglas Gifford, ed., *The History of Scottish Literature, Volume 3, The Nineteenth Century* (Aberdeen 1988), pp. 89-106. See also Douglas Gifford, *James Hogg*, (Edinburgh, 1976).

RECENT EDITIONS OF HOGG'S WORKS

The Private Memoirs and Confessions of a Justified Sinner, ed. John Carey (London, 1969)

Selected Poems, ed. Douglas Mack (Oxford, 1970)

Memoir of the Author's Life and Familiar Anecdotes of Sir Walter Scott, ed. Douglas Mack (Edinburgh and London, 1972)

The Brownie of Bodsbeck, ed. Douglas Mack (Edinburgh and London, 1976)

Highland Tours, ed. William Laughlan (Hawick, 1981)

Selected Stories and Sketches, ed. Douglas Mack (Edinburgh, 1982)

Anecdotes of Sir Walter Scott, ed. Douglas Mack (Edinburgh, 1983)

The Private Memoirs and Confessions of a Justified Sinner, ed. John Wain (Middlesex, 1983)

A Shepherd's Delight: A James Hogg Anthology, ed. Judy Steel (Edinburgh, 1985)

Tales of Love and Mystery, ed. David Groves (Edinburgh, 1985)

Selected Poems and Songs, ed. David Groves (Edinburgh, 1986)

A Tour in the Highlands in 1803 (Edinburgh, 1986)

Scottish Pastorals, ed. Elaine Petrie (Stirling, 1988)

James Hogg: Poetic Mirrors, ed. David Groves (Frankfurt, 1990)

The Private Memoirs and Confessions of a Justified Sinner,
  ed. David Groves (Edinburgh, 1991)
*The Shepherd's Calendar, ed. Douglas Mack (Edinburgh,
  1995)
*A Queer Book, ed. P.D. Garside (Edinburgh and London,
  1995)
*The Three Perils of Woman, eds. David Groves, Anthony
  Hasler and Douglas Mack (Edinburgh, 1995)
*Lay Sermons, ed. David Groves (Edinburgh, 1996)
*Tales of the Wars of Montrose, ed. Gillian Hughes (Edin-
  burgh, 1996)

*Works in the Stirling/South Carolina edition of James
Hogg, general editor Douglas S. Mack. This long over-
due scholarly edition aims to bring all of Hogg's works,
prose, poetry and plays, back into print. When complete
the edition will comprise thirty-one volumes.

The James Hogg Society produces a journal, *Studies
in Hogg and his World*; enquiries about membership
and journal should be addressed to The Department
of English Studies, University of Stirling, FK9 4LA.
Scotland.

COMMENTARIES ON HOGG

Edith C. Batho, *The Ettrick Shepherd* (Cambridge, 1927)
Alan Lang Strout, *The Life and Letters of James Hogg, The
  Ettrick Shepherd*, vol. 1 (1770-1825), (Texas Tech Press,
  1946). Note: volume one is the only volume published.
Louis Simpson, *James Hogg: A Critical Study* (Edinburgh,
  1962)
Nelson Smith, *James Hogg* (Boston, 1980)
Norah Parr, *James Hogg at Home* (Dollar, 1980)
David Groves, *James Hogg: The Growth of a Writer*
  (Edinburgh, 1988)

Glossary

a', all.

abe, let abe, let alone, not to mention.

aboon, above.

abraid, abreed, abroad, open.

ado, business.

ae, one.

aff, off.

afore, before.

agroof, prone, on one's belly.

ahint, behind.

aiblins, perhaps, possibly.

aikwood, oakwood.

aill, ails, afflicts.

aince, once.

airn, iron.

airt, direction.

aits, oats.

amaist, almost.

amind, in mind.

an, conj., although, if.

ane, one.

aneath, beneath.

anent, about, concerning.

aneuch, enough.

arle, money paid to confirm a bargain.

asteer, astir.

ata', at all.

athort, across, over.

atween, between.

aucht, eight.

aught, pron., anything; *vb.,* own.

auld ane, lit. old one, the devil.

auld farrant, old fashioned.

auld warld, old fashioned, ancient.

ava, at all.

awail: awail until, run to, rush to.

a-wastle, See *wastle.*

aweel, interj., ah well! well then!

awn, own.

aye, always, continually.

ayont, beyond.

back friends, secret enemies.

backman, follower in war, henchman.

bargrel, minnow.

bairn, child.

bait, to give food to.

baith, both.

ballant, ballad, song.

balluster, bannister.

ban, curse, swear.

bannocks, thick round flat cakes usually made of oatmeal.

barley, truce.

barn-door (fowl), farmyard (fowl).

barrowmen, men who carry bricks and mortar to a mason.

bassonet, light helmet.

basted, beaten.

bauchling, scorning, taunting.

bauk, beam of a pair of scales.

bauks, ceiling, flat roof.

bauld, bold, daring.

bean swaup, hull of a bean, anything of no value or strength.

bear, barley.

beardit, bearded.

bedesman, priest, confessor.

beef boat, pickling tub or barrel.

beeves, beef.

beguiled, tricked, disappointed.

behadden to, bound to, at the door of.

behand: to come well behand, to manage well.

beire, noise.

bellandine, squabble, broil.

bells, bubbles.

bellwether, inconstant person.

ben end, inner room in a two-roomed house.

bendit, fierce.

bent, open country; *to take the bent*, to flee one's creditors.

berkened, encrusted.

bested, got the better of.

bestedde, placed.

beuk, book.

bewiddied, deranged.

bicker, bowl,

bickers, quarrelling, fighting.

bide, receive.

bidden, stayed.

bield, shelter.

bien, comfortable.

big, build.

bigging, cottage, building.

bike, crowd, swarm, hive.

billies, fellows, brothers.

billyblinder, imposture, deception.

binna, be not.

birkie, fellow.

birns, scorched, dry heather stems.

birse, *lit*. bristle; *to set up one's birse*, to get angry.

birth, situation, berth.

blabbed, gossipped.

blackhag, morass, bog.

blade, someone weakened by overgrowth.

blatter, rattle, dash noisily.

blaw, *blawn*, blow, blown.

blethering, prattling, chattering.

blin', cease, desist.

blind bitch, bag used by miller to steal some of the meal coming down the milkspout.

blinkit, twinkled, flashed.

blirting, weeping.

blooter, *heather blooter*, bittern.

bluart, harebell.

blude, blood.

blyth, blithe.

boardly, stalwart.

boddles, *bodles*, copper coins worth two pence Scots each.

bodit, boded.

body, person.

bogle, ghost, apparition.

bog-stalker, idle worthless fellow.

bog-thumper, *bog bumper*, bittern.

bog-trotting, wild, idle, worthless.

bole, small opening in the wall.

boomb, noise made by a bird.

booner, upper.

boonmost, uppermost.

boots, behoves; *it boots nothing*, it is not necessary.

bore, pass over.

born-head, headlong.

bosky, wild, unfrequented.

boult, *bult*, hand lantern.

bouk, body, bulk.

bouking, washing.

bowie, bowl; *bowiefu*, bowlful.

brace, chimney piece.

bragg, boasting.

braid, broad.

brake, clearing.

brander, gridiron.

brattle, make a clashing, clattering noise.

brawly, very well.

breeks, trousers.

brigg, bridge.

brik, break, violate.

brochen, water gruel, thin porridge.

broken-men, outlaws, robbers.

broo, broth, juice.

brose, oat or pease meal mixed with hot milk.

brow, face.

brulzie, disturbance.

brush, *n*, rush, violent activity, onset; *v.*, rushed.

brusket, breast.

buckie, a refractory person.

buirdly, stalwart.

bumbazed, confounded, bewildered.

burd, maiden, young lady.

burden, lit., drone of the bagpipe, chorus.

bure, *v.*, bore.

burgonet, linen coif, helmet.

bursten, over-fatigued.

bur-throated, with a burr, i.e. *r* strongly sounded (as in Northumberland.)

bussing, linen hood or cap.

butt, extremities, bottom.

butteries, batteries (see note).

bygane, past, gone by.

byking, swarming.

ca', *v*, drive, pull, drag; *cawed*, driven.

cadger, carrier.

cairn, loose pile of stones.

callans, *callants*, lads, young men.

camstairy, *camstary*, obstinate, unmanageable.

cannie, *canny*, careful, prudent, gentle, safe, lucky, pleasant.

cantrip, charm, spell, incantation.

cants, sloping part, hind cants of the head, back of the head.

cap-a-pie, from head to toe.

cappercailzie, *caipercaillie*, woodgrouse.

carle, old man.

cast, *n*, lot, fate, chance; *v.*, tie.

castock, stem of colewort.

cast out, quarrel.

cates, choice food.

catwiddied, harebrained.

cauld, cold.

cawed. See *ca'*.

certes, certainly, without a doubt.

chafts, chops, cheeks.

chap, *v*, strike, knock; *chappit*, chopped.

Charlie-wain, the Plough.

chauntit, chanted.

chevysance, procurement, means of acquiring.

chiel, *chield*, fellow, man, stripling.

chopping, proceeding.

civis, misnomer for old English penny.

claes, clothes.

clagg, encumbrance, fault.

clap, press down, lie flat, crouch.

clanjaumphrey, low, worthless people.

clave, clove.

clawing, scratching; *clawn*, hit, scratched; *claws*, scratches.

clecking, lit. brood of chickens, family.

cleuch, narrow glen, ravine.

clippit, clipped.

cloake-bag, portmanteau, hence a complete collection.

clocks, beetles.

cloots, hoofs, feet.

clout, blow, slap; *clouted,* stitched, patched.

coble, small boat.

cock, to prick up; *cock-luggit,* prick-eared; *cock-strides,* a short distance.

cog, a bowl (usually made of wood).

coil, fuss, stir.

colley-shangie, uproar, squabble.

collop, slice, portion.

colly, a great admirer.

compeers, comrades, companions.

cooke, draught.

cope, vault (of heaven).

copper-nosed, red nosed.

corbie, crow.

corbie-messengers, messengers who either return too late or not at all.

corpulation, body, windbag.

coulter, coulter-nose, long beaked nose.

counterguard, narrow detached rampart, placed immediately in front of an important fortification.

coup, a good bargain.

coups, tumbles.

cout, young horse, term of contempt for man.

couthe, v., could, began to.

coutribat, tumult.

crabbit, cross, bad-tempered.

craboun, provocations; or obs. form of carbine, a rifle.

crack, gossip, chat; *crackit,* talked, spoke.

crackens, krakens, sea monsters.

craig, rock.

crannie, square or oblong aperture in wall of a house; *crannied,* slit.

crappin, stomach.

craw, croak.

cree, meddle; *cree legs wi',* meddle with.

creelfu', basketful.

crook, winding, corner, bend in a river.

croons, muttered prayers.

crossed, contrary.

croudy, gruel, porridge.

croups, bends, stoops.

crouse, brisk, lively, bold, proud; *crousest,* superl.; *crousely,* adv.

cuishes, armour.

currs, squats, cowers.

dabbed, pecked.

daft, foolish, mad, reckless.

darkling, in the dark.

dauntit, daunted.

davoch, an ancient measure of land, varying from place to place but usually about 416 acres.

dawted, petted.

deadthraw, death-throes.

deal, board, plank.

dean, hollow, small valley.

deaved, worried, bothered, deafened.

deemed, judged.

deil a bit, lit. devil a bit, not, nothing at all.

deire, deer, wild animal.

deray, disorder, uproar.

dicken, devil.

dimple, indent.

ding, beat.

dink, dinke, neat, trim.

divot, thin flat piece of turf used as thatch.

divot-seat, seat made of divots.

dizzen, dozen, twelve.

doit, a copper coin of small value, hence a trifle.

doited, foolish, in one's dotage.

dom, damn.

dool, sorrow, grief, misfortune.

doops, descends.

dorty, proud, haughty.

doubles, layers.

dought, could.

douk, bathe.

doupe, descend, lean down.

dour, stubborn.

douth, dull melancholy, gloomy.

dovered, stupified.

dow, dowe, dove (term of endearment).

downa, cannot; doesn't want to.

downfa', slope.

dowss, beat, thrash.

drave, drove.

dree, endure, suffer.

dreich, slow, tedious, wearisome.

dreid, suspect, fear.

drift, meaning.

drive, heavy blow, push.

droich, dwarf.

droule, bell (hart belling for doe).

drowthy, thirsty.

drumly, gloomy.

dumbfoundered, perplexed, amazed.

dunt-duntit, thudded.

durstna, dare not.

dust, disturbance, uproar.

ee, een, eye, eyes.

ee-brees, eyebrows.

e'en, even.

eenbright, shining, luminous.

e'en-down, straightforward.

effeckit, effected.

eild, old age, age.

eiry, uncanny.

elbowman, henchman.

elwand, ellwand; the king's elwand, i.e. Orion's belt.

elshin, a shoemaker's awl.

eneuch, enough.

enow, enough, sufficiently.

epocha, special event, beginning of an era.

ern, iron.

Erse, Gaelic.

eternitive, alternative.

ettle, ettling, aim, aiming.

fae, foe.

fa'en, fallen.

faderis, father's.

fain, I am fain to, I have got to.

fairly, certainly, quite, surely.

fairny-cloot, the small horny substance above the hoofs, said to be found only in sheep or goats.

fand, found,

fane, temple.

fash, n., trouble; *fashous*, troublesome.

fauld, fold.

fauld, lit. fold, as in sheep-fold, hence a yard.

fauldit, folded.

fawn, a white spot on moorland or on rocky ground.

fell, steep rocky hill, high land.

ferlie, wonder.

fie-gae-to, a great bustle.

fient, the fient ae, not at all.

fier, companion.

fishlight, bright light (used in night fishing).

fit, foot.

flail, beat, thump.

flasche, in flashes, suddenly.

flaught, hurry, bustle.

flickered, flecked, dappled.

fleg, frighten, scare.

fleysome, fearsome, terrifying.

flighters, flutters.

flim-flam, nonsense.

flinders, splinters, fragments.

flobby, large and heavy.

flow, small quantity.

fock, fouk, folk, people.

foreby, besides.
forespent, exhausted.
forrit, forward.
fouk. See *fock*.
foumart, polecat.
four-nooked, four-cornered.
foussomly, bulkily, copiously.
fraise, disturbance, fuss.
fray, terror, panic; *with the fray*, in panic.
frenauch, a crowd.
frene, pasture.
frith, firth.
frizzle, piece of steel for striking a fire from a flint.
fu', full.
fuffing, hissing, spluttering, sniffing.
gab, palate; impertinent talk, prating.
gae. See *gie*.
gaed, went; *gaen*, going.
gage, challenge.
gaindering, looking foolish, stretching the neck like a gander.
gait, goat.
galled, lamed, diseased.
gang, go; *gangers*, goers.
gar, make, cause to; *garring*, making; *gart*, made.
gate, journey, distance.
gaud, goad.
gavelocks, iron crowbars or levers.
gay, very; *gayan*, considerably.
gear, accoutrements, weapons.
geaving, staring, gaping.
genets, jennets, small horses.
gibe, mock, tease.
gie, give; *gi'es*, gives; *gae*, gave.
gillie-gaupy, foolish giddy fellow.
gillies, giddy young women.
gimmer, a ewe from one to two years old.

gin, if.
gin, trap.
girnel, meal chest.
girning, snarling.
glaikit, foolish, giddy, senseless.
glaiks, tricks, deceptions; *Gi'en me the glaiks*, given me the slip.
glaive, glove.
glamourie, witchcraft.
glebes, plots of land, fields.
gled, kite, buzzard.
glent, *n.* and *v.*, glance; *glentin*, glinting, glancing.
glime, look askance, glance.
glinting. See *glent*.
glisk, a quick look, a momentary view.
gloaming, twilight.
glooming, sullen, frowning.
glowring, scowling.
gluther, noise made in throat.
glyd-aver, carthorse.
goodman, man, master.
gorb, *gork*, rapacious, greedy.
gorbie, raven.
gorget, armour for the throat.
goud, *goude*, *gowden*, gold, golden.
gouk, fool.
gousty, desolate, dreary.
gowans, daisies.
gowden, See *good*.
gowpens, handfuls.
gaepit, examined, groped.
grains, prong.
greet, cry.
grene, long for, want to.
grews, greyhounds.
grit, great.
grumphing, grumbling.
Gude, God; *Gude troth*, a mild exclamation.
guidit, harassed, troubled.
gully, long knife.

gume, palate.

gust, n. and v., relish.

gustle, appetite.

gusty, tasty.

gutters, drains, ditches; *ding the brains out o' the gutters*, drive on.

gyte, mad, daft; *gaen gyte*, gone mad.

hadden, held.

hae, have.

haffet, side of the face, hair at the temples.

hagabag, huckaback, rubbishy.

hagg-hiding, hiding in the hollows of the moor.

haggies, haggis.

hairikens, hurricanes.

halde, dwelling.

hale, whole.

hale-head; wi' a chance o' a hale-head, with a chance of coming off unhurt.

halewort, the whole.

hallanshaker, knave, rascal, of shabby appearance.

happ, turn to the right (used in directing animals).

happit, wrapped.

hard, heard.

hard-rackle, headstrong, fearless.

harigalds, pluck of an animal.

harnpan, skull, brain-pan.

hauch, low, level ground beside a stream.

hauch-head, place at the end or head of a haugh (see *hauch)*

hand, *hold*, holding hauding, n., holding, possession.

hauld, habitation.

haut-stride-and-loup, hop, step and jump.

havering, talking nonsense.

hawkie, white faced cow.

hearte, hart.

heather-blooter, bittern.

heavit, came into view, moved, ran.

heffing, keep, maintenance.

hellicat, wicked creature.

herrie, ruin; *herrying*, plundering.

het, *hett*, hot; *hettest*, hottest.

heuch, steep slopes of a hill.

heveye, heavy.

hey-gae, extremely.

hiche, high.

hind, farm servant.

hinder-end, the end, close.

hinderlands, back-parts, posterior.

hing, hang.

hinney, honey (a term of endearment).

hirsel, flock.

hist, stop.

hizzy, hussy, housewife.

hobble, shake.

hopes, upland valley enclosed on upper sides by green hills or ridges.

horn-mad, raving mad.

host, cough.

hotched, shook with laughter.

hott, heap.

hough, thigh.

hout hout, interf., nonsense!

hovered, paused.

how, howe, hollow.

howked, pulled out, drew out; *howking*, digging.

howies, (?) a mistake for *sowies*, structures for protection of besieging forces.

humblin, threshing.

humphed, having a tainted smell.

hunner, hundred.

hurcheon, hedgehog.

hurkle-backed, hunch-backed.

hurlbarrowed, wheelbarrowed.

ilk, same place.

ilka, each, every, common.

ill-deidy, guilty of ill deeds.

ill-faured, unsavoury, unpleasant.

ill-tackit, wrongheaded, taken amiss.

intil, into.

izle, hot cinder.

jaud, jade.

jaumphed, fatigued, chafed.

jaupit, dashed.

javel, rascal.

jaw, talk, chatter, abusive language.

jee, move, stir.

jiffey, instant.

jink, amorous frolic.

jockey-coats, great-coats.

jurmummled, crushed.

Kail, colewort.

kane, rent in kind.

kebbuch, a whole cheese.

ked, sheep louse.

keekit, peeped, looked.

kelpie, water sprite, river horse.

kemps; striking a kemps, having a friendly 'flyting', bantering.

ken, know; *kend, kenned*, knew; *kendna*, knew not.

Ker-cake, cake baked for Shrove Tuesday.

ketch, toss, heave.

key, mood, frame of mind.

kipper-noses, hooked or beaked noses.

kipples, rafter beams.

kips, sharp pointed hills.

kink, faint convulsive cough; *to gae in ae kink*, to go at once.

kirning, churning.

kite, stomach.

kittle, dangerous, touchy, difficult.

kittling, tickling.

knab, blow.

knackers, flat pieces of bone or wood used like castanets; *shake my knackers!*, rattle my bones!

kythe, show, appear.

laiggen, bottom hoop of a barrel; *laiggens*, bottom, foot.

laigh, low.

lair, *n.*, bed, place to lie down; *v.*, put down; *lair'd*, rested.

laithly, loathsome, repulsive.

landward, boorish, rustic.

lang, long.

langkail, coleworts.

lang-shankit, long-legged.

laup. See *loup*.

lave, remainder, rest.

laverock, lark.

leal, leale, loyal, honest.

lear, learning, education, knowledge.

leeve, *v.*, live.

legbail, flight, escape.

leishest, most active, nimblest, supplest.

leuch, laughed.

levand, living.

levin, thunder.

libelt, long discourse or treatise.

licks, thrashing, punishment, deserts.

lie, lie to, aim for.

liege, vassal.

lift, oky.

lift, ill turn; *lend you a lift*, do you a mischief; *lifts*, raids, cattle-raids.

lingel, shoemaker's thread.

links, joints, rich ground in the windings of a river.

linn, cascade of water.

linned, ceased, rested.

lint, flax.

lippen, trust.

lippie, quarter of a peck, a bumper.

lire, udder, flesh, lean meat.
listed, chose.
lith, joint of the body.
logie, open space before the kiln fire.
loot, let.
loun, calm; *blaw loun,* calm down.
loun, rascal.
lounder, heavy blow.
loup, leap; *laup,* leapt.
low, n., flame, fire; *v., lowin,* glowing.
lown, sheltered.
lubbard, coward.
lubberly, sluggish.
luchts, locks.
lucken gowan, globe flower.
lucky, old woman, grandmother.
lug, ear, piece, bit.
lurd, lurde, v., would, would rather.
lyart, streaked with grey.
lycht, light.
mack, neat, tidy; *mack-like,* purposeful.
mae, adj., more.
mae, n., sheep, lamb.
mailin (g), farm, holding, rent of farm.
mair, more.
maist, almost.
maisters, masters.
make, n., figure, form.
marches, boundaries, borders.
mark o' mouth, indications of age by the teeth.
marshfire, will o' the wisp.
mart, cow or ox fattened and killed about Martinmas for winter use, pickled beef.
marth, marrow, pith.
maskis, mastiff.
massy, self-important, conceited.
maun, must; *maunna,* must not.

maut, malt.
may, n., maiden.
meldar, an amount of corn, used fig. as a large amount of good food.
mells, mallets, large hammers.
mends, compensation, revenge.
mense, honour, decency, thanks.
menseless, ill-bred, unmannerly, greedy, selfish.
merks, silver coins of old Scots coinage.
merled, mottled.
mess, meal, food.
midden, dunghill.
mids, middle.
min, man, a familiar form of address.
mind, v., remind.
minny, mother.
mint, venture, dare.
minnay, minuet.
mirk, dusk, night.
misbehadden, unbecoming, indiscreet.
misleared, unmannerly, mischievous, ill-bred.
misprision, abuse.
moldwarps, moles.
monyplies, intestines.
moorpoots, young grouse.
mosshag, place out of which peats have been cut.
mosstroopers, border freebooters.
mou, mouth.
moudies, moles.
moudiwort, mole; used fig. for an underhand or slow person, or a coin concealed in the lining of a coat.
muckle, much.
muir, moor, heath.
multure, toll (of meal) taken by miller.
mumped, grimaced.
murgeons, gestures, grimaces.

nab, peck, blow.

nadkin, disagreeable odour.

naigs, horses, stallions.

nail, lit. pain at forehead; *aff at the nail*, mad, wrong-headed.

nakit, naked.

nebbit, nosed.

nebs, noses.

neist, next.

neive, fist; *neive-fu*, handful.

neuk, corner.

nevel, a blow with the fist.

nice, fine, fussy.

nicker, neigh, whinny.

niff-naff, trifle, small person.

noddies, simpletons.

nolt, nout, cow, black cattle.

nouther, neither.

od, an expletive (for 'God.')

oon, oven.

or, until, before.

ought, pron., anything.

outgate, way out.

outlyers, cattle kept outdoors in winter.

outwale, n., refuse.

ower, over.

owsen, oxen, cattle.

paddo ck, frog, toad.

paughty, haughty, proud.

pawkie, pawky, shrewd, sly.

pease-weep, lapwing.

peching, hard breathing.

pell-mell, scrimmage, headlong rush.

pelting, fighting.

pelts, strokes, blows.

pike, prick.

pinching-bars, crowbars.

pincing, pinching.

plack, a small copper coin.

pliskie, practical joke, wild idea, disturbance, plight.

ploughgates, measures of land, varying from 40 to 104 Scots acres.

Ploydenist. See Notes.

pluffins, refuse of a cornmill.

plumper, n., an outstanding example.

pock-net, bag-shaped fishing net.

pots: gar one's pot play broon, to provide oneself with food.

pouch, pocket.

poutter, potter.

preceese, precise.

preclair, distinguished.

pree, taste.

preen, pin.

prick, fasten, shut; *prickit*, shut.

priminary, trouble, confusion.

prinkling, tingling.

prodd, stab, blow.

puik, pluck.

puir, poor.

quat, rid, free; *quat wi'*, abandon.

queys, heifers.

quhane, when (*quh* for *wh* being a literary archaism).

quhere, where (see above).

rackit, stretched.

raide, enterprise, expedition.

raiking, journeying, wandering.

raip, rope.

rairing, roaring.

raive, tore.

ranigalds, wanton, bold, impudent people.

rarely, excellently, capitally.

rascallions, low worthless fellows.

rattan, rat.

raux, stretch, reach.

raws, mountain ridges, rows.

reaved, stolen.

reavers, robbers.

red-wudd, mad with rage, furious, eager.

reek, smoke.

reide, council.

rhames, rhymes, rigmaroles, repeated phrases.

rhaming, rhyming.

riddled, mangled.

rig, ridge.

rigging, backs.

ring: ring on, rail on, pester.

rive, n., a piece torn off.

rock, distaff.

roop. See *stoop*.

ropy, rheumy.

row, v., roll; *rowing*, rolling.

rowting, roaring, bellowing.

rowts, roars, bellows.

ruggit, pulled, tugged.

rummaging, rampaging.

rummelgumption, commonsense.

rumple, rump, tail.

rung, cudgel; *piked rung*, spiked cudgel.

runts, old or small oxen or cows.

sachless, useless, feeble, innocent (? slip for *sackless*).

sack but, trombone.

saft, quiet.

saif, sauf, sauff, save.

sair, sore, sad.

sal, shall.

sanna, shall not.

sauf, sauff. See *saif*.

saut-faut, salt-cellar.

sax, six.

scaith, injury.

scaling, breaking, dismantling; *scaling hammers*, sledge hammers.

scart, wound, scratch.

scawed, scabbed.

scour, run, rush.

scowering, rushing.

scraigh, lit. screech, dawn.

scrieving, scraping, moving swiftly along.

scrimply, scarcely, barely.

scroggy, stunted, thorny.

seeds, husks of oats.

seen, obvious.

settler, conclusive blow.

sey, try, test, prove.

seymar, loose upper garment, scarf.

shakel, make to dance, jog, shake.

shank, leg, hence man.

shape, succeed, manage, contrive.

shard, break into fragments.

shave, slice.

shealings, husks.

sheile, hut for shepherds.

sheiling, cottage, shelter.

shifting, hesitating.

shift: be at your shift, hurry up, make a move, remove yourself.

shilpy, insipid.

shire, clear, separable.

shrieve, sheriff.

shurf, puny, insignificant person.

sic, such.

siccan, such.

sin, conj., since.

singit, singed.

single-soaled, with a single thickness of leather in the sole (a Selkirk speciality).

sinsyne, since then.

skaith. See *scaith*.

skaither, one who does damage.

skatched, fixed, skewered.

skebeld, mean, worthless fellow.

skins, hides, *sheepskins, fleeces*.

skraeshankit, having long, thin legs.

skrinkit, shrivelled, wrinkled, lank.

slack, slow.

slashing, juicy.

slaw, slow.

slee-gabbit, sly-mouthed.
sleeky, sly, crafty.
sloughs, skins.
slounging, lounging.
slubber, noise made in throat when asleep.
smoor, smother; *smorit*, smothered.
snapper, misfortune, scrape, entanglement.
sneck, latch.
sneckdrawing, *lit.* latch lifting, stealthy.
snell, keen, sharp.
snooving, walking carelessly.
snouking, sniffing.
soap, sup.
sodger-like, soldier-like.
sonsy, fortunate, sturdy, sensible.
soore, sure.
sooth: by my sooth, in truth.
sorners, spongers.
sotter, simmer.
sough, *n.*, moaning of wind; *a calm sough*, silence. *soughs*, *v.*, emits a rushing sound.
souple, *v.*, cudgel.
sow-house, pig-sty.
spairged, sprinkled, bespattered.
spauld, limb, shoulder.
speats, floods, spates.
speer, *speir*, ask, enquire.
splutter, fuss, disturbance.
spoolbone, shoulder-bone.
spuing, pouring forth, vomiting.
spulzie, booty, spoil, plunder.
spurring, kicking.
stack, stuck.
staincheons, stanchions.
stall up, steady up.
stamock, stomach.
stand, barrel.
stap, stuff; *stappit*, stuffed.
starns, stars.
staup, stave.

steek, shut, fasten.
steel-brander, gridiron, grilling iron.
sticked, spoiled in the execution, bungled; *sticking*, disobliging, unwilling.
stickleback, very small fish.
stoop, bent back.
stoop and roop, *phr.*, completely.
stound, stun; *stoundit*, stunned.
stoup, flagon, jug.
stour, *stoure*, strife, bustle, excitement.
stown, stolen.
straik, blow.
strait, *adj.*, tight, hard; *n.*, narrow pass.
stravaigers, wanderers, vagabonds.
streamer, northern lights, Aurora Borealis.
streek, stretch; *streekit*, stretched.
strick, strict.
stringing, moving in a single line.
strinkled, sprinkled.
sude, should.
supple, pliant, easily bent.
sutors, shoemakers.
swabble, tall, thin, overgrown person.
swagging, swinging to and fro.
swalled, swollen.
swap, blow, stroke.
swarfed, swooned, fainted.
swatter, splash.
swee, swing, balance.
sweer, reluctant.
swinging, swingeing, extremely hard or good.
swire, steep pass.
swuffing, breathing loudly in sleep.
tae . . . *tither*, one . . . other.
taen, taken.
tafferel, giddy, thoughtless.

tap, top.
tareleathers, shreds.
tauld, told.
tawpies, foolish, idle girls.
tent, notice; *tentit*; noticed.
thae, these.
thegither, together.
thir, these.
thirl, bound legally, subject to.
thole, bear, suffer.
thrangest, busiest.
thraw, wring, twist.
thresh, beat, thrash.
thristing, thrusting.
tichel, number, troop.
tiend, tithed, bound by tithe.
tike, cur.
til, to.
tummer, wooden.
tine, lose, forfeit; *tint*, lost.
tite, jerk, pull.
tittie, *titty*, sister.
tod, fox.
toom, empty.
tott, whole of any number.
toun, farm, farm steading.
towsy, *towzie*, shaggy.
tproo, ejaculatory noise.
traist, faithful.
trapt, ornamentally harnessed.
trash, riff-raff.
traupan, cheat, trick.
trow, believe.
tripe, term of contempt for a tall, lanky person.
tulzie, broil.
tup, ram.
twal, twelve.
tyke, cur.
up-putting, accommodation.
unbowsome, unbending, unyielding, stiff.
unco, adj., very, unusual; *uncos*, n., news.
unfeiroch, feeble, frail.
unsonsy, unlucky, ominous.

wad, v., would.
wad, n., pledge, wager.
wae, woe.
waif, v., wander, stray.
wale, pick, choose.
walise, case, bag.
wallets, bags for carrying personal items.
wallidraggle, feeble.
wall-i'-the-chamber, valet.
walloping, dancing, fluttering.
wally, beautiful.
wally, valet.
wally-dy, n., toy, diversion; as adj. diverting in ironic sense.
wampished, flourished.
wantit, done without.
wap, flap.
war, were.
ward, watch for, keep off.
wared, spent, expended.
wark, work.
warrandice, surety, security.
warrant; I'se warrant, I'm sure.
warst, worst.
wastle: a-wastle, westward of; *the world be a-wastle us*, may worldly cares be far from us.
watna, know not.
wauking, awake.
waul, roll.
waur, worse.
weaponshaw, muster of arms.
wear, pass, turn.
weathershaker, (?) a wild animal.
web, roll of wovencloth.
wedd, *wedde*, pledge.
wedders, wethers, castrated rams.
weel, well.
weelfaurd, comely, goodlooking.
weids, regions.
weigh-bauk, a balance.
weir, n., war; *weirly*, adj., warlike.

weird, fate, doom, prediction, prophecy.

wench-bairn, female child.

weste, waist.

weynd, turn to the left (direction given to horses).

whalp, whelp.

whang, cut, large slice.

whanger, whinger, a long knife used in fighting and at meals.

whar, *whaur*, where.

wheelbands, bands for hair.

wheen, a few, a party.

wheezle, wheeze.

whiles, at times.

whilk, which.

whing-ladders, ladders made of leather thongs.

whinyard. See *whanger*.

whittle, butcher's knife, carving knife.

whup, whip.

widdy, halter, the gallows.

wight, n., fellow, man.

wight, adj., mighty, clever.

wilycoat, undercoat, vest.

Willy-an'-the Wisp, Will o' the Wisp.

wince, prance, kick out behind.

winna, will not.

winning, giving of blows.

wist, knew, wished.

withergloom, the clear sky near the horizon.

witherweight, counterbalance.

wizen, gullet.

wordy, worthy.

wulcat, wildcat.

wycht. See *wight*, *n.*

wyte, blame.

yammering, whining.

yank, sudden, severe blow.

yanker, smart stroke, great falsehood.

yare, quick.

yaud, old horse.

ycleped, called, named.

yerk, a smart blow.

yestreen, yester-even.

yether, lash.

yethering, idle talking.

yett, gate.

yeuk, itch.

yird, earth.

yoket, yoked.

yon, that, those.

yont, yonder, thither.

SCALE : APPROX.

0   4   8 miles

Pentland Hills

Moorfoot Hills

Lauder

Peebles

Biggar

Innerleithen

R. Tweed

Gala Water

Galashiels

Melrose

Kindlyburn
Abbotslee
Cauldshiels
Loch

Lindean

Eildon Hill

Manor Water

Heights of Manor / Deucharswire

SCOTLAND

Carterhaugh

Selkirk

Hill of
Blackandro
Shielshaugh

Howden Burn

Yarrow

Copelaw

Otterdale
Aikwood
(Michael Scott's
Tower)

Hartwood

Dryhope

Yarrow Water

St. Mary's
Loch

Gilmanscleugh

Delorrin

Dodhead

Hassendean

R. Tweed

Grey Mare's
Tail

Bellandine

Hawick

Teviotdale

Ettrick Water

Blakelaw

Buccleuch

Burnfeet

Chisholme

Fiendhopehaugh

Mount Comyn
(Redhough's Castle)

Criblaw

Philhope Head

Slitrik Water

R. Annan

Moffat

Tema Water

Aitas Burn

Craik

Craik Corsa

Houseco

Howpasley
Borthwick Water

Commonside
Castleweary
Coulters Cleugh
Carlinrig
Ridge

Fanesh

Frostylair

Skelfhill

Penchrist

Peel Brae

Limiecleugh
Hills

Annandale

Bilhope Head
Reddeugh

Pass of
Hermitage

Tower of
Gorranberry

Ewes Water

Eskdale

Debateable

Glitters

Lands

Cleugh

CANONGATE CLASSICS

Books listed in alphabetical order by author.

The Land of the Leal James Barke
 ISBN 0 86241 142 4 £4.95
The House with the Green Shutters
 George Douglas Brown
 ISBN 0 86241 549 7 £4.99
Witchwood John Buchan
 ISBN 0 86241 202 1 £4.99
Open the Door! Catherine Carswell
 ISBN 0 86241 644 2 £6.99
The Life of Robert Burns Catherine Carswell
 ISBN 0 86241 292 7 £5.99
The Complete Brigadier Gerard Arthur Conan Doyle
 ISBN 0 86241 534 9 £4.99
Dance of the Apprentices Edward Gaitens
 ISBN 0 86241 297 8
Ringan Gilhaize John Galt
 ISBN 0 86241 552 7 £6.99
The Member and *The Radical* John Galt
 ISBN 0 86241 642 6 £5.99
A Scots Quair: (Sunset Song, Cloud Howe, Grey Granite)
 Lewis Grassic Gibbon
 ISBN 0 86241 532 2 £5.99
Sunset Song Lewis Grassic Gibbon
 ISBN 0 86241 179 3 £3.99
Memoirs of a Highland Lady vols. I&II
 Elizabeth Grant of Rothiemurchus
 ISBN 0 86241 396 6 £7.99
The Highland Lady in Ireland
 Elizabeth Grant of Rothiemurchus
 ISBN 0 86241 361 3 £7.95
Highland River Neil M. Gunn
 ISBN 0 86241 358 3 £5.99
Sun Circle Neil M. Gunn
 ISBN 0 86241 587 X £5.99
The Well at the World's End Neil M. Gunn
 ISBN 0 86241 645 0 £5.99
Gillespie J. MacDougall Hay
 ISBN 0 86241 427 X £6.99
The Private Memoirs and Confessions of a Justified Sinner
 James Hogg
 ISBN 0 86241 340 0 £3.99
The Three Perils of Man James Hogg
 ISBN 0 86241 646 9 £8.99

Most Canongate Classics are available at good bookshops. If you experience difficulty in obtaining the title you want, please contact us at 14 High Street, Edinburgh EH1 1TE.